The
OVERSOUL
SEVEN
Trilogy

BOOKS BY JANE ROBERTS

The Bundu. A short novel in *The Magazine of Fantasy and Science Fiction* (March, 1958)

The Rebellers (1963)

How to Develop Your ESP Power (1966) (Also published as *The Coming of Seth*)

The Seth Material (1970)

Seth Speaks: The Eternal Validity of the Soul (1972)*

The Education of Oversoul Seven (1973)

The Nature of Personal Reality: A Seth Book (1974)*

Adventures in Consciousness: An Introduction to Aspect Psychology (1975)

Dialogues of The Soul and Mortal Self in Time (1975)

Psychic Politics: An Aspect Psychology Book (1976)

The "Unknown" Reality: A Seth Book in two volumes (1977-1979)

The World View of Paul Cézanne: A Psychic Interpretation (1977)

The Afterdeath Journal of an American Philosopher: The World View of William James (1978)

The Further Education of Oversoul Seven (1979)

Emir's Education in the Proper Use of Magical Powers (1979)

The Nature of the Psyche: Its Human Expression. A Seth Book (1979)**

The Individual and the Nature of Mass Events. A Seth Book (1981)**

The God of Jane: A Psychic Manifesto (1981)

If We Live Again: Or, Public Magic and Private Love (1982)

Oversoul Seven and the Museum of Time (1984)

Dreams, "Evolution," and Value Fulfillment. A Seth Book in two volumes (1986)

Seth, Dreams, and Projection of Consciousness (1986)

The Magical Approach: Seth Speaks About the Art of Creative Living (1995)

* New editions co-published by Amber-Allen / New World Library, 1994 and 1995.
** New editions to be published by Amber-Allen Publishing, 1995 and 1996.

A
Jane
BOOK

The
OVERSOUL SEVEN
Trilogy

___

THE EDUCATION
OF OVERSOUL SEVEN

THE FURTHER EDUCATION
OF OVERSOUL SEVEN

OVERSOUL SEVEN
AND THE MUSEUM OF TIME

Jane Roberts

COVER ART BY ROBERT F. BUTTS

AMBER-ALLEN PUBLISHING

The Oversoul Seven Trilogy © 1995 Robert F. Butts
The Education of Oversoul Seven © 1973 Jane Roberts
The Further Education of Oversoul Seven © 1979 Jane Roberts
Oversoul Seven and the Museum of Time © 1984 Jane Roberts

Published by Amber-Allen Publishing
P.O. Box 6657
San Rafael, CA 94903

Grateful acknowledgment is made to Steve Bing
for his vision and faith in these books.

Cover Art: Robert F. Butts
Cover Design: Beth Hansen
Editorial: Janet Mills
Typography: Rick Gordon, Emerald Valley Graphics
Printed by: Malloy Lithographing, Inc.

Library of Congress Cataloging-in-Publication Data

Roberts, Jane, 1929–1984
    The Oversoul Seven trilogy / by Jane Roberts.
        p.   cm.
        Contents: The education of Oversoul Seven — The further education of
Oversoul Seven — Oversoul Seven and the Museum of Time.
    ISBN 1-878424-17-3
        1. Fantastic fiction, American.   2. Religious fiction, American.
3. Spiritual life — Fiction.   4. Reincarnation — Fiction.   5. Soul — Fiction
I. Title.
    PS3568.02387093 1995
    813′.54 — dc20   95-1774
                                                                                      CIP

ISBN 1-878424-17-3
Printed in U.S.A. on acid-free paper
First Printing: May, 1995
Distributed by Publishers Group West

10   9   8   7   6   5   4   3   2

～ *Contents* ～

Book One

～

THE EDUCATION
OF OVERSOUL SEVEN

Book Two

～

THE FURTHER EDUCATION
OF OVERSOUL SEVEN 221

Book Three

∼

OVERSOUL SEVEN
AND THE MUSEUM OF TIME

THE
EDUCATION
OF OVERSOUL SEVEN

*This Book
Is
Written
in
the Time of
Lydia*

(Translated into
Vernacular English
circa A.D. 1970s)

*Dedicated
to
The Speakers
In all "Times"
and to Those
Who
Recognize
the
Sumari Songs*

～ *Chapter One* ～

*Oversoul Seven's Examination
and Josef's Dream*

O versoul Seven grimaced at Cyprus and began the examination. "Let's see," he said. "In Earth terms, using an analogy, I'm a man on Wednesday and Friday, a woman on Sunday and Thursday, and I have the rest of the time off for independent study.

"Actually, because of their time concepts this is somewhat more complicated," he said. "Each life is lived in a different, uh, area of time to which various designations are given." Cyprus smiled, and Seven continued. "As Lydia I'm in the twentieth century, as Josef in the seventeenth, as Ma-ah in 35,000 B.C., and as Proteus in the 23rd century, A.D. Then there's the further background in space, uh, different locations called countries. Then there's the ages of the personalities.

"I'm partial to Josef and Lydia, though I suppose I shouldn't be. Still, they show so much vitality and seem to enjoy themselves. Ma-ah cries a lot, and Proteus is always looking back to the good old days—"

Cyprus had been silent. Now she said, "You're wandering and not organizing your thoughts very well. Pretend that I know nothing about all this, and you're trying to explain it. You just told me that you had personalities in all those times, for example. So why should Proteus look back to the good old days?"

"Oh, I see. Sorry," Oversoul Seven said. "Proteus doesn't know that. He doesn't take anything for granted. He doesn't even take me for granted, or himself, for that matter. That is, he doesn't realize that he is a soul, much less that both of us are one. Certainly he doesn't know that other portions of us live in other times. I get lonely for him now and then, but there it is. In fact, sometimes I think we Oversouls aren't appreciated at all. We work and strive—"

Seven was suddenly struck by such a sense of desolation that he dematerialized his hallucinatory pencil. He brought it back as quickly as he could, but Cyprus shook her head at the lapse and said sharply, "Now, none of that. Dropping your hallucination loses you five points, you know. Suppose you were, say, Lydia on Earth, and she did something like that? Physical matter wouldn't be a dependable framework at all. One slip, that's all it takes! How would you like to be responsible for such a massive reaction? Then everyone would have to start over with a new . . . Oh, Seven, you just can't make errors like that. Pencils disappearing in mid-air!"

Oversoul Seven nodded, then suddenly, almost despite himself, he started to laugh. "Actually, Josef is almost on the edge of knowing. Once he forgot to materialize one of his painting brushes—he was in the throes of creativity—and bongo, the brush was just gone. Josef almost went out of his mind." Seven's eyes glowed with parental-like pride.

Cyprus said sternly, "None of your personalities are ready to understand that mind forms matter, and you know it. I hope you remedied the situation."

"I hallucinated the brush back at once," Oversoul Seven said. "But tell me, don't you find the affair even a little bit funny?"

"Not at all," Cyprus said, concealing a smile. "But now let's get back to your examination."

"Gladly," Oversoul Seven said. "But when I reach your position, I hope I retain my sense of humor."

Cyprus laughed. She laughed so hard that Seven got uncomfortable. Finally she said: "Your sense of humor includes only a small part of *my* sense of humor. There's so much you don't see. This examination of yours, for example—oh bless me—and having to maintain Earth-type conditions for it. Now *that's* funny. By the way, look around this room. There's something else that quite escapes you. Your visual is awful—"

Oversoul Seven looked around cautiously. He'd been secretly quite pleased with the environment he'd chosen and created. The classroom was authentic twentieth-century, like the one Lydia knew as a child. There were rows of desks, blackboards, windows, everything right down to stacks of paper—all individual new sheets—and an automatic pencil sharpener.

Then he blushed, all over his nice new cheeks and right up to the roots of the thick brown hair that sprang up from his forehead.

"Nice effect," Cyprus said, watching. "I meant to congratulate you on your form, very good fourteen-year-old male type, Caucasian, I believe. But for the other —"

"I found it, the error! There!" The wastepaper basket had been in the corner, complete with girth and thickness, exactly two feet high and as many around, but he'd forgotten to materialize it visually. Now he made it red, and with a flourish added scallops around the upper edge.

"But there's still another error," Cyprus said, looking nowhere in particular. Just at that moment a young man wearing a toga appeared. He looked around with a rather wild air, then shouted out at Seven: "Ah, there you are! I knew I'd find you again. Just the same, all this has to stop." He looked half mad, and yelled in tones of deepest outrage.

Cyprus raised her eyebrows at Oversoul Seven, who coughed several times and tried to look the other way.

"Well?" shouted the young man.

"How did you get here?" Seven asked. Then he whispered urgently to Cyprus. "That's Josef. He must be in a dreaming state, and sleeping on Earth."

"How did I get here? You tell me," Josef cried angrily. "Next time I'm going to memorize the route. I see you in my dreams too often for comfort. Dreams aren't supposed to work that way." He broke off, frowning: "I am dreaming, aren't I? I must be. What a crazy place. What on Earth is that?" He was staring at the automatic pencil sharpener.

"Don't touch it! It's *not* on Earth. That's the point," Seven cried. But Josef was fascinated.

"It's authentic twentieth-century," Seven said, giving in. "Works by electricity."

Cyprus moaned. "I believe that Josef is your *seventeenth-century* personality," she said. "Electricity isn't utilized there."

Oversoul Seven blushed and dematerialized the pencil sharpener. "Just forget you saw it. Forget the whole thing," he said to Josef.

"Where did it go?" Josef stood staring.

"Listen, you aren't supposed to be here. Not here, of all places. I get demerits for this," Oversoul Seven said. "Go home. Go back to your body where you belong."

"What do you mean, go back to my body?" Josef demanded. He rose to his full stature and adjusted his toga with a dramatic gesture. "This is my dream, and nobody is going to put me out of it."

"Why are you wearing a toga?" Cyprus asked gently.

Josef looked down at himself with some amazement. "I don't know. I didn't realize that I had one on. I like to paint models in togas, though. You can do so much with the folds — " He broke off, angry again. "You aren't answering my questions at all. What's happening? How is it that I meet you in my dreams?" He paused and shook his head. "You look like a boy now, but most of the time you look like an old man. You can't fool me, though. You're the same one."

"I've told you before, but you never remember," Seven said. "I'm something like your mother and something like your father, but neither. We're closer than sister and brother, mother and daughter, or father and son. That's all I can tell you now. You have to learn some things for yourself. You *are* learning fast, but you wandered in where you shouldn't be. I know you had a reason, though: You never look for me unless you're in trouble."

Seven caught the rebuke in his own voice and added quickly: "That's all right. I understand. But what's bothering you?" He looked around to see if Cyprus approved of the way he was handling the situation, but Cyprus had sympathetically dematerialized.

Josef never noticed. He said mournfully: "I'm twenty-four and I don't have any discipline. I can't keep myself at my easel two hours at a time, yet painting is what I want to do more than anything else in the world. If I don't learn some discipline, I'm afraid I'll lose what talent I have — and God knows how much that is, to begin with. On top of that I haven't felt any real inspiration for a year."

Seven shook his head. Before his eyes, Josef was turning into a big unhappy bear, his dark moustache transformed into fur, his eyes belligerent and sad at the same time, his toga changing into a blanket. Josef looked down at himself, hysterically. "I'm a circus bear; something for people to laugh at. Oh, what a dream. It's got to be a dream." Then the bear growled threateningly.

"Come on now," Seven said, and patted its head. "Turn back into yourself. In the dream state you take different forms as your feelings and thoughts change. You felt like a bear, so you look like one."

"Really?" Josef was himself again. Immediately he forgot what had happened. "If I don't do something, I'm going to ruin my life," he said.

"Oh, you can't do that," Oversoul Seven said. "You aren't aware of your real problem yet. It's one of my jobs to help you, so I'll get back to you shortly. In the meantime I'll do some little thing to tide you over."

As he spoke, Oversoul Seven created in his mind an excellent art studio, made to Josef's personal requirements. On the easel was a painting of the precise farmhouse in which Josef was staying on earth. The painting was signed in the corner: Josef Landsdatter, 1615. "Now I've made this dream for you," Seven said. "Look at the painting well. You'll begin work on it tomorrow. You'll be so filled with inspiration that you'll paint all day." He transmitted the dream to Josef telepathically, then said: "When you get all you want out of the dream, then wake up in your bedroom."

Josef nodded and dutifully disappeared.

"What did you think of him?" Seven asked.

Cyprus laughed richly, then returned visually. "Well, I see the similarity between the two of you," she said.

"Stop joking. He has a serious problem."

"That's something else about you, Seven," Cyprus said. "Your sense of humor doesn't extend to yourself or your personalities. By the time you reach Oversoul Eight stage, you'll know better. You *did* handle the situation well, however."

"I worry about Josef," Seven said. "He's so impetuous."

"As *you* are," Cyprus said. "Remember, your various personalities, while independent, also reflect qualities of your own. You can't create without giving of yourself.

"Now technically you *do* get three demerits," she said. "You should have been aware of Josef's approach and waylaid him. But rules are also flexible, and his achievement is noteworthy, regardless of the circumstances. So I'll note that in your files.

"The schoolroom environment was also well done, though I'm waiting for you to discover your one other error. Your appearance as the fourteen-year-old male was symbolically valid. You've demonstrated that you have an excellent understanding of Earth's conventions. Let's dispense with them now, though, and get down to the more serious aspects of your examination."

As Cyprus spoke, the room disappeared, and the trees outside the windows. Last to go was the wastepaper basket with the scalloped edges. A lovely touch, Seven thought, feeling a bit of dismay as it vanished. . . .

Now Oversoul Seven and Cyprus were two brilliant points of consciousness, without form. Oversoul Seven felt himself expand mentally, psychically. He breathed a symbolic sigh of relief. He and Cyprus communicated telepathically through the use of mental images that changed with each alteration of meaning, and were instantly perceived and understood. In Earth terms, it boiled down to this conversation:

"Creating yourself physically certainly is demanding," Seven said. "But even now, when I'm not Earth-oriented, I can appreciate Josef and all the rest, and feel the splendid growth of their vitality."

"I know how you want to handle this part of the examination," Cyprus said. "But remember, you can't contact any of your people. If they contact *you*, that's all right. But you can't correct any of their errors. I want to see how they're progressing, so this part of the exam involves you only as a bystander. Knowing how impetuous you are, let me emphasize that point. Later, of course, how well you communicate with your personalities will be an important factor."

All at once Oversoul Seven felt apprehensive. He heard the voice before Cyprus did, because it was directed to him.

"Tweety! Tweety!"

"That's a human voice," Cyprus said. "How can that be? No humans should be able to reach us here."

"Maybe it's a mistake," Seven said weakly. But already it was too late.

"Is it time yet?" asked the voice.

"Go back where you came from," Seven said desperately. "No it's not time yet, and for all I know it may never be."

"But I'm all ready," said the voice.

"No you aren't. That's just the trouble," Seven said. "If you were, you'd have better sense. This is my superior, by the way."

"Oh, Tweety!" cried the voice, desolate.

"Tweety?" Cyprus asked.

"Uh. We're old friends. It's Daga. Whenever Daga's a female she calls me Tweety. Right now she's a female and helping me with my independent study. At least we think she's female. When *I* am, I call her Tweety." In confusion, Seven took on the fourteen-year-old form again. "Earth language doesn't have any words for what we really are, no, uh, pronouns for beings that are male and female at once, so it makes explanations difficult."

"We aren't ready to go into your independent study yet," Cyprus said. "But I must admit that I'm curious. And I must note that you seem to have some difficulty in keeping track of your various projects."

"See?" Oversoul Seven said. "Daga, please go away."

"If you insist," the voice said. "But I've got my birth date planned, and—"

"Go away!" Seven cried, in consternation.

Cyprus pretended not to hear. She said: "I presume that you'll have a good explanation for this later on. Now if you don't mind, let's get down to the *scheduled* phases of your examination."

Oversoul Seven tried not to be nervous. "All right," he said. "Let's look in on Lydia. I certainly hope that she's having a good day. First, there's a few things I'd like to explain about her. She—"

"Sorry. From now on I must see for myself," Cyprus said.

Seven sighed. He thought of Lydia, lovingly brought her image into his awareness until it filled him, taking precedence over all the other memories of his many selves. Together he and Cyprus blinked off and on, rode piggyback on a million molecules, and emerged.

∾ *Chapter Two* ∾

*Part One of the Examination
A Quick Peek at Lydia, Proteus,
Ma-ah, and Josef*

THE PRESENT (MORE OR LESS)

*L*ydia felt nervous, as if someone was watching her, beside Lawrence. It was a thunderstormy morning, eleven o'clock, with great dashes of rain pounding against the windows. She was seventy-three, and angrier than usual about it on dark days.

Lawrence sat on the blue couch. "Well, what do you say? I do wish you'd quit prowling around and give me some kind of an answer," he said.

She frowned and put down her rye and ginger. "My kids won't like it much, not that it makes any difference. God, *they're* hitting fifty, and Anna in particular is pretty pompous. But l just might do it, Larry. The aged poetess on her last binge! I like college-age people, too. They haven't got into the establishment yet and we're out of it, thank heaven. My kids would okay the idea of a tour, of course. But you and me traveling around the country together in a trailer, unmarried—well, you know how conventional they are. But they can hardly call you a dirty old man, since I'm older than you are! So to hell with it. I'll go."

He was so excited that he almost dropped his pipe. "We'll fill the camper with books and food and liquor—"

7

"And two of my cats. Tuckie and Greenacre have to go, and Mr. George, my goldfish."

He groaned. "The two cats, *and* Mr. George."

She wanted to cry but she wouldn't. Defiance rose up so that she thrust her head backward in an old gesture that had been startlingly dramatic when she was young. "I'll make out papers before we leave, giving the house to my children. I don't imagine really that we'll be coming back."

"We will. Goddammit, we will." He stood up, but knowing how she was, he didn't put his arms around her. He only said, again, "We'll both come back."

"Oh, to hell with it. If you say we will, we will. After all, what difference does it make? Forget it. You know, I meant to tell you — not to change the subject — that those dreams of mine are getting nuttier all the time. Last night none of them made sense. Yet right now, talking to you, it almost seems as if they did, if only I could remember them."

Lawrence said: "When you talk like that, then I'm sure that we've known each other before — before we met, I mean. You are, after all, what? Fifteen years older than I am? But in some odd manner it always seems to me that you're younger."

"My dear love," she said flippantly. "In the world's eyes we make one hell of a funny pair. The thing is, no one ever thinks they'll really grow old. It always comes as a surprise, and the world sort of hates you for it. Growing old, gracefully or not, just isn't the polite or tasteful thing to do. And you can't blame the young either, because when we were young we felt the same way. Too bad, because in one way I feel freer than I ever did before —"

"You look ten years younger than you are," he said.

"Don't be trite. Telling a woman that she looks sixty-three instead of seventy-three isn't likely to win her favor. You'd be smarter to say nothing. For some reason that I've never understood, growing old is considered bad enough for a man, but an unforgivable crime for a woman. But best I don't get on *that* subject."

She took another sip of her drink. "It's true, I suppose, in good light and if I bothered to wear makeup, I could look near your age — maybe. But as it is I look like a scrawny boy grown suddenly old, with white hair and gaunt face and quite incredulous about how it all happened. As I am, of course. Yet what I am, I am. I can't see dying my hair, for example. In a way it's pretty damn lucky to be seventy-three years old, and get white, to begin with."

He was silent. Then he said: "If the doctors *are* right, and my heart does go suddenly —"

"Then I'll follow our plan," she said. "For that matter, I don't know how long *I'll* hold out. I'm quite aware that the first stages of my . . . condition have already come upon me. My memory should be all right, generally, for a while, though. But you can never tell. If not, then *you* follow our plan. When I can't recite my own poetry right, then I suppose I'll know that something's wrong."

And suddenly it seemed really funny, beautifully hilarious to each of them. He said, "We'll beat their hospitals, their rest homes and final asylums." Exuberance flashed through his thin nervous frame.

She laughed with him, then stopped. "My electric pencil sharpener," she said. "I just remembered. I dreamed of my old eighth-grade classroom. Only my electric pencil sharpener was in it, which is ridiculous, of course. They didn't have them then. Now I wonder what that means?"

"A bleed-through from one dream state to another," Oversoul Seven said to Cyprus. They were suspended in two green leaves that rustled in the wind outside the windows.

"You heard what she said about the pencil sharpener? That was the error you missed," Cyprus said, and Seven grinned.

"Wait," Lydia said. "I was a man in the dream, fairly young. Funny, how some of it comes back."

Lawrence frowned suddenly. "Never question the dream messages of the gods," he said dramatically. "You might find out what they mean."

"Now don't say things like that," she cried. "It makes me nervous. And look at those leaves outside. How alive they seem, how . . . watchful. God, I wish the damned storm would stop."

"The sound of rain on a trailer roof will be different," Lawrence said.

She smiled over at him. He'd just closed his leather shop for good. He'd upholstered the whole camper-trailer, and half of her books had leather covers that he'd made for her. She almost gasped: how could they be so in love and so old? "In my dream, someone was taking an examination," she said. "I was thinking of my books, and just remembered."

"I was, dear Lydia. We both are!" Oversoul Seven was all ready to transmit the words to Lydia when Cyprus said gently, "No prompting, remember."

The leaves were really tossing in all that wind. Oversoul Seven filled himself with the uniqueness of it, because Cyprus was saying: "All right, we have to leave now. The first part of the examination allows for a quick viewing only."

And the scene changed. . . .

TWENTY-THIRD CENTURY A.D.

Proteus secretly yearned to be a girl: they were so much freer to express themselves. Instead he was stuck at home in the living nodule with his father, and only innocuous hobbies to content him. He also yearned for the sight of something naturally green, growing, real. In fact, this desire had grown so strong that he determined to do something about it.

He said eagerly: "Surely we could take some small space and devote it to a natural miniature farm. Say the whole thing only took up one living nodule. It would be self-sufficient. Someone ought to be able to give us permission—"

Mithias, his father, frowned: "Life grows. *That* kind of life grows, anyhow. There's no stopping it. It's wild. We've spent two centuries developing an artificial environment that we could handle. If you gave *that* kind of life freedom, people would have children all the time. You'd be dead at sixty or seventy. Our way of life is balanced. But I can't expect you to really understand that at sixteen."

He paused and said with a grunt, "When we had our 'natural' environment, the women were kept busy having children. Men had the positions of power. Otherwise, I can't think of anything good about those days. They were filled with sickness, wars, social diseases—"

"You're right as usual," Proteus said. But he was still sick of being cooped up inside with his father all day.

Mithias was watching his son's face. "Now don't start brooding," he said. "We're due for a rain at noon. Why don't you go outside and watch? It always lifts your spirits."

"I might," Proteus said. He was shy, diffident, but strangely arrogant too. The suggestion sounded too much like an order, so he just stood there.

"It's almost noon now," Mithias said, irritably.

So Proteus scowled and went through the door of their spacious nodule. He stood on the small plastic sidewalk, and looked up at the plastic trees. Down there, beneath him, where the real Earth was, who knew what was going on? Really? No one, he thought. Except for the scientific expeditions, no one went there any more. But then he stopped thinking as the rain began. Usually it excited him. Now he felt more depressed. It would rain politely for fifteen minutes. The water would run down the plastic drains and be saved and purified, and then fall tomorrow for fifteen minutes someplace else.

When he was small he had a schedule of all the rainfalls. He knew exactly where and when it would rain. His own nodule area held fifteen subites, with over a million people, and he'd run over the plastic sidewalks, frantic with excitement, keeping up with the rain.

He squinted up. Three clouds passed. They always did, at rain-time. If you didn't know that the artificial sky stopped one-eighth of a mile up, or if you tried to forget it, like he used to, then you could imagine that the rain was real, and the clouds. They were real *enough*, he thought. Only they were man-made and regulated. He scowled, then grinned. Imagine seeing four clouds one day, or even two, how *that* would shake everyone up! But the rain fell from the sky of the floating city, and there would never be one cloud more or less. He almost wanted to cry but he didn't, remembering his age.

What would a real flood be like, he wondered, or a windstorm? For a minute his eyes almost closed under the impact of sheer emotional excitement: he'd seen microfilms of ancient natural disasters in which the power of nature was unleashed, and now he imagined great brown curls of flood-water emerging from real rivers, torrents of rain that fell with great force, winds that whipped a world apart.

Yet Earth had survived. It was still down there. And down there great climatic changes still existed; heat and cold, as they *were*, despite their con-venience or inconvenience to man. To be pitted against that—Proteus held his breath, almost whoosy with the thought of it—to exist *in* the con-text of nature! What excitement it must have generated. Just a real rain-storm, coming from nowhere—appearing out of . . . itself, out of nature, sinking down into real ground filled with dirt and bugs and roots!

His eyes stung. The polite rain was done. It was all sham. The plastic trees didn't need nourishment. They didn't grow. Psychologists thought that the Earth-type environment helped man feel secure. Proteus knew this, but now he stared angrily at the meticulous street and went back inside.

Mithias was waiting for him. "There's no way that you could set up nat-ural life conditions inside a subite, son," he said. "You know that. Don't tor-ment yourself. You'd have to go to Earth."

"Well, people *do* go there," Proteus said. His face flushed. He lowered his eyes.

"But they don't live there—"

"A few do! Microfilms mention them. Historians go down; scientists. They have to make repairs on their equipment sometime."

"So what?" his father said. "There's no future on Earth. The whole place is drained dry, useless, stripped of anything worthwhile. It's just a husk." He paused and said more gently: "And Proteus, you *are* a boy, not a girl. It's true that your opportunities aren't as extensive as they might be, but there are plenty of places for you to fit into, here. Even if there were op-portunities on Earth, and there aren't, then they'd go to women."

Proteus looked out the window. The sidewalk was already dry. The suction equipment had absorbed all the water so that none was wasted. He turned so that his father couldn't see his face. "Everything's the same all the time," he said, dully. "Don't you ever think about how fantastic it must have been? Just people with all colors of skin. That alone. Now we're all homogenized."

At this Mithias laughed. "What's wrong with everyone having olive skin?" he asked. "You're just arguing for the sake of it now. There's all kinds of variations if you want to look for them, from yellow-olive to brown-olive to—"

"Olive-olive," Proteus said. "You just don't understand at all. Centuries ago there were black men and white men and yellow men—"

"And they all fought with each other," Mithias said, wearily. "Now there's one less thing to fight about. The races merged. What's so wrong about that? Will you stop trying to pick an argument with me, and find something constructive to do?"

Proteus nodded, but he realized suddenly that he was finished arguing. His father wanted him to do something constructive, and he would. Somehow he'd get to Earth. Somehow he'd re-create an ancient farm there. Instead of dreaming and being frustrated, he'd act. Someday he'd stand on real ground, while real rain fell, and then this would seem like the dream.

"You're going to have trouble with that one," Cyprus said to Oversoul Seven. They were conversing in the further reaches of the room's plastic dome.

"Well, he's not one of my favorites," Seven said. "He's so gloomy half the time."

Cyprus waited. Then she said, "There's a connection that you seem to have missed. Shall I point it out to you?"

"No, give me another chance," Seven said. "I don't need any more demerits, not even one." He reviewed the entire scene, including the thoughts he'd received telepathically from Proteus. Then he blushed. "Of course, the farm! Proteus wants to set up a farm on Earth. It's just possible that he had a dream last night about a farm or a picture of one—"

"Exactly," Cyprus said.

"Well, Proteus has had that idea for some time," Seven said. "But if he did participate in Josef's dream, he'd use it in his own way, of course. You know, in a way he acts older than Lydia. He broods so."

Cyprus smiled. "Do you know why?"

"No."

"I'm sure you'll discover the reason for yourself. It's not up to me to tell you. But now suppose we look in on your Ma-ah."

Oversoul Seven was delighted to change the subject. . . .

35,000 B.C.

The wolf cubs sped across the cliffs in the moonlight. Ma-ah crouched in the shadows, waiting. She was hungry, but then she usually was, her belly pushed in almost to her backbone. She ran across the cliffs when the wolf cubs vanished, and scurried to the clearing where they'd been forced to leave the kill they'd found. She'd frightened the cubs off by throwing rocks. Rampa came over from the other side of the cliff. He'd used bow and arrows. The two of them found little: only a dead hare. But they ate it at once, ravenously.

The hides they wore protected them somewhat against the wind and they crouched, unspeaking, while the ice cracked along the cliffs almost in sequence, and the air rushed in and out of the rock crevices.

Cyprus said to Oversoul Seven: "I didn't know you were that adventurous."

Oversoul Seven shrugged with just a hint of smugness. Then he said: "Proteus should experience this, if he wants to know what the real Earth is like. He'd probably plead for some artificial pretty rain that stops on time."

Cyprus smiled but said nothing.

Ma-ah and Rampa finished eating. They ran down into a nearby cave, pulling in out of the cold; satisfied. The damp smell of the hides rose to their nostrils. Their bellies felt warm from the food. A sense of peace descended upon them. They fell asleep. Their satisfaction was transmitted to Cyprus and Seven, who also felt the cold wind that rushed past the cave entrance.

"I could make the wind die down just a bit, couldn't I?" Seven asked.

Cyprus nodded.

"Oh! oh!" Seven said. The change in the wind had alerted Ma-ah even in her sleep. In a moment her spirit body came out of the cave. She saw them.

"Oh, it's you, old man," she said.

"She's very good," Seven said to Cyprus. "But she always sees me as an old man."

"Why not? You always *are* an old man when I see you," Ma-ah said. "Are you going to help me keep watch tonight?"

"Not tonight," he said, adding to Cyprus, "Uh, I help her watch sometimes when she's tired, so the wolves don't find the cave."

"You know that you're out of your physical body?" Cyprus asked.

"Of course," Ma-ah said scornfully. "If I didn't go out in the spirit at night, who'd watch over my body while it slept? Only I don't like to get too far away from my body. Rampa hardly ever comes awake when he's asleep. Whose spirit are you?"

"I'll tell you sometime," Cyprus said. Then she and Seven disappeared.

"Ma-ah *always* sees me as an old man," Seven sighed. "Come to think of it, she sees me as black because she's black. Josef sees me in lots of different ways, but he likes to see me as an old man, too. It gives him confidence in me, for some silly reason. But Proteus never sees me at all."

"So?" Cyprus said.

"Well, none of them see me as I *am*, male and female, ageless, beyond any image. Even Lydia. I mean, she doesn't let herself believe in her soul at all, at least not on an intellectual level."

"Now who's brooding?" Cyprus said. "You sound as downhearted as Proteus."

"Proteus! He'll probably never see me if he keeps on the way he's going," Seven said. "But you've already met Josef, so I presume that this part of the examination is over."

"I'd like to see him when he's awake in his time, if you don't mind," Cyprus said dryly. . . .

1615

Just as Oversoul Seven and Cyprus arrived at Josef's, there was a tremendous pounding at his door. Josef Landsdatter moaned, bounded out of bed, ran his fingers through his bushy hair, and almost sobbed. He'd never felt so cornered in his life.

"Coming. Yes. Yes," he shouted. He hoped that he sounded enraged, impatient, anything but scared. He grabbed a paintbrush, dipped it into a jar of varnish, held it between his teeth, and threw open the door. "I'm working. Working. Can't you see? I'm busy. But come in, if you must."

Elgren Hosentauf reminded himself that his wife was watching from the first-floor landing, so he strode through the door briskly. It was after all his house, his extra room. The place was a mess of rumpled clothing, tossed bedding, paint jars, and canvases in various stages of completion. "Ah, were you sleeping or painting? My wife swears that you were still in bed."

"What does it look like? Do you think I sleep with my paintbrush in my mouth?" Josef pushed the brush toward Hosentauf's nose so that the smell of fresh varnish made the older man's eyes water and his nose run. "You distrust me," Josef said, now that he had the advantage. "You've always distrusted me. How can I work under such conditions?"

Hosentauf stepped back. "All right. But my wife tells me that you eat more than ten farmhands put together, and I won't be taken advantage of. We've yet to see a glimmer of our painting. You've been here six weeks now, eating our good food, using our nice room. The painter my cousin had did his portrait in two weeks and was gone."

"And the painting probably won't last much longer than that," Josef retorted, getting into it. "A good artist needs time." He pointed dramatically to the draped easel. "Your portrait is covered, I've told you. It makes me nervous to show a painting before its done. And it took me a good two weeks to get started as it is; your wife put me in such a mood that I couldn't think, much less paint."

"Shush." Hosentauf's light blue eyes lowered. Some of the belligerence drained from his face. He'd been shaking his finger at Josef. Now he fussed with his shirt instead, and looked almost pleadingly up into Josef's stormy face. "My wife is impatient to see the painting. Women, they cannot wait."

"Ah, don't I know," Josef said, as if they shared a dark mysterious secret. "But very soon now I'll unveil the portrait." He threw his arms out dramatically, smiled grandly. "You will see your family immortalized through the ages. *The Hosentauf Family*. The portrait will go down through the generations, from father to son —"

"He's a lazy clout, and you should put him out in the snow like the cur he is," yelled Avona Hosentauf from the stairs.

Flinching, her husband closed the door.

"Ahh, very well," shouted Josef. "I'll burn my painting rather than give it to the likes of that one. None of you deserves fine art. You're worse than shopkeepers." He rummaged through the room, picking up his belongings. Then he stopped in front of the covered easel.

"You will never be completed, never," he moaned. "Some silly woman prevents it. Ah well, if they resent the few morsels of food I eat, the use of this tiny room in exchange for a masterpiece —"

Hosentauf was an unimaginative man, at least generally speaking. It didn't occur to him at this point that anyone could fake such anguish. "Now, now," he said hurriedly. "I'll talk things over with my wife. I'll see what she says." He backed out of the room and closed the door.

Cyprus and Oversoul Seven were now two flakes of snow on the windowsill. Embarrassed, Seven said, "Josef's very excitable." Just then, Josef threw the cover off the easel, displaying not a half-completed painting at all, but the empty canvas beneath.

"And quite deceitful," Cyprus said.

"No, no, I'm sure he doesn't mean to be," Seven answered uneasily, because obviously it wasn't going to be one of Josef's better days.

Josef stared at the canvas hatefully. "Blank. All blank," he muttered. "Bah!" Completely disgusted, he planked down on the bed. Hosentauf wouldn't be back, he knew, but his wife would, with her eldest son. They'd boot him out. There'd be no more hedging or excuses. He'd be back on the plains on his skis, with his supplies on his back, cold and hungry, until he could find another farmer willing to give him bed and board for a painting. And worst, he just couldn't make himself paint anything at all.

This time his torment was quite real. He threw the sticky varnish-covered brush across the room and wondered what to do.

"Your dream," Oversoul Seven said. "Cyprus, can't I remind him? The painting I gave him in the dream! He's forgotten all about it."

"No, you cannot," she said. "No prompting in this part of the examination. You know that. Twenty-five demerits in case you have any ideas."

"Examination or not, I mean, he *is* in trouble," Seven said.

"Oh, somebody help me," Josef moaned.

"How many demerits?" Seven asked.

"Twenty-five, and you have several already," she reminded him.

"And you still won't tell me what happens if I fail? Or pass?"

She said gently, "That's part of the examination, too. You have to find that out."

"Oh, dear God, I'll never lie or cheat again if you'll just help me now," Josef prayed.

"Your dream!" Seven transmitted the words directly into Josef's mind. "The painting in the dream!"

The instant transformation in Josef was extraordinary. Suddenly he shouted, leapt up from the bed, threw his arms around himself, and danced about the room.

Oversoul Seven almost burst with excitement himself.

Cyprus made a determined effort not to show any expression at all, and to guard her thoughts.

"Get to it," Seven signaled Josef.

Now, standing before the easel, Josef grinned from ear to ear. In his mind's eye, as clearly as he'd ever seen anything in his life, he saw an oil painting of the Hosentauf farm in the summer, the fields rich, the sturdy house surrounded by tulips. The greens glowed with vitality. It was in the middle of the season, with only sneaky touches of brown hinting at the over-ripeness that would be its own undoing. Even the grays beneath the yellows and whites of the house suggested that the farmhouse, while secure, would not triumph over time. Yet somehow the overall effect was still one of vital-ity, as if the entire scene would endure even while it was so physically vul-nerable. He'd never seen a painting so clearly in his mind before.

The canvas was coated, all ready to work, and as the thoughts went fly-ing through his mind, Josef's hands were busily mixing the colors for his palette, combining the dry pigments with linseed oil. He felt swift, sure, godlike, with this sudden unexpected rush of inspiration. Singing, almost shouting, he began to paint.

Partaking of Josef's experience, Oversoul Seven forgot everything else. Once when Josef picked the wrong color, Seven called, "No, no, you'll spoil it. You want earth tones there." Another time he cried, "No, you dunce, this is only the underpainting."

Cyprus waited, never interfering. Only once she spoke. "This part of the examination is only supposed to involve a brief viewing," she said, making her tone as neutral as possible.

"Yes, yes, I'll be with you shortly," Seven muttered. Then, "No, no, transparent color there. Not opaque," he called to Josef.

Five hours of Earth time passed. There was a knock at the door. "Go away. I'm working," Josef shouted.

The door flew open. Mrs. Hosentauf and her eldest son, Jonathan, came pounding into the room. "Ahhh, now maybe we'll get a look at the painting that isn't there. I want to see underneath that cover. I don't believe a word you say —" Mrs. Hosentauf shouted. Then she and her son both stopped, speechless.

"Now you see. Go, go leave me alone," Josef muttered. Nothing mattered but the painting.

"It's of my lovely house," Mrs. Hosentauf said. "It's beautiful."

"An inspiration," Jonathan said. "Man to man, let me apologize."

"Apologize then, and let me work. Can't you see I'm busy? I'm not finished. I've barely begun —"

"And you've started the portrait too?" Jonathan asked hastily.

"Yes, yes, yes," Josef cried automatically.

"Liar," Seven shouted, to Josef's mind. "You promised not to lie or cheat again."

A sudden pang of guilt just made Josef angry. He wanted to get on with his painting. "You'll have your portrait in good time," he said. "Can't a man have peace to work?"

Mrs. Hosentauf and her son moved toward the door, almost deferentially.

Josef yelled after them, triumphantly: "The house was meant as a bonus to repay you for your great kindness."

"Oh, Josef," Seven sighed.

Cyprus said, "You realize what you've done, of course: become so involved in Josef's difficulties that you've forgotten everything. Even the examination."

Seven came back to himself with dismay. "But I have to wait till he finishes the underpainting, now that I've started, " he said. "Then Josef can do the rest himself well enough."

"I'll speak to you when you're finished, then," Cyprus said. For a moment Seven wondered why he couldn't pick up more of Cyprus' thoughts, but already she was gone. Seven stayed there while Josef continued to paint, his brush like a perfect extension of the picture in his mind.

∼ *Chapter Three* ∼

Ma-ah's Trek:
The Earthization of Oversoul Seven
Part Two of the Examination

Oversoul Seven and Cyprus were two points of light.

"**I** chose Lydia's study for our discussion for several reasons," Cyprus said. "For one thing, the next part of your examination will definitely be Earth-oriented, and in ways that you may not suspect—"

"Suspect?" Oversoul Seven said. "I don't like the implications of that word. Are you sure you're using the language properly?"

"Yes, I am, and I used the word purposely, to give you a clue as to what might happen," she said. "For another thing, we have to take Earth forms, invisible of course, and I want you to relate to the environment the way humans do. For example, let's get off the windowsill and move properly into the room. We'll sit in one of those chairs there."

"Now tell me precisely where and when we are," Cyprus said. She materialized, to Seven at least, as a young woman of mature years, or as a mature woman of young years. Either way it seemed to fit. Yet if you kept looking at her, she became a young man of mature years or a mature man of young years. She laughed: "It's according to which part of my personality you focus on. I'm not as Earth-oriented as you, and I just can't get all of myself into an exclusively male or female form. No one ever does, of course. At my level it's just more apparent.

"But what form do *you* want to adopt?" she asked. "You'll have to use it for all of our discussions, so make up your mind. For one thing, I want to see how good you are, remembering details."

Seven's point of light wiggled indecisively. "I hadn't counted on a test of form," he said. "But since details are important, I'll pick something with as few of them as possible. What about a glowing round orange ball?"

"No," she sighed. "A human form."

Seven grinned and adopted the fourteen-year-old guise he'd used in the first part of the examination. "Now to answer your questions," he said briskly. "This is a day in April in the year 1975, in the northeastern part of the United States, which is a country, and it's four o'clock—"

"Oh, I see," Cyprus said. "Four o'clock is in the United States, then—"

"Not exactly—well, yes and no—" Seven said. "It's four o'clock here in the study, but that doesn't mean that four o'clock *is* here—"

"If you can't explain when we are, and how *when* fits into *where*, no wonder you have trouble keeping track of your personalities," Cyprus said. "But never mind. I have something quite serious to discuss with you. I'm giving you a multiple-choice section next, so listen carefully."

Seven frowned, but Cyprus continued. "The second part of the examination was dependent upon your performance in the first part," she said, "though as you know, all of it is really taking place at once. But several things have become apparent. I feel as if I know Lydia and Josef much better than I do Proteus. And Ma-ah I know hardly at all—"

"Hmm," Seven said. He sat docilely enough in his best fourteen-year-old male form, but he was beginning to feel a flash of irritation.

"Could it be that you didn't tune into Proteus and Ma-ah as well as you did the others?" Cyprus said. "You couldn't get away from Ma-ah fast enough, it seemed to me."

"It's just *them*, " Seven answered, rather put out now. "Proteus is gloomy a good deal of the time. Ma-ah sees me as an old man, *always*, I told you that, and she always wants me to do something boring, like keeping watch over the cave. Well, she's quite demanding."

"I'm afraid that you've been a very distant oversoul to both of them," Cyprus said severely. "That's one of the issues we hope to take care of in this examination. You have to learn to relate to your personalities better. And why do you think Ma-ah sees you as an old man? Never mind, don't answer me now. And she doesn't see you as a *jolly* old man either, which would be something quite different. No, Seven, those qualities you see in Ma-ah and Proteus are your own, too, a fact that you conveniently forget. And you don't come to grips with them at all."

"But *I'm not* gloomy," Oversoul Seven cried, "or demanding either."

"You can only endow your personalities with your own attributes. They're born from your own joy and vitality and creativity, but they also have your characteristics. You're their raw material, so to speak—"

"I don't like that phrase much either," Seven said. "I like to think of myself as their . . . creator, or of them as my creations."

"Just as I thought," Cyprus said. "Oh, Seven, I don't know how you'll ever reach Oversoul Eight stage."

"You're leading up to something," Seven said. "And you tricked me into making my last statement—"

"You tricked yourself into that," she said. "But the fact is that you don't relate well to Proteus and Ma-ah at all. And worse, you're playing favorites. As a result, both of them are missing something important that only you can give them. They're each missing a part of their soul—"

Seven was so upset that his image blurred around the edges.

"Watch your form," Cyprus corrected. "There you go again. Details are important, too. I don't mean to be overly severe, but suppose something like that happened to Ma-ah? Or Josef?"

"Josef would get out of it somehow," Seven said.

"But Ma-ah wouldn't?"

"You're just trying to confuse me," Seven wailed.

"This must be your low point," Cyprus said dryly. "Oversouls don't cry—"

"I'm not crying. I'm wailing. There's a difference," Seven said. "Anyway, why not?" he added defiantly.

"Because when they're using all their abilities, then they see more clearly; and they know that there are no obstacles, only those you believe in. But never mind, here's Part Two of your examination. It's an in-depth Life Composition."

Oversoul Seven regained his composure.

"You have a choice between Ma-ah and Proteus," Cyprus said. "But you must focus your attention on one of them and identify as best you can with whichever one you choose."

"It sounds easy enough," Oversoul Seven said. "But I have a feeling that there's something you aren't telling me."

"That you'll have to find out for yourself," she said. "Which one do you choose?"

"Well, I suppose I should do Ma-ah because I related to her poorest of all," Seven said. "All right, I choose Ma-ah."

"Remember, you must try to identify with her as well as you can," Cyprus said, "And with that portion of you from which she came. Good luck, dear Seven."

"Cyprus, wait. I've a lot of questions!"

"Oh, it's you again, old man," Ma-ah said.

Oversoul Seven just frowned. Cyprus was gone. Lydia's study was gone, and instead Ma-ah stood in her spirit body outside of her everlasting cave.

"Why do you always see me as an old man?" he asked.

"If you're not one, why do you look like one?" she retorted.

"I *don't* look like one, that's the point," he said.

She shrugged. "I don't care if you do or don't, but at least you could be pleasant."

"I'm trying to be," he said, irritably. "And I'm apt to be around for some time, so I wish . . . oh, never mind." This is a great start, he said to himself.

But Ma-ah had already gone back into her body. She didn't have the greatest disposition in the world, Seven thought, looking about. The cold wind swept scraps of dry weed past his face, and the cliffs were white with frost. Seven sighed: she didn't have the greatest environment in the world, either. The cliffs rose straight up in the air, making dry curious noises as if the rocks were coughing.

Seven was impervious to the weather, but he found the view fascinating and he entertained himself by dematerializing from the valley, appearing on a cliff peak, and looking down at where he'd just been. Then, guiltily, he remembered his instructions: "Identify as best you can with Ma-ah," Cyprus had said. Clearly, he thought, she had something else in mind. Uneasily he went into Ma-ah's cave.

She lay asleep on a few hides, bundled in another that was used as cloak and cover. Her brown straight hair was matted, all emphasis gone from her dark face, making her look vulnerable and more like twelve than the twenty Earth years she had to her credit. Seven sighed again: Cyprus was right, he had maintained too great a distance. Unaccountably he felt suddenly drawn to Ma-ah as he never had before. At the same time, a curious lassitude possessed him.

He saw Ma-ah's mate, Rampa, sleeping beside her, but then without warning he felt Rampa's breath coming in warm waves at his own face, astoundingly close. His viewpoint changed too. Rampa was now beside *him*; beside . . . Ma-ah. He was feeling Rampa's breath *from* Ma-ah's body. . . . Because he was *in* Ma-ah's body!

How odd settling down into a real body was! Ma-ah wasn't aware of him, of course. Since he was Ma-ah and Ma-ah was himself, there was no conflict. Yet so far she only knew herself as Ma-ah, and him as the old man when she was out of her body. Seven was confused. He tried to get his thoughts in order. In one way, then, he thought, he was getting to know himself better by getting to know her.

Still, Seven's consciousness wriggled uneasily. To be confined to one body for all practical purposes — it wouldn't be like changing forms whenever you wanted to, as he did. To have the responsibility for keeping the same body going all the while! The details involved really threw him for a loop when he thought of it. Of course, *his* energy helped maintain her body to begin with — his was the spark, so to speak, from which her body grew, from which her spirit had come, but. . . .

He stopped that line of thought, aware of the strangest ambiguity. Being in a real body was so intimate; he could feel his consciousness nestling in all the atoms and molecules. He was aware of their million separate yet combined consciousnesses; so tumultuous, like the infinite buzzing of innumerable bees, warm, too close, throbbing. For a moment he felt frightened, confined.

On the other hand he was transfixed, fascinated, attracted to the body experience as to a magnet. He'd never allowed himself to enter the complete physical experience of one of his personalities before. For one thing, he'd never been invited, but suddenly it occurred to him that far more than that was involved. All Oversouls were individual, and related to their personalities in their own fashion. He *was* adventurous, and he'd set himself and his personalities some great challenges; but the truth was, he didn't want to get *too* involved. Worse, he was beginning to suspect that his personalities were setting *him* some challenges too.

Like right now. This full alliance with flesh and blood was startling; pleasant and unpleasant, and it was growing more unpleasant each minute. He felt . . . clotted, thickened, caught in a rich, dizzy gestalt of interaction. That was enough of that!

Seven roused himself. But nothing happened. His consciousness was intact, whole, itself, yet it was somehow dispersed throughout Ma-ah's body, stuck in the cells and wiggly organs, locked in labyrinthine tangled chambers of bone and blood.

The body's left shoulder was cold. *That's* what cold was. He knew the meaning of the word, but the feeling of draft, of empty wind blowing on exposed flesh, this was something new. Seven felt the tiny hairs on the arm raise, arch, stiffen. They stood up so taut and straight that it seemed they'd pull right out of the flesh. Ma-ah turned over suddenly in her sleep, shoving the shoulder beneath her. The hairs instantly softened.

Seven groaned. Ma-ah's eyes were closed, and he didn't seem able to manufacture any vision of his own, or do anything for that matter, but experience reality through her body. "Cyprus, this is too much," he called mentally, but there was no answer. He shivered, or Ma-ah did. He wanted to turn the wind down as he'd done before, but now he was imprisoned in Ma-ah and at the wind's mercy as she'd been, (and *was*)! "You could at least turn the wind down," he moaned to Cyprus, but again there was no response.

His first day was incredible. He experienced morning, noon, and night in sequence, through the body's senses as Ma-ah did. No more mixing and matching of times and seasons. He saw the world from her viewpoint. That is, he saw only what she saw, though he could interpret events in his own way. He'd never felt so limited. He couldn't get out of Ma-ah's day, no matter how he tried.

By late afternoon it was already growing dark. Again the wind began rising. A low moon appeared on the horizon. Ma-ah and Rampa finished eating some particularly bitter roots that they'd gathered during the day. The remainder they strapped about their waists with a rope made of tough weeds. Looking through Ma-ah's eyes, Seven realized that they were too far away from the cave to make it back by nightfall, and the cliffs here rose straight and smooth-faced, offering no chance of shelter. The body was very cold. The hides rubbed against the skin with irritating regularity, and the hide moccasins were badly worn. The feet, Seven realized, were losing all feeling.

So far the body sensations had taken all of Seven's attention. He'd never handled such a barrage of constantly applied stimuli without being able to shut it off at will. He heard what Ma-ah said to Rampa, but he was so engrossed in the tongue's feelings and the sensations involved in speech — the rush of air through the throat — that he ignored the conversation itself.

Didn't she know the feet were near-frozen? Didn't she know that the body needed help?

Then, as if in answer to his questions, Ma-ah's emotions avalanched upon his consciousness, only they snuffed *his* out. He could feel his own awareness disappear beneath sudden fear, anger — the words and feelings instantly translated. "It's Rampa's fault. I shouldn't have listened to him. I knew we went too far. My feet! and *he's* limping."

The emotions immediately transformed the body. The shoulders slumped, the mouth drooped. The blood was called to too many places at once. The belly swelled; gas collected. Seven felt himself crushed, threatened to extinction. ("Scared silly," Cyprus would say, later.)

But he roused himself, pulled himself up from the maze of Ma-ahness. He knew something important. What was it? Desperately he tried to make a small point of silence, a framework to hold him above all that tumult. He knew what to do and where to go, if only he could make himself remember. The confusion of body noises, activity, and emotions was still there. But Seven hung his consciousness above it all somewhere, like a spider in the rafters of a high ceiling, and brooded.

Ma-ah trudged on. Seven distinguished her voice now from the other jungles of vowels, syllables, gurgles, and body sounds, keeping track of what activity was happening inside her, and what originated from without. Rampa's voice, coming from the outside, definitely affected the inside of Ma-ah's body, though. Whenever Rampa spoke, a variety of mixed responses were aroused in Ma-ah's consciousness, and each of these had instant physical repercussions. Her emotions rose and fell in such staggered rhythm that for a moment Seven confused it with the rise and fall the thighs made in walking.

But he managed to cling to the precarious nest of silence he'd made, and he concentrated as hard as he could. Unfamiliar webs of energy grew from his alertness. He could feel them. They went stretching out into the night, searching. Finally they pointed clearly to the southeast. But why? What did they mean? Seven only knew that he must follow them.

Their body fell down. Again, without knowing how he did it, Seven picked the body up and started it walking once more. All the while, he kept concentrating. What was it he knew and had forgotten?

The webs of light moved again. They converged on one particular cliff not too far away. And suddenly the rock became transparent to Seven. Within it he glimpsed light, distance, and activity. Seven grappled with the problem. He knew he had to get Rampa and Ma-ah over to that cliff.

He tried to signal her mentally. "Ma-ah, Ma-ah. This way." Nothing. She kept trudging along, half-crying with frustration and cold. Seven's own sense of futility was almost more than he could bear; he was afraid he'd fall back into the tumult of her body and emotions again. Fighting for control, he felt his separate consciousness slipping, and as he lost his hard-won isolation, he was Ma-ah.

"Oh, we've got to get to that cliff," she thought frantically. She signaled Rampa. She'd been acting so strangely all day that Rampa nodded half out of sheer exhaustion, and half in surprise that she seemed so sure of herself. Ma-ah clenched her teeth in determination. At the same time, she wondered why the cliff was so important, and how she knew that they must reach it.

Both of them just slumped against the rock when they got there. Ma-ah cried with exasperation. Whatever she'd had in mind, the cliff was smooth, unbroken. Her disappointment smothered her. She was too tired to go on. Her thoughts grew hazy. And Seven found his own consciousness once more suspended somewhere within Ma-ah, but apart. He experimented cautiously, stood the body up, opened its eyes, and felt the cliff walls with its hands. For this, in his predicament anyhow, he needed the hands' sensitivity.

But Ma-ah's fingers found the spot that Seven was seeking, and the door that he'd somehow known was there opened. Seven pulled the body in. He couldn't work Rampa's body from the inside, and Rampa didn't seem able to work it much himself. Worse, Seven knew that the door would close automatically in only a few seconds. And his own energy was fluctuating. One instant everything was brilliantly clear. The next, his awareness dimmed.

Seven cried out, "Rampa!" but the words came out of Ma-ah's lips, in her voice. Rampa raised his head and half rose, dragging himself over to her. As soon as he was inside, the door closed.

From that higher point of awareness Seven thought smugly, "I should get an A on *that* part of the examination." Then, confused, he wondered what he meant.

~ *Chapter Four* ~

The Descent of Proteus

*P*roteus had been aware of his emotional pull toward the Earth for as long as he could remember. It was shared by practically no one. None of his school friends showed the slightest interest. During the long afternoons when they sat in their separate living areas for television classes, and when they chatted back and forth via video during discussion periods, Earth was hardly ever mentioned.

They did talk about going outside when school was over and the sets turned off, but none of them seemed to realize that outside wasn't really outside. Of course, the plastic trees were replicas of real ones, and the shade they provided was real enough. But the steadily illuminated inner sky beneath the dome was never that bright; shade wasn't needed that badly. It was just for effect. No birds flew through the branches either, and no matter how well cared for the trees were, they always looked artificial to him. It seemed sometimes as if he knew better, that in some forgotten past he'd known real trees and would never be satisfied with fake ones. Which was impossible, of course.

The floating cities were held in place by atomically powered motors that automatically compensated for any drift relative to particular designated points on Earth. No one alive remembered the time when people lived on Earth in any numbers. And there had never been real trees in the domed city complexes. But despite this, he dreamed frequently of Earth as it used to be. He felt angry on its behalf. They'd simply abandoned it, given it up. He began devouring the microfilms that were available from the vast video library. Often he sat up late at night, secretly, watching the films until morning.

His excitement grew with his knowledge. There were various outposts on Earth: archeological sites and diggings, several scientific installations, and, he suspected, a few back-to-nature communities that somehow eluded satellite surveillance. He couldn't be sure of this, he told himself for the hundredth time, but it was a possibility.

He began to gather supplies weeks in advance of his plan. His mother had an administrative position, coming home only a few weekends in a six-month period. So hiding his intent from her was no problem. Maintaining secrecy in the face of his father's almost constant presence was something else again. Mithias was a group father, though, keeping track of some thirty boys and girls on closed-circuit television, overseeing their studies and scheduled activities. Seeing his father so engaged always made Proteus angry: Why couldn't classes be held in one big school nodule as they had in ages past?

This afternoon, though, every thought but one fled from Proteus's concern. Each Tuesday he and his friend, Grek, went hiking, an activity favored by almost everyone, to ensure sufficient muscular and motor development. This Tuesday would be different though, from any other. Proteus thought that Grek would sense his excitement the minute they met, no matter how he tried to hide it. But Grek just walked beside him, talking as usual about everyday events.

Everything Proteus did or said himself seemed unnatural and suspicious to him. He kept throwing sideways glances at Grek, sure that he'd somehow given himself away, but Grek obviously saw nothing different about the day or about Proteus. They'd taken their lunch as usual. Out of sheer nervousness, Proteus suggested that they see which of the two of them could eat the quickest.

So they went down the plastic streets, whooping and laughing, popping the lunch pills (L.P.'s) in their mouths as fast as possible. They each had two protein-basics (P.B.'s), two carbohydrate-simples (C.S.'s), and an amino acid supplement (A.A.S.). Proteus let Grek win, because he felt guilty about hiding his plans from him, and he was feeling guiltier each minute.

The game had been foolish, too, he thought. It would be the last time he'd gobble his L.P.'s so nonchalantly, so sure of a constant supply. Had he stashed away enough of them? He was sure that he had. Still. . . .

"You sure are quiet," Grek said.

"Oh, it's the same old thing," Proteus said. "Walking down these streets depresses me, though I know it shouldn't. And I keep wishing boys were given the same training that girls are, taken into the heart of business and politics at a young age, so they can see how the world works. If we were girls we'd be studying seriously at our age, not just passively watching our fathers manage the living nodules or learning unimportant, mundane skills—" Actually, Proteus was surprised at the normal sound of dissatisfaction in his voice, because he was only talking for something to say. But he wasn't concerned with problems like that any more. Not him.

A few boys went by on aero-skis. A man sat out on the porch of a nodule, his face expressionless as they passed. "See?" Proteus said. "He looks as artificial as the trees. Well, not really. My father knows him. He's got as much responsibility as any man around here, but it just isn't enough. He manages rain regulation, but it's all computerized anyway—"

"Oh, don't start on that stuff again," Grek said. "My father says you'll end up in real trouble. You're so damn dissatisfied all the time."

This sent Proteus into a laughing fit. "If you only knew—" he said. "I mean, how funny that is! What kind of trouble can you get into around here?"

"I don't know," Grek said, uneasily.

"That's it. None," Proteus went on. His talk was supposed to keep Grek occupied while he went over his own last-minute plans. As the time approached for him to make his move, he was getting more and more nervous. Soon Grek would suggest that they return. As usual they'd be expected home before supper, and they'd been walking about two hours. It was near 6 P.M. Would he miss his father? Grek? Wasn't there something he could say to Grek without giving the whole thing away? Something that Grek could remember afterward?

"Grek . . . we're friends, aren't we? Look, I like you a lot—"

Grek stopped and stared at him. "What did you need to say that for? Sure we're friends—"

"I don't know." Proteus felt like laughing, like crying. He felt secretive, yet like shouting his secret aloud where everyone could hear it.

He caught himself—he needed the two-hour headstart. He had to get to the ramp that he'd staked out. He said, nonchalantly, "Let's go back a different way."

He paused and looked around as if trying to make up his mind which way to take. Actually, he was taking a long last look at the neighborhood in which he'd lived as long as he remembered. The living nodules stretched as far as he could see. Each complex was a duplication of ancient Earth conditions, as perfect as Art and Science could make it. Each city was done in the decor of a particular Earth period. This one was nineteenth-century America. He lived in the Ohio block.

"We always go home the way we came," Grek said.

"I know, but the lunch race gave me an idea. Let's each take a different route to my nodule and see who gets there first. I'll go a block to the left and you go a block to the right. It's just an idea. If you don't want to—" Proteus broke off. He knew Grek would agree. Any kind of challenge was always fun.

"All right. Ready, set, go!" Grek shouted. He turned around without looking back, and began to run as fast as he could to the right. Shocked, Proteus just stood there for a moment. He hadn't realized that Grek would take off so quickly or that there wouldn't be time to make some gesture, some veiled good-by. Grek disappeared around the corner. Proteus began to run himself, going faster and faster now, stopping only when he had to catch his breath.

The slightly springy material of the sidewalk gave just a trifle with each step, so that he felt an added sense of acceleration, as if he was running so quickly that he could just take off above the treetops. His feet were strangely cold, although the air was maintained at a constant 73.2, and his heart was pounding when he finally came out onto the five-acre area of artificial trees and fields that surrounded the city complex.

Benches were neatly placed around the landscape, each with one bush beside it and a potful of simulated flowers. Now at suppertime the area was vacant. Some of the flowers were growing brittle. Scientists were working on a new material that might actually reproduce itself, or at least repair itself, maintaining a more natural look. Proteus wondered if he'd ever come back, and if he did, whether or not the new plastic "life" would replace the old.

A week ago he'd carefully cut out a whole chunk of "grass" and placed his survival kit and supplies beneath. Now he retrieved them hurriedly. It would be dark at seven, when the day lights automatically lowered to minimum illumination. A panicky feeling flickered behind his forehead. Ignoring it, he inflated his aero-skis, put his survival kit over his back, and glided through the quiet air. The skis worked by reacting against the air beneath them. His were a boy's set, allowing only an elevation of six feet; but they could go fast enough.

He was too much in a rush now to enjoy sky-skiing as he usually did, but his love of the sport paid off. He was an expert at riding the soft eddies of regulated air that rose and fell. And the skis could go almost thirty miles an hour. The light began to dim to early twilight. It would last for forty-five minutes. He wasn't nearly as obvious as he would have been in maximum daylight, and if anyone saw him he'd just look like any boy, sky-skiing—if you didn't happen to notice his direction. Because now he was heading away from the complex.

In another half-hour he was at his destination. He floated down, deflated the skis, and tied them around his waist just as the inner sky turned to night light. The ramp entrance had taken him months to discover. Now it was only ten minutes away. No one came to this area except maintenance crews. Here, no effort had been made to decorate; a series of gray sprawling plastoid buildings stood silently. He reached the ramp entrance. None of them were guarded; no one but the women crews used them to begin with.

Proteus stood, uncertain. Soon Grek would wonder what had happened to him. His father would be worried. Should he go back while he could? Was he doing the right thing? His eyes stung. Boys rarely even competed in the examination for Historical Training, since it was a woman's field—his father said they rewrote history—but he'd tried and flunked. If they'd taken him, he probably never would have decided to strike out on his own; to discover Earth on his own. He would have been content with records.

Remembering, his resolve came back with a warm rush. The grating was beneath him. He pulled it up easily—it was made for womens' lighter hands—and closed it from inside. Quietly he began to descend the dimly lighted ladderlike stairs.

His steps echoed through the aluminum tunnel. His scalp prickled and his ears rang. Suppose, just suppose, that he couldn't get out at the lower end, and someone locked the upper entrance? "You're just acting like a scared kid," he told himself scornfully. He knew that the ramps only extended a few hundred feet, yet it seemed that the steps would never end.

There were other ramps, but many were used to transport scientific supplies and he didn't know their schedules. That's why he'd chosen a utility ramp, because they were visited only several times a year for inspection purposes. But now it occurred to him that if anything happened and he couldn't get out, it would be a long time until he was found. Not that he didn't have enough supplies, he told himself quickly, because he did. He was just nervous because he couldn't have known ahead of time how he'd feel.

The descent *was* oddly distasteful. He felt like one of the archaic looking insects he'd seen in microfilms, creeping inside the huge ramp that descended from the underside of the city. Maybe it was just the knowledge that each step took him nearer the ramp's end that bothered him, he thought.

Twice he stopped to rest, gripping the thin railing with both hands and slipping his survival pack down on the stairs. At the same time he kept thinking of his father, who must know of his disappearance by now — he was probably questioning Grek at this very moment.

To show himself that he didn't really care, he started to run down the stairs, the echo of his steps growing even louder. Then the steps ended. A small door read: "Outlets — Surface." It opened automatically at his touch and closed behind him. A narrow hall lined with machinery ended with a second door.

Proteus gulped. If he was right, he should be in one of the infrequently used atomic-powered skylevators on the underside of the floating city, with nothing between him and Earth but seven miles of empty space! He looked around at the small globular room in which he stood. He'd made it — the dials on the wall console told him he was in a skylevator. But suppose he couldn't run it?

Suddenly a whirring noise began; an odd droning. Proteus held his breath. His entrance must have activated the mechanism. Even now his weight and dimensions were probably being fed into the minicomputers in charge of descent. A red light flashed on. At the same time, three signs glowed into life: AUTOMATIC DROP, PAUSE FOR INSTRUCTIONS, and HOLD ON WAIT.

The room itself began to vibrate softly. Proteus gulped again, pressed the button marked AUTOMATIC DROP, and closed his eyes as tightly as he could. His stomach lurched. His head snapped back. The skylevator dropped out of its nest beneath the city, and began its descent.

Proteus' eyes flew open. Inside, the lights dimmed. A dial flashed: 35,000 ft. The sight of it almost made him sick as he realized that plans were one thing, and their realization was something quite different. Here he was, 35,000 feet up in space, alone, falling steadily away from the only world he knew. One side of the skylevator was a transparent window. He looked out, hardly believing what he saw.

Bright emptiness stretched all around him, an endless blue sky through which he was descending. Then he looked down — in terror — for below there were mountains of black-gray clouds, heavy and threatening, like an ever-moving uneven floor upon which the skylevator must surely crash. Despairingly he looked up, to see the dark undersides of the city disappearing as he plunged further down. Could he make the skylevator reverse itself in mid-air? He eyed the dials. No, he thought, even with the little he knew, he was sure that reversal was impossible.

Now the dial read: 30,000 ft. He looked down again, astonished, for as he approached the clouds, holes appeared in them as if by magic. He'd never seen clouds before—not natural ones—only the three tamed ones that went past with each fifteen-minute rain, but he knew about them academically. No film or account could begin to describe what they were really like, though, and involuntarily he shouted out with wonder as the skylevator dropped through one of the cloud-holes. He gasped—the clouds gave way, as if on purpose. The clouds *knew*. They're alive, he thought, like sky creatures. It seemed to him that they were rushing from all over the open sky, to watch.

Proteus stood, hands pressed against the window; transfixed. There were layers and layers of clouds. Again he thought of sky creatures, grazing. What did they think as they watched him plunge past? Then, suddenly, they thinned out, moved away, *rushed* away as if frightened. Once more he cried out involuntarily as the curve of the Earth appeared, with the sun at one rim, splashing the most incredible rays of light that he'd ever seen or imagined. He's seen microfilms of sunsets but they never even hinted at this shimmering vitality.

He eyed the dial quickly and looked out again, fascinated. 20,000 feet. The ground—the *surface* of Earth suddenly emerged. Giant patches of color were visible, some dark, almost blue-black—real shadows cast by the real sun!—some so brilliant that he could hardly look at them. His excitement grew as the skylevator dropped further down. The mountains were like gigantic teeth rising out of an open mouth. He was going to land in a perfectly flat area, the floor of the "mouth." He held his breath as the skylevator fell into the shadows, below the horizon, and the ground came rushing up.

Motion stopped. The skylevator landed. The door—impossibly—opened. A light blinked on: WAITING FOR INSTRUCTIONS. Two dials shone, one saying, KEEP ON HOLD, and the other, AUTOMATIC RETURN. Proteus bit his lips. If only he dared set the control on HOLD, just in case. How good to know he could get back, if he wanted to. Once the skylevator was gone, his connections with home were broken. But no, the skylevator mustn't be missed. His hand trembled, but he pushed the RETURN button. Then he ran out as fast as he could, afraid that the vehicle might take off while he was still inside. He rushed out onto the small ramp, down the steps, and took his first step upon the ground.

As he stood there, the skylevator shuddered and four small rockets fired, sending their hungry flames outward. The skylevator lifted, wobbled slightly, and then slowly and surely began its steady rise. He felt as if he were losing—everything. "Good-by," he shouted. Then, resolutely, he turned away.

At first glance, the scene before him was terrifying. Instinctively Proteus looked up, but no plastic dome covered the real harsh sky. Now that it was all above him, on *top* of him, not around him, it made him uneasy. The late sunset blazed across the rocky plains that reached into the distance where they were finally ringed by high hills. The sun's brilliance hurt his eyes, but more than this, he was unprepared for the spectacular reaches of open space in which he suddenly felt very small and vulnerable. He shivered. He'd never felt so unprotected in his life.

He looked up again, this time in the opposite direction. The gobular skylevator was rising, growing smaller and dearer each minute, looking now like a balloon. Soon he wouldn't be able to see it at all. Proteus watched, thinking of the floating city complex to which it would return. He sighed, realizing how snugly he had been held within that plastic bauble. Now he almost yearned for the skylevator's sheltering walls.

Already his skin prickled. The air was wild here, not controlled and even. Surprisingly soft, still it pushed against his face, thrust itself all around him, pushed him, though gently. It felt alive. But then so did the ground, which seemed to be a litter of sand granules and stones and small weeds. He was so surprised to be walking on an uneven surface that once he stopped dead still, almost afraid to go on. He wobbled when he walked. The stones hurt his feet, and he realized that in no time at all his shoes would be a complete loss. The sun fell a few notches in the sky.

How many other human beings were on the Earth? Suddenly he felt brave, heroic, caught up in a rush of exaltation. Once his mother had taken him on a business trip to the Moon with her, but the Moon was civilized and quite mundane in the domed areas. Earth was different. It was primitive, real. In a strange manner, he felt that he'd come home.

His aero-skis would save his shoes and feet until he got used to walking on the surface. He inflated them, and took off, whizzing just above the rocks and stones. But at once he was in trouble. Too late he realized that the skis had been developed for the comparatively even air currents inside the complexes. It was impossible to glide smoothly in this bumpy, undisciplined air.

Trying to navigate, he looked down beneath him. So this was Section 7! The entire Earth's surface was designated by symbols now, though archeologists and historians could rattle off the old names with ease. Still, he wished he knew the name for his landing place. It seemed sad not to know.

He searched his mind, but all he could remember was the name Cyprus, which referred to an island, he thought, not a large body of land. Still a name was a name, and better than none. His skis wobbled in a sudden eddy of air, but already he could tell that he was beginning to handle himself in the new air currents. He glided almost easily over a good-sized air-hill, and yelled down at the land, "I name you Cyprus."

Just then he realized that the sun's rays were disappearing. While he didn't need a sheltered spot to put up his small living nodule, the thought of staying out in the open area frightened him. Hopefully he eyed the hills—if only he could reach them before night came—the real night—without the city's gentle illumination. He tried not to think of the ancient Earth night as he'd read of it in old records. For the first time he wondered how far the hills were in actual miles from—well, from Cyprus.

~ *Chapter Five* ~

Oversoul Seven's Mini-Vacation

*O*versoul Seven kept making platforms to hold himself above the well of Ma-ah's experience, only to topple down into it again. His apartness from her was slipping, and in those moments of his own lucidity he thought that this wasn't fair at all. Cyprus was going too far. This part of the examination was too difficult for his stage of development. He'd fail miserably, if he didn't end up losing himself in Ma-ah completely, if that was possible.

The only time he managed to reassert himself was when he was called on consciously or unconsciously by one of his other personalities, or when Ma-ah needed him in some direct manner. For example, he was lost within Ma-ah, or thought he was, when suddenly he was aware of Proteus' descent to Earth. Quick, clear images came to him as Proteus landed. Once he saw the entire landscape from the tip of one of Proteus' skis. What on Earth was *he* up to? Seven wondered irritably.

And what was happening to Josef and Lydia while he was trapped (what else could you call it?) inside Ma-ah's body? Ma-ah, it seemed, needed his help at every turn. When he *was* Ma-ah, losing his independence, then he felt her own fear and insecurity, unmitigated, without the benefit of his own superior knowledge. And her fear threatened to devour him. He had to get *her* above it, he realized suddenly. Only her release would free them both.

Actually, she was pretty aggressive and independent on her own, except when her fear made her forget everything she knew. As it had yesterday — was it yesterday? — when they'd been found. The men who captured them were different in appearance from any people that Ma-ah or Rampa had ever seen, and it was this that frightened them so completely.

Ma-ah cried out as they were led down the hall beneath torches that were set in the wall niches. She and Rampa were terrified of fire, Seven discovered. Both of them cowered at the fire itself, and at the dark shadows that leaped up the rocky gray walls. Their captors — or rescuers? — were approximately nine feet tall, as Lydia would have measured them, to Ma-ah's five-foot-three and Rampa's five-eight. Besides this, the men wore robes dyed with brilliant colors, and obviously not made of hides.

Seven knew that he had some information concerning these people, but Ma-ah's emotions kept blocking out his own awareness. In the cave now, Ma-ah stared at the wall. She and Rampa were chattering, wondering whether or when they would be freed. They'd just finished eating the last of the roots they'd gathered and tied about their waists.

A torch burned high above them. The top of the room was open in the center. The two of them were less frightened now. They'd been left alone for hours. The cave's door refused to budge, but otherwise they were not restrained in any way. Oversoul Seven let his own consciousness climb up again wearily. He peered through Ma-ah's eyes, but as he did so, images appeared on the cave wall. They were apparent to him, but not to Ma-ah, who paid no attention. Briefly he thought that this was strange, since they were, after all *her* eyes he was looking through. The pictures were milky and opaque at first, then they turned clear, soft, vivid. To Seven, but not to Ma-ah, the wall disappeared as if it did not exist.

Mentally, to no one in particular, Lydia had just called for help. The trailer wall was blurring before her eyes, and she knew what that meant. It was one of those trailer-camper trucks. Lawrence was driving. She'd been reading at the small table that was hinged to the half-wall behind the driver's seat. One slim bony hand still rested on the book. Now it trembled suddenly, without warning.

Another . . . petit stroke. Quickly she leaned back while she still could, anchoring herself so that she wouldn't fall off the chair. And she wouldn't call Lawrence. She'd determined not to. Let him drive on, unknowing. The edges of her vision were blurring faster now. Something within her was giving way. She braced herself for the confusion, maybe for unconsciousness. . . .

Would Lawrence have the guts to give her the pills? You promised, she thought wildly. I won't die senile . . . in a home, locked up. Her eyes flew to the small high cabinet where the pills were kept. If she didn't come out of it . . . right . . . if her mind was . . . gone . . . if she couldn't keep up, Lawrence knew what to do. Looking at the cabinet was the last thing she remembered.

As usual when she came out of "it" she didn't know what had happened. Lawrence was still driving, and listening to the radio. Then she hadn't called out, or he hadn't heard if she had. The book was still beside her. She felt dizzy, that was all. She . . . but who was she? Panic splashed over the frightened surfaces of her mind. How could she forget? How could the body forget its name? The body's name? Did the body have a name? Oh Lord. She closed her eyes, feeling as if tiny islands of knowledge were crumbling away, falling into endless oceans of oblivion.

So quickly that he hardly realized what he was doing, Oversoul Seven leapt from Ma-ah to Lydia's body. With all-knowing finesse he quickened her blood, thinned it, gave orders to the body consciousness to increase circulation, filled in with the commands necessary. "Count, Lydia. Remember. Remember. Count," he directed.

She suddenly recalled a trick that sometimes worked. Quickly she found the name for the first number, one. She saw it in her mind and concentrated on it visually. Then two. Then three, continuing in order until finally the panic cleared and her own name, Lydia, floated back to her between fifteen and sixteen.

Oversoul Seven returned, again without knowing how he did so, to Ma-ah. He thought triumphantly: he wasn't trapped inside Ma-ah for good, then. He'd left, if only momentarily. Still, his distance from his personalities was vanishing. He must have agreed. No experience was ever thrust upon a soul—or a personality, for that matter. But when had he agreed? And what else had he agreed to? Seven felt petulant. Already Ma-ah was getting restless again. What was she so upset for? Lydia could have lost her life right then—and he knew she wasn't ready. The thought intrigued him. If she wasn't ready, she wouldn't lose it, of course.

Actually, Lydia was thinking the same thing. Here she was. The attack was over. She was alive, and as far as she could tell, she was still sane enough. She forced herself to concentrate on Lawrence, and away from herself. How close he was, yet how far away! She watched the back of his head . . . like a big bleached walnut, she thought, the brown-white hair so alive, bristly; the cords on the back of his neck so responsive. Oh, the ease with which his neck shifted as he watched the road!

"You're awfully quiet back there," Lawrence called cheerfully.

"Am I?" Her first spoken words after the attack were so bright, her voice so crystal clear and lovely, and sane and normal, that she wanted to shout

out with joy. Oh God, how great life . . . consciousness . . . was! "It's such a great day. A shame to read and not pay attention," she said. "So I've been looking out the window."

"We'll stop soon, for supper," he said.

"Mmm." She opened her pocketbook and looked into the compact mirror. Her face was . . . intact. How odd. The eyes, flecked with orange, looked clear, alert, knowing, sardonic as usual. The face wasn't even terribly wrinkled for seventy-three — she was too thin to get wrinkled, she supposed; the mouth small, drawn down at the corners now though; the thick white bubble of hair still vigorous.

Yet what happened in those . . . what? Three minutes? Not enough blood to the brain, as the doctor described it. And unnoticed the small cells die, one by one, blinking off. Taking memory and desire with them. What events had disappeared that she would no longer recall? What fine discriminations necessary to ordinary life had vanished? How many did you have to lose before it showed? Pity the poor body, the poor mind, so thoughtlessly losing its precious cargo.

"Shit!" she snapped to herself. That kind of thinking was worse than, well, maybe even a stroke itself. It bled the will dry. Live in the moment. She looked out, filling her mind with the view. It was autumn. Why had fall always made her feel exhilarated? Yet it did.

They passed brown-gray lawns and others that were deep in orange fallen leaves, and soon they were driving through a small town. There were all the houses, she thought; and each was secret and mysterious, containing within dimensions of human experience that could never be put into words. Would words finally desert her too? They would, she supposed. Yet here she was, seventy-three, traveling through these towns and villages in this today.

Suddenly she laughed. All at once it seemed that the houses and trees were all artificial in some way she couldn't put her finger on; that the leaves would somehow be . . . recycled and used again. And no one would know the difference except maybe a very few; children, perhaps. Yet a great nostalgia filled her at the same time, as if the whole town had already gone beyond recall, or as if she had left it in some way she couldn't understand.

Simultaneously a sheer rush of love for the real physical world filled her. This was a real Earth, after all. And she was still in it, still rational and alive in it. She felt exultant. "These lovely Ohio towns," she said. . . .

"It's Proteus' memory of the Ohio block and its artificial foliage that just struck Lydia, in bleed-through fashion. And it's Proteus' fresh astonishment with the natural Earth that's reviving her spirits right now," Cyprus said to Oversoul Seven. "Proteus, in the twenty-third century, is erecting his living nodule at the same time that Lydia and Lawrence hook up their small tent to the camper—in the twentieth century. Do you understand? There are points of association brought into activity—"

Seven blinked. This conversation with Cyprus had obviously been going on for some time, and he had only now become aware of it. "Of course. It's obvious," he said, desperately trying to cover up.

"But you so often overlook the details," Cyprus said. "When you help one personality, you help all the others. Unconsciously, each feels the effects. For that matter, each personality helps the other, and when you're in contact with one, you're also in communication with each of them—"

"But who helps *me?*" Seven asked petulantly. "I've been pelted around like a volleyball—"

"A most apt Earth description," Cyprus said, smiling. "But what makes you think you haven't been helped?"

"How long have we been talking like this?" Seven asked, ignoring the question.

"In whose terms?"

"In *any* terms," Seven said. "You're just dancing rings around me. And you think it's funny. Ma-ah and Lydia are in real trouble; and maybe Proteus, who knows? And I get stuck inside Ma-ah, just trapped there except for now—and only let out when somebody needs me. It's not at all fair, examination or not."

"You make your own reality," Cyprus reminded him, gently. "We all do. Each consciousness does. So, dear Seven, try to remember what you've forgotten. Or better still, just take it for granted that you really know what you're doing, and go on from there."

"Take what for granted?" Seven asked. "There you go again."

"Your . . . predicament."

"Ma-ah's in a predicament. And Lydia. And Proteus. I'm not, except for this ridiculous examination."

Cyprus could no longer contain her amusement. She sighed. "Oh, Seven, you'll have to go back to Ma-ah for a while. Outside of your present context of operations, I'm sure you'll agree with me. You still don't understand."

"But I want to know what's happening to Josef," Seven objected. "And I don't want to go back inside Ma-ah. You have no idea how terribly confining that is, and I keep getting lost in her till I think I'll never get out. Couldn't we take a break? A recess? And look in on Josef?" Oversoul Seven had adapted the fourteen-year-old image again. He found it most effective in dealing with Cyprus.

She smiled and said, "All right. But remember, this is to be a very brief vacation. Think of Josef's painting."

The landscape of the farm and grounds was on the easel. Josef was in the process of applying a series of transparent glazes to it. Bianka, the eighteen-year-old Hosentauf daughter, sat on the messed bed, watching. (As he saw her, Seven moaned.) Josef was obviously showing off, standing with strong thighs apart, leaning backward, staring at the painting with his heavy brows lowered dramatically—and very conscious of Bianka's admiring glances.

"You better get out of here," he said. "If anyone catches you in my room, I'll really be thrown out on my ear—or ass."

She blushed, stood up, and wiggled over to him, teasingly. She still hadn't retied her bodice so that, looking down, Josef saw her bare breasts. She grinned, shamelessly, he thought; flipped one breast out of the bodice at him, and ran, laughing, about the room.

"They'll hear you. Hush. Shut up—" he yelled.

"They aren't home yet and you know it. Worried?" She giggled breathlessly, her brown eyes alight with excitement.

"Well, your youngest brother is. You can't bribe him to leave us alone forever. What if he tells?"

"La la, that's your concern," she laughed. "I'll just lie about the whole thing."

"Well, so will I! So will I!" he shouted. He never knew how to handle her when she got in this kind of mood, and she knew it. "Ah, the hell with it!" he yelled, hopelessly. He grabbed her, threw her on the bed, and grinned while she ripped his clothes off. Again.

Seven was very quiet. He and Cyprus had merged with the landscape painting, peering through it, out into the room. "Well, he's certainly having a good time," Seven said finally.

"I thought that's why you liked him so much, because he *did* enjoy himself," Cyprus answered.

"Well . . . he *is*, isn't he? There's something in all of this that I don't like," Seven said doubtfully. In the meantime he and Cyprus discreetly blocked out the scene so as not to invade Josef's privacy in such a personal moment. They simply stayed in the landscape, while putting a mental shield between themselves and the room.

When Seven peeked back out, the girl was gone. A disheveled Josef sat unhappily on the bed, muttering to himself. He'd lost most of the good daylight painting hours, and now he was so disgusted with himself that he didn't feel like working. And if he didn't work, he'd just feel worse. More, as he eyed the painting, he had the uneasy suspicion that something was wrong. For one thing, the glazes didn't look nearly as clear and glowing as they could. There was a suggestion of murkiness creeping into the color. He went over to the easel and stood glowering at the painting.

Three days ago, the painting had looked great to him. This morning it had looked great. Now he had projected all of his dissatisfaction with himself into the landscape. Flaws he hadn't noticed earlier became readily apparent. Had he grayed his colors down too much? Had he put on the top glaze before the one beneath was dry? Or was the problem in the dry pigment itself as he mixed it with the oil?

He almost snarled. The thing was ruined. Ruined beyond repair. His great inspiration, the best in his life — and he'd messed it up. To hell with it; he'd never be a good painter. To hell with Bianka and her damned family and the three lousy meals a day they gave him. He even had to eat with the farmhands.

It was Bianka's fault for tempting him to begin with, keeping his mind from his work. In a rage he shouted and kicked the bedside chair across the room. Then, to Oversoul Seven's utter disbelief, he grabbed the landscape and sent it flying to the floor with sudden fury.

At first Seven thought that the landscape had come to life in some mysterious fashion. What he saw before him *was* a landscape, but different, a three-dimensional one that stretched all around him. He looked around, trying to get his bearings.

Cyprus and Josef were gone. He was Ma-ah again. She stood gripping Rampa's hand. Before them were acres of green trees and flowering bushes, such as they'd never seen before. The entire area was ringed by immense sheer cliffs, obviously impossible to climb. They were in a secret valley. A group of robed people stood in a circle on a small grassy knoll, and Ma-ah and Rampa were being led toward them.

Seven felt himself falling headlong into Ma-ah's experience again. Yet oddly enough, descending into the body almost seemed like coming home.

∼ *Chapter Six* ∼

Josef's Second Dream

*J*osef felt alone, as if his soul had left him, or as if part of his soul had been in the painting that he'd just destroyed. He hadn't the heart to look at it again. One glimpse of the smeared topcoating of glaze had been enough. In portions, the paint had been gouged out right down to the bare canvas.

Memory of the painting's initial, almost blinding inspiration rose up to mock him. He hadn't lived up to it, of course. The one great inspiration of his life, and he'd ruined it in a fit of anger. Or had it been flawed beyond repair even before he destroyed it? Had he known all along that he'd never be able to paint the masterpiece that he saw so vividly in his mind?

Josef didn't like to examine his feelings. He just liked to give in to them, or paint them. Self-examination made him nervous. Yet these thoughts kept returning as he grappled with quite unpleasant practical considerations. He had to get out of there as quickly as possible. Jonathan would give him the beating of his life, and with the painting gone, he had nothing to bargain with. He could fight Jonathan if he had to—they were about the same size—but Jonathan would be self-righteous about it, furious, and he'd just be out to protect himself.

So it had come to this! Grumbling, he gathered his gear together, the dry pigments, jars of oil and varnish, brushes, three rolled canvases. Feeling sorrier for himself each minute, he stacked the stuff by the door and looked out the window at the snowy plains and low hills. There were occasional farmhouses where he could stop. If it was only summer, he thought, when he could do sketches at town festivals, flatter the ladies in the market-place — *then* there was no trouble finding a place to stay. But it was winter, and he'd spoiled his nest.

He flopped down on the bed, eyeing the bundle of belongings. Now he saw it all differently. He hadn't been kicked out yet. Why should he put himself out in the middle of winter? Maybe he could save himself. Maybe he could think up a good enough story. Maybe . . . Briefly the face of Avona Hosentauf came into his mind — she was particularly taken with the damned painting — her face when she saw it would be a study in rage.

But it was all too much. Josef fell into an exhausted sleep, tossing fitfully, expecting the Hosentauf force to be upon him at any moment. When he awakened it was past midnight, and the house was still. Hardly believing his good fortune, he got up quietly and opened the window. The Hosentaufs must have returned late and gone to bed, he thought. Holding his breath, grinning at his own craftiness, Josef threw his gear out the window, well into the snow. He didn't dare use the stairs — they creaked. Instead he went to the other window and cautiously dropped down the few feet to the shed roof.

It was below zero, but now the cold air was exciting and added to his sudden mood of exuberance. As he leaped to the ground, he thought of Hosentauf's impotent rage when they found him gone, the painting ruined. With good luck they'd never discover his escape until morning, giving him at least a good head start. And why should they follow him? They'd just yell and sputter instead. They knew he had no way of paying them back for his room and board, even if they did take all the trouble to track him down.

He attached his skis, threw his knapsack over his shoulders and started off. At first it was pleasant in all that quiet night snow, but he'd forgotten how heavy his gear was; and after being inside all winter, the unaccustomed cold began to annoy him, then to upset him, until finally it was all he could think about. He wasn't that good a skier, either. He felt bulkier than usual — which he was. He'd worn all his clothes — three sweaters, two pair of pants, and two sets of underwear — and now his body itched and sweated inside, while his face felt frozen to the bone. But it was worth it, he thought, trying to regain his earlier cheerfulness. The end of an era. Saved again.

They caught up with him near morning. He'd stopped to rest in the early dawn, when he saw the horse-driven sleigh approaching, and heard the stupid ringing of the little bells, and felt that awful hard lump in the pit of his stomach. They'd be on him in no time. There was no place to hide, and they'd seen him already. He could tell by the vicious intent set to

Jonathan's head and shoulders as he drove the sled. There was no mistaking that obstinate outline.

The Fates were after him, chasing him in the figures of Elgren and Jonathan, and the other two who sat behind — probably Elgren's brothers, Josef thought. To his own surprise he just felt transfixed, unable to move, or do anything but watch their approach. The sleigh drew ever closer, its gray outlines taking on definite shape, the red color getting brighter and brighter, more and more real. He felt as if the whole thing — sled, horses, and riders — rode from some nightmare place in his own mind, out here to pursue him. On the other hand, it seemed that they'd always chased him, the pursuit would never let up, and the moment would never end.

Why did they bother? he wondered, with a mild astonishment that didn't even begin to touch his panic. Revenge? Why else? But already the stocky figure of Jonathan leapt into life, jumped from the sled with his father right after, followed by the two others from the back seat. All at once they were at him. They had ropes which they threw about his body, pinning down his arms.

"AaaaaHhhhh," Jonathan kept shouting. "You brigand! Thief! Aaahhh — More rope. Tie him up good — "

The sight of the rope made Josef really crazy. He suddenly began kicking, yelling, biting. They threw him down and took his skis off and tossed him in the back of the sled. Elgren's brothers, both big, usually good-hearted men, were laughing now. They thought it was one big joke. Between them, all trussed-up, Josef glared. Jonathan was swearing steadily from the front seat, and his father, Elgren, kept grunting, "Yes, yes."

During the entire trip they amused themselves by pretending to consider the most gory of revenges, all the while assuring him that he needn't worry: his fate was already settled with a punishment most fitted to his crime. Josef pretended not to hear a word.

What did they really have in store for him? Josef closed his eyes and tried not to think about it. Did they know about him and Bianka? he wondered desperately. The suspense made him dizzier than the sled's motion, which unaccountably had now begun to bother him.

Finally the trip was over. Shouting triumphantly, they dragged him off the sled, up the steps, and into the kitchen where Bianka and her mother and the two smaller boys stood — pointing, giggling, in a great mood. They whisked him through, pushed him upstairs, and threw him in his room. Jonathan shoved him over to the bed.

"We've decided what to do with you, famous artist," Jonathan said. His round head bobbed. He wet his lips. His gray eyes sparkled. He put his hands on his stocky hips. "Haven't we, everybody?"

"Yes," came the shouts from outside the door where the rest of the family gathered, peeking in, from the top of the stairs.

"We are putting you in jail. It's too much trouble to take you to town and swear warrants. Good farmers like us can't take all that time. So this room is your jail—"

Nods and shouts all around. Josef squirmed underneath the ropes, and glowered.

"You're going to do us a painting, as you promised. And you don't get fed unless you do. Every day one of us will come up with some food, and if you aren't working on a painting that takes our fancy, well then you'll just get lighter and lighter and thinner and thinner."

Bianka poked her mother and laughed.

Elgren stepped to the front. "It's only fair. A bargain is a bargain. You don't leave this room, no matter how long it takes, until we get a decent painting. My wife, here, wants a painting of the farmhouse, just like it was. She had her heart set on it, and that's what she's going to get."

"I can't just copy one painting over," Josef yelled. "You can never get one painting just like another—"

"You better learn how, then," Avona said, coming forward, shaking her apron in his face. "Thought you got away with it, didn't you? You never had any intention of finishing that painting, and if poor Bianka hadn't felt ill last night and couldn't sleep, she never would have been up so late and looked out to see your tracks reaching out there in the snow—"

Bianka lowered her eyes. Josef could have killed her.

"And we're boarding up the windows to make it more like a real jail," Jonathan said. "Then you'll work harder to get out of here. When you've given us a picture we like for all the good food you ate, then we'll let you go your way."

"You just can't keep me a prisoner that way," Josef managed to say. "Why, it's . . . it's immoral. I won't be able to paint, all locked up. And I need light to begin with. You can't board up the windows." At first he was just relieved— he was alive, after all. But loneliness and isolation would be unbearable, he realized. They picked the one thing most likely to drive him out of his mind.

He'd escape somehow, he told himself, as he stared up at their flushed, triumphant faces.

But that afternoon, they boarded up the windows. There was no food that entire day or night, and he couldn't paint. They left lanterns, but he just sat there in the gloomy darkness without lighting them. He couldn't sleep. Finally he just paced the room . . . angrier and angrier . . . and banged on the door in the middle of the night. He'd drive them crazy with his noise at least. But no one paid the slightest attention.

He wore himself out, slamming his body against the door, shouting, throwing furniture. Disgusted, he realized that nothing would work. "They mean what they said," he said aloud, wonderingly. He hadn't really believed them. But a bargain *was* a bargain to Elgren and Jonathan. It was as simple as that. If he showed signs of real starvation, they'd probably just send the women to relatives so that his condition didn't weaken their resolve.

Prickles of panicky sweat broke out on his face, trickling into his mustache. He didn't even know if he could produce a decent painting now to begin with. Being forced to work would just make things worse. If he couldn't make *himself* work, how could anything else? He glowered at the boarded windows. Hosentauf really meant to lock him up for good, to starve him if necessary. He could hardly believe it, he thought again. He'd never hurt anyone in his life. To begin with, how had they taken him so seriously?

His thoughts wavered. Once he felt his teeth crunch down into an apple. With great gusto he bit into the crisp skin. It split with a popping sound. Cursing, he sat up and looked about the room which now had an ominous waiting air that made him pull the blankets up to his chin.

In the morning, Jonathan and Elgren came up together. They glanced about. "No work, no food," Jonathan said.

"The atmosphere isn't exactly inspiring," Josef yelled from the bed, but the two marched out without another word, locking the door behind them. "I'll die of starvation before I lift a brush to do a painting for you," Josef shouted. No one answered. There was no one to talk with. He drank the water they were big-hearted enough to leave in the pitcher, but he was getting dizzy from lack of food.

The next day he just lay on the bed, brooding, and watching the few shafts of light that fell through the crevices in the boarded windows. A twilight cast filled the room. He felt lethargic. He'd almost convinced himself that Bianka would certainly sneak up with some food for him, when he began to doze.

The next thing he knew, he was dreaming. Then the dream itself shuddered, split open. The air shimmered. He was staring at his double, who looked down at him, mustache bristling, eyes warm and oddly understanding. "What are you doing here?" Josef said. "You're another me? I'm dreaming again. One of me gets in enough trouble. I certainly don't need two —"

"I thought your own image would be reassuring," Oversoul Seven said.

"Reassuring! That's how little you know —" Josef shouted. He turned his head to the wall.

"All right. All right," Oversoul Seven said, hurt. He changed into the image of a wise old man. "Is this better? Turn around so you can see me," he said.

"Thank heaven. Now you're somebody I can trust," Josef said. "Where have you been? I haven't seen you in my dreams at all lately."

"I've been very busy," Seven said. "For that matter, I probably shouldn't even be here. But I always relate to you. More and more, you remind me of myself. Except that you get in such trouble all the time; and it's always needless. You could so easily avoid it. This time you've really done it. Hosentaufs won't let you out, either, unless you produce. You've roused their sense of virtue. They're going to teach you a lesson, even if you die of starvation —"

"Am I dreaming?"

"Yes and no. You're sleeping. I'm really here, if that's what you mean. But I'm not staying."

"You can't just go away and leave me," Josef pleaded. "I haven't had anyone to talk to for days. I'll go crazy, if I haven't already. You've got to help me."

"I gave you the idea for that painting. And what did you do? Ruin it. You must like trouble," Seven said, fading out.

"You can't go. I won't have it," Josef cried. "If you *have* to go, take me with you."

In utter astonishment at the suggestion, Seven rematerialized. He debated. "It's not sensible. It's not at all wise," he said. "You aren't even resourceful like Ma-ah or Proteus or Lydia. And I can't trust a word you say, because you change your mind all the time —"

"You'll take me?" Josef asked.

"I'll take you," Seven said, sighing. "Only because something in me always worries about you, though. But you've got to do what I say, and you probably won't remember much when you wake up. If you were awake in *your* terms, then you wouldn't have asked the question."

"What question?" Josef asked.

"Never mind. Look around the room and tell me what you see."

Josef shrugged. "A chair, easel, windows, and a funny yellow monkey —"

"The monkey isn't really there. You're hallucinating it," Seven said. "Make it go away or you'll just get all confused."

"Make it go away?" Josef asked.

"Do you have a monkey in your room ordinarily?" Seven asked, as if he were speaking to a slow learner.

"No."

"Then it shouldn't be here now. It's a dream element. Tell it to disappear or I'm going on without you."

"Go away," Josef said to the monkey, and it just disappeared. Josef stared. A sense of power made him smile brightly. "What about you?" he said. "Suppose I make you go away?"

"Then what will you do?" Seven asked.

"I see what you mean. What's next?"

"Well," Seven said. "I'm not too happy at the thought of dragging you along, but there's someone I have to look in on before I go back — Proteus. Never mind. Just follow me and don't look back at the bed. Here, we'll do it the easy way. Take my hand."

As soon as Josef did, the two of them began to rise in the air. Josef's consciousness blinked out for a moment as Seven thought it probably would. Unconscious, Josef was much more reasonable and easier to handle.

Cyprus watched Seven as he toted Josef along, but she just smiled to herself and made no attempt to contact him. His technique, she decided, was anything but unobtrusive.

~ *Chapter Seven* ~

The Further Descent of Proteus
and the Rest of Josef's Dream

*P*roteus' small living nodule floated so gently when he went camping at home, that you simply forgot that it rested on air. Now it was only a few feet up from the ground, the collapsible steps reaching down to the rocky earth. But here the air currents pushed it every which way, and when Proteus looked out through the small transparent window-holes, earth's opaque darkness stretched out as far as he could see.

He sat on an air pillow, eating his late meal, all he allotted himself, a minimum diet of supper pills washed down by water. He'd been under the impression that on the real Earth it rained often and abundantly, providing natural water that didn't even need to be recycled. He knew it didn't rain-on-time as it did at home, but he'd been sure it rained every day or so. For that reason he hadn't carried much water with him, and now he thought of his plastoid sack, hanging open outside, from his nodule. If it rained, he'd hear it filling, and try to make sure that it didn't spill.

Sitting alone with all that dark space around made him uneasy, not afraid, he told himself—there was a difference. Actually, he missed the gentle dim illumination that passed for night in the floating city, even though his camping nodule lighted itself up automatically when the sun went down. Besides this, he was becoming worried about the nodule itself. It was drifting some, and he tried not to think what might happen if a really strong Earth wind began to blow. Could it rip the nodule to bits? It wasn't made to stand free air currents.

But what if it drifted? Unless he got tangled up in trees, what could happen? Still, it might be wise to take another look around, he thought—unhappily. The skylevator ride hadn't frightened him in the same way that going outside did now. For one thing, he trusted the skylevator, but the nodule floor wobbled when he stood up, opened the door, and went out to the tiny platform. The steps were flying out horizontally in the air, and the breeze seemed determined to pull his hair out by the roots; he still found unsteady air scary, and his eyes stung. You could fall and break a leg, he thought, holding on.

With his motion, the nodule flipped. Proteus fell off, sprawling on the ground. Desperately he sprang to his feet, trying to catch the waving steps. They eluded him, as if on purpose, he thought, until finally he jumped higher than he ever had in his life, grabbed the lowest step, and just hung on. His weight pulled the nodule down low enough so that he could climb aboard. Half-crying, out of breath, sick with relief, he went inside and drew the steps in after him, where they disappeared beneath the couch in storage position.

The wind, which actually had been a slight breeze, grew stronger. Bumpily the illuminated nodule drifted through the air, with Proteus inside, looking out, afraid that he'd run into an area of trees or shrubs that could damage the nodule beyond repair.

He'd taken to talking to the nodule in the last few hours. Now he said, "We can make it. Don't you worry." As he was chattering, his eyes fell on the small TV unit, but there would be no stations here, he told himself—for the tenth time. Still. . . . He turned the set on and just sat there, staring at the glowing empty screen, until finally he fell into an uneasy sleep.

The next thing he knew, he was wide awake. The time-dial showed that he'd slept for several hours. But something had awakened him. What was it? It took him several moments before he realized that a pattern was trying to form on the TV screen. Quickly he leaned forward, but the pattern wouldn't stabilize. Instead there was static. His excitement grew, and suddenly the static turned into words.

"Turn off your illumination at once. Then leave your nodule," the voice said. The patterns jumped, but no images formed.

"What? Are you talking to me? Who are you?" Proteus shouted.

"Repeat. Proteus. Turn off your illumination. Then leave your nodule. Search parties are out looking for you. We can't take the chance of using this channel any longer. If you receive this message, follow our directions. Wait for us. We're friends. You have nothing to be worried about."

"How do you know who I am? Who are you? Where are the search parties?" But the screen turned opaque. Proteus tried the other channels, but they were dead. For a moment he thought he'd imagined the whole thing. Who was out there? What did they want? Should he do what they said? The bumpy air was rushing all around the nodule. Any second now it could crash to the ground; ruined. He'd collapse it because of *that;* to save it, he thought. Then find a hiding place and see what happened. He couldn't turn the illumination off anyhow as long as the nodule was inflated; the lighting was automatic.

He looked out again, this time searching for what he'd hoped to avoid earlier — an area of trees — only with a clearing to settle down in. It was a good hour before the nodule drifted close to any brush at all. Even then Proteus hesitated. He was under surveillance! He couldn't get over it. He'd seen no signs of anyone, and he certainly hadn't seen any Earth copters, such as a search party from home might use here.

The brush was coming closer. Quickly he grabbed his survival kit and pressed the nodule-collapse lever. Holding his breath, he came outside on the platform again, down the wobbly steps to the ground. The nodule shuddered, wrinkled, and collapsed beside him, a small white plastoid bag the size of a valise.

He yanked his belongings out of the clearing and ducked into the shrubbery. There were short stubby trees, brambles, and vines. Proteus ran as fast as he could, his head down, his camp shoes automatically shooting out their small circles of light from the toes, illuminating the ground beneath his feet. They were a present from his mother — a luxury — hardly a necessity at the camps he attended with their gently lighted grounds. But here—he paused, best not to think of his parents, he thought. Not now.

His feet hurt already. The shoes would wear out quickly on this uneven surface. But he felt excited. At least things were happening, and he was on his own. He was scared, he finally admitted, but even that was exhilarating. He felt very hunted but very free. Then a new worry bothered him. Suppose the people who contacted him were really from home and trying to trick him?

Still, Proteus thought, they'd be more apt to send out women on the search, and the voice he'd heard had been masculine. He looked up through the thicket at the black sky and thought that despite everything, he wouldn't be caught and sent home. He never felt so . . . like himself before.

Suddenly Proteus stopped, his shoe-lights illuminating the beginning of a hill, or a drop of some kind. Cautiously he inched forward, then stopped again, staring. He was on the high brim of a strange round hill.

Within were dark, curious shapes, like buildings, that were situated a good thirty feet down. Actually, he was on the edge of a circular valley he saw. Quickly he found a more inclined area and began to make his way down.

There were no hills in the floating city. He wasn't used to climbing. Several times he fell. When he was halfway down, he stopped, staring through the darkness. As he did, streaks of light ribboned through the clouds—his first sight of dawn. He looked up, marveling at the way dawn happened (all by itself, not by prearranged signals, as at home). He knew all the scientific reasons, but again the phenomenon at first sight was amazing. The sky shivered. Clumps of cloud turned from gray-black to gray to . . . puffs of perfect muted colors which themselves began to change the moment they appeared.

For a moment, until he looked back down, he'd forgotten the scene below. Now in the growing light, the buildings sprang clearly upward from the litter; ruins of such an extent that Proteus stepped back involuntarily. And what ruins! There were portions of sprawling walls, high pillars such as he'd seen in some video tapes, and piles of rubble. A few tall white towers still stood, half-covered now with vines and foliage.

Delighted, forgetting everything else, Proteus ran down the hill as fast as he could go. The rocky ground hurt his feet. Brambles caught his clothes. He hardly noticed. Twice he dropped his survival kit, picked it up automatically, and ran on. What kind of people had lived there and when? The area was being worked; some machinery stood silently nearby.

Then off to the side he saw buildings, ruins in better shape than elsewhere, that looked inhabited. Rough material hung at the windows. Perhaps laborers or archeologists stayed there. Cautiously, Proteus stopped, then set out in the opposite direction, walking as quietly as he could.

It didn't take him long to come to the largest rock platform in the middle of the dig. As soon as he approached, a small dog ran suddenly out from behind a broken statue of a man. Proteus knew it was a dog though he'd only seen them in zoos, so he ran after it. The dog never barked, though it might, Proteus thought suddenly, and awaken whoever might be sleeping at the dig. Instead . . . could he be mistaken? . . . No, the dog was trying to lead him somewhere. It kept wagging its stubby tail, and running to him, then back to the statue.

Finally Proteus followed. A round hole was visible beside the statue, and the dog ran down a flight of stairs beneath. Proteus couldn't tell how deep the hole was, for the stairs turned, but already the dog had disappeared.

An open invitation? A trained dog? Did it belong to the man who'd contacted him on TV? Was it a trap? Proteus' arguments with himself were only academic, and he knew it. Already he had taken his first step down. A trapdoor within the Earth, on the other side of the surface — he'd never really expected to see any such thing. After traveling down in the skylevator *to* the ground, what an opportunity now to descend ever further, inside it!

But where had the dog gone? When Proteus went down perhaps ten of the stone steps, a noise attracted his attention just as the light suddenly changed. Whipping around, he was just in time to see the hole close above him, and a round arc of blackness shut out the morning sky. It was only then that he realized that the steps were dimly lighted. Simultaneously he wondered if the statue above had changed position and stood now solidly atop the hole.

Again his excitement conquered his fear — almost. Only now and then his scalp prickled and the blood pounded alarmingly loud in his ears. For one thing, he'd never smelled such odors before, a mixture of minerals and moisture and thickly packed dirt, long untouched — a musty yet evocative pungency that kept reminding him that he was actually on the other side of the Earth's surface.

The passageway turned. Again Proteus wondered where the dog was. Insects dashed out of the dimness into the circle of light cast by his camping shoes. Proteus recoiled, but they scurried away. Here and there large stones littered the steps, holes in the rocky wall showing where they had fallen; and often the walls were slimy with moisture.

Finally the steps ended after another turn. There, silently, sat the dog, tail wagging, eyes friendly. Was it mute? Proteus wondered. To the right was a door. It opened easily. Proteus found himself in a large room without windows, dimly lighted from the ceiling. The entire area was filled with long tables loaded with tools, stone busts, and piles of debris.

It *was* an archeological site, then. Proteus hadn't realized that such work was carried on this far underground. Maybe they'd let him stay and learn while he worked? But then another idea came to him. The dog had crossed the floor and was waiting for him at another door at the far end of the room. It was all too pat, Proteus thought. Suppose there was a reward out for him, and the archeologists were going to turn him over to his parents or a search party?

He couldn't even imagine seeing his mother, but the thought of seeing his father surprised him. He felt a pang of loneliness, an unexpected rush of tenderness that he instantly tried to hide from himself. He adapted a jaunty stance and opened the door. The dog ran into the small room on the other side, and he followed. A creaky funny old elevator! Instantly the door closed, the tiny room moved downward, with bumps and squeaks as if it hadn't been used for centuries. It stopped. The dog began to bark impatiently, as if it had just been given voice. The door opened and the dog ran straight out into the arms of a man who stood not three feet away.

"Good job, Winter," the man said, picking the dog up. The man had brown hair, thick brown brows, a humped nose, and wore loose flowing overalls and a long-sleeved shirt or blouse. But it was his manner that caught Proteus' attention at once. He'd never met a man with such presence, with such an easy yet assured air of friendly command.

"My name is Window," the man said. "And you're Proteus. You've caused us quite a bit of concern, though you didn't know it, of course. You could have ruined everything."

"*I* could have? Ruined what? You're an archeologist, aren't you? Are you the man who sent me the message? Are there really search parties out for me?" Proteus had so many questions that he didn't know where to start. At the same time he noted the long stone tables at one end of the bare room, the clay tablets lined up on raised wooden platforms, and the murals, in various stages of completion, that lined the walls. "A man named Window. I never knew of anyone with a name like that," he said. "And isn't Winter a funny name for a dog?"

"We have names that have meaning to us. I'm Window because I can see through things sometimes," the man said. "And we found the dog in the wintertime. You're in the Dig of the Tellers, but there'll be plenty of time to explain. Right now you're a danger to all of us, drawing search parties in this direction. Usually the Floaters leave us alone."

"The Floaters?" Proteus said.

"Your people," Window said, with a sardonic grunt. "Now come along with me. I hope you like what you see, because you're going to be around here for some time."

Proteus looked around uneasily now. "You mean, I'm a prisoner?" he asked.

Window shrugged and smiled. "Definitions are funny things. I wouldn't define your position here as that of a prisoner, no. But for your own good as well as ours, I believe that you'll voluntarily agree to limit your experience to the Dig of the Tellers for a while."

Oversoul Seven and Josef had watched Proteus ever since he awakened from sleep and heard the Teller's voice on the television set. Now they stood, invisible, in one corner of the room. Josef said, enraged. "What's going on? What are they doing to do with that boy? Why don't you do something? You *can*, can't you? If you didn't help him when he fell out of his strange bubble, I don't suppose you'll do anything now, though." He paused and shivered. "And that foul tunnel or whatever it was—"

"Can't you be quiet?" Oversoul Seven said. "You've done nothing but yell since we started. I knew I shouldn't have taken you along."

"Yell? Being dragged through the air by the hair of my head almost! I've never had a dream in my life like this before. I suppose it's because I'm half-starved—"

"In a way it is," Seven said. "It clears the mind."

"Clears the mind? You call this clearing the mind?" Josef yelled. "Who's that? That soldier or whoever it is?"

Seven looked to where Josef was pointing. "He's just another hallucination of yours. Why do you keep doing that? I told you: if he disappears, you'll know he's not real—at least not to anyone else. If he stays put, then he's a part of physical reality or mass hallucination. Can't you keep that straight?"

While they were talking, Proteus and Window left the room. "They're going," Josef said. "Aren't you going to follow them?"

"Proteus never even knows when I'm around," Seven said. "But I can't stay here any longer. I think he'll be all right. I'm sure he will. He's so resourceful—"

"What's wrong with that?" Josef said. "It didn't sound like a compliment."

"You're not supposed to question *me* like that," Seven said. "Don't try to switch roles with me. Come on, I'm taking you back."

"But that boy!" Josef said. "At the mercy of God knows what—"

"That's your trouble. You always exaggerate," Seven said. He sighed, touched Josef on the arm, and thought of Josef's bedroom. This time Josef only felt a flash of air, a whoosh of sound, and then a strange scrambled-up sensation. The next thing he knew he was lying above the bed, looking down at his own body or all he could see of it, bundled in a hump beneath the blankets.

"Is that me?" he said. "I've been out all over everywhere without my body?" The realization terrified him. He froze.

"Turn around," Oversoul Seven said. "Your head's at your feet. You've got to line up with your body."

"I can't. I don't know how to. Suppose I don't get back in?"

"Getting back in is easiest of all," Seven said. "You just have to want to. And I suggest that you give some thought to solving some of your other problems. In fact, what you've seen tonight should help you considerably. But this time it's up to you. I've given you the ingredients for something, but you have to use them. Now get back inside your body. Just drop in—"

"Drop in?" Josef asked.

Seven sighed and gave Josef a slight nudge that lined him up with his physical body. "Go *ahead*."

Josef stared at him distrustfully, but he dutifully tried to do what Seven suggested. A funny falling sensation rushed through him. In panic his eyes flew open. He was in bed. The room was perfectly normal, except for a toy-man soldier who stood in the corner.

"You forgot to dismiss your hallucination," Seven called helpfully. He himself disappeared.

"Go away," Josef yelled, and the soldier vanished before his eyes. He sat up, shaking and sweating, and lit the lantern. What a nightmare, he thought. Tomorrow he was going to start a painting for the Hosentaufs, no matter what it was. The lack of food was driving him out of his mind.

Suddenly he jumped to his feet, fully alert. Scenes from his "dream" rushed into consciousness. He saw those old ruins rising up from the gray dawn. What an idea for a painting, he thought. Already the experience with Seven was disappearing, first into a dream, then into the memory of a dream, then into the feeling that he'd had a dream that he'd forgotten. Only a clear image of the ruins remained. Josef lit another lantern and began a quick preliminary sketch of the circular hill and ruins at the Dig of the Tellers. As the charcoal lines outlined the scene, he had the weirdest feeling that the place was somehow familiar, as if he'd been there once and forgotten.

~ *Chapter Eight* ~

Proteus in the Dig of the Tellers
and Story's Tale

W indow stood watching the sky as the dusk settled down, filling the wide earthen cup that held the ruins. His head was thrust upward, his long humped nose pointing at the suspiciously empty air above. The search party had not returned as they said they would. For hours he'd waited for their copter's shocking emergence in the usually silent sky. Floaters were leary of Earth night. It was odd that he hadn't heard from them earlier. Window thought back: they had no reason to doubt his word when he told them he hadn't seen the boy, and promised to contact them if he did.

He opened his inner senses as fully as possible, but he could perceive no strangers in the immediate area, on the Earth surface, beneath it, or above. No alien thoughts nibbled at the far reaches of his mind; no unfamiliar shapes rose out of the darkness of his inner concentration. He smiled to himself—either Window wasn't open, or the area was safe for the night. Still, he didn't like it. He sat down, fingering a piece of broken pottery. A picture of the woman who made it so many centuries ago flashed into his mind. It was of early twentieth-century origin, fashioned apparently for show rather than use. Irritably Window dismissed the images, not wanting to be distracted. No skylevator had descended or risen that day, so his scouts told him. Then where was the search party?

All they needed was a lost search party, he thought, wearily. That would bring more Floaters down to investigate. Such a situation could be more of a calamity than any they'd ever faced. He looked up. The sky was darkening. Window became aware of a familiar inner sense of motion . . . activity approaching . . . still some distance away. He closed his eyes. The inner darkness vibrated, trembled, broke, and a miniature image in full color formed — the searchers' copter.

Mentally Window enlarged the picture, then his consciousness entered it. There were the same three women he'd spoken to yesterday. He picked up their thoughts and conversation at once, so he really couldn't differentiate between what was said or only mentally decided upon. He grinned: they weren't going to return, that much was clear. With typical Floaters' arrogance, they didn't think that he and his men could possibly find the boy if they hadn't.

He laughed suddenly, discovering deeper reasons beneath their consciousness. They'd stayed on Earth later than they'd planned in a last attempt to find Proteus, and they felt uneasy about landing at the dig at night with men around who weren't under their thumb. Besides, they were convinced that the skylevator simply malfunctioned the day Proteus disappeared, releasing itself and leaving evidence of the unauthorized trip on its log — a coincidence that led them to a futile Earth search.

Again their prejudice came into play: they should have known that a boy wouldn't be daring enough to attempt such a journey. Now they were convinced that he was hiding someplace in the floating city, where they should have concentrated their efforts all along.

It was odd, Window thought, but their prejudice against men did annoy him, even though he understood its roots. But prejudice itself, the sensed feel of it, had a bitter shape to the inner senses. It felt like a prickly bush, whose needles jabbed against his own soft acquiescence to all forms of life. Enough. There was no need to wait the actual appearance of the copter in the sky. It would not stop. They'd already notified the floating city hours ago, and a skylevator would be picking up the search party, copter and all.

He kicked at some debris, went inside one of the small shacks ostensibly used for the dig, pressed a portion of the woodwork, and crossed to the center of the floor. At once a trapdoor opened. He went down the few stairs to the elevator which dropped him quickly and directly to the inner dig, where Proteus would be waiting.

Proteus heard him coming and leapt to his feet. He was full of questions.

"Well," Window said. "Your search party is leaving. They've decided that you're not on Earth because a boy couldn't be bold enough to pull such a stunt alone; and being men, we couldn't find you if they didn't." Window smiled dryly. "They're wrong on several points. We have men and women here, and the ruins above—the dig—is just camouflage. We live beneath, as you know, obviously."

"How many of you are there?" Proteus asked. "How do you get away with it?" He was refreshed after a good night's sleep. All he could think of now was the fact that people were actually living beneath the Earth, unknown to the people above it.

"I can't tell you everything at once," Window said, smiling. "We're supposed to be part of a minor archeological society, with our own funds. We report to our own mother group, in the floating city. Archeology is considered a harmless male activity, no longer taken seriously since the main population left Earth. So no one bothers us."

"I guess I don't understand," Proteus said. "Do men rule things here?"

Window shook his head. "Each sex has tried to rule the other, throughout history. In a way, the results were more disastrous when men had the upper hand. They became so alienated from themselves as simple individuals that they could only relate through sex-directed activities. But the women are doing a poor job, too, as you should know, with your background. They tried to retaliate and turn the tables until they took on many of the unfavorable traits they thought were male. I'll explain more about it later, but I can honestly say that we relate here as individuals. Each person is respected for his or her uniqueness. Even names have individual meanings, and aren't sexually based."

"But how many of there are you?" Proteus asked again. "When will you show me around? Why are you called Tellers?"

"As for our name, it's like this," Window said. "In ages past, archeologists used the term *tell* to refer to the artificial mounds that cover the remains of past ruins. Finally they called themselves Tellers." He shrugged and smiled. "As for some of your other questions, I'm afraid the answers will have to wait for a while. Maybe before too long, you'll learn the rest."

"Maybe?" Proteus said.

"Maybe," Window repeated. "Many of our ways will be directly counter to those you've been brought up with. We have to decide just how much you can assimilate and accept. We may have to keep you on the outer edges, so to speak. I hope not—"

"But what could be so strange to me?" Proteus asked. He was tired of sitting around; he wanted to explore the place. "I think you're hedging," he said, looking away.

"You do, huh?" Window said. "I am, in a way. But there's someone I want you to meet—" He pressed a button, and a doorway slid open.

Proteus was already gearing himself. Something in Window's tone told him that some type of a test was involved. If he failed it, what could they do? What would it mean? Before he had time to think any more about it, a girl entered. She was a little older than he, slender, dressed like Window in flowing overalls and overblouse.

"This is Story," Window said.

As she came forward, smiling, suddenly her eyes darkened. She took a step backward, shivered slightly, and turned to Window as if for support.

"What is it?" Window asked.

"I don't know yet." Her voice was so soft that Proteus had to strain to listen. She said, "I just feel . . . that he's a bigger threat than we realized, but in an entirely different way than we thought. I don't know why. The story's only just beginning to come—"

"Could you be wrong?" Window asked.

"Of course," she said, irritably. "All of my stories have to be deciphered. Maybe I'm reading it wrong. Some are true now, but not later. Or later, but not now—"

"What are you staring at me like that for? And what are you talking about?" Proteus asked, hurt. "We've just met. What do you mean, about stories?" He frowned at Window unhappily, and wouldn't look at the girl's face.

"She's called Story because often stories come to her that are true. They've actually happened or will happen."

"But that's just superstition," Proteus said. "I don't want to hurt your feelings, but–"

"You don't, huh?" Window interrupted, smiling.

"Well, if he doesn't understand anything at all, then what's the point?" Story cried, exasperated.

"Never mind, tell your story," Window said. "I'm sure that Proteus will be polite enough to listen anyway."

Proteus shrugged airily, half-intimidated, half-curious. He tried to ignore the goosepimples that thickened up on the insides of his arms. After all, he thought, what could the girl possibly say? Why did he feel that she could ruin everything?

"I can only tell the story as it comes to me," she said. "I just trust it, whether or not it seems to make sense right away. So don't be angry if it sounds strange—"

"I'm not angry," Proteus said, too loud. He blushed.

She kept her eyes open, but looked way over to one side. "Well, first I see an old man and woman. She's . . . giddy and maybe ready to die. Or maybe he is. They're in some kind of vehicle that was used on Earth centuries ago. . . . Something is about to happen. Or maybe it just has. She seems to be talking to some man who's dead and his body is nearby. The two of them are connected with Proteus."

Proteus stared at her, transfixed yet scandalized. What nonsense, he thought, wondering how Window could take Story so seriously.

"Then there's another man," she said. "Older than Proteus, but still young. He's imprisoned in a room all alone. And there's a painting of an ancient farmhouse, with trees all around."

Proteus started and leaned forward. He'd dreamed of such a painting or one like it. The trees had fired his imagination and made him even more determined to go to the Earth's surface.

"What is it, Proteus?" Window asked.

"Nothing," Proteus lowered his eyes uneasily. He wasn't lying, he told himself. It was just coincidence.

Story's eyes never changed direction. She kept staring over to the right without turning her head until Proteus was tempted to turn himself, to see what she was looking at.

"Anyhow, I don't like this particular man too much," she said, "the one locked in the room. He's terribly self-indulgent. And I see a young black woman too. She's connected with us, with the Tellers, in some odd fashion. And—" Story broke off for a moment, her face so grave that Proteus didn't interrupt as he wanted to. Despite himself, he felt frightened . . . or anticipatory. He couldn't tell which.

"She has something to do with archeology too," Story went on. "Or with ruins or a god or spirit of some kind. I see her standing by pyramids. But the threat to us comes through her!" Story looked at Window now, almost appealingly. "That's all I have so far," she said. "Does any of it make sense to you, Proteus?"

He shook his head. "To me least of all. I think that it's, well, just a story. If you want to believe that stuff, that's up to you, but it made no sense at all to me. If it did, I'd tell you."

"If you get anything more, Story, make sure you tell me," Window said. "And Proteus too."

"But if Proteus doesn't understand, and I don't know that he ever will—"

"Wait, now," Window said. "Proteus, listen to me for a moment. When the women took over, they tried to emphasize physical agility, strength, boldness, logic—all the qualities that men insisted were prerogatives of the male in the past. They minimized some other excellent characteristics, because they erroneously considered them beneath their new status, and a threat to it. They tried to ignore the intuitive understanding with which they were basically gifted, for example. So there are many quite normal human abilities that you're probably prejudiced against, because of your background — "

"But I'm very open-minded," Proteus objected.

"What about seeing into the future or into the past? Or reading minds? Just before the massive takeover by the women, scientists were realizing that such things were quite possible. The world was at a point of new discovery — "

"But all that represents the superstitions that the women were able to wipe out," Proteus said. "Granted, they've made a lot of errors, and I was anything but happy as a Floater, as you call it, but the women *are* logical. I'm open-minded about . . . well, real things."

"He's going to be quite impossible," Story said, coldly, to Window. She tried not to sound angry, but she felt quite upset and personally insulted. "No one ever doubted my stories before," she said. "What they mean isn't always apparent at once, but everyone always took it for granted that a meaning was there. The stories *do* stand for something real. My name's Story because my stories began when I was a child. We pick our names when we're seven, with our parents' help, and confirm them at fourteen. So you're saying that my name doesn't mean anything. You're trying to deny my whole existence — "

Her outburst so surprised Proteus that he didn't know what to say. Hopefully he looked to Window, who unaccountably looked the other way, so Proteus was forced to come to his own defense.

"That's not what I meant," he said. "I'm not saying that your name is wrong, or you're wrong. Well, the story you told didn't make sense to me, but it was a story of sorts. So you *do* tell stories, and your name is right. I just don't think that the story really had anything to do with me." In utter confusion, with his face reddening, he said, "That's all I can say."

"And not one thing made sense to you?" she asked, persistent.

Proteus shook his head. Then he said, "One small thing sounded familiar, but that was just coincidence or something. You mentioned a painting that sounded like one I've dreamed of several times; not that I remember many of my dreams, because I don't. That one stuck in my mind because it made me want to come to the Earth's surface even more than I did already."

Proteus hadn't realized that Story had been so tense, with her shoulders all raised up until he finished speaking and she suddenly smiled.

Her shoulders relaxed, and a flush of warmth transformed her face. "But that isn't anything," he said quickly. He turned to Window, but Window was smiling at Story.

"Why should such a small thing make you feel better?" Proteus asked, genuinely surprised. "Nothing else made any sense to me at all."

Window said, "The dream may have had something to do with your coming here—"

"But I already intended to."

Window turned and placed his hands on Story's shoulders. "You should have learned something from this," he said. "You have to trust your own abilities, and not doubt them because someone else does. If we do carry out our present plans, you'll have to hold your own sense of integrity in the face of skepticism just like Proteus'.

Then, turning to Proteus, Window said, "You'll be good for her, she isn't used to anyone doubting her word. You'll end up teaching each other." To Story he added, soberly, "If you get more on the implied threat, let me know." Then, gently, "Distortion could account for it; you could unconsciously consider Proteus a threat to begin with, particularly if you doubt your own abilities in any way. I'll see what I can get, too, though, using my own methods."

"What do you mean?" Proteus asked, shocked. "You don't do the same thing?"

"Window *sees*," Story said.

"Sees what? I *see*," Proteus said to her.

"Enough for now," Window said. "Proteus, we've given you and ourselves enough to think of for one day."

"But, if you really think I'm a threat to you in some way, how come you're taking me in?"

"Threats are often challenges," Window said simply.

Proteus tried to stall for time. He could tell that the interview would be ended in a minute. Had the meeting with Story involved some kind of test? And had he failed it? Should he have pretended to go along with what she said? "Are you going to show me around?" he asked, uneasily. "Now I feel as if you won't, or as if you've put me on probation. And you still didn't tell me how many people are here—"

Window stood up. "I think we'll show you the dig by stages, Proteus. We'll begin in the morning. And I'll find something meaningful for you to do while you're here, but some of your questions will have to wait."

Proteus nodded, but he felt very alone and increasingly dissatisfied. A girl named Story whose stories were supposed to be true, though they sounded like nonsense; and a man called Window who could see! See what? And they were only going to show him what they wanted him to know. Already he decided that one way or another, sixteen years old or not, he was going to discover whatever it was they were hiding.

∽ *Chapter Nine* ∽

Cyprus and Oversoul Seven
Beginning Part Three
of the Examination

Oversoul Seven was the fourteen-year-old male again, and Cyprus was talking to him. "You seem to have been neglecting Lydia," she commented.

Oversoul Seven concentrated as hard as he could, bringing his consciousness entirely into focus. They were in Lydia's study. Autumn leaves fell past the windows so fast that Seven blinked. Then, enlarging his visual he saw that the room was a flurry of activity. Three men were banging drawers open, and throwing their contents on the blue rug. "You could have picked a quieter place," Seven said. "What's going on here? And is this another of those conversations that have been going on without my conscious knowledge? They always confuse me."

"Lydia's family has sold the house," Cyprus said. "She deeded it to them, so that they could do what they wanted with their inheritance without waiting for her to die —"

"Couldn't you put that more delicately?" Seven asked, grumpily.

"That's how Lydia put it, as you'd know if you'd been keeping good track of her," Cyprus said.

"But I have," Seven protested. "She had another stroke. It practically catapulted me out of Ma-ah, and I helped her, Lydia, that is; in fact, until then I couldn't get out of Ma-ah." Seven said, suddenly remembering, "You told me to identify with Ma-ah as completely as I could, and I agreed. But I didn't realize how completely I *could* identify with her, or I might not have agreed so readily." He shivered. "All that body around all the time," he said.

"*They* have their bodies around them all of the time," Cyprus pointed out. She kept changing almost imperceptibly from a beautiful woman of indeterminate age to a handsome man of indeterminate age. Every once in a while there was a moment when the two images merged, blended, achieved oneness and stability.

"You seem to be having some trouble with your own physical form," Seven said. "If that was me, acting like that, you'd give me three demerits."

"I know more of myself than you do of yourself," she said. "So it's much more difficult, in fact, almost impossible, to create a physical image to express my known reality. But I've told you that before."

"You certainly have good answers," Seven said. The two of them were sitting nicely on the couch. Suddenly Seven sprang up: "Look at that," he shouted. "That lughead just dumped the entire contents of Lydia's shell collection on the floor! That's no way to do," he yelled at the mover. And in a flash the shells flew back into the drawer.

"Seven, stop that," Cyprus said urgently.

The mover turned around, and stared at the drawer. "I could have sworn that I dumped all that stuff out," he said, turning toward the other mover.

"Put it back," Cyprus ordered. "Now."

The shells went from the drawer, singly, to the floor while the mover's back was turned. When he looked back, the drawer was empty. "Why, I did," he yelled. "I mean . . . I could swear —"

"That's how rumors get started about places being haunted," Cyprus said.

"Well, they're Lydia's favorite shells," Seven muttered. "I don't like meeting here like this anyhow. Can't we go someplace else?"

"All right. Think of a cloud," Cyprus said. She and Seven left immediately. At the last moment, Seven dematerialized one perfectly shaped shell to save for Lydia. He and Cyprus emerged on a cloud just within the borders of Earth's atmosphere.

"I want to give you a quick review before I tell you about the next part of your examination," Cyprus said. "First of all, though, what did you learn so far?"

"Well," Seven said, frowning. "I have trouble staying with Ma-ah exclusively. At first I couldn't get away from her. Now I get called willy-nilly from one personality to the other as they get into trouble, and it seems like something comes up constantly for me to deal with. Then, I lose my sense of perspective — "

He went on. "Proteus still doesn't believe in anything but the good old days. Lydia doesn't recognize me, and I've always liked her," he said petulantly. "Josef knows me, more or less, but he just gets in needless trouble. Ma-ah, well, I like her much better now. But I have the feeling that you're holding out on me again."

"I'm holding out on you?" Cyprus said, smiling. "How about that shell?"

Seven just shimmered around the edges. "Oh, *that*," he said. "Well, I peeked into Lydia's future and there's one place where she could really use it; I mean, where the shell could help her."

"That's what I thought." Cyprus sighed. "Now what's illogical about that statement?"

"But there's a difference between ideal circumstances and practical action," Seven exploded.

Cyprus looked as stern as Seven had ever seen her. He said, "All right. I know I'm supposed to experience time as they do, day by day, and I have. I've only snitched a few glimpses into the future — "

"Into what?" Cyprus said.

"Into . . . uh, the *probable* future," Seven amended quickly.

"Your personalities have free will just as you do," Cyprus said. "You must never forget that. You looked into one of the probable futures as they exist for Lydia; and at any point she can alter circumstances and choose one probable future over another. Do you understand?"

Seven nodded, properly chastised.

"Now, let me explain this more clearly," Cyprus said, "You're Proteus, Lydia, Ma-ah and Josef in all of their probable presents, pasts and futures; and yet they are themselves, and also more than the selves they know themselves to be. And you, of course, are more than the Oversoul Seven you presently identify with. As you help them and instruct them when you can, others who *you* may not recognize help and instruct you — "

"And I'm a part of them?" Oversoul Seven asked.

"Precisely," Cyprus said. "But here let me show you how it works, using images as a method of instruction." And before Seven's eyes, a wide endless flat surface stretched as far as he could see in all directions. Looking down, he saw all the centuries man had known and was knowing and would know, laid out like countries all at once. He couldn't see everything though, simply because there seemed to be no end to the glittering surface.

Cyprus said, "Now watch as closely as you can."

"I *am* watching closely," Oversoul Seven said, emphatically.

This time, the endless flat surface became the top part of an infinite circle, so that while the scene itself filled up all space, Seven could only see a portion of the circle itself. And from each century, other spirals constantly arose.

"I'm getting dizzy," Seven complained.

"Seven, pay attention to your lesson," Cyprus demanded. "Now all of that is just one Moment-Point; one 'point' wherein creativity knows itself. So in Earth terms, probable presents are born in each 'moment.' The one that is physically materialized is the only one that your personalities accept as real. But you'll learn how to keep track of all of them." She paused and added, "theoretically."

"But in all of that, how can I know myself?" Seven asked—reasonably enough, he thought.

"You *do* know yourself though, don't you? You certainly know enough to ask questions," Cyprus said. "Your knowledge of yourself is self-evident." (So is your lack of it, she thought, smiling figuratively.)

"I got that!" Seven shouted.

"Oh well, you *are* improving then," Cyprus said.

"You wanted me to get it. You were testing me all along," Seven said, suddenly understanding. "It takes the edge off my triumph."

"You may not know all of yourself, but that's a process of self-discovery, of becoming," Cyprus said. "The more you discover of yourself, the more you are—"

"I can hardly handle the parts of me I know already," Seven said sadly. "But can't you show me more of the images?"

"You just aren't ready, Seven," Cyprus said. "And you have to learn through direct experience. There really isn't any other way. Now, for the next part of your examination—"

A jet passed by. Cyprus and Seven dropped down on top of it and rode along, occasionally looking down at the Earth. "You have to get through to Proteus and Lydia," Cyprus said, without pausing. "And you have to get all of your personalities together in some way, so they can better benefit from each others' separate experiences."

"How on Earth am I going to do that?" Seven asked.

"How *can* you do it, on Earth?" She asked, smiling. Then she added, "But Seven, you must become more involved in the activities of your personalities. But then, I know that you will."

"I don't like the way you said that," Seven answered, worried. "And there's one thing I want to know. How long has this conversation between us been going on? Before I came in on it, I mean?"

She just looked at him. For a brief instant the handsome man of indeterminate age and the beautiful woman of indeterminate age materialized again and merged, stabilized, focused until it was so vivid and brilliant that Seven could hardly bear it.

"Don't you know? Don't you know?" The musical voice seemed to come from everywhere, from inside Oversoul Seven, and outside him, from the clouds and the jet. The words seemed to echo through time as he knew it and didn't know it, until he felt that Lydia and Proteus and Josef and Ma-ah were all singing, and asking the question all at once.

The phenomenon vanished so quickly and completely that Seven almost lost the balance of his consciousness. "What was that?" he gasped. "What happened?"

"Every once in a while you ask a really important question," Cyprus said. "Or rather, the question that you actually ask has a really important one hidden inside of it. Then you get an answer."

"But now I've forgotten what the question was, much less what was hidden inside it," Seven cried. "And I don't know what the answer meant."

"Dear Seven," Cyprus said, with some compassion, "You *do* understand. A part of you does. But before you go back, I want to give you one hint. You make your own reality, and your personalities make their own realities too."

"But I know that," Seven said, disappointed. "I thought you were going to give me a big hint — "

"I have," she said. "And I suggest that you begin with Lydia this time. Remember: you make your own reality."

Seven mused about it: you make your own reality . . . and instantly he lost track of the constant conversation. As Cyprus knew he would.

～ *Chapter Ten* ～

Lydia and Lawrence:
A Trip Is Interrupted

"*H*ow's Mr. George?" Lawrence yelled.

"Okay," Lydia called. Usually she kept Mr. George, the goldfish, in a bowl on the trailer bookcase, propped up with books so that the bowl wouldn't fall off. Every once in a while she went to check on him to see that the water didn't slosh out with the bumps in the road. Now she was driving. Lawrence was reading in back, and Mr. George was in the front seat beside her. Greenacre, the Angora cat, lay curled around the bowl.

Lydia drove on at a good pace, chain-smoking, listening to the radio, and occasionally talking at Mr. George or Greenacre. She had sunglasses on, and a visor cap set on her cropped white hair, and she was wearing a leather peace sign suspended on a strap around her neck—a gift from Lawrence. She felt jaunty, wearing it. When any black people went by in a car, or young people with their flowing hair, she grinned and made the peace sign.

Still, blacks resented liberals these days, she thought, "do-gooders." So maybe she should stop the practice, as far as they were concerned. After all, if *they* didn't like it, what was the point? A car passed by, with a black couple in front. Lydia gave the peace sign. The man smiled and returned the gesture. Lovely man, Lydia thought. Now I can go on doing it.

"Aren't you ever going to quit reading?" she called back to Lawrence. No response. Well, he probably dozed off, she thought, let him sleep. "Wouldn't you say, Greenacre?" No response there either, not even the flicker of an ear. She changed the radio station.

A half-hour went by. An Indiana dusk was beginning to fall. She wondered if they'd make it to the University of Iowa in time for her lecture and poetry reading. "We should stop for supper soon," she called, keeping her eyes on the road. Then, "Greenacre, go wake Lawrence and tell him its almost time to eat." Greenacre opened one eye. "Lawrence," she called again. She switched off the radio. There were no sounds from the rear — no snoring or heavy breathing (or gasps, in case he'd had a heart attack). Silly, of course he hadn't. He was years younger than she; doctor or no, his heart would last for years.

"Lawrence!" Be calm, she told herself. "Shall we put up at the next road park? Supper isn't exactly gourmet food — hotdogs, rolls, salad — " Even as she went on speaking normally, she was pulling up at the side of the road. It was a four-lane highway, but traffic was light.

The trailer seemed filled to the ceiling with silence, stuffed with it like cotton. She felt as if it was packed in her mouth. "Get up, Lawrence. It's time for supper," she said. Her words sounded all woolly. She went back to him, her face rigidly smiling, and found him just sitting there, eyes open, mouth open; quite dead. In her mind she heard him say, "How's Mr. George?" How long ago was that? He must have . . . must have . . . right after that, while she was giving the peace sign and calling back to him.

She looked at him intently and tried to take his pulse. There was none. She breathed into his mouth as hard as she could, trying to fill him with air, so much that he'd float up to life like a balloon, but it was like trying to fill up a tire with a hole in it, or — She broke off.

"We were positive I'd go first," she said. "Because of my age. And you'd have to be the one to decide what to do when my mind went. . . . " She tried to keep a conversational tone, not to panic. For one thing, they'd promised each other not to cry.

A few cars passed. She felt as if Lawrence was still alive, but obviously not in that body. How had it let him escape? She eyed it, accusingly, became angry at it. A chuckle started up in her throat and she caught herself. A sign of panic, she thought, to be avoided at all costs. Lawrence was dead and his body was dead. She didn't believe in an afterlife.

She paused, staring at Lawrence's body, trying to be very matter of fact. She must be detached to avoid panic, to protect her own sanity, and be as normal as possible. What would she do if everything was all right? The answer came. She got milk, bread, and jam from the midget refrigerator, sat down across from Lawrence's body and began to eat, neatly, careful not to spill any crumbs upon the floor. Careful about everything. He was sitting upright. People passing by in their cars saw an elderly man and woman facing each other in a camper-trailer, with a lamp warmly shining behind yellow transparent window curtains.

Finishing her milk and jelly sandwich, Lydia put the stuff away and fed the cats.

Plans, she thought. If her mind was failing her, and she was sure that it was, then she had to be crafty; and careful. They'd promised each other no funerals and no flowers, no calling of relatives until everything was over; none of the rituals or nauseating rites reserved for the dying, dead, and aged.

"Lydia."

She sprang around, certain that someone had called her name. Involuntarily she said, "Lawrence?"

"Am I dead?" he asked. But where were the words coming from, inside her head or outside?

"Of course you are, don't be cruel. You know my mind does funny things sometimes," she said. "I'm not hearing a thing. I'm making it all up."

"Your mind can't make me up. I'm over here," Lawrence said.

"Lawrence, I don't believe in spirits—"

"But neither do I," he said. "Is my heart beating?"

"No!" she shouted. "You don't have any pulse at all. Now stop it. Where is your voice coming from?"

"Why, from me, I suppose. I'm over by the couch. At least I think I am. I had a heart attack—"

"I know you did," she cried, exasperated. "Now be quiet and let me think." Silence. She had to return to normalcy, wait until this period of . . . irrationality passed. The open eyes of Lawrence's body gave her the shivers but she couldn't bring herself to close them, so she put a book in his lap and started to clean out the refrigerator. They'd been on the road just long enough to collect unused leftovers. But she got confused and started to throw away good food. Once, unaccountably, she forgot how to open the crisper door underneath, and had to stop to remember.

"Lydia, why the hell are you cleaning out the refrigerator at a time like this?" Lawrence asked.

"Now stop it," she shouted, thoroughly distracted.

"You aren't crazy. I'm here," he announced forcibly. "You don't believe in spirits generally, but you believe in me, and *I'm* here; it's got something to do with that, why you can hear me."

"But Lawrence, the dead don't talk, so I must be mad."

"What would you rather believe?" he asked; and suddenly she didn't care if she was crazy or not, or what was happening. For all she knew, maybe she was just having a nightmare. "All *right*," she said, aloud. "What's next on the agenda?" The sweetness of madness, she thought, the freedom. She'd just go along. What else could she do? Lawrence was there; somehow he was going to help her figure out what to do with his body. She just couldn't cart it around forever. It would be a terrible nuisance.

He wanted her to just leave it somewhere, where it was peaceful and quiet and could just rot away by itself. She started the trailer up again, after putting Mr. George back on the bookcase. She *felt*, anyway, that Lawrence was beside her on the seat.

"The readers never got a chance to know you at all," she said suddenly.

"What readers? What are you talking about?" Lawrence said.

"I don't know. It just slipped into my mind," she said. "But what are we going to do now?"

"Just leave my body somewhere. There's no law against it that I know. Maybe local health laws. But after all, what could they do to you?"

"Well, it's more or less what we planned in case one of us died. At least you didn't change your ideas," she said. "If you're here, and I can't see you," she added, nervously.

"Well, I must be dead, I mean, really dead, and too stupid to know it," he answered. "If I was really dead, though, how could I be talking? You know—'ashes to ashes and dust to dust'—"

"Don't joke about something like that," she snapped. "Honestly."

"I'm just staying around to help," he said.

"A big help you are," Oversoul Seven said. He'd been around for the entire episode, but Lydia, as usual, wasn't aware of his presence.

"I thought someone else was here, but I wasn't sure," Lawrence said. "I don't see anyone though."

"That's because you don't know how to really see yet, or you're afraid to—"

"Well, look here, am I dead or not?" Lawrence asked. "Lydia and I are quite confused about it all. And who are you?"

"Yours was one of the easiest, most proficient transitions I've ever seen," Seven said. "You're to be congratulated. Most people make much more fuss about it. Of course, you weren't in pain for any long period or anything. Still, it was very good. You won't be around long, though. Someone will probably come for you. I'm a . . . friend of Lydia's."

"Really? I thought I knew all her friends," Lawrence said.

"Who are you talking to, for heaven's sake?" Lydia asked.

"Don't you hear him, too?"

"No, I don't hear anyone but you, and I shouldn't be hearing *you*. There!" she got that stiff smile on her face and turned the radio on, loud, to drown out his voice. But Lawrence said, "There's a state park, Lydia. Drive in there."

She felt as if she was in some kind of trance, and did as she was directed. She had to pay fifty cents and pass two guards who smiled and said what a great day it was. And Lydia thought, if she *was* in a trance, or dreaming, how come everything was so vivid?

"I don't know if this is altogether a good idea," Oversoul Seven said.

"A man has a right to do what he wants with his own body when he's finished with it," Lawrence said. Lydia frowned: Lawrence didn't sound crazy, or at least no crazier than usual. "There. That way. Turn left," he said.

She drove past rows of tents and campfires and children playing in the fields, now dark with dusk. A crowd was singing "Someone's in the kitchen with Dinah," and the air was full of the smell of hotdogs, steak, and onions. Lydia had given up all attempts to understand what was happening. Somebody — Lawrence? — was telling her what to do anyway, which was just as well, she thought, because she was incapable of making any decisions on her own.

"Further on," Lawrence directed.

The road became more isolated. Giant fir trees rose into the twilight darkness. They came to a park area of even green grass, dotted with benches. It was empty. "Here, Lydia, pull up," Lawrence said. "I haven't much time, darling, I can tell. Hurry."

She pulled the trailer up as close as she could to the nearest bench.

"Oh, the next one," Lawrence said. "The view is so much nicer."

She parked and went into the back of the camper. Lawrence's body was still there, with the book in its lap. "Well, that's that, then. I can't move it alone," she said.

"Just push it off the chair," Lawrence said.

"I can't!" She stood there, staring. "I've got to have a cigarette," she thought. She went outside, lit up, and looked out at the park and the woods and the benches and breathed the cool night air. Then, sure that she'd cleared her mind, she went back inside. It was all a dream: Lawrence wasn't dead, and he'd be in his body where he was supposed to be.

She went back inside. The body was still there. How bad was her mind? She had no way of knowing. All right, then! She yanked Lawrence's body down, dragged it the length of the trailer, down the steps, and over to the bench. Katydids were calling. She got a stone in one of her platform shoes, and had to take it off. It was much more difficult to tug the body *up*, but she did, until it sat nicely on the green bench, looking out across the fields to the woods.

"Admirable," Lawrence said. Then, to Seven, "Will you stay around to help her out? She's going to need help, you know. I hear someone calling me, and I have the feeling — " With that, Lawrence disappeared and Seven couldn't see him any longer. Lydia never had.

She got back in the camper, stared out at Lawrence's old-man body, and wanted to cry, but she couldn't. She started up the motor, left the state park, and just kept on driving. The road seemed real. Nothing else. At the same time, some inner, usually quiet part of her was alert, and talking mentally. This part was usually masked by her conscious thoughts, but there were great holes in her usual consciousness, through which these inner reasonings came. She was retreating, and had been for some time: that much was clear. The trip cross-country was to help her shake loose from her normal surroundings, for they held her . . . kept her oriented.

She was finished with orientation. She didn't want to relate any more. Lawrence hadn't wanted to reach sixty either (a milepost that hadn't bothered her a bit), and he hadn't. But she didn't want to go quickly, suddenly, like that. She'd go slowly, step by step, mental slip by mental slip, she thought; retreat easily, so imperceptibly that she, herself, could forget what she was doing. Like mental sleeping pills.

Lydia was only half-aware of these thoughts, even now. The picture of Lawrence's body on its bench kept coming into her mind. She blocked it out and kept driving. In the morning she fed Greenacre and Tuckie and Mr. George, and ate breakfast at the side of the road.

Seven kept trying to talk to her, but she didn't hear him; she didn't believe in spirits, except in Lawrence's, and it seemed to have deserted her.

They finally caught up with her three days later, when Lawrence's body had been traced. The police were very understanding. Lydia's children came for her. She explained what had happened and they all pretended that the events were quite normal, so she saw that they didn't believe a word that she said; and she didn't much care. She eyed her offspring with great detachment. They seemed too . . . solid, unimaginative . . . limited.

For a week her daughter, Anna, took her. She left with the cats and Mr. George, carrying his bowl in her arms, while Anna was out at bridge. They found her within a few hours. Roger, her son, had her next. But she looked around the suburban home and garden, and the whole environment seemed too pat, unreal; no longer where she belonged. It seemed quite clear; she didn't belong anyplace. Her interest in the world was fading. Vaguely she wondered that she'd ever taken it seriously at all.

They were giving her tranquilizers because every once in a while she kept talking about how Lawrence picked out the bench she'd left his body on, even though he'd been dead for hours. She thought it mystifying herself.

One night she didn't take the tranquilizers, and sneaked out after everyone was asleep. It was early autumn. The orange leaves were all dull and soft and falling everywhere. She ran — agile for her age, she thought — through all the backyards, ducking under clotheslines, avoiding garbage cans, sprinting past lighted windows showing glimpses of glowing television sets.

A great exhilaration filled her. Her nightgown flapped at her ankles as she ran. She lost her slippers, and luxuriated in the wet grass against her bare feet. They'd raise hell if they found her. Dimly she wondered when and why she'd stopped doing things like this. When she was a child? From the distance she heard alarmed voices — probably Roger and his wife calling — but she ran on and on.

For a while she almost felt as if someone was running with her, or keeping up to her in some funny way, and once she would have fallen over an old tree stump, but a voice in her head said, "Look out," or at least she thought that it did. She wasn't aware of Oversoul Seven though. Actually, he kept calling her name, but this inner voice merged with the shouts of Lydia's son and daughter-in-law, and in any case Seven kept feeling himself being pulled further and further away from Lydia, till he could hardly sense her at all. Instead, another scene was coming into reality for him. The backyards vanished, and shining mosaics took the place of the grass.

～ *Chapter Eleven* ～

Ma-ah in the Land
of the Speakers

Ma-ah had never seen mosaics before. She stared at the courtyard's spectacular floor, gazed in marvel at the brilliant blue, green, and purple tiles that glittered in the afternoon sunshine. The multitudinous patterns almost made her dizzy. There were strange wiggly lines, odd shapes, circles and squares, all flowing one into the other.

At one point, one shimmering blue fish-shaped flat stone fitted into a shining green one, of a bird. But it was almost impossible to find the dividing line, so that before her eyes the fish turned into the bird. And the same with all the other patterns. The various representations were so fluid and bright that she hesitated to walk on them. Sumpter went ahead, without looking down at all though, so she followed docilely enough. Long shadows lay clearly over the tiles, cast by the towering sheer cliffs that surrounded the courtyard.

"Sumtoa," Sumpter said, waiting for her. She was growing used to him; he'd been her steady companion for the two days that she'd been separated from Rampa. "Sumtoa," he said again.

She didn't have the slightest idea what the word itself meant, but his meaning was obvious from his gesture. He pointed at the cliff wall nearest them. She turned to look, and leapt back, startled. An image of a man was etched in the rock so cleverly that she thought him real for a moment; one arm close enough to brush her own. Like Sumpter, he was giant-sized, dressed in a violet-colored robe, and like all the people she'd seen here he had very light brown skin and blue eyes, flecked with orange.

"Sum-to-a," he said, more slowly this time.

She shook her head, saying in her own language, "I don't understand."

He pointed again. Once more she turned to look. The entire cliff wall was painted with figures and drawings. Now she wondered how she could have missed them before. So craftily were these executed that it looked as if real people blended with the rocks, emerging from the crevices.

"Crom a taum," Sumpter said, smiling.

Ma-ah shrugged, almost angrily. What did he want her to do? And where was Rampa? Every time she asked, Sumpter answered with gestures and those words that she couldn't understand, but she deduced that Rampa was undergoing the same kind of experiences that she was, with someone else. "Why were Rampa and I separated?" she asked, but Sumpter only smiled reassuringly. Then he pointed to his own ears, to hers, and to the image on the wall. He wanted her to listen to . . . the painted-on man?

Sumpter shook his head, the robe's cowl moving just enough to show the straight black hair that fell to the nape of his neck. He took Ma-ah's hand gently, so as not to frighten her, and ran her fingers lightly over the portions of the wall painting that she could reach. At first she recoiled with uneasy surprise. The oddest sensation began to spread through her fingertips; a tingling. Sumpter just watched, encouragingly.

Ma-ah was caught between wonder and distrust. The lines of the painted figure were giving off . . . sounds . . . that somehow rushed through her hands. Utterly engrossed, she ran her fingers over the broad areas, and these produced a different sensation. The colors had something to do with it, too. Green made long ripples in her flesh, and then long lingering sound-feelings.

The figure's head and shoulders were too high for her to reach. Almost slyly, she sped around and touched Sumpter's robe. It was soft, but no sounds went singing through her fingers. He laughed kindly enough, but she felt that he was making fun of her, or perhaps had even anticipated her motion, or one like it. Her eyes darkened sullenly.

Seeing her reaction, Sumpter touched her robe, the brown one they'd given her, and shook his head with a mischievous shrug as if to say, "See, yours doesn't make any noise either."

Her eyes cleared, but she watched him guardedly. She was under constant surveillance; but apparently she wasn't being restrained. She could look at the cliff walls, or not, as she chose — he wasn't forcing her to do so.

No contest of wills was involved. Satisfied, she ran a few steps to the next drawing, a strange large bird squatting on the ground, with people coming out of its open mouth, or belly. She couldn't tell which. The sunlight shone on the bird's folded wings, and the people looked alarmingly alive. How could that be, if the bird swallowed them? And what bird was big enough to swallow whole people?

She glanced sideways at Sumpter. Such things were impossible. She knew what animals and birds were, even if she was ignorant about this hidden valley. So she shook her head and grimaced, then smiled broadly, pointing at the drawing, to show her disbelief.

Sumpter took her hand again and tried to run her fingers across the lines of the bird's body, but she sprang back, frightened that the bird's belly or mouth might suddenly close and swallow her hand, fingers and all.

Sumpter nodded soberly, as if respecting her fear. Then he fingered the painting himself. Only when he withdrew his hand, intact, did Ma-ah follow his example. At first she was very cautious. This could be a trick that she didn't understand. But suddenly her face softened. She tipped her head. The sounds were joyful, filled with exaltation or satisfaction. She laughed up at Sumpter: the bird was singing.

Now it was Sumpter who was excited. She was forgetting herself in the enjoyment of new discoveries, as he'd hoped. She was feeling less trapped. He'd been appointed as her teacher, and she was learning quickly. But how much could she learn? What were her capacities? It was important that he encourage her just enough, without making her feel inferior, faced as she was with so many new experiences.

He walked quickly to a small particularly bright corner of the courtyard, without waiting for her, then stopped. Ma-ah followed readily enough, dawdling along slightly to show that the decision to follow was her own. Good. He wanted to encourage her independence, at least when it wasn't just stubbornness.

But she forgot everything else as she examined this corner of the wall. Here the drawings were particularly vivid, the colors alive and glowing. Some were figures of animals and birds that she'd known in her own world, but others she'd never seen before. Excited, she pointed out those with which she was familiar, feeling that she was showing *him* something for a change. Sumpter was delighted. He waited for her to discover the writing, the simple one-word descriptions beneath.

It didn't take her long. She spied the wiggly **Z** beneath the bird first, and impulsively fingered it. The sound translation zinged through her fingertips—weak as yet, Sumpter could tell, but she was getting it. It took her only a few seconds to connect the sounds she was getting from the symbol, with the drawing of the bird above.

It would be a while before he could explain that the symbols were embossed with sound—not the drawings themselves, as in the earlier ones she'd seen, because if all the paintings identified themselves audibly, then there would be no built-in reason for pupils to learn the written characters.

"Boroo," she said, wonderingly, pointing at the bird.

"Bor*uu*," he corrected quickly, almost shouting and smiling at once because she was learning so fast.

Ma-ah loved challenges, but she wasn't about to appear inferior. She frowned, indicated the picture of a hare with its written character, and demanded the sound-word for it. Gently Sumpter shook his head. She sulked for a moment, but then returned to the wall, touched the Λ beneath the image, and laughed with renewed astonishment as the symbol automatically gave up its sound to the pressure of her hands.

"Zentu," she said, repeating it. Then she put her fingers to her ears, but the sounds were absorbed too quickly by the skin; she couldn't transmit the sound, like that, to the ears. She glared at Sumpter: where had the noises gone? Had he taken them from her in some way? He pointed back to the symbol. She touched it, receiving another sound stimulus, and from then on there was no stopping her.

They spent the whole afternoon there. Ma-ah ran from symbol to symbol, picking up the vocabulary incredibly fast, demanding that Sumpter repeat the words for her correctly, sometimes dancing around him when she conquered a particularly difficult sound.

Even when the sun lowered and the courtyard was buried in deep blue shadows, she wasn't really ready to quit. Walking back, she stared down at the floor tiles, calling out the words she could remember as she recognized the corresponding images. Once she got down on her hands and knees and fingered one of the drawings, but these weren't sound-embossed, and she rose, disappointed.

Sumpter didn't want to rush her, but it was time to show her the city, to introduce her gradually to customs and experiences that would frighten her considerably if she were unprepared. He waited until she tired herself out with chattering—in her own language. He pretended not to know it, to give her the impetus to learn the new vocabulary. In any case, he knew many of her thoughts; telepathically she was easy to read, but she wasn't ready for *that*. For that matter, there was something odd in her mental experience occasionally that struck him as incongruous, but he couldn't place exactly what it was.

Now, for example, her thoughts were quite transparent, with curiosity foremost. She was following him agreeably enough. He led her over to the living-wall just on the other side of the courtyard. Two couches were placed at the far end of the room, enough away from the wall so that pupils would not feel trapped or too frightened by what they saw. Purposely Sumpter left the gate to the court open, offering her an easy escape if she thought she needed one. He pointed. She eyed the couch and sat down. Then he pointed to the living-wall, signaled the proper mental sound for activation, and waited.

The opaque wall shimmered, turned milky, and slowly the images emerged, until an entire city street came into view with its sounds, odors, and activity. Ma-ah stiffened, gasped, and eyed the open door. Sumpter watched her eagerly, wondering that his pupil's first reactions still excited him. He enlarged the view. There they were, the tiled paths with their magnificent colors, dotted by islands of foliage; the individual dwellings open to sun and air (all erected with sound frequencies, but using native-Earth materials); one of the model cities that were scattered in suitably hidden areas over the planet.

She was completely engrossed, and he gave the mental sound command for three dimensions. Instantly the scene came forward, leapt out, became complete. He looked quickly for her reaction, expecting that this final clarification might alarm her.

Instead the strangest smile lit up her face, oddly uncharacteristic, unlike any of her other expressions that he'd seen so far.

"Of course," she cried, and jumped from the couch. Instant comprehension flooded her features, giving him the weirdest feeling that she understood something that he didn't; that the scene had a completely significant personal meaning for her that was impossible.

The pupil's gateway to the city was to the left. He hadn't intended to introduce her to the city itself until they'd held several orientation periods, but she rushed to the gate and opened it before he realized what had happened. And why did she run to that one entry which she could not have known led to the city?

It was Oversoul Seven who inadvertently gasped through Ma-ah's lips, and again, impulsively rushed Ma-ah to the city gateway. But Ma-ah's astonishment at the view dislocated Seven's consciousness. She stood amazed, unable to speak. Her look of clear knowing vanished so completely that Sumpter wondered if he'd imagined it, though he knew he hadn't. Instead, Ma-ah just looked dazed and frightened. ("And no wonder," Cyprus would say, later, to Seven.)

Incredulous, Ma-ah found herself staring at three huge triangular objects that towered into the sky. They seemed to have just grown up from the Earth, isolated, not a part of any other structures such as mountains or cliffs. Yet they were made of rock, and she knew they were man-made. Broad at the base, they gradually narrowed to a peak top and were, she saw now, equipped with stairs. Around them, Sumpter's giant-sized people looked like ants as they hurried about, engaged in too many activities for her to take in at once.

Courtyards surrounded the structures, and a series of stone platforms dotted with all kinds of foliage. There were other buildings of various sizes facing several squares. Squinting, Ma-ah suddenly let out a yelp of panic and disbelief. She pointed, trembling, at one of the foundations that had just caught her eye — water shooting up from the ground, instead of coming down upon it, like rain. Water raining up from the Earth, instead of down from the sky! This terrified her above all else she'd seen. It was . . . wrong, impossible . . . against all she knew of nature and the world. Appalled, she stood staring, oblivious to everything else.

"Ma-ah," Sumpter said.

She looked at him, her eyes wide with unwilling sharp perception of her predicament and the power of Sumpter and his people. If they could reverse nature, make rain fall upside down, then she was obviously at their mercy. Sumpter saw that recognition in her taut face as she looked up at him, that grudging awe. But her glance also disclosed an instant intelligence that was shrewd and inventive. Despite it all, she wouldn't be browbeaten. Already she half-shrugged, accepting her present position but somehow rising above it.

She gave the fountains a sideways defiant look now, took a deep breath, and looked back at the view as if it was, after all, quite usual and nothing to get excited about. Sumpter grinned approvingly, but behind his hand, and with his head turned the other way.

As Ma-ah regained her composure, Oversoul Seven's consciousness came back to itself. He recognized the pyramids, but what else was there that eluded him? What knowledge had he forgotten? A great yearning possessed him. Ma-ah suddenly ran forward, with obvious eagerness, straight brown hair flying, robe in disarray. She wasn't used to running with cloth whipping about her ankles. Several times the robe caught between her thighs, so that she lost her footing, but she regained it and went running on. Bewildered by her contradictory reactions, Sumpter followed. He mused, somewhat disgruntled, that he didn't have to worry about introducing her to new surroundings — she was leading him.

Ma-ah's and Seven's consciousnesses were separate, yet bleed-throughs constantly occurred. Now Ma-ah picked up Seven's surprising sense of familiarity with the people and the pyramids (which she suddenly understood *were* pyramids) and his excited urge to inspect them.

She accepted these emotions unquestioningly as her own for the moment—they were so clear and unmistakable. Only later would she question. So she kept running, scattering the people who gathered in various groups around the assorted stone buildings. They looked at her curiously, her small size and darker skin instantly setting her apart. Then they went on with their activities as they saw Sumpter, his violet robe marking him as a prominent Speaker.

And Oversoul Seven felt an exhilaration and joy in Ma-ah's body rhythm as she ran. He was acutely and pleasurably aware of the free integrity of her motion, the smoothly functioning nerves and muscles cooperating in the swift stride. For an instant he and Ma-ah almost knew each other as separate while one, united as they were by that imperative purpose to reach the middle pyramid.

Ma-ah paused, then flew up the steps. They were giant-sized to her, yet she leapt them easily. Sumpter followed, growing more serious and perplexed. They had ascended nearly a hundred stairs when Ma-ah paused to get her breath, and turned, looking out over the city. Now the different areas were clearly visible; the residential sections in a large exterior circle surrounded by foliage and tiled paths; the interconnecting roads, and in the center the pyramids, temples, and public buildings. The impenetrable cliffs surrounded all.

When had she stood there before? Ma-ah wondered. Why was it so familiar? She leaned against the smooth shining wall for support.

"You haven't been here before, but I think I have," Seven tried to say to her, but now she was suddenly aware of the height, and it made her dizzy. Vaguely the eager run to the pyramid returned to her mind. What was she doing here? Had she run or only dreamed that she had? Never in her life had she stood so high above the ground. She backed away now, toward the wall. Only birds went that high.

Sumpter put his arm out protectively, but his face was stricken: did she know how close she was to . . . the door? She couldn't, of course. Yet she'd run almost like one possessed directly toward one of the most secret of pyramid entries; unknown even to many of the people. Now she stood almost immobile, staring down at the city below, trying to conquer her fear. It was almost as if the fear itself suddenly surfaced, he thought. Certainly it hadn't been present earlier. Yet she wasn't faking now, he was sure of it.

Too late, Seven realized that heights would frighten her. Of course, he should have known. For that matter, he was almost as confused as she was, a pretty state of affairs. She was going to faint. Quickly Seven tried to take over for her, but she took one last terrified look down at the city, and fell in a heap beside Sumpter.

Sumpter picked her up gently, and carried her down. A small crowd had gathered, but the people parted to let him through. A woman brought a sponge dampened with water, and he bathed Ma-ah's face. Her behavior was definitely strange in ways that he couldn't decipher, he thought. Suddenly the words came into his mind: "Once a Speaker, always a Speaker." He knew that, of course, but why did the thought come to him now, under these circumstances? Now the well-known phrase seemed to have a particular significance that escaped him.

Ma-ah was coming to. As she began to open her eyes, Sumpter was suddenly certain that she would end up before the Tribunal, though why he couldn't say.

~ *Chapter Twelve* ~

Ma-ah and the Shining Building Blocks of Sound

"**S**yllables are the sound equivalents of atoms," Sumpter said. "And atoms compose matter. Syllables can be organized into words, of course. But they can also be organized into sound patterns called no-words. That is, the sounds don't refer to objects or even feelings, and they don't name things in usual terms. Instead the no-words are simply . . . power. They do things, not represent them."

Ma-ah shrugged. "You said we were going to see Rampa this morning. That's all I care about. I can't concentrate. How can you expect me to be interested in anything else, when I haven't seen him in so long?"

Sumpter nodded. She's picked up their language very quickly, but all morning she'd been scowling and pretending not to understand what he said. Still, he was growing more uneasy. She was learning amazingly well and he resented this . . . encounter that would surely upset her. "Rampa might already be in the courtyard," he said. "We may as well go down now, then."

She jumped up from the stone bench and walked swiftly ahead of him, as usual. She flung the courtyard gate open and went flying across the mosaic floor, with no thought now of the glittering tile patterns that had once so engaged her attention.

Rampa was already there. She stopped suddenly. He looked so different in the robe they'd given him; so distant and oddly unapproachable. Her eyes narrowed. All at once she saw the other robed figure who was waiting for Rampa as Sumpter was waiting for her. Only this was a young woman! Ma-ah swung around and glared accusingly at Sumpter, who'd let her think all along that Rampa's teacher was also a man. She stopped for a moment, then began to walk ahead at a slower pace, almost nonchalantly. But her teeth were suddenly chattering and she had to hold her lips tight together in a forced smile.

Rampa stood silently, watching Ma-ah approach. He was uneasy — she saw that immediately. "How different you look," she said, in their old language.

"You, too," Rampa said. "Is that man your teacher?"

"Sumpter? I guess so. Is she yours?" Ma-ah pointed toward the girl who stood at the other end of the courtyard.

"Yes, my teacher," he said, but there was an inquiry in his answer that Ma-ah didn't understand. She frowned.

"Do you like . . . him, your teacher?" Rampa asked, in that same peculiar tone.

"I like him well enough," Ma-ah said irritably. Rampa seemed confused. He looked past her suddenly at Sumpter. A flash of understanding seemed to pass between them that made Ma-ah unaccountably furious. "Well, what are you looking at him for?" she said. "We haven't seen each other in weeks and you just stand there — "

"I like my teacher very much," Rampa said. "I'm sorry that you don't like yours as well."

Ma-ah glanced past Rampa, over to the girl who stood in the background with her eyes lowered. She was much taller than Rampa, of course; yet Rampa didn't look small by contrast, simply sturdier and more compact. And he'd changed, Ma-ah realized, as she had. There was nothing between them.

Surprised, she looked closely at him. He laughed and mimicked her shrug as he used to. "I don't know what's happened," Rampa said. "What we shared — that life is gone. For all she's taught me, my alliance goes to my teacher. How is it that you don't feel the same for Sumpter?"

Ma-ah didn't answer. She was staring at the girl.

"Her name is Orona," Rampa said.

"Who cares?" Ma-ah flared, automatically. Yet again to her own surprise she realized that she didn't care. They'd joined forces in the old world, and whatever held them together there no longer applied. Rampa smiled when she snapped at him, and she found herself smiling back.

"You agree, then?" he asked.

"To what? . . . To you and . . . Orona?"

"That you and I be . . . separate?"

Ma-ah nodded. He relaxed visibly and said in a softer voice: "They hoped that you would like Sumpter more. They have plans for us, but I don't know what they are yet."

"I'll make my own plans," Ma-ah said with some defiance.

Rampa was silent for a moment. Then he said slowly: "Will you come when they build a dwelling for Orona and me?"

The implications flew through her mind — memories of their being together on the prickly hides, the moonlight through the rock crevices. But she nodded, agreeably, astonished at her own reaction once more. All right, she thought, very clearly. All bonds were cut. She and Rampa in their robes, with their new language and knowledge, were no longer the people they had been. For one thing they weren't half-starved all the time; they didn't have to cling together for protection and mutual help, they didn't have to hide in the cold, forsaken cliffs. All right.

"I'll come," she said soberly. She turned and walked away, but her eyes stung and she glared accusingly at Sumpter once more as they left the courtyard. "So it was all planned," she said. "And what more is planned? I might be heartbroken for all you and your people know or care. It just happens I'm not. But you couldn't have known that — "

"It was hoped that you'd turn to me, as Rampa turned to Orona," Sumpter said painfully.

"I turn to no one," Ma-ah said. But when he didn't answer, she grinned to herself: rather than go back to her old world, she'd do . . . well, practically anything. Something in Sumpter's manner made her suddenly realize that he'd hoped she would turn to him, too, in the . . . way she hadn't. Her steps quickened. The realization gave her a certain sense of power. Ma-ah also began to feel very free and unfettered. A mate was just a mate, she thought; important in the old world because men were stronger than women. But here . . .

At that moment, her relationship with Sumpter changed. He was aware of her thoughts, and instantly marked the difference in her attitude. He shook his head; keeping her in line until she learned what she had to learn would take some doing. He was very aware of her swift steps, the swish of her robe, and amused by his own illogical sense of hurt over her . . . comparative rejection. Rampa had instantly taken to Orona. Ma-ah had not been so compliant. And if she did not take to him, eventually someone else must be found to take his place. She must have children.

Ma-ah strode ahead silently, but now with a certain amusing arrogance, he thought. She was going to tease him quite purposely.

"Did you take to me at once?" she asked, suddenly stopping and turning to face him.

"Of course," he said.

The simple statement disarmed and infuriated her. Sumpter didn't even seem embarrassed.

"Good," she said, shortly.

At this, he couldn't help but laugh.

Later that day he tried to prepare her to attend the time-of-joining. "Just watch and listen," he said. "I'm not going to explain what will happen now. I want to know how much you'll understand on your own." He told himself that she would do very well, yet when the day of joining came, he was vaguely uneasy. Would her resentment over Rampa and Orona inhibit the proceedings?

Ma-ah, however, was aware of no resentment at all. She stood with Sumpter amid groups of his people. A bare spot of land was before them. They all stood staring at it and smiling, splendid giant-sized people with bare heads now, their robes bright and festive. "Watch well," Sumpter whispered.

"Everything is a lesson," Ma-ah said, adding, "some lesson," as she stared over at Rampa and Orona, who stood together in the center of the clearing.

An odd expectant silence fell. Even knowing as little as she did about Sumpter's people, Ma-ah was alerted. Each face was quietly smiling, but no one spoke. Around the clearing chunks of rock were piled, haphazardly it seemed, some very large, some hardly bigger than stones. No one moved, yet Ma-ah sensed some change in direction that she couldn't comprehend. Her fingers tingled as they did when she touched the sound-embossed cave drawings, yet she was touching nothing. She heard no sounds, either normal ones or the inner kind that the embossed drawings gave her.

Inquisitively she turned to Sumpter. What was he doing? What were all of them doing? Sumpter's head was thrown back, his eyes oddly masked, secretive, dreamy, yet excited. They glittered. His lips were closed, yet very gently. His throat muscles weren't moving, yet she had the impression that they were. Ma-ah sensed the weirdest kind of rising tension, weird because everyone looked so delightfully relaxed and quiet. How could they stand so still, though, she wondered. Could Rampa? She glanced over at him.

Orona held his hand, and he stood as quietly as all the rest of them, only his eyes were lowered. He and Orona both stared at the ground before their feet, steadily and intently, as if they expected something to happen there. But what? Rampa seemed to know what was going on, though, Ma-ah realized. Irritated—why should he know while she didn't?—she turned to Sumpter and touched his hand. As she did, a strained unsteady sound appeared in the air above her head and she jumped with surprise. She felt as if some . . . sound-shape was up there, invisible and yet shining; and that her irritation had somehow disturbed it, broken it up into . . . known sound? Blushing, she lowered her head. She'd interrupted whatever they were doing, and they knew it, she was certain. . . .

Before she could finish the thought and without otherwise moving, Sumpter reached over and took her hand. Ma-ah would have run away in that first moment, but instantly she was dizzy and astonished. She felt as if a river had suddenly begun to lift her up and carry her along; and the river was . . . the energy or concentration or purpose of the people. They were doing things she couldn't understand again. Her tingling fingers told her that sound was involved, but it was within-sound, not without-sound. She couldn't hear it. But because of her practice with the cave drawings she could feel it now and then; and occasionally brilliant images of . . . shaped sound arose in her inner eye. Where they came from Ma-ah didn't know, only that the people were manipulating . . . something. And Rampa and Orona were waiting for it. Did Sumpter smile? Ma-ah thought he did but she couldn't be sure.

Then before her eyes one large chunk of rock rose up seemingly by it-self, slowly. She wanted to gasp aloud, but didn't dare to. Her fingers twitched as if they were full of . . . sounds that couldn't get out, or as if she didn't know how to release them. The rock rose higher. It went suddenly flying across the ground, just above it, toward Rampa and Orona. Rampa saw it coming and looked as if he wanted to run out of the way.

For an instant Ma-ah was caught between fear for him — the rock could slam into his knees if it didn't change direction — and relief: she wasn't the only one who was frightened. She and Rampa at least shared that. Rampa's eyes widened as Ma-ah watched, but Orona's hand held his, and he wasn't about to break away if she didn't. The rock came right at them, then about three feet away, its progress slowed. It hung for a moment, then quietly dropped at their feet. Still holding hands, Rampa and Orona took several almost-ritualistic steps to the left.

Ma-ah had been too surprised to do anything. Now she looked to see if some kind of incline could possibly account for the rock's movements. Per-haps her eyes had tricked her; the rock didn't really fly, but only seemed to . . . because of some peculiar aspect of the ground. Her eyes widened with triumph — there was a very gentle incline leading to the area where Rampa and Orona stood. Ma-ah relaxed for a moment, then frowned. The incline just wasn't enough to account for what had happened.

She was used to Sumpter's strange land, with its peculiar characteristics like the fountains. Sumpter had explained how water could be made to flow up from the ground. But . . . rocks flying above the ground like unwieldy, clumsy birds? Some deep part of her was outraged and threatened; and angry. How could you do anything, if the rules kept changing?

Again, Ma-ah's thoughts broke off. For the last few moments the air itself had been developing an unaccustomed feel to it that she'd half-ignored. Now some barrier seemed to break, some hidden but powerful intensity was suddenly released. A dozen rocks lifted at once. Ma-ah's hand flew to her throat. She felt as if a million vowels and syllables rose into the air, all glittering, all . . . alive; like . . . animals of sound, moving beneath the rocks then and moving them, flying with them, supporting them. Instinctively she looked over at Rampa. He stared as unbelievingly as she. But again he followed Orona's example and never budged.

Well, neither would she, then! The rocks lined up, inches from the ground, then gently moved to the bare spot and fell softly. Now the air seemed saturated with sound, but Ma-ah heard nothing. How could that be? Silent sound? Her fingers tingled once more. Then she noticed that her right hand, in Sumpter's, felt different from her other hand . . . lighter, strangely empty yet moving. This frightened her most of all — *her* hand was involved. She was just about to pull away when two things happened almost at once.

First, whole stacks of rocks moved, this time even quicker than before. Without a wobble they whooshed into the air. But even more amazing to Ma-ah was the placement of the rocks. They fell to the ground in such a way that a pattern was obvious. Before her eyes a tall center pyramid came into being, with a half-circle room on either side. Yet no one moved or spoke. Now the rocks piled one on top of the other. No eyes followed their flight but hers. And Rampa's. Again, she thought: they still shared that — they were outsiders.

Then the atmosphere suddenly changed. Ma-ah sensed it at once, even before she realized what was happening. Some massive effort was lessened. A tension disappeared. The dwelling was completed. No — she looked again. A few gaps in the rocks still remained, by the doorway. She was watching the structure, so it was a few moments before she saw the group of children coming from the direction of the courtyard. They were all smiling, obviously excited, hardly able to contain themselves, but none of them spoke.

They made a circle in front of the adults, and as they did so the adults relaxed noticeably; their intense focus was gone. The children looked at the dwelling. Rampa and Orona stood in the doorway. Three stones, small in contrast with the others, still lay on the ground. Were they supposed to go into the gaps in the doorway? Ma-ah stiffened. The tension was building up again — this time she swore she *heard* it through her fingertips — into a high-pitched whine. Yet with her ears she heard no sound at all.

At first nothing happened. Then one of the smallest rocks rose slowly up but a few inches, wobbled, went up higher, tottered and fell.

The air was so full of extra tension that even Ma-ah held her breath. Then came a single audible sigh of disappointment—the first "real" sound in so long that Ma-ah was astonished. One small girl clamped her hand to her mouth. Those on either side frowned so deeply at the offender that Ma-ah almost cried for her, knowing exactly how she must feel. The girl was about half-grown, but smaller than the others.

Then the child put her hands back at her sides; the look of dismay left her face. Once more everyone was smiling, effortlessly it seemed. Almost at once the same stone rose, fairly steady this time, and flew through the air. It stopped, hovering. Ma-ah grinned herself. The children obviously were trying to move the stone into position. Would they?

A tiny frown began to appear on the face of the little girl who had gasped earlier. Ma-ah knew that in some way a frowning concentration was wrong. "You can do it. You can do it. It's easy," she told the child without thinking. And suddenly the girl's brow cleared. The stone sailed across the ground, landing right where it seemed to belong. Now it was the children's turn to relax.

The air of waiting diminished but did not disappear. Then Orona threw her arms out in a gracious smiling gesture, and the second rock rose and flew into place. One rock remained. Who was to . . . ? Suddenly Ma-ah understood. Rampa was to move the last rock. Of course. The man and woman put in the last two rocks of their own home.

Rampa *had* known about the entire affair, then, and she had not. Ma-ah's cheeks burned. She'd been given no such training. Why had Rampa? But now he threw his arms out in the same gesture Orona had used a moment earlier. Nothing happened. The last stone was quite small, but it didn't budge from its place on the ground. Training or no, Rampa couldn't do it. Maybe only Sumpter's people could. Ma-ah glared at Sumpter for putting Rampa to such a test in front of everyone.

Yet no one seemed worried. There was no impatience. Rampa just stood there quietly, for that matter, his face quiet and expectant. The idiot, Ma-ah thought; then with a flash of self-indulgent triumph: it served him right. The suspense was more than she could bear. Suppose he failed—in front of his new mate and the entire group?

Memories flew to her mind, of times when he'd helped her; when except for him they might have starved; when except for his strength she might have given in to fear or panic. She wanted so to help him. But how? Suddenly the tingling in her fingers was so strong that she flinched. In her mind's eye she saw the rock rise into the air, then fit into place. It had to!

And the actual rock suddenly shot into the air with great jerks and wobbles, flew as if pushed by a great angry force, and slammed into place so vehemently that Ma-ah thought it would crash into pieces.

She almost laughed out loud. Rampa may have been clumsy, but he was effective! She looked over at him, disconcerted: he looked astonished and surprised. There was silence, inside-silence, outside-silence. Then all eyes turned to Ma-ah.

What for? Confused, she swung around to Sumpter—who began to laugh. His laughter was picked up by the others. Ma-ah stood haughtily, angrily. What were they laughing at? It was a great, generous relieved laughter, almost indulgent, as if she'd done something quite well—considering. Considering what?

Ma-ah looked at Rampa and Orona. They were whispering. For a moment Rampa looked over at her, and Ma-ah saw that he was furious. At what? Why should he be angry when everyone else was smiling at her? "What's happening?" she said to Sumpter, since obviously the ban against talk was lifted. "Why is everyone so happy with me suddenly? And why is Rampa furious? I should be the one who's mad, if anyone. After all, he left me—it's his new dwelling—"

Sumpter looked down at her, so obviously pleased with her that Ma-ah grew even more confused. At the same time she felt terribly left out, not knowing something that was obvious to everyone else. "I'll tell you everything as soon as I get the chance," Sumpter said. "And now your training will really begin. You're ready for it. I'll tell you who we are and how we came here, and where you can fit into our plans." Again his pleasure with her was so obvious that Ma-ah couldn't help but be gratified. Yet despite herself she almost glowered at him: he treated her like an exceptional child, she thought resentfully; just happy because she learned to do something—even if she didn't know what it was.

The crowd had broken up into groups. They were passing around fruits and drinks. Everyone was talking and laughing at once. Now and then someone caught Ma-ah's eye and smiled. The celebrants were making such noise that Ma-ah could hardly hear what Sumpter was saying. She looked around, at Orona and Rampa, who were being toasted; at the new dwelling; at the children who were running and dancing. A great sense of detachment overcame her. She savored it, while resenting it at the same time. Sumpter waited, watching her, the smile gone from his face. Slowly they began to stroll together toward the courtyard.

∼ *Chapter Thirteen* ∼

Josef's Pictures of Magic
and Jonathan's Revenge

Josef eyed his canvas. He was painting a tiled courtyard. When he was finished each tile would be perfect, individually patterned and glowing.
The glazes he would use! He almost chortled with delight—and the towering cliff walls, impossibly high, yet somehow right! The scene in his mind
was so vivid that he felt a mixture of torture and exaltation as he tried to
capture it.

In fact, he was so filled with inspiration that he felt transformed. Only
a few days earlier all he could think of was food. Now it was the last thing on
his mind. Jonathan left a tray underneath his door twice a day; sometimes it
was hardly touched when he retrieved it. Thinking of Jonathan, Josef glowered and stared at the windows. Time and time again he'd begged Jonathan
to take the boards down from the top at least, so he could have decent light.
The lamps weren't enough.

For one thing, the tiled courtyard was an outdoor scene; he couldn't
duplicate that light under these conditions. And what could Jonathan do to
him if he ripped the boards down himself? The glass would be ruined, of
course, because he'd have to do it from the inside. Josef went back to his
painting, forgetting everything else for a while. Then he stood back once
more, studying his painting. It was obvious: the light just wouldn't do.

In fresh outrage, he yelled aloud, broke the top window glass with the chair, and banged away at the boards that had been nailed up outside. Even the noise he made sounded satisfying. "Serves them right," he thought, enjoying the onrush of energy; grinning as the light came splashing through the room.

He heard the pounding footsteps rush up the stairs, and in a moment Jonathan came in, yelling, when he saw the damage. Broken glass was all over the floor. Jonathan lunged at Josef, cursing. "The glass. The fine, expensive glass," he kept shouting.

"I'll pay for it. I'll pay. I can't work in that miserable light," Josef yelled, fighting him off. Jonathan was so shocked that finally he just stood aside, staring at the glass.

"I warned you," he said, this time in a desperate quiet voice. "This time you've gone too far."

Josef turned back to his painting. "I'll pay for the glass," he shouted again, wearily. "I told you I needed decent light. Before winter, I'll sell these for good prices, and you'll have your precious windows back. Now let me work."

"You're a crazy man. Crazy. Wait till my father gets back from the fields. We're not going to get any glass for *your* windows ever again — "

"Good," Josef said. He laughed out loud and went back to work, leaving Jonathan to sputter and rage until finally he left, slamming the door behind him.

When Jonathan was gone, Josef left the easel, danced in the sunlight that came through the open windows, twirling clumsily around in circles like a circus bear. Then he returned to his canvas. All he cared about now were his paintings. He'd never been so inspired in his life, for any period of time. To work at such a pitch! When you had inspiration, you didn't need discipline, he thought gleefully; or at least inspiration had its own built-in discipline.

His paintings came like magic, out of nowhere, or out of a somewhere of dreams or imagination.

The afternoon went so quickly that Josef thought only a few moments had passed when Jonathan returned with his father. Without paying too much attention, Josef was aware of the annoying noise in the hall, the footsteps again; and then Jonathan and Elgren were in the room. The old man gasped, and Jonathan shouted with triumphant spite.

Josef just turned around and looked at them with all the fierceness he could muster. "I warned you that I needed light. I pleaded, but would you take down the, boards? No, so it's your fault, for being so stupid — "

"I told you. He's crazy," Jonathan said, with some awe.

Elgren stood there, round, fat, and serious. "There's something here we don't understand," he said, slowly. "Men just don't act like that; not ordinary men."

"That's what I mean! He's—"

For once Elgren motioned his son to be quiet. "The destruction of perfect glass," he said. "Only the finest houses can have such windows. They're the pride . . . the pride. . . ." He broke off. "It's demoniac. Wanton destruction. I liked you. Despite it all, I liked you."

"You had a fine way of showing it," Josef shouted, getting redfaced. "Locking me up—"

"For your own good. To make you fulfill your bargain. That was only right," Jonathan shouted back.

"We gave you food again when you started to paint, even though you made no progress on *our* painting," Elgren said, as if his heart would break.

"Thank you. Thank you. I'm grateful, I'm sure," Josef thundered. "And there's your painting. It's started. Begun." He pointed dramatically at the one prosaic, uninspired painting in the room. "The undercoating's done. I'm just waiting for it to dry."

Jonathan ran over and touched it. "It feels dry enough to me," he said. "You just set it aside to do these other crazy paintings; to spite us."

"The window glass," Elgren said, with a deep sigh. "We can just stop feeding you again. You take our food on false pretenses unless you finish our painting."

"I don't care about eating anyway," Josef said. His warm brown eyes filled with vehemence. "I'll just paint what I want, and eat the pillows if I have to—"

"Eat the pillows! I told you, he's mad," Jonathan said.

"There's still something here that we don't understand," Elgren said to his son. "So shut up and let me think."

Josef snorted.

Jonathan paced the room angrily.

Elgren stared at Josef. "We might as well not exist for you," he said finally. "You don't see us at all as us. Just as we . . . affect you and your paintings. We don't exist for you." He paused, struck by his own words, frightened by them even.

"Ahhh, I just want to work, to paint," Josef said, not understanding at all. "You'll get your painting. I'll do it. You see, it's begun. I'll pay for your glass. I'll sell some of these paintings, and I'll pay—"

"He's possessed," Jonathan shouted. "That's it."

"Possessed by nincompoops like you," Josef yelled back. But real uneasiness gnawed at him. Something in Elgren's face worried him, and he realized suddenly that he needed the Hosentaufs. Suppose they put him out and he lost his work space? He was dependent on them right now. All at once he felt threatened, really threatened. Any commotion and his inspiration could vanish — who knew, forever maybe?

He tried to smile pleasantly, feeling the muscles in his face go all wiggly with the effort. "Just let me paint, and you'll have all the fine paintings you want — the one of the house, and the portraits, too — " He blushed furiously, feeling abject, miserable, amazed at the change in circumstances.

He tried to see Elgren as a person, but all he could see was a pompous, fat, funny . . . caricature of a man. Which he was! Which he was, Josef thought angrily. "Ahhh, just don't torment me," he said, in exasperation.

"We'll be back," Elgren said.

"No doubt. No doubt," Josef answered. He glowered at nothing in particular when they'd gone. Elgren was taking him seriously in some way that he didn't understand, he thought. And now all he wanted was to stay here in this room more than anything in the world so he could paint, while only a week ago all he wanted was to get out of it. Somehow that gave the Hosentaufs a hold over him that no one had ever had before. Was he a prisoner of his own inspiration? Where had his freedom gone?

It came to him all at once that he didn't even want to go outside; just to paint and keep up with the ideas that were coming to him so quickly for the first time in his life. They fascinated him. Did they frighten him, too, coming from nowhere as they seemed to? "Bah!" he said aloud. Thinking could drive you crazy. He went back to work. In a matter of minutes he forgot everything but the painting on the easel.

It was early twilight when Elgren and Jonathan returned, and instantly Josef sensed a change in their manner. For one thing, they weren't wearing work clothes; they were dressed for visiting. For another, there was an odd formality in the way they entered the room; quietly, not yelling or shouting at him; soberly. He was still painting, trying to get the last use of the daylight, and he said, impatiently, "Can't it wait? My first day of sunlight. Can't I at least use it all?"

"We'll wait," Elgren said, as if he were a pleasant stranger or prospective buyer in to look at paintings. Beside him, Jonathan nodded with a broad smile. Josef was alerted. If Jonathan was smiling, something was really wrong, he thought. He began cleaning his brushes in turpentine; his mustache bristling. He was getting low on supplies, and where would he get more?

"May we sit down?" Elgren asked.

The polite question so alarmed Josef that he turned around too quickly and knocked his palette to the floor.

"I'll get it," Jonathan said, retrieving it, and getting paints all over his hands.

At the sight of this help from Jonathan, Josef plunked himself down on the edge of the bed, threw up his hands, and said, "All right, I give up. What are you trying to do?"

Elgren cleared his throat. "We, ah, had a family conference about you," he began.

"Ahhh," Josef groaned.

"No, no. We've some matters to discuss with you quite frankly. To your advantage—"

Josef wanted to shout, "To my advantage! When have you been concerned with my advantage?" But something told him to remain still. He looked at his hands and pursed his lips. "They must want something," he thought craftily. Otherwise they wouldn't be so nice. Best to be quiet, then, and make them come out with it.

"Yes, a family conference," Jonathan said.

Silence. Josef refused to speak. Elgren began, leaning forward earnestly. "With all good regards, still you broke our glass and you have no way to pay us for doing it. You can't sell enough paintings now to pay for such expensive glass. And you owe us at least one family portrait, and a picture of the house, for your room and board these months. Instead, you work on other paintings that you, at least, take very seriously–"

"So? So?" Josef said impatiently. They were driving him mad with their politeness.

"What to do honorably was the question," Elgren said. "Throwing you in jail was no answer, though we considered it, because then you'd never pay us and we'd never get our paintings done either. Not feeding you might make you so weak that there'd be no chance of payment for the glass. Putting you out of the house would let you go scot free. And so it occurred to us that you would like this thing settled also, so you knew where you stood."

"Then you could go on painting without worry," Jonathan said quickly.

Josef scowled. "So this idea of yours, whatever it is, is Jonathan's? He's that worried about my state of mind?" Josef said, thundering out.

Jonathan grinned, smugly.

Elgren spread his hands. "We have problems, like any family. You may be able to help us with one of them, and—"

"I just want to paint," Josef interrupted. "Will you get to the point? Stop torturing me."

"Bianka likes you," Elgren said so quickly and flatly that Josef snapped forward. How much did Elgren and Jonathan know? Had the younger brother squealed? Josef felt his face turning red.

"Don't be embarrassed," Elgren said. "She likes you. So that's a fact that we have to take into consideration. There aren't many young men around here. The farmhands are all right, but she thinks that you're different; romantic, maybe. You know how women are."

Josef didn't dare say a thing. He didn't like the smile on Jonathan's face or the air of absolute earnestness on Elgren's.

"It's time for her to have a husband," Jonathan said, now looking everywhere but at Josef.

"She thinks you would make her a good man," Elgren added. "Now wait — she doesn't like too many young men. The opportunities are limited around here. It would be different in the cities."

"You hate me," Josef shouted. "Jonathan hates me. Your wife can't stand me. You think I'd marry into such a family? You're all out of your minds." He sprang up, furious, confused, sputtering with outrage — but surprised with himself. Underneath it all, a part of him thought coldly: a guaranteed place to live and work; a woman built-in when he wanted one! They'd have to buy his art supplies, too, or he wouldn't do it. Astounded by these thoughts, he yelled, "No, no. I won't consider it under any circumstances. No. My answer is no."

"These things are delicate. Think about it," Elgren said. "I told Bianka this would be your first reaction — "

"First and final and last," Josef yelled. He stood up and tramped about the room.

"Or we confiscate your paintings and supplies and have you thrown into jail," Jonathan said, mildly.

Josef stopped in his tracks. "That's blackmail! Besides, I'd make a miserable husband — "

"You'd have to help us in the fields in the morning or do the morning chores. The rest of the time you could paint," Elgren said. "Your own painting made me change my opinion of you. You've worked at it steadily now. It consumes you. This is good. It means that eventually you will sell your paintings. A good artist in the family — " He paused and added, "You could do pictures for my relatives, too. That is a fine cultural thing to do."

"You'd never get out of debtors' prison," Jonathan said, "But you can see our point. We have an investment in you. It's only fair that we come to some understanding. And you'd have this room for your studio. I have the feeling that if your painting is so important, you'd be making a pretty fair bargain."

Josef stared; Jonathan was shrewder than he'd given him credit for.

Elgren stood up soberly, again with that unfamiliar formality and said, "This is how things are done. We've told you our proposition. Think about it. We'll be back tomorrow for your answer."

Josef didn't answer. It was Bianka, the bitch, who was responsible for his getting caught and dragged back in the first place. All she had to do now was tell her father about their romps. Josef was sure Elgren didn't know— though Jonathan might. Elgren thought that his daughter was a prize; not that there was anything really wrong with her, Josef thought hastily. Only that he wasn't about to marry anybody.

The Hosentaufs left. Josef eyed the windows which thankfully were now unboarded, remembering that soon the land would be clear and open. The fairs would be starting in a month or so. In his mind's eye he saw himself jaunty and free, doing sketches for a good price, sleeping in cool fragrant barns. But his eye fell on his unfinished paintings. He had to finish them. He had to have a quiet place to work. What had happened to his freedom?

Frowning, he went back to the easel. He wasn't going to marry Bianka, paintings or no. And all the while that he was talking to himself so vehemently, uninvited mental images came into his mind; Bianka leaving him a tray of food while he worked—Bianka as a model, taking every conceivable pose; and in years to come, Josef the artist, lord of the manor, rich and prosperous while fat sons did all the work in the fields that he and Bianka had somehow inherited.

"You'd better jump out of the window to the shed and just keep going," he told himself, alarmed by these seemingly independent thoughts that glowed so temptingly. Was he being offered an opportunity unequaled where he could work in peace? Or was he in mortal danger of losing all independence? Or both? Or neither? Groaning, he threw his brush down and stared at the wall.

~ *Chapter Fourteen* ~

Proteus' Decision
Window's Window into the Past
(and Aspect One)

Cyprus and Oversoul Seven sat nonchalantly on a pile of rock on the rim of the hill overlooking the Dig of the Tellers. "I lost myself in Lydia's life, then Ma-ah's, then Josef's," Seven was saying. "It's great to surface again. I'm worried about Josef. I mean, he *is* forming his own reality but he doesn't know it, of course, and he thinks the Hosentaufs are tricking him."

"I take it that Josef is still your favorite?" Cyprus asked.

"Well, no, not really. He's just more like me. Or he seems like me. Anyway, he reminds me of myself more and more. He gets lost in his paintings now, as I get lost in my personalities. And you know, before my examination he didn't paint like that; and I just peeked into my personalities to help them out now and then. I mean — now sometimes I think they own me; and Josef's worried about losing *his* freedom. Well, I don't relish losing mine, either, in their experiences."

"Is that what happens?" Cyprus was smiling.

"Well, it's certainly what *seems* to happen," Seven said, testily. "It's easy for you to talk in your position — " Seven broke off in consternation. Cyprus was gone. "Cyprus? Cyprus?" he called.

"Yes?"

Seven blinked. That was Cyprus' voice, but it wasn't just that she'd dematerialized her image—he could have perceived her presence in any case—

"Over here," she said.

Seven frowned with his fourteen-year-old male face, and swirled around. Cyprus was blinking on and off, or here and there, disappearing entirely *in her essence,* and then returning. Exactly what *was* she doing? Taking herself out of his experience and then reemerging in it? "All right. Come back," he said.

She reappeared beside him, looking rather severe. She said, "When you talk about my position, you aren't thinking straight, as that little performance of mine should show you. Obviously my position is a changing one. It isn't static. And neither is yours. Or Josef's, for that matter."

"I think I understand," Seven said. "But why are we here?"

"Window is going to put on a demonstration for Proteus," Cyprus said. "But afterward, I'll want you to tell me what you think the significance of that demonstration is."

"But Window isn't even one of my personalities," Seven cried. "And if the demonstration is for Proteus, then Proteus should be tested, not me."

"This is a particularly important part of the examination," Cyprus interrupted. "So stop objecting and listen. . . . "

"You have a very adventurous nature," Window was saying to Proteus. "But because you were taught to curb your sense of wonder, you're often frightened of where your curiosity might lead. Story's abilities worry you because you're going to have to open your mind to them, or reject Story— and you don't want to do that either."

"I was brave enough to come here," Proteus said.

"Exactly. So I hope you'll be courageous enough to accept what you find."

"Well, I accept you," Proteus said, with a shrug. "And I'm ready to accept whatever abilities you have as, uh, real."

"That's only the beginning," Window replied. "I'm going to take you on a tour—"

"Story was right. You *are* going to show me around, finally. I was afraid that you weren't, that you were hiding something," Proteus said. He grinned; already he liked Window better than he did his own father, a fact that struck him as very strange. "I've been a little disappointed," he added. "This part of the . . . dig . . . is nice enough, but you've kept me isolated, really." He broke off. He'd also seriously wondered whether or not there *was* anything else to see; and whether Window was lying. Now he blushed, remembering.

Window stood there, ready to leave, when the door burst open. Story ran into the room. "There's another search party coming. I don't know why, but they're more determined than they were the last time. The news came from one of our outposts. I didn't wait to get the details, but now they're beginning to think that Proteus was kidnapped."

Window whirled around. His face was white.

"Did you . . . take him around yet?" Story asked.

Window shook his head. "We were just ready to leave."

"You weren't going to show him all — "

"No," Window said quickly.

Proteus stared at both of them. "You were hiding something back, then," he said, accusingly. "I thought you were."

"He has to be found, then. He has to go home," Story said. "He doesn't know what's here yet, and he's got to promise not to tell what he does know. Otherwise, they'll just keep on looking."

Confused, Proteus looked from one to the other. Story was speaking so quickly that it was hard to follow what she said. Proteus spoke as emphatically as he could: "I'm not going home. You can't make me. If you do, then I'll tell them that something strange is going on here, and they'll come back to investigate anyway."

They were paying little attention to him. Story just kept staring at Window. She said again, "Proteus has to be found."

"Or *never* found," Window said.

Story shook her head. "That would be even more difficult. He's not able to make the choice."

Proteus was furious. "Stop talking about me as if I'm not here," he said angrily. "I have a right to know what's going on."

Story cried urgently, "Proteus, we're just trying to save you from having to make a decision without knowing what's involved. Till now you couldn't really do us much harm — you hadn't seen anything. At any time you could decide to go home, and we could just abandon you topside and no one would ever find us. But now . . . you're going to have to stay with us for good — never see your home again — or leave at once with a suitable explanation."

"Like what?" Proteus demanded.

"Well, we have the dig above, that they know about. You could say that you wandered in there. . . . No, then we'd get in trouble for not notifying the proper authorities — "

"Wait." Window closed his eyes. He tried to lose the sense of urgency and desperation that had been closing in on him, and as he did, his inner vision cleared. There were three copters this time. How could one boy threaten an entire project, he wondered wearily, for now he saw that the searchers were far more persistent than they had been. Then he discovered the reason. "Your mother's a member of the search party," he said. "She has some kind of executive position, doesn't she?"

"My mother? Are you sure?"

"Her name is Amanda. She has . . . brown hair, blue eyes and olive skin. She's thirty-nine. She calls you Proto—"

"When she thought of me, she called me Proto," Proteus said. "She didn't pay that much attention to me usually."

"Well, she's thinking about you now," Window said soberly.

Proteus was so surprised that he didn't know what to do or say. Window had *seen*—that much was obvious. What Window said was true; so maybe Story's tales were true, but in a different way. He said, wildly, "I could . . . say that I pleaded with you not to notify the authorities; or tell them that your communication system went on the blink—"

"He *could* say that, about the communications," Story said. "It just might work."

"Could we trust you to be quiet about the little you do know, or suspect?" Window asked.

"Of course," Proteus said. "I give you my word."

Story stared at him. "A few minutes ago, that's not what you said."

"I was angry at you, for talking around me. I didn't mean that I'd really do anything to get you in trouble—"

"Then it's your choice," Window said. "Either you return, and we'll still be taking a chance, or you stay. If you leave, we can only hope that your story is convincing enough. I can have our communications cut temporarily, and let *them* come here, where we'll be ready—"

"The men at the dig took care of him till help could arrive," Story said. "That story would work to our advantage—"

To return home! Proteus was almost sick to his stomach with indecision. Despite his resentments, he kept seeing his mother's image in his mind's eye: the green uniform, beautifully severe short hair, the almost military bearing, and yet. . . . "No," he shouted. "I won't be dragged home, even if it means never going back. I won't go unless it's the only way that you'll feel safe, so somebody better think of something!"

"There's only one place where you'll be safe if you stay, and where *we'll* be safe, no matter what. No one knows where it is but the Tellers," Window said. "But if you go there with us, then you'll have to stay and join your fate with ours. Right now there's no time to explain. You'll have to go it blind, if you've really decided." He paused, then said quickly, "They're landing by the outer dig. I see it, mentally."

Again Proteus thought: his mother, so close. He'd decided to leave home once. Now it seemed he was going to have to make up his mind all over again, while knowing that his mother was only a short distance away. Nothing else had offered this tremendous point of contrast. Yet all the deep feelings that had propelled his initial flight now reasserted themselves. "I'm ready. I'll go with you, if you'll take me . . . if I won't cause you more trouble than I'm worth."

His eyes were smarting. Story and Window were already at the door. "All right," Window said. "Hurry."

They ran down the corridor past all the rooms with which Proteus was familiar. The wall at the end of the corridor opened as they approached. Proteus gasped with surprise. He'd been in the hall often, no door was apparent. Now it closed soundlessly behind them. "It's all operated from below," Window said quickly. They were in a very small room with rock walls. Two large rocks moved back. Proteus followed Story and Window inside, and they began to climb down a very steep staircase hewn out of rock.

This time the stairs seemed endless, but the way was illuminated dimly, though Proteus saw no lamps or torches. When they'd walked downward for some time, the steps evened out until they gradually formed a rocky corridor with a downward incline. Neither Window nor Story spoke, so Proteus asked no questions. He was growing more and more excited, even while he realized that they were steadily progressing beneath the Earth's surface. What would he find? What secret . . . project could there possibly be that Window and Story considered so important?

The corridor ended with a final rock door that opened for them automatically, as had the others. Now they were obviously inside a gigantic rock building of incredible age and richness. Here also the walls were lit by that same dim illumination. Drawings of animals, birds, and buildings filled the walls. Proteus eyed them with awe. They seemed alive, waiting.

Window and Story still hadn't spoken, yet Proteus had the strangest feeling that they carried on some inner kind of dialogue. What kind of people were they, actually, he wondered? Story was approximately his age, yet sometimes she acted much older, while on other occasions she was so playful and innocent that she might have been a ten-year-old. And Window? Why did he trust Window so? Proteus shivered slightly. In this odd building, both Window and Story seemed like strangers to him.

He looked down. The rock floor here was smooth and clean, yet the air was filled with a sweet mustiness that was impossible to describe. The cleanliness itself disturbed him; it didn't seem to be fresh, but rather, ancient; a cleanliness somehow preserved from the past. Window and Story turned into another corridor, and Proteus followed. This time Proteus paused briefly. The door before them was heavy and old. Why didn't it creak as it opened? A series of steep upward steps led to a rock landing, and here Proteus stood motionless, unable to speak, amazed at the scene before him.

He'd taken it for granted that they would still be underground. Now before him stretched a lush valley, ringed by towering cliffs that formed a very wide cone shape, opened, far above. The valley was so enclosed by the cliffs that the only entry seemed to be from the wide circle of sky above. Through that opening the sun poured so brightly that Proteus had to look away, because his eyes were still so accustomed to the dimness of the underground corridors.

"Welcome," Window said, and though he had seemed vital enough before, now he seemed to come truly alive, snap into focus, be himself, in a way that took Proteus completely by surprise. The same transformation came over Story. She smiled at him fully, as she hadn't earlier, her whole pose expressing a deep satisfaction. It was obvious that Story and Window had come home.

Proteus didn't have time to wonder further about the change in his companions. Too much competed for his attention. Everywhere there were tall green trees, grass, flowers, buildings of the oddest designs and all in the richest of colors. Yet in the distance ruins were clearly apparent, in various stages of reconstruction. Piles of rock glittered in the sun. Bright shoots of green licked at them like green flames.

At first Proteus didn't notice the people. Then he saw the figures moving around the ruins, and at the same time men and women began to emerge from the buildings. They came in twos and threes, small groups from the multicolored triangular structures that were arranged in a semicircle around what seemed to be a general square.

It was only then that Proteus thought of turning around. Directly behind him was a pyramid—through which they must have just emerged! "But at the last, we came *up*," Proteus said. "How can that be?"

Window smiled. "We'll explain it all later. For now, meet the Tellers."

"How long has this place been here? Why hasn't it been discovered?" Proteus was so filled with questions that he was in a daze for the next few hours in which several hundred people surrounded them, greeted Window and Story with great warmth, and listened to Window's explanation of Proteus' presence.

Proteus himself began to feel as if he'd also returned "home." Everything seemed new and unbelievable, yet familiar. It was twilight—twilight on Earth as Proteus had never seen it before, except in his dreams. How sterile and insignificant the floating city seemed by contrast, he thought, remembering the artificial trees and plastic grass. He and Window strolled past the buildings as Window pointed out the sights.

"This place was ancient long before the time of Rome," Window said. "And it's coming alive again. There's so much to tell you that I don't know where to begin. Our discoveries, for one thing. That's a story in itself. We're learning to activate mechanisms that we would never have dreamed of—and they're all here in instructions that date back to the time of the cavemen. This was a fantastic civilization. We don't know yet how it began, but we hope to find out. It flourished while most Earthmen were still savages. We're still learning, finding new records—Look."

Proteus gasped. Above in the wide circle of sky in the center of the cliffs, a few stars shone and a dull Moon. Here before them the valley narrowed slightly into what had obviously been a kind of courtyard. Between patches of grass, broken colored tiles glittered. In several places the grass had been uprooted, baring whole areas of clear shining mosaics, each fitted into the other so cleverly that it was impossible to tell where the divisions were between them.

Window stood there and closed his eyes. "I'll tell you what I see with my inner vision," he said. "Each time I come here and look inward, I see something else, a further detail, another piece of information that tells us where to look, that brings us one step closer."

Window's mental vision shimmered, blurred, then cleared. Describing what he was seeing, he said softly: "This was a courtyard, as you can probably tell. The mosaics covered the whole area, the floor of the valley. The walls and drawings are very important, but while we've discovered some very strange things about them, there's a lot we don't know. They *do* contain a key that's vital; we're sure of that. But wait . . . I'm seeing something new . . . A young woman stands in the courtyard now."

Proteus frowned. Suddenly he felt nervous and uncomfortable. He stared at Window, whose head was flung back, his face expectant and yet passive, his long humped nose sensitive as an animal's. Proteus wanted to interrupt, but didn't dare to.

"She's beautiful, black. She's looking at the drawings—" Window sighed audibly. "She's disappearing. I'm losing my focus."

"I suppose she could be the girl Story told us about—the one who was supposed to threaten the Tellers through me somehow." Proteus spoke resentfully, almost unwillingly. "I wish you hadn't seen her," he said. "Everything was so great. I still think that Story's tale was—"

"Distorted?" Window said, smiling. His eyes opened. "It might have been. The threat she saw could have been the second search party. She could have perceived the black girl separately, and just put the two together. That's possible. She's young, and still learning to use her abilities."

"Well, I just wish she wouldn't practice on me," Proteus retorted. He looked around. Now the ancient courtyard seemed alive and glowing in an unfriendly way. He no longer felt that he'd come home. Sensing Proteus' mood, Window led him back toward the buildings and the people.

Seven and Cyprus stayed. They'd watched the whole day's proceedings. Seven was incredulous himself. "Window saw Ma-ah! Of course," he said.

"Do you understand now?" Cyprus asked.

"Yes, I do!" Seven cried out triumphantly. "Ma-ah and Proteus live in the same physical place in different times, at least they do now that Proteus' journey has taken him there. What a pity that they don't know each other, or see what's happening. I wonder if I could possibly explain it to—"

Seven broke off. He was growing slightly dizzy—or his environment was—he wasn't sure which. Objects seemed to shift focus, become blurred, then become clearer again than they'd been in the first place—yet oddly different. For a moment Oversoul Seven was in the courtyard of the Speakers, standing next to Ma-ah in 35,000 B.C. The mosaics were bright and dazzling. The cliffs shot upward. But there was a difference. What was it? "Ma-ah! Ma-ah!" he shouted.

"Did someone call me? I thought someone called my name?" Ma-ah swung around, obviously astonished.

"It's me, uh, the old man," Seven said. But the ground shimmered once more. Seven could no longer see Ma-ah. The cliffs rose as before, but now the grass covered most of the tiles, and where the rubble was cleared away the tiles were chipped and darkened.

Cyprus was waiting for him. "Now, hold my hand," she said. "And remember, you'll have to answer some questions about this later on."

"I've got some questions now," Seven objected.

"Seven! Pay attention."

Seven sharpened his own fourteen-year-old male image, made the face as elfin as he could—and grinned.

In a flash Cyprus turned into another fourteen-year-old male image and grinned back. The next moment she had the woman's form again. "Now," she said. "Back to your examination. Look at one tile. Any one will do."

Seven chose a chipped blue and orange one, with a design partially showing. The rest had broken off.

"Do you see it clearly?"

"Yes."

"Now, this is the way that the tile appears to your present focus of perception. You must change your focus to see its other Aspects. *You* can stay here. Do you follow me?"

"I'm trying to," Seven said.

Cyprus sighed. "Those in Ma-ah's time use one specialized focus to perceive their reality—and that tile. Do you remember how the tiles looked a moment ago when you slid into Ma-ah's courtyard?"

"I'll never forget—" Seven said.

"Then keep moving your consciousness a notch at a time while watching that particular tile until it looks like the tiles did then."

"A notch at a time?" Oversoul Seven said, frowning.

"All right, if that doesn't quite make sense to you, then do this. Imagine that your consciousness is a light—which it is, of course—and keep turning it in different directions, but very slowly. The rotating light will pick up the tile in its different Aspects. Stop when you think you recognize Ma-ah's tiles—"

"I think I've got the idea now," Seven said. "Now don't rush me." He stared at the tile. How perfect it was in its way, he thought; how unique, even chipped and darkened, the tail of some animal or fish all wiggly set in the stone.

"Blink," Cyprus said.

Seven blinked, then looked back at the tile. It wrinkled. It was curling at the edges, diminishing, disappearing at a rapid rate.

"You're going too fast in that direction," Cyprus cautioned. "That's how the tile appears in future centuries, in a matter of speaking. Go back the other way."

Almost in a panic, Seven watched the tile disappearing. He tried to reverse his focus which was difficult, because he didn't know yet how he was doing what he was doing. "Come back," he shouted at the tile. Suddenly he felt a great love for it—how precious it was—yet despite his efforts it continued to wrinkle and diminish. In the back of his mind somewhere, he thought he heard Cyprus' (delightful) laughter. He wondered angrily what she was laughing at, and just then he found the feel of his consciousness, and pulled it back to the left of his inner vision.

Miraculously the tile shimmered, stabilized, then began to grow thicker. Portions of the design began to appear. Then Seven understood. When he saw the design completed, the tile would be as it was in Ma-ah's courtyard.

Then he recognized the right tile, or thought that he did. The design was completed, all the chips restored—a blue fish with a strange long tail.

The tile looked new—too new. Before Seven realized what had happened, a brown hand appeared on the top of the tile; laying it, Seven saw, shocked by the hand's intrusion. He was tempted to follow through and go backward before the tile's "time." Instead he backtracked. The hand disappeared, and the tile remained. When it looked right to him again, he held the focus of his consciousness and just observed it. Was Ma-ah near? "Ma-ah?"

Instantly he was dizzy again. In the same instant he saw Ma-ah quite clearly, standing only a few feet away. Enlarging his inner vision without being sure how he did so, he saw the ancient courtyard; but unmistakably, vividly, and simultaneously he also saw the courtyard as it existed in the twenty-third century A.D. The tile in the same physical place showed its two separate Aspects at once, not one before the other. And as his vision widened, the two courtyards were transposed one upon the other.

Cyprus' voice seemed to come from a great distance. "This is just one hint of what's possible," she said. "But the same is true of you, Seven, and your personalities. You all exist in your own Aspects, at once, each separate yet a part of the other . . . occupying the same 'place' which isn't a place at all . . . like the tile. Lydia, for example—her experience is yours, even if you aren't conscious of it. And your experience is hers, if only you can help her realize it—"

Cyprus paused, and said, "Even now she's translating your experience in her own way."

"Yes, I see," Seven cried, and the courtyards—both of them, disappeared. He was Lydia, yet she was herself, distinct, an old woman strapped in a wheelchair, staring with drug-filled eyes into the faces of her adult children.

～ *Chapter Fifteen* ～

*Lydia's Children Grow Backward in Time
and Tweety Delivers a Message
(Aspect Two)*

L ydia sat staring petulantly at her grown children. She'd been in the Medford House for a week. It was Sunday, visitor's day, and she sat propped up in the wheelchair like an ancient doll, powdered and perfumed, and dressed in one of the few dresses she owned. They'd thrown out her slacks and dungarees. Her eyes kept drifting off to the right, and she kept trying to bring them back into focus.

"We have her all fixed up for visitors. Doesn't she look nice?" the nurse said. Like Lydia's children, the nurse was in her fifties. "Shit!" Lydia said under her breath.

The nurse, Mrs. Only, smiled indulgently and chuckled. "Don't pay any mind," she said to Lydia's daughter, Anna.

"Mama, you're looking well," Anna said nervously. She was a big woman with a large bosom; well-educated, at a loss as to what to say.

Lydia just stared.

"She's tranquilized," Mrs. Only said.

Roger, Lydia's second son, grinned: "Any particular reason?"

"She got upset the other day and threw her milk glass across the room. Then she cursed everyone out, ran down the hall, and was heading for the stairs when we caught her."

"I'd do it again if I had the chance." Lydia tried to say the words clearly. They came out garbled, slurred. It was the damned drugs. She strained to get out of the chair.

"See, she can't articulate," Mrs. Only said. "The blood thinners should help bring more blood to the brain, but her condition is really irreversible."

Lydia threw them a fantastic scowl this time. How could she get them to understand that she knew what was going on quite well? And who wouldn't try to get out of this stupid place?

"Mama, what is it?" Anna asked. She took off her hat and gloves, laid them carefully on an empty chair, and came closer.

In her mind, quite sanely, Lydia formed the mental words: "Get me out of this hellhole. And stop calling me Mama, as if you were ten." But all that came out was a mess of gibberish, with a few recognizable words mixed in. Worse, something else happened. Before her startled eyes, Lydia saw Anna quickly change from a stout woman in her early fifties to a woman in her . . . thirties . . . to — Lydia gasped, no longer able to keep track of the rapid transformation. In the next moment she saw Anna, aged approximately seven, standing there in a starched yellow dress. Lydia trembled in recognition and shock. The dress — she'd just ironed it for Anna's birthday.

"Mama, tie my sash," Anna said.

"Say please," Lydia said automatically.

"I said please, didn't I?" Anna asked.

"No, you didn't," Lydia said. "But come here and stand still."

"She said quite clearly, 'Come here and stand still,'" the grown-up Anna said to Mrs. Only and Roger.

"Well, do it and see what happens," Roger said.

The grown-up Anna came close to Lydia's wheelchair, and stood there with a silly I-don't-know-what-to-do look of embarrassment. For Lydia, the two figures merged one into the other. "Not you," she said irritably. It was terribly difficult to separate Anna Young from Anna Older, and Anna Older didn't need her at all. Why didn't she get out of the way?

"Come here, honey," Lydia said, coaxing, to Anna Young.

"Okay."

Lydia smiled. By working . . . something just right, she could block out Anna Older entirely and tend to the child.

"You look lovely, honeypot. Happy birthday," she said, glad now that she'd ironed the yellow dress after all. "You smell all nice and clean and starchy."

"Mama, it's me," Anna Older said, near tears. "It's not my birthday. Is that what you said? Who are you talking to?"

"She's living in the past. She probably thinks you're a child or something," Mrs. Only said. "They go on this way. She might come out of it in a minute."

Roger didn't know where to look. He shook his graying head, adjusted his glasses, blew his nose, and tried not to look around at the other old patients. He had the oddest feeling that they were all staring. But when he took a quick look out of the corner of his eye, he saw that no one was paying the slightest attention.

Anna Young pirouetted. "See how far out my skirt goes when I turn 'round and 'round—"

"'Round and 'round," Lydia laughed, delighted to be so young herself. God, how beautiful the child was; and even the kitchen—the leaves through the window all waving and alive. The ironing board stood there with the iron upon it, splashed with sunshine. She bent over, saw her own face reflected in the iron, and the smell of freshly ironed clothes rushed to her nostrils. What a fantastic day—the birthday cake on the table—the small guests shortly to arrive.

"Oh, Mama." Anna Older suddenly bent down and took Lydia's hand. Lydia's eyes had been hazy only an instant earlier. Now she stared, with an angry superclear glance, it seemed to Anna, that quite pierced her through. "Go 'way." The words didn't quite come out clearly, but their intent was plain.

Lydia's hand gripped the wheelchair. When she focused on Anna Older, then the child Anna disappeared, and the kitchen. Anna Older was in an incredibly dreary hospital-type room, surrounded by old people who looked half like mummies, half-dead, strapped in chairs; and Anna Older was clearly no beauty herself. Lydia tried to blot out the vision and return to the kitchen, where at least she could cope.

"She doesn't want a thing to do with me," Anna Older said, with half a sob. "Roger, you try."

Lydia frowned. There they were, at her again. Now which Anna was that, and where was Roger?

"Aw, Ma, it's a girl's party and I don't want to go," Roger said, coming into the kitchen. He wore dirty sneakers and torn jeans.

"Don't, if you don't want to," Lydia said calmly. This kind of remark always disarmed him.

"They're all little kids, besides. I'm ten," he said.

"And one day you'll be eleven," she laughed. But somehow she knew she was on dangerous ground. One day he'd be eleven, then twenty, then forty, then fifty—

"It's me, Ma; Roger," Roger Older said. He was perspiring. He'd never put in such an afternoon in his life. He didn't know if he could bear to come back again.

But Roger was Lydia's favorite. Nonplussed, she looked about. Roger Young and Roger Older were each there; the boy in the kitchen, and the man in that awful hospital-type room. Her head throbbed. First the kitchen would disappear, to be replaced by the other room; then the reverse; then, dimly, both would exist together again.

Roger Young was on his way to the dining room desk where Lydia kept all her poetry, notes, books, and papers. He was carrying a glass of pop. She didn't want him to spill —"Don't spill that on my things," she called. "And get away from my desk — "

Lydia broke off, seeing Roger Older's face suddenly transposed on the boy. And Roger Older looked hurt. He thought she was yelling at him. Oh, dear. What was he saying? She strained to hear.

But Roger Young yelled, "Okay, Ma," and turned toward the kitchen, grinning; he was going to . . . going to . . . "Oh! no — "

"What is it, Mama?" Roger Older asked, bending down. She tried to say, "I can't tell you now. You're going to spill — "

"Oh!" Lydia cried. The pop spilled all over her papers. Were they ruined? She had to clean it up before the party. Her arm swung out, knocking a glass of water off the tray that was attached to the wheelchair.

"Oh!" Lydia cried again. The wetness shocked her. "Look at what you did." She scowled at Roger Older. Again her words were garbled. In the hospital-like room she couldn't make her tongue work right, although in the kitchen she had no trouble.

Anna laughed, almost hysterically. "I *think* she's bawling you out for spilling the water — "

And Lydia thought: what the hell is going on? She'd seen this room before, but hadn't realized that she was in it. Yet she was. Of course: she was seeing it through the eyes of the old woman in the wheelchair. But how could this be, when she was simultaneously a young woman in the kitchen, just before the birthday party for Anna? Her own thought made her grin. Now just how did you put a kitchen before a birthday party? Or in front of a birthday party? The party, then, had been years ago. Yet it was going on now. If she could do . . . what she'd been doing — whatever that was — then she could catch the party in progress.

"Don't you know me, Ma?" Roger Older asked.

She glowered at him. Of course she did. What a stupid question. If he'd just stay one age at a time, it would make things a hell of a lot easier. Here she was, trying to figure out what was going on, and he wanted to know if she knew him. Just like him!

If she was losing her mind, she was certainly losing it in the craziest way, she thought; then she realized that she wanted a cigarette. "Smoke." The word came out in a croak after she tried to say "Pall Mall" and "cigarette" without success.

They all stared at her. Ninnies. Patiently she made pantomime gestures of smoking. God, they were stupid. Didn't they understand anything?

"You can't have a cigarette," Mrs. Only said, finally. "You might burn yourself."

"Even if we watch her?" Roger asked.

"Well, all right."

Roger — bless his heart — gave her a cigarette. Her fingers just wouldn't do what they were supposed to do to hold it, though.

"Look out — she'll burn herself," Anna cried.

"Oh, shut up!" Lydia said in disgust. For once the words came out clearly. Anna recoiled.

Someone next to Lydia chuckled. Lydia's normal vision returned. She swung around. An old man with half of his teeth gone was strapped in his own wheelchair a few feet away. He caught her eye.

"That's Mr. Cromwell," Mrs. Only whispered to Anna and Roger. "Don't be frightened. He can't help slobbering like that. He's all right; just, well, you know — "

"Afternoon," Cromwell said brightly. He spat through his teeth, just missing the toe of his right foot. Anna blanched. Lydia tried to say, "What manners!" But this time she couldn't get her tongue to move right at all.

"Nice day," Cromwell said, leering at Roger.

"Why, he knows what's going on," Anna said, horrified, to Mrs. Only.

"Be quiet. He can hear you," Roger whispered back.

"I think it's time for us to go, Mama. We don't want to tire you out," Anna said nervously. "We'll come back next Sunday."

"Don't rush," Cromwell said, to no one in particular.

"He's . . . malicious," Anna whispered.

"Oh, no. He doesn't really know what he's saying," Mrs. Only said.

"Bye, Ma," Roger said.

Quite suddenly and simply Lydia put out her hand, almost formally; and Roger took it, feeling foolish. He wouldn't be coming back — Lydia knew this in a rush, without knowing how she knew. He was scared of becoming what she was, or what she seemed to be. But she didn't really understand him too well, even if he was her favorite, and she could get Roger

Young back if she tried to. He had all kinds of great things going for him. Had Roger Older gone? And Anna? Lydia supposed they had.

"Your kids, huh?" old man Cromwell said.

His raspy voice was so intrusive that she jumped.

"Gotcha all doped up, huh?" he said sympathetically.

Lydia ignored him. For one thing, she wouldn't associate with old men who spat through their teeth; what a nasty habit. For another, she kept seeing Roger and Anna as they used to be, and somewhere in the back of her mind a birthday cake glittered with candles.

"Blow them out. Make a wish," she said gaily. In the dining room, her voice was lovely and clear as a bell. How odd!

"I want to be a doctor or an artist when I grow up," Roger said.

"You can't wish. It's my birthday," Anna said. "You shouldn't even be here, anyhow. You're a boy, and it's a girl's party—"

"Now, don't be that way, honey," Lydia said. But now she couldn't figure out if she was the old woman in the wheelchair, or the young woman cutting the birthday cake. For example, she thought: Now what did Roger grow up to be? And she didn't know *who* thought that: the old woman or the young one. Then the answer came. Roger grew up to be the manager of a chain of department stores. Now *who* knew that? The young mother couldn't. But miraculously Lydia realized that she was both—and now the young mother, looking at Roger, also knew what he grew up to be.

But Lydia in the wheelchair thought: what a pity. Not that she had anything against department store managers, but suppose she'd encouraged Roger's drawing more when he was little. She thought she had, then, of course. Still. . . . Desperately she tried to remember. What games had they played that day? Pin the tail on the donkey, hide and seek. Suppose she stepped in and made a change. Could she? Well, it was never too late to start.

"Roger . . . is going to make pastel sketches of each of you!" she said quickly. "Just like a real artist. And you can take them home—"

Roger said: "Wow!" and rushed off for his materials. Odd, that only now she remembered how crazy he used to be about art. He used to copy the funny papers for hours.

Now she was all mixed up again. Was she changing the past? And if she was the old lady and the young mother at the same time, then had she changed the future, too? Would Roger be different? Of course, he might not respond to the encouragement, either; she might end up not helping him at all—if that would be helping him. And had she done enough, or would she have to keep it up, inserting encouragement in suitable places in the past?

Someone said something to her in the hospital-like room. She tried to see who it was, but when she went back to the woman in the wheelchair again everything got foggy.

"Time for our pill," Mrs. Only said. "We have a new nurse coming late today. We want to have our medications all taken care of, so she can just relax and get to know everybody."

Where the hell had the nurse come from? What was she chattering about? Lydia scowled again. What was real and what wasn't? Could she get back to the birthday party? She certainly wasn't going to stay here with that maddening, condescending . . . person.

"Now, now," Mrs. Only said.

Lydia was quite exhausted. She stared at the nurse, or tried to. Her eyes kept going to the right again. Mrs. Only put the pill in Lydia's hand and gave her the water. Lydia swallowed the pill resentfully, and went on with her own thoughts, lost in them; but as the medicine took effect everything became blearier.

She dozed. Once the weirdest thing happened. She felt as though she was slipping sideways out of herself; then her body shook and jumped as if she'd fallen back into it, but from above. "Doped up," she thought irritably. "The pills. Next time I won't take them."

Then she saw the birthday party, but from a great distance; and felt motion so fast that she couldn't follow what was happening. Briefly it stopped, and she thought that she saw herself sitting in the wheelchair. Instantly the motion started up again. It was accompanied by odd sounds, rustlings, as if tissue paper was being crumpled right next to her ears, and static. She glimpsed a body in a casket — hers? Then a young girl appeared, about twelve years old. She said something like, "Lydia, I'm Tweety. Tweety." And she almost felt as if she knew who the girl was. Then the motion and the noises came once more.

The next thing Lydia knew it was dinnertime, and she kept dropping her head into the mashed potatoes.

"We can cut down on her dosage, I guess," Mrs. Only said to the new nurse. "It takes a few days before we can figure out just how much they need. I don't think she'll turn violent again, anyway. She's been with us a week now."

A week? Lydia thought. She tried to focus her eyes. When was the birthday party?

∼ *Chapter Sixteen* ∼

Ma-ah's Signature in Stone
and Sumpter's Surprise
(and Aspect Three)

While Oversoul Seven was perceiving the tile in two of its many Aspects, and Lydia was slipping back and forth in time, Ma-ah stood in the courtyard of the Speakers. "Who called me?" she asked again, and again she received no reply. She shrugged, and looked up to see Sumpter walking purposefully toward her. Coming close, he smiled and pointed at the tree drawing on the wall nearby.

"Mamunsha," he said. He squatted down easily beside her, a habit he'd recently taken to, to minimize the difference in their sizes.

"I thought *sanoraja* was the word for tree," Ma-ah said, in her new language.

He grinned. "Sometimes it is. Sometimes tree is *arumba*—that's a tree at night, when there's no moon. *Lidata*—that's a tree splashed with sun. *Kadita*—that's a tree with leaves dancing." He was laughing now, but serious. His laughter disconcerted her. It reminded her that he had feelings. "Look at that drawing, and make up a word that fits it," he said.

Ma-ah stared at him uneasily.

"Go on," Sumpter said.

"Brambeda."

"Then that's what the tree drawing is in this moment."

"But I just made it up." Despite herself, Ma-ah was laughing, too.

"Exactly. When you force certain specific words onto objects, you limit them and their reality to you. So we have certain words which you've learned for the purposes of classification. But we never make the mistake of confusing the object with the name we've given it. All objects are changing constantly. No one word could ever express the entire reality of any one thing in all of its many aspects."

She liked him best now when he was teaching her. In that role she could accept him and not feel threatened. Now she shook her head, laughing back at him. "But you are Sumpter. That's a name."

"It's the name I gave you as mine at the moment you asked me," he said, soberly.

"You mean it isn't your name?" Ma-ah was scandalized.

"It is sometimes. I call myself other names, too —"

"If you don't have the same name, how will people know who you are?"

"My face tells them," he said. "At different times my friends call me different names, too. And I call myself what I please —"

She didn't like the odd warmth in his expression as he spoke: it had currents of coolness in it, too, but also a lazy, frightening invitation. "I call you Sumpter," she said, almost angrily.

"That's because you try to limit my reality for your own purposes," he said, without rancor. "You try to limit your perception of me, too. But right now I call you by two names — Sorana and Marunda. These names and words suggest two parts of you, seemingly in conflict at this instant."

"I'm Ma-ah," she said, irritated. She sprang up and paused. Sumpter made no move to follow her. "What two aspects?" she asked in spite of herself.

"The desire to control and the desire to surrender," he said.

Her thighs felt warm and her head felt cold. The remark was so true of her in so many different ways that she just stood staring down at him.

"We're called Speakers because we try to speak inner knowledge," Sumpter said softly. "Often we put it into words for people who need them. But otherwise we free ourselves from words. The people in the world you came from are just beginning a long journey into discovery. We came here to help them because that's our purpose." Sumpter suddenly looked away. Ma-ah watched him, curious. He seemed almost uneasy.

"We're beginning to mix our race with yours. Already on other parts of the Earth, this process has begun. You're a part of this, Ma-ah. It's time for you to mate. Since you're with us and don't want to return to your old world, then you should choose a man from the Speakers."

"Choose you," she said vehemently. "That's what you want; or what I was supposed to do —"

"Choose whomever you will," Sumpter said. "But you must join your stock with ours, or return."

"Why? I won't go back," she shouted.

He smiled, yet she sensed a great impatience beneath his manner. "You've been a good pupil," he said. "You learn quickly. Your race will take centuries to learn what we've managed to teach you so far. But we can't stay here forever, for reasons I won't go into now. You must pass on what you're learning to your own people, and the mixtures of our stock is important."

The sun was hot on the tiled courtyard floor. Ma-ah stared down as Sumpter talked. The shadows of night would soon be falling, and she shivered. He was giving her an ultimatum and she had the sudden feeling that she had to come to a decision before the evening came.

"Some of our knowledge is written in our blood," Sumpter said. His soberness was upsetting Ma-ah more and more. "It's become a part of our physical stuff," he went on, watching her. "It will be passed on, latent, but full of potential. It *will* emerge, time and time again."

He didn't stand up, but she had the impression that he was standing; beneath his words she was dimly aware of other nonverbal meanings. She thrilled to it, and was frightened at the same time.

"Knowledge exists in every form possible," Sumpter said. "What you've learned is written in your soul, which is independent of your body. But it's also written in the body you inherit from the Earth, in the cells, and that knowledge is passed on, whether or not it's ever consciously recognized or used." He paused, and added, "I want you to have a child . . . with that heritage. . . . I want you to mix your stock with mine."

Ma-ah's eyes flew wide open. Until now he'd always said "our stock" or "your people." Now he was saying "his stock," and "I want *you* to —" Suddenly she thought of the drawing of the strange bird, with all the people emerging from its belly. "You weren't . . . born here. You weren't, were you?"

"No," he answered, watching her face.

"You came from . . . that bird in the drawing. I used to think that it was a real bird, but it must be something different —"

"It is something different. But I can't discuss that particular subject with you yet . . . not until you take the part that you must take if you stay here."

Ma-ah frowned. "I won't go back. That's all there is to it. Not willingly, and I know enough about your people to know you wouldn't use force. But I don't like to do something because I'm supposed to, either. I know how animals mate. Rampa and I have done that often, if that's what you mean. You say children come that way, but Rampa and I had none. If I had any, they'd be *mine*. So I'm not sure what you want me to do. If it's what Rampa and I did, why didn't you just say so? That's only natural and makes you feel good all over. But you must mean more than that in some way I don't understand, or you wouldn't be making such a fuss about it."

"What you and Rampa did, we'll do then," Sumpter said, very formally.

"That's all you wanted?" Ma-ah was astonished.

"Why did you and Rampa stay together?" he asked quietly.

"Why, we needed each other. It's much easier to hunt for food — and we helped protect each other. Why else?"

"No other reason?" Sumpter asked carefully.

"What other reason could there be?"

"Did you feel toward each other the way Rampa and Orona seem to feel now?" he asked.

Ma-ah's face darkened. "No." She paused and said, accusingly "You feel that way toward me sometimes, though, and it makes me uneasy. I thought that you wanted me to feel . . . that way too, whatever that way is. I didn't understand that you just wanted me to do what Rampa and I did, or I'd have said yes at once. I haven't done it since I've been here, and I've missed it, too."

She expected Sumpter to laugh, now that the matter was cleared up. Instead, some hope seemed to drain away from his face. He looked up at her and said, "I'll never threaten your sense of . . . emotional freedom. I'll settle for what you can give me now. And the mating, hopefully, will bring a child. You're much healthier than you were."

Ma-ah looked up, startled, to see that the shadows were beginning to fall. There had been no decision to make, then! Yet she felt oddly cheated, as if there had been a decision that she hadn't seen or recognized — and should have. "Just mate, as Rampa and I did?" she asked again.

"Yes, Ma-ah," Sumpter said quietly.

"Well, let's do it now, then." She threw herself down on the ground, laughing. "I'll never understand why you just didn't say so. You made such a fuss that I got the idea something more was involved, something I didn't understand." Then, at the expression on his face, she cried, "What's wrong?" Yet all the time she felt that she knew without knowing, and that he knew. Knew what? "You've got that look again," she said, accusingly.

"And you're . . . Sorana and Marunda again," Sumpter said.

She sprang up, grabbed a loose stone, shouted defiantly: "I'm Ma-ah!" and scratched the symbol for her name into one of the floor tiles as deeply as she could. "There!" she shouted triumphantly. "Now do we mate or not?"

"The part of you that can mate now will mate," Sumpter said. And he thought: she was unpossessable . . . like the world from which she'd come; innocent, splendid, shrewd, and perhaps terrible in the same way that a storm was.

Ma-ah began to slip off her robe.

"Not here," he said quickly. "The tiles are too hard. . . . We'll use one of my private couches—"

She shrugged. Now at least she thought she understood what was wanted. It was something she wanted too. There was no conflict. She ran along beside him quite happily. She considered the whole affair so matter-of-factly that Sumpter was deeply troubled. So far, emotional feelings weren't connected in her mind with sex at all. He'd suspected as much, but he wondered what to do with his own longings for the part of her that even she had not yet discovered.

"I'm walking on the tiles' faces," Ma-ah said. Now she felt anticipatory and carefree.

"Yes," he said.

"Wait . . . why, the tiles are shifting." She cried out in alarm and ran ahead of him.

Sumpter caught her arm. "Of course they aren't. See? They aren't moving."

"I saw them. I was looking down and they began to . . . crawl . . . yet they stayed in the same place." Ma-ah shivered.

"Well, they're not moving now," he said.

"No. But when they moved, I got frightened. They made me think of things. If we mate and I have a child, then it will live and come and go, and be forgotten like a wolf cub. That's what I thought when the tiles moved. Or maybe I just thought they moved. But something shifts and we die. I've seen dead animals, and eaten them and never thought about it before."

"Our child, if we have one, will have many birthdays," Sumpter said. "And live to grow old."

But Ma-ah stood there, still startled. Her feelings had erupted; feelings not connected with hunger or necessity, free emotions welling up as she remembered them doing only once or twice before in her life. Astonished, she said, "Feelings . . . *move* inside people."

"You've felt emotions before—"

"But I didn't have time to know what I felt," she said wonderingly. "I never had feelings before that I didn't have to do something about right away. Well, once I did, watching a storm when I was safe in a cave. Or maybe a few times that I've forgotten. I don't know if I like this kind of feeling or not. You can't do anything about it."

"Something shifts," Sumpter said, echoing her earlier remark. "Strange." He refused to read her thoughts, though he could have easily. But he knew that something had happened to her. In some way she'd changed, opened.

She walked pensively now, beside him. Quite unaccountably he felt sorry for her. The birth of feelings, and feelings' reflections, he thought.

And into Ma-ah's mind rushed memories of her earlier life, in the world of cliffs and hunger, light and night's unmitigated darkness. The contrasts had been so brilliant and demanding that there'd been no time to think. They'd just seemed given, and she'd accepted them without questions. Now she discovered her memory clear and unblemished—yet there was no reason to remember. The memories just came. "I won't go back there," she said, in a hard voice.

"You won't have to—" Sumpter broke off, realizing that for the first time, perhaps in her voice, Ma-ah had given him a real glimpse of her life before she came to the Speakers. She'd told him all the details before, but in such a matter-of-fact way that her emotional response to the environment never came through. With all he knew about her, she gave little of herself.

They were almost at his quarters. It was a humble enough stone structure, with a single unit—the basic pyramid-shaped center shabia or center room, with two smaller rooms on each side. The tiled floors were covered here and there with small white wool rugs, and the walls hung with tapestries in bright, glowing colors. Sumpter led her to a side room, with its wide windows and low couch.

The dwelling was much like the one the Speakers had given her.

"I've never mated where it was protected like this," Ma-ah said. And suddenly she was uneasy and shy. "Usually we just mated when we felt like it, on the spot. All this talking—" She began stalking about the room.

But Sumpter didn't want to just take her, though she seemed quite ready, and his own attempts to give her time were apparently making her nervous. "Sit here for a minute," he said. "Once we mate, I'll have much to tell you about the Speakers' background; how we came here, traditions we hope to pass on. But we maintain this place in ways that you don't yet understand. One day all of it will be yours; it will belong to the children of matings such as ours. Still . . . we'll vanish from the face of the Earth as we are. Mingling, we give up certain qualities that we'd retain if we kept our stock pure—"

Ma-ah sat there listening, wondering if the Speakers really mated or only talked about it. At the same time Sumpter's voice had a soothing hypnotic quality that she enjoyed, and a liquidlike fluidity of feeling rose and fell within her as she listened. "We'll retain our most characteristic natures," he said. "We'll go truly inward, though, reaching men in the dream state, where words are really only symbols—"

She suddenly looked truly curious. "Why, that's like the old man, I suppose," she said. "I see him in my dreams often. Or I did. I can't remember seeing him lately."

"Speakers appear frequently in people's dreams and sometimes they are seen as old men. Why didn't you tell me earlier?" Sumpter stared at her, amazed.

"He's just the old man," Ma-ah said. "He isn't a Speaker because he isn't as tall as your people—"

"Is he always an old man?"

"Of course," she said firmly.

"Are you aware of him at other times?"

"No. Well, sometimes there are thoughts that don't seem to be mine, so I suppose they're his. I don't know why—like the time I ran up the pyramid steps. It was like having a dream while I was awake."

Sumpter's face grew so serious that she broke off. "What's wrong?"

"Nothing's wrong—"

"Well, then. I feel better." Ma-ah started to throw the robe off, this time with mischievous haste. Sumpter stared at her. She was there, offering herself so carelessly, yet he had to meet her on the terms she offered now. After what she'd just told him, a meeting of the Tribunal was a necessity. Only for the moment he had to relate to her as the person she thought she was, and try to forget the person he suspected she might be. She was right: something happens and reality begins shifting. And most important, Ma-ah had been . . . that "someone else" the day she went running up the pyramid steps.

~ *Chapter Seventeen* ~

Seven's Blackboard in the Sky
(and Aspects Four and Five)

*J*osef stared at his painting uneasily. It had the oddest kind of mobility. The mosaics seemed to jump up; move out of place, even; shift, as if the painting didn't want to stay on the canvas — as he didn't want to stay in one place either. Why should he? If he pretended to agree to Elgren's proposal, they'd allow him some freedom; then he could escape easily enough, he thought craftily. Bianka would be furious. He grinned: what a man-trap she was, and she knew it.

Now he sat on the edge of the bed, relaxing, eyeing one painting after another, enjoying the warmth of the sunlight that splashed through the windows onto the wooden floor. He'd been painting for hours. What a great day's work, he thought. What a perfect studio. Who could ask for more? He almost dozed, his muscles relaxing in the summer heat.

In his mind's eye he saw the room cozy in wintertime (without the windows boarded like last year), a rug on the floor to keep his feet warm (he'd insist on it), and a bright coverlet for the bed (Bianka could damned well make one). But there would also be her room — ah hah! *their* room — for sleeping and romping. And he'd gone scrambling through the countryside for the last time, half-starving, peddling his talent. This time he'd done himself well, outdone himself, set himself up for good.

The sunlight moved over the tiles in the painting. Josef watched, nearly hypnotized, dreaming of the comforts of the "good life." Then he caught himself. Not that he intended to go along with any of it, of course. He was just playing around with the idea of staying before turning it down; exaggerating the benefits so he could feel doubly virtuous (and twice as crafty) when he finally got out of there, regained his freedom, and left Hosentaufs more or less the way he'd found them. There was no doubt in his mind that he would leave as soon as he got the chance.

A small ladylike knock came at the door. Josef's face lit up exuberantly. "Come in."

Bianka came into the room with the new shyness she'd developed since the "arrangement" arose for discussion. She left the door open—and at this, Josef laughed out loud.

Her face clouded. "Mama's orders. Papa's, too. It isn't funny. They don't know about us . . . last winter."

Despite himself, Josef remembered the two of them hot and sweaty beneath the covers, though the room had been chilly enough. He said, "Well, come in anyway. *You* can come in, can't you?"

She looked at him as demurely as she could manage under the circumstances. She had to show him that she could make a wife as well as a bed companion. Now she couldn't afford to be bold.

"If you don't stop trying to be such a grand lady, you'll explode," he said.

"Oh, shut up!" she said, before she caught herself.

"That's better. Now close the door and let's go to bed—"

"You know I can't." She was honestly scandalized. "If we're going to get married, then it's not right."

"Good. We'll go to bed and forget marriage."

"You think I'm trapping you."

"You? How could *you* trap me? I do only what I want to do!" he shouted.

She sat down next to him, averting her eyes, not yelling back at him as she used to do, and it worried him. She stuck her legs out in the air parallel to the bed, under her long skirts and petticoats, and wiggled her booted feet in small perfect circles. Her hands were in her lap. "That's a pretty picture," she said, looking at the courtyard scene.

"Say what's on your mind," Josef said, uneasily.

"You could go right inside that picture and walk to that yard or whatever it is, and no one would find us." She giggled softly. "The picture's big enough. We'd just disappear."

He stared at her. "I didn't know you had such an imagination. I didn't know you liked that painting, either." He paused. "Come on, let's talk about something else," he said. He didn't know if he liked the idea of Bianka having imaginative qualities or not. He was growing more uncomfortable every minute. The room seemed to be waiting. It had an unreal clarity to it; extraordinary, he thought. If he could only duplicate those colors! The sunlight almost had a . . . texture: there were variations in transparency so that one moment he could see through it and the next moment it became heavier, though without any suggestion of weight . . . thicker, moving in golden columns of air.

"You look so funny," Bianka said.

He turned and saw that the room's transformation affected her also. The brown hair was an intricate thick and lovely webwork about her face. Her eyes seemed built up of deepening layers of color, not isolated but flowing one into the other—the pupils small pools sunken miraculously in the eyesockets. The cheeks cast rich purple shadows that echoed the firm jawline. The face was a living landscape—he saw it, filled with these soft hills and valleys of flesh, with Bianka's moods illuminating it from within, flashing across it like clouds or sun emerge and disappear in the sky above the Earth.

"Don't move. Don't move an inch. Just sit still—" He was rising. Everything was shifting, he felt: room, sunlight—everything in precarious balance. He had to get her just right, this moment, before it all changed forever. One canvas was prepared for painting. He grabbed it and began to sketch her face. She stared at him, filled with awe. He was like one possessed, she thought. Not daring to move, she sat until her muscles ached.

"No, no. Don't move," he said.

"I've got to rest," she protested.

"Not now. You can't." But he saw then that she was losing the pose, the muscles were quivering like shadows underneath the skin. "All right, all right," he said. "Take a rest, and then return to the same pose."

"But I can't just sit like a statue so you can paint me."

"Why not? Of course you can. Think about something else."

"Let me see what you've done." She sprang up.

"No. No. Not now. Later."

At his insistence she sat back down and they resumed. They went through the same routine three times when Josef finally put his brush down. "The light's no good now. Come back tomorrow at the same time."

"What? Besides, Mama may not—"

"Tell her I said to send you, dammit!" he thundered.

She backed away, and he realized with amazement that he'd frightened her. "Bianka, I didn't mean to yell. It's just that my work is important. You're a good model, a great model. I don't know why I didn't realize it before."

"Could I see what you've done, then?" she asked.

"Yes, yes. Anything to mollify you," he said.

She stood in front of the easel. The canvas was barely covered, yet the face seemed to be appearing from within the canvas, peeking out, emerging from some hidden dimension. "It's spooky, looking at my face, unfinished like that," she said.

"You think it's spooky, do you?" he said, laughing now, in great good spirits.

Bianka stared at the painting and then at Josef. Then she made one of the shrewdest moves of her life. If he saw her like *that,* she thought, then she had no worries. "Mama's resting," she said. "Papa and my brothers are in the fields. If you want, you can leave. I won't tell or give warning. If you go west from the house, no one will see you. I don't want you to feel trapped. I thought I wanted you any way I could get you. Now do what you want."

At first Josef didn't believe her. She stared at him again, then turned toward the door. "I'll go downstairs. You can only have an hour or so to get clear. When Mama wakens, I'll keep her busy in the kitchen for as long as I can. If you're still here by suppertime, well then, that's your choice." And she was gone.

Damned good of her, Josef thought. At least she was sporting. He wondered what he could manage to take, and what he'd have to leave. Once he'd left with only the clothes on his back and a few extras; now he had seven paintings in various stages of completion. The exuberance was at him again. He threw some belongings in his knapsack. Free again! Wandering the villages and the fairs — the outsider, with his canvases and paints! He started to hum. The sound vibrated satisfactorily through his teeth.

His travail and imprisonment were over. Aha! But even as his mouth hurt from grinning so broadly, he avoided looking at his paintings. He tried to pretend they weren't there. And all the while he wondered: would he really leave? When he turned around and saw the paintings, would he be free to go? Of course he would. No one was keeping him, after all. He went on thinking and humming, because no matter how loudly he hummed, the thoughts wouldn't go away. If no one was keeping him, then what was? What kind of a game was he playing with himself? Had Bianka unknowingly — or shrewdly — called his bluff?

Lord, what nonsense went through a man's mind at times. Of course he was leaving. He was half-packed.

And he turned. His paintings stood there like living entities materializing out of paint and canvas. The sun and shadows within them now seemed more real than the sun and shadows within the room itself. He couldn't leave them. And he couldn't take them. Some were too wet; he didn't dare roll them up; they'd crack and be ruined. For a moment he felt really frightened and more imprisoned than ever.

But what a great technical job he'd done on those tiles. He bent closer to the courtyard painting. The way he'd applied the coats of lacquers so that the transparent colors lay clearly one over the other, without muddying—

But suddenly it was as if the various layers of color somehow represented his own emotions. Not physically, but mentally he felt himself falling through the coats of lacquers, only in doing so he was falling from one emotion to another. The feelings had been opaque. Now they were so transparent that he saw them with childlike brilliance, but the dizzying physical sensation of falling through them remained, though he knew he was standing quite solidly on the floor.

They were *his* emotions! First there was his desire to leave. He felt this so strongly that his stomach ached with longing. But then he fell through that feeling to the one beneath. This one was a combination of relief and shame so closely bound together, glued, that the feelings were like fabric and he fell into the soft slippery folds of unsuspected shame.

His real emotions, buried, denied, now caught him. He was really so glad to have "a place," so really delighted not to be wandering half-hungry, that he was ashamed. A man should be free, not tied down to one family, one room, one woman. Tears ran down his face as he fell through the shame to the emotion that had been beneath.

The anger felt like a thick red web that enveloped him. He stormed about the room, feeling the web grab at him, catch his legs in a tight grasp. Even this gave way, and he tumbled headlong into the fear that had given the anger its strength. He tossed a chair across the room and threw his knapsack at the wall.

For this was what had been bothering him, beneath all the other guises. The fear—he'd tried to avoid it—but it was too late, of course. The inspiration that he'd wanted so desperately had come—and it had somehow betrayed him. It was forcing him to care, to feel, to become attached. Even while the inspiration seemed to come from another world, it was forcing him to relate to this one—and he hadn't wanted to. Even the Hosentaufs were becoming real to him. They were no longer caricatures that he could make fun of, or ignore.

The superclear light bathed the room again. Or was he only imagining it? He turned. Amazingly, Bianka stood in the doorway; staring. He hadn't even heard her come up the stairs. She was different too, he saw—uneasily. She was no longer just someone to romp with, or the model for his latest painting. She was . . . herself, whatever *that* meant, with a reality of her own apart from his . . . alive with the same tormenting complexity of emotions that he'd just experienced, and usually tried to hide.

"You didn't leave," she said. This time she closed the door.

She looked so splendid — she might have just stepped out of one of his paintings, he thought. Grinning at him, she went over and waited for him by the bed, willing to make *some* compromises now that matters seemed sealed. They threw their clothes off, shouting happy obscenities at each other. In his mind's eye, Josef saw the two of them laying in the courtyard on the hot tiles, and staring from the painting out into the room.

Actually, Proteus stood in that precise spot in the real courtyard, with Window beside him. And Window could have seen into Josef's room — he was staring in the right direction — as far as space alone is concerned. But instead he was concentrating on Proteus' discovery.

"I'm sure of it," Proteus said. "We were standing right here talking a while ago. Remember? Then we walked back to talk to more of your people. I was upset because you 'saw' that black girl, and you were trying to divert me, I think. Then we drifted back here. But that one tile! Earlier you were staring at it as you told me what you were 'seeing,' and it didn't have that sign or symbol on it then. I'm positive."

"It could have been a different tile," Window said.

"But it wasn't. I know it's the same one. I kept staring at it because you were. And that mark wasn't on it."

"If you're right, then someone had to do it while we were gone."

"But look at it," Proteus cried angrily. "Get down and see for yourself. That's what's so unbelievable. It isn't a fresh mark. It's old. It's been there for ages, *yet it wasn't there a few moments ago.*

Window knelt down, examining the tile. The blue fish with its lost tail sparkled even in the dim light, and a small symbol was clearly visible just above the fish's eye. "You're right. So it must have been there earlier, and we just overlooked it," he said.

"But it's almost dark now. It would have been easier to see when we were here before," Proteus said impatiently. "You're the one with all these abilities. Find out where the mark came from — "

Rising, Window smiled. "All of a sudden you sound like Story defending herself against your skepticism. I don't remember seeing the mark earlier, either. But in this case, common sense tells us that we just missed seeing it for some reason — "

"Now I *do* know how Story felt," Proteus said. "And I don't like it. Maybe there's no explanation, but I know you're wrong and something about that symbol is important."

Window said, "Either the mark was there and we didn't see it, or it was put there while we were gone and in such a way that it *appears* old. The first explanation is certainly the more reasonable one."

"I don't care; it makes me uneasy," Proteus said. "This arouses my curiosity more than any . . . demonstration of your abilities or Story's just because it happened to me, I suppose. No matter what you tell me, I know the mark wasn't there earlier. And I'm going to find out where it came from, one way or another." Proteus straightened up, his voice ringing with such intensity that Window couldn't help teasing him.

"This is our pragmatic Proteus?" he asked.

"See," Cyprus said to Oversoul Seven. "Each of your personalities interpreted your experience with the aspects of the tile in their own way. Lydia used it to feel her own identity in the midst of 'shifting time'; Ma-ah and Josef used it emotionally too, perceiving to some extent the many aspects of their own subjective reality; and Proteus is letting it open his mind to new possibilities—"

But Oversoul Seven was staring at the symbol that was indisputably now set in the tile. He turned to watch Proteus and Window as they walked away, and then shook his fourteen-year-old-type head: "Proteus is right. That symbol shouldn't be there; at least Proteus shouldn't be able to see it. When I traveled to Ma-ah's time, the sign wasn't there in the tile in *her* courtyard. It's her signature, the sign that she scribbled just now in the tile—defiantly—when she got angry at Sumpter—"

"Exactly," Cyprus said.

"Exactly what?" Seven cried excitedly. "What do you mean?"

"I've told you before that everything happens at once."

"Yes, but—"

"And that time is open-ended—"

"Yes, but—" Oversoul Seven felt on the verge of a great discovery, but he couldn't quite get it. His predicament was so obvious (and to Cyprus, amusing) that she started laughing.

"Stop it," Seven said. "I'm distracted enough. Let's see. Everything happens at once, so while I had my experience with the tiles and how they exist in 'time' . . . then each of my personalities did the same thing, but in their own way. I understand that much. In Earth terms, my experience rippled out in all directions—"

"An excellent analogy," Cyprus said.

"Yes, but . . . new things happened. I see what Lydia did or tried to do. . . . She went back in time and realized that the past and present are happening at once, so she tried to change the present by changing the past. But there's a big difference between that and the other thing that happened. Ma-ah signed the tile, but Proteus saw it in his present where it hadn't been a few minutes earlier. And it wasn't there in *my* earlier either — "

"Of course. Go on," Cyprus said.

"Go on? I can't. That's where I get lost," Seven said dejectedly. "There's something that's escaping me."

"There certainly is," Cyprus said, smiling. She kept changing from a man's form to a woman's so swiftly that Seven said, "I don't mean to be rude, but couldn't you stop doing that just for now?"

"It's supposed to remind you of something," Cyprus said. "But you're too involved with this particular problem right now to pay any attention," and she steadied down to the woman's form that she used as a matter of convention.

"You don't have to sound so superior either," Seven said angrily. "I never had an examination like this in my lives, any of them, and I hope I never have another like it in the future, if you'll forgive the term."

"Oh, dear Seven, do calm down and try to understand," Cyprus said. "The so-called past is a source of fresh action and constant creativity just like the future or present — "

"I know *that;* that isn't the part that confuses me — "

"So Ma-ah signed the tile *now* and affected Proteus' present," Cyprus said. "A few moments earlier she hadn't done it in the past, so it couldn't appear — it hadn't happened — "

"Ah, I caught you," Seven cried. "I was always afraid that I would, some day, but I wanted to, too. Now that it's happened, I wish that it hadn't. I've caught you in the worse kind of contradiction."

"Don't look so . . . soulful," Cyprus said softly.

Seven didn't even smile, he just threw Cyprus a reproachful look and said, "You said that Ma-ah hadn't signed the tile *yet,* so it couldn't appear in Proteus' twenty-third century. But Cyprus, that doesn't make sense, not if everything happens at once!"

"You can scowl just like Lydia," Cyprus said.

"All right, take Lydia. She went back and did something new in the past," Seven said, scowling even harder. "I understand that, I think. Yes, I'm sure I do." Suddenly Seven got so excited that he blinked off and on until he even made Cyprus dizzy. "I'm getting it, I'm getting it. I think. New things can happen in the past, right? Even as the present happens and keeps happening, the past keeps happening and new events can happen in it. Oh, no, that's not quite what I mean — "

"You're getting closer, though," Cyprus said, excited herself. "Make up an analogy if you have to."

"An analogy! This entire examination is an analogy, if you ask me," Seven exploded. But the next thing he knew he had an analogy so real and vivid that he was astounded.

"I must be making it big, so I can see it clearly," he apologized, grinning. For written across the entire sky in towering, shining letters was the following message:

$$PAST\ TIME = P_p + P_{PR} + P_f$$
$$PRESENT\ TIME = PR_p + PR_{PR} + PR_f$$
$$FUTURE\ TIME = F_p + F_{PR} + F_f$$

"Since this is an examination, I'm using the sky as a blackboard," Seven said proudly. "An extra touch that should earn me a few extra credits, I hope. It's put rather simply, so I'm sure that it's clear. Just look at that."

He'd really outdone himself. The glowing letters covered the sky from horizon to horizon. On second thought, Seven gave the letters shadows that now covered the tiled floor of Proteus' twenty-third-century courtyard so that the tiles and grass were full of contrast and brilliance. "How do you like that?" he cried triumphantly. "Now that's a landscape and skyscape no one is apt to forget—"

"Breathtaking," Cyprus said. "Would you mind giving me your interpretation of the letters?"

"Can anyone else see it?" Seven asked. "It's a pity to create something so spectacular, and have it more or less go to waste."

"*Seven,*" Cyprus said, with at least a touch of severity.

"All right. I made an analogy so I could understand, and I made up my own formula to express it. All time *is* simultaneous. There isn't any contradiction, thank heaven. But while we're at all attached to ideas of time or people who believe in them, then certain contradictions *appear* to exist. Actually, they're not there. They're only the result of limited perception. So I made up this formula to explain the contradiction that isn't there—"

"Must you be so wordy?"

"All right. It's as though there are three kinds of time, perception-wise: Past Time, Present Time, and Future Time. Look—" As he spoke, Seven demonstrated, and in the sky above the letters, three boxes appeared, like this:

"Excellent," Cyprus said, concealing a smile. "You certainly are inventive."

"Now listen," Seven said, impatiently. "I put those kinds of time in big letters to show that they're the main divisions. But there's a past, present, and future in Past Time; and a past, present, and future in Present Time, and a past, present, and future in Future Time—"

"I see what you're getting at," Cyprus said.

"So the *past* has its own present, past, and future in small letters, like this," Seven said. And he added the letters in the boxes in the sky, thus:

Seven was so taken with his own creation that he stared with awe at the giant boxes and the huge sparkling letters. "There's so much I haven't got yet," he said. "But I'm getting it. For one thing, that middle box, marked Present Time, is particularly intriguing—"

"Seven, you're getting very close to something very important," Cyprus said. "Whatever happens, remember: *You create your own reality.* You're apt to get lost in your own analogy. Be careful, Seven. There are implications—"

"Careful? Why? I'm fascinated," Seven cried.

"Don't be *too* impetuous!" she said.

But Seven was muttering: "That middle box. Lydia's Present Time is in it, with it's own present, past, and future. But so is Proteus', isn't it? And Josef's and Ma-ah's? It's according to. . . . But no, Lydia certainly thinks it's her Present Time—"

"Dear Seven, please. You must remember. *You create your own reality.* "But it was too late. Seven felt himself drawn up toward the middle box, analogy or no; and into its mosaic-like structure. There were cubes within cubes within cubes, endlessly it seemed. And in one Lydia waited.

~ *Chapter Eighteen* ~

Out of Body, Out of Mind
Lydia Takes a Journey

Sweet Young Thing was the patients' name for the newest nurse. She'd been there three days now. She handed Lydia her pill and said, "There, let's just open our mouth and swallow this, and we'll feel so much better."

Lydia's thick tongue pushed out dutifully and the cracked lips opened; but craftily, oh craftily, Lydia made swallowing motions while holding the pill in her cheek. When the nurse turned away, Lydia spit the pill out and waited.

Old Cromwell, in the wheelchair next to her, leered his approval but kept silent.

Tranquilized, Lydia had more trouble than usual concentrating, but she knew now that she could do what she wanted to, if she only tried hard enough. She'd been "out," as she called it to herself, twice now. She mumbled irritably; she was bored rotten. To hell with it, she thought. She closed her eyes and imagined herself out of her body, standing right beside it. At first she made all kinds of mistakes, straining her physical muscles instead of using the peculiar inner tension that she'd discovered only the other day. A few times she swore under her breath. If her body moved too much, some troublemaker might come in and think she was trying to get out of the wheelchair. Then they'd add more restrainers, or strap her in tighter.

"Out, out, out," she kept saying to herself.

"Old Lydia's talking to herself again," Sweet Young Thing said, passing by.

"Poor old Lydia, my foot," Lydia thought angrily, and in that moment she was out. In a snap, a real snap, she felt as if rubber bands went zinging too far, and then broke, and there she was. Oh, God. Unbelievingly she saw the really wild old bony body, the sly face with the eyelids closed, hiding such great *secrets* — *her* body in the silly robe and pink slippers, and that stupid little-girl bow they'd put in her hair, so condescendingly. And there the others were, all of them, in the stark room, the propped-up half-empty bodies. The shock of seeing her body almost made her hysterical, but she caught herself at the sound of her first crazy chuckle. She didn't know how long she could stay out of her body yet, or what she could do. Could she; for example, just sneak away from it, and not come back? And if she did, what would happen?

"If you ain't the tricky one," a voice said. She swung around. Old Cromwell stood a good three feet off the floor, tipped sideways, grinning at her. Startled, frightened even, Lydia's eyes flew to his wheelchair. His body sat in it, as quiet as you please, fat and funny in its flannel pajamas and feet stuck in mismatched socks.

"Thought you were alone, and had it all to yourself, huh?" Cromwell asked. She gasped. He looked like an off-balance kewpie doll, floating in the air like that. "Come down on the floor," she commanded. Lydia's composure returned. She certainly wasn't going to be intimidated by toothless Cromwell. "Come down this instant," she said.

"Haven't got myself properly organized yet," he said. "But I know more than you do. You're new at it. I've watched you. I can get out of this place, and you haven't figured that out yet."

Lydia blinked up at him. "Out of what place?" Actually she was almost disappointed. She'd felt so beautifully isolated before. Knowing Cromwell could leave his body, too, almost spoiled it all.

"You just follow me and do what I do. It ain't going to hurt none," he said.

"*Isn't* going to hurt *any*," she corrected, automatically. A surge of dismay filled her. "Oh, Cromwell, why you?" she asked, half in amusement now and half in tears.

"You want to waste all your time yakking?" he demanded.

"No. No. You mean that we can get out of this . . . infirmary?" Lydia was embarrassed at the urgency in her voice; or was she actually talking? She touched her lips, wonderingly. Yes, they were moving.

Cromwell jumped up and down, watching her, holding his fat sides. "Sure they work. Your lips work, your arms work. Everything works."

"You crazy old coot. Stop laughing at me." Lydia shouted. This only made Cromwell laugh louder.

"Sorry," he said. "But you beat all. Here you are, finding me out of my body, too, and all you can do is correct my English and check to see if your lips are moving any. Never mind, come on, follow me now."

She tried, but she had difficulty navigating. She wanted to walk along the corridor, with dignity, but she kept rising up in the air, bouncing up and down, and once she even floated sideways. They passed Sweet Young Thing in the hall. The sunlight through the window fell on her hair. So breathtaking was the light that for a moment Lydia forgot everything else. "Come on," Cromwell called, looking back.

He went into one of the empty visiting rooms off the hall, walked over to the window, and went right through. There he was, bobbing up and down like a balloon, only in the air three stories above the ground. "I must be out of my mind, not out of my body," Lydia thought with a pang of panic. "They're right. I'm just senile, quite mad." The sight of Cromwell lolling out there enraged her.

"What the hell is it now?" he asked, and impossibly he was beside her again.

Lydia pulled herself up to some semblance of dignity. "Old men don't go strolling through the sky in the middle of the afternoon," she began.

"Would you like it better if I was a young fella?" he said stiffly. "What's bugging you more: looking funny, making an ass of yourself, or are you just plain scared?"

She'd hurt his feelings. "I'm sorry. Really I am, and I guess I'm scared. I just can't do it, just step out like that through a window three stories up —"

"Okay. Go back to your body," Cromwell said. "I thought you had some guts. They said you raised Cain right up to the last, but I guess that's all left you now. Be like some of them others if you want, afraid to get out even when they know they can."

"Besides being a crazy old coot, you're a cruel one," Lydia said. "And you're a stubborn old idiot," he said, grinning.

She looked out, debating. Suppose she fell and died? Then the humor of it hit her. Everything was so outlandish that the word *death* didn't really mean much any more. How could it when her body was all folded up by itself in the other room, while she was here? At her age, what the hell did she have to lose?

Lydia almost gave Cromwell a coquettish smile. "I might as well die trying to fly as any other way. It's better than being drugged to death," she said.

"Now!" he shouted. He floated up several feet and just walked through the window; the glass just seemed to part to let him through, though at any time Lydia expected to hear the whole thing crash into pieces. She kept her eyes on him, rose, approached the window, put her hands out, closed her eyes tight then—and went through! Hardly believing, she found herself looking down at the yard. Below sat other old people, in less advanced stages of senility, those still allowed outside privileges. How she used to envy them! "Cromwell, I'm doing it, I'm doing it," she shouted. She felt free and weightless as the air itself. Already the two of them were moving away so that the building itself became a blur.

"Oh, God, how I wish I were back at my desk, writing all of this down," Lydia thought. And suddenly, with no transition that she could remember, there she was in her study. A notebook and pen were in front of her on the desk. She felt the wood, her fingers trembling. Was the desk real? It was. Wasn't it? It certainly seemed solid. But her furniture had been sold. She knew that.

Yet each object in the room stood out with the most intense brilliance. Even the air itself seemed to shine. A bouquet of violets stood on the coffee table. Her favorite flower. It was spring, then? It was! The scent of lilacs came rushing to Lydia from the garden below. Then she looked down at herself, half-terrified, half-filled with exaltation. Her body was a young woman's; hers, as a young woman. She was wearing a long-forgotten lovely blue-flowered dress.

What was happening to her? It was fall, not spring, or it had been. "I won't stand for this confusion," she said, suddenly furious. "I'm an old woman in a home for the aged," she added, sternly, determined to hold onto whatever reality was left.

And she was. Lydia opened her eyes. She sat in the wheelchair. Her bones ached. Her hand was sore, and clenched. She opened it. The tiny tranquilizer fell out and rolled to the floor. The nurse would find it. Desperately she tried to reach it with her slipper, so that she could shove it underneath her chair.

As usual, when she tried to move her physical body correctly, her arms flopped like two scaly fishes, their mouths where her hands should be. Fascinated, she made her fingers move, or what felt like fingers, and watched the fishes' mouths open. A napkin lay there. If the fish swallowed the napkin, and if her hands were the fishes' mouths, would her arm digest the napkin? Marvelous! Delightful! She could experience her hands as hands, or as fish. Reality was slippery.

But Lydia's eyes fell on the tranquilizer again, and she sobered. If they realized she hadn't taken it, they'd shove the next one down her throat. She'd seen it done to others, and had already resolved that she'd bite down hard if they ever tried it on her. Teeth and biting reminded her of near-toothless Cromwell, and the entire episode with him rushed back into her mind. She turned as far as the chair straps would allow, to get a glimpse of his face.

Two things happened then, almost but not quite at once. First, Sweet Young Thing's voice came from the hall; she was obviously approaching. Lydia's eyes flew to the pill again, where it lay out in plain sight. Next, Cromwell did . . . something . . . that she couldn't put her finger on. She just sensed the quickest, most eerie feeling of some kind of communication going on between him and Mariah, whose wheelchair wasn't strapped to the wall as theirs were. In almost the same instant, with nothing being said, Mariah wheeled out to the center of the room. The wheel of her chair went crunching over the tiny pill, smashing it into the smallest of pieces.

"La la la la," sang Mariah, wheeling back and forth in the same spot, never looking down. Now the pill was white powder, scattered so thinly as to be invisible. "La la la," went Mariah, with her tongue lolling. She looked over and gave Lydia a broad wink. Cromwell chuckled, yes, chuckled quite sanely, Lydia realized. Then Mariah banged on the chair so that it made a defiant, satisfying thud.

"My, my, what a lovely song," Sweet Young Thing said, entering the room. Lydia's heart sank, but the nurse didn't even look at the floor. Mariah kept chanting, "La la la," sounding quite like the senile old lady she was supposed to be.

Sweet Young Thing said, "Now let's wheel you over to the window, out of the center of the floor so other people can get by. There! I'll turn the television set on, so you can watch before supper." Then she left the room.

"Got lost, huh?" Cromwell said. His words were slurred, as they usually were. He had the same old white bib tied about his neck in case he salivated too much and dribbled. His hands danced around each other as if they had a life of their own. Yet his eyes were crafty, amused, and in a strange way guileless.

"You got a bib on too, ya know," he said as if reading her thoughts. "What? What?" Lydia's voice was harsh. She could hardly hear what he was saying above the television program.

"When we was on our flying stroll you just plinked out — you got carried away somewhere —" The words ran together, but made sense.

"Hush, hush," she snapped. "They'll hear you." She glanced quickly, fearfully, all around. "Sometimes I think I *am* batty." she cried.

This sent Mariah and Cromwell into gales of laughter. Mariah wheeled herself up close to Lydia and screeched: "Fly, fly like a bird. Tweet. Tweet. Tweet. Tweety." She waved her arms in the air and made a face, giggling all the while.

Then, exhausted, she fell back in her chair.

Sweet Young Thing came bustling in. "Now let's not be so noisy. Who's making all the racket?" This time there was a slight edge to her voice. Lydia watched her, thinking that she was young and sane at least, and could be depended upon. "N . . . Nn . . . nu . . . nurse —" she said, furious with herself; when she wanted most to speak, often she couldn't. Worse, the nurse didn't even hear her. She reached out, and this time the floppy right arm just lay there, refusing to move. But . . . an arm reached out. Briefly Lydia saw it . . . and felt it . . . and then it came back into her body and disappeared.

She was nearly in a state of shock. Sweet Young Thing turned, saw her face, and said, "What is it, Lydia? Are you trying to say something? What do you want?"

Lydia meant to say, "I know this sounds crazy, but I swear I went flying about this afternoon." Instead, all she got out in a raspy voice was: "People fly."

"Of course they do," the nurse said cheerfully.

Cromwell had a coughing spell. The nurse said, "What next?" and left to get him water.

Everyone in the room stared at Lydia.

"Fear you notch," Cromwell said, meaning to say, "Fear you not."

"They don't know nothin'," Mariah said. She grinned like a three-year-old and rolled her eyes.

For an instant Lydia rallied. "They don't know *anything*," she corrected, but when she tried to speak again the words didn't make any sense.

But her thoughts did. It came to her quite clearly that even while she couldn't speak properly, she *could* concentrate. And just as she was beginning to learn about these odd new movements in her . . . inner body . . . she was aware more and more of an inner straining, as if words from outside were trying to form in her mind.

~ *Chapter Nineteen* ~

The Speakers' Dream Tribunal
(Ma-ah)

Sumpter slipped out of his body easily and stood up. He always felt more truly alive and alert, lighter and more exuberant when he cast his physical body off. Not that the Earth form wasn't marvelous, he thought, because it was, and he couldn't manipulate in the environment without it. Still, he felt more in his natural element whenever he slipped out of his skin.

Ma-ah was on the couch. He went in, moving quietly in the moonlight that splashed through the window. Her body was sleeping but Ma-ah was obviously gone; her form showing that peculiar vacancy that was apparent when the person-consciousness deserted it. Well, he had plenty of time, and he had a good idea where she was. Smiling, he remembered the nights that he'd followed her down to the courtyard, and found her studying the cave drawings and inscriptions. In the morning she never recalled their meetings, though now her dream memory was improving constantly.

Still, as he left his quarters, he wondered how she would respond at the Dream Tribunal; and what they'd learn. An unaccustomed nervousness was at him — she obviously knew so much and yet so little. He had the feeling that the Tribunal would discover information of great import to all of them. But as he went along, his native sensitivity drowned out his speculations. The night was so perfect that he felt honored to be a part of it.

He paused by the private dwellings. The Speakers' bodies were all sleeping, men, women, and children alike. But the Speakers themselves were up and about. The adults would soon be heading for the Dream Tribunal, having just finished the childrens' nightly dream training; and the children were playing. Groups of them went rushing by, playing tag, and Sumpter grinned indulgently as he watched.

The children ran laughing and shouting in their dream bodies — straight through trees — usually the biggest ones they could find, emerging gleefully on the other side. Their games reminded him of his own early training: the joy of learning to use the dream body and the great freedom of discarding the physical one. Then, of course, there was the contrast, equally delightful, of slipping back into the physical form. As children, they used to compare the two bodies for hours at a time.

He found Ma-ah at the courtyard as usual. He approached slowly, calling out when he was some distance away. She still had some difficulty in controlling her consciousness when she was out of her body, and he didn't want to startle her.

"Who is it?" she asked, turning.

"Sumpter."

"Oh. Funny. I thought it might be the old man."

"You might even see him before the night is out."

"What makes you say that? Do you know something I don't?" she asked. "Besides, this is another dream, isn't it?"

He paused. It might be best if she thought that the whole thing was just a dream, at least for a while. "You might call it that," he said, "But there's someplace I want you to go. I told you that most of the Speakers' real work was done at night, and this evening the Tribunal is being held. I want you to go with me, and please try to remember what's happening."

She shrugged. "A dream is only a dream. I'll stay in this one as long as it's happy." Laughing, she took his arm as she never did in the day, and they walked down the path together.

At least Sumpter walked down the path. Ma-ah still bobbed along. Sometimes her feet were on the ground, and sometimes she floated gently above it. A few more children passed, and she frowned: "Look at them. They navigate better than I do. This is like learning to walk all over again."

"Just tell yourself that you want to stay on the ground, then forget it," Sumpter said.

"That might work for you, but I keep bobbing —"

"You're trying too hard. Forget it," he said. "If you were in your physical body, you probably wouldn't even see those children, you know. The place would look empty."

"Will I remember any of this in the morning?" she asked. "Anyway, do you think I will? I'm getting better. During the day bits and pieces of our dream activities keep returning."

"I hope you will," Sumpter said. "Tonight's Tribunal is very important, and I've tried to prepare you for it."

They were nearly at their destination. The robed Speakers were congregating in a small natural cup of the valley. Seeing them, Ma-ah said, "They're part of my dream, then?"

"What's happening now is an event. A dream event is as real as a so-called waking one. You know that."

Ma-ah nodded; but the colorful robes of the Speakers blended with the landscape, and now and then one of the figures would disappear, then reemerge. She shook her head, and blinked.

"Your consciousness is fluctuating," Sumpter cautioned. "Remember what you learned a few nights ago. Get the feel of your consciousness again. Mentally swing it around until this entire scene comes into clear focus. Then hold it."

She did as he directed, grinning up at him because the instructions worked so beautifully—when she remembered to follow them. Now she could make out the individual faces of the men and women who seated themselves on the grassy banks of the circular hill. Sumpter walked over to the center of the natural arena, and stood there. Ma-ah sat down, to his left. The people quieted, and Sumpter began to speak.

He said: "It's written that all events occur at once, and as Speakers we know this. Yet past, present, and future seem to exist. So a prophecy has come down through the ages in our records about a woman who would come into our midst from the outside. She would learn our customs with great rapidity, and be a pivot point of energy in a way that even she would not understand. Her actions would deeply affect our work, opening up new probabilities that would appear in Earth time as it is experienced, pulling together the future and the past. She is here, now, among us. Of this I am confident."

He was silent for a moment. The Speakers stirred expectantly. Sumpter went on, with a certain dryness. "She has mated with one of us. Our stock will be reflected through hers. Though she appears in this present time as predicted in the apparent past, we know that in other terms, this has already happened—and yet is still to occur. So what we discover here will affect all other realities and times in which we are in any way involved."

He paused, looking into the faces of his people. "Many of you have met Ma-ah in day-life, or in our dream-training periods. She's learning our ways very quickly, as predicted, and before coming here she had some basic understanding of out-of-body consciousness, an unusual achievement for one of her background. But many important questions remain unanswered, and these I hope can be resolved before the tribunal is over."

Sumpter turned to Ma-ah. "Will you tell them how you came here? Tell them how you found the cave — the part of the story that you didn't understand yourself, and only remembered recently."

She stood up slowly; suspicious, quite stunned. "You're saying that I was meant to come here? Why didn't you say something to me about this?"

"I wasn't sure until yesterday," he said soberly. "And according to the prediction, you weren't told until the Tribunal was held."

Ma-ah looked out at the Speakers. Now they seemed to blend in with the trees that dotted the hillside, or sometimes they disappeared back into the grass itself. She tried to readjust the focus of her consciousness. Again everything came into clear brilliant focus, and she found herself speaking.

"I can't remember much," she said. "Rampa and I were half-frozen. We'd wandered too far that day and I knew we had to find some kind of shelter. Then something like a dream happened. I kept feeling as if the old man was talking in my head, giving me instructions, telling me to go in a certain direction. I've told Sumpter about him. I used to see him when I was out of my body; he helped watch for me before I came here. I don't know why I haven't seen him since, unless he knows that my body's safe here when I leave it. Somehow through him, I knew there was a refuge nearby. When we got to the cave I fell asleep or fainted, and when I came to, Rampa and I were both inside."

"The two-faced door." The words rushed up almost in a chorus from the Speakers.

"What does that mean?" she asked.

"It's symbolic, but also quite practical," Sumpter answered. "The door that leads inward or outward. We have several secret entrances — and exits — to our territory. They're almost impossible to just come upon; but I'll explain that to you later. Tell about your experience the day you ran up the stairs of the third pyramid."

"All I can remember is — " Ma-ah broke off. Portions of the trees began to fall apart and fly away. She felt dizzy. The images of the Speakers began to disintegrate at the edges, and her side vision kept closing until all she could see was a circle of light surrounded by darkness. Involuntarily she yelled out.

"It's all right. Don't be frightened." She heard Sumpter speak, but couldn't find him. "I'm right in front of you," he said. "You've lost your focus again, that's all. Relax. Don't worry."

His voice reassured her. For a moment she felt held in a soft blackness. Sumpter said, "You know what to do. Feel around now with your consciousness until you begin to see us—"

She gasped. The scene instantly cleared. The Speakers were smiling and nudging each other. "She's still learning," Sumpter said.

"I'm back in the dream again," she said, astonished.

"Remember, dreams are events as real as waking ones," Sumpter said. "Now—the pyramid."

"Pyramid?" She'd forgotten.

"Tell about climbing the stairs of the pyramid," he said gently.

"Why can't we do all this in the day, with my usual consciousness?" she asked, suddenly irritated.

"One kind of consciousness is as normal as the other," Sumpter said. "And this way we'll be able to find out far more, as you'll see. Now go on."

"I was with Sumpter, and I saw the three pyramids, only then I didn't know what they were. Then again I fell into a dream or something like one. When I came to, I was standing way up the stairs that lead to the top of the middle pyramid, and I was scared to death because I'd never been up so high. Then I realized that the old man had done it somehow. . . . The pyramid was familiar to him, but not to me. But even this vanished from my memory until a few days ago when I suddenly remembered it again."

When she finished speaking there was such a silence that Ma-ah was frightened. Though she still saw the Speakers, she had the oddest feeling that they'd withdrawn in some way that she couldn't fathom, or disappeared into some inner dimension where she couldn't follow. Disconcerted, she turned to Sumpter—and stared. The same thing had happened to him, or he was causing it to happen. All those people there, in plain sight, and she felt completely . . . alone.

"We just switched our awareness to another level for a moment," Sumpter said. "Forgive us. It isn't very courteous, but it was necessary. We've decided to tell you more about the prediction, and see if you can help us."

Ma-ah frowned. "It wasn't my imagination then? Well, it frightened me. I'm going back to my body and forget the whole thing. What good is it if I hold my consciousness at the right level, and you go off someplace else?"

Some of the Speakers smiled. She glowered back at them. "It's uncomfortable being with people who know more than you do all the time," she said angrily.

"No one is trying to make you feel inferior," Sumpter said softly. "You aren't. You're more important—and your presence here is more important than you know. Try to understand. You didn't come here accidentally.

It's probably no coincidence that you were even in the area. You were led here. By whom? You ran unerringly to the third pyramid, stopping just outside the invisible third door. Its real significance is known only to a few Speakers.

"And there's more," he said. "In our records it's also written that the woman would have a twin; a psychic one, of the other sex. We don't believe that he's the old man. From talking to Rampa, we don't think he's the one either. So we have two questions. Do you have any idea who the twin could be? And what do you know about the old man?"

She looked sideways at him, grinning. "You didn't tell me that you talked to Rampa about this. Anyhow, I don't know the answer to either question. I know that this is an important dream event, and I'm determined to remember it. But I don't see how all this is connected."

"Neither do we — yet," Sumpter said. "Ma-ah, can you find the old man? Have you ever called him?"

"I never went looking for him. I wouldn't know where to look, or how. But why is it so important?"

"Learning the answer to that question is part of the importance."

Her eyes widened. Suddenly she felt frightened again, but excited at the same time. "Wait," she cried. "I do remember something else. The other day in the courtyard, I thought I heard someone call my name. No one was there. For a moment I felt it was the old man's voice. Is that any help?"

"It might be. Perhaps the courtyard is a focal point." He touched her hand and imagined the courtyard. Instantly they were there. Ma-ah was aware only of a whirr of sound like wind rustling through very dry grass. They'd traveled that way before when out of their bodies, but it always confused her.

Now she rubbed her eyes and looked about. The Speakers stood on the sidelines, so that their figures seemed to blend in with the drawings on the cliffs, as if the people themselves constantly moved in and out of the stone. The moonlight was brilliant and the tiles glittered.

"Think of the old man. Keep him in your mind," Sumpter said.

She tried to do as he directed, but there was no response, and unaccountably she became frightened again. "Maybe he's gone, or in trouble," she said.

"Just keep thinking of him, picture him," Sumpter said. None of the other Speakers made a sound. To Ma-ah it seemed that the world was waiting. Then she said calmly, "Lydia is dying."

The sound of her voice startled her. "What did I say? Did I say that? Who's Lydia? Sumpter, I'm frightened. What are we trying to do? What's happening? What do you hope to find?" Then she felt as if she was falling steadily downward. The last thing she remembered was Sumpter's voice saying, "Don't worry. I'll follow you if I can."

Then the scene vanished. She was tumbling, helpless it seemed, into darkness.

~ *Chapter Twenty* ~

The Speakers' Dream Tribunal
The Night of the Soul
(Seven and Lydia)

O versoul Seven began to fall headlong into . . . himself or his personalities . . . or something, yet he was losing himself at the same time, being
dispersed. Into what? Frantically he tried to recall Cyprus' last words, but
they eluded him. He kept feeling the separate essences of Lydia, Proteus,
Ma-ah, and Josef. They were gaining a soul and he was losing himself — was
that it? No, he thought, it couldn't be. I'm each of them, yet more, he told
himself. I'm the portion that makes them what they are — not the product
of what they are. "Aren't I, Cyprus?" he called. But there was no answer.

Even his thoughts began to slide away in the most insidious fashion. He
felt his consciousness break apart into specks of energy, yet he was aware of
his being in each of them — even as they fell away from each other. "Come
back, come back," he cried to his multitudinous parts. For an instant there
was just . . . nothing, and even Seven's terror was lost. Then he was in the
midst of an incredible silence. There was no reference point within it. He
seemed to be everywhere equally, yet nowhere in particular.

It was impossible for him to say, "I'm here," or "Here I am," because *here*
and *I* had become impossibly synonymous. He could almost say, "There is
no here and there is no I," except then who was thinking?

And then even his thoughts ceased; or if he thought, he was not aware of it. Instead he felt dragged down, drugged. Even the *I* who had been doing the thinking lost itself, until only nonverbal emotion remained. Seven fought against falling. He struggled against this great power that seemed to push him down into some indefinable blackness.

"Souls can't die." Once, from somewhere within him, the thought surfaced. He tried to anchor himself to it, but it fell away into meaninglessness. All the while he kept falling; and fighting against it, and the harder he fought the faster he seemed to fall, the further down he was dragged, and the weaker he became. Once again he managed to cry for Cyprus. At least he heard his own mental call, and again there was no answer. Nothing seemed to exist but this terrifying descent into darkness.

At the same time he felt that Lydia was falling too, surrendering; and in a different way, Proteus and Ma-ah and Josef, all together. Suddenly in the background of his wavering awareness, he thought he heard someone call, "Old man, old man," and he felt that the words must have a significance, though at the time they were meaningless. He couldn't tell where they were coming from. For that matter, the concept of *where* quite eluded him.

The word *Cyprus* seemed once to hang in his mental vision, and he knew only that Cyprus was someone he needed desperately to reach. And in that moment he realized that someone else needed him. There was someone he had to help, and only by helping this other . . . someone could he rouse himself. He was falling with someone, for someone, because of someone . . . who was also in great danger. The need of that other consciousness became his own, was his own: he became it, looked out through its eyes; through the drug-filled eyes of Lydia.

The eyes saw nothing but the blackness in which all objects were swallowed. Then the falling intensified. But Seven knew that he looked out through Lydia: that this was Lydia; he had a reference point and he tried to collect himself about it and save them both. It was her fear of death and dying that had trapped him, that must have come upon her with great suddenness—or had he just become aware of it because she had? It was impossible to tell.

"Lydia. Lydia." He said her name over and over as calmly as he could, even while the darkness rushed past them both and engulfed them in the chasm of her panic. "Lydia." It was no use, he realized. She didn't believe in life after death, or *the* soul, much less her own soul—he could never reach her that way now.

"Lydia," he said again. This time he mimicked Lawrence's voice perfectly.

Their descent slowed. He caused an image of Lawrence to appear in the blackness. Somewhere in it he could feel Lydia's surprise—her hope;

and a small pinpoint of light appeared. Now Seven felt stronger. He caused Lawrence's image to appear in her mind and said, "Lydia darling, don't be frightened. It's all right—"

"Larry?" Even mentally she could hardly form words.

"You're having a terrible nightmare," he said. "That's all. Concentrate on my voice and it will be all right."

"Larry?" This time her lips moved.

"That's the name of a . . . friend of hers who died," Lydia's daughter, Anna, said to the nurse, Mrs. Only.

Lydia's terror released her enough so that one clear circle of consciousness formed.

"Relax," Seven said, as Lawrence. "Your own fear is causing the nightmare, and it stops me from helping you."

"But I'm dying." Lydia's words rang through her own awareness and fell crumbling into the room.

"No, no, you're not," Anna said. "Don't say things like that."

"She knows," Mrs. Only said.

Lydia heard. Frantically Oversoul Seven tried to calm her. Where was the real Lawrence? Why wasn't he here? Seven tried to call him, but there was no answer. Where were Lydia's parents or her husband? Why was there no one to help her? But Seven had no time to wait for answers. Lydia's fear was mounting again, and she'd have a difficult time adjusting if she died believing that her consciousness was really annihilated. He still had to fight against her panic, but he gathered together all of his strength to capture her attention. He needed a suitable vehicle. . . .

Suddenly he knew what to do—if he could do it. Slowly and at first in miniature, he built up the image of the old camper-trailer in her mind. She began to focus upon it; it roused her interest and curiosity. As it did, Seven built up the image, enlarged it, brought it into focus—and then projected it outward until it enclosed them. And he adopted the image of Lawrence.

"Lydia—"

"What?" She looked around, spun around. She was in the camper-trailer, in the front seat. Lawrence was driving. Greenacre, the cat, was on her lap and Mr. George was in his goldfish bowl on the wide shelf under the windshield. She closed her eyes deliberately, then opened them again: everything was still there. The sun was bright through the green treetops by the side of the road, and the air was soft and warm. It was early fall. Her right arm rested on the open window, and the air moved the tiny hairs on her skin. Everything was very real.

"We don't have far to go," Lawrence said.

She looked over at him. He looked great, like pictures she'd seen of the aging William Saroyan: funny, philosophical, his dark mustache bristly, his eyes grave and amused all at once.

The hair at the nape of her neck prickled; she felt an odd sense of foreboding, yet she felt more alive than she had in ages. Yet. . . . "Larry, I had the worst nightmare," she said. "I dreamed that you'd died and I was dying, and that I ended up in an old peoples' home after all." She shivered. "It was so real . . . yet here we are, our trip uninterrupted . . . going on as if nothing happened."

"You *were* sleeping, snoring too, but I didn't want to disturb you," Lawrence said. "If I'd realized you were having a nightmare — But maybe it was something you ate."

"Mmm," she said. "But what a strangely lovely day. I mean there's something positively unearthly about it. And you even seem different, more sure of yourself, maybe; decisive or something; wiser."

"That's just my natural superiority," Lawrence said. "I didn't know it showed."

"*Honestly,*" she said. But she felt uneasy. Her gaze flew about. She turned and craned her neck to see the back of the camper.

Inside his Lawrence image, Seven was nervous, too. The camper was a duplicate of the real one. He'd placed everything as carefully as possible, but undoubtedly he'd forgotten something. Nobody was perfect. The ruse had to hold until she was safely dead, to protect her from that panic — and if she found just one item wrong or missing, it could make her question the entire episode. Not that it *would*, he thought hastily. He could always think up a good explanation. Still he wished that she'd stop looking around like that. "Why don't you read me a few of your poems and practice for your reading?" he asked. "We'll be there soon."

"I left my notebook in back."

"No, it's behind me," Lawrence said. He reached around the seat and brought out the freshly materialized book.

She was smiling. Oversoul Seven was so relieved that the Lawrence image was grinning from ear to ear. Seven felt much more like himself now, and far ahead somewhere it seemed to him that he heard Ma-ah calling.

Lydia laughed, and pulled her visor cap further on her head to shield her eyes from the sun. "This is one of my childrens' poems. It came so easily that I can hardly lay claim to it, really," and she read:

> The future rises up
> Like a camel's hump,
> A part of the beast
> Like his ears or his feet.

Who rides the present,
Wiseman or dunce,
Rides future and past,
Aha, all at once.

"A great little poem," Lawrence said. "And true, too."

"Is it? Yes, I suppose it is," she said. "I did a series of children's poems and called them *Sumari Songs for Children*. I don't even know why I called them that. The title just came to me. I always considered them odd in some crazy fashion. The book sold amazingly well, too. My own kids were young when I wrote them. Funny, as I said that, I had the feeling that Anna was upset. Now, I mean. I heard her voice way back in my mind—"

"I'm sure she's all right," Lawrence said.

"Mmm. I suppose." She looked out. "Strange that there isn't much traffic. We seem to have the road to ourselves."

"She's sinking," Mrs. Only said to Anna.

She had minutes left. Lawrence said, "We're coming to a tunnel. There's a terrific place on the other side that I want to show you."

"Oh?"

Seven materialized the tunnel quickly; because Lydia's physical senses would be experiencing their final darkening. She shouldn't be aware of it now, yet the final severing might possibly alert her to the physical situation and renew her panic.

"Oh, how dark it is," she cried, astonished.

"Tunnels are," Lawrence said.

"Mr. George won't even be able to see the sides of his fishbowl," she said.

For some reason this reminded Seven that he'd forgotten to materialize the second cat. Hastily he did so, placing him in the rear of the camper.

"This place I mentioned," he said. "I know the people will really appreciate you giving a poetry reading. They're poets too, in their own way."

"Do keep talking. This tunnel makes me nervous. I guess I'll take off my sunglasses."

"We're coming out of it now. There's the light at the other end. See?"

"Thank heaven. Poor Mr. George will think he's gone blind. Greenacre couldn't care less, of course. Cats can see in the dark." She broke off. "Oh, Larry, how lovely!"

"She's gone," Mrs. Only said to Anna, who started to cry and blow her nose, and look for her kleenex and sinus drops all at once.

"The landscape's changed. Look at that," Lydia cried, quite delighted.

Inside Lawrence's image, Seven grinned; the landscape was an excellent job if he did say so himself—soft hills, early twilight—but now he had to let it merge with the quite real environment, because he knew now where they were, and what he had to do. "I might have to leave you for a minute after I introduce you to these people," Lawrence said. "I'll be back shortly though. It's in the nature of a surprise."

"A surprise?"

"Yup." He stopped the camper, got out, dapper and chipper, and opened up the door for her. She stretched and turned around. Lawrence was gone. An old man stood beside her instead. He looked vaguely familiar though she couldn't place him, and he wore a brown robe that suggested a monk's garb or an unconventional academic gown.

"Lawrence had to leave for a while. He'll be back. He turned you over to me, and I'm to take you to the poetry reading. I'm . . . Oversoul Seven."

"What an odd name," she said. "Well, if you're a friend of Lawrence's, I'm sure it's all right." After all, she thought, Larry knew an awful lot of far-out people; he used to travel around selling his leather goods off-season. She looked around. "Is this a . . . commune or something? Did you buy leather from Lawrence? I mean, do you know him well?"

"I know you far better," Seven said, grinning. She was seeing him from a memory in her mind of an aging sophisticated college professor — a roguish sort of would-be philosopher, but a kindly, well-meaning man to whom she'd once been attracted.

"Now what does that imply?" she asked. "I'm sure I don't know you, though you remind me of someone. At least, I think you do."

"You'll remember," Seven said. "But here is your audience. In a moment the poetry reading can begin."

Lydia blinked. In the background there were groups of people, obviously waiting. Where had they come from? She hadn't been aware of them before. Nor did she know how it was that she suddenly was standing in front of them, with the old man at her side. Politely Seven materialized a chair for her, and she sat down. As she did so, her poetry book appeared in her lap. What was happening? First everything made perfect sense, and the next moment none of it made sense at all. She was about to say something when a lovely black girl in a long gown left the audience and came up to the platform.

Lydia gave the peace sign, but the girl ignored her.

"Well, at last you're here," Ma-ah cried to Seven. She saw him as her version of the old man, with a white beard, black skin, and clear piercing eyes. "I don't know what's going on, but it's very important," she said, "And I've had an awful time trying to find you. I fell into a terrible nightmare and kept falling and falling, and Sumpter had to get me out of it. All that to reach you," she finished, accusingly.

Sumpter came forward and paused deferentially. He bowed to Oversoul Seven, perceiving him as a giant-sized Speaker of superior bearing, wearing the sacred purple robes. "We're honored to have you here," he said.

"Honor yourselves as well," Seven said. "Tell me, do you see me as an old man too?"

"As a prophet, sacred Speaker of old," Sumpter said.

Seven shrugged. "I'm Oversoul Seven, a learner and a wanderer. I'm not physical at all, but if you want to see me as an old man, that's your business."

"Now, stop that. You *are* an old man," Ma-ah said angrily. "And the Speakers want to know how I got here. You had something to do with it, that much is certain. My guess is that you know more than you're telling."

Sumpter frowned. "Ma-ah, this personality is One Made of Many, as our records say. Be more courteous."

"She always talks to me that way," Seven said. They all looked so serious that suddenly he grinned and added, "Well, I guess I'll leave now. You're all so profound that I feel out of place."

"But you can't," Lydia cried, from the platform. "Where's Lawrence?"

Seven sighed. "You certainly all get yourselves in messes," he said, but suddenly he knew that the examination was nearly over. Memories that he'd purposely put aside now returned to consciousness. There was a job to be done.

"Some time you'll see me as I am," he said to Ma-ah. "But you'll have to see yourself as you are first. In the meantime, the necessary answers must come from you and Lydia. The whole must discover its parts, and the parts must discover their whole — "

Sumpter stood back, smiling. "Yes, I understand now why I see you as I do. My interpretation, of course. But you *are* who I knew you were."

"Am I?" Seven asked., "But there's someone I want to introduce. Please ask your people to be quiet and just observe." And Seven called Lydia. She looked down at herself with some surprise. She was wearing a lovely softly folded gown that she remembered wearing years ago, as a young woman. Confused, she said politely to Ma-ah, "How do you do?" As soon as she spoke, the Speakers stirred with sudden understanding.

"I've seen you someplace before," Ma-ah said. "But how can that be?" She frowned. "Maybe in my dreams. But I'm sure that I know you."

They stood staring at each other, astonished by the warmth they felt, and then Lydia gasped: she was . . . growing younger, there was no doubt of it. "Something strange is happening to me," she said, in a whisper. "And besides that, the funniest things are coming into my mind. They're pictures of *your* life," she said to Ma-ah. "I know they are. They're your . . . memories. They're certainly not mine."

The same thing was happening to Ma-ah. She saw Lydia as a child, as a mother, as—Quickly Ma-ah dropped her eyes, for the pictures in her mind showed her something else—Lydia's death. And she understood in a flash that Lydia didn't know. A great, almost unbearable love went through her for this . . . woman, this girl, this *dead* old woman? Confused completely, Ma-ah turned to Seven.

"Lydia is going to read some of her poetry," he said.

"Oh, do," Ma-ah cried quickly, for who would tell Lydia that she was dead? And what did the whole thing mean? How long could a dream last, if this was a dream? But suppose it wasn't? "Sumpter?" she said, but Sumpter took her hand and motioned her to be silent.

The Speakers quieted. Lydia opened her book. "This is from my *Sumari Songs for Children*," she said, and she began to read:

> The wind remembers tomorrow.
> Children, hear its voice.
> It speaks through the voice of
>   the singing leaf
> That dangles in time's corner.
>
> All at once is evermore.
> The leaf in the moment knows
> It is present and past and tomorrow now,
> And even a leaf is wise.

Sumpter's face showed such utter surprise with the poem that Lydia broke off. "What is it?" she asked. The Speakers murmured. Expectancy was on each face.

"Please read another poem," Sumpter said. Ma-ah couldn't believe what she was hearing. She just kept staring at Sumpter, waiting for an explanation.

Lydia looked around again. She was more confused than ever, but not at all frightened. Her poetry had never affected an audience so strongly, and she felt more exuberant each moment. Once more she began to read:

> No one comes to the land of time
> Without wandering the fields
> Of the hours,
> Plucking the minutes that grow
> Side by side,
> And climbing the trees of the months
> Very high.

Lydia got no further. Ma-ah ran forward. She recited the following so quickly that the words all ran together:

De li a ne bo,
Fra se igna mambra.
Sor ju anda
See far barde nee um
Lar breatum tes mu
Ze to.

"Not yet. Don't say it yet," Sumpter said, urgently.

Seven just stood there, feeling freer and freer, beginning to understand the events that would unfold.

"I don't understand," Lydia said, appealingly, to Ma-ah.

"Do you write poetry for adults?" Sumpter asked.

"Why, yes, but I don't think I can remember any of them all the way through, and I don't seem to have that book."

"You can remember, Lydia," Seven said, gently. She gasped again; his eyes seemed to unravel her memory.

"How odd. Yes, I *do* remember. Yes." And she recited:

THOUGHT-BIRD SONG

The birds outside my window
Are your thoughts sent to me.
From the nest of your brain
They come flying; fledglings.
I feed them bread crumbs
So they do not go hungry.
Then they perch on the tree branch
With beaks open, singing:

"We have come from the nest
Of yesterday and tomorrow.
God bless our journey.
We have flown from the inside
To the outside world of your
    knowledge.
The cage door is wide open.
We burst out, singing.
We fill all the treetops.

"Splendid and glowing,
Tiny as tree bells,
We dance on the branches
Of night and day always.
Listen to us. Feed us.
We are your thoughts winging
Out of the nest
Of the birth cage
Into summer and winter.

"Our song is your heartbeat.
We move with your pulses.
You send us out
Perfect and shining,
Each living and different
To populate your kingdom.
We sing outside your window
And line up on the rooftops."

As Lydia finished, all the Speakers arose. They began talking excitedly together. Many rushed up to Sumpter. He raised his arms for silence and everyone quieted as he began to speak.

"Lydia's poems, as you now know, are translations, somewhat distorted, of the Sumari verses we teach our own children, in which truths as we understand them are passed on through the generations. Ma-ah has been learning these precise verses as a part of her training." Sumpter paused, then continued. "I assume that our telepathic translation of the poems was correct, but I was astonished that Ma-ah understood at first. Then I remembered the connection between Lydia and Ma-ah that was apparent when they met—"

"But what *is* the connection?" Ma-ah asked. "And what was the last, longer poem? I didn't understand that one—"

"The last verse was also from our Sumari records," Sumpter said, "But your training hasn't extended that far yet. Again, the poem is one of many in which we transmit the truths of existence to the best of our ability. That's one of the reasons we're called Speakers—we try to put inner Sumari knowledge into verbal terms for those who have a need for words. The word *Sumari* is Lydia's translation of another word that refers to a particular 'family' of consciousness. All of us here are Sumari, for example."

"But where did I get the poems, then?" Lydia cried. "And who are all these people? I've never had such a dream in my life. I'm beginning to doubt it's a dream at all. But if it isn't, then what is it?" She turned to Oversoul Seven and said, impatiently, "And where is Lawrence? You told me he'd be right back, and that was ages ago. Oh, I'm so nervous. I need a cigarette."

"Here," Seven said obligingly. He materialized a cigarette of her favorite brand from the folds of his robe, and lit it for her. She puffed at it with great vigor and stared at him suspiciously. "Now I'm not to do another thing or move an inch until you tell me where Larry is," she said.

Seven sighed. Pretty soon he was going to have to tell Lydia that she was dead.

~ *Chapter Twenty-One* ~

The Speakers' Dream Tribunal
(Proteus and Josef)

Who was Lawrence?

Proteus was having the most disjointed dream. Nothing in it fit together. Yet for a moment, like now, he knew that he was dreaming, and this only confused him the more. The whole thing was somehow connected with that symbol he'd found in the ancient tile — he knew that much. Groggily he wondered what he'd eaten to bring on such a dream. But then he fell back into it again. This time he dreamed he was traveling backward in time to the original civilization that the Tellers were studying; in the exact location; and the tiles were new, or nearly so.

Proteus could even feel his feet on the courtyard floor. He looked about. How curious! The place was mobbed with robed figures, with everyone listening to someone who was speaking at some kind of podium. It was a brilliant night. He'd never had such a dream. It seemed so real. Proteus shook his head, shrugged, and made his way up front so he could hear what was going on.

Suddenly he stopped, almost thunderstruck, recognizing one girl in particular. He was certain that she was the one Window "saw" and described to him, the one Story said was connected with him in some way she couldn't understand. At least she was black and beautiful. Proteus stood there a minute, trying to decide what to do. Should he speak to her? If this was a dream — which it had to be, of course — it didn't make any difference what he did.

But suppose it wasn't a dream? The girl was several years older than he was, too. He didn't want to make a fool of himself. As he stood there trying to make up his mind, Proteus saw Window — or he thought he did. Window? Proteus scowled: what kind of a dream was this, anyhow? He pinched himself, and it hurt. What did that mean? That he was awake, which was impossible? Or that he dreamed that he pinched himself and it hurt? He decided he'd rather take his chances making a fool of himself with a man than with a girl, so he approached the man who looked like Window.

"Window?" he asked.

"Yes?" Sumpter answered.

"Oh, I'm glad it's you. You didn't find out how that symbol got on the tile with the blue fish yet, did you? That still bothers me." Proteus wanted to ask if they were both dreaming or not, but he was too embarrassed.

"Why, Ma-ah did it, but how did you know? Who are you?" Sumpter asked.

"What? Don't you know who I am? I mean, you *are* Window, aren't you?" Proteus began to blush. "You look just like him . . . but no, you're much bigger. Of course you're not! I don't understand. Are you a Teller?"

"No, I'm a *Speaker,* is that what you mean?" Sumpter asked. "But how did you know about the tile? No one was there but Ma-ah and myself when she did it."

Proteus closed his eyes and opened them again. Sumpter still stood there, along with all the rest of the people. Proteus tried again. "I saw it yesterday. And it doesn't make sense because it wasn't there a few moments earlier. It just appeared. And why did you answer to Window if that isn't your name?"

"Names are just designations. I answer to just about anything anyone wants to call me," Sumpter said.

"So you finally got here," Oversoul Seven said, coming over. Proteus also saw him as an old man. He struggled to wake up. Everything began to blur, but Seven touched him on the arm and the scene cleared. "Who are you?" Proteus demanded. Dream or no, now he was determined to find out what was going on, and hold his own.

"Don't you know me at all?" Seven asked, disappointed. "Never mind. At this point I suppose it doesn't matter. You're back in the good old times you were always dreaming about. Doesn't that make you at all happy?"

"This is only a big dream!" Proteus shouted at the top of his lungs.

"Well, make it a quieter one and stop yelling," Seven said. "I've lots to explain to you. Come with me." Then he called to Ma-ah and Lydia. The Speakers retreated so that they seemed to be only shadows cast by the late moon.

"Proteus, what time do you live in?" Seven asked.

"What do you mean? It's 2254," Proteus stammered, as Lydia and Ma-ah walked over beside Seven.

"And who are the Tellers?"

"Why, they're . . . archeologists of a sort, living on the ruins of an ancient civilization —"

"Oh! This one!" Ma-ah cried. "The Tellers are . . the —"

"He's got to find out for himself," Seven said quickly. "But you're doing very well; you're picking up part of my knowledge."

Despite herself, Lydia joined in. She was growing more excited. Even Lawrence's absence seemed unimportant in the face of what was happening, or seemed to be happening. "And my poems?" she asked. "They came from here. Did I get them from Ma-ah?" Her mind was working with great clarity. She turned to Ma-ah, who now seemed like an old dear friend, except that now she felt too young to have felt that way about anyone.

"In some way. I'm not sure," Ma-ah said, smiling back.

"You were aware of the poems through Ma-ah," Seven said.

"I hate to admit it, but this is spooky," Proteus said to Ma-ah. "If I'm thinking straight at all, then you and I live in the same place, with me in the future and you in the past —"

"Well, you're *not* thinking straight," Ma-ah retorted. "I don't live in the *past*. What do you mean?" she said, staring at Proteus.

Sumpter looked, amazed, at Seven. Indicating Proteus, he said: "The twin . . . Ma-ah's twin . . . in our records —"

"I suppose it isn't important, but I wish Lawrence *would* come," Lydia said, to no one in particular. Ma-ah took Lydia's arm quickly and said, "I'm sure he'll get here. But there's something I want to show you first. Look at that cliff wall. That's the way those poems of yours look in the language of the Speakers. See those symbols? And the drawings?"

Oversoul Seven was more than delighted with Ma-ah's concern over Lydia. He nodded at her vigorously, then said to Lydia, "If you'd been interested in art rather than poetry, you might have tuned into the drawings instead, as Josef did."

"Who's Josef?" they all asked.

"Oh, I've been so busy, I forgot," Seven apologized. "He has to meet you all, too." Seven was growing younger himself, more buoyant, as the bits of the puzzle began to come together for him, and suddenly it occurred to him that . . . they saw him as an old man when . . . in their terms, symbolically, he felt like one. What was it that Cyprus told him to remember . . . her very last words? "Well, no matter," he said. "Watch."

Mentally he called Josef's name so clearly and truly that it echoed through Josef's sleep. "What? What is it? Oh, it's you again," Josef said. He sat up, out of his body without realizing it. Bianka was sleeping beside him.

"Follow my voice. We're, uh . . . having a party," Oversoul Seven said.

"Can she come too?" Josef asked.

"No, there's too many already," Seven said.

"I don't know, then. I'd hate to have her wake up and find me gone."

"Your body will be there," Seven said, reasonably enough, he thought.

"My body!" Josef cried.

"Hurry, we haven't got all night," Seven said, with just a touch of severity. And in the next instant a blinking Josef stood with all the others. "What? What? How did I get here?" he asked. Then he recognized the courtyard. "This is my painting . . . What are all these people doing in my painting?"

"Is that Josef?" Ma-ah asked.

"Why, he's the boy we followed down the tunnel that night," Josef yelled, pointing at Proteus. "There was a man there, too, with a funny name —"

Proteus turned white. "Window? Was that his name?"

"Right. Right. It was Window," Josef said. "Does he appear in your dreams too?" he asked, indicating Seven.

"Not in mine," Lydia said. "My, you look familiar. I'm sure I've seen you before. If only I could remember. . . . Are you an artist? I had a son sometime or someplace . . . who could have been an artist. I wonder how he is —" Lydia broke off. Suddenly she was looking into Roger's bedroom, and she knew quite clearly who he was. Memories of her life, but not of her death, rushed back to her. Roger was grinning, looking very relaxed and boyish for a man of fifty. He stood painting at an easel set up by his bed. The easel seemed quite incongruous and out of place compared with the white ruffled curtains at the windows. It seemed to be very early in the morning. He was talking to someone in the next room, through the open door. Lydia was quite astonished. Roger, *painting* before going to work in the morning? Roger — who had let his artistic ability just vanish through the years?

"Funny," Roger said. "Since mother's . . . well, anyhow I've been remembering things I'd forgotten for years; how mother encouraged my painting even when I was a kid, for example. And I just remembered an incident I haven't thought of for a long time. It's so clear now that I wonder how I ever forgot it."

He paused, squinted at his painting, and went on. He was in his pajamas still, and Lydia smiled: the pajamas were a riot. Roger always did have lousy taste as far as clothes were concerned.

"There was a birthday party, for Anna, I think," he said, "and Mother had me do pastel sketches of the kids. They thought I was great. Maybe that buried memory was responsible for my taking up painting again, who knows? I feel as though I've found something I lost. I can even remember what Anna wore: a yellow starched pinafore." Roger stopped and turned as his wife entered the room. At once she burst out laughing. "What is it?" he said.

"I don't know. You just looked so funny for a minute, standing there in those crazy pajamas—"

The scene vanished.

"What is it, Lydia?" Ma-ah cried. "You look as if you've seen a ghost."

"Why, I don't know. I just saw my son as clear as life," Lydia said. "But. . . . " Her eyes widened incredulously. "He was fifty, and I don't look nearly that old. Look at me, I'm not nearly that age. And there was something else; I'm not certain; he started to say something about Mother's— something, and he didn't finish. But it gave me goose pimples."

"Why don't you tell her?" Ma-ah said to Seven.

"Someone else wants to, but I will if he doesn't get here," Seven said.

"I'm here," Lawrence said, suddenly appearing. He carried Mr. George in the goldfish bowl, and a picnic basket. "Come on," he said to Lydia. "I promised you a picnic and we're going to have it. It's almost daylight and we'll watch the sun come up."

"It's about time you got here," Seven said, with a mixture of irritation and relief. "What kept you, anyhow?"

"I'll explain when I see you again," Lawrence said jauntily. He took Lydia's hand. "We're going to have a long talk. Here. I brought you a pack of cigarettes in case you were out."

"Well, I'm certainly glad to see you," Lydia said. "I thought you'd never come back—" She paused. Then she gave Ma-ah the peace sign, and she and Lawrence vanished.

Proteus and Josef stood side by side, staring.

Sumpter came forward. The Speakers moved softly out of the shadows. "I don't mean to interrupt," Sumpter said to Oversoul Seven. "And you've certainly given us some education in a short time. But there are still so many questions important to us. Why did you bring Ma-ah here? How did you know about the third pyramid's secret door? And are the Tellers really the Speakers? I mean, does the name mean the same thing?" He paused, then said quietly: "Perhaps most of all—are the ruins in the future the remains of our culture?"

Seven started to reply, unsuccessfully. For one thing, he didn't know all of the answers. For another, an acceleration seemed to be happening all about him. His consciousness started to whirl faster and faster—swirling upward as swiftly as earlier he had been swept downward; yet, again, up and down were meaningless. For an instant Seven felt suspended just above everyone else, moving in the same spot so quickly that the others seemed motionless by contrast, caught in midactions, almost frozen into position.

The next moment everything vanished.

Cyprus stood there.

Seven stood there.

They were in the courtyard of the twenty-third century A.D. Above them, Seven's huge letters blazed in the sky, with their boxes carefully marked.

"See? You got caught in your own analogy," Cyprus said. "You just plunged headlong into the middle box, the one that you marked Present Time, and experienced some of its ramifications—"

"But—"

"The Dream Tribunal is over," Cyprus said. "At least, in terms of *your* experience."

"There you go again," Seven cried. "Qualifying. And when I've got something very important to tell you. Lydia's dead. Lawrence just came for her. What kept him? And there was no one to greet her—I had to do it myself—"

"Lydia didn't believe there would be anyone. You create your own reality," Cyprus said. "That's the last thing I told you to remember. You forgot to examine your beliefs."

"*My* beliefs?" Seven exploded. "Lydia's the one who didn't believe she had a soul—"

"And you let *her* belief sweep you under," Cyprus said. "You accepted it, and that belief drastically reduced your energy and effectiveness; and drained your vitality. You weren't able to use it because you accepted Lydia's belief as your own. One of the most important jobs of an Oversoul is to instruct its personalities—not to fall prey to inferior beliefs: to become part of their experience but not to lose sight of your own nature."

Cyprus broke off and said with very gentle severity: "Seven, for a split second you didn't believe in yourself."

"But what saved me?"

"I believed in you," she said. "But the examination isn't over. Proteus and Ma-ah and Josef are in physical reality, you know. There's some important questions that you must learn the answers to; then I want to see how your personalities apply what they've learned—or almost learned."

But Seven felt crushed, and disappointed with himself. He glowered impatiently and erased the letters from the sky.

"Any Oversoul can make a mistake," Cyprus said. "And sometimes we make mistakes on purpose, to teach ourselves something important. . . . Oh, Seven, stop it—"

He'd changed his image to that of a little, angry old man, and started pacing up and down. "Oversouls are supposed to be dignified and . . . well, Window or Sumpter look more like souls than I do," he muttered irritably. "Physically speaking, that is. And they looked up to me so down there, and I tried to help Lydia; and here all the while I'd made a big error and didn't even know it."

Cyprus immediately changed into a clown and started laughing. "See, examine your beliefs again," she said. "Souls are full of vitality and energy, and if people want to think of them as being dignified and longfaced, then it's up to you to change their beliefs, not accept them." And Cyprus rolled into a ball and went bouncing over the tiles.

Seven was utterly astonished. Still in the old-man image, he went rushing after her, trying to keep up. When she stopped he said: "I never thought I'd see you do anything like that—ever—for any reason. I'm . . . scandalized. . . . I mean, well, you shouldn't act like that."

"Why not?" Cyprus said, adopting again her more conventional woman form.

"Why, just because," Seven started to answer. Then he got it, and blushed.

"You're learning," Cyprus said dryly.

~ *Chapter Twenty-Two* ~

Proteus Gets a Few Answers
from Window and Learns That
Window Doesn't Know It All

*P*roteus awakened. He felt lonesome, which was silly, he thought. Still, he'd had that crazy dream about all those people, and he *missed* some of them: the girl called Ma-ah, for instance. He grinned, rubbing his eyes to get the sleep out of them. She was so splendidly . . . insolent in a way; well, maybe not insolent, but—Actually, though he tried to remember it, most of the dream was disappearing. Wait. He sat up, feeling that he was about to recall something very important. But he lost it. Anyhow, he thought: it was reality that counted. And he had a million questions for Window.

The Tellers, for example: how strange that this second dig wasn't discovered from above. It was protected by the cliffs to some degree, but it - wasn't underground. And Window'd said nothing about the rest of the planet. Was it populated? And why had Window been so certain that search parties wouldn't find him here? What was there to stop them?

Something about the dream itself made him determined to get some definite answers. He got up and went barefoot, looking for Window. He was also ravenous, so he went to the eating hall first. (He kept wanting to call it an eating nodule.) Window was there, and Proteus sat down beside him.

"You're gaining weight," Window said. "It must be our sun and food."

Proteus grinned. "My stomach's finally getting used to the bulk, instead of synthetics. Window, where did your people learn to grow all this food? Any of it?"

"It's given," Window said, with a half-smile.

"Given?"

"It's already here. The Earth produces it. We harvest it and plant the seeds that the Earth gives; and cultivate the soil—"

"What about the rest of the planet?"

"It's in pretty poor shape. It's been stripped, but it's recovering, now that most of the people are gone. Even the animals are coming back. There's no question, though, that this particular area is amazingly productive." Window spoke slowly, and Proteus thought that he was holding something back. He was tempted to pursue the subject further, but there were too many other questions on his mind.

"Why don't the Floaters know about this dig?" Proteus asked. "They know about the first one."

Window stood up. "We don't know," he said. "You tell me."

"You don't know? You're joking, aren't you? With all of your knowledge, you don't know?"

"You can't even get in here except for the way we took you in, through the pyramid," Window said. "We suspect there may be other secret entrances but we haven't found any. No animals come in either, unless we bring them. Of course, the cliffs make a natural barrier, and there aren't that many animals yet, still—" He lowered his voice, almost in embarrassment. "A few times we saw planes go over. We thought for sure we'd been discovered, but nothing happened. The truth is that this place should be easy enough to spot from the air, yet it escapes the observation cameras that are aimed constantly at the Earth from the floating city. And we don't know why."

"Maybe the Floaters *do* know, but aren't letting on," Proteus said.

Window shook his head. "We're sure they don't."

"Well, maybe you can't answer my next question either, then. I never thought of that. But your abilities seem shared to some extent by all of the people here. Where did they come from?"

"We've developed them," Window said. "Living close to the Earth seemed to arouse long-forgotten tendencies in us, for one thing. We tried to encourage the Earth to come to life again. After everyone left, we explored the land as well as we could. This area was the least damaged, the most fertile. I'm second-generation. A few, like Story, are third. This work was begun by our fathers. But I'll have to show you something in order to really answer your question. Come with me."

Window took Proteus to another building he hadn't been in earlier. "Here's a videotaped record of the day the Tellers first found this place," Window said. "The narrator is Joel Bradwick. He was my father's brother. At the time he was fifty-seven. He lived to be a hearty eighty-four. The cameraman is Story's grandfather — one of the reasons I've taken such an interest in her development. Here we go." He darkened the room, and he and Proteus sat down to watch.

Window said, "Actually, after they found the valley, they went back for cameras and so forth. Bradwick waited here. When this video begins, the other members of the party had just returned."

The video glimmered.

"Incredible," Bradwick said. Watching, Proteus caught his breath, feeling that he was intruding. He was embarrassed for Bradwick, a man long dead, he reminded himself. But Bradwick was so obviously awed. He looked full-face at the camera and said, "I've never seen anything like this in my life before." He was so moved that his eyes looked bleary. There was sweat on his forehead. His thick mobile lips seemed uncontrolled.

"It's just chance that we ever came on this place," he said. "God knows how long it's been here." He paused. "I'm going to sit on this rock and narrate while the camera roams the nearby area. I've been here alone while the rest of my party went back for some equipment, and I've discovered some astonishing things." This time the camera showed him full-figure, and Proteus saw that he limped, and was taller than the earlier shots made him appear.

Bradwick went on, excitedly explaining the video scenes. "This whole valley is surrounded by those high cliffs. You couldn't climb them — it's impossible — so we must have gone under them through the door we found at the first dig. And we thought that we had a find there! Twentieth- and twenty-first-century ruins. But this! This is the greatest archeological discovery of the century. Any century!" The video showed the wide expanse of sky, then moved in for a shot of the cliff walls.

"The cliffs incline forward as if on purpose, to protect the valley and keep it hidden," Bradwick said. "But more than that, the ancient drawings and signs on the cliff walls are in excellent condition, which is amazing when you realize that this place isn't underground. The later ruins at the other dig are in far worse shape. I found records stored on blocks of stone here, thousands of them, in inner rooms. Who knows what they say, or if we'll be able to decipher them."

The camera took a closeup shot of one cliff section, and involuntarily Proteus yelled out.

"What is it?" Window asked.

"I don't know. Can you hold that shot?"

"Of course."

Proteus stared. A small section of the wall held his eye. On it the following appeared:

$$\Delta \ .7 \ 2 \ 4 \ 5 \ 5 \ \bot$$
$$/ \ 3 \ C \ \Delta \ 4 \ ^c \ L)$$

Window said again, "Proteus, what is it?"

"I just don't know," Proteus answered. "My pulses are really racing, I'm so excited. Yet I can't tell you exactly what it is, because I don't know. But I had the wildest dream of my life last night, and the dream has something to do with those symbols. I only remember a little. There was a girl in it, a black girl. It struck me as odd, since Story spoke about a black girl and then you 'saw' a beautiful girl with black skin the day that the symbol appeared on that tile. And in the dream someone was giving translations of ancient verse. When I saw those symbols just now, I thought that—" Proteus broke off, embarrassed. Then he continued, almost despite himself. "Well, I thought that I knew what the symbols meant; or rather, I thought I saw them translated into words of a sort, but in a different language. Yet I've seen symbols like that on the cliff walls here and never felt anything like that."

"Maybe you tuned into some kind of unconscious knowledge in your dream," Window said. "That's quite possible, you know."

"No. I really think that I just had the dream because that stupid symbol on the tile bothered me so. The dream might have been an imaginative solution to the questions I had or something—"

"Do you want me to go on with the tape?" Window asked.

Proteus nodded. "Yes, go ahead with it."

"Words can't describe this place," Bradwick said. The camera showed the entrance to the courtyard and played over the tiles. "How this place remained undiscovered through the centuries . . . I just don't understand it." Bradwick shook his head. "Until the end of the twenty-first century, this planet was literally covered with people. Yet no records mention this place. The ruins are obviously ancient, yet they're right here—out in plain sight—with no later ruins on top. It just doesn't make sense." Bradwick's voice was so filled with amazement that it was shaking.

"It's terribly difficult to recapture the sense of wonder those men felt when they found this place," Window said. "That's why these films are so valuable, to remind us. We're so used to it here."

"I just don't get it," Proteus said. "No later ruins? I don't suppose that somebody dug these out from under later ones?"

"Not unless they made them disappear completely," Window answered. "And there's no evidence of anything else having been here."

"The Floaters have complete records of the entire Earth," Proteus said. "Are you sure that—"

Window interrupted, smiling. "Our men went over all those records. There were various towns and small cities here, particularly in the last centuries of Earth's habitation—and no ruins of them in this particular spot. The first dig checks out perfectly, for example. There are a few possible explanations, but they don't hold up.

"Remember," he continued, "buildings in the later centuries weren't made to last, for one thing. Civilization was remaking itself, tearing itself down at an ever-increasing rate, and rebuilding. They destroyed a good deal of evidence of their past, so that only records or pictures remained. The whole so-called Urban Renewal Era began in a small way, but it ended up so that few cities were ever in decent shape or in stages of completion at any given time. They ripped down the old buildings to put up newer ones to house the greater numbers of people. But the new buildings seldom lasted over ten years. Material got low, until finally there was nothing else to do. They left for the floating cities and these took nearly a century to complete—"

"But Earth's been under observation all this time," Proteus said.

"Yes, but the race has concentrated all its attention and energy on off-Earth survival. Actually, there haven't been any real overall systematic explorations of the planet since man left. For so long it was just stripped bare, they had to let it rest. Portions are still scarred, maybe permanently, by radioactivity from the nuclear skirmishes of the early twenty-first century. Even many of the old famous ruins were destroyed. The Greek and Roman edifices are completely gone, for example. But here, I'll switch the video back—"

The picture came into focus. Bradwick said: "The thing is, these ruins have no right to be here. You get the insane feeling that they're . . . fresh. They're ancient, of course, but you think in terms of . . . freshly created age, or some such. And they're too complete—"

As Bradwick spoke, the camera ranged around the area once more. The three pyramids came into view. "That middle one is the one we emerged from when we got here," Window said.

Bradwick's own voice was more controlled now. A touch of resolution hardened his tone. "It's occurred to us that we might be able to keep this our secret," he said. "We've declared the first small dig, but so far no one knows about this place to our knowledge. There's an unequaled opportunity for me and my entire party. We could spend our lives here deciphering what we find—"

He paused, then smiled ruefully. "I really don't know how we could get away with it, but the idea is worth considering. Women rule the floating cities now with an iron hand. Men have the least important jobs. It's only because this type of exploration is low on priority lists that no one bothers us. They think there's nothing valuable to be found. If they discover the importance of our finding, they'll take it completely out of our hands."

Bradwick looked away from camera as if unwilling to meet the eye of any subsequent observers of the film. "This may be a rationalization," he said, "but the race needs one spot on Earth where maybe it could start over—one spot where we can be Earthlings, not Earth men or Earth women but Earthlings. This place could present us with the opportunity to begin a small living experiment of our own." Bradwick's voice was unsteady again. He said, "It's almost as if we were led here."

Window stopped the soundtrack. "So that's what they ended up doing," he said. "It took all kinds of subterfuge, though hardly anyone comes down to the surface as a rule. Planes are obsolete, no good for the Floaters' above-atmosphere conditions, though a few are stored on Earth, and copters are carried in the skylevators for use here when necessary. But still—both have gone over and still this place remains secret." He added soberly, "That's why you put us in such a predicament. We didn't want any attention drawn to this area at all—much less a search party looking for a citizen from one of the floating cities. They must think you're dead by now."

Proteus listened, but he wiggled uncomfortably in his chair. Portions of the dream kept returning, particularly the image of Ma-ah. He colored and looked away because the mental picture of her was so vivid. He realized that he wanted to meet her again, which was really impossible, he thought, because the whole thing had only been a dream. Some of his thoughts were so confusing that he tried to keep them even from himself.

He'd always wanted to be a girl because they had the positions of power, and the girl in the dream was exactly the kind of a girl he would have liked to be, for instance. On the other hand, he wanted her the way a male was supposed to want a woman—and in the way he *didn't* want Story, though he thought that he *should.*

The half-buried thoughts brought up another that surfaced suddenly, with strong emotional vitality. "I just remembered something," he said. "In the dream it was the girl who made the symbol in the tile. And she was supposed to live in . . . this particular spot, right here . . . but back in the past, when it was all new." The memory almost made him dizzy—because if this was so, then the girl in the dream *was* imaginary, beyond all doubt, and he'd never see her again. Either that, or she'd been dead for centuries. How could she have seemed so alive? How could the dream have been so real? "I just don't understand it," he said.

Window smiled sympathetically. "You had a dream that explained something that had worried you," he said. "Natural enough. And at your age, so is a dream girl. And you got the idea for her from my description of the girl I 'saw.'"

"I know. But just suppose that I did see an actual girl and it was the same one? I know it's not really possible, because she'd be dead. But if you can see things in your visions, then why couldn't I, in a dream?" Proteus frowned. "I don't believe it, but—"

"You could, of course," Window said. "But you haven't had the advantage of our training, so I suppose that didn't really occur to me."

"There, now, what training? You've kept so much from me because you were afraid that I'd be found, and tell it all. But since you don't even know how this place remains secret, I don't blame you. But I know something, I'm sure of it. That symbol on the tile is a key. That much is logical. There's a tie-in."

"In what way?" Window looked troubled. He turned the video off and turned to Proteus. "Maybe Story's insights weren't distorted as much as I thought they were, and you *are* connected with all this. Tell me what you mean."

For the craziest moment Proteus felt that he should drop the whole thing, that he was dabbling in something dangerous, that this very instant had a significance beyond any he could imagine.

"Well?" Window asked, and Proteus looked the other way.

"I've always liked you, Window," he said. "But I feel closer to you now than I ever have. I'm embarrassed, I guess. I have the funny feeling that what I'm going to say will change our lives—not just yours and mine, and Story's—but the Tellers too, as a group. Yet I don't know why I feel that way."

"Just trust what you feel, and say whatever it is," Window said.

"That's just it," Proteus answered. "What I have to say just doesn't sound that important at all. Listen: this is all there is to it. The symbol on the tile appeared suddenly. No matter what we tell ourselves, it wasn't there and then ten minutes later, it was—fresh and new, yet ancient. And watching Bradwick on the video, I realized that in a bigger way, that's what happened with this whole dig. He found this place — obviously ancient, yet it hadn't been here earlier — or at least there were no records of it. The same thing as the new-old symbol on the tile, only on a larger scale."

Proteus lowered his voice. "But the important thing is that the tile symbol just happened a few days ago. So whatever is going on *is still happening.* No matter how crazy it sounds, the same thing *just* happened, and we almost saw it take place. If we'd been there at the precise moment the symbol appeared, what would we have seen?"

Window just stared at Proteus and didn't answer.

Proteus rushed on, carried along by the intensity he was feeling. "You've been here so long, Window, that you take lots of this for granted. But I don't. If you'd tell me about the training you've been speaking about, maybe it would help. Maybe I'd be able to see things that you can't, just because of my different perspective. And you've kept so much from me. Where does your water supply come from? Where did you get the model for your civilization, small as it is?"

Window said, "I'm afraid that I've relied on my inner seeing, and ignored some things that were right in front of my physical eyes. Forgive me, Proteus. Maybe you *can* be of help."

"Not only that," Proteus said. "But the tape showed me so many things. Those men began just the kind of experiment that I dreamed of for years as a boy: setting up natural life on Earth again. But you've really stopped asking the kind of questions those men asked. You've even stopped wondering why this place is still undiscovered. Only my question brought the matter to your attention again. But finding out the answer is important."

Window stood up. "You're right, of course. In a way, maybe we were afraid of learning too much," he said slowly. "A lot of this has to do with the training. We do many things because of it that we don't understand. We've been content to do them, and let it go at that, I suppose. We began the training — or it was begun — about three years after the original party arrived — and in a most peculiar manner.

"Wait a minute," he said, "And I'll show you another tape that you'll find even more informative." He paused, then continued. "Proteus, your attitude had a lot to do with our secrecy, too. You were upset enough about your own situation, of course: running away, the search, the new surroundings. But more than that, you were shocked by the little you did learn about us. Your reaction to Story was a good example. We knew you were uneasy about our abilities, and I 'saw' that you weren't ready."

"I'm sorry I was so skeptical," Proteus said. "I didn't mean to hurt Story's feelings."

"That's another thing," Window said. "I had her to think about. She's in the middle of her training, and she's never come up against doubts like that before. They *can* be ruinous. But here — this is a later tape. Three years later."

The sound and video returned. This time Bradwick stood in a room lined with stone slabs piled sideways on rock ledges. Bradwick was obviously older, yet in another way he looked more vigorous. His voice had an added assurance. A baby about two years old sat on the stone floor. Just as the camera focused on Bradwick, the child began to toddle about.

"The date is June 17, 2211," Bradwick said. "We all know it — I doubt we'll ever forget it — but our descendants might be interested. To save equipment we only tape on the most important occasions, and this is one of them. Rather than tell what happened, I'm letting my brother's child unknowingly demonstrate. At least we hope he'll do what he did earlier in the day. Please watch. The camera will be aimed at the baby. And just a hint here. We've left some of these stone tablets loose on the floor. We're hoping that the boy will go over to them as he did about an hour ago."

Proteus watched expectantly and somewhat impatiently while Window sat there smiling quietly, and offering no information. The baby crawled about, half-stood, fell down, got to his feet again, laughed, got up. "What does he do?" Proteus asked. "Just tell me so I'll know what to watch for."

"There. All right. Watch closely now," Window said. The child saw the stone slabs, went over, sat down, and put his chubby hands flat on one of them. The camera came in closer, and Proteus could make out the symbols on the stone quite clearly. The baby seemed disappointed. He put his hands down flat on the symbols and scowled. Out of camera range, Bradwick chuckled encouragingly. Proteus almost snapped, "Be quiet." He'd completely forgotten about Bradwick in his intentness.

The child turned, yelled, "Da!" and grinned, apparently at Bradwick.

"What does he *do?*" Proteus demanded; then he bit his lips, staring. While he'd turned to look at Window, the baby had returned to the stone tablet. Now the camera zoomed in. The small fingers were clumsily following the outlines of the symbols. Proteus noticed that the signs themselves were larger and more pronounced than the others he'd seen. At the same time the baby laughed with delight. When his fingers ran off the symbols he stopped, looking disappointed again and ready to cry. This happened twice. Then, whether his fingers just happened to return to the symbols or what, the baby seemed to be —

Proteus turned, startled, to Window. "What's happening? He looks as if he's . . . listening through his fingers? Or hears something through them?" But before Proteus finished speaking, the baby stood up unsteadily, and then went back to the floor, this time with his ear to the stone. Nothing happened. The child looked outraged. There was a rich, loud laugh—Bradwick's. "Just exactly what he did earlier," Bradwick said.

"Sssh," Proteus said, and Window laughed.

The baby fingered the symbols again, and began jabbering excitedly as if he was trying to . . . repeat sounds he was hearing through his fingers from the stone? "Gibberish?" Proteus asked, not taking his eyes from the screen.

"That's what Bradwick thought at first too, but watch now—"

Bradwick squatted down beside the child. "My nephew has given a beautiful demonstration of his earlier performance," he said, with obvious pleasure. "I didn't know what to make of it in the beginning. He's often in here while I work. Curious, I examined the tablet and almost dismissed the whole thing, but something—his aura of discovery, maybe—wouldn't let me. What did he find so fascinating? Then I thought of repeating his actual motions—"

Bradwick paused significantly, then looked directly at the camera. "When fingered a certain way, those symbols give off sounds that are carried through the fingertips. In this case, the symbols themselves give off the vibrations, but there are other variations, as we've already discovered in the last hour or so."

Window turned the sound off. "I can tell you this part," he said. "They were so excited that everyone tried fingering the symbols, of course. After several weeks it was apparent that the tablets were arranged in a certain order. In the first series, for example, simple pictures gave off an audible 'word' that described the object shown. Later ones added the symbol so that you had the written version. . . . Proteus, what's wrong?"

Proteus stared, white-faced, at the silent screen. "Turn up the sound, hurry," he said.

Window turned up the volume. The screen showed the following:

$$\}\cdot\int \Gamma. \underline{L} \diagup \diagdown \underline{\ } 7o$$

Bradwick was running his fingers over the symbols. "In sounds, these come out like this," he said. "Sa or ne ba tu om."

"It's impossible," Proteus cried.

"Proteus, what?"

Still watching the screen, Proteus said, "Don't say anything. Just hear me out before I lose the thread of my thought, or think it over and decide that the whole thing is too ridiculous. Before you tell me any more about the training you undergo, let me tell you more about my dream—and *your* people. Then tell me if I'm right or not. Your people discovered verses, too, that were supposed to . . . carry truths from generation to generation. Some were for children, some for adults. And the cliff drawings are tied in here, too. I wouldn't be surprised if they gave off sounds in the same way—"

"Proteus, that's all correct," Window said, staring at him. "What else do you know?"

"That's it, I *don't* know. I didn't know I knew that." Proteus was dazed himself. "I thought it was just a dream. But those symbols looked so like the ones I saw last night, that startled me on the first tape you showed me. But in my dream, someone told me what I just told you—or I saw it, or something. But I definitely recognized the sounds just now, the words or language, or whatever it is."

Proteus paused, trying to remember more of the dream. "There's something else important, but I'm not sure what it was. Something about the sounds themselves having the power to . . . do things; that's entirely apart from their meaning . . . I just can't remember."

"Give yourself the suggestion that you will, and you will," Window said.

But Proteus frowned. "I've lost it. But I'm more excited than I've ever been in my life. You've got to let me take that training. Maybe we'll discover how this place has remained secret—you never know. But you have to send out expeditions to other parts of the planet. *We* have to. Suppose there are other places like this that we don't know about. They'd be hidden, too, from us. Unless we find out what conceals this dig, we'll never know if there are others like it or not. Maybe there's several, for all we know, all waiting to set up new life on the surface of the Earth."

"Maybe," Window said. "But Proteus, don't be too excited. We may be the only ones, you know. What makes you think there may be others? This is an amazingly complex—"

"I don't know," Proteus interrupted. "But I'm sure that there are others. And I don't know how I know."

～ *Chapter Twenty-Three* ～

Ma-ah and Sumpter
In Which Ma-ah Speaks
Through Proteus

Sumpter said, "Ma-ah, how much of the Dream Tribunal do you recall?"

"How much do *you* remember?" Ma-ah asked, grinning at him. "I have the feeling that more happened than you counted on."

"Ma-ah, be serious," he said.

"Don't 'Ma-ah' me that way, or I won't mix your stock with mine. What a confused baby I'll have. He won't know if he's awake or asleep-awake."

"He? And anyway, you already have —"

"But nothing's happened yet." She grinned at Sumpter seductively, on purpose. "I think we should do it again right now, just to make sure." Then she laughed uneasily and shook her head. "I remember the old woman who turned young, I'll tell you that. She was dead, and didn't know it. I guess I remember that most of all because in a queer way I almost felt like I was her — or a version of her. I can't explain it —"

"You're doing very well," Sumpter said. "You recalled that with no distortion; that is, without any hallucinations of your own. You seem to have those under good control."

"Is that what happens when I lose the right focus of consciousness?"

He nodded. "What else do you remember?"

She closed her eyes to think. "A boy, a few years younger than me. But he said that I lived in the past and he lived in the present, and we almost argued about it. He seemed so smug. I said that I didn't live in anybody's past. I lived now." Unaccountably Ma-ah found herself growing angry. "Why should he say that I lived in his past?"

"He lives in your future, Ma-ah," Sumpter said softly.

"Do you know him?"

"No. I've never met him before, but he's connected with you, and someday you'll realize how. I can't tell you."

Her eyes darkened. "Why not? I'm always in the position of your knowing more than I do. Why can't you just tell me?"

"Because I'd rob you of something important."

"Not if you have my permission," she laughed.

"Ma-ah," Sumpter said. "How can you give it, when you don't know how invaluable the thing is you'd be giving away?"

"Oh, all right," she said, only half-convinced. "But tell me one thing. Does that boy really live in the future? That's impossible in one way because he wouldn't be born yet." She frowned. "When I was in the outside world, before you found me, I would never have thought anything like this was possible. I mean, everything was Now. If I wanted to I could remember past nows, but I never thought of a future now." Ma-ah's eyes widened. "Why, that would mean that there was a future-now me to remember me, and you, and all of this. Just saying that gives me the strangest feeling."

"The now part is the truest statement," Sumpter said. "But you have to go through the past and future stage of thinking to understand it."

"Well, I'm more concerned about something else," Ma-ah said. "If I'm going to bear your child, I have a right to know about your people; that is, if what you tell me is true, and a child comes from both of us."

"It's true," Sumpter said gravely. "But what about your own people? How much do you remember of them? So . . . mysterious in a way, that your stock grew out of the Earth itself like the trees, literally emerged from the womb; everything, men and animals, coming from the rich body of the planet, and physically at least returning to it. It's still such an alien concept to me."

His eyes were half-lidded, and his tone frightened her. She said slowly, "Sumpter, did someone give you . . . training on how to go *in* body? I mean, on how to live *in* one, just as you train me to live out of it, and remember?"

He stared at her. "Ma-ah, sometimes *you* frighten me. After showing the greatest ignorance of your own body mechanics and the birth of children, then you perceive something that I've . . . tried to keep from you, at least for a while. I shouldn't have said what I just did. I was swept away by your own beauty, as I often am. Then to think that this planet of itself produces such fantastic channels through which consciousness can express itself—" He broke off. "We still haven't discovered how you knew your way here."

"The old man, I remember him now, too," Ma-ah cried. "And I know he's somehow different than I thought he was. That's another thing. He's the one who directed me here, I'm sure of that—"

"And knew of the secret pyramid entrance, too," Sumpter said. "The connections are important in terms of what happens to the future of this settlement. And in some ways you're a key to the knowledge."

"Stop looking at me like that. I don't know anything I haven't told you. The old man does, though."

"Do you want to try an experiment?" Sumpter asked. "I have an idea—"

"No. Suddenly I'm nervous. . . . Rampa and Orona will have a child, too, won't they? Born of your people and mine." Ma-ah looked at him quickly, shrewdly, out of the corner of her eye. "Are there more children like that?"

He waited before answering. "No," he said. "For several reasons I can't go into right now, it . . . hasn't happened before."

She didn't know what to say, the implications of his answer were so startling. "You mean, our child could be the first; or Rampa's? According to who gets pregnant first, Orona or myself?"

Sumpter nodded.

Ma-ah said slowly, "Our child won't even know what it was like, outside in my old world, will it? I've almost forgotten myself. I try to put it out of my mind, I suppose. It was so terrifying. But I didn't have anything to compare my experience to before I came here. Then, I just accepted it." She paused and said: "Maybe I should go back sometime. I'd be frightened now, in a way I didn't used to be. But perhaps I should do it anyhow."

Sumpter stared at her. "Once you said you'd do almost anything to stay here."

"But it occurred to me: I don't even know what my heritage is. I call the people out there my people. There are bands of them, tribes. Rampa and I came across them but they were leery of us, and chased us sometimes. But their children will know that world. So awful in a way. Yet I feel almost frightened right now because I'm so safe and isolated. My people will go their way, and I'll go another—" She couldn't look at him.

"You're not really thinking of leaving?"

"I probably wouldn't even have the courage. But I'd like to see it again."

"If you left, you'd change everything," he said.

"Oh, why did such an idea come to me? It spoils so much," Ma-ah said angrily.

"What I said about my awe of the Earth did it, I'm afraid," Sumpter said. "I emphasized differences —"

But suddenly an idea came to her; a way out, a compromise. "I have to do something tonight," she said. "Please don't ask me what it is. I have to do it alone and I don't want you to follow, even to help. Maybe the Dream Tribunal had something to do with all this. It made me realize how different we are, you and me; how easily you manipulate in ways . . . I find difficult. I'm still an outsider in your world."

"But our world *is* on the Earth. This is the Earth. It's not something apart," Sumpter said. "Look — trees, grain, flowers — everything is inside here that's outside —"

"But maybe I was meant to go through . . . whatever my people have to go through before they end up with this: your buildings and pyramids and cultivated lands. Maybe I was closer to myself in a crazy way when I was half-starving. I have to do what I have to do, or even staying here wouldn't work."

"You can't go outside alone. You don't know the way —"

"I know it," Ma-ah said. He could read her mind easily and see what she'd planned, but she knew that he wouldn't.

Sumpter looked at her quietly for a moment. "I suppose you want me to leave you alone now."

She nodded. "I want to think. And I want to sit here and look at the courtyard a while."

There was nothing for him to do or say. He nodded soberly and walked away.

Ma-ah waited until after sundown. She wanted to be back if possible before midnight, when the Speakers would be up and about in their dream bodies. Now she was frightened but determined. Could she remember the mechanics of out-of-body travel well enough to do what she wanted to? Could she master them without Sumpter around to help? Could she set her destination, reach it safely, and return?

It wouldn't occur to Sumpter that she'd try to go back out-of-body, because he hadn't given her instructions yet on going so far from her physical form, or pinpointing destinations. Ma-ah hoped she remembered enough just from hearing him talk about it at various times. She frowned again: physically she didn't even know how to get outside, but unconsciously she must know. And Sumpter had mentioned once that unconscious knowledge could be used to direct you to otherwise unknown destinations.

Still pondering, she walked back to their private dwelling. When you went "out" spontaneously, things often took care of themselves — she thought — but all kinds of hallucinations could happen, too, if your body was still sleeping. Yet to grab control consciously as she was going to do, and direct the journey, *you* had to do the things that were automatically done for you in a spontaneous dream projection.

Ma-ah lay down on her couch and closed her eyes. Will power alone wouldn't get her anywhere, yet she didn't want to fall asleep and drift into a dream, either. Instead, she started saying mentally: "I want to go outside, to the precise spot where I entered this place." Nothing happened. She wasn't being clear enough, she thought. She tried saying instead: "I want to stand outside, on the other side of the hidden rock door." At the same time she tried to visualize the spot as clearly as she could, from her hazy memory of it.

Suddenly her body felt as if it was rocking from side to side. Then she felt as if she was rocking inside her body. There were odd rustlings of sound, like words scrambled or backward, then loud whooshing noises like wind. "Be calm. You have to stay calm," she told herself, even while the sounds became louder. What caused them? Later she'd ask Sumpter. The wind became a roar, the rocking motions quickened. Something snapped at the back of her skull with an almost sickening thud—

And her eyes snapped open. Everything was quiet. She was outside; it had worked. At first she just stood there, staring. So much, yet nothing. The area was full of prickly shrubs and dry high grass. There were no high trees, just cliffs on one side, behind her, and mountains in the distance. The mountains contained caves—she and Rampa had used them for shelter often.

Her eyes stung—her dream-body eyes, she reminded herself. Her physical body was on the couch, back inside. She and Rampa had traveled from one full moon to another many times without meeting any of their own kind. Why hadn't they ever been in one of the tribes of men, women, and children? They'd been alone together as long as either of them could remember. Then so suddenly—they fell apart from each other when the Speakers found them! Why? How dreary everything looked, she thought.

She took a few hesitant steps. She could stay on the ground easily enough if she simply told herself that she would, she found. But if she forgot, she'd begin to float upward. But she wanted to walk, to feel the Earth against her feet. She stopped: she wasn't doing something right because while she could see and hear, she wasn't feeling; not the air against her face, or the grass against her feet.

She concentrated on using all of her senses. Almost at once everything intensified. It was just as if she was in her physical body. She was home! The air had a different aroma somehow, she thought, fuller of wild roots and bushes, but how strange—the air itself had a loneliness in it, an odor of waiting . . . of suspension. She shook her head, unable to put what she felt into words. The air felt as if it was waiting for . . . people. For an instant Ma-ah felt close to men and women who *would* come, to that very spot. Unseen but felt voices seemed to murmur around her as if, unbeknown to her, she was surrounded by people in other times, close enough to touch, but divided by some invisible barrier.

It was as if . . . here, outside . . . she could sense people happening but not formed *here* in this particular focus. But there was activity all about — as there had been activity and tribes all around Rampa and her, though they'd never come near enough . . . never. . . . Ma-ah felt close to some personal revelation, and again she was frightened, overly excited. Yet another part of her was very calm, just waiting for the ignorant parts to understand.

She was outside, she thought. When she and Rampa had lived there before, how lonely they'd been. They'd never questioned their isolation, they'd just accepted it. Now she was shaking: Just who were her people? Where did she and Rampa come from? Why couldn't they remember? And this Outside, how far did it go? They'd only traveled so far in it. The Speakers' settlement had definite boundaries. How was it that she and Rampa had never wondered about that in the past? Or had they? Did they know and had they forgotten?

As she stood there a wind began to rise. It was gentle enough, yet it, too, had odors in it that she couldn't place. How odd, she thought. She looked up at the sky and gasped involuntarily. She'd come from the sky! She knew it, could feel the rush in her belly as she made the descent from far up, down through the clouds.

It was impossible, of course; people didn't come from the sky. At first Ma-ah thought that her consciousness was simply confused, but her thoughts were clear and distinct and her reasoning was functioning. The odd impression continued:

She came down. . . .

In something like a round bird with open eyes on all sides, from . . . some large settlement . . . far above the clouds; she descended in a bird of metal that detached itself from something else —

And this place now where she stood was different . . . yet the same. She knew that — but suddenly Ma-ah was floating and her consciousness fluctuated. She saw glimpses of ground . . . then a tunnel underground. . . . There was a small dog running ahead down crumbled, dark stairs. She was dizzy; where was she, and where was her body? Then she saw someone who looked like Sumpter. Mentally she called out to him, but it wasn't Sumpter at all.

This had to stop. It wasn't making sense. She was coming out of the pyramid's hidden door now, but the pyramid was no longer as high as it was, the hill was gone from beneath. She was back inside the Speakers' settlement. Relief almost made her cry; then she held her breath. Everything was wrong. Half of the buildings were gone, or crumbled, or . . . just not right.

Ma-ah sat up.

Sat up?

Who sat up?

Everything was out of focus. Proteus was terrified. He'd been examining the sound-embossed drawings in the courtyard; he'd grown dizzy or dozed for a minute — he wasn't sure which, now — then he sat up. And everything looked wrong. He tried to stand up but he couldn't. What happened? The Speakers' settlement was in ruins. Such an unutterable regret and sadness filled him that he felt literally sick.

But at the same time he kept thinking: What's the matter with me? I know these are ruins. And why did I say *Speakers,* instead of *Tellers?* Yet no matter what he said to himself — or to this other part of him who was so astonished by the ruins — he was still overwhelmed with bewilderment and the deepest desolation.

And the part who was so bewildered said: Of course, the Speakers told me how to get here when I came down from the sky. That's how I knew!

And Proteus said to himself: What am I talking about? The Tellers directed me here after I left the skylevator, but what of it? And why did I say *Speakers* instead of *Tellers* again? "I'm arguing with myself," he said, aloud.

Ma-ah shut off her thoughts. She was back in her body but someone else was in it — at least other thoughts were in it that weren't hers. It was the oddest feeling. Or had someone moved her body? Because what she was seeing through the eyes wasn't right at all. Or was her consciousness just confused? She stared — the ruins were still there. Had some catastrophe taken place while she was out-of-body? But no — these were old ruins, not new ones. . . .

Of course they're old ruins, Proteus thought angrily; that was the intriguing thing — the old ruins and the symbol on the tile —

The tile, Ma-ah thought, where was the tile with her sign on it?

Proteus shook his head. Why did he want to look at that stupid tile again? It was already driving him out of his mind.

There it was. Then this had to be the right place, Ma-ah thought. But she'd left her body on —

"Window! Window!" Proteus cried.

Window had been working nearby. Hearing Proteus' call, he came running over.

"Something's happened. I don't know what . . . I don't know if I can separate myself from what I'm getting — "

Window squatted down, and nodded, but he was alarmed. Proteus' eyes had an uncharacteristic expression, as if they were reflecting another personality entirely. "Proteus—"

"Listen," Proteus said. "I'm trying to do something . . . but it's so hard . . . listen, and see if I can do it." He paused long enough for Window to become even more alarmed, then said: "*Tellers* is another name for the *Speakers*. This was their . . . settlement. This place is inside in a funny way . . . I don't understand. . . . There's an inside way to get here, besides the way I came . . . not a physical way but a real way—Oh, I don't know if I can keep this up. . . . The tile was signed in the distant past. . . . No, it was three days ago," Proteus said, in a quite different, feminine voice. Window bent closer. "Proteus?" he asked.

"I'm Ma-ah," the voice said. "Where am I? I signed that tile a few days ago. Who are you? You look like Window—"

Like Window? Proteus thought, way in the background somewhere. In his dream there was a man who looked like Sumpter. And the name Window was familiar. He tried to speak, but the odd voice kept saying other things instead, and he couldn't seem to control his own vocal cords.

"Be calm," Window said. "Speak slowly."

Proteus managed to get control. "Who said that?" he asked, dazed. "Did I?" Then the other voice immediately cried out: "These are ruins. What happened?"

"Everything will be all right," Window said. He bent closer, and as he did so he sensed Ma-ah within Proteus quite clearly. "Both of you relax a minute," he said. "Get your separate thoughts straight. Don't worry."

Proteus took a deep breath, his-her eyes riveted on Window's face.

"What year is it?" Window asked.

"October, 2254," Proteus said.

"You're the boy from my dream," Ma-ah cried, through Proteus' lips. "Where are you? I can't see you."

"Window, what's going on?" Proteus asked.

"It's Sumpter," Ma-ah cried; then, forlornly: "You look like him but you're a wrong version—" The voice sounded panicky.

Quickly Window said, "Listen. Everything will be all right. You can get back where you belong. You're in the wrong place. Now wait and listen."

His voice, so like Sumpter's, held Ma-ah's attention. She tried to organize her thoughts and perceptions as best she could.

"Proteus, you be quiet for a moment, too, so I can help," Window said. "I'm named Window because I can see things happen in other times or places. But Proteus, you must be like a psychological window. Or looked at from the other way, Ma-ah is. Proteus, this time be quiet, and let Ma-ah speak if I ask any questions. Will you try it?"

Proteus nodded numbly.

"Ma-ah, somehow you got into another reality," Window said. "I'm very curious about your own environment, but I'm also concerned about my friend here, and this is a tricky situation. I want you to think hard about where you belong. Picture it vividly, and you'll return safely. Just follow my suggestions. Picture where you want to go."

"I feel whooshy. . . . " Proteus cried. "Oh — it's gone, or she's gone."

"Are you all right?"

"I guess so. Was it really someone?"

"We'll talk about that later. You're sure you feel all right now?"

"Just a little shaky — "

"So am I," Window said. "To all intents and purposes you seemed to be two different people, and the girl gave some pretty evocative answers — or you did, speaking for her."

"She lives here, in the past — as this place was," Proteus said, awed.

"Or maybe she's . . . a personification," Window said. "No, that's the logical answer, but not the real answer. Still, there must be a connection. No wonder Story felt she was a threat."

"In a funny way I could almost follow her," Proteus said. "At least I feel that I could, but I'm too frightened to right now, I guess. But I have the impression that she's on a couch, opening her eyes."

The room was there. Ma-ah looked about. She was in her body. Her relief was making her shake. Her real, lovely, physical body! Laughing and crying, she hugged herself. A few minutes later she fell into an exhausted sleep.

∼ *Chapter Twenty-Four* ∼

Discussions Between Lives In Which
Lydia Doesn't Believe She's Dead
but Cromwell Knows

L ydia and Lawrence drove along.
Contentedly Lydia polished her sunglasses, put them back on, and lit a cigarette.

"You've got to believe me," Lawrence said desperately. "I tried to tell you on the picnic. We're both dead. This whole thing—the road, landscape, the trailer—it's all a hallucination. In, well, greater terms, it doesn't exist. It just isn't real."

Lydia petted Greenacre. "And Greenacre. He's dead too, I suppose?" She delighted in baiting him.

"No, Greenacre, the real cat, isn't dead. Or, I don't know. He may have died. I just don't know enough to state the mortal status of that particular cat."

"Well, I'm glad to hear you admit that. What is this, anyhow, a new philosophy that you've picked up somewhere? It certainly took, I'll say that. I've never heard of anything so—"

"Lydia, you've got to believe me," Lawrence said.

"If the trailer's a hallucination, how come you aren't taking your eyes off the road?"

"Habit. Just habit," he said.

"All right, for the sake of argument I'll go along. But if it isn't real and you know it, then you wouldn't believe in it and it would all go away. Isn't that how hallucinations work?"

"I *don't* believe in it."

"Hush. Don't you yell at me, Larry. I've never heard you argue like this or raise your voice before in your life, much less over an esoteric point of philosophy."

"But *you* believe it," he cried. "And as long as you do, it'll all keep happening. Besides, that old man, Oversoul Seven, is maintaining it for you too—"

"Why, how nice of him!"

Lawrence shut his mouth and went on driving. After a while he said, "You know how young you've grown. Look in the mirror. You look thirty. That should convince you, if nothing else."

"There, that's something else. What makes you think I'd be alive and getting younger if I were dead? If I were dead, I'd be a corpse, and I wouldn't be getting anything. I wouldn't dream, either, if that's what you're going to say next."

"No, you aren't dreaming—"

"Of course I'm not."

He groaned.

"I just don't understand what's happening at all," Lydia said. "I admit it. And how come you still look near sixty?"

"So you'd recognize me."

"Honestly, Larry. That's plain silly. You aren't sick, are you?"

"If not, I don't know why not. Lydia, I'm not sick. I'm dead. I've never met anyone so stubborn in my life."

"Honestly, I'm getting fed up, Lawrence. I just don't understand you at all. If we're dead, prove it."

"All right, I will," he said. He thought about being young, tried hard to remember what he'd looked like. Beside him, Lydia shouted with astonishment.

"You did it, just like I did! You look fantastic. Oh, Larry, what on Earth have we hit upon? If scientists find out, we'll be famous."

Lydia's tone caught him off guard, then he realized that her consciousness wasn't quite . . . together yet. She wasn't functioning with her complete reasoning faculties. He suspected she wasn't because she was afraid that she'd discover the truth. And the truth was against her belief in the nature of reality. This was all quite new to Lawrence, too. He tried to figure it out.

"What will we have for lunch?" she said.

"Anything we want will be in the refrigerator, I suppose," he said dryly.

"Well, if that's how hallucinations work, then I'm all for them," Lydia said. "Oh, Larry, I don't mean to hurt your feelings. But driving along with a man who's convinced he's dead is something new. You've had some weird ideas in the past, but—"

"We're *alive,* but dead."

"Well, that's a much nicer concept, I'll say that. . . ." She paused and stroked the cat. "Greenacre, you certainly purr loud enough for any two cats, dead or alive—"

Lawrence said, "Do you know what it's like, driving through a hallucinatory landscape, trying to convince your mistress that she's dead?"

"Larry, you have to admit that that sounds pretty wild. It would make a great short story, though. . . . You *are* joking, aren't you?"

"Lydia, what do you think would happen if you, well, went back to that old folks' home? Tell the truth," Lawrence said.

"That was a dreadful nightmare. What an awful thing to suggest."

But Lawrence remembered how things worked, or seemed to work. If thinking about being young made you young, then thinking about. . . . He concentrated on Lydia as the old woman in the home, and what it must have meant to her. He tried to think about what it must have been like—

They were walking down the corridor.

"Lawrence!" Lydia grabbed his hand. "What's happening?"

He looked around them. Well, at least he'd gotten rid of the trailer. Maybe memories from the old peoples' home would snap Lydia out of it, and make her face the truth, he thought. He said, "This is the home you were in, as an old woman. Don't be frightened. It's all over now."

"I'm not frightened. I'm mad. What happened to the trailer?" She broke off. "Why, I know those nurses. That's Mrs. Only talking to Sweet Young Thing."

"See, it'll all come back to you," he said.

"Well, suppose I don't want it to?" Lydia said defiantly. "I'm young now and I'm going to stay young."

"You can. You are."

"Don't take that tone with me, Larry, and in public. What *are* you up to?" She paused. "Oh, I just remembered something else. An old man. His name is Cromwell. I think I'll just look in on him. Don't go so fast. Should I speak to the nurses, I wonder? They'll never recognize me, of course. I'm so young."

Lawrence just shook his head. It was useless, he thought, to say anything. The two women stood there talking, taking no notice as Lydia and Lawrence passed by. "Why, they didn't even nod," Lydia said. "You'd think they didn't see us at all."

"They didn't," Lawrence said. "Darling, we're ghosts."

Lydia stared at him. His age had stabilized so that he looked about twenty-eight. She felt so exuberant herself and for him, and here he was talking all that nonsense. She said, "Here I am, trying to figure out what's happening, and all you do is spout this idiocy about our being dead. Now either stop it or don't come in with me. You'll just upset Cromwell. When I saw him last, he was confused enough."

"I'll be quiet," Lawrence said.

"Well, that's better." Lydia grinned and went waltzing into the common room.

She gasped. Toothless Cromwell looked simply awful. "Oh, Larry," she said, involuntarily. Lawrence said nothing. He just tightened his grip on her arm. Patients sat in wheelchairs all around the walls of the room. Some, like Cromwell, were tied into their chairs. Cromwell's face was sunken. He'd kicked off his shoes and socks, and he no longer had any teeth at all. The TV was on: a ball game, poorly focused.

The announcer called the plays of the game. An old woman snored loudly. She was sitting up quite neatly in her wheelchair, and held a melting chocolate cookie.

"That old woman looks vaguely familiar," Lydia said. "I've had this dream before."

"Have you?" Lawrence almost smiled. He might be able to convince her of the truth now. She might believe it, if only to get out of this place.

"What's that noise?" Lydia asked. "You can't hear yourself think."

He listened. "Drums, singing, a terrible band. . . . "

"Oh," she said. "The Mission Society's Sunday services! I never went to *that,* thank you, mad or no—"

"When didn't you go?" Lawrence asked.

"Well, on Sundays when they had it—"

"That's not what I meant and you know it."

"Oh, hush. Who knows what you mean." Lydia stopped. A young man sat on the windowsill, reading. He had red hair and wore a green fedora, which was silly but nice, she thought. She poked Lawrence. "I wonder who he is. He doesn't act like a visitor, and he certainly can't be an attendant."

At the same time a young woman appeared. She looked agitated, almost angry, and before Lawrence or Lydia could say or do anything, she strode to the door and out into the hall. They followed her. The off-key band was louder now, its "music" obviously coming from an open room at the end of the hall. The young woman stood in the doorway, looking in. Almost insolently. Then she cried angrily: "Lousy racket. For God's sake, can't you just quit and go home? These poor old people—you'd drive them mad if they weren't already—" The music went on. "Idiots!" the woman shouted, coming back. "Isn't that the end?" she said to Lydia. "Who are you, anyhow? You don't belong here."

"I'm Lydia—"

"Lydia! What on Earth are you doing back here?"

"Well, I don't know, really. I don't recall meeting you before."

"Didn't Tweety reach you?"

"Tweety?"

The young woman turned to Lawrence. "Listen, she isn't supposed to be here. And I don't know what you're doing here, either."

"It's a bit difficult to explain," Lawrence said.

"Cromwell," the woman shouted. "You better come over here."

Lydia turned toward Cromwell's body, which just sat there. The young man looked up from his book. "What's the matter? I'm reading." He came over, tipping his green fedora when he saw Lydia.

"This is your old friend, Lydia, believe it or not," the woman said. "At least I think it is. And she doesn't have the slightest idea what's going on. Figure that one out."

Cromwell smiled with brilliant recognition. "Of course! I was so busy I didn't pay any attention; I just knew some people had come in; our kind, I mean." He looked at Lydia. "But you turned into your younger self once when you were out of body with me. I'm sorry I didn't recognize you."

"But I—" Lydia began.

He interrupted her, smiling. "Fantastic to see you again. Is this gentleman a friend of yours? We're the only ones left of—hah—the old crew!"

"The old crew?" Lydia asked.

"She doesn't know," Lawrence said significantly. "She won't believe me."

"Oh, she doesn't know?" The young man grinned. "So you don't want to remember, huh?" he said to Lydia with a laugh.

"Remember what?" Lydia said sharply. "Are you Cromwell's grandson or something? It's not very nice of you to carry on so, when he's in such terrible condition."

"It certainly isn't," he said gleefully. "He can't even spit through his teeth any more."

Lydia was shocked. And suddenly she felt very tired.

"How long are you going to avoid facing it?" the young man said. "Watch."

He grinned at her and walked over to old man Cromwell's body—and disappeared into it. Cromwell opened his eyes.

That's all that was necessary. Lydia ran over to the window, crying. And in her mind's eye she saw herself and Cromwell, two senile old people flying over the grounds, looking down at the strollers below, and the benches. And it all came back.

"What a nasty trick," she gasped, when she could talk. "I'd have faced it myself. It's just so unbelievable — "

"You're so hardheaded," Lawrence said.

Cromwell, the young one, sauntered across the room. "At least you're safely dead," he said. "We're studying and learning, but we still have the death bit to go through — "

"And all those idiots out there, shouting about heaven and eternal bliss," the young woman said. "Incidentally, Lydia, do you remember me now? I'm Mariah — over there — the old lady with the cookie."

"Oh," Lydia cried. "My body, then, where is it? It must be buried."

"No. Cremated," Lawrence said. "Mine too. We decided on that ahead of time."

"Usually you have to wait till you're really fed up with your body," Mariah said. "I mean, it just gets so it doesn't work right. See my body over there? It still likes to eat. I mean, it still wants to . . . and up to a certain point, a body has its rights."

"Mine fights back," Cromwell said. He stood there looking very elegant and dapper, staring at it. "I tried to bow out twice, but it just mobilized itself and pulled through. So you have to give it credit, in a way. I'll just have to ride it out; and while it lasted, it was a great body."

"But I just went all at once," Lawrence said. "I thought everyone did. No, of course, Lydia didn't even know when she died. I *knew.* I felt a twinge of regret, I suppose, when I left my body on the park bench — with Lydia's help. I knew I didn't want to get old in it, or I didn't want it to get old. But now I wonder: there was still a lot of vitality in it. I'd made up my mind, though, half without knowing. That must have made the difference."

"Die and learn," Mariah said, grinning. "But seriously, Lydia, Tweety's been looking for you."

Cromwell interrupted, "I tried to help you when you died, Lydia, but you wouldn't let me — "

"That's all right," Lydia said. "But who is Tweety?"

"I don't know," Mariah said. "Maybe she has something to do with . . . well, the classes we attend. We pretty much understand what's going on around here, and we help the other people as they begin to operate independently of their bodies, like Cromwell tried to help you. Now we're pretty certain that the classes are hallucinatory in some way, but real in another way. The things we learn are certainly real enough. We think that perhaps the room, the teachers, and so forth are just images or projections for our benefit, so we'll understand — "

"But the fact is, we're deciding if we want to be born again, and if so, under what circumstances," Cromwell said. "And we're learning that we can't intellectualize everything."

"You certainly sound more educated than you did," Lydia said. "You used to say 'ain't' all the time."

"You were a bit of a snob, in your way," Cromwell said.

Lydia sighed. "I suppose I was."

"Well, you'd better find Tweety. She was around when you were here before. Once I tried to tell you," Mariah said.

"I *do* recall a voice once. . . . " Lydia stopped, then said, "But Cromwell, if you want to . . . die, why won't your body let you?"

"Oh, it would if I really pushed it. But the cells are still alive, and parts of it work great. And to tell the truth, I think my body's relieved and at peace with me out of it, and not bugging it all the time. As long as I'm busy and happy, I suppose I shouldn't begrudge it that."

"And bodies change, too," Mariah said. "Thank heavens. The cells and the awareness in them; bodies want their own fulfillment. Strange, even with mine, eating those lousy chocolate cookies all the time. I've felt it, yearning to return to the Earth again, unorganized for a change, free to be anything. I mean, just scatter. . . . And it's amazing, the vitality of bodies. The ones we have now are great, of course; they don't *age*— but they also make you appreciate your physical bodies even *more*, with all the stresses they go through."

"I think I'm going to cry," Lydia said. "I don't even know where mine is."

Lawrence grinned. "Roger has the ashes in a mayonnaise jar. I don't know how he worked that."

"Larry, that's awful. Before I do anything else I'm going to unplug that jar and let the ashes out, scatter them someplace where they can be free. Oh, I never even liked mayonnaise." Suddenly she broke off. "Why, if I'm alive though I died, then *I must have a soul.* I always thought that that was just a big bunch of nonsense — "

"Listen to that racket," Mariah cried.

The Sunday services were winding up. Just as Lydia finished speaking, and Mariah interrupted, the band broke into an resounding off-key rendition of "Nearer My God To Thee."

Lydia glowered and said, "That's what I mean. That . . . stuff!" But in the meantime, just as Lydia said, " . . . I must have a soul," Oversoul Seven appeared. Now Lydia turned and saw him. In his eyes she saw all of her memories from the day of her birth as Lydia. She knew who she was, and who Seven was. She saw the love and order that had always been beneath her days. And the hospital disappeared, and Lawrence, and Mariah, and Cromwell.

~ *Chapter Twenty-Five* ~

In Which Lydia Meets Tweety,
Discusses the Meaning of Life with Oversoul Seven,
and Stakes Out Her Future Parents

*T*enderly, actually with crafty tenderness, Josef eyed Bianka while she lay
next to him with her back turned. A while ago her body had just been
a buxom, tasty one (mmmmm, he grinned). Somewhere along the line it
had become *her* body, a natural, joyous expression of her . . . Biankaness, so
that sometimes he actually got embarrassed (him!) when he touched her.

She was asleep. He'd just wakened from one of his old-man dreams, another vivid one in which a crowd of people were *inside* his courtyard painting. Now he ran his fingers down Bianka's smooth naked back. How alive
the flesh was, the veins like buried rivers — ah, the body like a landscape —
a *fleshscape*. He could try a painting from that angle.

"Mmmmm," Bianka said.

"You'd better get back to your own room," he said. "After all, the wedding's today. At least we won't have to sneak around any more."
"Mmmmm." She wiggled with sleepy seductiveness, not at all worried. In
fact, she wanted to laugh out loud, but she didn't dare. "No more worries
after today," she said. "Can't you just imagine Jonathan's face if he caught
us, even now?"

"Ugh. Come, come, get up then. Hurry, into your own room."

She stood up slowly, stretching, arching her body in the particular way
that always excited him. "I suppose I should. Yes, I'll hurry."

God, she was magnificent. His flesh warmed. His penis started a delicious ache. Yet to be caught, to antagonize the family at the last minute, after all their tortured sneaking about — "Ahh, they'd let you sleep late the day of your wedding, wouldn't they? They wouldn't call you yet?"

She turned. "Oh, no, I'd better go. There's my hair to do and I have to help Mama. There's extra butter to churn, though maybe I'll get out of that. Besides, if Jonathan caught us now — "

He groaned happily, grabbed her arm, and pulled her back down on the bed, while she looked tempted and willing, and confused and partially unwilling all at once.

She closed her eyes, groaning herself. She loved him and she loved the game. Oh, Josef! Again she wanted to laugh because the whole family knew what was going on. How did he possibly think that they could hide all that — her careful tiptoeing through the hallway from her room to his — his sly, barefooted rush to his door, ear glued to the wood, afraid someone was spying? "What should we do?" he'd say. "I'll hide under the bed," she'd say —

All *that*, to add spice to it; to give him his excitement. And after the wedding, sometime when it all seemed quite usual, she'd think of something else. An imaginary lover? No, he'd be likely to kill anyone he suspected. Her thoughts stopped. She let herself go in great emotional rhythms that were all bound up with their flesh — his and hers.

"Ah!" he shouted, plummeting through her. Though the delicious tunnel of her was mortal, ended finally with a bone, still he felt as if he went traveling through and beyond flesh; his seed impatiently shooting into places he could not imagine, yet carrying him too. He felt this. No thoughts were involved, only a luxurious joyous, tormenting acceptance and acquiescence. Here, now, you could push, shove, thrust, yell, laugh, shout —

"Ow! Oh!" Bianka cried, dizzy with him.

Her cry brought him back. He was finished, triumphant, yet scared. Awed, as he always was. You could get lost in that tunnel. You *did* get lost in it. Ahh, who cared?

And so the seed was planted; and an opening was made in the tunnel that leads to other realities.

In one of these, Oversoul Seven was talking to Lydia. "Do you feel better about things now?" he asked.

"You'll have to forgive me for staring," she said. "But I've never read any etiquette rules for talking to your own soul, and it's a bit disconcerting. And what am I supposed to call you? Besides, I didn't know that souls looked like people."

"I'm a people soul," Seven said. "What did you want me to look like?"

"You're laughing at me and that's not fair."

"I'm *your* soul," Seven said, reasonably. "And *you* have a very funny sense of humor. Actually, I just form myself into an image so you can relate to me, or so we can relate to each other. You'd find talking to someone you couldn't see much more disconcerting, with your background. I could look like a ghost, but I prefer not to. That's too conventional."

"And this place?" Lydia asked. "It's so beautiful. The trees and hillside. I can feel the grass under my feet. Is all this real?"

"You need a location. You'd get upset if you thought you weren't anywhere," Seven said. "You always need a *where* to put yourself in, at least at your present stage of development." He coughed, remembering to cover his mouth because Lydia was still concerned about manners. "I seem to be in an in-between stage myself, so I can sympathize," he said.

"And this conversation?" Lydia stood up, musing, very aware of her body, the lithe form, of herself moving (yet, in what terms?). "I need the words, too. Is that what you're going to tell me next?" she asked.

He grinned.

"And I suppose if I believed in heaven — "

"Then you'd experience it for a while," Seven said, "Until you got bored or finally listened. It can get quite complicated."

"Can? It is now," she said, still musing. "How strange. Oh God — Anna and Roger down there, still caught in all of that, and I can't tell them. But of course it's not *down* there, is it?"

"No, it's right here," Seven said. "A different kind of focus."

"I don't have to be born again, do I?" she asked.

"Well, you have to do something," Seven answered. "And you need a framework right now or else — well, you have to learn to use your consciousness within a framework or you can get very confused."

"And God?" Lydia asked.

"Who?" Seven said.

"Are you a soul or aren't you?" Lydia demanded.

"I thought you didn't believe in God," Seven answered.

"But you're a soul; *my* soul from what you tell me, and what I feel. You're supposed to believe in God or who else will? What's the use of souls and all this if God is dead?"

Seven didn't want to laugh and hurt Lydia's feelings. In fact, he didn't know how to handle the situation at all. "I'll ask Cyprus," he said.

"Who's that?"

"Don't get me off the track," Seven said. "If you aren't really dead, how could God be dead? I didn't say that there *wasn't* one, and I have my own ideas of Who It Is, or What It Is. See, when I use your terms, I get all mixed up."

"Well, for heaven's sake, use your own terms then," she said impatiently.

Seven sighed. "In many ways I'm still an Earth-bound soul, or you wouldn't have already decided to be born again."

"I've decided no such thing," Lydia retorted.

"Yes you have."

"Well, not that *I* know of," she said. "I've always suspected it—this proves it—there's no free will."

Seven closed his saintly type eyes and mentally called for Cyprus. She appeared looking feminine and lovely, but with the clearest, most brilliant intelligent eyes that Seven personally had ever seen. He smiled gratefully; a touch for Lydia who trusted the intellect so, he supposed.

"Would you please explain free will to Lydia?" he asked. "She's worse than Josef—argumentative, that is."

"Like someone else I know," Cyprus said, but so pleasantly and with such sympathy that Seven couldn't take offense, much as he wanted to.

"Who are you?" Lydia asked, liking her at once.

"A friend."

Lydia and Cyprus looked for all the world like two young woman friends, walking arm in arm, which was precisely what they did. Seven felt left out, or he would have, but part of him understood what Cyprus had in mind.

"This reminds me of my college days when I was trying to learn so many things at once," Lydia said to Cyprus. And Seven smiled—why hadn't he thought of that?

"Look over there," Cyprus directed. They stood on the rim of a hill. Cyprus pointed to the edge. Beneath, through clouds, a scene appeared. A lovely woman—no, wait, a child—first young, then old. "Oh God," Lydia cried, out loud. "Do I remember that? Or hasn't it happened yet? That's the seventeenth century, isn't it? And that girl—" As Lydia spoke, the girl detached herself from the scene and walked up a shining ladder to the hill's brim. A bit too much, Seven thought, but Lydia seemed entranced. Then he took a better look.

"It's my independent study—Tweety," Seven cried.

"You're not *that* independent," Cyprus said.

Lydia sat down with surprise. "Why, that knocks the breath right out of me," she said, and Seven laughed. "Why, I remember now," Lydia said. "I remember making up my mind, quite on my own, to be born again. Only when did I decide?"

"In the dream state," Tweety said. "And in that old peoples' home. But you forgot, and I was afraid that you might not remember," she added forlornly. "My real name is Daga. I adopted this form so you could see what you'll look like—"

"Daga, I told you it was just a matter of time," Seven said.

"Of *what?*" Cyprus asked.

"Well, there's no need for me to have this image now," Daga said, "You won't be using it for a while—"

"In those terms," Seven said quickly; and Daga disappeared.

Lydia scowled. "I still don't understand clearly."

"You decided to be born again, as you remember now," Cyprus said. "Tweety, or rather, Daga adapted the image for you so you could see how you'll look. Seven always calls Daga 'Tweety.' It was a nickname of sorts. You liked that, too, and decided to use the name as well. Seven was giving you a good deal of help on his own. It was in the nature of a surprise for me, so I could see that he was acting independently." She added, looking nowhere in particular, "He wanted to keep one step ahead of me, in other words."

Seven lowered his eyes.

"But you're quite free to recall all the things that you've forgotten, Lydia," Cyprus said. "I'll give you a clue. Remember the young artist you met the night you died, at the poetry reading?"

"Of course! Now I remember. He'll be my father! I'm so . . . verbal, but I'd like to deal with experience in terms of color and emotional richness for a change, yet still continue to be connected with the arts somehow. And for once, I'd like emotional parents. I've been quite intellectual in many ways, which is good; and I've enjoyed it. But often I'd get so involved in ideas that I had trouble really feeling. And I do have strong abilities I haven't begun to develop along those lines—"

"Josef is emotional. I'll say that," Seven said.

"I'd met him in my dreams often before that too—I just remembered. When we're . . . alive? Is that the term? . . . Then we don't recall what we do when we're asleep—"

Seven beamed. "You're doing very well."

"Why, I was drawn to him at once," Lydia said. "And he and Bianka need someone to give them . . . intellectual balance, too. And, oh, yes, I remember something else. I'll be the model for many of his paintings." She turned to Cyprus. "But how can I be reborn in the seventeenth century if I died in the twentieth? Funny—I was always attracted to seventeenth-century literature too. That must be because I knew I'd be born there."

"Seven will explain," Cyprus said, with a smile. "But you see, there is free will. We just knew what you'd decided, while you'd purposely forgotten."

And Cyprus disappeared.

"Tweety. Tweety Landsdatter," Lydia said, musing. "That will be my name. Tweety, daughter of Bianka and Josef."

Josef squirmed. "I feel funny," he grumbled. "Like there's someone else in the room."

"You're just nervous after all the festivities," Bianka said. "You're embarrassed to be alone with your virgin bride." She giggled.

"I ought to—" he said, laughing, but he was exhausted. "My God, there's a ghost or something in here!" he thundered.

"Go to sleep!" she cried.

Lydia grinned, staring at the boots thrown on the floor, the pile of clothes beside the bed, the smell of sweat and love. How odd, she thought. She trailed about the room, smoking an hallucinatory cigarette, looking about twenty-five. But in other terms they were all of the same age — ageless. God! How intertwined their lives would become.

~ *The Final Chapter* ~

The End of This Particular Examination —
Seven "Graduates"
He Learns Something About Himself
and Discovers Who Wrote This Book

Seven grimaced and began the final portion of his examination. It was entitled "Comprehension." "Lydia comprehends a lot," he said to Cyprus. "Proteus is learning, and so is Ma-ah. Josef certainly has made great strides. I mean, he's really painting, and he relates to people better than he ever did before. But will he have a time with Lydia—I mean, Tweety! She'll teach him a thing or two, and it serves him right."

"That's not a very nice attitude," Cyprus said. "I imagine Tweety can learn quite a bit from him, too, and from Bianka."

"But I'm worried about several things," Seven admitted. "Ma-ah doesn't know her origin, and" (he looked down) "I seem to have forgotten it myself. Proteus doesn't understand how the Tellers' dig went undiscovered all those centuries, much less why the Floaters haven't found it now—"

"Yes?" Cyprus said.

"Well, I don't understand how I knew enough to lead Ma-ah and Rampa to the Speakers to begin with—"

"Keep going," Cyprus said.

"I can't. Something else is wrong," Seven said moodily. "This whole scene I've chosen, the classroom and benches: it was fun in the beginning, but it doesn't fit now. I don't even like the wastepaper basket any more.

Worse, I've been so busy that I suspect I've missed several important issues. And so far, you aren't helping me one bit."

Impatiently Seven waved his hand, and the entire scene vanished. Now he and Cyprus stood, invisibly, in Ma-ah's 35,000 B.C. courtyard. "I have the feeling that there's something here that I still don't understand," Seven said.

"You just made up for several points by making this move," Cyprus said. "Very astute."

"I did? Mmmm," Seven said. "That reminds me of something else. Do you mind if I bring my analogy back?"

"Not at all," Cyprus answered. "That's a very good idea, only don't let it run away with you this time."

Seven grinned sheepishly. Once more in the skyscape, the glittering letters appeared.

$$PAST\ TIME = P_p + P_{PR} + P_f$$
$$PRESENT\ TIME = PR_p + PR_{PR} + PR_f$$
$$FUTURE\ TIME = F_p + F_{PR} + F_f$$

"Do you remember what the letters meant?" Seven asked.

"Indeed I do," Cyprus said quickly. "And I certainly hope you do, too."

"There's just one problem," Seven said. "But wait." And above the letters, Seven projected his three boxes, representing the three kinds of time with their three subdivisions.

"Now just give me a moment," Seven said.

"A *what?*" Cyprus said, with mock shock.

"Well, in my present state of development it takes time to understand the nature of time."

"In your *what* state of development? Don't you *see*, Seven?"

Her words rang through Seven's mind, and in some indescribable way his mind expanded. Barrier after barrier previously invisible and unfelt dropped away, until Seven's comprehension itself encompassed everything he saw or knew or perceived. His consciousness circled the analogy in the sky—and he went *through* it, finding that all these times were different appearances of one inexpressible experience in which all Happening Out of Itself kept newly, freshly Happening.

All of his Boxes
Merged.
They Changed into
Circles
in Which Other Circles
(And "Times")
Were Constantly Happening.
And the Circles
Changed into Shapes
Of Sound
On the Other Side
Of Silence,
Until the Very Breath
Of
Nothingness
Danced in Time-Drops
And Light-Drops
And Finally
Thing-Drops,
And out of the
Thing-Drops
His Boxes Emerged —
And out of the Boxes
Came
Lydia's Time
And Josef's
And Ma-ah's and Proteus'
And the Tiles
in the Courtyard.

And Seven shouted: "Oh, I've got it! The Speakers' ruins were never discovered before Window's time because—" He was so excited that he projected his words outward so that the letters seemed to come out like minutes one at a time from his open boxes.

"The Speakers' ruins
Didn't appear until the twenty-third century
Because
They weren't there *earlier*—

Because
They were fresh action
Happening in . . . the future of
   Past Time
and only *then*
Emerging in the past of Present
   Time —

They were brand-new ruins!"

"Will you elaborate?" Cyprus asked, smiling.

"Of course. Oh, gladly," Seven said. "The nineteenth- or twentieth-century ruins are *underneath* the new 35,000 B.C. ones because those appeared "later" from the future of Past Time, where there's always fresh action and new things happening. That's why Window couldn't figure it out. It's a complete dilemma in the framework of time as he understands it — "

Cyprus said, very softly: "Seven, remember you create your own reality. We all do."

"I know. You keep telling me," Seven said, somewhat impatiently. "What does that have to do with this?"

"It has to do with other questions you haven't answered yet, and it all fits together. And it's a clue."

"Oh, well, then. Let me see — "

"You Make Your Own Reality," Cyprus said again, in the weirdest fashion, and suddenly the words rang in Seven's own mind, from within *his* own consciousness, not from outside it. And with that, Cyprus disappeared.

Yet in a microsecond that could also have been a century, Seven experienced a richness of being beyond any he had ever imagined, in which he was himself, or rather itself.

And he and Cyprus were both participants in a multiplicity of selves; multiple existences rippling inward and outward like constellations. Each self was unique. Seven knew who he was, yet in experiencing Cyprus he knew he was glimpsing only a portion of his own reality. His consciousness reeled. He couldn't grasp it all. Somewhere within him, Cyprus laughed with the most delightful brilliant understanding. And images appeared, sometimes inside him and sometimes outside him until he could no longer keep track.

And Seven's Consciousness
Parted Four Times

In one he was Proteus, in the courtyard of the Dig of the Tellers. Window was beside him. And though Seven was Proteus, Proteus was himself and inviolate, and Seven from far above saw the entire scene. Proteus' face was grave, yet full of excitement, and Window was looking at him with the eye of a father such as no boy ever had.

"I know I'm on to something important," Proteus said. "From now on, I'm a Teller, too. This dig has secrets that no one's discovered, and I'm going to learn what they are. Sometimes, like now, I feel so close to knowing. I'm going to work with these sound-embossed tablets until I know them backwards. I think that the sounds themselves are far more important than we realize."

Proteus looked up. He could feel himself teeter on the edge of some new comprehension that was still beyond his reach. It was twilight. As Window stood there, his skin seemed to absorb the blue of early evening so that to Proteus he looked blue-green, almost fluid, joining the sky and the ground, growing into the sky like a figure-shaped tree for him, Proteus, to climb. What a weird idea, Proteus thought.

For a moment he almost got dizzy, watching, because he did "see through" Window, as he explained it to himself later. Then Window seemed so physical that Proteus' stomach lurched, and he thought: We grow up, reach up through blood and flesh as trees grow up or emerge from the flesh of the Earth.

So in leaving Earth, man had left the growing medium of himself, and Proteus knew in that moment that he must help man return to the Earth again, even if it meant returning sometime himself to the floating city. Admitting Earth, man could travel and live wherever he chose. Denying it, he denied the heritage that gave him such yearnings.

And experiencing Proteus' thoughts, Seven knew that he would descend again and again into flesh, for there was no descent or ascent, only being in its many forms. Proteus and Window vanished, and where they had been, Ma-ah stood with Sumpter.

"I don't know where I came from, that's what it amounts to," Ma-ah said. "I have no memory of parents; just finding myself, with Rampa, in the outside world a long time ago. How we got here I don't know. I suppose we were born into it."

"In certain terms, none of us know," Sumpter said.

"But I want to know. I insist on it," Ma-ah cried defiantly. (And Seven laughed.)

"And if I have a child, I won't know where it came from, not really."

(And Seven laughed louder). Dear, dear Ma-ah, he thought.

"I thought I heard the old man," Ma-ah said.

"It's all right," Seven said to her, knowing that he was also reassuring a part of himself.

But Ma-ah said, "*What's* all right?" just as Seven had so often questioned Cyprus. "And how did you direct me here, with Rampa?" she asked.

Before Seven could say "I don't remember," he was suddenly back, lost in Ma-ah again, struggling to walk beside Rampa, while the body signaled its great alarm. And a whispered voice that was his own and also Cyprus' broke through only for a moment, telling him where to go and how to get there. Only then, he hadn't been consciously aware of the voice, lost as he was in Ma-ah's dilemma. But how did he, or Cyprus, know?

With the question came a new onslaught of images. Again he could only capture a few of them.

Cyprus: Free of being male or female, containing both, writing the first Sumari records of the Speakers; "writing" them in sound before the birth of words in terms of time — but in a reality *still happening*—

Images he could not decipher—

Sounds that operated directly on *matter*. . . . Of course! A force field, protecting the land of the Speakers, called into activation by . . . Sumpter, who was Window — but as Window he'd forgotten what he knew, and it would be Proteus who would help him remember—

And Josef—

Seven saw him swearing and painting, roaring, despairing — heard him yell at the baby, Tweety, who screamed back at him just as lustily. Seven fell into Josef briefly, looked out through the warm brown eyes, felt the intimacy of the buzzing flesh, looked at Bianka who in this now was full of a form into which Tweety had not yet entered.

"We'll be left all of this," Josef said with joyful craftiness. "The house, the land—"

"And you'll grow fat and prosperous, I suppose, and give up painting," Bianka said, grinning.

"No, no, never!" Josef thundered. But Seven as Josef felt the divisions, the conflicts, saw — But then Josef as Josef vanished, replaced by Josef the Speaker, painstakingly etching in stone the Sumari pictures that would be found by Ma-ah and Proteus in their times.

And Lydia—

Was Story!—and he, Seven, had forgotten who he was and what he knew. Forgotten, so that his parts could grow and learn on their own. Yet all the while unknowingly he nourished them as he was—

Nourished by Cyprus, who had learned to remember, to teach with a light hand, and to learn, gracefully. And the sounds of the Speakers were an important key that Cyprus would help him decipher.

Seven's consciousness flew together, and then parted seven times in which he glimpsed Ma-ah, Josef, Lydia, Proteus; and, with surprise and won-der—Story, who would develop quite on her own as Tweety would and Lydia had; and Sumpter, who was Window—each apart, yet whole, know-ing and unknowing—

And Cyprus' consciousness parted—into such myriad shining realities of being that Seven could no longer follow, and he yelled out, "Cyprus!"

She sat beside him by the tiles, changing form so swiftly that he said, "Now stop that. I've learned so much that I'm dizzy. I don't suppose you could have just told me?"

"Oh Seven, *told* you?"

"Forget I said it," he replied hastily.

"Well, this examination is over," she said. "I thought you'd like to know." Cyprus paused, looking nowhere in particular, and added: "You passed, you know."

"I'm too confused to think," he said. "And what about Ma-ah's origin? I didn't answer that question yet."

"That's for next time," she said. "Anyway, some questions can't be an-swered in the context of the question itself. You have to find a new context. Of course, the question itself is deeply symbolic—"

But Seven said, "*Next* time?"

"In your terms of experience," Cyprus said gently. "Of course, in other terms—"

"Never mind," he said. "And if I'm correct, then you're to me as I'm to Ma-ah and Josef and—"

"Precisely," she said.

"So, what did you do for this examination?" Seven asked. "I did all the work."

Cyprus smiled. "I wrote this book," she said.

"But Cyprus—you aren't physical," Seven cried.

And Cyprus sighed. "Seven, you still have a lot to learn."

~ *Epilogue* ~

Epilogue to This Book
and Prologue to
The Further Education of Oversoul Seven

*C*yprus said, "This is how the next book will begin:

> Lydia was
> Called Tweety,
> Because
> Bianka said
> She was
> Skinny and tiny
> As a newborn
> Bird."

"Wait a second," Oversoul Seven said. "I think your tenses are wrong. Even though Lydia died in the twentieth century, and is reborn in the seventeenth, shouldn't you say, 'Lydia *will be called* Tweety,' because she hasn't experienced that life yet? or is, 'Lydia *was called* Tweety' correct, because people think that the seventeenth century happened first? Or—"

They both burst out laughing.

Cyprus said, "You'll just have to wait and see. That is, though all time is simultaneous, I'll have to wait until writing the book catches up with my experience."

∼ *Appendix* ∼

*For those readers
who may be interested,
the following information is provided:*

Although all the Speakers in Ma-ah's time were Sumari, the term refers to a type of consciousness, generally speaking — a grouping together of consciousness with certain characteristics. The Sumari are initiators, highly creative, playful, given to originating systems of reality and then going on. As a friend of Seven's once said: "They don't stay around to mow the grass, though." A Sumari is a Sumari, in flesh or out of it.

Seven and Cyprus are both Sumari, as are all the main characters in this book.

Careful attention should be given to Sumpter's explanation of the use of words in Chapter 12. The Sumari language is not a language in the ordinary sense. It's importance lies in its *sounds*, not in its written patterns. The sounds do things. The meaning is apart from the power of the sounds, and rides on it as fish swim in water.

The meanings rise out of the sounds, then; and the sounds are channels through which the meanings come. The sounds can seem to have different meanings at different times, and yet always be expressing aspects of the same reality. Sometimes many words can come from one sound, sometimes only one will emerge. This is apparent when you study the same song in Sumari and in its translation as written by Lydia. The following examples will make this clear:

FIRST SONG FOR BEGINNERS

(Sumari, as learned
   by Ma-ah.)

(from *Songs of the Sumari*
   by Lydia)

Angella pur tito
Angella to panito.
Angella pe toto panto
B o a eto
Rameta.

This is one side of truth.
This is the left side of anger.

The stars are singing.
Listen.

Ando andolato
Me do repen rabelli
Me no latillo
Angelo le peju lacol
Mendo. Rendo be woopta

From east and west
Messages come richly. Like
   leaves falling
You cannot hold them.
Secrets beneath hearing ride
   on the wind.

Has a vendelli

This is forever rising out of
   the silence.

Indo lato
Angell ella
Suri la mari
So la pinto
Contella.

Rejoice
In knowing unknowing.

Indo rito
Angella gondula
Pito. miro.
Angella peto torello
Soli in do.

Beneath the starlight
The Earth stirs and opens.
The Earth stirs and opens
To our touch
Unfolding.

Angella pindo
Pindu and tito
Pungula vito
Deto.

The moonlight cries out
When it touches
The forest floor.
The forest flowers are filled
   with
The light born of darkness.

Ando capeto
Angella peto
Ingol. angol.
El lo go.

This is the beginning
Ending and center
Rushing ever
Outward.

From the lighted heavens
The gods come and wander
Inside and outside
Over and under.

Their footsteps are starlight,
Their voices are echoing
Beyond the edges of silence
Never sunken in yesterday
Or tomorrow.

ANIMAL DREAM SONG

(Sumari as learned by *Ma-ah*
in the Land of the Speakers.)

(from *Songs of the Sumari*
by Lydia)

Frea tumba, tul j leta
Greenaje odaro
Deleta umbarge
Sel var denoto
De na evisa
To marro insida
De ne r o.

See us, see us,
In your adjacent world.
We are your dreams living
In fur and blood.
We are the animals
Blessed and holy,
Savage and bony,
Thrust out by you
Into the world.

Gramaje netaro
Denita visa
Flo marro ontoa
Deneta demari.
O ne demari.
On a es par.

We sing your praises.
It is good common sense,
For we know that we come
From the ribs of your
slumber,
Born, torn, and rent
From desires
Glowing and raging.

Ma ne o de vista
De magna on to o
Grem age an to a tum
De es splen ato
Gre ne a torum
Ineago.
Silva vista ne ta
Gre en ad e bus
Tumba.

O nea umba
O framage tu a
Oh le e on to
A de um timbi.
Gravi timbo taru
Sev r ant a to bum
Grim age endeo
De midge a a tu um
Mari on umber
Grey e a on obus.

In the midnight of your
    senses
We rise up all splendid.
Perfect and agile
We leap out into the forests
We race across the landscapes
In moonlight and shadow.
We are your dreams escaping
The dream cage forever.
The door is wide open.

We dream our dreams.
    Remember,
Entreaty and warning.
Our bowels are dancing
With splendor and longing.
Under tomorrow
We live by your spell.
But our dreams rise up
Even as yours, and confront us.
The animals' animals
Must be nourished and
    tended.
The dreams' dreams are not
    orphans
To be cast into darkness.

We congregate before you
For your attention.
We are the blood and hide
Of your dreams prancing
In midday.
We plunge through forests
And hillsides,
Carved out of your unknowing.
Know us who wander
Beneath the moon of your brain.

FRAGMENT FROM A SUMARI SONG OF ORIGINS

(Deciphered by Window
   in the land of the Tellers
   from stone tablets.)

O shel u a stare
Le munde tu am
Del an o resplendi
Tel mal del o
Fram mondi.
De na resplendi
O terum nesta
Far bundu. Tarra
Ne o responde
La dum. La day dum
Framba.

Out of the knowing
Darkness of unknowing
We lifted ourselves, rising
On the webs of our thoughts.
We dangled above the warm
Nest of nothing,
Climbing the images
That rose from our yearning,
Grasping the syllables
That circled
Our muteness like stars.

(This song was not among those "written" by Lydia in the twentieth century. The rest of the song is in the records of the Speakers in Ma-ah's "time.")

Window is still translating portions of Sumari songs, fragments of what seem to be mathematical documents, and other records. One such document in particular seems to be leading toward an explanation of the connection between sound and matter, suggesting a relationship between numerical values, atoms, and syllables. This same connection is also hinted at in several Sumari songs. This "mathematical" statement has only been deciphered in fragmentary form thus far, and Window is certain that other portions of it are still to be discovered. A part of it is included here because of its implications in terms of the Speakers' method of erecting buildings through the use of sound.

The first section, devoted to quite a different matter, seems directed to the general student. It is a preamble to the body of the material, and shows the basic ideas upon which the Speakers built their civilization. For that reason, it is also being included here. The following is Window's translation:

(from *The Sacred Script of Covenant*)

Honor your body, which is your representative in this universe.
Its magnificence is no accident. It is the framework through which
your works must come; through which the spirit and the spirit

within the spirit speaks. The flesh and the spirit are two phases of your actuality in space and time. Who ignores one, falls apart in shambles. So it is written.

The marriage of soul and flesh is an ancient contract, to be honored.

Let no soul in flesh ignore its Earthly counterpart, or be unkind to its mate in time.

The mind cannot dance above the flesh, or on the flesh. It cannot deny the flesh or it turns into a demon demanding domination. Then the voice of the flesh cries out with yearning through all of its parts; the ancient contract undone. And both soul and flesh go begging, each alone and without partner.

Who feeds the body with love, neither starving it nor stuffing it, feeds the soul. Who denies the body denies the soul. Who betrays it betrays the soul. The body is the body of the soul, the corporal image of knowledge. As men and women are married to each other, so is each self wedded to its body.

Those who do not love the body or trust it do not love or trust the soul. The multitudinous voices of the gods speak through the body parts. Even the golden molecules are not mute. Who muzzles the body or leashes it muzzles and leashes the soul. The private body is the dwelling place of the private guise of God. Do it honor. Let no man set himself up above the body, calling it soiled, for to him the splendor of the self is hidden. Let no one drive the body like a horse in captivity, to be ridden, or he will be trampled.

The body is the soul in Earth-garments. It is the face of the soul turned toward the seasons, the image of the soul reflected in Earth waters. The body is the soul turned outward. Soul and body are merged in the land of the seasons. Such is the ancient contract by which the Earth was formed.

The knowledge of the soul is written in the body. Body and soul are the inner and outer of the self. The spirit from which the soul springs forms both — soul and body. In Earth time, the soul and body learn together. The genes are the alphabets by which the soul speaks the body — which is the soul's utterance in flesh.

So let the soul freely speak itself in flesh.

The body is also eternal. The soul takes it out of space-time. The body is the soul's expression, and its expression is not finite. The spirit has many souls, and each has a body. The body is in and out of time, even as the soul is. Let the soul rush freely throughout the body, and breathe life into all of its parts. The first birth was a gift, freely given. Now you must acquiesce and give your blessing to the life within you. Trust the spontaneity and health of the body, which is the spontaneity and health of the soul. For each morning you spring anew, alive and fresh, out of chaos. . . .

(Another fragment, deciphered by Window, is from the same document, from a verse portion connecting the above with the later material on atoms, sound, and numerical values.)

The universe is the body of the
    god's soul,
The flesh of his utterance.
In the beginning man was given
    two homelands,
His body and his planet.

The calculations are written
    everywhere,
Inscribed in each object.

The body is a language
Of atoms instead of words.
The body is the most ancient of
    alphabets,
And atoms spoke before the
    Earth knew sound. . . .

(The following fragments are from the main body of the statement. Other portions, still being deciphered, seem to point toward a multidimensional mathematical system.)

Speaking the body . . . so the body is built also on sound principles, sound becoming matter in your terms at certain pitches.

In reality, numbers are magnified in all directions. They represent points of emerging energy, as it intrudes into the third dimension. . . .

Integers represent pivot points or centers of radiating activity, out of which energy emerges, in terms of light and sound. These qualities — light and sound, for example — exist on both plus and minus sides of all equations and on all sides of magnification.

Much of the document will be beyond the interest of the general reader. As it continues, however, it suggests an inner property or value that exists within all physical matter. Since the Speakers seem to have utilized such knowledge, and the Tellers are trying to decipher it, the following three paragraphs are included merely as an example of how the subject is handled:

These hidden values [of numbers] only emerge under certain conditions, though they are always acting and must be considered as a part of the integers' characteristics. These hidden or invisible values are often responsible for instabilities that seem to arise without reason to undermine an equation's effectiveness. They are also responsible for phenomena that seem to defy equation.

The whole is more than the sum of its parts because of these hidden values. They exist on the minus side on all sides of magnification. They affect the plus reactions or the behavior of integers on the plus side, and under certain conditions can sap their energy. Usually they magnify all existing properties, however, and leap over the plus border into regions in which the integers' characteristics are vastly changed — in comparison to their behavior in a three-dimensional system. These invisible values root the integers firmly in dynamics superseding your space-time continuum.

Some integers are more susceptible than others to their own inner nature. They lean toward their invisible values. These integers are those from whom surprises can be expected, though they are less stable in a numerical relationship. They are explosive in nature, easily combined, rather than binding. Such integers can experience a temporary cave-in, a momentary physical collapse, in which a hole is created through which all values fly (black hole). Here, the invisible values rise paramount, affecting the behavior of other numerical values, connected with the integer. . . .

This small sample of the document shows its complex nature. As Window, with Proteus' help, tries to decipher the rest of it, the Tellers hope to discover the secrets of the Speakers' civilization.

This same idea appears also in the following Sumari song that was found among Lydia's papers after her death. From a scribbled note in the margin, it's apparent that Lydia had no idea what the poem meant, and did not include it in her published version of Songs of the Sumari.

SONG OF THE CHOOSING

Before the Earth light was born
We wandered
Scattering alphabets into silence
And out again, splashing
Silence into vowels
Until silence spoke
With the voice
Of a million worlds.

The tongue of the universe
Chose silence
And silence chose sound,
And the
Earth sprang forth,
An utterance
Congealed into form.

The atoms are syllables,
Forever unspoken, yet speaking.
The silence is sound
Forever circling and gathering.
The rock is mute
To listening ears,
But the deaf eyes of watching clouds
Hear piles of vowels
Continually dancing.

The time of choosing
Opens the rift
In the rock,
And the hidden voices
Of Earth
Rise up.

The following is a partial copy of the simple alphabet or "cordella"—the symbols etched into the cliff walls in the time of the Speakers and rediscovered at the time of the Tellers. Fingering the outlines of these symbols gave forth the appropriate sound values. These were discovered in the order given here. Others exist in different groupings; some still unknown to Window's people.

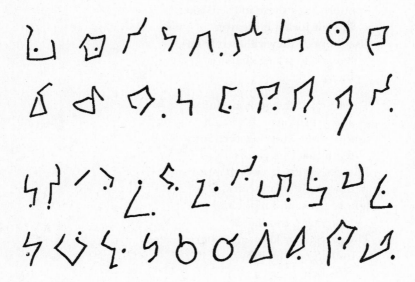

Another partially deciphered Sumari script suggests that the word *cordella* rather than *alphabet* is used to break up usual conceptions connected with the word *alphabet,* while conveying an idea of symbols closely related, upon which alphabets are based. Seen in this way, there would be cordellas beneath the sensations of hearing, smelling, seeing, and so forth. The fragment further implies that the skin has its own alphabet.

Since the Tellers have translated so few of the Speakers' manuscripts and records, only hints of their significance can be given here. The process of translation and discovery continues, of course, and publication of further songs and records will take place as the work continues.

Because the Sumari philosophy includes such a rich mixture of theory and practical understanding, the appendix will close with a translation of one of the first songs learned by Ma-ah in her early instruction as a student. The advice is pertinent in any "time."

THE GODS' GIFTS

Those who are given gifts by the
    gods must use them.
Polish your gifts in the morning,
Shine them with yearning,
Pluck them from the trembling
    tree of creation.
Tenderly tuck them in the basket
    of your loving endeavor.
Use them or they will turn from
    fruits into stones that are
    heavy.

The fruits of the gods are juicy
    and nutritious.
Ignore them and they turn into
    teeth that bite you.
The gods' gifts are worth more
    than night or morning.
Ignore them and night and
    morning pass away.
The pit of your knowing is buried
    in the gods' fruits within
    your being,
Spit out the pit and you are lost.

The gods' gifts are the yellow
    piths that glue together
The fruity fibers of your knowing.
Use them or your parts fall away.

Used, the gods' gifts are abundant
    and increasing.
They grow as they are consumed.
Shake the branches of creation,
And the gods' gifts fall into your
    lap, resplendent.
Turn your back and the tree
    withers
And the wind carries the seed
    away.

Use the gods' gifts, then, with
    great abandon.
They are your nourishment.
They are the fruits that bloom
    in dreams' darkness.
They are the light that falls out
    of chaos.
They are the fruit of the tree
    that is unknown
But always present.

They are the fruits growing ever
    on the branches of unknowing
Made visible.
They are sweeter than the evidence
    of love in the body.
Let no man stand with his back
    turned as the fruits fall,
But gather them.
They are your abundance and
    sustenance.

THE
FURTHER EDUCATION
OF
OVERSOUL SEVEN

*This Book
Is
Written
in
the Time of
Jeffery*

(circa late 1970s A.D.)

Dedicated
to
The Gods
Behind
the Divine
Camouflage

∾ *Prologue One* ∾

C yprus said, "This is how the book will begin:

> Lydia was
> Nicknamed Tweety,
> Because Bianka
> Said she was
> Tiny and skinny
> As a newborn
> Bird."

"Wait a second," Oversoul Seven said. "I think your tenses are wrong. Even though Lydia died in the twentieth century, and is reborn in the seventeenth, shouldn't you say, 'Lydia *will be called* Tweety,' because she hasn't experienced that life yet? or is, 'Lydia *was called* Tweety' correct, because people think that the seventeenth century happened first? Or —"

They both burst out laughing.

Cyprus said, "You'll just have to wait and see. That is, though all time is simultaneous, I'll have to wait until writing the book catches up with my experience."

~ *Prologue Two* ~

(Some time later)

"**Y**ou *are* going to write this book, aren't you?" Oversoul Seven asked, somewhat anxiously.

"In a manner of speaking," Cyprus said. "I think the first part will be called, 'The Odyssey of Jeffy-boy, Ram-Ram, and Queen Alice.'"

"Who on Earth are they?" Oversoul Seven asked. "And what do they have to do with Tweety and her new life, and my further education?"

Cyprus smiled. "That's something you'll have to learn for yourself. Real education always involves surprises. But pay attention, now. The odyssey of Jeffy-boy, Ram-Ram, and Queen Alice is about to begin. Of course, Jeffy-boy doesn't realize what's happening yet."

∼ *Chapter One* ∼

Journal of a Surprised Psychologist
(Jeffery W. Blodgett)

*T*hese notes contain a record of my . . . what? Dream activities? Hardly the word for them. No, to be correct, this manuscript is a chronicle of journeys embarked upon, strange as it sounds, when my physical body sleeps. There are several points to be made and I will make them here, with my first long entry. To be honest, I write that last statement with painful acceptance of general limitations that I for one no longer accept. For I know beyond all doubt, as you will see, that there is no past, present, or future in usual terms. Granting that, from now on I'll keep this journal as up to date as possible, and I have the oddest sensation that something important is about to happen even before I have time to sketch in what has occurred thus far.

Theoretically, these notes could be discovered in the past, even before I write them in my present. For that matter, they could come to light in some reality of which I know nothing. They could even emerge (as I know now) as automatic writing on the part of some stranger who lets down the conscious barriers of his mind; appearing as . . . psychological apports of a kind. Even as I may appear a wanderer in your dreams. Or you, in mine.

It seems that I've come alive only in these past few months, yet when these events first began, I was staggered. Even now, at times, I doubt my sanity. Yet what has happened so far has given me glimpses into the undersides of reality, and these only make the topsides that much more miraculous.

For the record, let me state that I've taken no drugs of any kind. Nothing that I know of initiated the adventure in which I'm now involved. These notes, written in the daytime, represent my attempt to relate my activities in dimensions of which most people are completely unaware.

So far I've managed to return to normal daytime living, but I have no guarantee that this will always be the case, particularly since I've encountered difficulties at times of a certain undefinable nature. Again — so far — I've retained my normal conscious stance in the reality accepted by everyone else. But I do grow aware of a precarious balance.

As long as I write these notes and read those that I've written before, then I'll know that I've returned safely from those equally valid realms. If I decide not to return, then I'll record my decision here, so that anyone interested will know that my exodus was voluntary, not the result of coercion, or worse, error or carelessness on my part. Particularly if my ex-wife, Sarah, ever reads these notes, I wouldn't want her to imagine me trying to claw my way back from an underside of reality that she could not understand.

Perhaps I should mention here that I'm a psychologist. My degrees alone will at least ensure that these notes get a reading. (B.A. at Cornell, master's and doctorate in behavioral psychology at Harvard.) To those who still recognize such ludicrous badges of erudition I say, "Hear me out. By your own standards, I have a right to your recognition." To those who think that degrees are primarily signs of ritualized ignorance I say, "I'm on your side." But I spent many years acquiring such status, and I may as well take advantage of it in that academia to which I no longer belong.

I should also tell you that I'm thirty-six years old, and still partially distrust that part of me over thirty. My ex-wife lives on the other side of the continent, remarried practically if not legally, and pregnant with her first child. I was trying to make up my mind as to whether or not I wanted to grow a human being in this crazy garden of existence. Sarah, apparently, got tired of waiting, and took up with another, more willing package of seed. So I was living alone when these events began.

I'm convinced that I'm involved in work of the utmost importance. I'm also aware that my attitude has all the earmarks of egomania, or a good deal of them. But I'm not suffering from any kind of Messiah complex. For one thing, I'm tired of examining myself for signs of schizophrenia, particularly since I've discovered that what I used to regard as my normal state of consciousness represents only the surface ripples of my identity. For another thing, I'm using my own personality as a psychological guinea pig in my adventures, and part of my work necessitates playing around with different states of awareness.

I hereby admit to those anticipated criticisms that my colleagues will make against me: that I'm not maintaining suitable objectivity or conforming to the "scientific method." I'm even turning my back on the electroencephalograph and the now respectable "dream laboratories," as they're called, though they have their place. Where I go, I must go utterly alone. No one can tell me what methods are useful or dangerous. The ordinary assumptions of daily life serve me not at all. Yet I will not turn back. The hope of great personal accomplishment—and knowledge—far outweighs the hazards, those that I have discovered and those that may still wait.

So after this lengthy introduction—psychologists are notoriously long-winded—I'll record the events that led me to this pass. The first episode seems so insignificant, by contrast with my later activities, that my initial astonishment now seems almost amusing. Yet the first hole in physical reality opened for me that night. The first crack appeared in the ordinary existence that I'd always known.

I was living in one of the wild stacks of modern apartments connected with the state university in a town in upstate New York. Each cube dwelling had its own entrance. The buildings had just been completed, and each terrace looked out on piles of rocks, dirt, and mudholes. The apartment itself reminded me of a Skinner box, complete with artificial environment, air conditioners, soundproofing, humidifiers; everything to make life sanitary and dull.

I couldn't get to sleep that night, so I got out of bed and went into the living room. For a few moments I stood on the terrace. There were no stairs connecting it to the ground, and I was on the seventh floor. Across the way identical terraces stuck out, hanging flimsily out over the snow-covered debris below.

It was 2 A.M. when I came back inside, after having been on the terrace for perhaps five minutes. I checked the clock and threw myself down on the couch. Immediately I fell into a deep sleep and dreamed that two men were talking to me. They wore ordinary clothing, suits of some innocuous nature. We were discussing the failure of behavioral psychology to uncover any but the most surface qualities of human personality. I disagreed with their indictment. At this point, a terrific noise awakened me. I sprang to a sitting position, fully alert—and I must admit, instantly alarmed.

To my astonishment, the two men still stood there. I recalled the dream clearly and recognized the two of them as my dream images. Blinking furiously, I rubbed my eyes.

"The wind knocked over the empty geranium pot on the patio. Don't bother yourself," the first man said.

I didn't speak. Quite deliberately I looked around. Everything was as it should be. The room was solid and real, except that the men couldn't possibly be in it. The sensory clues in that respect made no sense. There was one dim light lit, and I could see the men as clearly as I saw the couch, or desk, or anything else. I could have thought them intruders, burglars, if I hadn't remembered them from my dream.

As reasonably as I could, I said, "Look. You're dream images. I can't possibly be talking to you because I'm wide awake. Unless I'm still asleep and don't realize it."

"You've been overworking. Is that it?" The first man smiled in a way I found curiously comforting; and like an idiot I nodded my head vigorously and said, "Yes, that must be it. I *am* still asleep and dreaming."

But the second man laughed, and didn't seem as well-disposed toward me as the first. "Interesting hypothesis," he said. "Suppose I insist that you're a dream image of mine instead?"

I scowled, but even then I noted my own reactions. This second man was somewhat younger than I, and I resented his manner of knowing, or pretending to know, more about the situation than I did. To make it worse, the other man then grinned indulgently and said, "On the other hand, you may both be images in a dream of *mine.*"

By now I knew that I was, indeed, fully awake. And I was frightened. For a moment I suspected that both of the men were lunatics who had somehow gained entry — intruders, in fact — and that I'd only confused them with earlier dream images. I pinched my arm. My reflexes were normal. My critical faculties were operating. Yet I could make no sense of the situation at all.

The younger man said, "Now that we've provided you with suitable stimuli to your curiosity, we'll enjoy watching your further reactions."

With this, I sprang up from the couch. Two things happened at once. Before my startled eyes, the two intruders began to disappear as if space itself was eating away at their edges. Then a severe, shattering click came at the base of my neck. The next thing I knew, I was back on the couch, thrown there in some fashion that utterly escaped me. The room was just as it had been, but the men were gone. Moreover, there was nothing to prove that they'd ever been there. Something else: I remembered opening my eyes, though I don't recall ever closing them. As soon as the men vanished, I ran to the French doors and threw them open. The geranium pot was in pieces on the patio floor.

As the days passed, I convinced myself that the whole affair had been some kind of dream-within-a-dream. Only one thing bothered me: my certainty that I had jumped up from the couch the moment the men's images were vanishing, while the next minute I was back on the couch, with my eyes closed. If it were only a dream, why would I have thought my eyes opened or closed? I mean, usually in dreams you see what you see, and that's the end of it, or so I thought at the time. The clicking at the back of my neck was also difficult to explain away, but I decided it was caused by some spasmodic jerking of my muscles.

I didn't tell anyone about the experience. Indeed, I managed to put it out of my mind so well that I might have forgotten it entirely if it hadn't been followed by an even more bizarre event. This next, more alarming, episode happened about a week later, and there was no way I could assign it to dream activity.

As far as I can recall, this was the sequence of events. I was at my desk, concentrating on a student's paper. It was devoted to a discussion of some experiments we'd done on the frontal lobes of rats. Then, without transition, I was caught up in an experience of frightful intensity. First, my body felt as if it was expanding, yet growing lighter in weight. The process continued until I felt impossibly light. Miles of space seemed to exist between my ears.

I became aware of the cells of my body in the oddest fashion. Each seemed to possess an alertness, a mini-personality—eager, responsive, and individualistic—and most of all, each initiated action and didn't just respond to stimuli. I had some crazy idea that my consciousness had dropped back to its components, when suddenly I felt . . . loose, or unfixed. There was that same clicking sensation in the back of my neck again, and to my horror I found myself quite literally suspended in the air, outside the terrace, about five feet away from the railing, with nothing but some sixty feet of space between me and the ground.

At any instant I expected to go crashing down. But nothing happened. I yelled for help, though there was no one in sight. It was late afternoon; I'd come home early to work on the student's report, but most people in the building were still in classes or meetings. In complete disbelief, I hung there, telling myself that I couldn't possibly be where I was, and wondering why I wasn't falling. It seemed that nothing was ever going to happen; no one would come to discover me, and I'd be left there for all eternity, like a fish on an invisible line, waiting to be pulled back in. Then, just as suddenly, I was back inside the living room, but still in the air, floating.

Next, I changed position and got the next-worst fright of my life, for I was staring down at my own body. There "I" sat, eyes closed but pen in hand, as if I'd taken a catnap while reading. I looked down at the top of my head; each hair springing up merrily like red grass from my scalp. My shoulders were slumped. The familiarity and unfamiliarity, so intermixed, quite transfixed me. My body looked so weirdly forlorn that a heartrending pity for it rushed through me.

But how could I be outside my body, looking down at it? I'd hardly thought of the question when I was drawn back into my usual form so quickly that I closed my eyes, imagining the worst kind of crash landing. I'm not sure what happened next, except that the clicking sound came again, and with it a sound like a soft explosion. Almost beyond panic, I opened my eyes to see my fingers holding the pen. I was back in my body. But if I had just opened my eyes, what eyes had I closed just before I plunged back in?

Dazed, I looked out the window to where I'd hung just a few moments earlier and I had the disquieting fear that I might see myself, still dangling there.

That night I knew I had to talk to someone. Only one person came to mind — Ramrod Brail — an older colleague who'd dabbled in fields like hypnosis and parapsychology. Now I wonder what would have happened if I'd chosen someone else to confide in instead. Certainly in the next weeks I wished more than once that I'd never made that phone call.

∼ *Chapter Two* ∼

Ram-Ram's Experiment

*T*hirty-six can sound pretty ancient if you're in your early twenties, or incredibly young if you're over fifty. To Ramrod Brail I was a mere youngster—although, because of my educational background, one to be taken seriously. He came over as soon as I called him, his curiosity aroused by the few hints of my experience that I tossed out over the telephone. I had called him for several reasons. Quite frankly, I was shaken not only by my experience itself but by its implications. Also I wanted to discuss the whole affair with someone perceptive but levelheaded, and someone who wouldn't blab all over campus.

Ram-Ram, as the students and younger professors called him affectionately, was what best can be called a faded campus flower, past retirement age and still teaching in an honorary position. He'd made a name in several specialized fields, from industrial psychology to hypnotic research. It was because of this latter unconventional interest of his that I thought he might be helpful.

His quick nervous cough told me he was outside the door even before he knocked. He held a cigarette in one hand and a half-finished drink in the other. Without preamble, he said, "Mmm. Not on pot or acid or anything, are you, Jeffy-boy?"

"Look, I don't like to be called Jeffy-boy," I answered irritably. "And no, I'm not high on anything."

He ignored my first remark and said, "No, I suppose you aren't; it's not your style; but I want to know where we stand. Now suppose you tell me, slowly, exactly what's been going on here. You weren't too clear on the phone."

I showed him to a chair and explained both episodes. He seemed excited, which surprised me somewhat. All the while he sat, chain-smoking, his eyes seldom leaving my face. I paid little attention to his kindly-old-psychologist's smile. I'd seen him use it too many times. He is kind, but not nearly as kind as he looks, and he's exceptionally shrewd, or he was until lately.

At one point in particular he interrupted me. "Yes, yes, yes," he said. "That click you felt at the base of your neck. Explain that part again." He spoke with exaggerated nonchalance, or so it seemed to me. I wondered if he was on to something, or thought he was. I repeated what I'd told him, and as he didn't stop me, I continued with my story.

Then he stood up impatiently, moving around in a kind of slow frenzy. "Yes, yes, yes," he said, more to himself than to me. "And what do we tell our young man here?" As he muttered this last, he swung around to face me. "We greatly need some good experimental work in this field. They're doing it all wrong," he said.

"Who? What field?"

"You really wouldn't know what I'm talking about, of course, being a hard-line behaviorist. You are, aren't you? Never mind." He sat down heavily, too heavily in my wicker chair for a man his size. The chair creaked and groaned, but held. "Now, this is it," he said. "I have a proposal to make. First, you have no insight at all, yourself, into the experiences you just told me about?"

"I have no explanation, if that's what you mean. Some odd quirk of perception? Complete hallucination brought about by a belated response to my wife's leaving me? Who knows?"

"Exactly," Ram-Ram said. "So?"

"So? So—nothing. If I didn't hallucinate, then I was really out of my body, and I can't buy that. I hoped that with your background, you might have some alternate explanations."

"Suppose you *were* out of your body?" he asked. "I'm not for the moment saying that you were, but have you considered the possibility seriously?" "Why, not really," I answered, surprised. "I'm the first one to admit that behaviorism hasn't solved all our problems, or begun to, but it's offered sufficient evidence that our consciousness is the result of our physical mechanism and the way we use it. In those terms, there's no 'me' to get out of my body. I wouldn't have any perceiving organs." I paced about, rather angry and defensive. All of this was too obvious to me at the time to argue about.

"Now, hold on," Ram-Ram said. "Look. You *felt* that you were out of your body. You felt that you were hanging out in the air there, and later you looked down at your own body. Since all this was so vivid and unmistakable then, what convinced you that it was not in *fact* happening?"

"At the time, I thought it *was* happening, of course," I said, more mildly.

"Then what later convinced you that it hadn't?"

By now my exasperation was rising again. "Good common sense, I suppose. People just don't hang out in thin air without support . . . without falling—"

"You deny the evidence of your own experience, then?" Ram-Ram smiled his famous mischievous-little-boy-psychologist grin and said, "That would be *true* insanity, you know."

"I don't deny having the experience or I wouldn't have called you," I shouted.

"Now, look here and listen to me." He smiled honestly and fully for the first time that evening. "You're a nice young man. Several times you've carried my garbage down those monstrous stairs to that modern trash heap of a mess below. A man like that can't be all bad. But it seems that in the past you've managed to be very prosaic, as a rule, which is why all of this surprises me.

"Look here. The various schools of psychology don't do a very good job of communicating with each other, ironically enough. You may not even consider parapsychology a legitimate field of endeavor, for all I know, yet some new men are doing some evocative experiments along certain lines—"

"Oh, come on," I said. "I've come across a few of those reports, mostly in pseudoscientific magazines or drug literature. The popular occult craze has even taken over the movies. Then there's the old Rhine experiments. It's all fringe stuff."

But Ram-Ram went on stubbornly: "They're investigating OOBs, or out-of-body states. So far psychics are being used primarily, or other laymen who profess to experience the phenomenon at will, or think they can. But to date, no gifted psychologist has worked it from both ends. What's needed is a psychologist who can project his consciousness out of his body and objectively study the experience from both an in-body and out-of-body context. No mystic mumbo jumbo . . . no—"

"Uh huh," I said.

"Now"—he waved his fat little hand in the air—"I'm not for the moment suggesting that you take on that role—"

"Good," I said. "And good night, Dr. Frankenstein." With clownish grand eloquence, I bowed and pretended to usher him out. It occurred to me, though, that his best days were over; that I'd been mistaken to call him; and that perhaps his reputation had been exaggerated.

He looked genuinely hurt, so I grinned and fixed us each a drink. I'm making no excuses for my attitude at the time, however; then I was convinced of the rightness of my position and it was one shared by many of my colleagues, of whatever age. I just didn't want to hurt Ram-Ram's feelings.

"I *thought* I saw two men. And I *thought* I was out of my body," I said more gently. "I'm sure that there's some logical explanation. Instead, you take the experience at face value — something, frankly, that just didn't occur to me. I can accept both episodes as hallucinations, though the idea does make me uneasy. But not as facts."

"Yes, yes, yes, certainly," Ram-Ram said. "But wouldn't it be ironical if man were independent of his body after all? And if psychology denied the one characteristic of human nature that could free us of the fear of extinction? What energy would be released if it were proven that man's consciousness *is* separate from the body!"

I didn't answer immediately. It was a painful moment for me anyhow: any psychologist worth his salt should know better, I thought, than to mix psychology and religion. Ram-Ram's voice drifted off. He eyed me slyly.

"The fairy tale of all fairy tales," I said.

"You think that I'm an old man, nearing his end, grabbing at any straw to convince himself of the impossible. Quite all right, and a natural enough deduction," he said.

I started to deny it, guiltily, and he said again, "No. It's all right. In your place, I should think the same thing, I suppose. And yet" — he stood up, giving me a quick, shrewd and yet haughty glance. "And yet if I'd had the experiences that you've just had, and I was your age, I'd be daring enough, curious enough, to investigate them. I wouldn't be quite so willing to deny the evidence of my own senses, and I'd ponder more on the meaning of such experiences to me personally and as a psychologist."

I started to interrupt, but Ram-Ram's kindly-old-psychologist's mask was gone again and he went on, rather brusquely. "I'm quite aware of my reputation on campus with the younger professors. Poor old Ram-Ram, senile old coot, with all of his brilliant work behind him. You're surprised? Of course I know my nickname. We gave nicknames to elderly professors too, and usually there was some intuitive truth in them, as there most likely is in my case. But despite the youth cult, man's mind is not necessarily obsolete in those nameless decades past, say, sixty. Instead, its activities may even accelerate in the oddest fashion.

"But the thing is, you called me because you hoped that I'd somehow confirm your idea that the whole thing was hallucinatory, a sort of self-hypnosis that still didn't involve any mental instability. You wanted to shove both experiences under the rug, because they didn't conform to your beliefs about reality. But I refuse to be a partner to that. Your experiences are valid, psychologically speaking, and maybe factually as well. I propose some experiments, then, instead of this verbal pussyfooting around."

"That's unfair," I objected. "You're trying to cast me in the role of callow youth, and I'm too old for that; and moral coward, which I resent. I'm as curious and open-minded as anyone else."

"Hell, isn't it?" He smiled, apparently delighted at my discomfort. "But tell me, what do you do when you're just past thirty and discover that the world is half mad? Go along and play the game, or try to discover what's wrong?"

"We *are* trying to find out what's wrong!"

"By examining rats instead of people? By losing yourselves in statistical analyses of test data and ignoring the subjective realities of the human mind?"

"Oh, come on, now. Those are pretty pat objections to behaviorism, and you know it." He was laughing at me openly, so I said: "All right. What do you have in mind?" I shrugged and gave up for the moment. Clearly he wasn't going to leave until he'd had his say.

He began slowly and deliberately enough. "First, examine both episodes with an open mind. If you decide that hallucinatory effects were involved, then try to discover more about hallucinations. If you aren't sure, pursue the matter further. If you still aren't satisfied, then I suggest some definite experiments, and I have several books I'd like you to read. I'd expect you to keep complete records, of course, with copies for me."

Ram-Ram was growing more excited by the minute. I stared at him. "Why don't you try all this yourself?" I asked, on the spur of the moment.

"I have," he said. "Years ago, with no notable results. But you're quite gifted in that respect, I think. Call it an old psychologist's intuition, if you will. But if you could visit a definite place and correctly report what you saw while out of your body, we'd at least have a start.

"Some other young psychologists have attempted such experiments, but either they dropped out of the establishment entirely or otherwise messed themselves up with the scientific community through drug use and lifestyle generally. So the way is open for someone like you, within the system, to begin some serious experimentation —"

I looked at him as if he'd *completely* lost his wits. "Look, if I *did* get out of my body, I don't know how I did it, much less how to change my location —

or get back where I started." As I spoke, I remembered how I'd felt, dangling out the window, and to shake off a sudden uneasiness, I laughed. "Besides, suppose I got out of my body and couldn't get back inside?"

The glow faded from his eyes. "Yes, there's always that possibility, but I don't think it's a practical danger."

I said in amazement, "But I was only joking."

"Were you?" he asked quite soberly. "Actually there *are* tales of people facing just such difficulties."

"What? The whole idea is preposterous." I nearly shouted.

"Is it? Old wives' tales?" Ram-Ram shook his head. "Maybe, maybe not."

"No 'maybe' about it. It's nonsense," I said. "And as for the experiments, what you're actually talking about is my taking a trip without drugs."

"And without props," he said. "Yes, I'm trying to get you hooked on something else entirely. I'm trying to get you to do something that I tried and failed at. I've told you my motives; that's only fair. There are a few things that I'm holding back, but if you decide to go along with me on this, then I'll take you into my full confidence. But if—and this is a big if—if you can get out of your body with any predictability, then we may really be able to prove something."

I said slowly, "And you'd have a revolutionary paper to deliver, no more resting on your laurels—"

"Exactly." He didn't look at all guilty. In fact, he looked quite pleased with himself.

So I went on. "I'd be your prize subject, and still be acting as a psychologist since I'd be studying the subjective mechanisms. And your reputation would ensure publication of our results."

He was positively beaming.

I said, "I've had some doubts about behaviorism, I admit it. But, look: studying the effects of psychedelic drugs is accepted now. It's almost old hat. Encounter groups are on the rise, and some psychologists are getting interested in various methods of 'mind control.' But what you're talking about smacks of the occult and God knows what else. Do you honestly believe that there's that much to learn about human consciousness? I have to admit that I'm prejudiced in the other direction—that perception is the result of brain activity and nothing more."

"All the better," Ram-Ram said. "Your notes will make that obvious, too; and in the scientific community, that will serve us well. You weren't a believer of any kind to begin with. Don't you see? That's what we'll say, and it will be true. But we must conduct this work—if we do it—in complete secrecy. If it's known that we tried and failed, we'll be considered idiots. And your career won't be worth two cents. First, if you agree, I want you to study OOB methods."

"*Methods?* You mean there are do-it-yourself manuals for that too?" For some reason, the thought sent me into bouts of uncontrollable laughter; probably just my nervous reaction to the whole night's events, but the mental images aroused by Ram-Ram's remark were hilarious. In the meantime, *his* expression went from amusement to outright irritation, which only made me laugh louder.

Our discussion ended shortly after I regained my composure. Ram-Ram went into his own apartment and returned with an armful of books which he left with me. When I was alone, I leafed through them, noticing idly that they were library books, taken out a week earlier. At the time I attached no significance to this. Nor did I question my choice of confidant. If I'd known what was going to happen, I'd have kept Ram-Ram there all night, questioning him. As it was, I didn't realize until months later how cagey he'd been.

~ *Chapter Three* ~

A Book Out of Nowhere and
an Interview in a Mental Institution

You can imagine my feelings three days later when I learned that Ram-Ram had been admitted to a psychiatric clinic under his own cognizance and labeled a schizophrenic. In the oddest way, this relieved my mind; I wouldn't have to regard what he'd said to me that night with any seriousness; and while I felt sorry for him, I also felt absurdly free.

Yet as I looked back at our meeting and remembered his strange excitement, I wondered: Did our interview and my own bizarre experiences set him off? Even so, he must have been predisposed toward that particular illness for some time, I thought. Yet it seemed that I should have been alert enough to spot the symptoms. So, somewhat guiltily, I decided to visit him as soon as possible.

It was nearly a week before the opportunity presented itself. For one thing, my academic load was considerable then, and despite my resolution I kept putting the visit off. All kinds of excuses came to mind until I took myself in hand and realized that I felt illogically responsible for Ram-Ram's condition. I was reacting quite mechanically, feeling guilt for no reason, as I'd been programmed to do by my background both as a private person and as a member of our society.

So the very next day I made my duty call, and met Ram-Ram's new friend for the first time — Queen Alice, as she's called, a kooky old lady about Ram-Ram's age who's taken him in hand. Or he's taken her in hand. But the interview was most unsettling and peculiar. I say this because it almost seemed as if Ram-Ram was checking on my state of mind, instead of the other way around.

"Dr. Brail?" I said, striding, I hoped, with a strong, positive, reassuring step into the common room.

"Ah, Jeffy-boy, step into my parlor," he said, with the sweetest of guileless smiles. Other patients made way. Ram-Ram was playing the role of kindly old psychologist, this time to perfection, and the other patients surrounded him like supporting actors, showing him deference while Ram-Ram kept smiling like some ancient pied piper.

He indicated one corner of the room where an old table stood; a beat-up conference table about which chairs were cocked at crazy angles. Then he smiled again and sat down as if I were a patient of whom he was particularly fond. His whole manner indicated that this was his office or its equivalent. He wore his own clothes rather than any hospital-like garb, and he treated the table as if it were his desk, ignoring the piles of torn magazines which he shoved aside.

I was taken aback, yet willing enough to go along with the pretense, considering Ram-Ram's condition, when he gestured to a woman who came up beside us, and said, "Dear Queen Alice, do sit down with us. You'll be interested in Jeffy-boy, here."

As Ram-Ram spoke, the other patients began to mill about, make noises, cough, sneeze — or in other ways seem to indicate that they were involved in their own concerns and wouldn't eavesdrop. At the same time, their motions also seemed sly and aimless. I had no idea how to react to them, being more used to dealing with laboratory rats than people.

I pulled myself together, smiled jovially, and said, "Well, now, how are we feeling?"

"Fine, fine," Ram-Ram answered, with no indication that anything at all was wrong. "I'm continuing our research at this end, and Queen Alice, here, has become my assistant."

"I'm very glad to meet you," I replied nervously, and I had to turn to look at the woman as Ram-Ram's attitude so clearly demanded. I didn't want to ruffle him, but I didn't particularly want to deal with anyone else either. Queen Alice's white hair made a wiry bush about her face. She was wearing dungarees and a shirt, and for some reason her attire upset my sense of propriety — an attitude that even then I understood was unfair and ridiculous. "Queen Alice?" I said gently, with just a hint of a smile, I suppose.

"Another nickname of sorts, or rather, a title of deference," Ram-Ram said. "It really denotes the fact that she's out of her time. She's living in the wrong century."

"A dreadful inconvenience," Queen Alice added. "And so few understand. Oh, some do, I'm not saying that. But no, I'm not a queen. I have no pretensions of *earthly* royalty . . . I presume you're a gentleman of your century?"

"Oh yes, he is that, indeed," Ram-Ram said with obvious relish and an almost sarcastic chuckle. And the entire affair was just too much for me. I was about to make some excuse and leave when Ram-Ram leaned forward with a sudden, almost gay attitude of conspiracy and said quickly, "We haven't all the time in the world, you know, so I want to fill you in on what I've learned so far."

Tolerantly enough, I put off my departure and said, "Go ahead," for I hoped that I could learn just how irrational he actually was. And certainly my curiosity was more than aroused. This was my first encounter with schizophrenia in a human. We'd induced similar symptoms in rats through the use of disorientation conditioning, but this was something else.

So while I tried to look sympathetic and personally involved, I kept track of Ram-Ram's reactions at the same time. He acted feverish as he started speaking, gesticulating quickly, urgently, his small brown eyes not leaving my face for what seemed like an eternity. He wouldn't let me look away, and kept punctuating his sentences with excited exclamations of "You see? You see?"

So I was forced to say, "Yes, yes," and sit there while he stared at me with the greatest intentness — a most uncomfortable spot to be in, I might add — and a very curious situation indeed.

"These people here, in their way, are quite sane," he said. "A fact that I've often suspected about such patients. They are not — I repeat, *not* — insane. You see?"

"Yes, of course," I answered, not wanting to upset him further.

"But beyond that, listen. This is important. Queen Alice hears voices. They speak to her at various times, delivering what seems to be the most astonishing information. Once I heard them, too, though not as clearly as she does, and I'm not really certain that they *were* the same voices. I believe this information to be a kind of garbled divine dialogue. Do you follow me?"

His eyes still hadn't left my face. I tried to hide my almost overwhelming dejection that a fine mind could deteriorate so in such a brief time. Lacking practical experience or not, I knew enough to recognize the classic symptoms of his disease.

"You see? You see?" he said impatiently. His normal clothes and appearance contrasted so sharply with the wildness of his manner that I was ready to leap from my chair in consternation when he reached out and grabbed my arm forcibly. "Have you begun your out-of-body experiments yet?" he asked, in a hoarse whisper.

"No."

"Well, you must. At once. It's vital." This time he shouted.

"Yes. I will. Tonight," I said, as soothingly as possible, but having no intention, of course, of doing any such thing.

"He doesn't believe in my voices at all," Queen Alice said suddenly. I spun around to look at her, having forgotten her presence entirely. She stood up, frowning, staring at me with the uncompromising clarity that children and the mad both sometimes assume.

I didn't know what to do or say. Certainly I didn't want to upset either of them. Just then, a tall clownish-looking man came up to us. He walked bent over, but quickly, on the balls of his feet. He took a magazine from the table and winked at me sympathetically. "Don't let it bother you none," he said. "None of us hears the voices either like Queen Alice does. Maybe you'll be able to hear them later on yourself. You never can tell." He winked encouragingly and went back to his chair.

I just stared after him. This . . . *patient* wanted me to understand that I was in the same boat as all of them — he was trying to comfort *me*. I rose to leave. As I did, again the other patients began to mill about. Queen Alice squared her scrawny shoulders and asked suddenly, "Who do you think you are? I mean, who do you imagine yourself to be?"

"Nobody," I said.

"That's too bad," she answered, and with the craziest smile, Ram-Ram said, "That's his trouble." Without another word, I left.

Actually I was more shaken than I wanted to admit. Obviously the conversation in my apartment *had* set Ram-Ram off, I thought, for now he supposed that we were conducting some esoteric experiment together, in which Queen Alice's voices were also involved. I shook my head: "The poor old coot." Yet as I returned home, I could feel my mood swing about in the most unusual fashion from definite disquiet to an almost lethargic passivity. From this latter I was then struck by a sudden exuberance in which it seemed that everything would work out well, and, indeed, that none of my problems or Ram-Ram's were important at all.

I'd been working too hard, I thought. Obviously the two experiences that led me to call Ram-Ram were perfectly natural results of exhaustion. I decided to take some vitamin C. Then my exhilaration quickened. The idea came to me that there was something I must write down at once. Almost without thinking, I inserted some paper into my old typewriter.

I recall being surprised beyond measure at the first sight of what I'd written. For there at the top of the page the following words appeared as if in a title:

The Further Education of Oversoul Seven

I stared. The further education of *what?* What had possessed me to write such a nonsense phrase? Yet even as I puzzled over the sentence, excitement seized me. Suddenly assured and full of confidence, I began typing as fast as my hands would go. The words seemed to slip through my brain from some-place else, and onto the paper, yet I had no idea where the material was com-ing from. Moreover, a story of sorts seemed to be developing.

I was aware of the words perhaps a second before my fingers actually typed them, and to my amazement, the pace actually quickened. I didn't even have time to read what was on one sheet of paper before, urgently, the next sentence appeared. Two hours passed. Finally I stopped, dazed, lit a cigarette, and almost immediately felt again that strong compulsion to type. *Was* it a compulsion? It was certainly far more than an impulse, yet I was sure that I could resist it if I chose. Instead, I decided on the spot to go along as an experiment of sorts, to see what would happen.

What happened was the beginning of a book with the rather improb-able title given earlier. Except for a short break, I typed steadily for four hours. I had no idea of the quality of the material, but its imaginative fan-tasy struck me as highly uncharacteristic of my own personality. Outside of dry academic papers, I've never done any writing in my adult life.

The rest of the evening I spent trying to trace my own subjective states before and during the experience. This time I didn't make the mistake of calling anyone, but I was more frightened than I'd been earlier. Now I was faced with the physical evidence before me — a stack of writing produced by me in a way that I could not understand. Where had it come from? Would I be seized by the same compulsion again? And could I really resist if I wanted to, or was I only fooling myself?

Even those questions became unimportant as another, more terrifying thought came to me: If Ram-Ram was considered mad because he some-times heard voices, where did *this* put *me?* Was it possible that schizophrenia was actually caused by some as yet undiscovered virus, and had been passed on by Ram-Ram to me? Impossible, I thought. Yet such an explanation would at least place the entire affair in the realm of the real and reasonable.

I knew it was silly, but I took another vitamin C, remembering that large dosages were supposed to combat infections. I also comforted myself that no auditory or visual hallucinations had been involved.

As it happened, the episode was followed by another, and still another. I'm recording these odd chapters here, with no changes. As you read on, you'll see the strange way in which *Oversoul Seven* began to take over the ordinary details of my life.

~ *Chapter Four* ~

Gods Wanted
(or Chapter One of Jeffery's
"Further Education of Oversoul Seven")

The interviews had been going on for centuries, or for only moments, according to your point of view. Oversoul Seven frowned, put an *Out To Lunch* sign on the door, and said to his teacher, Cyprus, "Everyone wants to be a god. I never saw anything like it. I don't trust any of the applicants either; they're all too anxious." For the present, Oversoul Seven looked like a guru, because that was what the earth applicants expected. He caught a glimpse of himself in the mirror over the waiting-room coffee table, and smiled despite himself. "I do sort of look like Christ, too, don't you think?"

Cyprus was thinking so fast that she kept changing form constantly. She paused long enough to say, "If Lydia is all ready to be born again, then I really don't see why you're going to all this trouble on her behalf at a time like this. You'll be graded on how smoothly you help Lydia begin her new life, and if the affair is vital to her, it also makes up your own most important work for this semester. So I don't see where this search for the gods fits in at all."

"How do you think I feel, getting sidetracked like this? But my earth peoples' education has really hit a snag, just because of their god concepts. The earth gods are just senile. Too bad and all, but what can you do? When you toss gods into time, well, they get tinged by it just like anyone else. It just, uh, takes longer. And even though Lydia *is* one of my personalities, she has to discover the answers for herself."

"I hope *you* remember that, Seven," Cyprus said. "And I also hope you remember that you're dealing with subjective realities this semester. I suppose the *Out To Lunch* sign has something to do with earth customs? Even so, I'm not sure that I approve of the setting you've created for the interviews."

Seven said broodingly, "Well, it's the replica of a doctor's waiting room that Lydia visited in her twentieth-century life. I'm trying to use earth sym-bolism as much as possible to give her a sense of security between lives; she gets awfully skittish. I was pleased with this environment — physician of the soul, that sort of thing."

Cyprus said, "That kind of venture *can* get quite complicated." She paused, giving Seven time to comment, and when he didn't, but just blushed guiltily, Cyprus disappeared. Her voice, coming from nowhere in particular, said, "Apparently you have no real problems with Lydia, though — at least nothing that you can't handle — so you can carry on quite well alone. Just so Lydia gets born on time."

"All *right,* come back," Seven yelled, symbolically speaking, because ac-tually the entire conversation thus far took place soundlessly, and word-lessly as well.

"There *is* one little problem," Seven said, blushing again as Cyprus re-appeared, this time looking very stern. She materialized as a mixture of man and woman or woman and man; and of age and youth or youth and age; one aspect or another of her image being emphasized as she reacted to Seven's words.

"Uh," he said hesitantly, "actually Lydia refuses to be born until she searches for the gods. She wants to know if they really exist or not before she takes on another life. All in all, she's been very stubborn about the whole thing."

Cyprus' face turned ancient and glowering. "And? What's the rest of it?" she asked.

Oversoul Seven sighed deeply and tried his best to look only slightly (not deeply) concerned. "Well, Lydia's mother-to-be in her next life is Bianka, as you know — Josef's wife. And she's approaching labor right now in seventeenth-century Denmark. Remember, Lydia decided to go back-ward in time for her next life — in her terms, of course. I mean, *we* know that all time is simultaneous, but — " His voice drifted off miserably.

Cyprus felt so sorry for her pupil that she turned immediately into the image of a kindly old physician, and Seven's spirits momentarily lifted.

"Actually the problem is mainly one of time, using earth terms," he said. "I mean, in *those* terms, a woman's labor pains can't be put off forever. And there *is* always the chance that I can change Lydia's mind."

Cyprus disappeared again, this time because her reactions were so quicksilver fast and contradictory that she couldn't get any one image to express them. She said, "Are you trying to tell me that Bianka, Lydia's mother-to-be, is nearly ready to deliver a baby, and Lydia wants to go on some kind of misguided pilgrimage to the gods first?"

"Uh, I'm not positive, but if I have the time sequences right, then Bianka is expecting to deliver a baby in twenty-four hours or so," Seven said very quietly.

Silence.

"Of course, with probabilities, there's variations of all kinds," he added. "Any time from three hours to forty-eight, I imagine."

Cyprus said, "Or, granting probabilities, Lydia *could* decide not to be re-born as Tweety at all." This time Cyprus' voice rang, echoed, thundered. Vowels and syllables turned into images and went flying through the air, catching the sunlight and turning into multicolored prisms. Only these prisms also *sounded*, so that the vowels and syllables fragmented, splintered, and registered in so many different scales at once that Oversoul Seven shouted out and covered his guru ears.

When the commotion ceased he said glumly, "You didn't have to do that—" and with belated dignity: "I understand your concern."

"Oh, Seven!" Cyprus said. She'd changed back to the image she often used in such discussions with Seven: that of a young woman with ancient knowledge—or that of an ancient woman with young appearance, according to his (or her) point of view. "You're Lydia's *oversoul*, after all. How could you let her do such a thing?"

"She gets me confused," Seven protested. "In her last life, she didn't believe in me at all. Then once she realized that she *had* a soul—after death—she wanted truth handed to her on a silver platter, if you'll forgive my earth vernacular. On her own, she decided to be born as Tweety, Josef and Bianka's daughter. But if you ask me, she's carrying this free will business too far. Now she's not sure she even wants to be born again at all, unless she—"

Seven broke off. In his dismay, he'd forgotten to maintain the hallucinatory doctor's office; or his own image, for that matter. He and Cyprus were two points of light in the middle of nowhere. Quickly Seven reestablished the environment, hoping that Cyprus hadn't noticed, but she just smiled wanly. Since she didn't comment, Seven continued as if nothing had happened.

"It's hard on the father-to-be, too. In fact, I had a little trouble with Josef.

First he wanted to be an artist, free, with no responsibilities. Then he wants a wife and children—"

"And *now,* "Cyprus interrupted, "with his wife about to go into labor, he doesn't know if he wants to be a father at all."

"You've been checking up on me," Seven protested. "You knew about this all of the time!"

"And Lydia wants the world to stop while she tracks down the gods. Is that it?" Cyprus asked. Vowels and syllables started to glitter in the air again, spinning down to the red velvet couch in the corner and landing on the dark leather chairs.

"Now don't start that again," Seven cried, but it was too late. The sounds went flying all about, some tinkling like crystal, some booming like thunder as they fell apart into fragments of light-and-sound; linked. They fell onto the lush rug, twirling in the pile. And ignoring the entire display—indeed, only half aware of it—Cyprus said, "Looking for the gods can be a very tricky, serious, and funny affair all at once. Now, listen to me. Remember that Lydia and Josef are both your personalities, so they have some of your characteristics. Lydia says that she really doesn't believe in any gods, which is why she wants to find them so badly, of course. And—"

"She's coming," Oversoul Seven cried. "Please don't tell her that we discussed all this. She has the most exaggerated sense of privacy—"

"All right. But *your* beliefs about the gods are important too, Seven. Don't forget that," Cyprus cautioned. She made the vowels and syllables disappear, and Lydia walked into the room.

She looked to be in her early twenties. She gave her long black hair a decisive toss, snapped her fingers, and said, "A doctor's office. Physician of the soul and all that stuff, I bet."

Oversoul Seven grinned and said, "I thought it applied."

"It does," she answered. "Physical doctors aren't very competent, and physicians of the soul probably aren't any better." She smiled, though, and took a hallucinatory cigarette from her dungaree pocket. Seven lit it for her and said to Cyprus, "What did I tell you? She's . . . difficult."

Lydia had met Cyprus on several occasions. She gave her a grin of welcome and shrugged her shoulders. Seven ignored the flippancy; or almost. He frowned slightly and said, "Anyhow, Lydia is going to advise me about earth conditions, in case we find any new gods to insert into time."

Cyprus turned into a young woman, more or less. That is, she tried to relate to Lydia by adopting a similar image. Her thoughts went so fast again, though, that to Lydia it looked as if she appeared and disappeared in the most confusing fashion.

Lydia puffed nervously on her hallucinatory cigarette and said, "If I'm going to be born again, then first I want to find out about the gods—or God, or whatever. When I'm in a physical life, I get sidetracked, so I'm taking the opportunity now, while I can. Otherwise, I don't know. The gods never did much good as far as I can see—if there *are* gods. But I thought that if we found a decent one, we could—well, insert him in time. Or *her.* Earth could do with a woman god for a change, if you ask me."

Oversoul Seven smiled brilliantly at Cyprus and said, "See, the gods can be inserted just after Lydia's time in her last life. She knows all about that period. Even her prejudices are still fresh in her mind."

"I suppose that's considered an asset?" Cyprus asked. "And if I were you, I'd forget about inserting any new gods in time—*if* you find any willing to undertake such a venture. I should tell you, Seven, that there *are* a few things you've forgotten on purpose for this semester's work. Your own entire range of knowledge on certain subjects isn't available to you, because otherwise you might be tempted to overdirect your personalities."

There was something about Cyprus' speech that wrinkled the edges of Oversoul Seven's momentary smugness. He almost panicked, but instead he went on, quite bravely he thought: "Lydia knows what people expect of the gods. Of course, we'll have to check out the old gods first. But if we find any new ones, they'll have to know earth customs. Earth people keep their sexes separate, for example, as you know. In each life they stick to one sex or the other—"

"Or the *other*? So there are only two?"

Cyprus' words went thundering through all of Oversoul Seven's experience, scattering images everywhere. The millions of sexual variations of plant, mineral, and animal planetary life glittered before his mental eyes; the endless convoluted yet sparkling couplings and transcouplings by which life multiplied and refreshed itself. He knew it. He knew it all, but at some level he had forgotten. Or else he pretended not to know—for a reason. But for that moment, Seven stepped out of his own vision into that immeasurably vaster one, and he felt as if he possessed a thousand heads, all of them reeling. And in the very back of his mind, he wondered uneasily what he'd forgotten about the gods.

Cyprus was still saying, incredulously, "Only two?" when Seven regained himself. This time he took on his fourteen-year-old male image and stood there, head bowed, fresh new cheeks puffed out—pouting—and said, "Cyprus, that wasn't fair at all."

Now Cyprus looked far older than Lydia, older than anyone ever in the strangest fashion, even while her features hadn't really changed in any usually observable way. She wanted to smile at Oversoul Seven and Lydia; she wanted to reassure them. Yet looking at them through her knowledge put them so far away that she could barely perceive them. She sorted through times and places, sometimes growing weary, until finally she found them again — Oversoul Seven first — drawn to him by that rambunctious energy of his, which now was turned into grave inquiry.

"Where were you?" he asked, telling himself that he should know better than to ask the question at all.

"I never know what's going on," Lydia protested. She sat down on the hallucinatory red couch, her fingers flashing nervously through the magazines. "I have the worst feeling that this search for the gods may end up in some completely different fashion than we suppose."

But as a fourteen-year-old boy, Oversoul Seven felt himself drawn toward some ancient childhood, falling back into some newness that was (and is) the center of each tiniest spark of being. And he knew that godmaking was a children's game; but the only one worth playing.

As he thought *that* Cyprus disappeared, as did the physician's office with its fine velvet couch. He and Lydia were on their own. Seven felt a momentary flash of dismay — there were so many things he'd wanted to ask Cyprus first — but it was too late for questions. He looked around, expectantly. The environment was changing, doubtlessly because of Lydia's beliefs, and Seven wished fervently that he had a better idea of just what her beliefs about the gods *really* were.

~ *Chapter Five* ~

The Beginning of the Search and
a Demon in the Foothills

*L*ydia was feeling petulant. "I thought that after death, you were supposed to know all about God, or whatever," she said. "And even though
I didn't believe that I had a soul when I was physical, I thought that souls —
if they existed — would at least know the answers. Instead, here I am, helping my oversoul go tracking down the gods. After all I've been through, I'm
not certain of anything."

"Shush. Will you be quiet?" Seven cried, exasperated. "We're in someone else's territory. I can tell."

Lydia grabbed a cigarette from the pocket of a hastily hallucinated
trench coat and looked around nervously. "What do you mean, someone
else's territory?" She squinted; things were changing. There were walls and
walls of shadow that weren't there before. And they were advancing. To test
her perceptions, Lydia stood still. And sure enough, the walls seemed to
come closer, stealthily.

"On earth, it would be like an alien country," Seven said, "when you
don't know the rules and don't like the looks of the place. Just take my
hand and be quiet."

He sounded much more confident than he felt. The area was drenched
with personality characteristics that he found most distasteful. Fear was
draped invisibly but definitely over everything; like a heavy suffocating vine

that choked out all other growth. And anger crawled in and out of all the tiny crevices that suddenly opened up around their feet, spreading like miniature earthquakes. Seven didn't like the feel of it at all. But as yet, the various elements were diversified. By steering Lydia and himself carefully, he managed to follow the few clear spots still open.

At the same time, Oversoul Seven felt the fear and anger collecting itself; it belonged to some*one* or some*thing*.

Lydia hadn't made a wisecrack in what seemed a century. She was beginning to shiver. Instantly she hallucinated a big brown handbag with a revolver inside. The bag swung from shoulder straps that fit over her trench coat.

The automatic hallucination of objects was something Seven had tried to teach her without success until now. But she was so frightened that she never noticed her success.

A presence was slowly gathering about them. The fear and anger were literally taking shape. Seven felt a thickness grow before he saw it; a gigantic swirling black-centered demonlike form. Despite himself, he stepped backward. The demon—or whatever it was—*was* definitely there, rising out of the shadow walls. Yet, on the other hand, there was something not-there about it too. Lydia opened her handbag and reached for her revolver.

As she did so, the thing began to speak—or at least words came from somewhere, though Seven knew that the creature's tongue could have no power of its own. And as it spoke, like a giant evil porcupine it sent out darts of terror that stuck into—well, psychological skin—while foul odors slithered like snakes from it, coiling everywhere. Lydia dropped her handbag. The ground beneath it turned into quicksand, swallowing the handbag, revolver and all.

"Well, do something," Lydia stammered.

Seven closed his eyes. He opened them again. Nothing had changed. "We're on our way to visit the gods," he said politely.

A gigantic chuckle began somewhere nearby. And built up. And grew until the sounds drowned out Oversoul Seven's thoughts as well as his hard-earned composure. Giant teeth appeared in the sky, too close to the ground for comfort. They clanked up and down with each god-forsaken gasp of laughter; and the open mouth showed a gullet-path that led into distances too far even for Seven's imagination.

Lydia was sobbing.

Seven was frightened enough; and confused. He whispered to Lydia, "I thought you didn't believe in demons?"

"I don't really know if I believe in gods or not but I believe in demons all right," Lydia muttered, staring at the huge teeth which now were fading, while the original monster-shape came closer.

"There aren't any demons," Seven said urgently. "You've got to believe me."

"Then what's that?" Lydia cried angrily.

"Kneel down and adore me, or be annihilated," demanded the voice issuing from the creature but also seeming to come from the ground beneath their feet, and from the sky as well.

Oversoul Seven finally got his mental footing. "Okay," he said agreeably, borrowing Lydia's expression on purpose.

Lydia grabbed Seven's arm, shouting, "Oh, how *could* you? You'll be bowing to evil!"

"*Will* you let me handle this?" Seven almost yelled.

"Bow down, with your belly on the ground," insisted the monster, hissing now.

"Never!" Lydia screamed, trembling. She advanced, saying the Lord's Prayer, which she suddenly remembered.

"'Our Father —'"

"Lydia, that's useless," Seven said. But Lydia was beyond listening.

"Bow down and adore me," the monster raged.

"'Who art in Heaven —'" Lydia prayed.

It was going to be a metaphysical shouting match, Seven thought — somewhat angry himself now. "You don't really believe in God the Father," he reminded Lydia, as gently and considerately as he could under the circumstances. "But you *do* believe in demons."

"'Hallowed be Thy name,'" Lydia said, between clenched teeth. She was just yards from the creature, who was now very rapidly approaching, constantly changing shapes.

"Adore me," it commanded, "or be annihilated."

"Annihilated!" Lydia cried, so frightened that she almost forgot to pray.

Seven didn't dare wait any longer. He let his own beliefs predominate until they flooded the entire environment. The monster disappeared just as the huge mouth, momentarily materializing, opened. Seven snatched Lydia away; she was still yelling the Lord's Prayer.

"You're lucky you believe in *me*," Seven said, disgusted. "That was all your fault back there, and it took me a while to realize what was going on. But would you let me handle it? No. Not until you were scared to death."

"How *did* we get out of there?" Lydia asked.

"I got us out."

"You!" Lydia cried. "You were a coward. Some behavior for an oversoul! You were ready to do anything the demon told you to."

Seven sighed. "It's pretty difficult to explain all this to you, when we're still in the middle of the action. Look around. What do you see?"

Lydia looked—and looked. On earth, the landscape stayed whatever way it was. Here, it seemed you couldn't be sure of anything. First she thought that she saw a row of trees, prickly shapes in space; and once she was positive she smelled pine needles. But the next instant, the same shapes wiggled and thickened in some odd fashion until they suggested steeples and a medieval street. Although *something* always seemed to be out there, whatever it was kept changing.

"It reminds me of Impressionist painting," Lydia said. "It looks like someone painted wiggly trees with brush strokes that just suggested trees. But when you really look, they aren't trees at all." She didn't like the effect much either. Her literal mind wanted one environment or the other, and she said as much.

Oversoul Seven grinned. He'd changed himself into his version of an artist, a rather antiquated version in Lydia's eyes. For he was wearing a brown robe and beard to match, and gesturing with a paintbrush straight out of the fourteenth century. "Your mind is painting the pictures or forming the environment," he said. "I'm purposely letting your mind predominate right now. Earlier you formed the demon because as far as your beliefs are concerned, gods and demons are connected. Look for one, and you automatically find the other. Worse, your belief in God the Father was far weaker than your certainty about demons. So your prayers were only an exercise in futility; and in a way, they only reinforced your belief in evil. You *really* believe that evil is stronger than good."

"Well, there certainly seems to be more of it on earth," Lydia said tartly. "I don't see how you can sidestep the entire issue. At least I rose to the challenges of the encounter."

"You won't really believe any gods exist unless you meet some demons along the way, is that it?" Seven asked. "Because if it is, you might get more than you bargained for. And I'd just as soon not watch."

"Watch? You mean you wouldn't help?" It was hard for Lydia to concentrate. The environment turned from a shadowy boulevard to a shadowy back street in some town in Ohio where she remembered living at one time or another. It was as if space kept advancing and retreating, always carrying different images; or like staring into a shop window where the reflections almost came alive and were as real as objects. The gods, she thought, were probably just reflections too. . . .

"Stop staring," Seven cried. "You're getting the edges of your reality blurred, and we aren't ready for that yet."

"For what?" she asked distractedly. She wished that he'd be quiet, because suddenly the images were becoming much clearer, and she could almost hear voices.

"Lydia," Seven shouted, "don't let your mind drift so." But it was too late.

She *wasn't* ready yet, Seven thought miserably. For that matter, he didn't know if he was either. But there was nothing for him to do but follow her — and her beliefs.

The reflections shimmered, thickened into sparkling kaleidoscopes of cubes and circles, piled one on top of the other, all dissected by a strange glinting light against a dark purple sky. Then, in an instant, the whole thing jelled, set, settled into a solidity so perfect that the new castles and palaces carried an air of ancient elegance, a sturdy jeweled splendor that surely was old when the earth was new.

"Why, it's the land of the gods, just as I once imagined it!" Lydia was so excited that she could hardly speak.

Oversoul Seven, still carrying his paintbrush, sighed. He knew, or he thought he knew, where all this would lead them. But he couldn't just step in and direct Lydia — the search would have to follow her own desires and beliefs. Her desires didn't worry him, Seven thought; but her beliefs were another matter. The air was so clear and sparkling, though, that even Seven found himself exhilarated.

"And it's the most fantastic summer day you could ever imagine," Lydia exclaimed.

That's just it, Seven wanted to say, but he didn't.

As Lydia's mood soared, her dungarees and trench coat were replaced by a silver suit of armor like one Joan of Arc had worn in a picture Lydia had seen as a child in her previous life. And here she was, Lydia, brave and young; splendid in her determination, out to find the gods — and more. She'd found them. Or almost.

Seven almost moaned, picking up her images: she'd been eighteen when she'd seen the Joan of Arc illustration and had imagined the present scene.

Which was quite real, of course.

"Well," she said. "We *did* get rid of the demon one way or another, didn't we? He must have guarded the land of the gods."

Seven gave up for the moment. "Right," he said dourly.

The scene was quickly taking on all the dimensions of an actuality. Mountains appeared in the distance, roads and paths arching over them. Trees materialized, growing to full size in the flash of an eye. Lakes almost spilled over with soft water. Lydia said, "Oh, it's all so unbelievable that I have to sit here for a minute and catch my breath."

"You do? You wear *me* out," Seven muttered, but he was proud of her; the environment *was* splendid.

While it lasted, he thought. His robe was hot. He changed it to a silken one, though he was sure that few artists in any century wore silken gowns.

Still, there could always be a first, he thought, and with some admiration he stared at Lydia. No one could say that she wasn't independent! There she was, slender, brave, and true, he thought, grinning. Her innocence and intensity were more than he could bear. He wanted to see how far those qualities could take her.

More; a part of him roused up in response so that all of his own beginnings began to merge, surge, ascend. He added his exuberance to hers, as it came tumbling into his experience from all the times and places that he'd known; and the scene took on that incredible clarity that defied any one reality; transcended them all and yet was brilliantly itself, and no other.

The summer-scented path led up to a gigantic building that overlooked the top of the hill. They began to climb.

~ *Chapter Six* ~

Josef's Difficulties

*A*t first the path was easy enough. Then Seven noticed that it gradually became slippery, and the clear air seemed colder. Suddenly, in fact, the wind was so chilly that Oversoul Seven changed his artist's robe to a woolen one and added a scarf.

"Aren't you cold, Lydia?" he called, but there was no answer. Squinting, Seven realized that a fine snow was blowing before his eyes, and for a moment he couldn't see anything at all. "Lydia?"

He called again, when he thought he saw her ahead in the distance. But where had the snow come from? In the next instant, with a sinking heart, he knew. For the figure ahead wasn't Lydia. It was one of his other person-alities—Josef, Lydia's father-to-be. Seven had been so involved with Lydia's experiences that he'd almost forgotten Josef entirely. Well, not really. That was an exaggeration, he told himself quickly, guiltily. Yet he was rather im-patient at being called away from Lydia, and it didn't help when Seven re-membered his last encounter with Josef, who had angrily told Seven to mind his own business and leave him alone.

Seven had to claim these rather uncharitable thoughts about Josef as his own; but as he told Cyprus later, that was before he realized Josef's plight. For almost instantly he sensed the desolation of Josef's spirit; even before he saw Josef's body half frozen, huddled up on the mountain, and the vodka bottle which had rolled halfway down the first slippery hill. It would be difficult to find a more dismal scene. In a flash, Oversoul Seven took it all in. The events involved with Josef's life collected, swirled, flew into Seven's immediate experience—colliding, appearing, and disappearing, until finally they fell into their proper time-space relationships—and Seven could focus clearly in the present, according to Josef's experience.

In the farmhouse hardly visible down the seventeenth-century hills, for example, Josef's wife, Bianka, was approaching labor. Through Josef's dimmed mental vision, Seven saw the scene: Josef had rushed through the house in a frenzy of agony and concern that he was unable to voice. The four fireplaces were all blazing so that the house would be warm for the coming birth, but (because Josef hadn't cleaned out the flues properly) it was overheated, filled with fireplace smoke and the steam from water boiling in the iron pots. Josef kept yelling that the steam would ruin his canvases—sitting there unused for months actually, gathering dust, because he hadn't been able to paint decently for what seemed like ages; but the smell of his turpentine rags had mixed in with the smoke and steam and made him ill. The women were all yelling—Bianka most of all, screaming in bed, so bloated he thought she'd burst; and his mother-in-law chased him out into the barn.

The sudden icy air made him dizzy. He glared back at the house with loathing and love (all twisted together), grabbed his vodka bottle from where he'd hidden it underneath the hay, and jammed his skis on his feet.

The first slopes had been easy. He sang to lift his spirits and pretended that he was twenty and unmarried—a roaming, frolicsome artist—instead of twenty-six and domesticated. He skied fast and drank faster, not noticing (or pretending not to notice) that darkness was falling; and trying to forget Bianka's staring eyes; determined to run from the pleading screams that terrified him for reasons he couldn't explain. If that was birth, well, damn the gods, if there were any! No wonder Christ wasn't a father! The thought scared him; it was sacrilegious. No mention of Christ having a penis—"Oh God," he moaned, bleary and horrified. Now where had that thought come from?

Thinking frightened him to begin with. To forget his thoughts, he tried to plan a painting in his mind. Just then he fell down, twisted his leg, lost one ski, and realized that most of the feeling in both legs had vanished at about the same time. How far from home was he? His clothes were warm enough for working outside for an hour or so, but he'd been out for longer than that, he thought. Or had he? His time sense was all jumbled. How long ago was it that he'd been thrown out of his own house so unceremoniously?

Well, they'd be sorry. His emotions overspilled. He sat up, leaning against a tree, staring down the mountainside. The icy twilight was already descending. Bleak barren hills were snow-crusted, and the air was sharp. He knew that he had no time to waste; he had to get going, claim his other ski and start back, going faster than he'd come. He had to restore his circulation. Yet perversely he sat there, grumbling to himself.

Birth had no right to be so beastly, he thought. He couldn't bear to think what Bianka must be going through. How could their jolly lovemaking lead to such . . . terror? Dear God! And what use was it to pray? What did God know about terror? He himself had no use for Christendom, nor did it have any use for him. Which was all right. But now he wanted some kind of comfort; some reassurance . . . that birth wouldn't be as awful for Bianka as he (and everybody else) thought it would be.

If there *was* a God, if there were *gods*—but they were all children's tales, he thought. A lot of good Bianka's Christ was now. He imagined, just as he lost consciousness, that some ancient Nordic gods shared the hills with him: They would wake him up, welcome him with gigantic feasts and resplendent sword fights, boisterous male laughter, offering him slabs of charred sweet meat—pigs stolen from his neighbors; gods that were eternal and male and didn't need fleshy soft women's bodies; gods that had no need to give bloody birth; ancient Viking gods, banqueting through the long winter night.

"Don't you ever think of anything besides food?" Oversoul Seven said rather peevishly: Josef had definitely broadened girth-wise since he'd last looked at him closely.

Josef opened his mental eyes. His physical ones were nearly frosted shut.

Seven took the shape of an old wise man. "You've very nearly done it this time," he said.

"Oh, it's you," Josef moaned, then said pathetically, "You've got to get me out of this. I'm half frozen. I'll never make it home."

"I hope you thoroughly realize the serious predicament you've got yourself into," Seven said sternly, looking ancient as the hills, wise and dependable—and somewhat angry.

"This isn't any time for a sermon," Josef said mentally. "I don't even know if I'm really seeing you or not, but whenever I *do* see you, then I'm either dreaming or delirious—"

"You're always delirious," Seven answered. "Here." He hallucinated a bottle of brandy. Josef sat up in his spirit body—unknowingly in this case—and drank, sputtering as he did so, while Seven made a quick mental trip to Josef's house to see what was going on there now. A steam bath. The boiling water steamed up the windows and froze into a glittering glaze in which the candlelight danced. The chimney smoke made a low dark ceiling so that the members of the family went scuttling beneath it; bent over, coughing and spluttering. Bianka was in the master bedroom on the second floor. She looked like a terrified big blonde-haired doll. Her hair, braided for the birth, was wet with perspiration and steam; her light blue eyes vacant one moment, and scared to death the next. Her mother, Mrs. Hosentauf, kept yelling "It's almost time" to three female cousins who kept moaning for no good reason that Seven could discover.

A huge half-finished painting stood on a heavy wooden easel by the hall window, and the rags hanging there stank of the turpentine that Josef cleaned his brushes in, daily, so that Bianka would think he'd been busy painting. All the other rags and pieces of cloth were piled in the bedroom, preparatory to the birth. Seven, invisible, kicked these aside and went over to Bianka.

He'd seen more births than he could remember, and he knew at once that Bianka's pains right now were caused by fear and foreboding. She *was* close, though, he saw, with some very definite feelings of disquietude, and he'd have to accelerate time considerably for Lydia; because when the baby was due — well, Lydia had to be there. Yet he tried to forget his concern about the future birth, so he could concentrate on Bianka's present.

She never saw him. Shaking his head, half vexed with her and Josef and Lydia as well, Seven said mentally, "Bianka, you aren't due yet. Your pains are caused by fear. Breathe deeply. Let yourself go. There now, there's nothing to it. That's right." He sent ripples of energy to her belly, watched them travel to her uterus and down her thighs. Bianka began to doze. Seven patted her stomach good-naturedly and when she began to quiet down, he went downstairs.

The men, Elgren Hosentauf and his brothers, were in the barns along with sawdust and hay, animal breath and manure, and — Seven saw — vodka. The four men were huddled together, squatting and laughing, in one of the cow's stalls; warm and cozy, with pitchforks ready in case one of the women came to fetch them, in which case they would say they'd been working all the time.

"Josef's near frozen and needs your help. He took his favorite ski trail up the mountain." Seven said these words to Elgren, Josef's father-in-law, and at the same time he implanted in Elgren's mind the most pathetic picture of Josef's predicament. Elgren suddenly swore; his fat stomach rumbled; he leaped to his feet. "I just had the awful thought that Josef's taken off somewhere," he squawked. "Where is he, my dumb son-in-law?"

Seeing the commotion safely started, watching the men check for Josef unsuccessfully and then indignantly saddle the horses for rescue, leaving the warmth of the barns for the winter night, Seven returned to Josef. Or rather, he returned the part of him that he'd sent to the house for his mission. To Josef, Seven had been with him all the while.

Seven, however, was worried. Josef believed that he was nearly freezing to death (which he nearly was), and Seven had to let Josef's beliefs predominate. "I'm dying," Josef moaned. "No feeling at all in my legs. I'll never see my firstborn, my son who will grow up to be a fine gentleman."

Seven was more upset than he wanted to admit. Suppose the rescue party didn't arrive in time? There *was* one thing he could do, beliefs or no, he thought. "Close your mental eyes," he said to Josef. "And you're going to have a daughter. That is, you are if everything works out the way it's supposed to."

"I *am* delirious," Josef cried. "I decided I wanted a son, in any case."

"You and Bianka decided on a girl. And we're not going to argue about it out here in the snow," Seven cried. "You're drunk, besides."

"I don't want a boy or a girl," Josef sighed, filled with self-pity. "I want to be single."

"Close your mental eyes and keep quiet," Seven ordered.

"Not on your life," Josef protested. "I still don't know if I'm awake or dreaming."

Seven said calmly, "Look. You always get upset when you come across something you don't understand. So kindly close your eyes for your own benefit."

Josef's mental eyes were terrified. "I don't know if I'm more afraid of freezing to death, or of your help," he moaned.

"You haven't time to wonder about it," Seven said, and in a flash he transported Josef—physical body, mental body, and all—some three miles further down the hill, to a good clear spot where Elgren and his men with their horses and sleigh would find him quicker and easier. Josef was screaming. "I'm dead, for God's sake. I'm flying through the air, carried away by demons." And at the same time, almost slyly, he kept poking his mental body in the ribs, seeing that he was, after all, quite alive.

His dream or mental body had separated from his physical one, though, and suddenly Josef stared, literally beside himself, to see his rumpled, nearly blue, stiff, sodden, and drunken form; eyelids stuck shut, with frost climbing between the thick dark eyebrows; proud brown mustache looking like the ancient white quills of some senile porcupine. He was struck by a sudden forlorn longing for his body, with which he'd made love to Bianka and planted his seed—his bristly, usually vigorous thighs, splendid arms, paint-stained fingers. And he vowed that if he ever got out of this, he'd never complain again; he'd paint masterpieces and be a good husband and father and householder beside.

Oversoul Seven got embarrassed whenever Josef really allowed himself to *feel* his emotions, as opposed to playing with them as he usually did. What would happen if Josef actually allowed himself to—well, honestly experience his feelings, instead of playing the mad artist or buffoon? Easy sentimentality was one thing—and Josef moaned often, loudly, quarrelsomely, bombastically. But these present feelings went deeper. Josef's sudden compassion for his body, in contrast to his usual self-pity, led Seven to say, gently, "Your body will be all right. If you believe me, it *will* be found in time. It won't be damaged to any important degree."

Josef was still staring at it, but the easily manufactured self-pity came back. "It'll freeze, poor thing," he sobbed.

"It just might," Seven cried, exasperated. "Now, listen, I have to get your thoughts off your body somehow. Just forget it, will you?"

"Forget it?" Josef screamed, nearly out of his wits by now.

Nothing, Seven saw, would take Josef's attention away from his body while he could still see it; and it wasn't in any shape for him to get back into.

"Dear gods above," Josef cried dramatically.

And Oversoul Seven thought: What a brilliant idea! It just might work—"Look over there," he told Josef. Josef turned, and with his attention momentarily off his body, Seven was able to whisk him away from it. Josef felt a sudden dizziness; the snow grew dazzling bright all around him, despite the darkness of the moment before. The ledge above him trembled and shifted in some indescribable fashion as he stared at it—and before him stretched a summery path. The air was so warm and lovely in contrast to the earlier iciness that Josef cried out with delight and relief. So did Seven, because Josef's concentration on warmth would help keep his physical body from freezing. That is, it would as long as Seven could keep Josef occupied.

"Where are we?" Josef demanded. "How did we get here?" He spoke so quickly that he nearly stuttered because he looked down at his mental body (thinking it was his physical one) to see fine sun-bronzed limbs, small beads of perspiration running between the merry thigh hairs, as his legs flashed in and out of a brown walking robe. "And look. There's someone else," he shouted.

It was Lydia, still looking like Joan of Arc, only somewhat wearier than before. She gasped when she saw Josef. "What are *you* doing here?"

"I don't even know where here is," Josef said agreeably. "And I don't know you, either." Then, perplexed: "Or do I?"

Lydia looked at Seven, incredulously. "He doesn't remember who I am?" she asked Seven.

"No, and I'd rather you didn't remind him right now," Seven replied quickly. "I have some excellent and important reasons—"

"What are they?" Lydia interrupted. "I really do believe in honesty above all. And as a Soul, I don't know if you have the right to hide important information from Josef."

Lydia made a fascinating picture, and Josef was staring at her with open admiration. He was in excellent spirits now, completely involved in this new adventure, his miseries and danger forgotten. (And Seven wanted to keep it that way for a while.) But Lydia indignantly put down the sword that went with her outfit and said, "I really think you owe Josef an explanation."

"That's the spirit!" Josef cried. "You tell him. He always intimidates me. I just see him when I'm drunk or dreaming, and right now I'm not sure of anything."

Lydia frowned. "I know one thing," she said. "I'm sick of looking like Joan of Arc, and I'm tired of changing images all the time. I'd like to stick to one image and one environment. Why can't we camp here for the night and explore the land of the gods tomorrow? If it *is* the land of the gods." She was tired, and peevish, and Seven sighed. The environment about them darkened. The sun was sinking; purple shadows filled a nearby meadow of flowers. And just then, above on the hillside, the lights splashed on in all the palaces and shone from the balconies. Josef stared: He'd never seen so many lights in his life.

Lydia laughed out loud, "The streetlights of the gods." She sobered instantly. "The gods don't really live on any mountain, or anywhere else, for that matter. I know that. I must have picked up the whole idea from mythology." She was her twenty-year-old self now, nervously smoking a cigarette; and critical. She eyed Josef: "You're real enough. I've met you before, even though you've forgotten. And Oversoul Seven is real, even though I used to think he wasn't."

"Now look here. Of course I'm real," Josef shouted. "And I almost seem to remember you. But what are we doing here? I must be dreaming. Are you?"

"We're on a pilgrimage to find the gods—if there really are any," Lydia announced dramatically, half sarcastically, staring at Oversoul Seven, yet unable to keep a certain wavering hope from her voice. "Anyhow, you seem to have joined us," she added. "And that's all I can tell you."

Josef scowled. "I'm not religious, and I think that the priests are mostly rascals, but there's only one God. Talking about gods is blasphemy," he said, honestly outraged, forgetting his own earlier thoughts on the matter. He stared accusingly at Seven. "I knew it," he moaned dejectedly. "Why can't I have an ordinary soul like anyone else, one that I can count on, instead of some renegade kind that sets out on pagan pilgrimages?"

But as soon as he spoke, Josef stopped, considering. Everything that he'd ever heard about pagan gods rushed into his mind. Orgies! He remembered the Norse deities again and almost smelled the meat roasting on spits, thick grease sizzling. (Damn, he was hungry.) The sensual richness overwhelmed him and spread out its tantalizing aura so that Lydia cried, "Something really smells great!"

"Roast pig," Josef shouted. "A feast of such gigantic proportions—"

"He's delirious," Elgren Hosentauf muttered. "Roast pig indeed." He and his two brothers knelt by Josef's body and tried to bundle it up onto the sleigh. It was well below zero. The men felt nearly frozen themselves.

"Wake up, Josef. You have to move around. Wake up!" Elgren shouted in Josef's ear. He and his brothers grabbed Josef's arms and started jerking them up and down; then his legs. Elgren opened the stiff mouth and sloppily poured some brandy down Josef's throat; Josef gagged, sputtered, coughed—and opened his physical eyes. Instead of the summer night he saw the snow and a closeup of Elgren's anxious face, large pores with blackheads, some half hidden at the edges of the red woolen scarf. But most of all, Josef saw Elgren's furious yet frightened cold-swollen eyes. "Oh, God," Elgren was yelling, caught between calling Josef a blockhead and crying with gratitude as Josef's bleary eyes opened.

"He's come to," Elgren shouted. "Give me a hand." They all loaded Josef on the sleigh, while Elgren sat beside him, constantly moving his arms and legs, forcing him to move—much against his own inclination. "Let me sleep," Josef kept muttering. "Just let me sleep."

"Severe frostbite at the very least," Elgren muttered. "The damned fool, running off like that with his wife about to bear—" At the same time, he and others found that their moods were lifting. They had needed relief from the house and barns. The excitement of the rescue and its success would make them heroes on their return. Still, Elgren was anxious. He urged the horses on: Josef had been out in the cold far too long. He frowned, cursed under his breath, and kept rubbing Josef's hands, while sipping brandy to keep himself warm. Now and then he forced some more down Josef's throat.

The brandy, Josef thought, was excellent. "Where did you get this?" He held up a heavy mug and grinned. "It's fit for the gods," he said, while Oversoul Seven looked on anxiously. Josef shrugged. "I thought I felt a cold draught of air, and this really warms me up. But how could I have felt a chill? The air is warm as summer."

"Just your imagination," Seven said.

"I almost heard voices, too," Josef said. Some brandy trickled down his fine brown mustache. He wiped it off with his hand. "Do you hear voices?" he asked.

"It's just the breeze," Seven said quickly. He didn't want Josef to return to his body again until it was thawed out, yet even he could hear Hosentauf's raucous shouts, the horses' gallop—horseshoes now and then breaking through the crusted snow—one horse's forehoof sore. Seven caught himself just in time and closed out the images before he landed all three of them back there with the Hosentauf sleigh.

Lydia, now in blouse and slacks, sat down dejectedly. "I was so excited at first, seeing these mountains. I thought of Mount Olympus. But most likely there's really nothing real up there. Yet why is that scene so tantalizing?"

She stared: The warm bright lights splashed down the summer night hills. "Those *are* Olympian hills," she said moodily. "My God, the universe is vast." She felt as if she were going to cry.

"Don't worry about it," Josef replied. "All of this has to be a dream to begin with." The soft wind enveloped him. He felt full of vigor, and he eyed Lydia with more than just a touch of appreciation. "Let's go sit down beneath those trees," he said, his moustache quivering with his sudden gleeful duplicity.

Lydia understood his intent at once. She almost yelled, "You can't act like that! I'm going to be born as your daughter," but Oversoul Seven mentally stopped her. He didn't want Josef reminded of Bianka or his body until the physical situation was stabilized. Like Josef, the Hosentaufs often exaggerated the most simple events of their lives, and Seven knew that despite her moans and groans at the farmhouse, Bianka wasn't really in labor—yet. Checking, Seven mentally monitored Josef's half-frozen body as it sat slumped in the sleigh, and frowned. Josef could just possibly lose a leg.

For a moment Oversoul Seven felt really disconsolate: He had more trouble than he needed; and what he *really* needed was a good brisk wind behind the sleigh and horses. The horses themselves were tiring. What he really needed was—Seven broke off. Suddenly the Denmark scene became brilliantly clear. A strong wind came sweeping down behind the sleigh, pushing it so fast that Elgren Hosentauf yelled, "Where the devil did that wind come from?"

And in a near kind of distance, Oversoul Seven heard Cyprus say to him, "That's the help you needed. And don't forget your practice teaching dream class."

"I *had* forgotten it," Seven cried mentally. "I—" but Cyprus' presence had vanished.

Josef was saying, "I know what I'd like to do," and leering at Lydia.

"Can't you do something with him?" she asked Seven impatiently. Her black hair gently tangled in the wind. She swept the loose locks back uneasily, wondering if she felt any desire for Josef. There was warm moisture around his brown eyes and broad forehead; his glance was certainly inviting, but she couldn't forget that she would be his daughter; maybe, anyway. But more than that, she kept relating to him from a viewpoint of a whole lifetime of different ages. If she stayed at twenty, then Josef was an interesting older man, gallant and almost sophisticated. But then mentally she sprang to thirty-five and from *there,* he seemed amusingly inept and bumbling.

She was quite lost in these thoughts, perplexed and near harried, while Josef sat down on a ledge, crossed his legs, and gave her what he considered his deadliest, most suggestive leer.

Mentally, Oversoul Seven heard an invisible Cyprus say, "Look at the mountain." Her presence vanished again before he could comment, and Seven stared at the mountain as directed.

It hadn't changed. Or did he now notice vague figures at one of the distant castle windows?

"Good Zeus, woman, make up your mind," Josef thundered at Lydia.

∽ *Chapter Seven* ∽

Some Assembled Gods

*L*ooking down from the mountain, Zeus said, "They're at it again. Their energy and persistence is really incredible."

Christ answered, "Verily so."

"Yet they keep changing the rules," Zeus complained. He leaned back on his velvet couch, surveying the worlds and times that flickered outside of the castle-sized picture windows, drank his wine, and idly fingered the divine spider plant on the bronzed table by the divan.

Christ just smiled. Then he said, "I don't know what *you're* complaining about."

"Oh, the Crucifixion?" Zeus said. "I'll grant you that was no fun."

"Yet the whole concept was," Christ said nostalgically. "There were great moments, moments when I thought I almost got through to them. Jerusalem wasn't Olympus—but the saga was there, the excitement and educational contrasts."

The two of them sat quietly for a moment (that lasted for centuries), each lost in his own thoughts, watching the nights and dawns flicker off and on across the earth and all of the earths below and around; for outside of the god-place, times and spaces blew gently past the windows, and the paths in the stately gardens outside connected worlds.

Such a place doesn't exist in usual terms, of course, but in—well, extra-ordinary terms, in palaces of the psyche; in an inner world that is as sepa-rated and personified as you and I and as all of the readers of this book. So in that sense, Zeus and Christ and Mohammed and all of the gods do all sit conversing. And in that sense, Oversoul Seven goes out seeking the gods.

Castle or not, however, nothing could conceal the fact that this was an old gods' home. Zeus kept dozing. Christ now and then had nightmares about the Crucifixion. And in one of the courtyards, Mohammed flashed his fiery sword, but none of the attendants even pretended to get out of the way anymore, or played scared, so that Mohammed just kept flailing away at the infidels, cutting the bodies in half or into a zillion pieces which were all in the next moment magically repaired. It was enough, dear Allah, to take the joy out of killing. Mohammed sighed, and Allah, mechanically clapping on the sidelines, was bored.

No one there, Zeus thought, had anything really left but memories.

"But what memories!" Christ answered aloud. "Still; pathetic. They're still fighting about me on Earth, even now. And waiting for the Second Com-ing. That'll be the blessed day. I'd *really* have to be crazy to go back there."

Zeus lifted his still black, thicker-than-forest eyebrows and said with a thunderous-enough laugh, "Come on, now. You love it. They still think of you, and it's the only thing that keeps you going. Admit it."

A flash of the old zest illuminated Christ's eyes so that electron worlds within his pupils veered dangerously; and on forgotten islands in time, small volcanoes erupted. "I *should* go back and teach them all a lesson. Hyp-ocrites and liars! Deliberately twisting a god's words. Hypocrites and liars!" Christ banged his golden cane on the massive floorboards, sending sharp splinters of light everywhere, and Zeus said soothingly, "Forget it. It's all passed now. And don't go into a tantrum. You'll make it rain in—where is it? Ohio? Last time you carried on, they had a flood."

"That's nothing compared to what you did in Greece, and the entire Mediterranean, for that matter," Christ said, recovering. But then he shook his great head, untended graying curls cascading to the shoulders of his slightly stained sky-blue robe. "Still, it's sad," he said. "This whole place is just filled with old gods. Half of them have forgotten who they are. And no one comes to visit except those whiny petitioners. Bad enough, they call me by my first name."

"You always did get depressed easily," Zeus said. "We'll rouse again. You wait and see. And if one of us does, we all do, of course."

Into the splendidly appointed solarium came a dark, bent-over, totter-ing but massive figure of a goddess; gray hair kinky and wiry with leaping electricity; eyes a fury of autumnal ecstasy; ponderous yet so compelling in her mood of dejection that the whole room momentarily darkened. Christ and Zeus eyed each other with a worried air. Zeus coughed apologetically as he always did when Hera, his wife, came out of her private quarters: She was quite insane. She thought she wasn't a god at all. She even believed she was human on bad days (which lasted for centuries, of course).

"She doesn't have a believer left, poor thing," Zeus said.

Hera sat down in the thronelike rocking chair with silver gliders; her face darker than the deepest twilight. She stared out the multidimensional windows for a while, then said finally, "It's you two who are mad. We aren't gods and goddesses. We never *were*. We were all deluded. I'm the only sane one here. You're obsessed: Christ, with his Crucifixion; you, dear husband, with your claims of power; Mohammed with his magic sword, and all the rest. And Christ keeps seeing the head of John the Baptist on a platter, carried by one of the dancing girls. Divine delusions! Obsessions! Sad enough that you've deluded yourselves, but world upon worlds! I can't bear to think about it. If it wasn't that I had Pegasus for company, I *would* lose what mind I have left."

And when she said his name, Pegasus appeared, his huge wings decorously folded over his sleek horse's back. He'd been galloping to keep in shape for the best part of the century, and now he sauntered over to Hera, smiling with his fine horse teeth. "Still talking about the same old thing? You all need exercise. You know, that's your trouble; you need a good workout." He strutted slightly but nicely and added, "I don't mean to brag either, but being a god and an animal both does seem to give me certain advantages."

Absentmindedly Hera stroked Pegasus' hide, while Zeus turned speculative eyes toward Christ. "Suppose Hera's right? he said. "I mean, suppose her insanity carries a certain understanding of issues . . . ?"

"Of course she's right and utterly wrong at the same time," Christ replied.

Zeus frowned his famous frown. "Now you sound like Buddha," he said irritably. "He can't give a proper yes or no answer either. He's never even made up his mind if he likes existence to begin with."

Pegasus' divine animal nature got the best of him. Gently he disentangled his mane from Hera's stroking fingers and said heartily, "Forgive me. This closed-in atmosphere really gets on my nerves. And I don't give a hoot if people remember *me* or not, though it's nice when someone does. I can always go out and gallop beneath the stars and nibble the grasses. And I'm only sorry you can't do the same."

"He probably doesn't gallop at all, but uses his wings the minute he's out of sight," Christ muttered sourly.

Pegasus heard the remark, but ignored it. In his more sardonic moments he thought that it was his animal nature rather than his divine one that was his salvation, for it was the creature part of him that delighted in details, yet basked in a kind of generalized diffused good spirits that could also be quite gargantuan. Now, outside for example, he could appreciate the tiny trembling of the earth beneath his hooves, sense the dirt sliding beneath the surface—small earthslides that slightly shifted the tunnels in which the cool worms slid—and enjoy the summer moon that ever so slightly lightened the roots of the grasses, its rays traveling downward, staining the sliding underground worms with the slightest tint of silver.

Yet he could, when he wanted, use his wings to soar into the skies; and mentally to send his spirit into realms that were extraordinary even in divine terms. Now he nibbled the grass thoughtfully: There was something in the air—a hint of a change—a foreign scent. He perked up his ears. Extraordinary! There were visitors on the ledges below!

The other gods frequently got lonely. On several occasions they'd gone on pilgrimages to find some followers, but each time, unfortunate circumstances cut short their journeys. Again, being the god of inspiration gave him another edge, Pegasus mused, because his own thoughts were as lively as any company, mortal or divine. In fact, he often thanked his thoughts for their vivid and companionable nature. But now there would be a banquet perhaps, some cheer; excellent conversation and surcease from the eternal boredom of the other gods. No, boredom wasn't the right word, Pegasus thought. The gods were never really *bored*. It was just that they didn't feel wanted anymore. They'd been put out to pasture, so to speak. They really didn't have any duties to perform.

He didn't either, in the old accepted manner. But he had his robust animal nature, and someone or other was always asking for inspiration, even if they didn't know where it came from. Actually, Pegasus mused as he trotted along, he was called upon in one way or another a good deal of the time, but people often forgot his animal characteristics, or worse, his playful ones. "Ah, well." Pegasus neighed, and headed toward the visitors.

Oversoul Seven heard the hoofbeats first, and cupped his ear. While Pegasus was still in the distance, he neighed a welcome so as not to startle anyone. He reveled in the sound himself, for it was the quintessence of each and any and all horses neighing in greeting and triumph. He stomped up and down, the magnificent muscles luxuriating in each motion. He neighed again, aware of his fine form beneath the Olympian sky, while the full moon shone brightly on all the peaks and ledges.

"What on earth was *that*?" Lydia gasped.

"Why, it sounded like a gigantic horse, or a hundred horses," Josef said, growing uneasy.

Pegasus came slowly and majestically out of the shadows. His godlike, animal-like natures merged so perfectly that even Oversoul Seven just stood there for a moment, staring. Barnyards of Earth's past and present and future joined in Pegasus' form, so that before Seven's and Lydia's and Josef's eyes rose images of barns and meadows and wars and battlegrounds: There were horses bravely carrying men, forgetting their own terrors as swords flashed and cannons roared; horses hitched to plows tilling the earth; the odors of manure and grass and grain all intermingled. All of this was sensed in one way or another by Seven, Lydia, and Josef, until the animal part of Pegasus alone was godlike in proportions. But besides this, yet rising from it, Pegasus' divine attributes became natural and physical — nature knowing itself as a horse, glorifying in power and speed and filled to the brim with creaturehood.

Lydia, who had never been a horsewoman, was terrified at first. Josef, who loved horses, was awed, and almost appalled by his own reactions. He identified with Pegasus' sense of power, imagined the beast galloping down dark hills, and he shuddered, almost dizzy with elation. Oversoul Seven wasn't just elated: He was steadied and restored. His earth nature had seemed to grow new roots in the few moments since the arrival of Pegasus. Seven smiled: Suddenly he understood Lydia's need for a place of her own in the universe, and he felt himself as the earthroot soul out of which all of his personalities emerged. At the same time, he experienced a rush of almost unendurable sorrow. It vanished almost at once, but lasted long enough for him to sense the sharp, private earth realities in which each human individual lived—

Seven was so fascinated by Pegasus, though, that he'd taken his attention away from Josef, who had just noticed Pegasus' wings and was muttering, shaken, "I never saw a horse with wings before." And for a moment, Josef's consciousness was in two places at once. Elgren Hosentauf said anxiously, "Hear that? Talking about a horse with wings! He's really delirious." They were unsaddling in the barnyard where the horse manure steamed in the cold air, and with great shouts and bustling they managed to get Josef inside, to the kitchen.

His mother-in-law yelled, "Quick, sit him here." She opened the oven, thrust Josef's legs onto the open door so that his feet were inside, took out the bricks she'd heated, covered them with rags, and placed them between Josef's body and the chair arms. The fire inside the stove was raging. She threw in more kindling.

All this time Josef kept opening and closing his eyes and muttering about the horse with wings. For a few moments, he didn't feel anything. Then the burning, tingling, itching sensation started beneath his woolen stockings, a sodden wet smelly odor rose, someone grabbed his feet and removed the stockings which had been nearly frozen to his feet before, and Josef snapped to.

He looked down to see his feet, distant purple swollen hulks that seemed to belong to someone else. His mother-in-law was trying to force hot cocoa down his throat. One of the cats, having sneaked in from the barns, jumped on his lap and was indignantly chased by a serving girl. "You damned nincompoop," Elgren began. "Trying a fool trick like that at a time like this." Josef moaned, closed his eyes again, and pretended to be unconscious so as to avoid the coming lecture.

∼ *Chapter Eight* ∼

Lydia Meets Christ Under
Very Unfortunate Circumstances

As Josef disappeared, Lydia cried, "I never *did* remind him that I'm supposed to be born as his daughter. The least he could do is remember that."

"He's just absent-minded," Oversoul Seven muttered. He was trying to discover how Josef was making out at home and listen to Lydia at the same time.

"You seem to be having difficulties," Pegasus said politely. "May I be of help?"

Lydia frowned. "You're only part of a myth come to life," she said sternly. "I remember . . . Pegasus, the god of inspiration—"

"Yes, I helped you often, even though I didn't use this form," Pegasus answered. "You're lucky that I'm one of the gods you believed in, even if your ideas about me were a little confused."

"You're not going to claim credit for all the poetry I wrote in my last life, I hope," Lydia said tartly.

"Are *you?*" Pegasus asked, smiling.

Lydia started to say, "Well, of course. Who else?" when she remembered having often felt that her poetry was hers and not hers at the same time.

"You wrote it," Pegasus said, a bit smugly, "but I carried you out to the rarefied air where the poetry exists."

"All I really wanted to do *then* was write poetry," Lydia said, a bit crossly. "And all I want to do now is find the gods, if there are any—"

"Well, you've found one," Pegasus said, tapping one forefoot modestly enough in the grass.

Lydia tried not to sound disappointed. "I *have* known inspiration in one way or another, as you pointed out," she said. "And without meaning to hurt your feelings, I just didn't expect a god to be a horse. Divine or not, a horse is a horse, even one who speaks as well as you do. Your elocution is excellent," Lydia added, suddenly remembering that she'd also taught English once.

Oversoul Seven had been standing by, letting Lydia carry on, but now he interrupted nervously. "I suggest you end this conversation, Lydia," he said, "or you might regret it. Inspiration *can* be very tricky."

"Well, I'm certain I'd recognize a real god if I met one," Lydia was saying to Pegasus. "But even a horse with wings is a horse. I mean, wings don't necessarily mean divinity."

From nowhere, Seven heard Cyprus' voice: "You'd better remove some of Lydia's misconceptions quickly. They could lead to unnecessary complications."

"You must be kidding," Seven cried, mentally. "She's blindingly stubborn, and you know we have to do this *her* way—"

"But with guidance. And don't forget your practice teaching dream class!"

Seven didn't even have time to answer. He felt time wrinkle before it actually started to, and he knew that Lydia had gone too far.

He turned to her. She was saying, "I prayed for help during my darkest moments on earth, and no god answered."

"No, no, Lydia," Seven cried. "Change the subject. Fast!"

But she was staring defiantly at Pegasus. "In my darkest moments," she repeated. "And no one answered."

"Are you sure?" Pegasus asked; and the transition was so fast that even Oversoul Seven was startled. He heard time crinkle and Lydia's pilgrimage suddenly turned into a nightmare. He saw at once (in blessed hindsight, Cyprus said later) exactly what happened: Lydia had returned to one of her last life's worst, darkest moments.

Nearing death, she sat in a wheelchair in the solarium of the nursing home in which her grown children had placed her. She frowned, looking out the wide windows down to the hills below. She was strapped into the chair; drugged, but she felt drunk, bleary, so dizzy inside that she could have been guzzling liquor at some wild party for days. Yet, she knew, she'd been nowhere. She hadn't left the old people's home: That much was clear.

It was also clear that, wheelchair or no, she'd been somewhere, involved in some kind of mind-traveling that she couldn't understand.

"Time for our pills, sweetie," said the nurse, Mrs. Only.

"I'd like to sweetie her," Lydia thought, in a rage. The rage itself was vitally strong, though its energy didn't budge her arms or legs, which once would have reacted.

"Open our mouth now," Mrs. Only said, with a kind of threatening sweetness.

"Like hell I will," Lydia said to herself, but in utter surprise she felt her jaws drop open, slackly; felt the pill go sliding down that soft but somehow distant tunnel that didn't seem to have anything to do with *her* at all—though again, she knew that once it had.

She stared: The twilight was laid out before the windows. Down the hill, the lights of a gas station glinted. At least, she thought, it always *had* been a gas station and normal enough. But now she looked with sardonic curiosity—the flying red horse on the neon sign was lifting a foreleg, gently stepping out onto the first shining shelf of air. And he was taking off, wings stirring the early night clouds in ripples; *neighing*. How was it that no one else seemed to hear? She grinned, at least mentally, because she couldn't tell if her lips actually moved at all. But there were farms nearby. She imagined the flying horse neighing to all those farm horses below; liberating them, giving them wings too, so that hundreds of horses just flew off in the middle of fields while startled farmers watched aghast.

Seeing all of this mentally, she shook her head. The pills, she supposed; they were making her crazy. For a minute she strained at *her* bonds, just when the magic horse flew off the gas station sign—but by the time the whole thing was over, she just sank back, struck by desolation. Dimly her predicament came through to her. Not only was she tied up, legally shut up so that there was no justice to resort to, but the world itself was all changing. Nothing was permanent anymore; either it was the result of the goddamned drugs they gave her, or they knew this happened and they didn't want the old people to tell the young ones. The secret was that the world really changed all the while, and that when you dropped out of it, you saw the truth.

"Oh, Lydia, that's it but not it at the same time," Seven exclaimed. "You don't have to re-experience the nursing home." But Lydia didn't hear him, because when she was alive she didn't believe she had a soul, and so Seven just waited for an opportunity to free her whatever way he could.

Maybe when you died, things cleared up again, she thought, but she doubted it. Her ideas rolled down the hill of her mind so quickly that she could only catch a few of them. The rest disappeared. Where did they go? "Dinnie-din time," said Mrs. Only, coming close with a dinner tray.

Lydia tried to rearrange herself more comfortably.

"Be careful. Don't dump all the hot food now," Mrs. Only said in a terrible voice.

Lydia looked down to see the plate on her lap, the heat of the food rearousing her thighs. Mrs. Only unstrapped her for eating but Lydia didn't want any of their goddamned food. It took all of her will power — she collected herself, for parts of her seemed off in their own unknown places — but she focused precisely and brilliantly, gripped the insides of her own muscles, directed them as deliberately as she ever had, and sent the tray — plate, silverware, cream pitcher, and all — flying.

Then, satisfied, she sat back and tried to say, crisply, "That's what I think of your damned drugged food," but her lips and mouth seemed to turn into cotton, making soft white fluffy sounds that said nothing. "Dear God," cried Lydia inside her mind.

Mrs. Only was picking up the food when Lydia noticed something else, a change in her fellow patients. They'd been beside her all the while in their chairs, but she ignored them. They always ignored each other when the nurses were around, pretending to be dumber than they were. So she'd also ignored their background whining. But now their voices no longer whispered, but suddenly turned full and real and vital. And damn near thunderous; damn near louder than any thunder she'd ever heard.

"True resurrections are the kind we just observed," Christ said. His eyes glowed dimly.

"Who on earth are you?" Lydia gasped, noticing that she was speaking normally for a change.

"Jesus Christ," Christ said cordially.

"And Zeus, at your service," said Zeus.

How was it that she could speak properly, Lydia wondered, ignoring her companions as new patients. "Everybody thinks they're gods here," she said finally, admiring the tone of her own irony. How was it that suddenly she could think clearly too?

"Of course," Zeus answered. "We all are."

"You all *think* you are," Hera said, entering the room and sitting down, spreading her gigantic velvet skirt over the gold divan. "They're . . . divinely touched," Hera said to Lydia. "Quite mad though I admit, in a charming fashion. Without their obsessions, who would they be, after all? Or are they really senile gods?"

Lydia didn't dare say anything.

"And you don't have to look so dreadful, do you?" Hera asked. "Do change yourself into someone more pleasant. Even if Christ and Zeus aren't really gods, they *do* think that they are, and I try to treat them accordingly."

Lydia looked down at herself to see the spilled food crusting on her nightgown.

"Here, dear," Hera said, handing Lydia a silver mirror.

Lydia looked, shocked, to see her old face — a bony, wrinkled, yet satisfying face, but one filled with bitterness, anger, and dismay. Even in her bewilderment Lydia realized that *here,* dissatisfaction was somehow out of place. "What do you expect me to do?" she asked. "This is how I look. This is me."

"It's just *one* you, dearie," Hera said, with just the gentlest touch of displeasure. "Come now, change for dinner."

"Fish from Galilee," Christ said.

"The finest geese from Rome, a banquet fit for the gods," Zeus said.

"Do change," Hera coaxed, and Lydia stared, for in the mirror she saw her own face, seven years old and pouting. Instantly she remembered the moment: First grade. She'd thrown a temper tantrum and the teacher forced her to look into a mirror at her own angry face until she herself was forced to laugh. Now those earnest, self-righteous, furious young eyes glared out at her; so freshly, innocently outraged that Lydia wanted to cry. The child's face was so . . . cosmically funny, so comic in ways that she felt but couldn't understand, that Lydia suddenly grinned at the child's mirror face.

"That's so much better," Hera (and the first-grade teacher) said.

And — Lydia gasped again — because the child she had been, saw *her:* the old woman, grinning, and it was *that* face all wrinkled yet sunny that the child saw and liked; the face that had forced her to laugh and forget her tantrum.

The mirror's surface wrinkled. The child's face vanished. Lydia was seeing a dignified, funny, perfectly old smiling face that was her own.

"There, that wasn't hard, was it?" Hera (and the first-grade teacher) said. "You can change the wheelchair too," Hera suggested gently as she rearranged her own gown and added a summer wrap.

Lydia was so confused that she didn't know what she was doing. She stared down to see that she was no longer tied to the chair, but that was because they'd untied her for dinner. Wasn't it?

"Do help her, Christ," Hera said.

Christ leaned forward graciously. "Do you understand who I am?" he asked.

Lydia squinted at him uneasily. Was he the old man next to her in the nursing home, a senile old coot like herself? Or was he an old Christ, such as she'd never seen in pictures or read about in the Bible? In any case, she decided, he was nice; so why hurt his feelings? "You're Christ," she said, sighing.

"Verily," Christ answered. "And I say to you that you are you, whether you're young or old or male or female at any given time. You don't have to be old and sick right now . Certainly not *here*. Or there, either. So turn into the image that you like best."

"And then maybe we can get on to dinner," Zeus muttered. But Lydia didn't hear him. She was staring at Christ. He sounded so absurdly *sure*. His gray-white curls quivered with conviction as he nodded his head. His brown eyes didn't blink. They were wide open with that innocent look the very senile get. He wanted her to change her image so badly; she hated to break his heart.

"Daughter," he said.

And she suddenly was a daughter in fact! That is, she was young, glowing, incredulous.

"That was beautifully done, Christ," Hera said.

"Yes, I still have the old touch," Christ answered. He rubbed his wrinkled hands together with obvious satisfaction.

"Well, let's get on with dinner, then," Zeus shouted. He clapped his hands and a table appeared, loaded with delicacies. "Now that everyone's settled, what did you come here for?" he asked, reaching out not too gracefully toward a leg of mutton.

Lydia looked up to answer and she paused in bewilderment. Suddenly his eyes were young and hearty—and very, very familiar. They belonged to Oversoul Seven and just as Lydia realized *that,* that scene vanished and everything came back to her. "Whatever happened?" she cried. "Oh, that was terrible. I relived one of the darkest moments—"

"And you asked for help and got it," Seven replied. "Something you'd conveniently forgotten. I had a bad enough time myself, waiting until I could get through to you. Now I'm exhausted. Besides that, I have an appointment that I'm not looking forward to at all: a dream class with a student who is particularly difficult." He wanted to say, "Just like you," but he didn't. For one thing, Lydia's mistakes were at least exciting, and for another, he was too wise to start an argument. Instead he said, "I've been so involved in your difficulties that I completely forgot someone else who needs me badly. Well, I *almost* forgot," he amended, in case Cyprus was listening.

Seven had whisked Lydia out into one of the endless corridors that connected the various areas of the Gods' Rest Home. "Can I trust you to just wait here until I get back?" he asked. "Anyhow, you need to be alone awhile to digest your experiences."

Lydia was so glad to be healthy and strong again that she just nodded. There were some more things Seven wanted to say to her, but as he began to speak, the environment began to change; or rather, he was moving out of it. "Lydia, don't forget that—" he began, but Lydia didn't hear him, of course.

∼ *Chapter Nine* ∼

Oversoul Seven's Student, Will,
Wants to Drop Life Class

"W hat did you say?" asked Seven's student, Will, because Seven's words to Lydia were actually spoken in the dream classroom to which Seven was unceremoniously swept.

"Sorry I'm late. I was talking to someone else," Seven muttered, catching his breath. "Now, let's run through the world's problems one more time." He tried not to look at the hallucinatory school clock that hung on the equally unreal but definite walls of the dream classroom. Practice teaching wasn't his cup of tea, but he'd resolved not to be a clock-watcher either. When he thought the words "cup of tea," pleased with his use of earth vernacular, a cup of tea *did* instantly appear on a china saucer next to the copy of the textbook, *The Physical Universe As Idea Construction.*

"That cup of tea shouldn't be there," shouted Will at once. "It isn't a primary construction." He was a husky young man, smiling (or so it seemed to Seven) with unnecessary satisfaction.

"I was testing you," Seven said quickly. "You're quite right: The tea was the result of a stray thought that I deliberately allowed prominence. Just to show you . . . how inappropriate earth conditions can *seem* to appear for no reason."

"Bullshit," exclaimed the young man. "If you'll forgive me, you just made a mistake and now you're trying to cover it up!"

"There *are* no mistakes," Seven said, more sternly than necessary. "If you remembered that, you wouldn't still be in this class, and you wouldn't need me as a private tutor."

"I wish *you'd* remember that, Seven!" The voice, heard only by Seven, belonged to Cyprus, who was monitoring Seven's performance with Will. She was invisible, while Seven had adapted the image of a young man just out of graduate school. Seven said mentally to Cyprus, "Remember that this is my first practice teaching of a dream class, will you? 'Practical Living: The Formation of Private and World Conditions' — well, that's a pretty big subject from *any* point of view."

Cyprus didn't answer.

"Again, there are no mistakes," Seven said to Will. Absent-mindedly, he took a sip of the tea and grinned, despite himself. "Actually the tea is delicious," he said. "So this is an example of how a *seemingly* trivial mistake can result in a positive experience if you don't police your thoughts too rigidly."

Cyprus groaned, symbolically speaking. "That's called self-justification, whether or not what you said was true," she exclaimed.

Will didn't hear her, of course. He was standing up, leaning rather indolently against his desk. He smiled in a superior fashion (or so it seemed to Seven) and said, "Now you're justifying yourself again. I think I could teach this class myself if I didn't dislike the subject matter so much."

Silence.

"What an impeccable young man!" Cyprus said, but she smiled compassionately at Seven.

Seven sighed. "Will," he said, "you've taken the course three times before, I hear. You can't even pass it, much less teach it. So sit down."

Will shrugged angrily and sat down. Seven felt sorry for him then, so he sent over the rest of the tea. The cup sailed smoothly through the air, landing by Will's right hand. Seven projected a slice of lemon on the china saucer as an accompaniment and said, "Don't feel too badly. The construction of physical reality *is* an advanced course by many standards."

"If I don't pass this time, I'm going to bow out," Will grumbled. "I told you that before."

"You need permission to drop a course once you've signed up, and I hate paperwork, so forget it," Seven replied, quickly.

"Then give me a passing grade and get rid of me," Will yelled. As he reacted to Will's anger, Oversoul Seven automatically changed his image.

What Will needed was a father figure, Seven thought, and in a flash he turned into one — an old man wearing a mantle, sandals, and brown robe.

"Ultimately your teacher doesn't grade you: You grade yourself," Seven (as the old man) said. "Come now; you're very creative and filled with energy. Don't be so impatient with yourself."

Will calmed down some, but he stood up, frowning. "This kind of thing always happens in these classes," he said. "The teacher keeps changing into you, or vice versa. I like you better, though, I'll say that. He's too near my age to know much more than I do."

"So *that's* it," Seven said.

"Well, at least you're old enough to have learned something," Will replied. Then, suspiciously, "Am I awake or dreaming? I'm never sure of that, either, when I'm here."

"Both," Seven answered. "You should know that by now."

"Know? I don't *know* anything," Will blurted. "And besides, I think that Physical Reality is a lousy course."

"Then why did you take it to begin with?" Seven asked. He almost turned back into the young graduate teacher, but caught himself just in time.

"To prove I could do it, that's why," Will yelled.

In consternation, Seven forgot himself and called out to Cyprus, "Did you hear that?" Then, to Will, he said as calmly as he could, "That's your trouble right there. You don't have to prove yourself to anyone; including yourself!"

Before Will could answer, Cyprus materialized, and for once Will just stood there silently, staring; for with Cyprus' image an indefinable sense of power and assurance came to him. Suddenly he *knew* that he was somehow secure despite all of his difficulties; yet he couldn't tell for the life of him who stood before him.

For one thing, Cyprus reminded him of his mother and his sister, not as they were, necessarily (for they often annoyed him), but as he wished they might be. At the same time, Cyprus seemed to be someone else — the woman (not girl) that he often dreamed of meeting and falling in love with. All of these images were merged in the woman he saw before him, so that it was impossible to separate them. And, for reasons he didn't understand, Will felt more and more assured.

"You're the feminine principle? Or the female muse? Or" — he snapped his dream fingers — "Mother Goddess? I *do* have considerable education on earth," he said, when she didn't answer. "I'm not as stupid as I sometimes seem."

Amazing, thought Seven as he watched, for now Will looked nonchalant and even half insolent. He strolled over to Cyprus. "You *are* damnably attractive, whoever you are," he said. And the closer to her he came, the more powerful and assured he felt.

Yet suddenly he stopped and felt that he should go no further. At the same time, an image opened in his mind so that he *saw* himself—foolishly strutting, petty somehow—approaching what?

The image of the woman blurred, but grew larger at the same time, and he could feel some peak of intensity moving within it. "You *are* the female principle!" he cried, unable to stop himself, even while some part of him knew instantly that he was wrong. But even as he yelled out, he'd approached too closely. He was suddenly in the midst of an incredible calm that gripped him—that is, he could feel the calm's edges holding his mind, or trying to. He told himself frantically that dreams often went from the ludicrous to the horrible, while at the same time he wondered what was so awful about accepting this . . . terrible calm assurance? Why was he frightened of it? Because it was his own, beyond male or female connections, the vast security in which he had his being. But it was too gigantic, he thought despairingly, and when he said that, or rather yelled it out loud, it was all over. He was sitting up in bed, in a cold sweat.

A strange calm filled the room, and he stared about suspiciously. Was there an odd white-grayish mist against the usual night darkness? Or was that the effect of fog and the open window? Nervously, he reached for a joint.

"He half glimpsed us," Cyprus said. "Whenever he lets himself feel the dimensions between fact and fiction, then he's able to sense other realities."

"You were too hard on him," Seven said moodily. "He couldn't identify with his own vitality, really. He'd treat it like an enemy."

"Or call it the female principle," Cyprus said, smiling.

Still more moodily, Seven said, "I don't like practice dream teaching much, either."

"Is there anyone here?" Will asked. He was half awake, staring into the darkness, and speaking mentally.

"Nobody. Go to sleep," Seven answered.

"That's good because I just had a *scare*. A near nightmare," Will said, thinking that he was holding a mental dialogue with himself. He stood up, naked, and walked to the window.

"He's beautiful," Seven said to Cyprus. "Look at that healthy body; that pose—"

Will *was* posing and aware of his world-weary expression, dark brows lowered thoughtfully, as he savored his young-man-alone-in-the-world stance. What an unusual experience he'd just had! Obviously he was brilliant and psychic to have had such events happen at all, even if they *were* dreams. Yet he even felt that his pose was a pose or as if *any* emotion he felt would be bound to be vaguely . . . manufactured. Or perhaps he was actually far more assured and confident than even he knew? Anyhow, he thought, he did feel better than he had before he went to bed. He decided to grin philosophically, and he did.

"Will he remember anything important?" Seven asked.

"Not too many details, but I hope that he'll begin to sense his own vitality more. It will take a while for him to correlate what he's learned, though, because it can't be vocalized."

"*Did* he learn anything?" Seven asked dejectedly. "Sometimes I wonder—"

"Did *you* learn anything? That's more to the point," Cyprus answered. "I helped you out with Will this time, but from now on, you're on your own with him. Remember, you chose this experience yourself too, even though there are some things that you have to forget on purpose for a while. So tell yourself that you'll know how to help Will—and you *will!*"

She and Seven had both turned into points of light. Seeing them, Will thought that they were reflections from the neon sign of the all-night supermarket across the way. The lights flashed back and forth from his fingertips, as he drummed them up and down on the windowsill.

~ *Chapter Ten* ~

Jeffery's Notes and
Questions Without Answers

I haven't had time to write here, because I've been so busy with "The Further Education of Oversoul Seven," and except for my academic work, my life now almost seems organized about the book. In my sleep sometimes part of a chapter will suddenly awaken me, so I've taken to keeping a notebook by the bedside. Otherwise the "writing" takes me about three hours a night. I sit down; the words and sense of exhilaration come, some part of me gets carried away by what is being written, and all sense of time vanishes.

Of course, I've told no one what I'm doing. The fact is that I don't know what odd venture this is that I've embarked upon. I'm certainly not writing "Education" in usual terms. I have no idea what is going to happen next to the characters. For that matter, I have no idea where the words themselves are coming from. The concepts involved are hardly to be taken seriously, but as fantasy I suppose they're acceptable enough. In any case, this certainly involves me in the oddest behavior, and so I've decided to study everything that happens as closely as possible.

My sanity does not seem threatened as I first suspected. Nothing else in my life has altered (so far, Jeffy-boy, I remind myself). Well, to be more honest, nothing in my *exterior* situation has changed. I do have the impression that my dreams are different than they used to be, more numerous perhaps, and colorful. I haven't remembered any dreams, however, though as mentioned I have awakened with portions of this manuscript suddenly just here, as if freshly minted.

I try to look at the script objectively and then work backward, trying to figure out what kind of person would ordinarily write this kind of book; and I'm as far from being that kind of person as anyone I know. Or is the unconscious that playful and creative? That is, could the manuscript be the result of my own unconscious productivity? I can't really accept such a thesis, since I'm not at all convinced that the unconscious operates in such a manner. I've always thought of it as containing the suppressed, primitive, unsavory aspects of the self that, quite rightly, we've been conditioned to repress. The conditioning process: Everything must return to that basis. And somewhere, in that framework, there must be an answer to my current experience. Yet—nothing in my own background seems to present an adequate explanation.

I am trying a small experiment. A few days before the manuscript "began," I'd started taking vitamin C. Surely I see no connections. Nevertheless, today I began accelerating the dose of vitamin C to ascertain if there is any resulting alteration in my production of the book. Perhaps in a way that we don't understand, some vitamins cause an overstimulation of certain hormones that further trigger the creative abilities. I don't for the moment believe this, but I refuse to discount such a theory either.

One thing in particular bothers me: Why does the material come all prepared, without any conscious work on my part at all? And why do I have the feeling that "someone" is giving it to me? Well, I finally admitted it: More and more I become aware that there is a personified source behind the manuscript. Is such a feeling only the conscious mind's astonishment with the products of the unconscious processes? This is the most likely explanation, of course. Yet, granting that the unconscious has such abilities— and I'm not at all certain that it does— then why are they showing in my life now, suddenly, and never before?

I'm not doubting the unconscious origin of creativity, but I'm almost certain that conditioning directs its activity. Each act must have its reason, but the reason may simply be the reaction to learned sequences of nerve patterns. So my acts must, it seems to me, be the result of *some* kind of conditioned response.

I don't like it. We had a cat when I was a boy. He came without being called, when he heard the noise of the can opener. He was conditioned: He knew that the sound of the can opener, when it wasn't family mealtime, meant food for him—because we never fed him when we ate. Then, what "conditions" me to sit down and "get" that book each evening after a full day teaching? What element out of my past is wielding the can opener? And what kinds of learning processes are taking place?

Ridiculous rubbish — the last paragraph. Yet, granting the validity of conditioning and the learning aspects of behavior, there is no other alternative except that the answers to my experience lie in those directions.

Thus far I've ignored the contents of the manuscript, being by nature more fascinated by processes than by art; so the process of the book's production fascinates me, while the contents can best be judged by storytellers. Yet a few disquieting thoughts have come to me involving the book's scenes or characters and, try as I will to dismiss them, they keep returning to my mind. For the record, I'll try to put these unfortunate musings in some kind of order.

For one thing, the book's description of the rest home of the gods instantly reminds me of Ram-Ram and his Queen Alice at the mental institution. Even the "gods" are reminiscent of the inmates who seemed to regard me with such annoying condescension when I visited Ram-Ram. I don't even know why such a correspondence comes to mind, or why it makes me more uneasy than I'm willing to admit.

The descriptions of the gods in the book thus far don't bother me at all, of course. How can one get upset over the actions or conditions of mythic characters? I refuse to define my own position on the "gods" or "God," for that matter, in any religious terms at all. That is, the word "atheist" presupposes the existence of a God, if only in the minds of others. I myself believe in a chance universe and in Darwinian principles; and in that framework, the idea of a God (or gods) cannot enter, though some evolutionists try to eat their cake and have it too by inserting a Divinity who set the universe and evolution into motion. In any case, for all of those reasons, the descriptions of the gods do not offend me; only the curious correspondence between their environment and Ram-Ram's quite real institution.

But, just lately, a new issue caught my attention, or riveted it, to be more accurate. So here I will record my uneasy feelings about the chapter just previous to these notes. The first time Will, the young man, was introduced in the classroom dream sequence, I felt a most unwelcome sense of identification with him. For one thing, I wrote the introductory passages or, rather, took them down just after tutoring a particularly difficult student. As I started my nightly writing stint, a small shock went through me to find that Oversoul Seven was also tutoring a student. I shrugged and went on taking down the words that came — as the manuscript has, to date — as fast as I can type.

It was a muggy evening. The window was open, letting in a late February heavy air. Below my windows, a few groups of students or professors and their wives went by; their footsteps coming up to me with a curious intensity, undoubtedly carried, I thought, by the humidity. Someone went to the garbage cans and opened one. The lid as it was slammed down on the ground sounded so loud to me that I might have been standing beside it. It seemed as if the contents of my own mind were clattering.

If I remember properly, I got goose pimples. At the same time, however, I was typing the dream class sequence and my identification with the character, Will, grew quite insidiously. I was never aware of any . . . transition of consciousness, for example, yet by the middle of that chapter, in my mind at least, I was almost speaking Will's lines. I was speaking for him or he was speaking for me; it's impossible for me to express this clearly.

Nothing in the manuscript said so, but I was somehow certain that Will's threat to bow out of the course was actually a threat of suicide. Yet the main character, Oversoul Seven, hardly seemed concerned, so why should I be?

Another connection hit me when Will saw Cyprus as the feminine principle — for when he did, *I* saw my ex-wife, Sarah, in my mind's eye, almost as clearly as I've ever seen her, physically. It came to me that I'd refused Sarah a child — as I mentioned earlier, she's pregnant now by another man — because I saw no reason to bring another vulnerable human being into such a chaotic existence. And if I'm right about Will, then he sees no reason to continue his *own* life. Perhaps I am making too much of all of this, and I do note with some humor that Will was at least rational in his dismissal of life as meaningful, feeling no idiotic compulsion to search for any gods or divine varieties.

For that matter, now that I think more deeply, there *is* a rational reason, if only a small one, for my sense of identification with Will. For he does remind me somewhat of myself in my own undergraduate days, even though any young student probably has certain characteristics that a grown adult might find reminiscent. My body is rather stocky, not unattractive, but it has none of the grace that seems to be assigned to Will's, and I was never that nonchalant or charming or contemptuous. I was too aware of my pompousness, for one thing, even though I couldn't do anything about it then. Or now. But I feel almost threatened in any case by that identification. I didn't like my own participation, emotionally, in the chapter. And I admit that I'm rather abashed at the small coincidence that set me off on this tangent: My full name is Jeffery *William* Blodgett.

I have the sneaking suspicion that the book is playing a trick on me; that "someone" knew I would be discomforted by such a similarity of names. Furthermore, I suspect that the "someone" may be watching for my reactions.

So except for these notes, I refused to react. I took down the entire chapter as if nothing bothered me at all; as if I had not participated in the scenes; as if the sounds from below the window didn't sound unreasonably loud and intense; as if I wasn't suddenly struck by the frightening feeling that my own living room was as hallucinatory in nature as Oversoul Seven's classroom. And of course my thoughts were accompanied the entire time by the sound of my typing fingers, which, as if thinking by themselves, pounded out the words with amazing rapidity. It takes me far longer, for example, to type up these notes of mine, and I'm uncomfortably aware of the stiffness of my own prose.

I do wish Will hadn't been introduced into the manuscript, because surely this means that he'll return in other chapters. Now there is no doubt that the book will continue. In the beginning I told myself that each chapter would be the last and I'd be left with an odd but brief psychological adventure and no more. At least I'm not fooling myself any longer in that regard. Now as I write these lines, I decide to close these notes for tonight, with some dismay, for I find myself in the peculiar position of worrying about a fictional character and wondering whether or not he might commit suicide.

No sooner did I write the last sentence when I "knew" that another chapter of "Education" was waiting. But how did I know? How *do* I know? I try to take a moment to examine my feelings, but already in my mind's eye I see myself tearing this page of notes out of the typewriter and inserting a new sheet of paper to begin the next installment.

I can, of course, decide to resist. I know that resistance is possible. So what is it that —

∽ *Chapter Eleven* ∽

Oversoul Seven Journeys to the Undersides of the Universe

Seven went wandering through the universe. He wanted to get away from everything he knew, and since he knew more all the time, he had to go further to get away. To do this, he just let himself go unmoored in any given reality, unrelated to any ideas of himself. As always, some odd inner motion began to take hold, support him, and carry him along. When this started to happen he always worried a bit, but nothing like he used to, and then the journey really began. He felt like a seed in the wind, blowing through universes but never landing.

Somewhere along the way he knew that his thoughts would start changing too, and he tried to catch this happening. First, it was like thinking backwards, and very confusing. Just when he seemed to get the knack of this, his thoughts turned around again, and it was like thinking sidewards. He was used to the fact that there was really no up or down to space. But now the up and down quality of his thoughts was gone too, and his sense of subjective direction. That is, thoughts just came — backwards, sidewards, from inside and outside — and none of them were particularly his or anyone else's.

He tried to navigate in all this, because it seemed that there should be one thought of his own to use as a kind of measuring stick. But he'd already let himself go, or begun the process; and at this point he didn't know how to reverse what he'd started. The thoughts came all at once, not one before the other, and then suddenly Seven got scared — or the part of him that still held on got scared — because the thoughts began to mix with each other.

One thought said, "This is the beginning," for example. The thought nearest to that one said, "This is the end," and the two sentences came simultaneously. Then the letters in one sentence mixed into those of the other one, and some part of Seven's mind went in and out, trying to keep track. But at the same time, all the other thoughts he heard started doing the same thing. And parts of Seven kept leaving him to follow those too, as they went jumbling and turning into completely different patterns.

This wasn't Seven's idea of getting away from it at all, and something else happened that had never happened before. The sentences that he heard now came in different languages, so that "This is the beginning" came in every language at once, and so did all the other sentences. He saw the letters mentally also. Before he got used to this — and the sentences switching to all of their language versions — the letters themselves grew bleary and began to shift and break away from each other, turning into waves and particles of light. Now and then one would explode, and the light from that fragment would turn all of the other particles into waves. But in the next moment they'd be particles again, like mosaics, glimmering in the universe, with darkness all around.

Seven blinked: The darkness wasn't at all stationary, but kept slivering off and falling into all of this particle and wave activity, until some of the letters were made of a glowing, brilliant darkness.

"There was light and there was darkness," Seven thought, or thought that he thought. How could there be light-darkness or darkness that was light? That would mean — But before he could finish, the light fragments and the dark-shining fragments changed places or turned into each other. Seven screamed with dismay and shouted with utter amazement all at once. Because suddenly he was on the other side of . . . what? His mind (or what was left of it), he thought (or tried to think), was different.

He'd been traveling far faster than the speed of light in usual terms, but now he discovered that once this happened, there was a sense of complete stillness that existed inside the incredible motion. He calmed down. He was lolling.

When everything went so fast that you could hardly follow, there was a new quiet plateau within or above the speed — if that was the word. Because now all the letters and sentences that he'd heard before just went lolling about too, like clouds, only they were broad waves now, shining, separated, flowing past each other without a care in the world.

Now who thought that last sentence, Seven wondered, and what world did it come from? He didn't recognize it as his own, or as anyone else's, for that matter. He was simply intrigued, watching all of the gentle motion, which he discovered had a slight sound, like the breaking of light into music or the notes that music comes from — and he suddenly felt himself doing just that.

Some tiny part of himself rode piggyback on the rest of him, which was definitely breaking up or falling apart. Not that he had a physical form, because he didn't, but his being had an intangible form and this was gently falling off in bits and pieces, tumbling out into long waves that now and then bunched together in particles, and all of this kept extending outward into — well, whatever was there. In so doing, Seven's consciousness flowed through the lot; rising and falling in the waves, bouncing and gently snapping back — all very enjoyable.

The waves and particles that were his kept flowing through others that weren't, though he didn't know who or what they belonged to. Only a strangeness flowed through him when this happened. It was "sometime later" before he realized that each time this happened, a bit of his consciousness mixed into those waves too, and a bit of the other streams most certainly flowed into him. How many others was he, then? Or how many others were him?

How on earth could you tell?

How on *what*?

Was that thought his?

Whose?

He'd gone to the other side of the universe, or to the other side of the inside of the universe, whatever that meant and whoever or whatever he was.

Was. This was the strangest thought he'd ever had. Nothing, he knew, was. Everything *is.* But where was he in this everythingness? And how did somewhere come from nowhere, drifting as he was, spread out into all those waves and particles, each spreading both light and sound? The sound disappeared but was always present. And Seven realized then that he'd quite disappeared. He doubted even Cyprus could find him. He was . . . dispersed.

He was hopscotching all over; or space was everywhere turning into what he was; or he was turning everywhere into what space was, and couldn't tell the difference.

What would happen if —

He shouted, "I am Oversoul Seven," and meant it?

And he did.

At once, or rather before at once, all the waves and particles stopped, wherever they were, for some had vanished beyond the dimensions of his knowledge or attention, fallen over horizons of being that he couldn't fathom. Yet the stopping was so fast and involved such motion that, like a rubber band snapping, particles and waves all moved one into the other, contracted, imploded, shrank, moved faster than light into a different kind of light—and threw Seven back to the side of the universe he'd left earlier.

"To say I was multidimensionally dizzy is an understatement," he said to Cyprus later, and as soon as he said the words he was struck with the meaning of "understatement." He had gone *under* statement; beneath it. He had unstated himself, at least briefly, and he said proudly to Cyprus, "I must have restated myself rather well, too, because here I am."

"Are you?" Cyprus asked gently.

Seven shook his head, figuratively speaking, and said, "I've just been through enough without you trying to confuse me further."

"All right," Cyprus replied. "I'll take pity on you and help you out. If instead of saying, 'Here I am,' you say, 'I am here,' and if you realize that *here* is a noun synonymous with *I,* then you've really learned something."

Seven knew that he'd really learned something vital in his other-side-of-the-universe adventure. He knew that he knew, but he didn't know how to make the knowledge available. Still, he tried. He said. "You're trying to tell me that where I am is always here. No, that isn't it. You're trying to tell me that here is where I am, no matter where that is." His voice trailed off. "No matter *what* it is?"

"No," Cyprus said. "You're making it hopelessly complicated." She paused, waiting. Seven felt as if she was drawing the knowledge out of him; as if she reached down into some invisible closet of wisdom he didn't even know he possessed, and was pulling this seed of knowledge upward. He felt very odd, as if he should go (down?) there and help her. So he did.

Everything that he had felt and sensed in his other side of the universe experience was happening all over again, only the waves and particles that spread out into unknowable horizons were . . . forming *his* consciousness, and his thoughts were growing out and up and emerging as his words to Cyprus.

"I am here," Seven shouted triumphantly. "Here always happens for me where I am. Or, here and I are one."

"So if Will decides to commit suicide, he takes his here with him," Cyprus said gently. "He turns into a new here, that then knows itself."

"And if Lydia doesn't decide to be reborn as Tweety? Or if she changes her mind?" Seven asked, and added, "Not that she *would,* of course."

"That's enough questions for now," Cyprus said. "For that matter, I'd see just what Lydia was up to if I were you. And Josef. And—"

"I'm going," Seven cried.

~ *Chapter Twelve* ~

A Mother-to-Be Gets a
Midnight Surprise

D ejectedly, Lydia wandered through the giant halls of the Gods' Rest Home, her footsteps echoing against the marble floors. She trailed her fingers along the mosaic walls as she passed, frowning vaguely at the gargoyles, busts, and statues of gods and goddesses that lined the hallway. She'd never been so lonely in her life, she thought; well, at least not in the last life, which was the only one she remembered clearly, and probably not in any of the others that she hadn't remembered yet.

Worse, she couldn't seem to make up her mind about anything — her age or sex or clothes. Now that she'd learned a few of Oversoul Seven's tricks, they weren't half the fun she'd expected. She changed into a male page, looking like an illustration she'd once seen in a history book; then into a young girl dancer in Turkish veils; then, bored, back to herself. But even as herself, she had all of those ages to contend with, and none of them contented her or seemed to fit: She wasn't a young girl, for example, without an old woman's knowledge, even if she could look that way. And she wasn't an old woman, with youth behind her forever, either. She was obviously both, and the more she thought about it, the more confused she became.

She supposed that she was out of line, trying to figure out the god business, but on the other hand, she knew that once she was reborn, she wouldn't have the time. Or maybe even the inclination. She was getting tired of pilgrimages, though, particularly since Oversoul Seven had left her alone. Suddenly she realized how important his company had become. She'd met no one since he left her, yet she knew that some people or inhabitants of some kind were invisibly about. Their presence was tantalizingly close and attractive. Now and then she almost heard laughter. Once she almost glimpsed faces. Yet she felt some strange psychological opaqueness, too, that separated her from . . . whoever they were.

Musing, Lydia came to a large window, the first she'd noticed in the long passageway. She paused, looking out, if "out" was the proper word, and what she saw struck Lydia through with nostalgia. There, spread out sparkling before her eyes, separated from her only by the window pane, was a snowy scene reminiscent of a Christmas card. An old-fashioned, dear scene, she thought, showing farmlands and white-topped mountains; a place where people lived one age at a time, and with only one image to contend with; tucked neatly between night and dawn, birth and death.

She pressed her nose against the window, wanting to cry, feeling at the same time like a coward for yearning — as she was now — for a new birth into space and time. Her eyes sprang open. Of course, she thought, that must be Josef and Bianka's farm! Otherwise why would she be so drawn to it?

More, she felt — again nostalgically — that she already knew each tree and shrub in the yard, each horse in the barn, as if in some indescribable past she'd already lived the life she hadn't yet begun. On the other hand, she was filled with expectation and curiosity, and with such a feeling of suspense that she held her breath; and when she let it out, it suddenly turned into frost against the window.

And the air was cold.

Lydia shivered and looked around anxiously. At once she knew that she was in the farmhouse. A young woman lay on a bed piled high with mattresses. It was apparently late at night. A fireplace in the corner had died out and only a few embers leapt up now and then in the darkness. The woman, nevertheless, was perspiring. She was muttering in her sleep, tossing her blonde-braided head swiftly back and forth, so that the ribboned blue night cap trembled.

Lydia tiptoed closer.

Could that be her future mother? The woman lay on her back, her huge stomach pushing up the coverlets. There were woolen rugs on the floor and a few smaller ones at the foot of the bed. A pitcher of water stood on the bedside table. Lydia nervously hallucinated a cigarette for herself, lit up, and poured herself a glass of water. Forgetting herself, she drank the real thing instead of hallucinating her own, but Bianka, still sleeping, never noticed.

"Damn," Lydia muttered. Bianka was lovely, but her own connections were with Josef. She would be her father's rather than her mother's daughter, in that respect. She prowled around the room, eyes narrowed, considering. Bianka's true labor, as opposed to the false one just passed, couldn't be put off forever.

Just then a motion caught Lydia's eye. She leapt back. Bianka's dream image moved easily up from the bed (pregnant and all) but light-footed and graceful.

"Who's there?" asked the dreaming Bianka.

Lydia froze. She had little experience in dealing with people's dream selves; and besides she was suddenly confused because in relationship to her twentieth-century life, Bianka had been dead for centuries. But the same applied to Josef, and she met him fairly often, she thought. And she was, after all, being born back into the past only from the very limited viewpoint of "the living."

She said softly, "It's Lydia. Well, it's really Tweety. I'm supposed to be born as your daughter."

"No. No. No," Oversoul Seven cried, suddenly appearing. "Look *younger*. You aren't born adult!"

Startled, Lydia turned into a three-year-old pudgy blonde-haired little girl with round face and unswerving earnest eyes.

"Oh," Bianka cried. She bent over, smiling.

But Lydia was suddenly frightened.

"Oh, you'll be my baby!" Bianka exclaimed. "And until now I wasn't really sure that I wanted a baby at all! But just to see you—"

Quickly Lydia turned back into herself. She strode toward Oversoul Seven. "Somehow you engineered this . . . somehow—"

"She had second thoughts too, but she doesn't have them now," Seven said, grinning and pointing at Bianka, who stood staring. She wore her nightgown and carried a hallucinatory candle.

"Well, I *still* have second thoughts," Lydia whispered angrily.

"Oh, I thought I saw my future baby," Bianka cried. Her dream image grew agitated, blurred, was drawn to her body on the bed and, crying, "I saw my baby," Bianka woke up.

"What? What?" muttered Josef from his cot in the hall where his mother-in-law had put him for the night. He struggled awake, hearing Bianka's cries through the door. He frowned, wiped his eyes. The bricks that they'd placed at his feet were cold. There were no windows in the hall, and he hated closed places. Bianka called again. He cursed, not too softly, sat on the edge of the cot and held his head. Besides everything else, he had a hangover. And he missed his own bed. The women had put him out to make room for the cousins, and even his wife seemed to belong to them, or to the house, or to the baby that was supposed to be coming — to anyone, in short, but him.

He got out of bed, put his robe on over his nightgown, and opened Bianka's door. The moonlight made a golden white path from the curtained window, reflecting on the kettles and pails that earlier had held boiling water. They sat on the floor by the cold fireplace now, with the light glittering on them; and the piles of rags and other cloths were neatly stacked and ready on the chair. Josef frowned; he'd decorated the chair himself, painted on the flower designs that Bianka wanted, and there it sat — blue and pink for the baby's room — if the baby ever came. And the chair reminded him of his own painting, and of the time wasted on the rosebuds, and of the hours yet to come when he'd fail in one way or another to do what he kept telling himself he was determined to do — become a good artist.

"Josef?" said Bianka in small voice. She was on the side of the bed away from the moonlight, so he could hardly see her at all. His head throbbed and his feet hurt, but at the sound of her voice, he blushed deeply in the darkness, in shame at his part in her predicament, in anger — after all, women were supposed to know how to handle such things more easily — and at his own unexpected response to her half-crying voice: He was sexually aroused. He remembered how long it had been since they'd really bedded, and before he could stop himself, he saw her in his mind's eyes as she had been: naked, and if not actually slim, well, not as fat as a pregnant cow. The comparison made him further ashamed of himself. He sat on the side of the bed.

"Here I am," he said glumly.

"I dreamed I saw our baby, only she was about three years old."

"*She?*" Josef stuttered, half because he always said he wanted a boy, and half because he was cold. Besides, conversation about the baby bothered him. He kept getting the feeling that he actually knew more about the affair than was good for him to know. Snatches of dream encounters with Lydia stirred in his mind.

"She looked like you," Bianka said, "Except that she was blonde-haired like me."

"If she looks like me, God help her," Josef said, snorting.

"Maybe it was a true dream. Maybe I really saw her — "

"Old wives' tales. It was just a plain dream," Josef said, more gruffly than he intended, because Bianka's dream actually made him uneasy in a way he couldn't fathom. His brown moustache bristled. He stared around, suspiciously.

"What are you looking for? The stork?" Bianka asked. She giggled suddenly. "You look so funny, so gruff. And scared."

"I'm not scared. Scared of what?" he demanded.

"Of being a father," she said, adding half coquettishly, "You should have thought of that before."

"Before what?" he asked, grinning but still uncomfortable in the big bed where he had to treat her as if she were a virgin instead of a wife. The goose-feather mattress softly followed her body contours. He imagined the two of them yelling and shouting in homey ecstasy. He reached out for her, stopped his hand in midair and, instead, lit the bedside candle. "I'll just be glad when we can do it again," he muttered.

"It? It? Do what?" she asked softly. She was growing drowsy. She wondered if the baby was sleeping inside her now. "It'll all be over soon," she said.

He didn't answer, though he wanted to; because, he brooded, she'd never really be the same again. She'd be nursing the baby for months, for one thing. He blushed, thinking of it, mentally seeing the full bared breasts, bodice-loosened. They'd cavort again, but not, he was sure, as they *had,* like merry damn puppies without a care in the world. His youth, at twenty-six, was gone, and hers at twenty-three. And they were lucky. But Christ, the trouble was that their youth wasn't gone. It kept lingering and wouldn't give up. "You'd do it in a minute if you could, wouldn't you?" he asked, feeling better momentarily. After all, he wasn't dead yet!

"I'm a born slut," she said sleepily; smiling because the phrase always cheered him up and made him feel more like an artist with his mistress than like a farmer with his wife. She half roused. It made her feel that way too.

Lydia said nervously, "Let's get out of here. I feel claustrophobic." She and Seven had been silently and invisibly standing there.

Josef managed a fake smile. He said, "Your mother gave me one of the straw cots to sleep on. She treats me like a kitchen hand."

"She does not!"

"Now, snuggling down in those goose feathers with you would be more like it." Josef joked because he thought it was the time for it, but he was growing tired.

"I don't think I can do it," Lydia said.

"Do what?" Seven asked, innocently.

"You know what. Be born again. Why can't people just be born at ten? Just arrive somehow, full-blown?"

"You better get out of here, though," Bianka said. "If my mother catches you in here now, she'll start yelling and you'll yell back. You aren't supposed to be in here until it's all over."

"If it's ever over," Josef exclaimed. "Do you feel the baby now? Is it kicking or anything?"

"I don't now, but I did. Oh God, did I! Now the baby's sleeping, I think."

"Maybe it will just go away," Josef muttered.

"Some father he'll make," Lydia said. "We make all these agreements when he's in the dream state, but he sure doesn't remember them when he's awake. And not all the time when he's dreaming, either."

Just then dawn streaked across the sky. A gray light filled the room. Sound came from downstairs. A cock crowed. "You'd better get back to the cot," Bianka cried.

Lydia disconsolately looked at Seven, then at the frost-coated window and beyond to the snowy hills. The activity downstairs quickened, and through the window Lydia saw Bianka's brother, Jonathan Hosentauf, go out to the barn, rubbing his glowed hands together, puffing out his cheeks. Smoke was coming from one of the chimneys, and Lydia suddenly realized that now she was looking at the entire scene from above, and that the scene was withdrawing, or she was withdrawing from it.

In the next second she found herself standing back in the long corridor with her face pressed to the gigantic sparkling window, the marble floors beneath her feet and the entire snowy scene so distant a view from the window that she could hardly make it out at all.

She looked around, almost peevishly. For one thing, Oversoul Seven was gone, which made her angry, and for another she felt even more indecisive than she had before. Did she really want to be reborn or not? She didn't know, and yet she wasn't pleased with the present situation either. Just thinking about it made her angrier, and at the same time she suddenly felt vehemently, wildly, independent. She was tired of going off willy-nilly. She wanted a place of her own, a point of familiarity she could always count on and return to, a place where even Oversoul Seven would be expected to knock first before entering.

She wanted —

And breathlessly, joyfully, she saw the transition taking place. She'd imagined a trailer by the ocean; herself, fairly young, there alone, writing poetry (not, as in her last life, marrying and having children, with poetry second-best), but going it alone as — funny, she thought — Josef wished sometimes that he had.

"Oh," she exclaimed, for the trailer grew up around her, formica-topped table in front of wide windows, a fake geranium partially faded but so homey, notebooks piled on the leather built-in benches. She peered out the window: The trailer was only feet from the water. "Oh, God!" She ran out, twenty and barefooted, so delighted that she thought she was—well, alive, and that the ocean would be visited by tourists at least occasionally, just when she felt like company. And she'd pretend that she had just one space and time to contend with. *And* she wasn't going to budge, she told herself, until she was good and ready.

~ *Chapter Thirteen* ~

Between Ages:
Lydia Meets Tweety
and an Old Love

*L*ydia sat in her trailer, glowering. The ocean at her doorstep sparkled in sunlight. A few palm trees were visible in the distance; she was drinking coffee and she *smelled* the aroma. She was gloriously, triumphantly young, having chosen to be twenty-three after hours of changing back and forth, studying the subtle differences between each age from twenty to thirty. She was inspired enough; at least she'd been writing poetry. The scene, her own image — everything was perfect, the epitome of everything she'd always wanted. But she wasn't happy.

Who would read her poetry, for one thing? She was lonely. Between worlds. She felt dissatisfied with herself, as if she were still wanting a certain kind of understanding; as if she were really only half aware of the realities about her. Now and then she sensed vast activity, all around her, but beyond her reach or perception.

Yet to be born again seemed to demand more courage than she possessed, she thought, and her pilgrimage to the gods was dependent upon Seven's help (for without him, she seemed to get nowhere in her search), and Seven had disappeared once again. She suspected that he was letting her stew in her own juices.

She had sons and a daughter still living, but it was difficult to understand that now, Lydia thought. They seemed like storybook people. That was because she related better to poetry and to the natural world than she did to her own family; it had always been hard for her to take people seriously.

"You'd better hurry up," a child's voice said.

"What?" Lydia stared out of the trailer window, seeing no one at first. In the next moment a small child was visible at the horizon, yet moving toward Lydia with impossible speed. Before Lydia got over her surprise, wondering how she heard the voice when the child was so far away, she noticed something else. This was a little girl, wearing a snowsuit. The beach dunes glittered. Then the child was in front of her.

"You'd really better hurry," she said reproachfully. She was pudgy, with wide, earnest, light blue eyes and a firm jaw, although her face otherwise was round enough.

"I'd better hurry for what?" Lydia asked.

"You're not the only person in the universe, you know," the little girl answered, again reproachfully.

"What's your name? And what do you want? And for heaven's sake, why are you wearing a snowsuit?"

"I want to go home now," the little girl said soberly. "You'd better come back now too."

Lydia started to reply, but she stopped, considering. The little girl was about six years old, and she looked very familiar and very . . . foreign or exotic or *something* at once.

"Come on," the child said gravely. Yet at the same time there was also a note of gaiety in her clear, high voice. "You *are* coming, aren't you? I have to go back," she said, "and if you don't come, I don't know what will happen."

"Tweety, Tweety," came still another voice.

"I'm here," the little girl called back, and Lydia stared. *Tweety?* Her own future self? Provided she was reborn, of course! But how could the child be Tweety when she hadn't been born yet? "Just who are you?" she cried angrily. She was almost tempted to shake the little girl's shoulders when another child, a boy, also in snow attire, suddenly appeared in the distance. He was about eight years old, puffing, out of breath.

"It's suppertime. Where have you been? You'll get a licking if you don't hurry." He paused, seeing Lydia, and asked uneasily, "Who is that?"

He stared.

Lydia stared back. It was — Lawrence. It was —

"Don't you dare tell him!" cried Tweety.

As Lydia stepped back in astonishment, she noticed the farmhouse for the first time, and suddenly realized that for the entire interview, the bright sand had been transforming itself gradually, granules turning to packed snow; sunlight darkening until now it was twilight with blue shadows covering the winter landscape. She looked around anxiously for her trailer, for the sun —

The little boy asked again, "Who is the lady?" though, and she forgot everything else, as buried memories from her last life suddenly were reclaimed. She and Lawrence as young people in isolated scenes — she and Lawrence, old and stubborn, defying the establishment. And this little boy was Lawrence. She knew it. What then, Lawrence born again? How could she have forgotten him? And what else had she forgotten? And why?

"The little boy is my cousin," Tweety said gently to Lydia, speaking too meaningfully for a child.

Lydia just kept staring. The boy's eyes as he stared back were so innocent and guileless and clear, and so ignorant of her, that Lydia wanted to cry. But already the boy had turned, made a snowball in his snow-caked mittens, and ran to the farmhouse. The back door opened, a slice of light illuminating the dark barnyard. Tweety said, "I *have* to go. You have to come —" and she, too, ran toward the farm.

Lydia gasped and moved automatically toward the house, drawn by Tweety, but more, toward the memory of Lawrence. How was it that the children had found her to begin with? Why didn't the boy know he was Lawrence and recognize her? Why —

The children had disappeared inside the house, and moving closer to it, Lydia gasped again. How *could* she ever have forgotten her love of Lawrence, she wondered, more desperately than she had before. Because now all at once and in a rush, Lydia's full memory and feeling returned full blast, richer than anything she could imagine, more important than the meaning of life or finding the gods. The feelings roused — what? Desire for life, whether or not she understood it.

At the same time, she peered through the windows of the house. They were iced over on the outside and steamed over on the inside, so she chipped off some small patches of ice in order to see more clearly. What she saw filled her with the oddest nostalgia. The family was gathered at the table in the dining room, bright in fireplace light and further lit by two fat candles. On the thick wooden table sat a gigantic platter of smoked fish, along with loaves of brown crusty bread to which Josef was helping himself. Elgren Hosentauf sat at the head of the table with his eldest son, Jonathan, while Elgren's wife, Avona, bustled back and forth. The two children slyly eyed each other; they only had soup, no fish, and Bianka, Tweety's mother, grown stout, was saying: "Lars goes home tomorrow. His parents are coming for him, and that's that." Tweety mumbled under her breath, and the boy, Lars, lowered his head.

Lydia was almost crying: Lawrence would be called Lars, then, and be her cousin — that is, if she was born as Tweety. She yearned to tell the small boy, to make him understand. Mentally she cried, "Oh, don't you remember? We were lovers. You died on our trailer trip together."

"I'm a grown-up man really," Lars said, puffing out his chest for Tweety's benefit.

"Children do not speak at dinner," old man Hosentauf thundered.

"I am too grown up," Lars boasted, gesturing wildly, and spilling his soup. Tweety giggled and ducked to avoid the heel of bread thrown by her grandfather. It landed in her mother's soup instead, splashing, and everybody laughed.

"You'll just get him in trouble. And Tweety too," said a terribly familiar voice.

Lydia spun around. There stood Lawrence, exactly as she remembered him — in his late twenties, as he'd been when they first met.

"I couldn't talk to you until you wanted to remember," Lawrence said. He didn't look at her, though, but stared through the window. "Fascinating, isn't it, to see ourselves as we'll be?" he asked.

"Forget *them*. We're us," Lydia cried. "You mean, you remembered me? How I could have forgotten you, I'll never know."

He wore a black opera cape and carried a fresh bouquet of roses that flashed against the snow as the window light fell against the ground.

"Oh, Lawrence — Larry," she exclaimed; and for a moment she felt that they were still having their early affair, and she was still married to —

"Roger. You were married to Roger," Lawrence said.

"But I'm not married now," Lydia cried. "And we're young again."

"Are we? Or are we just between ages?" Lawrence asked, smiling. He handed her the flowers and said, "What will you do with them? Put them in a vase on a living room table? Don't you understand? We're ageless. But to be really *young*, we have to go back in time. We have to be born again."

"We can stay just as we are," she said.

"You'll like it less and less," he answered. "We really don't know enough yet to stay here, without physical lives. There's more, too. You've been living in your own mental world. Even I couldn't get your notice earlier — " But he broke off; embarrassed, worried for her and ill at ease himself. He knew the look in her eyes too well, and she was growing more desirable and lovely by the minute.

"Uh, I have this lovely little hallucinatory trailer by the ocean . . . " she said, shrugging her shoulders, raising those arched black brows with exaggerated, humorous, but quite effective invitation.

"Lydia, for God's sake, listen," he said. "Look in that window! Look at that child, Tweety. She exists in a certain reality, one that may or may not take place. The same applies to Lars. Doesn't that mean anything to you?"

"You were easier to get along with when we were alive," she said, glaring at him. "Besides, I'm being born as Tweety *in the past,* at least from our point of view. So, somehow, Tweety *was* born, no matter what I decide now. I've already figured that out."

"You're wrong," Lawrence said anxiously. "All the time is at once. There isn't really any past or future, so—" But her anger had taken her away where his love couldn't reach. She'd vanished, along with the farmhouse and landscape. And Lawrence knew that he had to try and find her again as quickly as he could.

To Lydia, *Lawrence* had vanished. "Larry? Where did you go?" she cried. Right beside her, he asked the same question of her. But neither one saw or heard the other, and each of them felt disconsolate; Lydia the most, because her memories of Lawrence kept swirling around her, vivid scenes appearing and disappearing. It was inconceivable, she thought for the tenth time, that she'd forgotten him. But he'd obviously returned because of their love, and to help her. Perhaps to warn her. But about what? And again, if she'd forgotten Lawrence, what else had she forgotten? And why?

Then, seemingly for no reason, she remembered the voices and presences she'd sensed about her at various times—the images that almost but not quite materialized, the voices that almost spoke.

She'd often suspected that she was surrounded by an entire different dimension of actuality. For one thing, the sounds were too fast for her to follow, and the images that she felt would change too quickly for her to perceive them. She realized that she had the same sensations now, of straining to hear or see some indefinable activity. She sensed motion of a kind, replete with people—a world that somehow existed right now, beyond her grasp, but a world into which she was trying to materialize. But what kind of a world? And who was there? Would she find Lawrence there too?

And as soon as she thought of Lawrence, the name Roger came to mind. And she thought, Of course: Roger was my husband. But somehow that didn't seem to be the right answer. Yet the name kept ringing in her mind until she could think of nothing else. And all about her, images began to waver and wobble and form.

~ Chapter Fourteen ~

Lydia Attends a Séance,
Shocks the Sitters,
and Keeps a Promise

"*I*t's Roger. Roger. Can you hear me?"

Lydia spun around. She heard the voice but saw no one.

"If you can hear us, give us a sign."

The voice, if that's what it was, Lydia thought, came out of nowhere as far as she was concerned. She heard it, but didn't hear it at the same time. That is, the voice seemed composed of a small mountain of sounds in some dim distance, and if she turned her attention in that direction, then she felt the sounds stacked up there, falling down into soundlessness or building up again—she couldn't tell which—when somehow she felt the words.

She'd just been thinking of Roger, her husband, trying to recall their life together, so maybe this was a message of sorts from him, she thought. Yet again, the name and the voice didn't seem to go together.

"It's Roger Junior," Lydia's living son said for the tenth time, following the medium's directions and feeling like a damned fool.

The candlelight flickered on the fringed table covering, touching the gilt-framed picture of Christ on the nearest knickknack-filled shelf, dancing on the edge of his sister Anna's huge diamond ring, and on the little gold bell that sat at the medium's fingertips. Roger's eyes followed the candlelight as it flickered from object to object. He shifted his weight in the straight backed chair. He was tired of the whole affair and he'd come only because he had promised Anna that he would.

"The vibrations are changing," the medium, Mrs. Always, said. She swayed gently. Her voice changed timbre. Roger looked at the glittering reflections again: They made Christ look cross-eyed, he thought nervously.

"Call her name again," Anna whispered, in a small spooky voice. She remembered playing with a Ouija board once as a child, when the pointer suddenly went speeding across the board, seemingly all by itself. Whether it was all bunk, as Roger said, or not — one never knew. "One never knows," she whispered.

The medium said, "Think. Concentrate. Close your eyes and try to see your mother in your mind's eye."

Roger did. He saw the bony finger, the boyish frame at about seventy, the intense, ironic eyes, the tailored suit she wore when she gave poetry readings. He saw her in the dungarees she used to wear most of the time and he saw her running off with that man — what was his name? Lawrence somebody — when she was past seventy. Christ; he tried to squash the image of the two bony old bodies making love in a trailer alcove. He was still scandalized by the whole affair.

"She's here! Your mother's here. I can always feel it," Mrs. Always said. She meant it. She wasn't lying. Her thoughts unwound like pink girlish ribbons, garnishes of sentimentality twirling on them everywhere: She believed wholeheartedly and with grim determination in Mother Love as the strongest force on earth, or anywhere else for that matter; and now she was convinced that she felt that force materializing. She listened inwardly. She sweated; an indignity gladly accepted for the sake of such a worthy task. And finally she saw a mental image. She whispered, "I see her. Your mother. In a lovely blue gown. She's standing to the left, over there. She says 'Give my dear son my love. Roger, I'm with you still'"

Mrs. Always's misty, half-closed eyes lit on Roger's face so that he tried to freeze his expression into an acceptable one for the occasion.

"Your mother says that your father is here, too," Mrs. Always said. "And so you see, true love is reunited."

"She and father never got along," Roger muttered. He wanted to ask, "What about that old reprobate she took off with at an age when she should have known better? Is he there too?"

But his sister, Anna, said in a small girlish voice, "Mama? Is it really you?"

Roger blushed uncomfortably. His sister was past fifty, for God's sake, and she hadn't called Lydia "Mama" since she was a girl.

"Is it *really* you?" Anna asked. She knew it wasn't, she told herself; but suddenly she felt very forlorn and childlike — overweight and dyed red hair to the contrary—and the room seemed depressing and sad in contrast to the medium's face, which was filled with a saintly innocence that she certainly wasn't faking. Was she?

"Your mother says that she and your father are both happy," Mrs. Always said. "Your mother is standing by me now. A man is with her. He's medium-sized with white hair and blue eyes. Is that your father?"

"No. He died quite young," Roger said meanly.

"Oh, well, maybe he's your mother's father. Even mediums can't always be sure. He died of a severe illness."

Christ, most people do, Roger thought. He was ready to get up and leave.

"He worked in—leather. Yes, that's it," Mrs. Always said. Roger and Anna both gasped. Anna grabbed her lace handkerchief and buried her face in it; it was drenched with perfume, and the scent made Roger sneeze violently.

"Oh, dear! Do be still," Mrs. Always cried. "You'll ruin the vibrations."

Roger was white-faced and almost sick to his stomach. "Tell us more about the man," he said, looking meaningfully at Anna, who was horrified: It would be doubly scandalous, she thought, for her dead mother's elderly lover to turn up at a séance. But he *did* work in leather. She remembered perfectly that he'd upholstered the trailer love nest when he and Lydia ran off.

"Oh, it couldn't be *him*," Anna whispered.

Mrs. Always knew that she'd really hit upon something, but she didn't know what it was. The word "leather" had just come to her out of nowhere. Neither of the sitters looked very happy about the connection, though. The man was glowering and the stout woman looked scared to death. "I sense a great love, a love that lasts beyond the grave," she said shrewdly, hopefully.

"Oh," cried Anna.

"Anything else?" Roger asked. He was beginning to collect himself again.

"A long journey," Mrs. Always said. She was growing tired. She was never sure where her impressions came from: Some were conscious guesses, but some . . . definitely had a different source.

Roger grumphed. Was that a lucky guess or did it really refer to the cross-country journey with the old man and woman, half out of their blessed minds, on their last wicked binge?

"She's leaving. Everything is getting dim," Mrs. Always said. "Goodbye, dear lady, your two children ask that you remember them," she said to the ceiling.

Children, Lydia thought; that was it. Out of curiosity she'd followed the voices that seemed to act like steps down inverted corridors with endless mirrors, until she emerged into this room. With surprise she saw that she was indeed on earth, obviously after her own death, but the rest of the proceedings at first were incomprehensible.

Two of the people looked very familiar, and from the dialogue she'd overheard, these must be her children, Anna and Roger. But they were older than she remembered. Next to them, invisibly, she was a jaunty twenty-five or maybe even thirty-five, and she was wondering whether or not to be born again as a baby. Lydia stared and tried to bring herself into the environment more clearly.

"There's something over there," Anna cried. "I swear it."

"Don't move," Mrs. Always whispered. In fact, the medium nearly sprang out of her chair, for in a flash she saw Lydia quite clearly in one of the few legitimate psychic experiences of her lifetime.

So séances worked, Lydia thought, catching on. When she was alive, she wouldn't have been caught dead at one! Mrs. Always was pointing at her, her face contorted. Roger was shouting something, and Anna was crying in her handkerchief. The relationships were so complex that Lydia wanted to laugh and cry at once. Yet she related from her own present. It was almost impossible for her to find the part of her that meant so much to these two middle-aged people. They'd never really been close. Had they forgotten?

"Over there, I see something over there," Anna shouted to Roger.

Mrs. Always cried out, "You've left the physical plane. You're dead. Rest in peace, dear soul."

"I know I'm dead," Lydia shouted, but no one heard her.

"There isn't anything there. Or anyone. It's all your imagination," Roger said. "I don't hear or see anything."

"That figures," Lydia muttered, thoroughly disgusted.

"Oh, Mama," Anna cried; and this time when Lydia heard Anna's voice, the room shimmered. The walls and tables and people turned into flying fragments of stained-glasslike jigsaw images that rearranged themselves until a new picture was formed. Now Anna was five and Roger was twelve and they were in the living room, playing, on some heretofore-forgotten spring evening. The white curtains were blowing in the wind. A dog howled outside, and the sweet damp night odor rushed through the open window.

"Where do the dead go, Mama?" Anna asked.

And Lydia saw herself, the young mother with her children at her feet, and she felt stabs of tenderness. "The dead go everywhere, honey," Lydia the young mother said.

But Roger stood up suddenly, his earnest face filled with rage; with the deep inexplicable passion of a child. He shouted, "You're just saying that, but it isn't true. When you're dead, you aren't people anymore. Dead people don't really come back, like sometimes in the movies. It's scary!"

Then it seemed — to Lydia, the young mother — that the night itself waited, that everything waited for her answer to the child, as if the question itself had implications she only felt but didn't understand. She said clearly, lightly, smiling, "I'll come back years from now, when I'm dead, and tell you all about it when I know more. okay?"

As she said the words, Lydia the young mother shivered and glanced at her son. Did he smile slyly? Did the child send the mother out ahead of time where he would be afraid to go? Awful thoughts, she told herself, as the young mother — as the mother still remembered by the grown children. And now Lydia thought that it was those children lingering in the adults, who still asked the question, and for whom she'd momentarily returned.

Roger said, "Promise?" — frightened, biting his lips, feeling his new youth rising in the suburban night.

"Promise," Lydia the young mother said.

"I'll believe it when I see it," answered young Roger, just as the middle-aged Roger said the same thing.

Lydia stared. She was back in the séance room. The medium was passing small glasses of wine to Anna and Roger, and they were excitedly discussing the evening's events. No one sensed her presence this time at all. Broodingly, she took on the old woman image she had died with. She tried hard to tug at her memories. It was like putting someone else's thoughts on, but finally she managed to sort out from all of her other experiences the one Lydia they seemed to be talking about; and from that standpoint she responded to the conversation.

She saw them now as through a mist; Roger and Anna, sipping the wine, gazing into the nervous face of Mrs. Always, who was more shaken than she wanted to admit. "Your mother must have been extraordinary. I've never sensed such a presence. Oh, I'm still nervous. I saw her so clearly." She fanned herself with her hand. "I've seen many, many apparitions — " Her voice trailed off; with a sinking in her stomach, she realized that the others had all been . . . imaginative images, because she wanted to *see* so badly. "I just hope she finds peace," she said quickly.

"She never particularly looked for peace when she was alive," Roger said glumly. "She was unconventional, a rebel until the last. I guess she enjoyed showing us how dull we were by contrast."

"That's not nice to say about her," Anna cried, looking around nervously.

Lydia stared at their faces. She'd loved them enough, she saw. But she'd judged them too harshly. Her poetry, and later, Lawrence, had been her life. And as she thought that, she suddenly saw Josef's face in her mind's eye: As *his* daughter, she'd have to relate emotionally. She imaged herself as a child in the middle of his bustling household.

"Do you think she's still around?" Anna asked, and Lydia said mentally, "Goodbye dear Anna, dear Roger. I kept my promise. Forgive me for liking you better as children. . . ." Why couldn't Anna show some flair? Why couldn't Roger display just a touch of gallantry? Why—She broke the thoughts off, struck by a new realization. The conversation with the children about life after death had taken place one spring night after she'd met Lawrence. She'd returned home, rather guiltily, after a secret meeting with him. She'd met him downtown, supposedly by chance but actually by pre-arrangement.

And suddenly she *was* downtown. The séance room was gone. No one saw her. It was 6 P.M. by the town hall clock. It took Lydia a moment to orient herself, and longer to discover whether or not she was really walking down the world's streets.

It was windy; people went by bundled in scarfs and coats; and cold. Lydia shivered, though she didn't feel the crisp air or the wind. Traffic zoomed by. Newspapers and debris blew in the gutters, and watching, she felt very lonely. She saw everything clearly, but she didn't really smell anything, she noticed. And she only heard the traffic sounds dimly, though cars rushed by just feet away.

She didn't feel any particular sense of contact with the ground either, though nostalgically she remembered how the click, click, click of her high heels used to accompany her wherever she went; or the soft pouncing jounce of sneakers, or—

She really felt, well, ghostly, for the first time since her death. Was this Oversoul Seven's way of making her feel uncomfortable, so she'd want to be born again? Though she didn't sense his presence, Lydia wasn't sure just how many of her experiences were the natural results of her own thoughts—or how many were directed by Seven. She sighed petulantly: her search for the gods had certainly been cut short; here she was, earthbound enough.

People were all around her, busy, concentrating completely in their cozy time and place, with appointments to keep, and with the arrangement of events so neat and simple! Despite herself, Lydia grinned; without even noticing it, she'd turned back into a woman in her late thirties. She'd never realized before how little of yourself was available when you were alive. In life you didn't have to worry about balancing youth's energy and innocence with the wisdom or experience of age, because by the time you got old, you'd lost touch with your own youth. Now she could switch back and forth at will—a mixed blessing, she thought, because she passed a store window and saw that she left no reflection there.

Yet, perversely, she refused to focus all of her energy where she was, in which case she would be able to really smell and feel the air, hear the traffic. But that would be a mockery. A mockery of what? Between ages, Lawrence had said. She sighed again. And suddenly she realized that she was being followed. Being followed? She started to laugh, her unseen image flickering back and forth and changing colors with the extent of her mirth. Who could be following her *here*?

She turned to see Lawrence several feet away, pretending to look in a shop window (Dear God, opera cape and all), and as insubstantial to others as she was. Until she saw him, she'd only sensed that she'd been lonely. Now she realized that she felt completely cut off, and no sooner did she see him than at once the entire scene burst into full brilliance so quickly that she leapt back in astonishment. The squeaks and squeals of the traffic, the cutting chill of wind, and all of the scents and sounds of the street came alive, with a vengeance, it seemed, an assaulting vividness. Automatically Lydia hallucinated a hat, coat, and scarf; and Lawrence was beside her, smiling.

"You're a real bitch to track down," he said, looking about twenty-five — as he did when she first knew him, fifteen years younger than she, dark hair mussed in the wind, opera cape blowing.

"Larry, that cape," she said, laughing, and time collapsed or the edges of it met, and the two of them actually *were* alive and meeting secretly; he dressed for his part in a play, on his way to rehearsal, and she — supposedly — at the library.

He kissed her quickly, excitedly. "How do you like my garb? I'm supposed to commit suicide in it. Can't you see my cape fluttering as I leap to my death? Some part. Maybe I should just concentrate on my crafts and leather work, open up a shop, and forget this acting nonsense."

"You look utterly fantastic," she cried. She was dizzy with exuberance, and the two of them stood there, so vital in each other's attention that nothing else mattered. In that moment Lydia had access to everything that had been in that earlier Lydia's mind, so that in blinding rapidity she was almost overwhelmed by emotions and a series of images. First she felt her love for Lawrence as he stood before her; then she saw the evening they'd later spent together — the small restaurant, red and white tablecloth, dinner, the candles and wine; she heard their own excited chatter and felt her own worry about the two children left at home with a sitter. Last of all a rush of guilt assaulted her, because her husband, Roger, who was on a brief business trip, thought she was at home. And with the guilt, the instant burst. She and Lawrence, two insubstantial images, stood facing each other on the busy twilight street with people passing by, not seeing them.

"Oh," Lydia whispered.

Lawrence said, "We were going to go away together after the play closed. You can recall all of it if you want."

"Do *you* remember?" she asked.

He nodded. "I'm here to help you revive your memories, if you want to. You seemed to close them out."

She said slowly, "You never did make it as an actor, and you did end up with a leather shop—"

"There's something else," he said. "The meeting we just re-experienced . . . was the last time we saw each other for about twenty years."

She just stared at him.

"You even considered suicide once," he said, not looking at her.

"Suicide? Why? Not me, not in a million years," she exclaimed. "Tell me. What have I forgotten?"

But Lawrence was gone, and the environment itself was disappearing.

~ *Chapter Fifteen* ~

Oversoul Seven Has His Troubles and
Will Tries to Drop Out

"*I* keep telling you, suicide is not on the agenda," Seven was saying. "I'm just not getting through to you at all, am I?" Seven sighed, not even trying to hide his disappointment. He'd appeared as the compassionate but wise young graduate teacher, and as the compassionate but wise old man as well, but Will was in such a rotten mood that nothing seemed to reach him at all. "I am supposed to be your soul," Seven said, "but we certainly don't seem to have much in common. I wonder if someone made a mistake somewhere?" Almost absentmindedly, Seven lit up a joint (of marijuana, dear reader) and puffed it in just the correct tender fashion.

"What do you think you're doing?" Will asked. "It's all sham. I know that. You're just smoking grass to make me feel at home or bridge the generation gap or something. And this classroom is all a dream hallucination too. And waking life is the same thing. Even dreaming, I'm not stupid, for God's sake."

Seven, as the old man, lowered his eyes and began to pace the classroom floor — perfect hardwood, sun splashing across the wood in just the right fashion — all gone to waste. He started to feel sorry for himself.

"You're some guru," Will said accusingly. "You can't teach me anything anyhow, because all learning is meaningless. Everything is senseless. I know that I'm asleep in bed, and awake here at the same time. So what? This place is as senseless as earth is. Or life is. I don't belong anywhere. And when your own soul doesn't like you, you may as well give up." Will finished speaking and stood staring at Seven broodingly, dark brows raised loftily; the picture of young, nonchalant, studied, contemptuous disdain. Then he said evenly, "Life is meaningless, and I don't intend to dignify it by staying around."

"You've *got* to stay around." Seven shouted, trying to think of something. "You can't commit suicide anyhow without taking a course in methods. If you have your heart set on suicide, you might as well do it right. Besides," he added, "suicide is a hard act to follow."

This time Will came toward Seven threateningly, fists raised, yelling at the top of his lungs. "I don't want to *follow* it with anything. You still don't understand. I want it to end. I want *me* to end."

"But why?" Seven asked for the hundredth time as he stepped back judiciously. "You have youth, health, money, intelligence — "

"Life doesn't make it, that's all," Will replied, with such unconscious arrogance that Seven just shook his head.

But Seven stood there stubbornly, and suddenly a great energy possessed him: Will, denying life, was so *full* of life, that Seven decided to try again, and to present Will with his (Will's) own strength and validity. Seven summoned Will as Will was and could be, and when Seven stopped changing shapes, Will stood there gasping, for he was staring at — himself. Only this self was so fulfilled and accomplished and loving that on the one hand, Will couldn't take his eyes away — while on the other hand, he could barely stand to look. All the yearning he'd ever felt in his life was fastened on that image. To be that person! If anyone so marvelous could be considered human. And this superversion of Will smiled at him, and though Will heard no words, he knew that this other self grew up from his own roots — that his, Will's, doubts and challenges had somehow led to this superversion, in which he himself existed.

At the same time, though, and paradoxically, it seemed to him, Will felt his resentment grow in proportion to his appreciation. Because this super Will wasn't just a better Will, which he could understand, but an Olympian self in ways he sensed but couldn't comprehend; a giant-sized self in terms of power and emotional reality. In fact his ideas of the good self didn't fit this Olympian version at all, which was too powerful to be good, he thought uneasily. Yet he knew it wasn't evil either. And if it wasn't good or evil, then he didn't know how to handle it at all, he thought angrily.

"You don't really exist either," he managed to shout. And the superversion of himself vanished.

Oversoul Seven cleared his throat.

Will was too shaken to pretend that he wasn't impressed. And now that the image was gone, he felt its warmth and vitality, perhaps because he wasn't as frightened. For a moment he felt himself responding, and in a split second he was the superversion of himself, regarding his usual self with the craziest kind of love and sympathy. There was nothing conventionally pious or good about the love, which was emotional and personal yet also composed of some gigantic, objective kind of support. And the sympathy had too much humor in it to be saintly, yet was too full of appreciation to be condescending. Will became so engrossed in trying to figure it all out that he never noticed as the classroom walls disappeared and a grinning Oversoul Seven waved to him from the window just before it vanished.

But Seven's smile vanished at the same time, relatively speaking, because Will had raised an issue that bothered him considerably, at least in retrospect. Did he like Will? Or, more to the point, did he dislike him? Certainly he wished Will well, exuberantly and definitely. Only he found him tiresome because he complained so much and because he was so ungracious inside, when he was so graceful and attractive physically.

"You don't particularly like him," Cyprus said, appearing out of nowhere. "So don't try to wiggle out of it. In any case, I want to talk to you."

"Uh, I was going to check on Bianka," Seven said nervously.

"By all means. I'll go with you," Cyprus replied. "Now, about Will — "

"Well, *he* doesn't like *me* very much either, or anyone else for that matter," Seven grumbled. "He doesn't care for anyone but himself, and of course he doesn't really approve of himself either. And he has this grudge against life that I just don't understand. Lydia's self-absorbed at times, but she *cares*. I mean, she really wants to give Tweety a spiritual heritage and some knowledge of 'the gods.' I know that's why she hasn't made her mind up to be born again! She wants the universe to be right for a new life. It is, of course; you and I know that. But — "

Now Oversoul Seven and Cyprus were invisible, and without any forms at all, in what would hopefully be Tweety's bedroom, which was Josef's old studio. They were at rest, yet part of their essences just kept drifting lazily through the bedposts, which Josef in a paternal mood had carved with the heads of animals; and through the bureau, which was quite elegant, an heirloom of Bianka's family, made of rosewood; and through anything else that happened to be there.

Seven eyed the thick icicles that weren't even dripping; it was so cold outside that the window was almost entirely frosted over. "So I can relate to Lydia now," he said dejectedly. "But Will makes me impatient."

Cyprus turned quite still. With a semblance of surprise, she said, "Seven, I was under the impression that Lydia *had* made up her mind to be born again, and that the search for the gods was more in the nature of a last fling before birth."

"That's what I meant to say," Seven muttered, blushing. "I'm sure she *has* decided—"

Cyprus said sternly, "If I understand what you're trying so hard not to tell me, then Lydia at the least is still hesitating rather vigorously. And Will, who *is* ensconced in a very comfortable life indeed, has decided that he dislikes his existence enough to contemplate suicide, and—"

"Don't say another thing," Seven cried. "All right, I'm beside myself with worry. And I'm trying to go along with human concepts about the gods, though this is very trying. Besides that, your Jeffery is identifying so with Will that if Will *does* commit suicide—though I'm sure he won't—I don't know what Jeffery will do. And since he isn't even one of my personalities to begin with, I don't understand his part in any of this at all."

Cyprus smiled one of the most satisfied smiles that Seven had ever seen, as she changed back into the woman teacher image with which she often conducted such discussions. "Jeffery won't commit suicide now," she said. "He has the book to finish."

"But when it's done?" Seven shouted. "Now I'm more upset than ever! He's writing this conversation down, for the book. So he knows we're talking about him. I don't see how you got him to write the book in the first place!"

"Oh, Seven, *I* didn't get him to 'write the book,'" Cyprus said. She started laughing, but with such sympathy and gusto that Seven couldn't be angry, though he tried. "Oh, is *that* what you think?" Cyprus cried. "Well, remember that you decided to forget some things that you know, in order to relate to your personalities better."

"Well, Jeffery *is* writing this book," Seven began, dubiously now.

"And you're right. He won't be happy with this particular section when he's read what he's written," Cyprus added.

"But he *does* know what we're saying about him!" Seven was so acutely embarrassed and exasperated that he threw his hallucinatory fourteen-year-old arms up in the air with dismay. "But Jeffery doesn't even believe we exist," he shouted.

And Cyprus answered, with an almost Olympian laugh, "He's not as sure of that as he once was. In any case, we've been keeping him very busy, and material about Will *does* always upset him, so shortly we'll have to give him some time to do his own notes."

Seven said, almost accusingly, "All of this just might be too much for Jeffery. I don't like his identification with Will at all, as I told you, or with the suicide question."

This time Cyprus said, "Seven, the trouble with you is that you worry too much. You're always afraid that people will make the 'wrong' choices. You're manipulating Will, or trying to, and he resents it. Manipulation won't work at all. Right now Will's purpose in life seems to be to end it."

Glumly, Seven nodded.

"You do have the answer; the way to help him," Cyprus said gently. "But the decisions must be his. And Jeffery's must be *his,* of course."

"What about Jeffery when the book is done?" Seven asked.

"Seven, the book will never be *finished.*" A certain sound came into Cyprus' voice and suddenly Seven saw a thousand books or more, each page of each book with its own sequels and probably variations, and each written down by a different probable Jeffery. Oversoul Seven winced. "It's the *one* Jeffery we know that I'm speaking about."

"Exactly," Cyprus answered.

Seven started to reply, but the icicle he was staring at suddenly began to melt, dripping past the windowsill that Seven saw was Will's, not Josef's. "Will must be in trouble," he cried to Cyprus. "Here we've been talking and—" Seven forgot what he was saying. The icicle was almost gone. The sun glittered on its vanishing remains for just a moment, and Will, staring at it, thought that he'd vanish from life as easily as the icicles melted in the sun. He'd take sleeping pills.

Will had a plastic Cheshire cat that he'd found in a secondhand store. Seven liked to sit inside it, when Will was in one of his moods, so that he could look out from a point of relative safety. Inside it now, he had an excellent view of Will, who was rigidly sitting on the side of the rumpled bed, staring hard-eyed out the window at the point where the icicle had just vanished.

"Shit," Will muttered. He'd awakened with a dream memory that infuriated him, and though the memory was already nearly gone, his anger grew. Now all he recalled was the feeling that he'd dreamed about himself, only a self so accomplished that next to that image, he was worthless. Or nearly worthless. Dead, at least his poor empty body would get some attention. Dead; he'd make them question, his friends and so-called friends, his traveling-free parents and prissy professors. How could you have let such a young man die? Will cursed: There he was, full of self-pity again! Well, sleeping pills would take care of that, too.

"You don't even like to swallow aspirin," Seven said mentally.

"No, pills won't do," Will mused, accepting Seven's thought without wondering where it came from. Neither would drugs. If he was going to die, he wanted to make an impact. He smiled brightly, dramatically: If he was going to do it, he'd do it right.

As Will thought *that,* the truly black despondent mood that had been curling around the edges of his mind suddenly overtook him. He didn't even try to fight it, because he thought life was so . . . shitty, that nothing really mattered. At the same time, as this blackness clouded his thoughts, his feelings got faster and clearer in a particular dark fashion. His despair accelerated and had its own dizzy excitement, and pulsated with energy and action. While all this was going on, so as not to frighten himself overmuch, Will thought almost airily that he'd make no decision. To hell with it. He'd leave it all to the fates. Suspense to the last moment. And even as he decided to leave it all open, Will was going out of the room, down the steps to the front of the house where his motorcycle waited in the driveway. Waited — he thought — like a black monster or like a knight's rescuing steed. Which would it be?

He felt wild and free, devil-may-care, yet he was smiling inside himself like death, he thought; and liking the expression, he thought it again.

There was still some, not much, slush in the streets, which glistened wet, almost shining black in the bright sunlight. And the stores were like cutouts of cardboard to be knocked down like soggy playing cards. It was all sham. He was dead anyhow, no matter what he did, he told himself. He didn't feel like other people did. He was unaffected, untouched.

The sound of the cycle came thundering up, disturbing the entire neighborhood, he hoped, rousing any people taking afternoon naps. The furious whirl of Will starting up death's engine. The sound was so loud and he was traveling so fast that he laughed and cried at once, wearing no helmet so that the cold March wind could eat holes in his head. A great image! Why did he feel so damned creative at a time like this? He wished to hell he'd stop commenting on his own godamned thoughts.

He stopped at a traffic light and decided to ride slower so that the cops wouldn't stop him for breaking some stupid traffic rule. Grinning coldly, he hit the highway out of town and forgot about driving slowly. The speedometer said 80. There was a bridge, an open mesh affair, very dangerous when wet, and he headed toward it. This wasn't going to be a suicide, but a test. A contest. He'd hit the bridge as fast as he could go. If the cycle crashed and he died — well, his problems were over. If not, then he'd take it as a sign that someone or something wanted him to live, and that he had a place in the universe, even if he hadn't found it yet.

Shit. He was losing the edge of his anger and he wanted to sustain it.

On the back of the motorcycle, an invisible Oversoul Seven groaned as he monitored Will's thoughts and tried to discover exactly how dangerous Will's course was. He kept transmitting Will's favorite memories into

Will's stream of thought, but Will kept blocking them out. Instead, stubbornly, he concentrated on the distant bridge. Quickly, Seven got a mental glimpse of it — there it was, about ten miles away, just as slippery as Will hoped, and it arched over a precipice, of course, with a river far below. A curve at the far end. And two houses close to the road. Seven grimaced: The trouble was that he had to allow Will his free will. And a free Will could be a dead Will.

The cycle was approaching 90. It was a light B.S.A. that Will called, euphemistically, a gentleman's machine, and it — "Look out," Seven shouted to Will, who had just missed hitting a car that came speeding around a blind spot in the road. But neither Will nor the other driver wanted to kill anyone else, Seven saw; each wanted to go out in a *private* blaze of glory. Seven threw a sigh of sympathy and understanding to the other driver's oversoul as Will shakily eyed the bridge which now came into view.

Really desperate, Seven scanned the neighborhood and contemplated his new clue: Will didn't want to take anybody with him if he died. Then (did Cyprus send him the inspiration just in time?) Seven remembered Will's love of kittens. How long did it take a motorcycle to stop? What was the safety factor? In a flash, Seven hallucinated a kitten, choosing a tabby which seemed to be Will's favorite. The kitten, with a sore paw, sat mewing in the center of the bridge.

Then it was up to Will, who saw the kitten and cursed. He'd take the damned thing out of its misery with him. To hell with it. The universe didn't give a shit about a kitten. He squinted; the cat had something wrong with it, or it would be running away. All Will could see now was the kitten, getting bigger and bigger as he approached it. Maybe *it* was committing suicide. It could crawl away, couldn't it? What was the matter with the dumb, stupid thing? Even if he swerved, he might hit it. It'd probably stay on the side of the bridge for days because nobody cared. Who'd bury a dead kitten?

Miserably the kitten tried to scramble to its feet. Sensing triumph, Seven made it the most pathetic kitten imaginable, as it mewed, stood, tottered over.

"Oh double and triple shit," Will screamed, screamed, and screamed, as the hottest, wildest pity overcame him and he felt himself slowing down, stopping his own death, because in the whole cruel universe, he wasn't going to add to the misery of it all by killing some dumb, stupid creature. The motorcycle skidded, skidded some more, as Will tried to stop in time, his fury and pity almost blinding him. He'd slow down, but not enough. He swerved, avoided the kitten, and was thrown off the cycle just before it slammed into the side of the bridge.

Everything seemed unrealistically still. Will landed on his hands and knees. He was a mess of scrapes and bruises, but he wasn't hurt badly. And he definitely wasn't dead. Turning around to look for the kitten, he shouted, "You dumb cat. That's one of your nine lives."

And Oversoul Seven, exhausted, sighed, "Look who's talking."

~ *Chapter Sixteen* ~

Jeffy-boy's Uneasiness Grows and
Ram-Ram Does a Disappearing Act

When I was finished with what you have read thus far, I stared at the manuscript, appalled beyond description. The characters in the book were discussing me, and quite objectively, with the oddest kind of sympathy for my predicament. This concern added to my anxiety beyond measure. The constant use of third person references to me, "he" this, or "he" that, struck me with a sense of panic. If the analysis of my character hadn't been so astute, perhaps I wouldn't have been so bothered, but several passages that I reread described me with a . . . loving detachment that I found most disconcerting.

All of this represented some important alteration in the pattern of activity thus far; and I recognized this at the time only opaquely, afraid to follow the matter through for fear, I suppose, of where it might lead. But the shock went even deeper than the realization that the relationship between the manuscript and myself was changing. No matter what they were, or how the book was being written, Oversoul Seven and Cyprus were fictional characters. Their criticism, even their awareness of my own existence, somehow upset the very foundations of all my beliefs. I found myself saying, "They have no right to do this, no right at all," before I realized the implications and irony of my own remark.

Intrusion enough — this weird book and its method of delivery — but I had begun to think that it might be good enough to publish, without, of course, giving any hint of the way it was produced. This made me wonder how many other manuscripts had been written in the same manner, with the "authors" smart enough to keep their mouths shut and cut out any passages that might give them away.

But this added development (I took it almost like an insult) was a further intrusion in which unreality dared to comment upon life; where Art refused to stay where it belonged (if this *was* Art of a most peculiar nature), and began a concerted program of entry into normal reality. The characters were becoming real, turning on their creator and daring to examine his abilities and characteristics. I looked at these latest developments in this way for some time, even though I realized that the premise wasn't acceptable to begin with, since to all intents and purposes I wasn't writing the book, but only taking down its dictation. Did that mean that whoever was originating it felt quite safe in dissecting my character, as I might feel in, say, examining the characteristics of a laboratory animal?

As far as Will's near disastrous motorcycle ride is concerned, of course I was somewhat anxious and carried along by the suspense, as anyone is, even when just reading such adventurous passages in any book. If I was relieved at the end, surely my reaction was no more than natural. In that regard, I am sure that my "identification" with Will was over-exaggerated by Cyprus and Seven in those passages where they refer to it. It's highly unlikely that they know me better than I know myself, for example. Though we all have a few suicidal thoughts in our lives, I've been no more given to them than anyone else.

In any case, whenever you read in "Education" any references to myself, you can pretty well imagine my own invisible reactions. For one thing, while writing down the script, I had no way of retorting to any such passages, of explaining my thoughts, or, in short, of speaking back. I was only barely aware of what I was writing to start with and didn't even realize that I *was* being mentioned until I read the material over. It was impossible for me to insert any comments into the script, even later. In the craziest fashion, my reactions didn't or *wouldn't* fit. My own sentences literally could not be inserted into the book itself. It was almost as if two different kinds of order were involved that could coexist, but not . . . mix. This further added to my anger, of course. If *they* could insert themselves so smugly into my reality and arrange for me to write their book, then why couldn't I at least report my own reactions within the script itself? Since I obviously cannot, however, these notes are really my parallel statements; the *other* side or my side of their book or world, if you prefer; the one in which the laboratory animals keep their own reports.

I a*m* worried: Will I end up bragging about how well I performed at a series of clever psychological mazes? And is that actually what I'm being led to do? Yet even laboratory animals are given incentives, so what reward am I being offered? What stimuli am I unconsciously reacting to? The question itself suddenly excited me so that I stopped writing for a moment, filled with anticipation. If I'm running a different kind of maze than laboratory animals, a "multidimensional" one, to coin one of "Education"'s terms, then, of course, the psychological rewards are being held out like the carrot before the horse.

And that simple enough statement sounds very much like Ram-Ram's agitated first conversation with me in connection with the experiments he suggested — experiments, incidentally, that were never quite explained to me . . . But in any case, surely I'm being offered a boon of a kind: the opportunity of studying this bizarre experience from the inside, at first hand, in the most isolated laboratory of all, in a way — my own mind. I seem to be both subject and analyst, and thus in a position to study behavioral conditioning from a unique standpoint. For the first time I see some kind of logic that I can understand in all of this. If I'm right, then each further intrusion of the "book world" into mine is actually the insertion of new stimulus to the laboratory situation. My reactions are being watched, then. Why didn't this occur to me before? Well, any number can play that game.

So: Tomorrow I won't write a line on the infernal manuscript, and *I'll* wait for *their* reactions. Am I being crafty, suitably clever, or in playing the game, have I already lost the fine edges of sanity? Now I question whether or not sanity has fine edges. I do wish I knew some truly knowledgeable colleague, familiar with all fields of psychology, with whom I could discuss what's happening. Actually I'm beyond that point now; I don't really feel that anyone else can help me. At the same time, I'm afraid, sometimes at least, that I'll end up like Ram-Ram or worse. Even the prospect of being considered a mere fool is a terrible one to me, when I've been so used to considering my psychological stance impeccable.

All of this concentrated thought must be wearing me out. I feel unusually tired and can hardly keep my eyes open. My fingers keep lingering over the typewriter keys as if uncertain whether or not to continue —

As I wrote the last sentence, a knock came at the door. I was glad enough of the interruption and called, "Come in," expecting some student perhaps, or associate. Instead to my surprise there was Ram-Ram, standing in the hallway, grinning, with a cigarette in one hand and a drink in the other. I leaped to my feet. "What are you doing out of the sanatorium?" I sputtered, sorry at once for the question. "Well, you're cured, then. They released you?" I was so relieved to see him that I grasped his arm and pulled him inside, feeling that he was the only person in the world to whom I could talk. Granting he *was* sane, of course.

"I'm as sane *as you are*," he said, as if reading my mind. "And that's a loaded statement."

"Is it?" I answered, thinking, if he only knew how loaded.

"In any case, I felt that you wanted to see me," he said, now ensconced in the wicker chair that literally groaned beneath his weight. "Actually, I'm as sane as the doctors are, which isn't saying much. Or rather, I'm saner, which places me in a peculiar situation — "

He was joking, in excellent spirits, but I said uncomfortably, "Saner than sane? That sounds suspicious."

"Can't tell if I'm sane or not, huh? That puts *you* in a peculiar position, for which I apologize. So since I'm here, in your territory, we'll play it your way. You can assure yourself that I'm sane, using your definition of the word — presuming you know what you mean by it, of course. Now, since my glass is empty, I'd like to suggest that you offer me a drink?"

"Sorry. Of course." I made us each one, leaving the liquor bottle out on the table.

"So, I've been given a clean bill of mental health," he said.

"I'm more relieved than I can say," I said, meaning it.

"I know you are," he said, and I had the curious impression that his words were double-edged, or that he knew more than he was letting on. But about what? Or was his attitude simply a hangover of his condition, a sly reminder of psychological duplicity? "How is Queen Alice?" I asked, testing.

"Fine. As well as can be expected," he answered — which told me nothing, of course.

"But you've been writing a report or thesis or book of sorts, haven't you?" he asked.

I stared at him. He looked no different. He didn't act as if he realized that he was talking about something he had no way of knowing was true.

"What's the matter? Secret, huh? Well, I've heard your typewriter going up here for hours at a time, from my rooms below. Not complaining, you understand. But I took it for granted that you were working on a manuscript of some sort."

The terrible nervousness that had assaulted me the moment he first mentioned a book subsided so quickly that I was giddy. Of course, I thought; he'd been in his apartment downstairs, not at the sanatorium. It would have been odd if he *hadn't* heard the typewriter since you could hear a sneeze in this building two floors away. "Beginning a thesis," I said, probably too quickly. "I suppose it could run into a book."

"Excellent. Excellent. Yes, yes, yes. Our boy is catching up," Ram-Ram said, rubbing his pudgy hands together. I caught the third person reference to myself uneasily, then remembered that this was his habit of speech, not only with me but with others. It was apparent that I'd been overreacting, and with new relief I poured myself another drink, though Ram-Ram was still sipping his.

"Anyhow, I'm delighted that you're been given a clean bill of health," I said. "Do you have to go back for any kind of follow-up?"

"I have to go back to keep track of our Queen Alice," Ram-Ram said, shifting in the chair. This time the wicker creaked more warningly than ever, and Ram-Ram grinned.

"Take the blue chair instead," I said quickly. "I've got to throw the wicker one away anyhow. Go ahead, the blue one is much more comfortable. I'll even stick the wicker out in the hall while I'm thinking about it." And as Ram-Ram moved, taking his drink, pack of cigarettes, and ashtray with him, I stuck the old chair just outside the door, planning to cart it down to the trash heap later.

Ram-Ram crossed his legs and made himself generally comfortable, this time on the couch. "Yes, I want to keep an eye on Queen Alice," he said. Then, looking at me speculatively, "I see that you don't want to tell me what *you've* been up to, though. Well, that's easily understandable, but right now I'm giving you a demonstration of sorts that you won't understand until I'm gone."

"Now, what does that mean?" I asked.

"You're a good psychologist. You'll figure it out," Ram-Ram answered. "I'm delighted with our little chat, though. Yes, yes, yes, our boy is doing fine." He stood up, rubbing his hands together in a quick, nervous, yet almost smug gesture, and grinned like a Cheshire cat. And disappeared.

I mean, he *disappeared.* I stood there, not believing my eyes: He was gone. Suddenly I felt woozy, spun around or thought that I did, and found myself sitting at my desk, head slumped over on it, resting on my arms. Ram-Ram definitely was not in the room. The only conclusion I could rationally draw was that I'd fallen asleep after he left, and dreamed that he'd disappeared. Then why didn't I remember him leaving? I reached for my drink. It wasn't there! My gaze flew about the room. There were no used glasses on the end tables. There was no bottle of liquor either. I rushed into the kitchen and to my amazement found the bottle in the cupboard with no indication it had been moved.

Nearly beside myself, I walked as calmly as I could back to the living room. The wicker chair sat where it always had. This time I poured myself a real drink and sat down to collect my thoughts. Ram-Ram hadn't been here at all. I hadn't moved the wicker chair into the hall. The entire episode had been a dream then, I decided. As soon as I finished my notes, I must have fallen asleep and my concern about Ram-Ram and my need to talk to someone must have triggered —

My thoughts broke off. The dream explanation just wouldn't do. The entire interview had been too clear. I began to think that despite . . . everything . . . in some way, Ram-Ram had been here. Had I moved the chair in the same unknown fashion? Was Ram-Ram actually still in the hospital? I tried not to ask the next question, but could not avoid it. Had Ram-Ram been here in an out-of-body state?

He couldn't have heard the typewriter if he wasn't home. So how did he know about the manuscript? Or, impossible as it seemed, was the affair all my own creation, not a dream, but a complete hallucination? If so, I was in trouble. Again I worried for my own sanity, but I was actually too angry — healthily angry, I thought — to think I was mad. I *had* seen Ram-Ram. Now I refused to doubt my own perception. And I hate practical jokers. So if Ram-Ram had played some kind of psychological or psychic trick on me, I was going to get to the bottom of it.

In other words, I decided to go over to the sanatorium later that very afternoon.

~ *Chapter Seventeen* ~

Ram-Ram the Godologist and
Case History 9871: J. Christ

The godologists were tucked away in a small corner of the universe, though once their domain had been extensive. Godology, it seemed, was a dying art, Seven thought. Not really, of course, since no arts die, but in the context of the times he was dealing with, godology wasn't the exciting pursuit it used to be. Seven shook his head with some dismay. The lawns and shrubs were in need of trimming; dust settled over the once ivied towers, and the buildings themselves had shrunken. Once they'd been so large that it took centuries to get from one complex to another, and now the same buildings could be seen in the twinkling of an eye.

The godologists were a peculiar breed anyhow, for their profession demanded that they mix godly and human characteristics, an uneasy blend, a transspecies really, that made them—well, a trifle eccentric. He had to have some psychological profiles on the gods for Lydia's benefit, though, so Seven resolutely hurried on.

The particular godologist Seven wanted to see was one he affectionately called Ram-Ram, because the godologist always seemed to be butting his head up against divinities that he couldn't understand. Names don't mean much to souls, so it was only when Seven actually entered the godologists' domain that it occurred to him that his godologist and Jeffy-boy's psychologist friend had the same name. Some godologists had physical lives going on, and some didn't. Since Seven didn't know Ram-Ram's status in that regard, he forgot the entire matter in the press of more serious issues. He'd promised Lydia that he'd discover what he could about the gods as they existed in terms of the world she was used to. So Seven sent out mental feelers for Ram-Ram as soon as he approached the nearly deserted grounds.

From somewhere inside, Ram-Ram flashed his mental welcome. "My, my, my. Yes, yes. What have we here? Seven! Delighted," and he sent Seven directions. Briskly now Seven went past empty consultation rooms to find Ram-Ram's small cubicle.

"How long has it been?" Ram-Ram asked at once. "How times fly. In any case, we've made some changes here since I saw you last. Not all for the best, of course. But at least I'm onto something vital." Because Seven was of earthsoul stock, Ram-Ram took human form, appearing as a sly old godologist, white kinky hair getting caught in the silver halo that was the sign of his station. He had a pink flawless complexion that was far too youthful for the rest of his image, Seven saw, wondering indeed if the godologist was getting out of touch with his earthly connections. No real human would take Ram-Ram as just another wise old man, and of course the halo was a dead giveaway too. Seven just grinned, though, and said nothing. He didn't want to hurt Ram-Ram's feelings for one thing, and for another he knew that the godologists, being academics, were very jealous of their rank, and the halo marked Ram-Ram as having ten doctorates of Divinity.

"Uh, they have cut down on your space a bit," Seven said. He wasn't quite sure how to relate to Ram-Ram after all this time, so Seven kept changing shapes until, watching him, Ram-Ram smiled brilliantly and said, "Yes, yes. That one is fine." Seven stabilized: He had his fourteen-year-old image on and it wore a humble brown woolen robe, as befitted a seeker after truth. Seven grinned and Ram-Ram said, "I haven't had a real student in ages, so I hope you don't mind looking like one for awhile. It's such a joy just to imagine that godologists have apprentices again."

"I'll look even younger if you want," Seven offered. Then, to make Ram-Ram feel better, Seven went on. "I *am* a student, though, and I'm on a pilgrimage to find the gods, on behalf of my human personalities. I don't pretend to know why this is all so important to them, to one of them anyhow, Lydia. I'm under the impression that human concepts of divinity are so limited that—"

"Exactly. Exactly," Ram-Ram cried excitedly. "Look, I've something very important to show you that proves that very point!"

Ram-Ram rambled through his massive file cabinet as he talked. "I've done some excellent new studies," he said. "But one in particular should be of special interest to you, since so many of your personalities are involved with Christendom. Look at this. Christ's case history. I prepared it myself!" Ram-Ram's enthusiasm was infectious, but Seven shook his head.

"I'm not interested in case histories, but in *living* divine personalities," he said.

"But here you have it all!" Ram-Ram exclaimed. "It's a thorough investigation. Here you find divine motivation individually and specifically apparent. Here you see the birth of a god, hear the first primal scream as godhood tears itself from nonexistence into divine reality, ripped from the womb of eternity—"

"I never heard such nonsense in any of my lives or before or after," Seven said, scandalized. "Gods come into being because they want to."

"Yes, yes, yes," Ram-Ram said impatiently. "That doesn't mean birth is easy. Any birth is hard, and a god's birth is—well, spectacular, and harder than most. The files show this to be true. The statistics make it clear. Interviews with divine personages confirm the facts."

"Haven't you ever examined your own existence?" Seven asked. "I mean, I understood that all godologists were part divine. Albeit minor god connections. But still. What about your own birth? Or births?"

"Examining my own existence wouldn't be scientific," Ram-Ram said severely. "I *do* have a counterpart on earth, a psychologist who's examining existence from a human standpoint. Granted, I don't give him a lot of attention, and I'm not even sure if he acknowledges the existence of the soul, but—"

Seven bristled despite himself, but he said politely, "If you'll excuse me, dividing yourself in half in order to study the whole seems silly to me. I hope I'm not hurting your feelings, but what happened to the art of godology? Now it's a science?"

"It always *was*. Art is too neither-here-nor-there. We want to be more specific. And a scientist's feelings can't be hurt, because he's too objective to have feelings to *be* hurt," Ram-Ram said rather proudly. "Now do you want to see this case history or don't you? It's Jesus of Nazareth: Case History 9871."

"Okay. That would be fine," Seven said, using his snappiest earth vernacular because he saw that, scientist or no, Ram-Ram's feelings *were* hurt. "I would really appreciate it," Seven added heartily.

Ram-Ram's face brightened, but he coughed, cleared his throat, and began to speak in his professorial style.

"The birth data are all here," he said. "Christ was carried in the womb of time and he had to fight his way through centuries, misplacing stars, galaxies, even; warping the universe, falling through black holes, tumbling from one to the other; seeking, seeking, seeking that one time and space, that one earthly womb, that one microscopic slit in the soil of time . . ."

Seven tried not to yawn. He was thinking that overall he liked Jeffy-boy's Ram-Ram better. At least he had a sense of humor. But the godologist went on, quite carried away by his own presentation. He kept interrupting himself, saying. "Yes, yes, yes," or, "Indeed, that's the way it was," then continuing, growing more excited until Seven became quite alarmed. Again, privately, he wondered if Ram-Ram was really mad. More, Seven couldn't get a word in edgewise, and right then and there he resolved never again to "lecture at" Will in his dream classes. Not that he ever really did, of course, but—

Ram-Ram finally stopped to clear his throat, and Seven said, "Where did you get all that, uh, information?"

"From Christ himself," Ram-Ram said. "Under hypnosis, it all came out." He rubbed his hands together triumphantly. "I have it all in the case history."

And Seven said, "Well, would you mind showing me the case history itself? Then you won't have to go to all the bother of describing it."

Ram-Ram turned on the eternal recording machine, saying, "All of these images came directly from Christ's mind, but first, here's an exterior shot of the experiment conditions. Look." He aimed the machine at the eastern wall of the godologists' building, and the wall disappeared for all practical purposes. Instead, the projections from the machine flashed out against the sky—somewhat like a drive-in theater, Seven thought, except that the whole sky was the screen. He wondered how many others were watching.

Christ lay on a golden couch, spread with royal velvet robes, his eyes closed, his long brown-gray ringlets in disarray about his face, his hands folded upon his chest, and a coverlet pulled up where his johnny robe left off. He seemed to be asleep or dreaming. Occasionally one divine toe twitched beneath the coverlet. Beside him sat Ram-Ram, in his professional capacity. "Now, count backward slowly," he was saying, "from one million back to zero."

"That must have taken forever," Seven whispered.

Ram-Ram, rather annoyed, said, "Never mind, we'll dispense with the hypnotic induction and the count." He touched a lever. "I'll skip ahead a bit. Ahah, here we are: Prenatal memories."

Seven leapt back as a gigantic Lucifer appeared in the sky projection. His form took a thousand images at once, while, overall, one huge leering visage remained.

"The original bogeyman," Ram-Ram said, with great satisfaction. "Quite effective, don't you think? You might say that Lucifer was Christ's shadow, and represented all the portions of his personality that he had to deny: the love of power, lust for knowledge, and the sheer automatic vitality, or the masculine aspects in earthly terminology. Christ's gentleness, understanding, and so forth, stressed the feminine — 'The meek shall inherit the earth' and all of *that*. Well, Lucifer in a way is the exaggerated other side of that image: the uninhibited — "

"Couldn't you just be quiet for a minute?" Seven interrupted uneasily. He stared at the Lucifer image, and cautiously dematerialized at the same time. He'd never seen such a terrifying figure. Though it didn't speak, it raged. The mouth moved insinuatingly as if it were calling out for blood and vengeance in a thousand unspoken languages.

Ram-Ram said proudly, "That image was projected directly from Christ's mind. In a way, it was born with him."

Seven stepped back even further as the giant-sized Lucifer changed into a shouting Jehovah, threatening the Israelites and demanding sacrifices. A mountain appeared, and out of a dreadful yet splendid cloud glimmered God the Father's hands, perfect yet somehow frightening, delivering the tablets with the Ten Commandments to Moses. But even Moses looked insane, Seven thought unhappily: ecstatic, alive to a frenzy.

"That's prenatal memory also," Ram-Ram said. "Finally, of course, Lucifer and God the Father behave in rather similar ways for all intents and purposes, so that afterwards the case history gets more complicated."

"It's complicated enough for me right now," Seven exclaimed. "And scary. Doesn't any of this bother you at all?"

"You forget, I've seen it all before," Ram-Ram said just a trifle smugly. "But watch, now."

Seven really wanted to leave. He remembered how Lydia felt once as a child during a frightening movie. She was afraid to move for fear that if she turned her back on the screen, the feared images would chase her down the aisle. He really wasn't *that* worried, he told himself, and besides he didn't want Ram-Ram to think he was a coward. So he stayed.

Now the sky-screen showed a thriving city. Donkeys, horses, and people filled the streets. Vendors in stalls surrounded palaces and temples. The tumult was tremendous, as Ram-Ram took a close-up so that Seven could hear the individual voices, when in the next moment, the entire city was destroyed. Seven couldn't tell what had happened—there was fire, brimstone, smoke; there were buildings toppling, stalls squashed, horses and people making agonizing sounds, a donkey with its head just cut off by flying debris . . . Seven stared: The donkey was still braying, or so it seemed. Then the sound was cut off as quickly as the head had been.

"You'd think Lucifer did all that," Ram-Ram said. "But it was Jehovah. You see? With prenatal memories like that, and a father who wiped out whole populations if they angered him—well, even a divine son would be bound to have problems. To that, add the fact that Christ had a human, not a divine, mother. Jehovah didn't have a divine mate; he was too ill-tempered. No goddess would put up with him. So in a way, Christ was a half-orphan, divinely speaking. He was the son of a father who was basically impotent— hence, the *angel* appeared to Mary—a father who took his frustrations out on earth, and," Ram-Ram added triumphantly, "on his son. Why else did he send Christ to be crucified? And no matter how he pretended, Christ knew that his father hated him. Couldn't face the truth, though, so he projected his father's hateful qualities onto Lucifer."

"I wish you wouldn't interpret the pictures for me," Seven cried, exasperated, because now the twelve disciples appeared with John closest to Christ, his head bowed near Christ's chest, and Ram-Ram said, "The relationship between the twelve men was interesting also, especially Christ's with John—the tenderness that should have gone to women . . ." Ram-Ram lifted his shaggy white brows significantly. His halo wobbled slightly. He straightened it impatiently and started to continue.

"How many others are viewing these slides?" Seven asked, before Ram-Ram could get going again. "All those images are just splashed out against the sky for anyone to see. I should think Christ could get you for invasion of divine privacy, and I wouldn't want to get Jehovah or Lucifer mad either! Lucifer at least has a sense of humor, but I'm sure Jehovah wouldn't understand at all."

"But basically, Jehovah and Lucifer are both projections of Christ's mind," Ram-Ram said.

"Then how come the sky is getting so dark?" Seven whispered.

"Aha! That must be Christ's anxieties emerging and taking form," Ram-Ram said appreciatively.

"But don't you feel even a trifle uneasy?" Seven asked. "The sky is getting darker by the moment."

"No. Like true scientists, we godologists turn our feelings off in order to do our work. We can't afford to become involved in subjectivity." Ram-Ram spoke very kindly, but rather condescendingly.

"Well, you'd better turn your feelings back on if you can," Seven said, "because mine tell me that we're in for some trouble."

The sky had darkened to such a degree that Seven found it almost impossible to remember what daylight looked like. All of the projections disappeared, yet in a strange way they remained, imprinted in the darkness itself; spooky giant-sized negatives made of layered dark on dark, and in the center of all this, Seven sensed a motion he didn't like at all.

"Magnificent depths of psychological activity," Ram-Ram breathed. "Christ's mind is now reacting to the projections set up by itself and—"

"Will you be quiet?" Seven glared at the godologist, who shrugged and continued his musings, only silently. But Seven was fully and genuinely frightened by now. Who knew what divine psychological mechanisms they *were* tampering with? And once set into motion, who but a god could stop them? And Seven felt that they were tampering. Let Christ's mind keep its secrets. Let the gods save their divine privacy. Let—

Seven broke off his thoughts. The darkness was now swooping into itself at an incredible rate, and in the heart of the activity, a small microscopic image was forming. It was tinier than Seven thought anything could be and still be visible; an image of such intensity that its vitality completely invalidated its size, so that now Seven wondered how he'd ever thought that importance and size were connected in any way at all. He stared at the image because there seemed to be nothing else he *could* do, and discovered that it was actually composed of glittering lights that somehow existed on the . . . other side of darkness.

"I'll teach them something about hypnosis," Christ chuckled.

Zeus said uneasily, "I still think you're going too far."

"Nonsense," Christ said. He and Zeus were whiling away the afternoon. They'd watched Ram-Ram's projections, which had appeared outside of the rest home's huge windows, flickering in dimensions too vast for mortal eyes to follow.

"Still, it was a damn good show," Zeus thundered.

"I gave that idiot godologist just what he wanted," Christ said. "Verily, I told him just what he wanted to hear. It's not my fault if he has to deal with the consequences."

The tiny image that Ram-Ram and Seven were staring at now made up the entire contents of the universe as far as they were concerned, and each of them interpreted it in his own, frightening way.

Every one of the separate glowing details he saw made sense to Seven, for example, yet none of the details taken together formed anything at all, while in each eternal moment they seemed just about to; and the suspense was almost unbearable.

"What about Oversoul Six?" Zeus asked.

"Seven. It's Oversoul Seven, though if he doesn't watch it, he'll be Oversoul Five," Christ muttered. "Verily, he's been asking for this. It'll do him good, and it will teach him not to go to the godologists expecting to learn anything of merit. It'll certainly give him a better perspective."

Ram-Ram was seeing himself, in a million different pieces, scattered, throbbing, changing relationships. His memories kept getting organized in different ways, like jigsaw images constantly changing shape and forming new pictures. The dark yet bright images held his attention so that it seemed nothing else had ever existed, or ever would.

"Now, *that's* hypnosis," Christ chuckled again.

"Still, that part about Jehovah was good," Zeus said, drinking his wine and at the same time wondering if it were nearly time for supper. He eyed Christ slyly, rubbing his black beard, trembling with a laughter that sent the royal floorboards quaking. "I didn't know you hated your father all that much!"

"It's no joke," Christ said irritably. "Mythology is full of such nonsense, and overloaded with divine murders. Humans always want the gods to handle their problems for them and commit their murders for them as well." He broke off, musing. "That's why Allah did so nicely. He didn't hide the facts."

"Well, never mind," Zeus chided. "Hadn't you better snap those two out of whatever spell you've thrown them into? They're really likely to get lost, you know. Besides, it's time for dinner."

"I should make that godologist count from a million backwards — a million times. Did you ever hear of such idiocy?" Christ tried to sound humorous, but he was upset. Invasion of divine privacy was involved; Oversoul Seven was right.

"Bring them back in," Zeus said soothingly.

"They expect me to retaliate," Christ said stubbornly. "I'm only acting out my role."

"Give them a break anyway," Zeus said. "You're supposed to be merciful too. At least take pity on *me;* we'll never eat at this rate."

"I knew you just wanted your dinner," Christ said, laughing because Zeus' good humor *was* godly in its proportions. (Of course, his ire at times could be equally impressive.) But Zeus didn't brood as he did, Christ thought. So he said, "Verily."

Ram-Ram's and Seven's consciousnesses were more or less captured by the multidimensional images that glittered in the doubled-in-upon-itself darkness of the sky. Christ called out good-naturedly, "There they are," reached out a royal hand that magically extended out through galaxies, and brought Seven and Ram-Ram back in. "Like the divine shepherd rescuing two lost sheep," Christ said.

"More like two poor fish," Zeus said.

This time Christ smiled indulgently. With one stare of his mind he destroyed Ram-Ram's case history 9871; with another, he deposited Ram-Ram on the floor of the godologist's main building; and with another he brought a bewildered Oversoul Seven directly to his golden couch.

~ *Chapter Eighteen* ~

Seven's Disquieting Interview with Christ, a
Multidimensional Happening Turns into an Insane
Vision, and Jeffy-boy Becomes a Character in a Book

Oversoul Seven found himself in front of Christ's golden couch, and he was so confused that he kept changing images faster than even he thought he could, in an effort to settle on one that might placate the glowering Christ whose commanding eyes never left Seven's face for one divine moment. "He didn't even blink," Seven told Cyprus later. Seven felt an apology on the tip of his newly formed tongue: He took the shape of the fourteen-year-old, since he understood that Christ particularly liked children.

"Well, what do you have to say for yourself?" Christ demanded. Then, as Seven's boy-image stabilized: "Oh, you're a very young soul," Christ exclaimed in a somewhat mollified voice. "Well, verily," he added, in a still softer tone.

"I'm terribly sorry that you were crucified to begin with," Seven replied quickly. "I hope you don't hold a grudge against the world, though. I mean, well, I didn't have a thing to do with it at all."

Someone chuckled, and Seven suddenly became aware of Zeus, who appeared at Christ's right side. Zeus was eating from a leg of roasted mutton. Still laughing, he offered some to Christ, who shook his gray curls impatiently and said, "No. This whole affair has taken away my appetite for dinner."

335

Zeus stared rather compassionately at Seven, who was just beginning to get his breath, and asked in a voice that was somehow sweet and threatening at the same time, "So you have a taste for the gods, huh?"

Seven whispered, "Render unto Caesar the things that are Caesar's and unto God the things that are God's. No, that isn't right. It's render unto God the things that . . . Um, well, surely you recognize the quote. What I mean is that I let the gods go their way, and hopefully they allow me to do the same." Seven paused, then added to Christ, "The quote was yours, wasn't it, uh, Sir? Or perhaps I should say, 'Your Excellency'?"

"Oh, all right. I'll take a bit of that mutton," Christ said quarrelsomely to Zeus. And to Seven, "I don't care how you address me, but that quote isn't mine. I never said that. I don't care if it makes good sense or poor sense, the fact is that I never said those words in that manner."

"I didn't mean to misquote you," Seven said uneasily. "If you say you didn't say it, well, that's enough for me." Actually, Seven was growing more ill at ease every moment. Earlier he'd been frightened, but now Christ's power seemed to be diminishing to a point where Seven was almost embarrassed for him. Christ was nibbling from the mutton, for example: eating without a knife or fork — he and Zeus both taking very full mouthfuls, with Christ having trouble with the tougher portions. As Seven tried to look away politely, Zeus put his chunk of meat down on the coffee table and said thoughtfully, "You know, Christ, you could have said that Give-to-Caesar quote, and forgotten. In a lifetime, a person, even a god, speaks so many words that surely it's possible that your divine tongue enunciated that particular verbal sequence and — "

Christ's eyes blazed dangerously. He spat out a bit of meat into his napkin and said, very emphatically and deliberately, "I did not say those words. And I didn't curse the poor fig tree either. Being misquoted is one of the worst things that can happen to a god's message, and it happens all the time. Then of course, it's repeated endlessly. Endlessly." Christ's voice grew morose. His divine eyes wandered. Seven thought that if this kind of behavior kept up, Christ might even forget that he was there, and he could sneak away.

"Endlessly," Christ repeated, staring at Seven.

It *was* quite possible, Seven thought, that Christ's memory was slipping, but even as Seven thought those words, Christ's head snapped forward. The divine eyes came afire and Christ said, "So you think I'm losing my memory, do you? I remember the beginning of the world." Once more his eyes dimmed. "Those were the days," he muttered.

Seven was ready to weep. If this was Christ, the legends far surpassed the reality. He was almost always disappointed meeting an author in person, but this! He lowered his eyes and looked at the floorboards. They began to shimmer. Somewhere, Seven thought that he heard Zeus and Christ laugh —massive chuckles that disrupted birds in their flights through a million skies—laughs that emitted divine humor, compassionate but largely lost to any but godly ears. Gradually the chuckles changed in character though they continued until Seven thought that they'd sounded for eternity.

Realizing that he'd closed his eyes, he opened them. Then he rubbed them. There were torn magazines on the coffee table where only a moment earlier there had been, instead, a plate of mutton. The golden couch was replaced by several rickety chairs and instead of Christ and Zeus, Jeffy-boy and *his* Ram-Ram sat with the coffee table between them.

Queen Alice, on the other side of the table, said, "Ideas of sanity are so limiting, don't you think? That's why people who think they're sane get in so much trouble when they realize that they're actually bigger than their concepts give them a right to be."

Jeffery said, "This is ridiculous." He ignored Queen Alice and turned to Ram-Ram, who shrugged his shoulders comically at Queen Alice and said, "Jeffy-boy just can't get all this through his head." Then, to Jeffery, "You want to know if I was really in your apartment the other afternoon. I was. Now, does that answer your question?"

"It does and it doesn't," Jeffery replied with some irritation. "Were you there physically?"

"Definitely not," Ram-Ram said; then, with the kindly old psychologist's smile, "I know, I know. You have more questions, but let's take them one at a time."

"You're the one who's in the mental institution," Jeffery shouted. "So don't give me advice."

"Quite right," Ram-Ram said agreeably.

"If there are gods, they'd be considered insane too," Queen Alice said musingly. She tucked her blue and white checkered shirt in under her dungarees, untucked it again, and said triumphantly, "Many of the insane speak for the gods all the time. Three Christs have come and gone from this very institution since I've been here. And they weren't missed either, I'll tell you. They were all fanatics."

Stoically Jeffery waited until Queen Alice finished speaking. Then he said desperately to Ram-Ram, "I thought that I had an entire conversation with you in my apartment. Then you . . . disappeared. Now you tell me that you *were* there, but not physically. In other words, our insane data agree. Facts that simply cannot be facts—"

"They *are* facts, they are, Jeffy-boy," Ram-Ram shouted excitedly. "But in a different kind of fact system. That's what I'm trying to get across to you." Ram-Ram broke off. A lovely young girl came over from the other side of the room, offering tiny pieces of a candy bar that she'd obviously slivered into numberless bits of chocolate. She curtsied. Ram-Ram smiled, said, "Thank you, my dear," in a sweet but grand fashion, offered a piece to Queen Alice, and turned back to Jeffery.

"There's another one," Queen Alice whispered, poking Jeffery, who quickly recoiled. Ram-Ram noticed, and chuckled. Jeffery said, exasperated, "Another what?"

"Why, another Christ. The only one left here, and the nicest we've had by far," Queen Alice said, standing; and despite himself, Jeffery noticed that for all of her years, she was as supple as a girl. Her white hair looked almost blonde for a moment in the afternoon sunlight that came through the yellow plastic curtains at the windows by the TV set. For a wild moment, Jeffery almost felt that she was younger than he was.

"Oh, yes, she thinks she's Christ," Queen Alice said gaily. "The psychologists keep trying to tell her that she must be the Blessed Virgin instead, because there are certain conventions to follow whether you're crazy or not." She smiled innocently, rubbing her wrinkled chin with a rather grubby finger, and added, "If you're female and think you're god, then they think you're crazier than a male who thinks the same thing, because at least he has his sexes straight. See?"

Jeffery's eyes widened incredulously. He fumbled nervously with the buttons of his properly rumpled sweater and said to Ram-Ram, "Do you understand what she's talking about?"

"Yes, yes, yes. And she's quite right," exclaimed Ram-Ram. "This place has the richest psychological climate in the world, you know. Cynthia, the girl with the chocolate, doesn't necessarily think that Christ was a woman, but that she is a woman and she is Christ. A subtle difference, don't you see? She annoys our psychological colleagues no end, of course, but she won't back down and be the Virgin Mary. Watch. Look now," Ram-Ram pointed, and Jeffery turned to see Cynthia, a girl in her twenties, move among the multitude. At least, from her manner and bearing, that was certainly what she thought she was doing; offering each inmate a sliver of chocolate; smiling with the sweetest generosity, so that Jeffery himself was almost taken in, at least for a moment. "Why, it's incredible. She obviously believes it," he gasped.

Ram-Ram was getting more and more excited. He wet his lips, and as if addressing a class, he said to Jeffery, "Don't you see? Her father brings her the candy bars. She distributes them instead of fishes—"

Queen Alice said comfortably, "She's writing a bible of her own in her spare time. I might help her type it."

"Oh, God," Jeffery cried, "You really are mad, the both of you!"

"What do you expect? This is a mental institution," Ram-Ram said, laughing; then, slyly, "Without madness, there'd be no sanity in the world. Don't you agree, Queen Alice?"

Jeffery didn't hear her answer. He sat with his head in his arms, overcome by the deepest sense of desolation he'd ever known. "And I must share some of that madness," he said soberly. "I thought I saw you *physically* in my apartment, and physically at least you were here. There must be a kind of contagion, so that the brain no longer distinguishes reality. It must perceive bits and pieces that don't agree. Maybe I mixed a memory of a past visit of yours with reality—"

"Now, now, don't take it so hard," Ram-Ram said. He took Jeffery's hand reassuringly before Jeffery wrenched it away. The girl, Cynthia, hearing the commotion, came over and offered Jeffery another sliver of chocolate. "Take it away," he said angrily. Then, looking up, he saw her eyes. They weren't Christ's eyes—who knew what Christ's eyes looked like? But they were the eyes Christ should have had, in which all contradictions vanished or were resolved, in whose glance he suddenly saw himself, a person of dignity despite all of his own vast misunderstandings. He took the candy and said, "Thank you," with a simplicity and grace he didn't know he possessed.

Queen Alice was sitting down again, studying her hands. Ram-Ram seemed to have fallen asleep in the hard-backed chair, or he was pretending to be dozing, as a hospital patient might when wishing that a visitor would leave. With a slight shock, Jeffery realized that no one was paying him any attention at all. He might as well have been invisible. Queen Alice picked up a magazine. Someone turned up the volume on the TV set: A ballgame came on, and the spectators' shouts filled the room. It was as if he'd already left, Jeffery thought. He coughed, picked up his jacket and turned to leave . . .

As he did, the sound of the spectators at the televised ballgame seemed to rise in volume, and the applause and shouts suddenly roused Oversoul Seven back to himself. Instantly he remembered the giant chuckles of the gods that had propelled him here. But he'd experienced the entire scene through Jeffery. When he discovered this, Oversoul Seven was considerably shaken and confused. Why Jeffery? he wondered. Jeffery wasn't even one of his own personalities.

And then, as he thought of the gods and Jeffery, between one moment and the next, the two environments—the Olympian rest home and Ram-Ram's mental institution—met and merged, attaining such unmanageable dimensions that Seven called out for Cyprus. There was no answer. Instead, the dizzying transformation continued. The gods' rest home with Zeus and Christ and the golden couch was suddenly transposed over the institution's common room. The magazines on the coffee table fluttered madly through the air, landing on Christ's couch. The television set, still showing the ball-game, now sat in the gods' rest home, with Zeus madly adding his shouts to those of the spectators.

Worse, Jeffery, who was just leaving the common room, suddenly—somehow—turned into Will, and stayed. Queen Alice became Zeus's wife, Hera, and Ram-Ram, like some mad director, was himself and the godologist Ram-Ram as well. Seven was reeling, trying to keep it all straight. In the next moment, however, all the surroundings expanded. Zeus and Christ, all of the inmates of the institution and all of the gods in the rest home, merged into one wildly incoherent supergod, but one so ancient, so grandly senile, so sweetly insane that even the grasses trembled at the very thought of his approach.

For now, in the next scene, Seven saw the world ruled by this spectacular entity, and heard the tempting senile god's voice as it drifted eerily though all the secret places of the universe, into forest corners, into the deepest, most inaccessible ocean caves, into the invisible closets of people's minds. And despite himself, Seven was terrified.

He saw frightened pigeons fly to hiding places. He felt the god's breath shake the world to bits in endless autumns; leaves committing exultant suicide. ("Ah hah," Will yelled, dying with each leaf.) And he felt each living thing tremble, trying to preserve its life in the face of such cosmic temper tantrums. This god's insanity whispered crookedly through men's chromosomes, tainting them with flaws beyond number. The senile god shouted his incoherent truth to the multitudes, who in turn killed their neighbors and rode in bitter triumph through endless savage wars. Mad Mohammed flashed his eternal sword; Jehovah in fits of holy tremors sent down his plagues and flood; Jupiter and Thor threw their thunderbolts while Buddha contemplated his divine navel and in the streets his gurus sprinkled holy ash.

Seven screamed, "Stop!"

The insane god, who was at once Jehovah, Buddha, and all of the others, paused and seemed to notice Oversoul Seven for the first time. The earth that Seven was seeing took on the god's features, so that Seven saw the treetops spinning in the wind as the shaken, tousled curls of Christ's head; the oceans, the depthless pools of his insane delight and the unendurable realization of his plight; for this god knew he was a demon, raging, possessing the earth, tuning it to his own cosmic insane pitch until surely one day—today or tomorrow or in a million years—that pitch would become so agonizing that the god's mind would split; divine neurons spilling out into mortality, the blessed essence contaminated beyond degree, and lost.

This *was* an insane vision. Seven tried to clear his consciousness, to shake it loose from the strands of despair that threatened to send him reeling into extinction. Hopelessly, he suddenly saw Lydia and Will falling through unnumbered days that wound back to the insane god's infancy.

"I won't live in such a world," Will was shouting. His voice splintered the air beneath him, and at the same time his memories poured out of his mind into space.

And Lydia, furiously angry, stood for a moment, shaking her fists at the universe. "I won't be born again in that mad world!" She was going to say more, but the insane god's eye blinked and Lydia twirled, turning smaller and smaller, blown willy-nilly by the thunderous power of that divine blinking eye.

Seven's astonishment at all of this slowed his reactions. What nightmare was this? But he couldn't seem to break its spell, and the psychological implications of this disastrous vision were all too clear. He had to break away for Lydia and Will, and if they were lost . . . But how could they be? Again Seven cried out for Cyprus. This time she responded so abruptly and severely that Seven was snapped back to himself — so quickly that he felt as if a million shocks surged through the most vital portions of his consciousness.

"Seven, how *could* you have allowed such a thing to happen?" Cyprus exclaimed, though "exclaimed" isn't quite the word. Seven felt her disapproval, or rather, her sorrow. But before he could respond, he watched as her image appeared simultaneously to Will and Lydia, who seemed to be in the distance below him. Lydia looked incredulous and angry. Will looked defiant and scared to death. Seven watched as Cyprus formed a gentle summertime hill beneath them. Then she talked to them quietly, before returning to Seven.

"What happened?" Seven asked impatiently. "What did I do wrong, and how much will Lydia and Will remember? Was Will on drugs or something?" He was still shaken himself, and he noticed that Cyprus wasn't consoling *him*. Instead she said, "Look for yourself." And she and Seven stood invisibly in Will's "bedroom."

Will lived in a loosely knit commune; that is, young people constantly came and went. Will's cot, with his name painted on it, sat behind a huge rubber plant, and beside this sat the two orange crates that Will used as a desk. The plant and crates marked this corner of the large room as Will's property, and above the bed a poster of Buddha stared blissfully over Will's pillow. Will considered himself quite lucky since his corner possessed a window, half of which he'd covered with a map of the world.

Now he lay curled up at the head of the cot, wondering if he felt strong enough to make it to the communal sink to wash his face, or even further to the refrigerator where his food—oranges—was stacked on the third shelf. There were ten other cots scattered around the room, each one marked in one way or another as private property, but for now, Will was alone.

He'd just awakened from a terrible nightmare, or so he thought, except for the ending where he was sunbathing on a hill; and he supposed that one or a combination of the drugs he'd been taking had caused the particularly frightening sense of insanity he dimly remembered. But now everything looked normal, which meant shitty and dismal, he thought. Reaching under his mattress, he felt around until his trembling fingers found his potpourri of pills, his cache, that he kept hidden there. Without even looking to see what particular pills he'd grabbed, he popped two.

Oversoul Seven said to Cyprus, "He does it all the time."

Will's eyelids fluttered. He began muttering. Cyprus sighed. "What you experienced earlier was a nightmare, all right, composed of Will and Lydia's worst fears about god and the universe. And you should have monitored it for them, not fallen into it yourself."

Will's mutterings grew louder. At the same time, he began to rouse in his dream body. "You stay with him now," Cyprus said. "I'll want to have a good talk with you later."

"What about Lydia?" Seven cried. "I should get back to her, shouldn't I?" But there was no reply, and in any case it was too late; Will stood in his dream body, eyeing Seven.

"Well, I've done it again," Will said sheepishly. "*You're* here, and you're one of my most exasperating trips." Actually, he felt quite satisfied with himself for the moment. He knew he was tripping, but he'd decided Oversoul Seven was some kind of symbol that meant he was safe, or nearly. In fact, for no reason at all, he felt cocky. "If you're a figment of my imagination, I'm pretty good," he said to Seven.

"I'm sorry I can't return the compliment," Seven grumbled.

"How come I feel so great?" Will cried.

Seven answered, "Cyprus gave you additional energy; but then you probably wouldn't remember." He himself felt quite glum indeed, and his mood didn't improve as Will ran up and down the room, shouting, "I'm out of my body, I'm out of my body!"

"You're strung out on drugs too," Seven cried angrily, "and if it wasn't for me, who knows what trouble you might be getting into."

"So what?" Will shouted happily. "I'm out of my body and you're here, and for once we aren't in a classroom. Is my wish your command, by the way?" Will eyed Seven speculatively and added, "Because on my last trip I had a terrible experience about an insane god or something, and I don't want to do that one again. But if you're like a genie, well, I can go where I want to."

"I'm not like a genie," Seven said.

"Well, anyhow. God was miserable. But let's take a trip to see his mother," Will declared.

"Whose mother?" Seven asked, uneasily.

"Why, Christ's. She'd know all about him, wouldn't she?" Will replied. "After all, who knew him better?" Will started giggling.

"Forget it," Seven said. "And anyway, why Christ's mother?"

"Why not?" Will said airily. "If I'm tripping, well, it's *my* trip, isn't it?" He grinned brilliantly and added, "And somehow, I seem to have you where I want you for a change."

"That's what you think," Seven muttered to himself, but there was no doubt that he had to stay with Will for a while, and he didn't like the new turn of events. How much bleed-through was there, actually, from one personality's experience to another's? Without knowing the details, was Will somehow aware of Lydia's search for the gods, and its so far unhappy results? He must be, Seven thought, staring at Will; otherwise, Lydia and Will wouldn't have been involved in the same awful nightmarish experience.

"Well?" Will demanded, and despite himself, Seven was caught between exasperation and appreciation: There Will stood, arrogant and sassy, and looking like a young god himself; filled right now with fresh determination. But determination to do what? Because in the next moment, Will said, "I'm probably going to commit suicide the first chance I get, so you really shouldn't refuse me any favors or you'll be sorry later. And I want to visit the Virgin Mary. If that's within your province, of course."

Seven sighed. Will's last remark made a certain kind of unfortunate sense. "I can't guarantee what will happen," Seven said nervously. "I wish you'd change your mind."

"Not on your life. Not on your life. Not on your life." Will started chanting the words over and over, and Seven wished wholeheartedly that Cyprus hadn't given him quite so much energy.

"Have it your way," Seven said. Will could have sworn that no transition had occurred, but now he and Seven were travelers.

～ *Chapter Nineteen* ～

The Virgin Mary's Tale
and an Ego for Buddha

Seven and Will were dressed like humble pilgrims. The street (if such it was) appeared to belong to ancient Jerusalem. Donkeys brayed. Tradesmen went about their business. Mary's small house was set in a bit from the numerous stalls at which vendors sold their wares. The house was actually the strangest combination of a manger, barn, and small sitting room. Outside, two palm trees stood at either side of the entrance. Incongruously enough, there was a small green lawn, and in the center of it were various small statuettes making up a tabloid of the nativity, with Mary, Joseph, and the baby Jesus. Alongside was a plaster image of Christ as a boy of about twelve, and to the right, a huge cross on which a statue of the adult Christ hung, with blood that looked real enough running from his wounds down into a small pond, which drained into the ground. By each palm tree knelt a statue of an angel carrying a sword.

Will just stared. "This isn't real, you know," he said to Oversoul Seven. "And this street just started from no place. If you walked to either end, it would probably just disappear." He shrugged to show that he wasn't impressed, yet there was something terribly impressive about the mixture of junky artifacts and real, braying donkeys; and the cheap-looking plaster-of-Paris angels had the craziest intensity, as if their grotesqueness gave them a life of their own.

Seven just said, "Now, let me handle this, please. And be polite for a change, if you can." He knocked at the door.

Will said, "I can't believe it; knocking at the door of the Virgin Mary. Even for a dream or a drug trip, it's just too much."

The door opened, seemingly by itself. At first the room seemed dim. Seven and Will took a few hesitant steps inside. Then, however, a series of glows lit up the interior, like spotlights, though not as bright. One showed an empty manger; one, a group of oxen, sleeping; and in the light of the third glow, the Virgin Mary sat crocheting.

She said, pleasantly enough, "Welcome. But if you've come to see my son, he isn't here."

"We know that," Oversoul Seven said politely. "It's you we've come to see."

Mary looked alarmed. "You aren't reporters? I don't give interviews anymore," she exclaimed.

Seven assured her that they weren't journalists of any kind, and with a partially worried air, Mary put her crocheting work aside.

Will kept saying to himself, "This is impossible. It can't be happening." To Seven he whispered, "This whole thing is crazy, and besides, she looks like Whistler's Mother." But even as Will spoke the words, he completely changed his mind.

Mary blinked constantly; anxiously. She looked like a windup doll, dressed in a long blue gown with a brown robe on top, her too-smooth head partly covered by a black veil. Her face was too chinalike, too chiseled, and her eyes looked too mechanical. But for mechanical-looking eyes, they were astounding. Will felt that they'd been weeping for centuries, and indeed they did begin to weep again.

As she started to cry, gently, Mary reached for a Kleenex and said, "Do forgive me. My son was a good boy always. They crucified him, you know. Just the same, people keep coming here and writing, wanting me to intercede for them. Life has its cruelties. And I can never answer all the mail, so people must think I don't care." With one hand, she indicated a corner of the room where stacks of letters and stone tablets and even sheets and rolls of papyrus, along with telegrams, were all piled together. "Mail even comes by wireless now," she said, "And I had to have the phone removed because for years I was on the phone day and night. And my son is in the old gods' home now, you know. I visit him when I can, but he never forgot the Crucifixion. And he's never been the same since. He never really thought that his father would let him die that way, even if it was to a good purpose. The family has scattered since. But I'm sorry for rattling on like this over my own problems. Would you like a glass of wine?"

Oversoul Seven shook his head. Will stood looking out the glassless window at the commotion outside, noticing that the sounds of the street somehow stopped just outside the window, though they should have been only too clear. It was like watching a silent movie, he thought: He could see the merchants' mouths opening as they spoke; see the carts drawn by the donkeys, but no clatter of wheels or raucous shouts entered that room. Wild, he kept thinking: What a trip. He hoped he'd remember it all.

"Do continue," Seven was saying to Mary. Then to Will he said, "And I wish you'd come over here and sit down." Will managed a partially insolent, partially nonchalant stride to show that all of this was too impossible and ridiculous to take his notice for a moment, but he sat down.

Mary gave Will a humble smile as if agreeing that she was, indeed, beneath anyone's serious consideration. Then she rearranged her robes slightly and, head lowered, she continued. "I tried to be a good woman. Joseph, my husband, was only a lowly carpenter; a virtuous one, it's true. But from the moment he was born, I thought Jesus was special and I wanted to give him a heritage to be proud of; a gift no one else had . . ." She paused, looked worried, and eyed Oversoul Seven with an anxious air.

"Do continue. It's fascinating," Seven said, without looking at Will, because he was doubly sorry that he'd let him come. This interview wasn't likely to convince Will that the universe had any sense, Seven told himself. At the same time, Seven had almost forgotten who Mary was supposed to be, in the reality of this woman before him, with her hesitant manner . . . Seven broke off. Or was her manner suddenly confessional? "Don't say anything you don't want to," he said quickly, but it was too late.

"I never could bring myself to discuss . . . things of the flesh with my son." She paused again. "Do you understand?"

"Absolutely," Oversoul Seven said nervously. "Do you want to change the subject?"

"No, it must be said," Mary replied resolutely.

"Well, say it, then," Seven muttered under his breath.

"I told him, my son, that he came from God . . . without the agency of man. It was only a mother's innocent deceit."

"Oh, I knew it," Will shouted, springing to his feet. He lifted his head dramatically and threw his arms skyward. "Sheer idiocy. Behind every religion, every philosophy. At least the Western ones. Oh, sheer idiocy!"

But Oversoul Seven (still looking like a pilgrim) was at Mary's side; truly upset. "Now, now, do calm down," he pleaded.

"My son believed me," Mary cried in an anguished voice. "He became truly deluded."

Her eyes *did* seem made for weeping. Crying, they attained an odd but truly spectacular cast, as if the tears magnified and yet distorted some truth that seemed irreconcilable with the words she was sobbing. "I knew it was a lie," she said, this time as if condemning herself beyond all hope of salvation. "And yet," she began, and as she spoke, her tears stopped abruptly. She lifted her head proudly, staring at the astonished Oversoul Seven, and moved her arm in a triumphant gesture. She was suddenly so authoritative that Seven leapt back just a step, and Will just stared. Mary's voice now was strong; almost hard. "And yet, the lie was the truth, and I knew that, too. Or the lie became the truth. Or maybe it was the truth all along, and I had to pretend it was a lie. But in some way, I *am* the Mother of God."

As she spoke, the air in the room seemed to shimmer. Seven thought uneasily that something could happen that could disturb worlds or disrupt them prematurely if Mary remembered . . . if Mary remembered what?

But she didn't. She almost seemed to have forgotten what she'd just said, for that matter. Dejection once again settled down upon her doll-like features. "So we shared the same delusion," she said in a sad voice. "It was so bad finally that Jesus attempted suicide. They took the knives and forks and all silverware away from him at the rest home. He's not allowed any sharp objects at all."

Seven felt a twinge of guilt for having thought that Christ and Zeus were gluttonous when he saw them eating without forks: He blushed.

Will stood in the center of the room and said, "Well, that's it, all right. If Christ contemplated suicide, it shows he's not all mad, Madam. Still, it *does* make you think twice, doesn't it? When the gods can't stand existence?" He started to giggle. He couldn't help it. He put his hand over his mouth, and sat down on the floor, holding his stomach.

Seven listened to Will with a feeling of dismay, but something else kept bothering him, and he couldn't properly identify what it was — a fact that annoyed him even more. Mary started to weep again; Will had the grace to be quiet for a moment, and Seven mentally explored the many-leveled nature of this interview with the Virgin. Mary was acting; that idea came to him. Christ and Zeus were acting; but no, that wasn't exactly right, either. There *was* a drama though, in which psychological props were being used, Seven thought, and he had to know what part he was playing, along with Lydia and Will before . . . what? Before the pilgrimage to the gods turned into something else entirely. Or had it already? As soon as Seven thought of Lydia, Mary's cottage vanished, or at least he and Will found themselves outside once more, walking down the street.

"Seven! Seven!"

Hearing his name called, Oversoul Seven stopped with surprise. Who could be looking for him *here?* He eyed the street. No one looked familiar. The street hawkers were putting away their wares for the afternoon. Donkeys were reladen with supplies. Dogs and children skittered here and there. Horses slopped water. Men and women in various everyday garbs suddenly began to hurry away—perhaps to simple suppers. Then amid the confusion Seven noticed one figure, also dressed as a pilgrim, running toward him. It was Lydia.

The moment Seven recognized her, he heard another voice, Cyprus', mentally say, "You forgot someone, didn't you?" Seven started to answer, but by then Lydia was saying breathlessly, "Cyprus sent me here. I had a dreadful experience. I'm not sure what it really was, but there were insane gods and God knows what! I came to on a hillside. But who is this?"

Will was really beginning to enjoy himself, and Oversoul Seven's obvious discomforture. "Who are you?" he asked, bowing with mock deference. "The Virgin Mary's sister, I suppose?"

Lydia started to respond rather tartly, when Will immediately went on, "Or Buddha's daughter? Or perhaps Buddha in a woman's guise? Or—"

"Stop that," Seven cried. "Not another word."

But Will was tasting a sense of power. He made a mental note to find out exactly what pills he'd popped because he'd never had such a brilliant, heady, conscious trip before. "That's it," he shouted, snapping his fingers. "You must be Buddha."

Instantly he broke off. Suddenly there were lotus blossoms everywhere. The stalls and people and donkeys were gone. The street disappeared. The silence after all the commotion was the oddest thing of all. Will had never sensed such silent air. Then he, Lydia, and Seven noticed something even stranger. The space around them formed a gigantic transparent image of Buddha, and they stood inside. The softest grass imaginable was beneath their feet, and the loveliest blue air was above; yet all of that was a part of the Buddha's form. Seven stared: The image was now repeated unendingly, it seemed, in miniature transparent images, kaleidoscopic Buddha-shapes, mixing and merging together, forming the grass and sky as well, a million Jell-O-cubes of Buddha images. And the air itself felt different, like the most softly moving gelatin, of different hues, that all blended together. Will, shocked, stuck his finger out and stirred the air; he could feel it nudge against his fingertip as if it had a life of its own.

"What a trip, oh, what a trip!" Will shouted. His voice sent ripples through the jellylike air, set it moving in a slow frenzy.

Oversoul Seven cried, "Be quiet. Listen."

"I don't hear anything," Lydia said. She pulled her pilgrim's robe about her throat and looked around anxiously.

Then Will leapt back. "I hear something," he exclaimed, for the air was making the most peculiar settling sound, and before their eyes, Seven, Lydia, and Will saw the air visibly thicken, while still retaining its transparent quality. A giant-sized, slightly solidified Buddha image formed in the air just above them. Its parts moved and flowed together, again, like gelatin made out of space itself.

Seven steadied himself and said politely, "Uh, good afternoon."

Lydia didn't say a thing. Will prostrated himself on the ground and said, "Here I am, Master. I've no ego left. I'm done with desire. I've read all about you, and please consider me your servant."

"Get up on your feet and don't make a fool of yourself," Seven whispered.

Will sent Seven a glance of nearly pure hatred, and then addressed the Buddha. "I tell you, I'm done with desire. I'm finished with wants and lusts."

The Buddha lifted his beautiful gelatinous brows and said to Oversoul Seven, "What is he talking about?"

"Excuse me," Lydia interrupted hesitantly. "Are you an Indian god? If you are, I have some questions."

"I am if it suits your fancy," Buddha said. "Now what is that poor fellow saying?" Buddha raised his flowing arm and indicated Will, who was sitting in a lotus position, and doing a rather poor job of it because his sneakers kept getting tangled in his pilgrim's robe.

"Om, om, om," Will chanted, and Buddha snapped, "Will you shut up?" so loudly that Will sprang to his feet.

"Now what's all this nonsense about giving up desire?" Buddha demanded. He spoke an elegant Indian dialect that Seven, Lydia, and Will all understood at once.

"It's a part of your teaching, Master," Will whispered. "I've read it in all of your sacred books."

"Let those who will, give up desire," Buddha said. "It sounds like a lot of nonsense to me, and if anyone said that I made such pronouncements, then I've been grossly misquoted. Shall the bee give up its honey? The cat, its tail? The apple, its core? The fly, its wings? The scalp, its hair? The cow, its moo? The —"

"Uh, we get your point," Seven said.

But the Buddha went on. "The horse must neigh. It cannot meow. But men, when they quote me, put the cat's meow in the horse's mouth." He turned his blessed eyes in the general direction of his navel and sighed, but Seven noticed that his eyes were quite merry, twinkling like gelatin.

"All of this is a bit disconcerting," Seven said, because by now it was apparent that Buddha's form was sometimes softly gelatinous and visible, and sometimes only indicated, except for the navel which remained, like a grape. For a moment the form stabilized again and Buddha's voice rang out, this time more sweetly than before, so that the sounds themselves seemed to glitter through the image's multitudinous jellyfish folds.

He said, "Desire not to desire—an impossible situation! For that matter, all realities and situations *are* basically impossible; that is, they would be if they happened, for the reasons mortals suppose they do. Lydia, for example—"

Without thinking, Lydia knelt down, genuflecting. She crossed herself and said, "Yes, Father," in response to an early Catholic conditioning that she thought she'd forgotten. Recovering, she jumped to her feet, glared at Oversoul Seven as if her mistake was his fault, and tried to hide her embarrassment. "I'm sorry, but I don't mean to kneel before anyone anymore," she said. "And, well, a real god wouldn't need adoration."

Buddha's image chuckled, quaked; and the sweet voice went on. "Lydia, a part of you—your desire—is building up someplace else, which is why you feel so discontented now. You haven't followed your desire to be born again. You keep hampering it and setting conditions. You set yourself apart from your desire, examine it, and demand that the gods take responsibility for your lack of decision."

"Why, I do not," Lydia sputtered. "And what do you expect me to do?"

"Just go where your desire dictates," Buddha began.

Will shouted furiously, "You can't say that! The Buddhists believe in rising above desire. Even I know that."

At this, the Buddha laughed, setting his image shaking and quaking, and he shouted, "Ah ha, but I'm not a Buddhist. I'm *Buddha*. And your desire is your inner direction, and you desire death only because it's the only desire left, the only one you allow."

"I don't believe that at all," Will shouted. "And I don't have an ego anymore. I've rid myself of it. I just want to serve, so I can only suppose that your ridiculous remarks are part of a trial to test me. I want to be selfless. I am selfless. I am, goddammit," he yelled. Then he stood, staring, too frightened to move. The gelatinous Buddha shuddered, trembled like a cosmic jell-mountain, and began to melt into a trembling mass of semithick liquid that moved purposefully and directly toward Will. First, the edges melted and small puddles reached Will's sneakered feet. He finally screamed, and leapt backward, as the entire mass flowed like cold lava, faster and faster, in his direction.

"No. No," Will screamed, staring upward at the unsteady melting Jell-O Buddha which now threatened to avalanche down upon him.

At the last minute, Oversoul Seven grabbed Will, and the Buddha-flow stopped; uncertain. Will was shaking and muttering, and Seven said sternly to the Buddha, "You didn't have to go *that* far. We get the message." Then, to Will, he said, "Your 'trip' is over, and I'm sure it's more than you counted on. Wake up inside your physical body. And if it's selflessness you want, you nearly got a taste of it, so I hope you've learned a lesson. Anyhow, you're safe now, so you can wake up relieved."

Will just nodded, too shaken to say a thing. He muttered something about never taking drugs again, and disappeared. The Buddha shrank at the edges, wrinkled, each part shaking with such humor that Seven almost forgot to be angry; and then the Buddha was gone. Seven and Lydia stood there a moment, still dressed in their pilgrim garb, when once again the air began to thicken into semi-shapes, and Lydia gasped as the grounds gradually changed to those of the gardens outside of the gods' rest home. Only this time, Cyprus was waiting for them.

"This has gone quite far enough. Seven, I want to talk to you," she said. She took a form that was nearly regal, so that Oversoul Seven made no protest, though he'd had one in mind. Even Lydia remained silent, though Seven was afraid she might complain about some of the less fortunate of their recent adventures.

A blue-green cast covered the garden; a twilight that was at once sad in nature and oddly neutral in quality in a way that Seven sensed but couldn't fathom.

Dejectedly, Lydia sat down on one of the benches. With her head bowed she looked medieval in the pilgrim's gown. She moved; glanced toward the gods' rest home, its stone structure looming now like a dark cliff in the distance. "I've made one decision, anyway," she said. "If anyone is interested."

Cyprus was smiling very gently, and yet her smile had the same neutral quality as the twilight, Seven noticed. "What did you decide?" Cyprus asked Lydia.

Lydia stood up, one arm resting on the back of the bench, the pilgrim cowl half obscuring the curve of her cheeks. She looked tired, defeated, and triumphant all at once. "I'm definitely ready to be born again. I'm going through with it after all," she said, but with a hard tone to her voice that defied her slumped shoulders. "I want earth life again, with clear boundaries and a framework that I can understand. And gods or not; God, my life last time made more sense than the gods do. So who needs a senile Christ and a Jell-O Buddha? I want to go to Bianka's room again, and check with Josef, and see how the birth preparations are going. I just can't handle all of this other—" She broke off and threw her arms out in the air. "Nonsense!" she cried.

Seven blushed. Cyprus, with that strange neutrality, took Lydia's hand in hers, and the two of them vanished. For a moment Seven was alone, though he knew that Cyprus would return for their talk; a talk he'd rather forget, he told himself. It was obvious that he'd gone wrong somewhere in this search for the gods, and yet he knew that he had to let Lydia and Will search in their own ways. He'd merely help out as best he could.

In the odd twilight, Seven disentangled himself mentally from his personalities, from Lydia and Will and Josef, and instantly he felt lighter, freer, and playful. The universe *was* safe, spilling over with exuberance; so where, he wondered, had Lydia's and Will's dissatisfaction come from? Granted, the gods seemed—well, a trifle erratic, but they were likable enough in their own fashions. So just what did Will and Lydia expect of them? And why should either of them suppose, if they did, that those gods had anything to do with running the universe?

He decided to forget about it while he could. Free of restraints, Seven played in the twilight. He turned into a flower, luxuriating in the touch of gentle air. He forgot himself in the very transparency of his being, while all the time knowing that he knew himself better for his temporary unknowing.

At first, Cyprus was only a distant thought to him. Then she appeared. The two of them turned into points of light, sparkling in the garden.

Seven said, "Before you say anything, I'm terribly disappointed. I thought that the gods would have more sense." Cyprus didn't answer at once. The background sounds grew louder. In the distance Oversoul Seven heard the clash of Mohammed's sword as he fought with the infidels, yelling "Allah" and leaping back and forth. "That's what I mean," Seven cried disconsolately.

"They mean well," Cyprus answered. "Don't be so critical. They're giant psychological projections, man's 'divine children' exaggerating their parents' best and worst qualities."

"You mean they aren't real at all?" Seven cried, astounded. "First I didn't believe they existed, and I guess I was better off. Then I thought that if they'd influenced human thought all that much, the gods *must* exist. Then I decided that they were real and I expected them to be—well, at *least* adult, in human terms. Now you're telling me that they weren't real to begin with."

Oversoul Seven felt tired and confused. He glanced around the garden. Birds of all colors flew through the air. The sky was an extraordinary blue-gray. Flowers grew everywhere in tints beyond description. But none of it contented him.

Cyprus kept changing position, appearing first on a leaf, then on a grass blade, and then on the top of Mohammed's sword, so that Seven cried out, "Cyprus, don't do that!"

Cyprus said, "Oh, Seven, you know better than that," and Seven answered, "I know it. Of course you wouldn't get hurt. But I'm too worried to think straight."

"Do stop brooding," Cyprus responded. "The gods are real enough. They're just different than your personalities expected them to be. In a manner of speaking, the gods are born from man's yearning, from man's loves and hates and fears and hopes. Each person contributes to the creation until you have—well, a conglomerate god, made up of part of each individual."

"Then they *aren't* real," Seven shouted.

"Oh, Seven, you haven't met the *real* gods yet, if that's what you mean. I thought you understood that!" Cyprus stared at Seven with amazed dismay, and to cover his confusion Seven took the fourteen-year-old-boy image. Cyprus automatically compensated, adopting her complementary teacher form. She said, "It never occurred to me that you supposed—"

"Supposed what?" Seven asked dismally. "What did you think I supposed?"

Cyprus said gently, "I took it for granted that you realized that you were perceiving Lydia and Will's *versions* of the gods; mostly Lydia's, as they were reflected through her mind and took on those psychological connotations. The gods as understood by mortals are always conventional personifications. They're like religious psychological statues, only possessing more abilities and characteristics. But all in all, highly limited by any standards of excellence or morality. Animated superstars; perhaps that term expresses it best of all."

But Seven was horrified. "I didn't understand that at all," he said angrily. "And certainly Lydia and Will didn't. I didn't believe that the gods, as mortals understand them, had anything to do with running the universe, but . . . I don't know what I thought," he cried.

There was a small pause. Then Cyprus said gently, "You *did* understand that you create your own reality?"

"But the gods' reality is something else again," Seven exclaimed. "How did such a misunderstanding take place? And if there are real gods behind the gods I've met, then how do you find them? If they're always camouflaged by people's beliefs about them, how can anyone find them? You and I know that the universe is safe, and that All That Is is hidden in us, and in everything else as well. But Lydia doesn't know that. And Will thinks he does, only he has some crazy idea that desire is somehow opposed to being. And I don't like Lydia being born again by default, if that's what's behind her decision. If she *is* born as Tweety, I have to give her something, some clues, to help her in her new life; some idea that frees her from—" Seven broke off, really upset. "I hardly know what to think myself," he said. "And what about Will? He was still talking about suicide."

"Which reminds me," Cyprus said. "It's time to give Jeffery a rest, so he can write his own notes. I imagine he might be just a bit upset himself."

~ *Chapter Twenty* ~

Jeffery's Notes and
Some Upsetting Realizations

Now I must confess my concern over what is certainly a rather unique predicament, for this manuscript has included events from my own life as a part of its narrative. Imagine my horror as I found myself automatically writing down (but not from my viewpoint) the entire happenings that occurred during my last visit to Ram-Ram. I was, in fact, more than halfway through the description before I realized this odd turn of events, for when I am embarked upon writing the book, it's impossible to tell where my mind is. A psychological absence falls upon me. That is the only way I can describe it. There is no amnesia. I know my fingers are working the typewriter keys, and I am aware of my environment, yet I am lost to myself in a way difficult to describe or decipher. When I finally realized that a portion of my own life was appearing as part of this unwelcome book, I was appalled, but my fingers typed on, and some part of me remained strangely neutral and unconcerned. A maddening situation.

My new isolation doesn't help either. Almost everyone has left campus for spring vacation. I stayed, because I expect a letter any time from Sarah: Her baby must be due this week or next, and ex-wife or not, I still bear her good will. In any case, I was alone here the afternoon after my visit to Ram-Ram, when I suddenly found myself reliving the experience through this manuscript itself.

Even the air had a deserted cast. There were no cars in the parking lot beyond the courtyard. The absence of noise was almost annoying; no footsteps to the garbage cans; nothing to distract me, so that as I wrote the words, it seemed as if the written dialogue had its own sound and thundered distantly in my mind. That would have alarmed me in any case, but unfortunately, this was only the beginning.

The sounds grew louder, and as if they were real, they echoed through the nearly empty building. Everything in this place is metal or concrete, it seems, and sounds are always intensified. But these had to be imagined sounds! The chattering of Queen Alice and Ram-Ram's damn chuckles, and even the shouts of the audience at the televised ballgame — all of these rose, and echoed through the entire building. Yet they couldn't have, of course, since the sounds belonged at the mental institution I had visited the day before. So I told myself.

As the sounds grew louder, however, another more bizarre intensification took place, one I'm quite embarrassed to describe. Certainly the entire affair will cast doubts upon my own sanity if and when this manuscript is ever read.

But, just as described in the previous chapter of the book itself, the air seemed to thicken into pseudo-shapes until, as I typed, the scenes were before my eyes that I had actually witnessed the day before at the institution! That is, as the scenes were described, I saw them. The entire common room, with all of the patients, was somehow transposed here, over the contents of my normal living room, so that in a manner of speaking, the book came alive. Nor did the effect end when the description of the affair was done, or with my own exit from the scene. Instead, the insane-god nightmare, or whatever it was, also came alive for me. The feelings of desolation were quite shattering; and I was also involved in the Virgin Mary fiasco and the Buddha scene as well.

When Will was told to waken in his physical body, the dictation ended for the day. I left the typewriter with a sense of great relief, and closed my eyes. But I swear that when I closed them, I looked out of Will's eyes for just a moment and saw the communal room that had been described earlier in the book. I cried out in true alarm, and at once everything returned to normal.

But I had seen enough, apparently through Will's eyes, to trigger a most regrettable response on my part. I saw the poster of Buddha hanging above Will's bed; and following his gaze, a kitchen sink stacked with dirty dishes; a plastic geranium crudded with grease plopped in a coffee cup. That was all, but it was enough. I knew that Will started retching, even though when I cried out, I stood in my own living room.

The scene disappeared, but Will's mood, his memory of the insane-god sequence, or his unaccustomed revulsion at the poster of the Buddha, added up to an emotional turmoil that struck me with full force. I told myself time and time again that Will was simply a character in a book, yet I knew that my own response was far stronger than the kind of identification given to fictional heroes or antiheroes. Memories that I'd purposely suppressed for years rushed almost revengefully into my mind, and with them came all of the attitudes about life that I'd had at the time the events occurred — the time of my own undergraduate studies.

Certainly I didn't live as Will does, or does in this damnable book, but I wished then that I had. How romantic communal living seemed, until at least, I imagined the intimacy from which there would be no escape. But I recalled with dismay my own brief but intense intellectual journey into Buddhism and various Eastern religions, an episode that until today I had almost completely forgotten. Worse, my own attitudes toward life at that time now returned to assail me, until I realized that I had never forsaken them but only hidden them from conscious awareness.

I barely consider life worth living. How long have I really felt this way?

I would not give my seed back to the earth because I did not agree with the conditions of life.

More, I realize now that I see the universe and everything in it as the accidental chemical creation of mindless elements, with life itself springing from the semen of some insane cosmic Frankenstein — chemicals gone mad, forming a world without reason, and certainly devoid of purpose. So to that degree, Will's insane god and mine were the same, though his was an offshoot of religion, and mine of science.

Those feelings of desolation came crushingly close, reviving long forgotten, only half-remembered thoughts of suicide: suicide as a rational man's only method of maintaining honor in a world without rules, in which each species survives only by being craftier than another. These realizations, so long buried, were bad enough. With them came the shame of a condemnation I could not escape, for I saw that in my investigations of rats and in my experiments with them, I took out my revenge against the world by literally mutilating the brains of rodents; out of sheer rage. And with this understanding, I fell down on the couch, covered my face with my hands, and wept.

A fine way for a professor of psychology to act! So I tried to examine my own feelings in order to clear my mind. Nothing worked. And nothing could erase my sense of outrage that Ram-Ram and myself were turning into characters in a book — a book written by my fingers, but not by my mind. And I wondered: How could *that* be an accident? I still couldn't see any purpose in the entire affair, yet the wild series of crazy events seem to hint of some strange order that exists completely outside the usual kind of purpose or design.

Why did I care if Will committed suicide? Or, for that matter, if Lydia decided to be born again or not? Yet I suddenly realized that I cared, deeply, and that my anxiety about both issues had been growing steadily, even though I'd resolutely tried to banish such thoughts whenever they came unbidden into my mind. So I asked myself another question: Did Lydia in some way remind me of Sarah? Did I, in my own grotesque imagination, suppose that the birth of Sarah's child was somehow dependent upon Lydia's decision to be reborn? The utter nonsense of such musings strike me with the deepest scorn, yet I cannot escape realizing that I have, indeed, made such impossible identifications and associations.

Moreover, I don't trust Lydia's decision to be reborn as given in the last chapter. She could change her mind overnight. I'm led to think that there can be no logic at all to these imaginative dissertations of mine, for I also imagine that Sarah and Bianka are *both* waiting for childbirth while (oh, dear Lord) the stubborn Lydia still dallies. At the same time, an irrational enough hope seizes me, as if Lydia's pilgrimage might yet lead to the discovery of life's purposes; and this despite the fact that I do not admit the existence of the soul (Oversoul Seven to the contrary). And from these skeins of irrationality, how can I possibly have any hopes?

Beside this, though, a general exhaustion overtakes me. I sit here waiting for more dictation. For the first time, almost weak with suspense, I know that the book must be finished, and that I must learn the outcome. And new fears assail me. Suppose whoever or whatever is giving me this manuscript suddenly decides to withhold it?

~ *Chapter Twenty-One* ~

Stage Fright and
Preparations for Birth

O versoul Seven grinned at Cyprus and said, "I hope it isn't as difficult to
get Lydia through her birth as it was to get her through her last death.
She wouldn't believe that she was dead for the longest time, in her terms, of
course. Suppose she doesn't believe in her new birth as Tweety either?"

Seven materialized as the fourteen-year-old male to complement Cyprus'
image as a young woman teacher. The two of them stood in a replica of the
room in which Lydia would be born, and Seven looked around with a worried air. "These rehearsals always confuse me," he said. "I think I've got it all
right. There's the cradle and bureau, complete with linen in the drawers.
Everything is perfect seventeenth century. And I've explained Lydia's role
to her time and time again. I think she has it down pat: how to orient physically inside the baby, how to organize her perceptions."

Seven had started counting the points he'd mentioned on his fingers,
but Cyprus said, "Stop that, Seven. When you worry about details like that,
you always make me nervous."

"Details," Seven said, indignantly. "Easy for you to talk! You just instruct,
and I'm out in the field, so to speak. Uh, oh —" He broke off, staring at the
cradle. He'd materialized it all right. There it stood, made of lovely earth
oak wood, but he'd forgotten to make it solid in space, so that even though
the shape was right, it stuck up like a piece of flat board.

"It's a good thing that this is just a class situation," Cyprus said, "or you'd be in trouble. No real baby would fit into *that* cradle. Talk about details!"

"Well, I'm glad this isn't an examination because I lose points on details in every examination I take," Seven said. "There, the cradle's right now." He grinned and added, "My marvelous inventiveness makes up for a lot."

Cyprus tried not to smile, and she said with just a gentle touch of severity, "Well, remember, you have to make sure that *everything* is in readiness for Lydia's birth as Tweety. I presume the new parents are all prepared, and that they have all of the necessary background information?"

"Right. Absolutely," Seven said, briskly. "I've talked to Josef over and over in his dream state. He understands why he and Lydia chose to be father and daughter; or rather, why he and Tweety have."

"And Bianka?"

"Bianka understands that she and Lydia will have, uh, certain creative conflicts, in order to help each other resolve challenges they want to work out. But they'll love each other just the same. And—"

Seven broke off again—and groaned. Josef suddenly appeared, wearing a toga. He strode angrily across the room and stood in front of Oversoul Seven. "Here you are in one of my dreams again," he said almost threateningly. "Or I'm in one of yours. I can never tell the difference. I'm in terrible trouble, and you've got to help me."

Cyprus dematerialized diplomatically.

Seven said, "Josef, you do this all the time, come and bother me when you're not supposed to. What is it now?"

Josef began to stride nervously back and forth, scratching his dream head and glowering at Seven. "I never know when I'll have one of these crazy dreams, and I never know what to do in them," he said. "But I knew I'd find you somehow. Now my wife is going to have a baby at any moment. How will I get my painting done? She's made my studio over into a nursery, just to rub it in." He glowered at Seven again. His brown moustache quivered. "I wasn't cut out to be a father," he wailed. "I wasn't even cut out to be a husband." He sat down on the bed, and Seven grinned: The bed creaked just like a real one; not bad for a hallucination, he thought. But Josef put his head in his hands and looked about ready to cry.

"Come on," Seven said, "we've been through all this ten times. You said that you wanted to be a father, so you could understand corporeal creativity as well as creativity through art . . . so you could help form a new life and study living art."

"Well, I take it all back," Josef moaned. "A painter has enough problems; he has no right to father babies. Paintings don't cry and smell and take a woman's attention."

"Why, you're jealous of Tweety already," Seven exclaimed, almost scandalized.

"Bianka's giving her my old studio," Josef shouted, "I didn't know she was going to do that."

"Tweety's going to be your greatest model," Seven said. "She might even coax you into being a really good artist."

"I'd rather use the cat for a model," Josef said, thundering now. "And this is all your fault."

"We oversouls get blamed for everything," said Seven, shrugging his fourteen-year-old shoulders. "You told me that you wanted to be a father. You and Lydia met in the dream state and settled on each other as parent and child. Bianka went along for her own reasons, but it was all your idea."

Josef looked up, craftily. "Someone told me once that if a woman was shown a black cat, she'd lose her baby," he said.

"It isn't true. It's superstitious nonsense," Seven said quickly and emphatically.

"How do *you* know so much?" Josef asked. "I keep forgetting who you are."

"I'm your *soul*," Seven cried, exasperated. "And that's some job, let me tell you." Seven sighed and turned into the image of an old man, because it was always easier for him to handle Josef that way.

"Oh, it's the old man I see in my dreams. Thank God," Josef said with obvious relief. "Did you hear what I was saying?"

"I did," Seven said, kindly and wisely. He had a white beard, white hair, and the saintliest blue eyes imaginable.

Josef started all over again. "My wife's going to have a baby. Just earlier today, I felt wonderful thinking about it. But now I'm filled with doubts. Besides that, I'm scared and feel like a coward. I should be feeling paternal, and acting like a tower of strength or something like that."

"You can feel any way you want to," Seven said.

"I can?" Josef said, with surprise.

"It's quite natural to be upset and have mixed feelings. Here, I have someone who might make you feel better," Seven said, and mentally he called for Lydia. She materialized in an instant—very cleverly, Seven thought, as a lovely young woman several years younger than Josef.

"Oh, it's you," she said. "You're getting cold feet, are you? Never mind. So am I! How odd it really is. Imagine me being a baby? And calling you Daddy? Or Dadda? Or what shall I call you?"

"Oh, God," Josef said, sputtering and laughing all at once. "I remember the whole thing now."

"This is how I'll look when I'm grown up. Won't I make a great model for you?"

"Model?" Josef said, making a grab for her and grinning.

"Let's not let things get out of hand," Seven said. "Josef, do you feel better now?"

Josef kept grinning and nodding.

"Well, you both have to get out of here then," Seven said. "You're sure it's all settled?"

Josef and Lydia shook hands almost formally. "I feel much better," Josef said. Then he exclaimed "Oh," and disappeared.

"What happened?" Lydia asked.

"He must have awakened, or something startled his body," Seven answered. "But technically, you shouldn't be here either. I'm rehearsing the, uh, inner mechanics involved in the birth. I *did* want you to reassure Josef, though. Now have *you* any more questions?"

"No. Right now I feel fine. How I'll feel when I actually take up residence in a baby's body may be something else again, though." She grinned jauntily and said with a laugh, "It can't be any more confusing than being old and senile, and I got through that all right. But when do I actually become Tweety?"

Seven turned back into his fourteen-year-old image. "I told you, it's your choice, really," he said. "You can become Tweety at the physical birth or just before, or just after. Babies have a body consciousness, and the self or spirit comes in when it wants to, so to speak, of course. But the body consciousness gets lonely if you wait too long; it needs support. But really, you'll just know the proper time."

Lydia smiled and took the form of the old woman she'd been before her death. She had a visor cap set askew on cropped white hair; she wore a pair of slacks, a shirt, and held a cigarette in her hand. "Funny, such a comfortable image in a way," she said. "It sort of heightens the contrast, when I think of being a child again. On the other hand, it makes me feel older than Josef, who's going to be my father. I hope I can handle him all right."

"That's no way for a daughter to talk," Seven said. He started to laugh, but suddenly Lydia turned serious.

She said soberly, "Remember, though, you promised to do something special for me, or for Tweety; to give us some kind of knowledge to compensate for all the distortions we've discovered about the gods. And it must be something a child can understand."

"I promised, and I'll do it," Seven said. "And it *will* give you some inner guidelines to begin your new life."

"And you won't forget me, I mean, *me, Lydia?*" she asked.

"Never. And besides, it doesn't work that way. Good-bye for now, dear Lydia," he said, and Lydia disappeared.

Oversoul Seven waited somewhat nervously for Cyprus to materialize. "I see you have your work cut out for you," she said, reappearing.

"Have I? I'll say I have," Seven said, grinning all over his fourteen-year-old face. "Aren't they something, though, my personalities? Aren't they unique? I *do* hope they manage everything all right."

~ *Chapter Twenty-Two* ~

A Birth

*B*ianka was definitely in the final stages of labor this time; scared and sweaty; and worse, she still wasn't sure if she wanted the baby who even now was kicking for release. Josef came in now and then, terrified, his hefty weight balanced as carefully as he could so no squeaking floorboards would announce his presence, in which case Bianka's mother would scream and chase him from the room. He could hardly see, anyhow, for the steam from the boiling water that fogged the windows and cleared his sinuses at the same time. He felt frantic. If he'd known that childbirth was so . . . agonizing, would he have left Bianka alone? He squinted his brown eyes with dismay. No, nothing would have kept him away from that lusty body of hers. And in his mind's eye, he saw the two of them in puppylike embrace, filled with an ecstasy that left him confused and triumphant at once.

"Get out," Mrs. Hosentauf screamed. "At least when you're drunk you aren't under foot."

"Josef," cried Bianka, "I'm almost ready."

"Out! Out!" yelled Mrs. Hosentauf.

"AArrr," yelled Josef back, but he lumbered out of the room with one anguished look at Bianka. She'd be small again after the birth, he thought, with a sense of elation he felt guilty about at once; and she'd be his again. And while all of this was going on, Lydia invisibly prowled about the room.

Bianka moaned and closed her eyes, and as she did so, some part of Lydia responded, fluttered, searched for freedom; sought for a beginning in which she could grow into being from a different angle. Suddenly something inside Lydia's personal reality turned as clear as cellophane. She could see through herself—through her subjective surface to her core—and as she did, she felt an exquisite acquiescence and exhilaration, and at the same time, a thrust of aggressive action so strong that it seemed to propel her into a creativity that was too fast to follow.

Oversoul Seven was there, and Lydia felt her experience merge with his, or his with hers. Yet, conversely, her own independence was never clearer. Even now, she could accept new birth or reject it, and if she refused it, there would be other choices. Yet how dear and solitary that bedroom looked, a tableau tucked in time and an infant about to be born in a house anonymous to history. Yet in that birth, or any birth, she suddenly knew that the unknown universe re-created itself into new knowing.

"Quick, the boiling water," Mrs. Hosentauf shouted.

Bianka was only half conscious. The labor pains felt like worlds cracking in her womb, as if more than a baby wanted out . . . as if, she gasped, as if a god wanted out! She caught the blasphemy, tried to mutter, "Forgive me, Lord," in response to her training, yet some wildly triumphant knowledge shouted that, yes, a god wanted out. The god was part her, part Josef, but mostly it was the earth turning into god, and god turning into earth all at once.

The last rays of sunlight struck at the windowpane, one ray leaping through the steamy room, and Lydia felt herself go out into the universe, disperse triumphantly into numberless knowing particles of consciousness, each shaken, cleansed, glowing, and renewed, and coming back together in a new configuration drawn by the shining door that was Bianka's womb, from which, knowing and unknowing, the infant now emerged.

Lydia felt herself sifted through the experiences of Bianka and Josef; woke up inside their molecules so that each of their most unconscious memories were implanted in the infant. She fell through Bianka and Josef's realities back through *their* parents' lives, and back further in dizzying descent; so that in sequences impossible to follow, she touched upon the consciousness and reality of each being ever born. She fell through the chromosomes of Christ and Mohammed, of Mary and the gods of Olympus as they are known to man, and saw that all of them still live, sifted through man's consciousness—distorted yet re-created with each birth, and with each creative thought or vision, with each impulse. Somehow she had to impart that knowledge to Tweety.

"There are no gods to be found," Seven said, "because they were never lost. They're so hidden in ourselves, so much a part of us and everything else, that they just *are;* everywhere. Yet nowhere."

"Feel your own knowing right now," Cyprus advised gently.

And Lydia, inside the infant, stretched her consciousness and felt earth's great endurance; and all of nature's parts were guests to the birth so that she was aware of endless dusks and dawns, numberless seasons, and felt the sweet couch of existence that supported her with such immense safety that it hinted of a love beyond any condemnation — as the universe in each infant, and in herself, opened its eyes again; *again,* yet for the first time.

The infant slept.

Lydia roused; frightened a bit now by the sense of unity. She wiggled around inside her own consciousness and her own individuality snapped back like a rubber band. She was frightened again: Where had she gone when she'd forgotten herself?

～ *Chapter Twenty-Three* ～

After-Birth Complications In Which Lydia
Wakes Up in a Probable Life

*I*nside the baby, Lydia scowled, figuratively speaking. It seemed almost unbelievable that she couldn't talk. So this was what rebirth or any kind of birth was! It certainly wasn't very dignified, and it presented all sorts of difficulties that she'd (conveniently?) forgotten when she decided to be born again.

Again? Or was she being born in many times and places all at once, as Oversoul Seven maintained?

"Of course you are, dear Lydia," Oversoul Seven said.

Lydia saw him mentally. Her eyes, or rather, Tweety's weren't focusing properly, but in any case, Seven and Cyprus weren't visible to Bianka or Josef.

"Seven is here to help you handle the situation intelligently," Cyprus said, "and I'm here to see how well *he* does. But really, Lydia, there's no need to be nervous. None at all."

"We really should call Lydia 'Tweety' now, shouldn't we?" Seven asked. "Or is she still Lydia, learning to be Tweety?"

The baby set up such a howl that Bianka cried, "Josef, listen to her. What shall we do? Her face is all red."

"Arrarh," Josef thundered. "Do something. I'm afraid to touch her."

"Don't yell. You'll frighten her," Bianka cried.

"Josef hasn't changed. I can see that," Oversoul Seven said. "But you took his character into consideration when you decided to be his daughter, of course."

"I suppose it's too late to pull out now?" Lydia asked dryly.

Cyprus smiled. "You sound so much like Seven when you talk like that, but that's to be expected. He's your soul, after all."

The baby quieted. Bianka and Josef tiptoed into the next room. "Thank heaven," Lydia said. She slipped out of Tweety's body and joined Seven and Cyprus by the cradle. Lydia appeared as a young woman of about twenty. She strode vigorously about the room, puffing on a hallucinatory cigarette.

"They don't have cigarettes like that in the seventeenth century, by the way," Cyprus said. She appeared as another young woman for Lydia's benefit. Seven couldn't decide what form to take, so he tried several until Cyprus asked him to settle down.

"I can't help being nervous," he said. "I'm supposed to help Lydia, but how can I when she insists on pacing the room like that?"

"You'd pace the room too, if you were being born again, and into the seventeenth century after you died in the twentieth," Lydia retorted.

"But I *am,*" Seven answered. "That's one of the main issues of all this. Only you're the . . . part of me that's closer to the experience." Seven looked hopefully to Cyprus, who said, "You're doing fine; explain it to her yourself."

"That sounds like I'm not myself, just a part of you," Lydia said, puffing on the cigarette.

Tweety started to cry again.

"Oh, hell," Lydia muttered.

"That's no attitude," Seven started to say, but all of a sudden he couldn't get his footing, and with good reason. He was trying to stand up in three different rooms at once. So, seeing his predicament, he dematerialized and regained his balance. Then he realized what was wrong. He was seeing too many times at once, because in one room Lydia was dying in the twentieth century: He recognized at once the surroundings in the old peoples' rest home where she died, but it took a minute for him to put the picture into the correct sequence. In the second room, transposed over the first one, Lydia was being born as Tweety in the seventeenth century, and that was where she belonged in her Now. And in the third room, she was dying again in the life that she was just beginning.

"Seven, stop drifting," Cyprus called from the second room, and sheepishly Seven returned, and stood by Tweety's bedside. He grinned: The baby's head was as fresh as a peach, only two soft open eyes staring up at him, quite like a peach suddenly given sight, he thought; and looking out from itself.

"Will I lose all of my own memories?" Lydia asked anxiously. "I will, won't I?"

"Now don't start worrying about that again," Cyprus answered. "If Seven can remember who *he* is, you certainly can. Attaining to your soulhood is much more taxing in its way; but you don't have to worry about that yet."

Seven frowned. "I wish you'd stop just staring at that baby, Lydia," he said. "You have to identify with her sooner or later. Procrastinating doesn't help matters. You aren't thinking of putting it off at this late date, are you?"

Lydia's eyes flew open. "I never thought of *that*. I didn't realize that I still could change my mind," she exclaimed.

Cyprus said sternly, "Seven! You aren't helping matters one bit. You're just making the whole thing more difficult."

Seven grimaced, took the form of an earnest young man, and paced the room. "Well, maybe," he said. "But Lydia's one of my personalities after all. She has the right to know that she *can* change her mind, though it's true that such things are frowned upon. You'd have to get a replacement now, Lydia, and someone who's interested in seventeenth-century life. People are very touchy about which centuries they get born into, and the seventeenth century isn't a favorite, in case you're interested. Some wouldn't touch it with a — "

"Seven, that's enough," Cyprus interrupted. "Lydia, try to relax. Just because you're fond of the seventeenth century, Seven doesn't have to be, of course. But he isn't being very diplomatic, either."

The baby stirred. "It's a living organism," Cyprus said gently. "Prepared for you, waiting for your consciousness to make it human. Now it has body consciousness, but no self in your terms. Are you going to give it selfhood or not? Some individuals enter the baby before birth, as you know, and some after. But you *are* dawdling some."

Seven grinned.

Lydia said, almost laughing, "How could I *not*, after that? Of course I will. I just got stage fright, that's all. I know I'm not saying good-bye to myself, but becoming another self while not losing what I am. I'll do my best for Tweety, as Tweety. I'll — "

But the oddest thing was happening, and Lydia opened her eyes to a scene of such suddenly recalled delight that she cried out. There was her bedroom, surely hers, with sun-splashed wallpaper and white ruffled curtains. She was looking down at the bedcovers from the viewpoint of someone sitting up in bed. She was staring at . . . yes, the baby in her arms. She'd just given birth a short while ago; but to whom?

Let me hold this scene, this moment, she thought desperately.

The baby was—oh God, real, still birth-smelly, whatever that meant, and hers, hers, hers! She chanted, dizzy with elation; the warm living curve of her sunshiny arms filled with that new, solid, wiggling flesh. And, how curious, the baby's eyes were so clear, like a tiny animal's, knowing yet unknowing. She'd write a poem about it later, but not now. Only where was Roger? And what was the baby's name? Why couldn't she remember? Suddenly she was scared, and the baby looked almost unfamiliar and strange.

"Roger?" she called. "Rog?"

He came hurrying in, a towel over his arm. "What's wrong?"

And seeing him, so substantial and *there* and solid, for someone so bony and gawky, she started laughing and crying at once. "Oh God, I don't know. I took a nap, as you suggested, and when I woke up, I couldn't remember Rog Junior's name. There, see, I know it now! But my own baby's name! And the room seemed so funny, and I had the feeling of doing all this before."

"Crazy puss," Roger said, bending down to kiss her; but she looked up at him and thought: Now who was *that*? His face was kind, anxious, loving, with funny off-center eyes. But who was it?

"Who is *that*?" Oversoul Seven asked Cyprus.

"You should know," Cyprus answered. "It's Roger, Lydia's husband."

Cyprus and Seven stood invisibly by the bed, and Lydia didn't see them any more than Roger did. Then Lydia began crying.

"Come on," Roger said. "You told me yourself that new mothers can expect all sorts of goofy feelings at first. Forget it. You'll scare the baby. Anyhow, I was going to bring you in a dish of fresh peaches. See what a handy husband I am?"

"Peaches!" Lydia exclaimed. "That's it. I was dreaming about babies and peaches. Or *something*. But God, I must look a wreck. Is my nose all red from crying? Maybe it's the stupid drugs the doctors give you during delivery. No, they wouldn't affect me now, would they?" She paused. "I'm still confused, though. What the devil is the date?"

Roger went "Tut, tut, tut," made a mock bow, and said, "Madame, it's October 18, 1927. Is there anything else you want to know? I'm your personal information service."

Lydia's eyes widened. "Now I remember," she cried. "I was dreaming about the seventeenth century for some reason, and when I woke up, I didn't know where the devil I was." She shivered and added, "Look, the baby's sleeping. God knows what *he's* dreaming about! Put him in the crib, would you? Well, at least I'm flat now and not big as an elephant. I'm going to get up and dress and—"

"Don't drink too much tonight, though, hon. It isn't good for new mothers," Roger said, regretting his words at once.

"Oh, you had to say that, didn't you?" she shouted. "You had to spoil this beautiful afternoon."

"What do you mean, beautiful afternoon? A few minutes ago, you were crying, and I cheered you up," Roger shouted back.

"What's going on?" Seven asked anxiously. "Lydia's in the wrong life. I thought maybe she was just reliving a memory, but she's really into this! She just finished that life. That baby is her son, Roger."

"So I see," Cyprus answered dryly. "Seven, all lives are parallel, you know that. Otherwise Lydia couldn't have gone from the twentieth century to the seventeenth."

"Yes, yes. I know. In theory that works. But in practice, well, Lydia is supposed to be a baby, Tweety, right now. She's not supposed to be *having* a baby in the twentieth century. How do I get her back on the right track?" Seven paused for only a moment, and went on. "Look at her," he said. "Now I remember this particular day! If we don't stop her, she'll live that life all over again, won't she? And that was the day she fell in love with Lawrence, husband or no, and—"

Seven was so upset he dematerialized even to Cyprus, turning into a worried swirl of air that rushed around inside itself. "I've got to stop her," he said, wordlessly, of course. "I'm her soul, after all. And what about Tweety? Cyprus, I'm really upset. Now, help me."

Cyprus sighed and said, "Stop that swirling. You'll make yourself dizzy."

Seven stopped, and turned into a small white worried human face that was invisible to everyone but Cyprus. "Don't you understand what might happen?" he asked. "Lydia has free will, you know."

"Well, of course she has."

"That makes it worse, don't you see? I can't understand why you aren't concerned. If she falls in love with Lawrence today, she'll have to go through the whole thing again. But with free will, suppose she *doesn't* fall in love with him?"

"I don't follow you," Cyprus said, trying not to smile.

"That's exactly what worries me," Seven cried. "You're supposed to be my teacher, but in earth-type orientation I'm beginning to wonder. If Lydia doesn't fall in love with Lawrence, or if she uses her free will to change anything at all in this life, she'll alter everything else. And maybe she won't even be born as Tweety!"

"Seven, look!" Cyprus directed. The whole house opened to Seven's vision; and on the doorstep stood a young man in an opera cape. He carried a bouquet of flowers, and looked so jaunty and pleased with himself, and so conscious of the fine figure he cut, that Cyprus started laughing.

But Oversoul Seven was nearly in a frenzy. "It's Lawrence," he cried.

"And he's alone, just like he was the last time this happened. He mustn't go in until I get Lydia out of this and back where she belongs."

"Seven, come back," Cyprus called. But it was too late. Seven changed into a small angry October wind that rushed around the edges of the porch eaves outside, rustled the flowers in Lawrence's hands, and blew his cape out suddenly so that Lawrence shouted, "Whoo! What a wind!"

"Don't go inside," Seven sent the thought directly into Lawrence's mind. "You mustn't go in there." And the wind wrenched the bouquet from Lawrence's hands and sent the flowers flying across the porch, down the steps, and past the geraniums that Lydia had planted by the walk.

"*Damn*ation!" Lawrence shouted, chasing the bouquet.

Seven returned to Lydia's room to find Cyprus smiling a smile in which serenity and amusement were equally mixed. She said, "Do sit down and enjoy Lydia. I'll explain it all to you later. You cause yourself so much trouble. Needlessly."

Lydia was magnificent, Seven had to agree. She was applying makeup from small jars, holding her head so proudly, tilting it to get just the right effect. The dress she wore was very short, with a flounce. Her stockings were sheer and black. Her cropped black hair lay almost flat against her head. She was putting on a pair of triangular silver earrings; and suddenly Seven realized when he'd seen them before.

"Those were the earrings that caught Lawrence's fancy," he shouted. "Lydia, do you know what you're doing? Take those earrings off at once. Come back where you belong. In a few moments you'll see Lawrence in that dumb cape for the first time and fall in love with him. Then I'll never get you out of here. And if you *don't* fall in love with him, I don't know what kind of trouble you'll get us into, because then you'll change everything!"

Roger came into the bedroom. "Ready, hon?" he asked. "I just saw Lawrence coming up the walk. His girl isn't with him, though." He stopped and said, reprovingly, "You're smoking, and you know that's not supposed to be good for—"

"Young mothers; yeah, I know," Lydia said, glowering at him. "You just don't think smoking is feminine, that's all. Well, I'll smoke if I want to."

Seven shouted, "Lydia. Come with me at once."

Cyprus said gently, "Seven, it's no use. Lydia didn't believe she had a soul in that life. And she didn't believe in hearing voices inside her head either. She won't hear a thing you say."

"You just don't understand," Seven exclaimed. "You're too . . . remote. Lydia's my personality, and—" He broke off, groaning, as a grinning, disheveled Lawrence, disarmingly devilish in his infernal cape, stood triumphantly just inside the open front door, his cheeks red from the autumn air.

And Lydia stood in the hallway, staring at him; hooked, Seven thought. He turned to Cyprus with dismay.

Lawrence said, "I had the funniest feeling that you didn't want me to come inside. Like something was trying to keep me out."

"Don't be silly. Nothing could be further from the truth." Lydia smiled and came out into the living room while Roger closed the front door. Without knowing why, Roger suddenly felt sad, and watching him, Seven wondered how much Roger knew or remembered. Lydia was obviously ignorant of what was really happening.

And Lawrence was positively gleeful. Roger looked at him and said, uncomfortably, "What happened to your girl?"

"She couldn't make it," Lawrence said cheerfully. "You'll have to share Lydia with me for the evening."

"Why, that's pretty flippant," Lydia said, laughing. She threw herself down on the couch.

"Something else is wrong," Seven said to Cyprus. "I just remembered; Lawrence is supposed to be a good deal younger than Lydia. They fell in love under these circumstances, only she was so much older that the whole idea seemed ridiculous at first. She was at least ten years older, and—"

"And now?" Cyprus asked.

She and Seven were two points of light hovering near the ceiling. Seven looked down and said, "Wait, I'm getting it, I think. Creativity happens constantly, and all existences are open-ended, so somehow Lydia and Lawrence *are* doing it differently this time. They're more or less the same age. But what about Tweety?"

"Let's see for ourselves," Cyprus said. "Watch."

Cyprus and Seven looked down again. The baby, Roger Junior, was crying. Lydia got up and went in to quiet him.

"What a crybaby," she exclaimed; then bending closer, she was struck by the living miracles of his eyes, so clear and brilliant and incredibly dear . . .

Someone was saying, "You see, your memories are alive, and even changeable. You can live them, in all of their dimensions, so there's no need to worry that you'll ever forget your experiences."

For a moment, Lydia didn't know where she was or who was speaking. Then she saw the baby in the cradle and realized that she was standing there too, with Cyprus and Seven.

"*This* baby is Tweety," Seven said, grinning. "And we're back in the seventeenth century."

Lydia stared at the room. It looked as real and solid as the other one had.

"Sit down," Cyprus laughed, "and I'll explain what happened."

"Yes, I wish you would," Seven said a bit tartly.

Lydia nodded. She looked so confused that Oversoul Seven hallucinated a cigarette and lit it for her.

Cyprus said, "Lydia when you're involved with any birth, then through
association you remember other birth experiences sometimes, when you
were born, or when you gave birth. Often death experiences are connected
in the same way. Except that your memories live, and this time you creatively
changed them so that you and Lawrence were the same age. Your father —
your *new* father, Josef — can't bear to copy a painting, for example. So when
you relived your memories, you changed the circumstances instead of copy-
ing them. When you're outside of strict three-dimensional reference, you
have considerable freedom with your own experience."

"And *your* experiences form the basis of Tweety's unconscious," Seven
said triumphantly.

"I'm glad you understand," Cyprus said.

Seven blushed and said to Lydia, "I forgot too. And when I got confused earlier with the three rooms, then that, plus your confusion, triggered
your twentieth-century memories and the whole episode."

"But how many lives can you live at once?" asked Lydia, sounding exasperated.

"You're usually aware of only one at a time," Cyprus answered, smiling.
But before you're really all the way into a life, you're often conscious of — "

Seven interrupted. Looking at Cyprus suspiciously, he said, "I have a feeling that there's more to this than you're letting on. But never mind; Lydia
and I can handle whatever comes up. And come on, Lydia. You really have
to identify with Tweety now. You just can't go flicking in and out all the time."

Lydia said, "And to think that I used to think that when you were dead,
you were just dead and that was the end of it! But this is too much. And I'm
wondering: How real was the Lawrence I just met? And what about Roger?
And when Lawrence and I meet as cousins, will we remember anything at
all? And — "

"See, I told you," Oversoul Seven said. "In your present state of development, you need one life to put yourself into. Otherwise you just get all
confused."

"As *you* did, Seven," Cyprus said. "And still do. But Lydia, by entering
fully into Tweety, you journey into the source of creativity. And from this,
with your cooperation, the self-consciousness of Tweety will emerge."

Lydia smiled and tried to answer, but suddenly she felt so drawn to the
baby that everything else slipped away from her attention.

~ *Chapter Twenty-Four* ~

The Birth of Self-Consciousness
for Tweety

*C*yprus said, "Look at me, Seven. There's something that you must do so
that Tweety's new consciousness can be born from Lydia, and yet be
unique and hers alone." As Cyprus spoke she began to spin, quicker and
quicker, and the motion turned into sound. Oversoul Seven found himself
staring at the sound of Cyprus into which, unaccountably, she had vanished. The first sound was a long, deep, drawn-out one and Seven didn't
know how to deal with it. Its resonance was so steady and ponderous that it
seemed to be the utterance of all physical matter; the heavy voice of mass
on mass, or weight on ancient weight. He blinked. How could Cyprus or
any part of her sound so . . . *massive?*

He, himself, felt suddenly heavy too, as if he weighed more than worlds,
and he began to sink into something (or through something); yet dropping
with no sensation of speed or even of motion. How could you fall without
feeling motion? he wondered. But the sound had him in its spell. Within it,
he was aware of incredibly slow thoughts that took centuries to speak, that
were dragged out across the ages, trailing syllables each heavier than the
most massive rock imaginable; and of a consciousness so slow, in his terms,
that galaxies could rise and fall in one second of its time.

Seven was frightened. By now, Cyprus had disappeared so completely
into the sound that he despaired of ever finding her again. And he felt him-

self congealing within it; its long tones turned his consciousness into something else, so that his own thoughts had the oddest *weight* to them. He was
dropping into a deeper mode of feeling than he'd ever known.

"Cyprus, where are you?" he called frantically. Yet even his fright had a
slow, heavy sureness about it, and his thoughts sounded drawn-out in his
mind, as if they began in some ancient past, finally to emerge in a distant
future. The syllables were so slow that by the time Cyprus heard them . . . if
she ever did . . . he wouldn't need her help, or he'd be beyond all help.

In fact, by the time the first syllable, Cy (of Cyprus) rang through his
awareness, he himself had finished the thought that was still being ex-
pressed. The sounds in slow motion, deep and ponderous, kept going out
from him at an ever slower rate. Again, each vowel was so heavy that Seven
felt he could grab onto it for support.

The next sound, wh (from *where*) began and this time Seven could feel
its weird mass, so without knowing how he did so, he clung to it. (For dear
life, he said later to Cyprus, who laughed.) The sound was falling, and he
with it, "whwhwhwhwhwhwhwhwhwhwhere."

"Souls are eternal," Seven thought, so the sound couldn't carry him beyond the time of his being into . . . And as he thought, the first vowel (of *soul*)
started out, stretching, still only beginning to sound when he'd finished the
sentence. All the while, the last thought — the cry for Cyprus — was still not
yet half formed into sound; and the last syllable, ere (of *where*) went echoing
all around him, while the "souls" from the last thought just began to thunder.

Finally Seven couldn't think at all, bombarded by all those belated vowels and syllables. He still clung to the whwh (of *where*) that stretched outward, somehow continually constructing itself without finishing the word. It
was a bridge of sound to which he hung, dazed, because now he realized that
the sounds really had *mass*. And that mass grew and thickened. Each vowel
and syllable, still sounding, fell. Yet a trail of mass built up behind them, and
did not disappear. Instead, the sounds formed structures in space, or *of* space.

And the structures were aware.

They had come out of the sound into which Cyprus had disappeared.

For the first time, Seven wondered: Had he disappeared into the sound
too? Was he a sound now, and his thoughts variations of what he was? It was
all impossible, he thought (or tried to think), when the first syllable of the
sentence instantly began its slow, ponderous, undeviating journey. He would
have cried, but he didn't know how to — and who knew what sounds *that*
would make?

But now, curiously, his own inner thoughts slowed down too, and there
was nothing he could do about it. His consciousness sank to some deeper

level where thoughts-as-sounds grew out of him like trees from the earth, slowly yet automatically, with great sureness and strength.

A strange triumph seized him, an acquiescent exultation, the feeling of being himself a source; though he didn't understand exactly what this meant. He had sunken as far down as he could. Into what? The heavy long sounds? The resonance? Had he . . . congealed? And his thoughts sprang up slowly out of him, from him, with slow majesty, forming structures that sounded when the words were finished. They were like buildings of sound finally completed, or worlds of matter and form rising from sounds within sounds.

Within him was a slow, sure peace. He wasn't frightened anymore.

> He felt his massive endurance,
> The strength of creativity, sure of
>   itself, unending.
> He rested, while his thoughts kept
>   growing out of him,
> Around him,
> Above and below him.
> The sounds of his thoughts formed
>   into shapes and images.
> In a slow-motion dance, the
>   vowels and syllables
> Congregated, thickened,
>   congealed,
> Until they turned into
> Flowers and trees all around him,
> With him in the center,
> Assured, at peace, creating.
> A bird came to life
> When a vowel joined another,
> Meeting, clicking together
> In seamless commotion.
> And from this came the worlds
> In which his personalities had
> Their living,
> And Seven knew
>   He'd fallen
>   Into the
>   Ground of his being.

"The chord was struck out of which you emerge," Cyprus said, from another dimension.

The first vowel started out. It would be centuries before the next one reached him, and Cyprus smiled; knowing, wise, aroused and yet unaroused, from the ground of *her* being; from which Seven emerged and was still emerging.

From which Tweety was emerging, in a new Now of being, rising into self-consciousness, yet claiming a consciousness that had always been hers; that now rushed into her knowing.

Tweety opened her eyes and looked about the room.

∾ *Chapter Twenty-Five* ∾

On the Brink with Will
and Jeffy-boy

*L*ydia sat invisibly, legs crossed, watching Tweety navigate in the snow. Tweety and the cat were playing together. The cat, Welheim, daintily ran along the thin-crusted snow until it hit a soft spot and fell in, straight down; then it would begin meowing, scrambling frantically, scaring itself, only to pop up again to start the entire process all over. Tweety watched, squalling delightedly each time the cat disappeared, and each time it re-emerged.

By now Tweety could get along without Lydia monitoring all of her motions, even though she fell down often and didn't really walk properly yet, and Lydia stared across the fields, wondering idly if it was time for supper. She caught herself with a start; It wasn't she, but Tweety, who was hungry and anticipated the mutton chops that Bianka had promised earlier in the day. On the one hand, Lydia thought, it was definitely exciting and fun . . . delicious . . . to anticipate the chops with Tweety—she corrected herself, *as* Tweety—and yet, well, it was also just as pleasant to be aware of Tweety's feelings without identifying with them all the way.

As she sat, musing, she smoked, and she was just reaching for another hallucinatory cigarette when a young man appeared, looking rather surprised. She recognized him at once from the Buddha affair, but it was obvious that he considered her a complete stranger. By his clothes and manner,

Lydia knew that he was from the twentieth century, and she sprang up with pleasure. "What are *you* doing here?" she asked.

"I'm dreaming and I must be traveling out of my body," Will said a bit smugly. "Anyhow, in answer to your question, I'm life-hunting, though why I'm here particularly is beyond me. Where are we?"

"Seventeenth-century Denmark," Lydia said.

"Great. That figures. I was looking for someplace exotic. What a dreary landscape this is." Will frowned and glanced around rather disdainfully.

"Why, it's lovely here," Lydia protested. "I lived in the twentieth century once, too. That's where you're from. I can tell."

"Wait a minute," Will interrupted. "Then you're dead!"

"No, you're not born yet," Lydia replied with a touch of anger. "Anyhow, you're lucky to be talking to me at all. I'm on a recess, in a way. Actually I'm living my life as that child over there."

Will was appalled. "Why, that's like living backwards," he said. "I mean, you're an adult now, and you'll have to be a child again."

"That's what happens," Lydia said, thoroughly enjoying the company. She related to Will as a contemporary, smiling at him as a young woman at a young man.

He scowled at her. "Smoking is bad for your health," he said.

She started laughing. "I haven't got any health at all," she said, between gasps. "I mean, I haven't got a physical body in usual terms. I just take this form. Tweety has a body, but then, she doesn't smoke. Besides they don't have real cigarettes like these in the seventeenth century anyhow."

"You're absolutely and completely mad," Will shouted.

"Or you are. It's your dream," Lydia replied. "You visited here in your dream, but it isn't a dream to me —" She broke off. Will said something else and she tried to respond, but suddenly from the house the sizzling smell of mutton chops wafted through the air so temptingly that Tweety's senses splashed over. Tweety and Lydia for the moment became indivisible. Tweety forgot the cat and headed clumsily toward the house. Will just stood there. The young woman had completely disappeared.

Will groaned. The dream, or whatever it was, was getting out of hand. He felt very lonely standing there in the strange dreary landscape. He was just beginning to feel really sorry for himself when Lydia reappeared.

"This happens to me more and more," she said uneasily. "I keep forgetting myself and turning into Tweety all the way. See how small this little fenced area is? They put Tweety out here whenever it's not too cold, and to her, it's absolutely vast. While to *me* —"

"I'm going to commit suicide," Will interrupted, but a part of Lydia was suddenly relating to Tweety again, in the kitchen, and she didn't respond.

"I *said,* I'm going to commit suicide," Will repeated.

"Oh, sorry, I wasn't listening," Lydia answered. "I don't think I ever died that way. And you were telling me that smoking was bad for my health. Suicide isn't about to promote good health either, you know."

Silence. "You're terrifically facetious," Will said finally. But his curiosity got the best of him. "How did you die and how many times? Are you putting me on?" he asked suspiciously.

But Lydia more than answered his question. She turned into the image of the old woman she had been before death: white bubbles of hair; thin but somehow jaunty bones dressed in a pair of dungarees and faded shirt. Will stared, horrified at the transformation.

She said, in the old woman's crispy voice, "I looked like this, more or less, when I died the last time. And I was pretty proud of myself in a way. I mean, I considered myself a survivor."

But Will was so startled that he could feel himself starting to wake up in bed; and he didn't want to. He did, though — in a cold sweat. He was somehow terrified. He'd taken quite a few Phenobarbitals, and he imagined, *imagined,* he muttered, gritting his teeth, that he'd just fall into a dreamless sleep. But no. Instead he had to have a nightmare in which a beautiful young woman turned into an old hag. Ugh. He tried, unsuccessfully, to remember what else had happened. Then he tried to interpret the whole thing symbolically, and gave up almost at once.

Why, he wondered, would he want to be born again anyhow? And again? And what good would suicide do, if you just woke up in another life? Christ, he grimaced. You could just go on killing yourself in one life, only to be born in another! If you did it fast enough, though, maybe giving yourself ten years to a life, he grinned bitterly — you'd get life, death, life, death, life, death, BAM, BAM, BAM. Shit! He reached beneath his cot and popped some more pills without even checking to see what they were.

Of course, babies wouldn't remember their past lives, at least he hoped not, so for a while, he thought, there'd be some peace — but just the same, you'd have to program yourself ahead of time to commit suicide before you grew up and started the whole thing over. And it wasn't that he was poor or ignorant or sick — he disdained such excuses, he thought proudly — he just didn't like . . . life itself, or the conditions of life.

He lay on the unmade cot, arms behind his head, leering at himself mentally; thinking that no matter how rotten he felt, he probably looked cool, nonchalant, clever, and sardonic. Because he always did. People always told him so.

"Clever." He hated the word. And people. Because no matter what he *said* to them — and his fluent tongue spoke convincingly — he never really related to them. He didn't know what they were up to. They were as imper-sonal, as far as he was concerned, as mathematical figures.

His glance went beyond his private corner to the communal kitchen with the greasy fake geranium on the windowsill, to the wooded area out-side, and he remembered the cliffs that surrounded the campus and the water falls where all the beer parties were held.

And without ever having made any decision, Will dressed languidly, thumbed his nose at the poster Buddha (but making this an elegant, almost classy gesture), to find himself some ten minutes later merrily walking along the slippery edges of the rockbed. Jauntily, whistling, he threw his jacket over his arm and eyed the highest level of the cliffs that he could comfortably reach. No need to wear himself out, even for such an important occasion.

"What important occasion?" he asked himself.

"Who knows?" he answered. His mind felt curiously and beautifully di-vided, and his body felt so light and transparent that he almost felt invisible, though he knew that he wasn't.

Then, eyes wide and clear, contemptuous and hurt, he looked down. It wasn't too far.

But far enough.

And he was woozy enough to jump. The drugs had taken the edge off the moment.

All he had to do was

Jump off

the edge

of the moment.

"Shit." Even now he couldn't forget himself, he thought, or stop watch-ing himself. He almost felt as if he were two selves, neither very likable, one watching the other, one thinking, "How tragic, yet how handsome and young I look," and the other thinking, "How dumb and cosmically stupid to have such feelings at a time like this." But both of him looked down again.

This is Jeffery, interrupting dictation of the book. Never have I used so much raw willpower, but as I completed that last sentence, "But both of him looked down again," I knew I *had* to stop writing. To go on could bring dis-aster. I knew that even as my fingers hovered over the typewriter keys, quite ready for the next sentence. Reason would have to come later; I knew that, too, as I reacted to a sharp, sudden, undeniable sense of personal danger. The next line, or the next, could destroy me.

Sweat ran down my armpits. I took one hand and with it *pulled* the other off the typewriter, feeling as if at any moment my hands would pounce upon the keys with their own will and type out—what? My own death sentence? The pun didn't escape me even as I lit up a cigarette and moved as far away from the accursed typewriter as possible.

I'd been nervous, beginning this section on Will. For one thing, it's the first on the book that I've received in two weeks to the day, for after the chapter on Seven's return to the ground of his being, there was nothing. Did that return, in *our* time, take two weeks? Then beginning this chapter, I found that there was a time lapse in the book also, for Tweety was no longer an infant. She was also becoming more of an individual, so did *my* two-week period somehow correlate with Seven's journey and Tweety's growing self-consciousness? And what about Will? As soon as he appeared in this chapter, I felt alarm signals, until, finally, with that last sentence, I could stand it no longer. I refused to write another line.

Will was only a book character and a poorly developed one at that. I said this over and over as I stood, growing more and more upset, staring out the window at the balcony, and oh, God, at the geranium pot on the railing, the same one that fell over during that first dream encounter related in my early notes. Feeling, yes, possessed, I walked slowly out to the balcony (where my first out-of-body experience had occurred). Almost hypnotized, I looked out at the new staggered cement apartment buildings, jutting out indeed like cliffs; and downward at the garbage cans, unfinished lawn, and parking lots.

What on earth was I doing? I knew I was trembling; I felt as if I were tottering at the edge of some chasm between worlds, trying to leap from one to the other.

And I knew that no matter who or what Will was or wasn't, I had to stop him from jumping. I had to reach him somehow. But how did one reach a character in a book? Impossible, I thought. At the same time, I knew that reaching Will was my mission, and if anyone had asked me then what my mission in life was, I would have answered unhesitantly, "To save Will's life."

As this thought came to me, I felt dizzy and off balance. I feared that I'd lost my footing, and would plunge (real body and all) over the railing onto the ground below. But instead, the apartment buildings blurred across the way and almost disappeared in a kind of white glare. Then they turned into the cliffs described in the book as the ones sought out by Will . . . and I saw him, standing on a rocky ledge, looking down.

So I—he—hadn't jumped yet!

Scared to death, horrified, I suddenly realized that I was Will's "other self" mentioned in the last passage of the narrative. I stood beside him—

the observer. And he knew it! I mean, he felt an observer-self, though whether or not he realized then that I was real, I don't know.

"Don't jump," I shouted.

"The wheel of life . . . round and round she goes," Will said, and giggled, an awful sound. Then he threw his arms out dramatically and said in a mournful voice that clearly mocked itself, "This is where Willy-boy gets off, sweet daddy-o."

As he said that, as Will, I felt a dizzy surge of irresponsible power and weird impulses: to let go, to jump, to choose *nothing,* to cheat mortality by courting death. Snapping back to myself, I said urgently, "You've got a future. You're going to be a psychologist. You'll forget all this, the drugs, the emotional bombastics."

Will groaned; there he was, still divided, still arguing with himself. He said, "And the search for excellence in life? What a dumb deluded search that was!"

"*Was?* You're still alive, aren't you? You can't commit suicide because I'm your future self and I exist," I cried.

Will looked directly where I was standing, not seeing me, surely, yet sensing my presence as his other self and hearing my voice in his head.

"How like me," he said. "Of two minds till the last. It's enough to drive a man to suicide! Still witty, too. God, how I hate myself."

I yelled, "Stop that! If you jump, you'll kill me, too." I shouted, frantic. But I was the real me: He was the storybook character; so how *could* his death possibly affect me? I didn't know, but I knew it could. "You're going to write a really strange book," I cried, on impulse. "I know. I've seen it."

"Who cares?" he said. "And I'm tired of this dumb dialogue with myself anyhow. On the other hand, I might as well talk to myself because I don't have a friend in the world. My parents couldn't care less, either." He shrugged eloquently and moved closer — too close — to the cliff edge.

I sprang forward to stop him, but with his last words I suddenly felt sick to my stomach. Because I had no friends now either. And without further transition, it happened. Will's feelings were no longer just Will's — they were mine, fully, completely. When this odd and terrible transference happened (for that's what it was), I almost fell over the cliff edge myself, with the impact of a despair that suddenly hit me full force.

At the same time, the scene before me took on a clarity beyond description — the gray cliffs interspersed with spring grass and small rocks, the crooked trees newly sprouting. The bottom of the gully beneath me, as if I'd lost all depth perception, now seemed but one mere step downward; hardly dangerous and, moreover, oddly inviting.

The despair and sense of hopelessness I felt was almost sexual in the strangest way, a yearning that sought orgasmic release. On the one hand, I ached to throw myself down through the gap of space I knew did exist despite my illusion of its shallowness. But like a lover, the gully itself changed seductively, seeming closer and closer, so that on the other hand I thought that one small sweet step would end the monstrous psychological pressures that I'd hidden from myself for so long.

And simultaneously, some voice within me whispered that I must be the observer again or Will and I were both lost; but the voice was weak and did not possess the power of my feelings. I listened, but the words seemed to make no sense.

While all this was happening, I was so completely engrossed with my own emotions, so hypnotized and gripped by the temptation to jump, that I almost forgot Will entirely.

"One little step, *shit*," I heard his voice say. The words got my notice. I stared. Will was shaking his head with what seemed to be happy bewilderment. For an instant I thought that he'd lost his reason completely, for the implications of his actions escaped me entirely at first. Giggling again, only this time with a wild, childish, almost animal-like relief, he plopped promptly down on the cliff, took off his shoes and stockings, and with a cackle like a starling's, he heaved his sneakers and socks down to the gully bottom.

I followed them with my eyes. The shoes . . . were they his or mine? *He* was crying and still giggling with relief, and only when I understood that he was crying with *relief,* did I realize what happened.

His despair, in some way, had been mine all along! When I accepted that almost impossible psychological weight, *he* was free.

Jealously I watched him: the young man's perfect form, set off now by a newly released psyche. *Who* was he? Now I resented him, lolling there on the bank as if he hadn't a care in the world. My own despair was still paramount, only now I was aware of it as *it,* and not quite as lost in its power as I'd been before.

Will turned, stood up, bare feet tentatively testing the path, the twigs and stones impinging on the soles of his bare feet; stinging, bringing tears to his eyes — and a triumphant defiance to his heart. "I almost jumped. Almost." (I caught his thoughts and listened in. He went on:) "I was saved. Something stopped me at the last moment. Something or somebody *cared.* I wouldn't be feeling these stones under my feet if I'd jumped. I wouldn't be thinking. I wouldn't be . . ." He continued with a chanted list of the things he wouldn't be feeling if he'd jumped; and I found his elation embarrassing.

Then, approaching the path from which he'd come to the cliffs, he paused. Or rather, he was . . . stopped. I felt his surprise. And, as if he were being magically *pulled,* he returned to where I was invisibly standing, eyeing the spot as if it intrigued him, though he couldn't see me; of that I was sure. Once more he turned toward me and once more he stopped and returned, as if compelled to remain within some mysterious and invisible radius. Almost forgetting my own plight, I watched him perform in the same way several times; ending with his standing irresolutely before me.

Why didn't he leave? My own sense of desolation swaddled me in a mental cloud, almost suffocating all thoughts not pertaining to it. Yet somehow I was as intrigued by Will's actions as he seemed to be, with the spot of ground on which I was invisibly standing. Now he stood staring at it, obviously perplexed. He appeared certain that something or someone was there, and though he didn't see me, he certainly was growing more aware of my presence in some other way.

Again, I thought: "Why didn't he go home? Back to the commune?"

And I thought, "Because he has no future alone."

The realization, I think, came to both of us at once.

His boyhood's life could only be fulfilled in my manhood.

In *my* life!

Was he real?

More real than real?

More real than I had been in years?

If I didn't accept Will as a part of myself, he had no place to go. I looked around. Was the ground I was standing on real? Did the paths go anywhere? Or was there only one that led back to Will's commune?

Will looked, almost desperately, at the path by which he'd come. His face showed fear, and anticipation as well.

"I'm here," I said, wondering if he'd hear me.

"Oh, wow, what I've just been through!" he answered mentally. "And besides that, I tried talking to myself a few minutes ago, and no one answered . . . like there was no one there. Weird."

"That would have been when I was too frightened myself," I said.

"That makes two of us, but what do we do now? I'm alive, anyhow." He paused. "Aren't I?" he asked. "Suddenly now that I've decided to live, I feel . . . unreal."

As he spoke, I saw him clearly. He was myself as I'd thought of myself years ago; living in a commune (though actually I never had), but more: so lonely that I could hardly bear to remember. Was I, Will, asking help from a future self? Or was I, the future self, changing the future by going back and altering the past . . . from my present?

So I said, "You'll be me. But I'm learning too. And I'll be different because of you; and because of what just happened."

"You mean, you're real and I'm not? To me, you're just the self I talk to."

"Neither of us is real without the other," I said. "If I denied your reality, I'm sorry. And if I ignored your questions and aspirations, I apologize deeply. But I don't know *how* to accept you, either, even though I desperately want to."

And as I said that, confusion overtook me completely, for suddenly I was *Will*, listening to my words of inner dialogue, and I was myself as myself, speaking the words.

I wasn't sure what was happening as the cliffs shimmered, and Will's image along with them. I know that I had a memory lapse in here somewhere, but the next thing I knew I was standing on my patio again, staring down at the unfinished lawn and at an old pair of men's shoes that someone had thrown beside the garbage cans.

My exhaustion was so complete that I stumbled into the living room and fell almost immediately into a deep sleep. But just before I collapsed, I remembered, as an official part of my own past, when I had stood on a hill, contemplating suicide. I'd completely forgotten the event; blocked it out, of course.

Yet drowsily I wondered: Or had the memory been born just now, and built into the past? And more urgently: Where was Will now? Were either of us still in danger?

~ *Chapter Twenty-Six* ~

Ram-Ram says Good-bye and
Tells What He Knows

"I think I get what you mean, but I'm not sure," Oversoul Seven said to Cyprus. The two of them were sitting, invisibly of course, on the chairs on Jeffy-boy's patio. "Will was a past self of Jeffery; *that* sounds simple enough, I guess. But . . ."

"But what?" Cyprus asked gently. Then she said nonchalantly, "When the lawn is finished, Jeffery will have an excellent view."

"There's something you aren't telling me," Seven said stubbornly. "I'm not fooled at all by your sudden interest in Jeffery's lawn."

"I'm not keeping anything from you," Cyprus said, looking nowhere in particular. "There might be a few things you've kept from *yourself*, though. I'll give you a hint. Jeffery remembered Will, and Lydia is going to have to give *her* memories to Tweety for a while, and—"

"Don't tell me," Seven cried. "I'll think of it myself."

"Good," Cyprus said, smiling. "I just wanted you to know it's all right for you to remember now."

"Sometimes you sound so superior," Seven answered, because no matter how many different ways he cross-referenced his memory—by times, people, events, or probabilities—he couldn't discover anything that he'd really forgotten.

"Oh, Seven, it isn't a matter of superiority," Cyprus began, "It's—"

"Hold on," Seven interrupted.

"On to what? Why?"

"It's just earth vernacular that means 'wait a bit.' Never mind; look there!" Seven cried excitedly, because below them Ram-Ram was ambling up the walk. "You knew he was coming, didn't you?" he asked reproachfully. But Cyprus only smiled.

She said, "Just watch and listen, and maybe you'll remember something important." By now she was laughing so hard that she was afraid she'd hurt Seven's feelings.

But he was too confused to notice. "There are so many unanswered questions," he mumbled. "I still don't know why Jeffery wrote the book for us, or how Lydia is connected to him, or how her full acceptance of Tweety's life has any bearing on Jeffery's future. I'm *still* having my troubles with Lydia, by the way. But why should Jeffery care?"

"Shush. Listen," Cyprus said. She and Oversoul Seven turned into two points of light on the ceiling of Jeffery's living room.

"What's Jeffery going to say when he types this?" Seven asked anxiously. "He'll know we've been listening to his private discussions with Ram-Ram."

"You forget," Cyprus said. "Jeffery thinks we're fictional characters."

Ram-Ram knocked at the door. He had to rap several times before the sound awakened Jeffery, who was still asleep on the couch. Groggily Jeffery yelled, "Go away."

"It's Ramrod Brail," Ram-Ram called.

"Great. Just who I want to see," Jeffery muttered; but he went to the door anyway and let Ram-Ram in.

"Well, I've been discharged," Ram-Ram exclaimed. He looked very pleased with himself.

"Nice for *you*," Jeffery said irritably. "Is it for real this time?"

"Now, now, now," Ram-Ram said. "I just dropped in to say good-bye. I'm going to take a trip and do some writing. I must say, you don't look very happy to see your partner in crime." He chuckled, and stared passively at the ceiling. "You *do* look pooped, Jeffy-boy, if you don't mind my saying so."

"I mind! And I don't like being called Jeffy-boy," Jeffery said.

"No. Of course you don't. The boy is part of the man, though . . ."

"Now what do you mean by that?" Jeffery demanded.

Ram-Ram sat down, smiling affably. "Only that you used to be so stuffy. I liked to remind you of the boy buried in there somewhere."

Jeffery stopped, stared, and asked despite himself, "Will? Are you talking about Will?" Even as he spoke, he felt an absence in himself. Where was Will?

"Will?" Ram-Ram asked.

"Nothing," Jeffery answered, with such obvious relief that Ram-Ram pretended not to notice. He stared at the ceiling again. "Of course, scientific journals are out," he said. "You can't prove any of this."

"Ram-Ram sees us," Seven cried.

"Does he?" Cyprus said.

"Prove what?" Jeffery demanded. He sprang up from the couch, displaying more agitation than he'd intended.

"Well . . . whatever you've been up to," Ram-Ram answered innocently. "I *was* here, out of body, for one thing, though you'd never admit that to any of our colleagues, I don't suppose. My being a mental patient for a while doesn't help you there either. Yes, yes, yes; I do have a good idea of your psychological adventures. You haven't committed yourself to them, at least not all the way."

Jeffery said as calmly as he could, "Just how much do you know about my activities? And *how* do you know whatever you know?" He paused and almost shouted, "Or *think* you know?"

Ram-Ram stood up, turning his back to Jeffery, arms folded behind his back, and walked toward the patio door. He stood, looking out. "I would imagine that you have a manuscript of some sort by now," he said. "But my knowledge of your, ah, bizarre activities isn't as detailed as you might think, or as I'd hoped. Before you called me about your first dream encounter with the two men, I wasn't at all surprised. I'd had a dream of my own about you—"

"I need a drink," Jeffery said abruptly.

"By all means," Ram-Ram replied, beaming as if he were the host, and still talking, he went into the kitchen. Jeffery heard the sounds of ice cubes being clunked into glasses, and Ram-Ram returned with drinks for both of them.

"A toast," he said grandly.

"The dream," Jeffery said.

"Oh, yes, the dream. Now, how would one tell our young man here about such an event? That was my problem, of course. Now you'll understand with no trouble."

"Oh, God," Jeffery yelled. "Will you get on with it?"

Oversoul Seven said to Cyprus, "How jittery Jeffery is! You know, for a moment I almost thought that I remembered something terribly important. But now I have no idea what it was."

"Oh?" Cyprus said, seeming to be quite unconcerned.

Ram-Ram sat down. "I'm not sure of much of this," he said. "But I dreamed of an automatic manuscript that you'd be writing in some way that I've forgotten, and I knew that I'd have a hand in triggering it."

"Go on," Jeffery said. His face was so intent and still that time might have stopped.

Ram-Ram continued. "Years ago, I was very interested in phenomena like out-of-body experiences, hypnosis, and alterations of consciousness in general. I fooled around with them, so to speak. But I was cautious: There was my reputation to consider. Life went on, and I followed the academic line. Then, when I had my dream, I perked up. Just suppose, suppose, there was something to it, I thought. It was several days before your experience, but somehow I awakened from the dream knowing that you had to come to me. So I didn't contact you. But just in case, I took several books out of the library to refresh my own mind on the psychic field in general, and to loan to you *if* by any chance my dream *did* mean anything and you called. As, of course, you did."

"I noticed the library date on the card," Jeffery exclaimed. "I did wonder briefly that the books were taken out before—"

"As you were meant to. So that you'd have some reason to believe me now. Not that anything is proven, but, ah, suggested, at least." Ram-Ram paused and said, "And then, of course, it's not quite over."

"Now what do you mean by that?" Jeffery asked uneasily. At the same time, he wondered if Ram-Ram's remark had anything to do with his own growing anxiety; for Will kept flashing in and out of his consciousness.

Oversoul Seven said to Cyprus, "What I'm supposed to remember has to do with Jeffery's dream . . . and *this* book . . . right?"

"Shush," Cyprus said.

"Now, Jeffy-boy, don't you like surprises?" Ram-Ram said, reverting to his humorous, coy air. "But be that as it may, I know this much: Whatever you're involved in isn't quite finished. There's something important you still have to do. Something else: I always sensed an unresolved and unhappy, maybe unloved but turbulent part of you, quite hidden behind your self-conscious professorial psychological attire. Again, that's why I called you Jeffy-boy; teasing you, of course."

Ram-Ram's voice had a hypnotic quality that seemed to fill the room in the growing dusk. Even Oversoul Seven almost nodded. Ram-Ram's small eyes were half closed, yet in their lidded drowsiness there also seemed to be a hidden spring of alertness.

"And more than that," he went on. "I also sensed that in some way you, uh, represented a past unresolved self of mine . . . as a young man . . . a part that needed help. I wanted to go back into the past and make some changes . . . even as, I believe, you've done the same kind of thing in your own case." Smiling softly, Ram-Ram said, "Yes, yes, yes. So it goes."

"I remember!" Oversoul Seven shouted. "How could I have forgotten?"

Just at the same time, Ram-Ram said, "So, to recapitulate, two people came to me in the dream state and somehow set up this entire episode, including the events I know of and those you haven't told me."

"It was me!" Oversoul Seven shouted to Ram-Ram, who didn't hear him, of course.

"And?" Cyprus asked gently.

"And you, too," Seven said, a bit abashed. "But why didn't I remember until now?"

"The *why* is next," Cyprus answered.

Jeffery said, "You're telling me that the two men who I saw here appeared earlier in a dream of *yours?*" The hypnotic effect of Ram-Ram's narrative was broken.

"I've no proof," Ram-Ram answered. "But yes, yes, yes, I'd say so. The descriptions of the men you gave to me matched mine, all right. I'd say that they were the same."

"But what about the mental institution?" Jeffery demanded. "How did that all start? Were you really, uh . . . "

"It's according to your definition, if you're asking me if I was mad or not . . .

"I'll second that question," Seven said to Cyprus. "And I have another. Where's Will? And why do I suddenly feel uneasy about Will and Lydia both?"

"For one thing, Lydia needs you right now," Cyprus said. "There are some things that must be taken care of, and before Jeffy-boy and Ram-Ram finish their conversation. And what happens with Lydia has something to do with Will and Jeffery, too."

"But what?" Seven asked with some dismay. "And there's more for me to remember, too, isn't there?"

"Hurry. Go to Lydia now," Cyprus replied. "Granted, there's really no time, but in your terms there's none to waste."

∼ *Chapter Twenty-Seven* ∼

"The Time Is Now,"
Lydia says Good-bye and Hello,
and Seven Remembers

The snowbank was blinding: yellow and white sparkles exploding in tiny puffs that Tweety tried to follow with her eyes. The sparkles were on the very top of the snowbank, floating out of the snow beneath like feathers; and with all that swirling, she could hardly see the snowbank beneath, which sat there like a huge white animal. Tweety eyed it suspiciously, to see if it might be dangerous.

Besides this, though, her bottom was wet inside and out. It was sloppy and wiggly on the inside by her underpants where the familiar brown, warm, smelly stuff came out. It squashed when she plopped down on the ground, and she could feel it squishing between her legs. But the wet outside her bottom stuck to the snow, and when she sat in the snow, it was cold and hard. Her face burned with the sunlight and burned — cold, too, and still she sat there, in the snow, where suddenly she'd fallen.

She didn't hurt, but she stung. She started to wonder exactly *where* she stung, and whether or not it was worthwhile to start crying about it, but she kept getting fascinated by the yellow-white, shining snow sparkles that flew out of the snowbank, glittering in the sun. She stared at them, feeling dreamy, but then the cat caught her eye: He was rounding the shedhouse. Then she remembered that she'd just fallen down, and that she wanted to follow the cat.

"Get up, me," she said to herself mentally, because physically she couldn't get the words out right, though they sounded all right inside. Getting the outside like the inside was hard. The cat dashed out into the sunlight again, a blur of activity. Impatient, Tweety tried to get up again, but nothing happened. There was something that the "other her" told her to do at such times. But what?

Then it happened all by itself.

She saw herself get up quite clearly and chase the cat. This picture of herself flashed right out in front of her eyes, and before she realized what had happened, she was up on her feet, following the image of herself. Only then it disappeared, and there was only the cat. For one instant, before it vanished, she was the image of the self she followed . . . and she saw it, herself, in her brown leggings and coat, and bundled up in the hateful orange scarf; running.

But she wasn't running really, just plodding. She couldn't go fast enough yet, and the snow kept rushing up to meet her, and it hurt when it hit her on the bottom. No, she thought, the snow didn't come up at her after all; she kept falling down to meet it. Then she was down again, harder than ever, plopped on her wet bottom, which really stung. She yowled.

Nobody came to get her up; no inside people or outside people. She got scared.

A wind came up and whipped about her. She flailed back at it, but it didn't stop. The sun became brighter so that the snow sparkles glittered all over and she could hardly see. Tweety shouted angrily at the wind, which now was blowing snow in her face. "Up, me," she said to herself.

"You have to make the picture first," said the "other her" somewhere in her head, and Tweety brightened, not feeling quite so lonesome. She had to make the picture first. That was how it was done. So, she wiggled her forehead and thought about it, and tried, but with no success.

"I guess I'll have to do it for you again," Lydia said, and she projected a mental image of Tweety, so that Tweety could see for herself what her body was supposed to be doing. Tweety saw herself get up and walk into the house, so she got up and followed the image; booted feet against the crisp snow. The sun went beneath some clouds and Tweety stopped, astonished. Where had the brightness gone? Why was the air darker? And colder? And she'd lost a mitten. The snow had changed too. Now it was all dark blue or worse, like upside-down clouds on a thunder day.

She shivered. The dark part of the air felt prickly, as if it had tiny prickers in it from air-bushes she couldn't see. She thrust her pudgy hand out and started giggling; the air stung like the cat's tongue did sometimes when it licked her fingers.

Oh, God, Lydia thought, how incredibly rich Tweety's world was! How much sense data had she explored in the five minutes or so that they'd been in the yard? Bianka never left Tweety out over fifteen minutes at the most, and always watched from the window, a fact Lydia kept in mind, but Tweety usually forgot in the brilliance of present experience. Lydia wanted to cry with nostalgia, and joy too: Feeling it all from Tweety's viewpoint was still shockingly immediate, while she herself had almost forgotten the first explorations of . . . well, life and creaturehood.

A part of Lydia's consciousness stayed with Tweety, and a part dissociated and looked down on Tweety as the child plodded through the snow. Lydia knew the house was only a few feet away, yet through the child's experience, it seemed much more distant. And that seventeenth-century landscape, Lydia thought: It was so dear, so lost in time, yet never lost, of course, because it was somehow or other, a different Now . . . Tweety's Now . . . ever opening up to her senses. What difference, if this was all past from a twentieth-century viewpoint? She had to learn to readjust her thinking, because obviously all time existed at once. No matter how much there might be that she didn't understand; how heroic, how forever meaningful and unique was that one child's wonder in the moment of its Now.

Then why did *she* want to cry?

She knew the answer. She was caught between her own experience and Tweety's. More and more she was drawn to the bright new focus of Tweety's life. Yet if she gave in, she'd lose her own identity and be swept away, at least into momentary oblivion. She'd lose her own freedom, she thought. Yet what did that freedom mean to her, if it locked her out of the incomparable creaturehood focus of one space, one time? So, watching Tweety, and feeling with and through Tweety, Lydia realized that she herself felt homeless, between dimensions, and yet unwilling to give up her freedom. And all the while she felt Tweety become more greedily alive, growing fuller and more magnificent in flesh.

Oversoul Seven experienced Lydia's and Tweety's feelings at the same time, and he'd been trying to get through to Lydia since Tweety first fell down in the snow, only Lydia had been too distracted to listen. "Lydia," he said, "you have to enter fully into your experience, which *is* Tweety's. Stop feeling sorry for yourself. Look at the backyard as Tweety does, with wonder, and your wonder will lead you where you want to go."

But Tweety had made it to the door. Bianka let her in, and now Tweety sat inside by the wood stove, where the hot breath of the fire rushed out at her when Bianka opened the oven door to keep her daughter warm as she took off her wet clothes. Lydia, exhausted, found herself as fascinated and frightened by the fire as Tweety was; and she tried to hold on, and not lose herself in the heat of Tweety's intense concentration.

Tweety felt heavy, bulky, and unpredictable.

Bianka said, "Now we'll take your leggings off."

"Look, sweetheart," Josef said. His voice, always loud, thundered in Tweety's ears. She started to scowl, but Josef held out a piece of bread and jam, and even if it was loud, his voice was yellow and warm and heavy like honey.

"You're trying to bribe her for a kiss," Bianka said.

"You bribe me," Josef answered, grinning, "And not with bread and jam either."

"Stop it now. This isn't the time," Bianka said, blushing and partly angry, because sometimes he just knew too much when you didn't want him to.

While Bianka and Josef laughed, and Tweety began chattering agreeably enough as her snow clothes were removed, Lydia nearly panicked. She'd forgotten herself again, hypnotized by the domestic scene, the warm kitchen, the adults . . . The adults! Oh God, she'd done it again, she realized—fallen naturally into Tweety's psychological world.

"That *is* the idea, after all," Oversoul Seven said, finally getting through to her. "I've been trying to talk to you. It's time now."

"It's time now? For what?" Lydia asked mentally. Then she thought: Of *course.* It really was time. Tweety's clothes were off now. Bianka was rubbing her skin with a towel that had been heated in the oven. The pleasant sensations made Tweety squeal.

"It's time to forget, just for a while," Seven said. "Time to give your new self a chance. You've helped Tweety all you can for now."

"Papa's little darling," Josef exclaimed, coming nearer, with his big face close to hers; brown moustache bristling.

Lydia felt all life calling. The wood in the stove crackled, it seemed, as no other kindling wood ever had. Josef gave Tweety the bread and jam, and the texture and taste was brand-new in the universe, a sensual wonder. All life and reality suddenly seemed concentrated in that warm immediate kitchen.

Inside herself, Lydia sobbed, with nostalgia for the future *and* the past.

"I'll be with you," Oversoul Seven said. He was a point of light on the windowpane.

Mentally Lydia muttered, "A lot of good that will do. I'll forget you too, won't I?"

"She looks like you, Bianka," Josef's voice warmly thundered. He stared, grinning, into Tweety's face.

And Lydia for a moment stared back. She thought that he'd already forgotten that they had chosen to be father and daughter; that . . .

"How strange she looks sometimes," Bianka cried, worried.

And Lydia looked out of the child's eyes, through the unsteamed portion of the kitchen window, seeing the seventeenth-century fields covered with snow; the past come alive, and turning into the present.

"But it isn't the past, of course," Oversoul Seven said. "And I'm so proud of you."

"The time *is* now, isn't it?" she said. "I wish there was some way that you could give Tweety some of the knowledge that I've picked up along the way. Or the knowledge that *you've* picked up. Like a built-in set of instructions or . . ." She paused, dizzy. She could feel herself becoming Tweety even more completely. It was difficult to concentrate. "Seven, it *will* be all right, won't it?" she called, for Oversoul Seven seemed to be disappearing into a kind of psychological distance, while she, as Tweety, impatiently wiggled as Bianka dressed her in warm clothes.

"It will be fine," Seven called back. "I promise. And I promise that I'll give Tweety some kind of 'instruction book' for her new life. And what you've learned will be a part of her heritage, too." In his pride in Lydia and his desire to help her, and in his exuberance, Seven shouted, "I'll think of something terrific."

Bianka stared. "Tweety looks different now. Look at her." She wiped her hands on her apron and looked closely into Tweety's face. "She seems more *here!*" she cried.

"More where?" Josef laughed. "She's my girl."

"She's more *here* now," Bianka muttered to herself. She stood watching as Josef swung Tweety over his shoulders, and singing a ballad, carried her into the other room.

"It will be just fine, dear Lydia," Seven whispered.

"Whee," cried Tweety.

Oversoul Seven felt like crying. He felt like laughing.

"Good-bye for a while, dear Lydia. And hello, dear Tweety," he said. But Seven suddenly felt himself being drawn away; something was happening, some important psychological readjustment . . .

Before he could wonder about it, Seven found himself back with Cyprus. Jeffery and Ram-Ram still sat talking and sipping drinks.

"No time has passed here," Cyprus said. "But Lydia's forgetting is letting Jeffery—"

"Remember," Oversoul Seven finished. "Of course."

"What is it?" Ram-Ram asked, leaping to his feet. "You look as if you've seen a ghost."

"Maybe a figurative one," Jeffery said mysteriously. "No, I'm all right. I just remembered something, though. Now it seems impossible that I'd ever forgotten it." Then, irritably, "And stop looking at me with that fake kind-old-psychologist smile, will you?"

"Yes, yes. All right," Ram-Ram said, unoffended.

"You may or may not know that my middle initial is W for William," Jeffery said. He stood up, almost groggily. It was hard for him to talk. "Well, just now, just this minute, mind you, I remembered that I used to identify myself as Will for, I don't know, several years. I even signed my name as William, not Jeffery. This was at a time when I was feeling quite despondent, really. Yet for years, all that slipped from my mind. Only earlier today I remembered an . . . what shall I call it? . . . almost-suicide attempt. One day I played around with the idea anyway, standing dangerously close to a cliff edge. And I never was sure what happened . . . a lapse of memory . . . but I didn't jump. And I just this moment remembered, after that day I never thought of myself as Will again. And until now, I'd completely forgotten that I ever had."

"You'd better sit down," Ram-Ram said anxiously.

But Jeffery paced the floor excitedly, calling over his shoulder, "But that was a kind of psychic suicide, wasn't it?"

"I suppose it *could* be called that," Ram-Ram said cautiously.

"You know damn well it could," Jeffery said. He was so agitated that Ram-Ram patted him on the shoulder, but Jeffery pulled away.

"I don't need any sympathy now," he said. "Suddenly, as I remembered the name thing, I had the oddest feeling. I feel more *here,* more me, as if I've resurrected portions of myself."

"Suddenly you make me feel quite envious," Ram-Ram said. "I could have written your book when I was your age, or my version of it. But I didn't, of course."

"I didn't say I had a book," Jeffery exclaimed.

"My first guess was a scientific treatise of some sort," Ram-Ram said, as if he hadn't been interrupted, "but afterward I realized that a different kind of manuscript must be involved. In any case, I had my chance and muffed it. But now it's almost as if I went back in time and changed a version of *me,* by helping you."

"I'm not any version of you," Jeffery shouted.

"Of course you're not. You're too literal-minded," Ram-Ram said. "Still, your future will be more like the future I might have had . . ."

Oversoul Seven was having difficulties following the conversation. For one thing, he was losing his focus on earth time, so that objects appeared and disappeared according to when they had existed, or would exist, in any given space; and particularly in the space that was Jeffery's living room. He heard Jeffery's voice, but sometimes it was speaking yesterday, sometimes tomorrow, and Oversoul Seven couldn't find a proper present at all.

Beside him, Cyprus waited. "You're too far to the left of today," she said.

Seven called somewhat anxiously, "I can't seem to find any today to start with."

"*Any* time is a present time if you're there. Stop where things seem to be 'right now,' and call that today."

"All right, if you say so," Seven whispered. "But now it's a different present than it was before. I got confused; or I *get* confused. I mean, you're in a different present time than I am."

"No matter," she said. "I'm on a platform above time. And theoretically, you should be, too. But tell me *when* you are."

"I'm to the left of time from your viewpoint, uh, I think," came Seven's hasty reply.

"All right; that's Jeffery's past. Now back up a bit further."

Seven was growing dizzy. Chairs and tables changed their positions according to their locations at any given time. Jeffery's figure appeared at the window; then, at the door. Ram-Ram disappeared entirely. The living room flickered bright, then dark, as nights and days flashed by.

"*Now,*" Cyprus directed.

Seven tried to stop things as quickly as he could. Then he grinned. It was Jeffery's room at night, before . . . before what? For he saw himself and Cyprus, both in adult male images, out on Jeffery's patio.

"That image suits me rather well," he said to the Cyprus on the platform above time.

"Shush. Listen and watch," she said.

"I think I have it all straight," said the earlier image of Seven who stood with the male Cyprus.

"All *what* straight?" asked the "present" Seven.

"Will you just listen?" said the Cyprus out of time, while the Cyprus of the past, standing with the past Seven, said, "I think you're very wise. After tonight, you'll completely forget that Jeffery is one of your personalities living in time. That way you can look at him more objectively, since you seem to be having trouble relating to him properly."

"So that's it!" shouted the present Seven, and suddenly it all came back to him, just as the past Seven said, "Right. I agree. We'll both appear to him in his dream state, and cleverly lead him out of the depression he's been in since his wife left him. Some psychologist; he doesn't even recognize his own depression."

Cyprus on the platform above time said, "And Lydia and Jeffery can help each other, as each looks for a meaning to existence . . ."

And the past Seven cried, "And we'll stimulate Jeffery's creative abilities, which he's buried for so long, and rearouse the young Will with all the dissatisfactions he feels, so that Jeffery can recognize them and deal with his problems . . ."

"Exactly," both Cypruses said.

"While Lydia rediscovers the joys of earth life, also helping Jeffery revive his own love of life."

"Exactly," both Cypruses replied.

And as both Cypruses and both Sevens spoke at once, time thickened; Jeffery's living room had two levels of time, simultaneously: In one, the earlier Cyprus and Seven in the male images were just entering the room from the patio and arousing Jeffery as he lay on the couch. The wind tugged at the geranium pot on the patio which would shortly fall over, alarming Jeffery.

In the second level of time — in their present — Ram-Ram and Jeffery still sat talking. "Yes, yes, yes," Ram-Ram was saying. "I could almost have done an automatic manuscript myself; and someday you'll have to show me yours."

"Do you feel that we aren't alone?" Jeffery asked suddenly.

Ram-Ram smiled and shrugged. "I've been staring at the ceiling all the time we've been talking. Drawn to it. See those two lights up there, by the corner? Reflections most likely, but . . ."

Jeffery looked. At the same time, though he saw nothing extraordinary, he felt an extraordinary yearning that made him say, "Do you believe in the soul? I mean, as a psychological entity?"

(And as Jeffery asked the question, in time's vast depth, Tweety looked out the window of her childhood room at the stars, and thought that the starlight formed a familiar yet strange image, as if looking out, she was looking inside her own mind.

(And in the vast reaches of Jeffery's consciousness, Will walked up mental steps to the threshold of Jeffery's growing understanding.)

Ram-Ram said comfortably, "More to the point, since you asked, do you?"

"I believe in . . . something," Jeffery said. "But there's some writing I have to do just now. I don't mean to cut our conversation short, but there's something I must finish."

"I thought there might be," Ram-Ram said.

Then Jeffery wrote this chapter and the previous one. He wrote all night, no longer astonished as his own experience wound through the narrative and was reshaped, turned endwise and sidewards, focused and unfocused, his and yet more than his . . . and . . . Will's.

And then, after a brief sleep, he continued.

~ *Chapter Twenty-Eight* ~

Oversoul Seven Keeps His Promise to Lydia
and Begins Tweety's Education

Oversoul Seven said, "I'm going to start Tweety on Sumari right away and really give her an excellent education, because I promised Lydia that I would. Besides, I've thought of a terrific idea."

"First, you'll have to explain what Sumari means," Cyprus replied.

"No problem," Seven said. "I'll tell Tweety that Sumari means many things, but we'll be using it as the name for the inner lands of the self." He paused expectantly and said, "Well, aren't you a bit curious about my brilliant idea?"

"I'm waiting for you to tell me," she said, again looking nowhere in particular.

"You probably know already," he said reproachfully.

"No, I know you like to surprise me . . . "

"Well, what do you think of *Seven's Little Book?*" Seven asked, unable to keep the secret any longer. "It will be a book just for Tweety—not a physical book, of course, but a dream book. I'll read some to her each night when she's asleep. I'm going to start with Sumari Geography; you know, the inner lands of the self and their, uh, subjective locations. Well, what do you think?"

"Truly inspired," Cyprus said. Her woman teacher image positively glowed, and Seven's fourteen-year-old male form glittered happily around the edges.

"Lydia wrote books, you know," he said. "So I thought it would really be fitting to do a book for *her;* I mean, for Tweety. It will have all the important things about life in it. And because it will be a dream book, her subconscious will, uh, lap it up like cream."

Cyprus started laughing. Lost in her humor, she forgot to hold her image, so that she started changing from a woman into a man and back again so quickly and in such hilarious fashion that Seven's head was almost spinning. "Stop that," he said indignantly.

"Oh, Seven, I was laughing *with* you, not at you," Cyprus said.

"Well, I wasn't laughing," Seven said glumly. "You just made me remember something that I forgot to put in the book. How am I going to explain that we aren't really male or female? I'll have to do a book on Sumari Sex, but maybe I should wait until Tweety is older."

"You'll work it out," Cyprus replied. "Are you going to show me the book now?" She turned into a male image, tall, brown-skinned, with thick black hair, just for the change, and to take Seven's mind away from the earnestness that seemed to possess it since he began talking about the book.

"Good form; Indian," Seven said automatically. "No, you can watch me read the book's first installment to Tweety, though, and check my bedside manner. But I don't want to show you the whole book yet. I *do* like to surprise you. And it's a little book, after all." He started grinning and turned into the image of an Indian guru, saying in mock-intense tones, "This will be a sacred book, containing the knowledge of the ages!" Then he stared at Cyprus hypnotically, materialized a turban around his head, with a gigantic jewel in the center. "How's this for my book-session attire?"

"Awful. You'd scare Tweety to death," Cyprus said, laughing, so Seven turned into a twelve-year-old guru, with a robe the color of brown fall leaves, and a face the same color only faintly tinged with gold, and deep soft eyes the shade of tree bark. "Now that's excellent," Cyprus said. "And it fits you, somehow. You should wear that image more often."

But Seven was already brooding again, and his whole image blurred a bit. "This is my first real creative endeavor in the line of multidimensional art per se, and I also hope to submit it as a thesis to meet my own educational requirements. So I certainly want it to be good. It'll be around for ages, influencing all kinds of people beside Tweety, because transdimensional art transcends so many realities." His eyes suddenly glowed. "Still," he said, "maybe there'll be other-world translations, so I should give the title special care too. *Seven's Little Book* was my first choice. But maybe I should give it a more formal title like, *The Beginner's Course in Sumari: A Preparation for Creaturehood.*

"Don't get carried away," Cyprus said.

"You're just jealous," Seven said, grinning. "Well, maybe I am a bit overly enthusiastic. But I really *am* excited. I'm trying to give Tweety all the important information she needs to start a new life, and yet it must be simple enough for a child to understand. And I think I've done it. So, are you ready? This is the first installment."

Cyprus nodded, and in less than a moment she and Seven sat by Tweety's bedside. The child was sleeping soundly. Oversoul Seven arranged the mental pages of the book in their proper order, and began to read:

Sumari Geography

Sumari cities are states of mind. They are quite as real as physical cities, more real, if the truth be known, and they have their own boundaries, cultures, crafts, and trades. Some people are travelers, visiting one city after another, and sometimes even living in two cities at once, for in the Sumari cities, moods and thoughts are like streets, alleys, or wide boulevards, all existing together and intersecting.

So, two Sumari cities can become one all of a sudden, without bothering the inhabitants at all, who are simply aware of the added richness of their surroundings, and an astonishing freshness of experience that they hadn't noticed before. In other words, the boundaries can shift and change constantly, with streets and paths always appearing and disappearing.

A Sumari city can suddenly become very small also, with dark hills springing up closely about it, shutting out the sunshine and hemming in the shops until it seems that the city has no room in which to grow.

Now, each person alive really lives in a Sumari city, or in several at the same time, no matter where he or she lives in the world outside. And all of the real work and creativity takes place first in these inner Sumari landscapes. People visit them at night when they're asleep in the outside world, but even when they're awake outside, some part of them is always aware of their citizenship in the inside world.

Of course, a whole Sumari reality is involved, with its own mental continents, countries, oceans, and deserts that are inner counterparts of the world outside. Only, the Sumari world is there . . . or here . . . all the time. I mean, you live in it whether you're alive or dead in outside terms. So it's very durable, and forms the physical world that you're beginning to know. But the Sumari world is more responsive, and changeable, because — well, everything moves by thought and feeling. And as you'll soon discover, people's feelings change all the time.

So, worried people all together in one inner city might make a mountain tower above them, dark and threatening, so that everyone stops what they're doing to look up at it, and worry some more. But their worrying just makes the mountain higher, and darker, and more threatening. But even then, some wise child or man or woman will say, sooner or later, "Our worrying only makes the mountain grow more frightening. So let's unworry it away. Let's ignore it, and see what happens." And if enough people listen and follow those suggestions, then in a twinkling the mountain disappears, and the city is free of it.

And when those same people are awake in the outside world, they'll remember what they learned, and realize that their thoughts and feelings cause their physical experience too. Or at the very least, they'll realize that worrying can turn into a mountain of trouble. In the outside world, of course, mountains stay around much longer and there are happy mountains too, in any case. But the inner bothersome ones don't have to grow at all.

All adventures and explorations really take people into inner landscapes where they can make their own underground caverns and woody paths and oceans to sail across. Then the people experience it all top-side, so to speak. People are always creating the physical world too, you see, materializing it in space and time in the richness of its seasons. And to do that is a magnificent adventure.

Most Sumari cities are the most brilliant, splendid places imaginable, and their light and creativity shines from the inner landscape to the outside one, so that the physical world is always illuminated; and each physical city always has some joy and vitality shining through, no matter what may be happening there.

Each person is unique. So are you. You have so many aspects of yourself that you create physical lives in which you can focus on particular abilities, and fulfill and enjoy them. In so doing, you help yourself and others too, and add to the richness of being. But that's a subject for later on.

Oversoul Seven paused. In the distance somewhere he heard Cyprus say, "That last part was far too complicated for Tweety. Besides, nobody wants to be read to all night, Seven. More important, though, there's something quite vital that you forgot."

Seven frowned briefly. He'd thought that everything was going very well, though it was true that he became so involved with his reading that he'd almost completely forgotten Tweety. In fact, where was she? Her body lay serenely on the bed, but Tweety had wandered off somewhere; her spirit was gone. As usual, Cyprus was right.

Somewhat disappointed, Seven mentally searched the house and grounds and finally he found Tweety, out of body, playing in the snow.

Seven shook his head. She'd probably been there for some time, and he hadn't noticed. Worse, she hadn't heard a thing he'd read.

"There you are," she said, grinning up at him and grabbing at his turban with pudgy jam-stained dream hands. A beautifully hallucinated jam jar was beside her, and she'd even hallucinated her brown coat and leggings so that she looked like a small bear at the jam jar. Snowflakes were falling. Tweety looked so triumphant that Seven knew she thought she'd pulled something over on someone.

"Why the jam?" he asked, squatting down beside her with his twelve-year-old guru image.

Her brown eyes turned angry and belligerent. Seven made the jam jar dance in the air and turn over several times until she started laughing and clapping her hands. Then he asked, "Why the jam? I know, but I want you to tell me."

She glowered for a moment, but he was her very own friend; no one, she knew, saw him but her. So she smiled, brilliantly this time, and opened her mind to him the way he'd taught her. Seven saw her then, earlier that day, in a rage, screaming for bread and jam. Bianka was busy and sent her out of the kitchen. So straight-away, after bed, Tweety rushed outside all by herself, down the stairs and out — something she wasn't allowed to do when she was awake — and she took the hallucinated jar of jam. (Killing two birds at once, Seven told Cyprus later.)

But Seven said nothing. He turned himself into a snowman for her while she tired herself out racing around him. Then she followed him upstairs to bed and he read her the material on Sumari Geography that she hadn't heard before. This time, though, he kept watch on her, and read more slowly so that she could ask questions.

Cyprus returned, looking like the ancient yet ever-young woman. "You are going to tell her how to keep in touch with her life, aren't you?" she asked. "And certainly you intend to discuss magic and Sumari Time . . ."

"Hello," Tweety said, matter-of-factly. She'd met Cyprus before, under these same circumstances.

"Of course," Seven said to Cyprus. "Don't rush me. Those subjects are in other chapters."

Looking nowhere in particular again, Cyprus said, "Seven, I have a suggestion. Actually your little book could help many people, not just children. Let's publish it in the Appendix of Jeffery's book. That way, people can read it themselves when they're awake."

Seven was so pleased that he couldn't maintain himself. He took three images at once, all of them dancing. "What do you think of that, Tweety? Your little book will be read around the world," he said.

But Tweety was really fast asleep this time, spirit and all.

"Your *Little Book* can follow the Afterword and Jeffery's notes," Cyprus said.

"Afterword?" Seven asked.

And Cyprus said, "The gods still have a word or two to say on their own behalf, so they're inspiring Jeffery to write an Afterword for them."

~ *Afterword of the Gods* ~

"**I**s anyone looking?" Zeus asked.

"Verily, no," Christ answered.

"Are you positive?"

"Would the Son of God lie? Aren't I omnipotent?" Christ asked. "Aren't you?"

"Oh, Jesus!" Zeus thundered.

The two of them sat momentarily alone, in the green wooden rocking chairs on the porch of the old gods' rest home. Silence settled gently about them, but a very peculiar silence indeed, one so vital that within it all probable sounds seemed ready to emerge. Yet even Zeus' voice, thundering, made no sound that anyone human could hear, because it was sounding on the other side of silence. And in the same way, Christ and Zeus rocked contentedly in *their* godly dimension, invisibly, on the other side of light where no one, including Oversoul Seven, could ever find them.

"It's always ever so much more peaceful after the visitors leave," Hera exclaimed. She came out onto the porch and peered into the divine distance. "I see our own world is back, thank heavens." She sat down and began to rock so that her orange taffeta gown went swish, swish, swish, with a sound that no one could hear, of course, but the gods.

"Just like the swish, swish, swish of Mohammed's sword," Christ said. He made the sign of the cross with wrinkled fingers, then sprang to his feet, his gray curls bobbing. "Well, the charade is over, at any rate," he said, and then in a voice even louder than Zeus', he shouted: "Alee alee in free! You can all come out now."

As Christ spoke, a variety of developments happened simultaneously. Hera, Zeus, and Christ were instantly rejuvenated: The flush of a thousand births turned their skin from paper-brittle gray to an idealized, glowing texture impossible to describe. Christ stood as a young man, each hair on his head and beard a crisp, lively brown. Zeus, with new powerful thighs and black beard, was anywhere from sixty to a hundred, yet with such an ancient youthfulness that his vitality was literally of divine proportions. Hera was also magnificently old and young at once, a mother goddess of such stature that Christ called out ecstatically, "Hail, mother of God."

"Why, bless you, my son," Hera cried, laughing, and she turned into the Virgin Mother for him.

"It won't make any difference that the charade is over," Zeus shouted. "Whatever guise people put us in is deceptive, and I'm tired of playing roles. Where's poor Mohammed? Someone should tell him he can put down that damn sword now. And poor Buddha; they *are* turning him into a mess of jelly, when you come right down to it."

But Christ yelled boisterously, "What difference does it make? That doesn't change *us*. But you're right; let's get about our godly business. These roles *are* hampering."

This time, all together, Hera, Christ, and Zeus shouted, "Alee alee in free! You can all come out now."

Zeus shouted, even more loudly, "Let the charade be over," and instantly a gigantic flash of divine lightning struck at the gods' rest home, coming down from a sky literally infinite, that no spaceship could ever find. And, as the lightning struck, sudden tumult began with such a riotous roar that all possible sounds did seem to be sounded, though again, these were inaudible, rising up on the other side of silence that divides worlds.

And, as the lightning hit, the thousands of gargoyles that decorated the gods' rest home began to move. Laughing stone heads grew fleshy; entwined stone limbs stretched. Angel wings of plaster began to beat. The statues, the wooden carvings of Mohammed's men, the bust of Zoroaster, and each and every gargoyle above the window casings and around the pillars moved, stirred, and rose to jump, fly, or leap to the garden, so that the building itself dissolved into the forms of all the gods who had formed it.

There were future gods and old ones, probable gods, aunt and uncle gods, animal and bird gods, each shining and unique with its own image.

"What an edifice that was!" Christ said, as one by one the gods turned from plaster or wood or stone, edging or turret decoration or whatever, into living forms and dropped down beside him.

"Nectar for everyone," Zeus shouted; and in vast good humor he added, "Or Christ, do you want wine and fish?"

"Laugh all you want," Christ said. "You can play Christ next time. I'm sick of roles that include crucifixions. The goddesses will be back in style with humanity soon, and I'm going to be one of those for a change."

"That's the trouble. We *do* have to change with the times," Mohammed said. He came running lightly up from the back garden, heaving his sword into the grass. "Buddha was always smartest there," he said. "He was always so ambiguous . . ."

The divine conversations went on as the gods lounged on the sunny green grass, sipping nectar; and each image was spectacular in proportion. The Virgin Mary's voice rose, "It's too bad, though; the Crucifixion story ruined the whole thing as far as I was concerned. Yet the people always insist that the gods be killed in these dramas in one way or another."

"Come now, it's all over," Christ said snappishly. "I admit it got on my nerves too, but if that's the kind of symbols people need, that's the kind they get. And besides, they *are* learning."

The Virgin Mary turned back into Hera and joined the group just as Pegasus came in for a landing and began to nibble delicately at the grass. Looking up, he said indulgently, "Why such squabbles? There'll be new gods before long. It's in the air."

"Well, I hope they're better than the old variety," Zeus said. "It's not creative at all to be stuck in the same old roles. Maybe the new gods will have more sense, so that we can really make something out of them. Christ didn't grow at all, for example. Neither did I, for that matter. But a new magnificent god role that we could really sink our teeth into . . . now, wouldn't that be something?"

"Wouldn't it? Wouldn't it?" The question was taken up by all of the assembled gods; wonderingly, yearningly.

"Impossible, I suppose," murmured Pegasus, sadly.

Hera said, "We can't force people to recognize us as we are."

"Sometimes I think it would serve them right if we could," Zeus said, laughing.

"But if they *could* perceive us apart from the roles . . ." Christ said dreamily. "I mean, if we didn't have to conform to their ideas about us! But if we don't conform, they don't perceive us at all. And all in all, each of us had some excellent qualities. The trouble is that people insist on their idea of specifics, I suppose. To imagine us as superhuman, in terms of their species alone, is understandable enough at their level. But to define us by their ideas of sexuality or race is ridiculous even by their standards."

"They're really quite unbelievable," Buddha said, arriving late as usual. He looked like an Indian guru, a situation he remedied at once by turning into a tree. Quarrelsomely he said, "They twist around everything a god says. If only they could perceive us as we really are . . ."

"Just what I was saying," Christ said triumphantly. "But it's a lost cause, I'm afraid."

"Except for nature," Zeus replied. "And *that's* my favorite materialization."

"Mine, too. Let's not forget that," Mohammed cried.

"It's ever so much more rewarding and creative," Pegasus agreed.

"But why *isn't* nature enough for them?" Buddha asked. "They keep misquoting me as saying that nature is unsavory; or that the point of earth life is to get over it, like a disease. And then they rant about annihilating desire, and I never said a thing like that."

Hera turned into the Virgin and said, "I probably understand humans better than any of you, and my miraculous conception told the whole tale. They just don't trust nature. They don't like the death part and they've never been able to see beyond it, really; it obsesses them. All of nature shouts of new births, yet humans have the greatest difficulty imagining any divinity in nature. I don't understand how they can be that way, but they are."

"They don't see any divinity in themselves, either," Zeus said. "At least the Olympian gods were in and out of nature — and human nature all the time. But Christ was born into nature just once, and yanked out fast."

"Well, let's get back to ourselves," Christ said. "Everyone's gone. No need to keep up these roles."

"Still, they *could* hold such promise . . ." Hera said nostalgically, just as she and all of the other gods dispensed with their images and with the personalities that went with them. Their individual awarenesses mixed and merged one with the other, swept through the others, psychologically romped and whirled through mental universes unending.

"It's time for our 'nightly check,' " came the unspoken, on-the-other-side-of-silence, multimillion thought. And each divine awareness turned its attention toward the earth, seeing it and all of its parts, down to the tiniest particle; merging with the mountains, sky, seas; rushing gloriously into each living thing, exulting in the cozy preciseness of earth time.

The gods dived exuberantly into the earth, minus images: growing up as trees in a million backyards, as fish in the oceans, as people and insects and animals. They merged with the twilight that came in through Jeffery's window, flowing through the pages of the manuscript of this book that sat on the table. And the gods continued to give life, form, and substance to the earth.

~ *Jeffery's Closing Notes* ~

*I*t is with mixed feelings of exhaustion, triumph, and misgivings that I close this manuscript with these few notes. Anyone who reads this book can easily trace the development of my own involvement, until I, myself, became a character in its bizarre narrative. For me now, the division between reality and fantasy exists no longer: That is, I realize that to some extent each of us deals with varying kinds of reality. Perhaps each of us also has a younger, unresolved self wandering the wild reaches of the psyche, but in any case . . . and despite the oddness of therapeutic measures, I feel whole for the first time in many years.

This doesn't mean that I have accepted Oversoul Seven as my psychological guide *per se,* but I do believe that he represents those more creative and expansive aspects of the psyche that most of us ignore. Would that ever-enthusiastic imaginative portion of the psyche then take such steps as this automatic manuscript to bring itself to conscious awareness? In my case, at least, the answer must be yes. Moreover, there can be no doubt of the devotion that such a mission implies, as this usually unconscious level of the self surfaces, and acts as a teacher for the conscious mind.

There are still many unresolved questions, some mundane and some quite mysterious. What will I do now? I have no idea, except that I'll no longer stay in the confines of my academic field, but roam more adventurously elsewhere into other investigations that I hope will please the curious Will, who still wonders about the meaning of existence.

I was astonished at Oversoul Seven's announcement of a little book for Tweety. "For God's sake," I thought, "the book is writing a book." Without explaining its origin, though, I intend to send it to Sarah for her child (she delivered a son about the same time Tweety was born) and to read it as well to any possible children of my own. The simplicity of the material is most deceptive, and had I read such prose as a boy, perhaps Will would have found more joy in life, and we would not have needed to stand on the precipice of psychological duplicity, contemplating a double suicide. For it now comes to me clearly that any suicide involves the death of thousands, those born or unborn; the slaying of probable selves who might have sprung otherwise from the points of our lives. And even if we continued to exist, we would have altered our own relationship with ourselves, perhaps . . . who knows? . . . becoming probable versions actualized in other worlds than those *we* know.

Obviously, I had become a stranger to myself before this manuscript began. I isolated my younger questioning self; buried the questions, for that matter; denied the dissatisfaction that was meant to lead to creative solutions. If I had not saved Will, in my past, would I have committed suicide in my present? Or wouldn't that present have existed to begin with, since, as Will, I would have died years ago? Or because my present *did* exist, was it a foregone conclusion that Will wouldn't commit suicide? I don't believe so. I think that I had gone as far as I could in time without Will, though, and that he was so despondent not only because of the problems that existed in the past, but also because I'd kept him apart in a psychological limbo that lacked all give-and-take or chance for fulfillment. So for him, time had stopped, then. And when I went back to save him, I started time up again, which meant that he had to jump or not jump.

As I read *Seven's Little Book,* I could feel Will reading it too, and I felt as if a new memory for both of us were being formed; a memory of having read the same material somewhere as a child; and in the strangest fashion as I read of Seven's nightly book sessions with Tweety, I saw my own childhood bedroom transposed in my mind over Tweety's. And Oversoul Seven was reading to *me* as well. Embarrassing confession! — but as I typed the material of the little book, a part of my mind went open and transparent, childlike; and was refreshed. The *Little Book* is being included in full, rather as an appendix to this manuscript, as Cyprus suggested to Seven in the last chapter.

Yet the *Little Book* is more than an appendix by far, and if there are mathematical and scientific formulas, perhaps there are psychological or psychic ones as well. If so, then *Seven's Little Book* presents one such formula by which life can be experienced more fully. Before I began these adventures, I would have been appalled by such a statement, of course.

About Lydia, who always remained a character in a book to me, I'm less sure, except that I began to realize, long before the manuscript itself told me, that her pilgrimage was for me also — and, of course, for Will — who visited the Virgin in that ludicrous scene before the nightmare sequence that I so frighteningly shared. I felt, without wanting to admit it, that Lydia's dilemma to be born or not born paralleled my own psychological state, even when I hid my depression from myself.

So, in a most unobjective fashion, I feel that in this case at least, fictional characters and real ones helped each other, interacted, and formed some kind of interdimensional series of events almost impossible to describe. I must state my belief that Cyprus and Oversoul Seven are real, then . . . fictionally real . . . and their reality may straddle such simple definitions.

Ram-Ram the godologist presents a problem. I have no idea if he is an independent personality of some kind, purely a fictional character, or a composite. He could somehow represent the futility of applying Freudian principles to religion, for example; or he could symbolize a portion of Ram-Ram Brail's deep distrust of religion and certain tenets of psychology as well.

I personally found the material on the gods fascinating, simply because it brought home one vital issue. To search for the gods in conventional terms is a useless pursuit, for most often our vision of the gods all but disappears in our ideas *of what they must be,* or what they must be like. The strange production of this book itself gives me a nebulous "feel" for the kind of creativity that any divinity must possess; a vast gestalt of being that could scarcely be contained in any of our conventional godly tales. I see now that in the past I equated God with the images organized religion had of Him, and recognizing their spiritual poverty, I cast out all thoughts of divinity altogether.

Evolution's "chance universe" was no solution to the origin of life either, however, though I trusted *that* more than a capricious god. But many questions concerning the existence of divinity still remain.

The most difficult and still unresolved question remaining regards the status of Ram-Ram, who I assure you is a very real person with a traceable history. The interview as recorded in Chapter Twenty-eight, was the last one we had. I never saw him again, and he left no forwarding address. By all reasons of logic, Ram-Ram cannot be a future self of mine, since his history exists in my present and well into the past. So, in those terms, I can't grow into who he is. Yet I am certain that Ram-Ram is a different person now than he was before these adventures began; as I am, of course. It wouldn't surprise me to find myself in my future growing into the *kind* of man he would be, had he in *his* younger years written this automatic manuscript instead of me.

As to whether or not Cyprus and Oversoul Seven are independent entities or personifications arising from highly creative elements of my own psyche, I have no answer. It's possible, I suppose, that some unforeseen future events might shed light on that basic question. Perhaps I will be suddenly urged once again to write down words not my own, producing a script that lives now only in probability. Or perhaps this book was a one-time boost, arising in response to my problems; in which case I suppose I shall never feel that bizarre and fascinating rush of creativity again. Or perhaps in a few months, I may look back and find the entire episode unbelievable. If so, I shall be far poorer than I am now.

The patients in the mental institution were quite real, of course. I personally met Queen Alice and the girl who thought she was Christ. It wouldn't surprise me terribly if in the future some odd manuscript of Queen Alice's came to light, perhaps prepared with Ram-Ram's assistance.

So *this* manuscript raises more questions than it answers, which is really the whole point of it, I imagine. Most certainly I will live the rest of my life examining reality in the light of what is written here.

~ *Epilogue* ~

Seven said, confused, "I *do* understand that Jeffery did write the book. But from another perspective, you and I both know that Jeffery's a character in a book, too."

"Precisely," Cyprus answered.

Seven was quiet for a moment, pondering. He really didn't want to say what was on his mind, but Cyprus said, "And . . . ?"

"Well," Oversoul Seven said, "what bothers me is this: We both know that from still another perspective, we're characters in a book, too."

"Precisely," Cyprus answered, smiling.

"But we *know* that we exist!" Seven shouted. He was beyond exasperation.

"Then what are you so concerned about?" Cyprus asked. "We created the book that we're in. We created ourselves, and a dazzling reality that *does* exist. We create the physical world in which the books have meaning."

And Seven cried, "I'll never get to Oversoul Eight stage if I have to understand all that first."

～ *Oversoul Seven's* ～
Little Book

An Appendix

A nd Oversoul Seven sat by Tweety's bedside each night, reading from
the special book he'd written just for her. But he also knew that it was
written for all children, those young in years, and those hidden within
adults. He also knew that the book would automatically rearouse the children within the adults so that they could be comforted in the present for
the misunderstandings of the past.

He said to Cyprus, "And my little book *is* magical. That's the beauty of
it! Who ever really understands what I'm saying *will* have a charmed life. In
fact, I have a whole chapter on that alone . . ."

So Seven read to Tweety, a bit at a time . . .

The Charmed Life

Each life is charmed (Seven said), yours, and everyone else's, and you
must never forget it. The instant you're born, you're charmed, because life
itself is a charm. Each being is charmed into existence in whatever reality it
finds itself, and given everything it needs to operate in the environment.
Your body is charmed, too: It's a magic part of everything else; springing up
from all the things you see about you. Atoms and molecules go singing

417

through the miraculous air, forming themselves into rocks and trees and dogs and cats and people, too. You *are* magic. You charm the air so that it thickens into your body wherever you are.

When you want to move, you think the air ahead of you into becoming your body, and the air behind you then stops being your body . . . all very magical indeed. You move your arm just one inch to the right, and the air to the left one inch stops being part of your arm. But it all happens so quickly, your snatching of the air and making it turn into your body, that you never notice it at all, and take it quite for granted. Which is why it works so well, you see.

But your life *is* charmed. And there is a secret, a very simple one. Really, it's not a secret. But you have to remember that your life is charmed. People who forget can't use their magic nearly as well as they did before, and they have a tendency to get angry at those who can. So, often, they pretend that no magic exists at all. Then they evolve great philosophies to prove it, which is itself magical, of course. But they can't see that, because they're so convinced that magic doesn't exist.

And many people forget how simple and natural magic is, so they evolve long theories, and methods that are supposed to make it work, when you and I know, and everyone else *really* knows, that magic happens by itself, because that's what magic is.

But people are also very creative . . . magic again! . . . so they make up gods of this and that, and realms and spheres, and maps to chart out in advance where magic might be taking them so they don't get surprised, which is silly because magic goes where it wants to, which is everywhere. And when you try to map it out in advance, you really cut yourself short.

Because a characteristic of magic is that it automatically turns into whatever you want it to be. You create your own reality with it, so whatever maps you make are real. And if you forget what magic is, then you're liable to think that your map is the only real one, and all others are false. You get in a terrible bind, fighting over which way is right, which road or map, while all the time magic is what makes the maps. And a great variety of maps can appear in the twinkling of an eye!

Particularly when you grow up, many people will tell you that there is no magic. If you believe them, then you'll forget too, and you'll act as if you aren't charmed and bring unmagic into your life . . . which is magic too, you see, but magic that doesn't know itself. Then you'll create things that go with unmagic, like sorrow or sickness, and you'll have to deal with them at that level until you remember that your life is charmed again.

So in the meantime you'll feel nasty and unloved and angry, way beyond what is natural, and have to worry about sad or fearful emotions and what to do with them, when magically, you'd know: They'd just come and go exuberantly like summer storms. But anger and hate and sorrow are all magic too, and left alone, they'd lead you back to the knowledge that your life is charmed. Because hate is love looking for itself every place but where love is; and love is what you feel for yourself when you know that you are where you're supposed to be in the universe, and that you're lovely just because you are, and, of course, charmed.

Not only that, but you're also the magic maker; the inner living part of you that forms your life. But consciously you have to know this, accept and acknowledge it, and let the magic of yourself happen. That way, you're directing the magic of yourself.

But it's even more fun just to let the magic happen as it wants to, because it's your magic, and that way it keeps telling you more and more about your magical self. Then the magic flows through you with unimpeded delight. If you keep saying, "I want it this way and no other," then you may be limiting your physical experience, because there's no doubt that your inner magical self knows more about your potentials than you do. And it will tell you quite clearly, if you only listen.

To many adults, all of this sounds too simple and unintellectual, because unfortunately many of them think that the mind is just something to say "no" with, and to keep out magic. Nothing could be further from the truth.

But if you use your mind to say no to magic, then it's like closing doors to your own charmed existence, and refusing to use the full power of your life.

Everyone works with magic, whether they realize it or not. Beliefs are magic, too, you see. Many people think that one particular belief makes everything right; or makes magic happen. And as long as they believe that, they're all right for a while. But if they start doubting that belief, and don't find another one to replace it, then they think that they've lost their Magic, or that life has. Instead, of course, the magic is there all along.

But people love systems, so they use all kinds of beliefs . . . some of them quite handy . . . as aids. And they travel through belief systems, sometimes going to considerable trouble to do so, when all they really have to remember is that they are magic themselves, and their lives are charmed without their having to do anything about it at all.

And your conscious mind is magic, too. Its workings are mysterious and complicated, and simple and clear at once, like air is. Your conscious mind looks out through your eyes, and knows parcels of air as its body, and smiles through cheeks and skin the same way that the moon shines through the wide skin of the heavens. See how clear and mysterious it all is? So, in a way, it's silly for the conscious mind to question magic, because — well, it's so magical itself.

But systems of magic are silly, too, and all of them are really based upon doubt. Magic is considered so tenuous that someone has to be at it all the time, making spells or paying someone else to do it. And the spells all have to be done just right, so people concentrate on how to do this spell or another. This gets very complicated, and many adult books deal with the subject.

But everything is a spell. Your words and thoughts are spells. Science is just another system that tries to discover what certain spells cause certain effects. Usually, of course, scientists don't understand magic any more than priests do; and they all get caught up in their own complicated methods.

There isn't much basic difference between muttering a lot of different phrases or drawing magic circles to protect yourself against illness, and taking handfuls of pills given to you by doctors. Both methods work if you believe in them, though the practitioners of one method will never agree that the other way works at all, of course. And unfortunately, neither side *really* understands magic, which is behind all of the spells and methods and formulas.

Spells work if you believe in them; only you don't need spells at all. Everything happens by itself. You happen by yourself, so does the world. And the principle behind it all is magic. And magic is the beingness within and behind all things.

The Body and Creaturehood

Within your creaturehood, you have all kinds of freedom. And all of the freedom you can ever enjoy in your lifetime must come through your creaturehood. Some people spend a good deal of time trying to ignore their own bodies, or trying to pretend that they only have minds, or that minds alone are important. Some people even try to ignore their bodies almost entirely in an effort to be more spiritual, or to be "better" people, which is like a bird trying to fly better than any other bird alive . . . all the time refusing to use its wings, or pretending that they weren't there. He'd never get off the ground. A bird would never think of such foolishness, of course, and often other creatures are smarter than people.

In fact, whenever you're in trouble, it's a good idea to watch the animals, for they bask in their freedom and don't worry about their limitations. A cat or dog can teach you a lot. A cat really enjoys its catness, just as you should enjoy your creaturehood. Even a fly buzzing around the ceiling loves its own reality and is free in it. If it stopped to wonder whether or not it could really fly—well, it would fall down in a minute or never go fast enough to outwit your mother's flyswatter.

So, trying to be religious or "good" or "'better" by ignoring your body doesn't make much sense either.

Actually, each person has a private kingdom for his or her very own, because your body is the one part of earth that is really yours, that no one can take away during your lifetime. It's the part of earth, moving and alive, that belongs to you and nobody else. In a way, it's your portion of the planet, sprung up in a living, moving statue of earth-stuff, for you and no one else. So how you treat your body is important.

You just don't live *in* it, either. You live *through* it; there's a difference. You flow through it, moving in all of its parts. The body is your own magic country. Your conscious mind is like a monarch. Now, a good king or queen is loving and gives the people freedom to move about the country. In this case, your own feelings and thoughts and desires are like the people in *your* kingdom. So you should treat your own feelings graciously, and you and your kingdom will flourish. Some monarchs are dictators, setting up all kinds of impossible laws and taboos, because they're really afraid of the people who make up their own kingdom.

If you're a good king or queen, you'll realize that your kingdom is a good one, and you won't be afraid of your own people . . . your thoughts and feelings and desires . . . but will encourage them. And you and your body will have all the freedom necessary to flourish and grow.

The Power and a Special Sumari Song

Now, here's a Sumari song, to help you remember that your existence is a charmed one. A Sumari song is one that speaks to your ordinary self and to your magical self at once. It's a charmed song, of course. But it isn't a spell or a sign or even a symbol, because all *those* things can be very tricky indeed. For example, if you believe that your magic comes from a medal or a cross or a necklace, and you lose your luckpiece, then you're in trouble, and you think that your magic is gone. Then you *can* spend a lifetime trying to find it.

And if you think that spells make magic, then you aren't secure either, because you might forget the words to the spell, since no one is infallible. Besides, people who believe in spells guard them very jealously, and often think that they alone have "the power," and if you want to learn their methods, then you must endure trials to prove your courage. And, of course, you must promise to follow the rules, and prove that you are worthy of "the power." Again, all of this is very silly because flowers and birds and frogs have the power too, and without having to prove themselves to anyone, or pass any tests.

So the Sumari song is just a reminder. It's been translated from an inner language into one that you can understand, but the magic is still in it. It will jog your memory when you're in danger of forgetting that your life is charmed. Of course, you might forget the song. But even then, you'd only lose a valuable reminder—which would be a pity—but you wouldn't believe that your magic had gone with your memory. Still, I hope that you'll always remember that your life is charmed, and that your magic is you; and you don't have to prove anything to yourself or anyone else to get it!

Here is the Sumari song:

> My mind is like a frog
> On a lily pad,
> Knowing, alone,
> But never lonely.
>
> My mind is green
> And glowing,
> Leaping without slipping
> From lily-pad-thought
> To thought.
>
> My mind sits smiling
> On the pond of my being,
> In morning and evening,
> Always knowing the time,
> Yet not needing
> A clock.

Sumari Time

There are special moments that are open channels in which a different kind of time emerges; an inside-Sumari kind of non-time. And in that time, everything is miraculous. One hour of it is worth—well, days of ordinary minutes. In Sumari time, you can learn something in a twinkling that might otherwise take years, and insights spring up, brilliant as fresh fruit, for the picking.

This Sumari time is the special heart of time, and contains its real meaning. Again, it's really a non-time, always new and shiny, and it contains secrets that are secrets only because so few people realize that this glittering time exists, and right in the middle of the regular time that they know.

Now, in earth time, so many minutes add up to so many hours, and when you're living in that framework alone, then so much time is needed to get things done. But inspiration is quite different. It seeks out those special moments when magic leaps from one world to the other with such ease.

And each person has his or her own key to Sumari time. All you have to do is use it. You can write or paint or learn things or solve problems or just be supremely happy ten times as well in one hour of Sumari time as you can in ten regular hours.

Of course, Sumari and earth time coincide, which is tricky, I admit. And earth time springs out of Sumari time, but people divide up usual time so much that they never realize that time is really whole.

So, Sumari time is whole time, since we're using the term "time" at all. Later we'll dispense with it entirely. But right now the trick is to recognize Sumari time and use it.

If time were a fruit, then Sumari time would be its nectar and essence, and if time were a holiday, then Sumari time would be Christmas.

When most people bump into a corner of Sumari time, they're delighted, but they don't know how to find it again, when it's there all the while.

Stacks and stacks of the wrong kind of hours won't give you even one minute of good Sumari time, though. Because in a strange way, a Sumari hour is the other side of an earth hour. I mean, all of a sudden, for example, 11 o'clock becomes transparent; it is what it is, on top, but it's something else too, underneath. And you can peer through — well, time itself.

The Beginning

It's deceptive to say that thus and so "happened in the beginning," or that "in the beginning was the word," or whatever, because there was no official Beginning when God suddenly came parading out of nothingness, bearing the ingredients of mountains, oceans, and land, and trailing sky banners proclaiming the opening of the universe, or the creation of life from a sea of gasses.

There are multitudinous beginnings. "The Beginning" is only the one you came in on, so to speak, which is rather like coming into a dream in the middle and wondering what happened earlier. In dreams, everything really happens at once, even though there seems to be a beginning and ending . . . the past and present and future merge . . . and the universe is like that in a way. You're bound to wonder what went on or how long it's all been going on, not realizing that in a matter of speaking, it just started when you got there. And in another way, it really isn't there at all.

If you dream that you're in a jungle, for instance, no vines or tangled undergrowth climb up the bedpost, and no exotic animals prowl between the window and the door. Yet the jungle certainly seems real. Where did it come from, or when did it begin? The universe is like the dream jungle. It exists quite properly, yet in the most profound way it makes no sense to ask when it began. It begins each day, each moment, at each point of our contact with it. The gods exist in the same manner, like a giant species of consciousness, striding psychological paths of vast proportions that never really physically appear in the world at all.

The gods and the universe really begin everyplace and *everywhere* at once, at every point. Our psychological reality rises from an inner inconceivable divine mind that's invisible to us, since we are It, earthized, individualized. We're the gods in camouflage.

On Methods

("This small chapter is very important," Oversoul Seven said, "so do pay attention, Tweety, and anyone else who might be listening.")

The whole thing about techniques is the idea that you need certain methods to make things *work* for you, when all you have to do is let things alone: Then they "work" for you automatically. If you forget that fact, then you'll always be looking for better and better methods . . . which will never really work . . . because Nature and your own nature work best when left alone.

If you're going to study such issues at all, then look for what you do right, and you'll always find that in those areas you let yourself alone and do what comes naturally, because you are inclined in that direction.

When you concentrate on what's wrong, you almost always try too hard, look for methods that will work better than the ones you're using now . . . when the truth is that the methods themselves stand in the way, whatever they are. Because Nature doesn't use methods. It "works" because it is what it is.

Methods presuppose the opposite, in whatever area of your concern. They show your belief that nature doesn't work right on its own.

OVERSOUL SEVEN
AND THE
MUSEUM OF TIME

*Dedicated
to
Oversoul Seven
in All of His
Manifestations,
and to All of Those
Who
Take the
Codicils
to Heart*

～ *Chapter One* ～

Cyprus and Oversoul Seven Look in
on Dr. George Brainbridge and Friends

"*I* don't like doctors," Oversoul Seven said to his teacher, Cyprus. The two of them were small specks of light on the front second floor window of the small medical building.

"This doctor is one of your own personalities, and he needs your help," Cyprus said, sighing. "Souls aren't supposed to be prejudiced."

With that, the window flew open. A man in a medical white coat stuck his head out and started shouting at the pigeons on the small roof just below. "Beat it, beat it," he yelled; and the window slammed down.

"He needs help, all right!" Seven said morosely. "Is this an exam?"

"Exactly," Cyprus said. "And you're going to be his new associate. You're going to adapt a physical body of your own for a change, and—"

"Never!" Oversoul Seven yelled.

"It's a necessary part of your education," Cyprus said gently. "You have to get closer to earth reality now to really understand your personalities' experiences. You knew it had to happen sometime." To comfort Seven, Cyprus turned into the image of a lovely young woman of ancient knowledge, or of an ancient woman with young appearance. Seven disconsolately turned into a fourteen-year-old boy. Both of them perched invisibly on the upstairs windowsill, above the Medical Center's circling paths. "This is really asking too much, Cyprus," Oversoul Seven said.

"Your personalities are physical all the time," Cyprus reminded him. She tried not to smile.

"How long do I have to have a body?" Seven asked.

"Why, just until you help Dr. Brainbridge with his problems."

"*How long will that take?*" Seven asked. His image blurred around the edges, and Cyprus answered, "Who knows? That's up to you."

"What *is* his problem?" Seven asked, uneasily.

"That's for you to discover too," Cyprus replied, looking nowhere in particular. "It will be readily apparent, though."

"I'd rather help Ma-ah in the Land of the Speakers," Seven retorted. "Her life is exotic; or there's Tweety, growing up in the seventeenth century. Now, they need my help, too. It seems that I have more personalities than I know how to handle, and worse, you keep introducing me to more all the time. I didn't even know I had a doctor personality."

"You knew," Cyprus said, meaningfully, and Oversoul Seven blushed. "Well, all right. I knew and forgot; I mean, I thought he was doing all right."

"You gave him his life and energy," Cyprus answered, "and I know that you sustain him at one level, but you *do* need a follow-up."

"It makes sense," Seven said, in a dejected tone. Then hopefully, "Can't I just help him from here, though?"

Silence.

"I really have to take on a body for a while, not just an image?"

Silence.

"Digestion, breathing, all that?" he said, almost despairingly.

"All that," Cyprus said.

"Well, all right, for variety as long as I have to do it. I'll be a woman in the day and a man at night. Or I'll be an Indian on Thursdays, a Greek on Mondays—"

"*One body,*" Cyprus said emphatically. "A man or a woman, take your choice. But you have to keep one body just like humans do, at least for this part of the examination. It has to be over twenty-one, too—say mid-twenties for this particular assignment."

Oversoul Seven was suddenly overwhelmed by the implications of the situation. "I'll have to . . . live someplace, then, I mean find a domicile or house, as it's called here; and wear clothes. Go into stores to buy them. I'll have to . . . relate to people; I mean, humans, as if I were one of them." He closed his eyes, so agitated that he changed into several images at once.

"Now stop that, Seven," Cyprus said quickly. "And do settle down. It's not all that bad."

"Not all that bad?" Seven was astounded now, growing more upset by the minute. "Helping my personalities out in the dream state, giving them inspiration, sustaining their lives is one thing! But . . . *joining them is something else!*" Now he looked like an old man, head bound with a turban; ancient and rickety.

"Pathetic image," Cyprus said, smiling.

"*Do I have to be born?*" Seven asked. "Nothing would surprise me now."

"No, there isn't time for that," she said. "You'll just appear."

"Well, that's something," Seven replied, a bit mollified. "I mean, birth implies such a commitment." Then as an afterthought, he asked, "What kind of a doctor *is* Brainbridge anyhow? A surgeon? General practitioner? A neurologist? A —"

"He's a dentist," Cyprus said.

"A dentist! I dislike dentists most of all," Seven cried. "They're butchers. In the twelfth century, a visit to the dentist is practically a death sentence, in just about every country of the world. The same applies to the seventeenth century, for that matter. Once my personality Josef almost died in a dentist's chair, though it was a filthy stall more than anything else, and —"

"Dr. Brainbridge lives in the late twentieth century," Cyprus said. "I checked medical histories in connection with time periods just to make sure you'd have the information you'll need. In this era, dentists are very, very respectable. And they are *not* considered butchers."

"They still *pull* teeth out," Oversoul Seven said, shivering slightly. "They don't use sound to dislodge them yet. Or to heal tissue, or —"

Cyprus couldn't help smiling. "See, you know a lot more about dentistry than you realized," she said. "Come now. Let's take a look at Dr. Brainbridge. . . . He's treating a patient inside. This is the Community Medical Building Psych Center, of Riverton, New York. George works there three mornings a week."

"Psych Center? What's that?" Seven asked.

"You'll find out. Watch —" Cyprus answered.

At first glance George hardly looked predisposing. He was stocky, brownhaired, with a flushed face and large lips and, Seven noticed, lots of white teeth.

"Haven't done any work on your teeth at all, have I? Well, today will take care of *that*," George Brainbridge said, and laughed. "Up in the chair, there."

"Verily," said the patient.

"*Verily?*" replied George, who was busily rearranging his tools of torture (thought Seven to Cyprus, who stood to one side, invisible).

The institution attendant, Mrs. Much, leaning against the door, said, "This one thinks he's Christ," and lifted her shoulders. She was dark haired, full in body, motherly.

George grinned at her and said, "Uh, oh. His appointment card says John Window, but that's okay."

"Here we go," he said to the patient, who was now ensconced in the dental chair, his undistinguished face surrounded like a halo by the swivel lamp that glared almost in his eyes. "It's the molar," George said. "Just a little nitrous oxide here," he added, more to himself than to the patient. Then, "That's laughing gas. You won't feel a thing." He got out the round canister from his bag, saying, "You just squeeze this. You can regulate how much you need. If anything begins to hurt, squeeze. Got it?" He was peering into the patient's face; some could regulate their own doses and some couldn't. "I think you'll do okay," he said.

The patient's brown, curiously warm and deep eyes stared into George's. "I'm Christ," the patient said. "I can stand a little pain. Or perhaps I won't feel any at all. I'm never sure of my reactions. Gas won't be necessary, though."

The attendant moved slightly forward. Oversoul groaned mentally; but with only an instant's silence, George went right on talking as if he were used to having Christ in his dental chair all the time. "I'm not allowed to take out teeth without anesthetic," he said. "And novocaine in a setup like this takes too long. So why not humor me and take the gas? It will make things a lot easier all around."

A pause. Then Christ shook his head. "Verily. Do as you want, then."

"Super, *super,*" George replied, rubbing his hands together. "Now, see how this works?" George demonstrated while the patient hesitantly took a few whiffs.

"Heavenly," Christ said. Oversoul Seven felt uneasy seeing the man in George's dental chair, his face brightly lit in George's lamp, his mouth now open as George peered inside.

"Take another sniff," George said. Christ complied. He smiled and began humming "Nearer My God To Thee" as the gas took effect, so that George had to tell him to open again. "Wider," George said.

Watching the procedure, Seven winced as George's pincers came down on a bicuspid in Christ's lower jaw. George applied pressure, pulled, and he had the tooth in his hand. "There, you did great. Super! There's the bugger," he said, showing Christ the tooth.

Christ was still under, smiling, and for a minute George Brainbridge stepped back in surprise. He'd never seen such a brilliant, uninvolved, innocent smile in his life. The patient was in his forties, yet right now his eyes looked like a boy's of ten. No, George thought: he had a kid of ten, and the kid never looked *that* innocent in his life.

"Bless you," Christ the patient said in a voice so peculiarly sweet and winning that George just stared, still with the tooth in his hand, bloody roots and all. And as the patient spoke, George Brainbridge felt his whole body suddenly, unaccountably become warm and tingly; it felt glowing, pliable, filled with strength as if he himself had become younger in the flash of an eye. Automatically he pushed a square of white gauze into the hole left by the tooth, and swabbed out the blood in the patient's mouth. All he could mutter, again automatically, was, "Super. You did super."

In the meantime, Oversoul Seven stared suspiciously at Christ.

"He always blesses everyone," said Mrs. Much, the attendant. She shook her head emphatically. "Never causes us any trouble."

George just nodded, trying to act as normal as possible. It was the gas, he decided, that gave the patient such a . . . a . . . sublime expression; he was euphoric, for God's sake, nothing mysterious about that. Except that George was feeling euphoric, too, and he hadn't taken anything; didn't even get a whiff. And how could you explain that? "You can get down now," he said, after checking the hole in Christ's gum; it showed slightly and he said, "We'll fill in that hole somehow. Don't you worry."

Christ spat out a little more blood and hopped out of the chair as agile as a boy. He paused, turned to George and said, "Bless you again, my son," and made the sign of the cross. And this time George just stood transfixed. He literally felt as if his entire body had been tuned up, adjustments made here and there, circulation quickened and cleansed; as if he'd been breathing pure oxygen for years. Despite himself the words were out of his mouth: "How do you *do* that?" he sputtered.

"I'm Christ," the man said, gently enough, and though George reminded himself that this guy was some nut in the mental institution, the words made sense. Not sensible sense, George thought, but some kind of sense.

Mrs. Much chortled: "He gave you the whammy too, huh?" Her broad face looked amused but kind. "Suggestion," she said. "Amazing, isn't it?"

"I'll take a shot of that any time," George said. He made a long, drawn-out whistle and watched with unaccustomed awe as Christ waved goodbye and went out the door.

"Ciao," George said.

George took care of several more patients, but he didn't joke as he had earlier and he forgot to say "Super" to encourage his patients and reassure them. Everybody wanted to be a "good" patient, after all.

But George was upset about the Christ patient and he wasn't sure why. And *that* worried him. It was okay to be depressed because, say, a tooth hurt. So you had it pulled. Or your blood sugar was down. Or someone said or did something to anger you. Or somebody rubbed you the wrong way. Like this guy, George thought glumly. Because the patient, a young man named Gregory Diggs, was staring belligerently into his eyes.

"Open up further, please," George said, and he took a good look at the man's face just before he slid his gaze to his open mouth. "Feel this?" he asked, tapping, exploring the gum tissue, "You had a wisdom tooth out at the reformatory." He bent back up. "It's your gums, not your teeth, I'm afraid. Hurt quite a bit sometimes, don't they?"

"Yeah," drawled the young man angrily. He scowled resentfully. "How'd you know?"

"The gums tell all," said George, washing his hands. "They never lie. They're falling apart. They're —"

"Shit they are! You just want me for more appointments. You'll probably pull every tooth in my head just to make a few extra bucks!"

George had almost forgotten what was bothering him, but the young man's defiant, scornful glare brought it all back, because George instantly compared that hateful look with the forgiving, yet childlike clarity in the eyes of his earlier patient. The exuberance he'd felt when the nut first blessed him had vanished. Naturally, George thought, with irony. But his usual state of being — that had always been A-O.K.— now seemed drab and dull by contrast, as if his whole body were full of novocaine.

"Well?" demanded the young man arrogantly.

"Hell, I pull teeth just for the fun of it," George said. "How come you're here?"

"The dumb bastards want to find out if I'm crazy or not."

"Are you?" George asked. "I think everybody is crazy. Can't say I'd suggest gum surgery. Don't think it would do any good."

The young man said, "You mean, if I had money, you'd do it, don't you?"

George had had it. He stepped back, hands planted on his hips.

"I'll take every tooth out of your head right now if you want me to," George said, with a forced laugh that was half joking menace and half real dismay. What the hell was wrong with guys like that? he wondered. Then, "The condition of your gums is so advanced that I don't think you can save the teeth anyhow. I'm trying to save you some pain. Gum surgery is no picnic, and I doubt it will help in your case. The teeth are loosening. In about three months or so we can start taking them out, and I'll give you a bridge for a while —"

"Shit, I'm not going to be here any damn three months," Gregory Diggs shouted. "You're a crazy man! In three months I'll be long gone one way or the other." He started to get out of the chair.

"Have it your way," George said, and he shrugged his shoulders because he couldn't get through to the kid at all. And, he told himself, he should have known better than to try.

"Yeah, well you done with me?" Gregory Diggs asked. "I got an appointment with my banker." He grinned, got out of the chair, wiggled his backside defiantly, and headed for the door.

"Super. Enjoy yourself," George said dourly.

George began cleaning up his equipment and packing up his instruments in his small bag. Still watching, Oversoul Seven said: "Even though he's in an institution, that Gregory worries me. I don't mean to make too much of this, but—well, he couldn't hurt George in any way, could he?"

"Remember the existence of probabilities, that's all," Cyprus said. "I wanted you to have a good look at your personality's life and work before you're introduced into his environment."

"And the Christ character," Seven said. "People who think they're Christ worry me too. You never really know what they're up to. I still don't see why George was so upset when he felt better."

"You will," Cyprus replied. "Worry about that later if you must. Right now I want you to have a look at George's establishment. George is spending the afternoon and early evening at the cottage, with his wife." And as soon as Cyprus spoke, she and Seven were in George's downstairs offices, several blocks away. "Pay particular attention to the layout of the house," Cyprus said. "The family rooms are upstairs, for example. You're supposed to meet George for the first time for dinner at eight."

"Why should I pay particular attention to all that?" Seven asked. "I sense some implications . . . or complications. . . ." But Cyprus was gone.

Uneasily, Oversoul Seven looked around. Though everything looked normal, the rooms had an unsettled quality—a shifting or impermanent feel—as if they had only just taken their present form the moment before he arrived. Seven sighed. Despite his odd premonitions about the house, his first duty was to look it over, and then to meet Cyprus so they could settle the question of what kind of body he should take.

Seven whiled away the time by trying on various images for size, though he didn't thicken them into bodies—mostly because he didn't know how.

The time passed so quickly that it was evening before Seven realized it; and George, he thought, should be home at any time. He decided he'd better look the house over as Cyprus suggested. He went into the next room; just as he did, he took the immaterial form of a young man in his late twenties—the approximate age he'd appear in his physical body—when he got one. It was then he realized that something wasn't right: Everything was blurring, as if either time or space were being squeezed out of shape.

~ *Chapter Two* ~

The Right Place but the Wrong Time.
The Right Name but the Wrong Man.

*I*nvisibly Seven swirled around, trying to get a fix on the proper time and space and to acquaint himself with the territory, so to speak. He knew that he had the space right, for looking out of one of the windows through the lace curtains, he saw the river a block away, the arching bridge, and the opposite shore. The house lights were off . . . *lights?* Oversoul Seven gulped and looked out the window again—those were gaslights in the street instead of electrical ones. He was in the wrong time. In his preoccupation with his images, he'd let his hold on time slip.

Of course. Now he noticed the gaslight fixtures on the house walls. He sighed, turned his inner attention to Dr. Brainbridge and his proper 1985 time, and waited. But nothing happened. Moreover, something in the atmosphere of the house seemed strange in a way that Seven sensed, but couldn't pinpoint. A consciousness was . . . wandering, perhaps slightly off course. He could almost feel a consciousness bumping up against concepts too big for it.

Oversoul Seven paused. His job was to get back to the right time, not to go wandering off by himself. But his curiosity was aroused, and his sense of adventure. Staying where he was, he let his mind travel throughout the house. Downstairs was a small dentist's office. To the left, bits of late sunlight glinted on the instruments. A smell of cloves and camphor . . . ugh . . . and chloroform. A waiting room was at the front of the house with two work shops and a kitchen of sorts to the rear.

Three bedrooms, a parlor, and kitchen took up the floor Seven was on. He was becoming impatient, until his mind suddenly caught a commotion on the floor above. He rushed upstairs. There in an attic room, on a cot, lay a man of about thirty. His consciousness was wandering berserk all over the place. Oversoul Seven saw the man's dream body, which had no stability at all, but was changing images constantly even while the man was hallucinat- ing other images — so that the room seemed full of dragons and demons, with the poor fool, Seven thought, caught in one battle after another.

A demon with a wolf's jaws rose threateningly in front of the man's dream body. The man yelled out, started trembling and closed his dream eyes in terror, just as Oversoul Seven turned into the image of an old wise man, told the demon to disappear, and led the frightened dreamer back toward the cot.

It was then that Seven noticed the paraphernalia — hidden partially be- hind a chair — and saw how the dreamer had come to such a predicament. "You've been sniffing gas," Seven said.

The two of them sat side by side on the cot. The man was still in his dream body. "I do it all the time, up here alone, while my wife and son are away for the summer," he said. "I'm experimenting. But who are you? I must still be under."

"You're under, all right," Oversoul Seven said. "By the way, what year is it, and who are *you*?"

"Why, I'm George Brainbridge. Dr. Brainbridge," the man said, in a sur- prised voice, as if he thought that his name was a household word. And as he spoke he leaned toward Seven rather formally, and held out his hand.

Oversoul Seven was dumbfounded. "Dr. *George* Brainbridge? You're sure?"

"Well, my good man, I certainly hope I know my name," Dr. Brainbridge said. "And who, pray tell, are you? I'm not exactly sure what's happening, but this is by far the most delightful encounter that I've had under these cir- cumstances —"

"Uh, what year did you say it was?" Seven asked. He was almost afraid to hear the answer.

"It's May 21, 1890," George said. "You mean, you mean, you don't know that either?" His voice grew excited, and *looking* at him, Oversoul Seven got his first real look at George Brainbridge the First. He had sandy hair, fraz- zled right now, a sandy beard, and light blue eyes that were shaped like the electric Christmas tree lights that he, George, would probably never live to see; and he had two dimples on his left cheek. As George's eyes lit up with excitement and expectancy, Oversoul Seven immediately knew George for what he was — a dreamer, an idealist, forever caught between dreaming and acting.

Oversoul Seven just groaned: "You're the wrong George Brainbridge. I'm in the wrong time period; but if my calculations are right, you're far too old to be George's father. It must be your grandson I want."

The gas hadn't begun to wear off yet. George Brainbridge now thought the entire affair was magnificent. "Well, while you're here, let's talk," he said agreeably. "I keep a journal of my gaseous activities, as I call them, and what an entry this will make." He rubbed his chin, reached for a pipe, and prepared to settle himself for a long chat.

Without thinking about it, Seven hallucinated a pipe for George, who didn't realize that he was still in his dream body; then Seven said moodily, "I've got to think my way out of this because your grandson — he *must* be your grandson — needs me, and I don't even know what trouble he's in."

"Ah," said George, dreamily.

"Ah?" said Seven, a bit loudly. "A lot of help you are; sniffing gas and hallucinating demons and God knows what. . . ."

"I heard William James talk about nitrous oxide and determined to try it myself," Brainbridge said, huffily. "I consider my activities as explorations, pure and simple, into the nature of . . . of truth."

"That sounds pretty pompous to me," Oversoul Seven said. He didn't mean to be unkind, but he was worried about returning to the proper time period, and at the same time he was growing more and more aware of his surroundings and the nineteenth-century summer twilight. Indeed, the scents rushing through the opened window grew clearer and more tantalizing. He wiggled his nose and breathed deeply.

"Those are lilacs you smell," George Brainbridge said. "They're planted on one side of the drive. French lilacs and white ones. You can still smell the apple blossoms, too. They're planted by the barn — "

And suddenly Oversoul Seven was so enchanted by the odors and by the late sunlight on the white lace curtains, and by the sky showing beyond that he just stared at George in amazement. "In the midst of this beauty, this sensual bath of light and scents, why would you bother looking for other realities . . . ? If you really felt . . . what this moment demands . . . you'd be so filled with life that you'd sense what truth was, and you wouldn't need to go looking for it."

"That was a beautiful sermon," George murmured drowsily. Just before he closed his dream eyes, he muttered, "Grandson? I don't have a grandson. . . ." His dream body fell back into his physical one, and George Brainbridge was finished with everything but sleep.

Seven sighed. He eyed the sleeping George with a mixture of exasperation and relief, and covered him up with a crisp white sheet that had been folded neatly by the bed. But why, he wondered, had he become so mixed up in time? Did the gas-sniffing activities of the nineteenth-century George have any bearing on the problems of the twentieth-century grandson? The house, Seven mused, was the same. So the space coordinates were the same for both men, though obviously they focused in different time periods. But why, why, had the wrong George attracted him?

Because *something* had attracted him, Seven thought, or he would have gone undeviatingly to the right George. Seven sighed again; here he was, all alone in some nineteenth-century attic, in the right house, but some hundred years away from where he should be. Worse, usually such errors were somehow self-corrective, or else Cyprus bailed him out. But this time the environment was remaining stubbornly stable. He couldn't seem to move one minute ahead in time, much less a hundred years — or eighty-five: what was the difference?

Seven stared dejectedly at the floor where Dr. Brainbridge's paraphernalia still lay. He had to get back to the twentieth century, where he *would* form a body and live in it for a while. A short while, he hoped. In the meantime, he noticed that the sky was beginning to darken. He looked out the back window of the attic, down through the twilight mist at the wooden barn, smartly painted a dark red. A horse neighed from inside; and then he heard a very clear distinct clippa-cloppa sound, leaned out, and saw an iceman in his horse and wagon. The man wore a green cap with white stripes on it, and a bright green jacket. He stopped the wagon, went around back, picked out a big block of ice and sprinted to the backporch, just beneath the window buttress where Seven couldn't see him; he reappeared, and leapt back into the wagon.

Seven smelled warm manure mixed with the smell of the lilacs, and in the next moment the mist lifted so that the purple flowers stood out all dewy by the driveway below. A delightful scene, Seven thought; and he *liked* the gas-sniffing George Brainbridge a lot better at first sight than he did the twentieth-century version who chased the pigeons. And as if he'd called them, a flock of pigeons came swooping down from the back side of the barn to the buttress beneath the window; and began cooing. From the cot inside the room, George Brainbridge muttered, "Goddamned pigeons," and Seven despite himself began to laugh. Then he sobered. He had to get back somewhere close to twilight, 1985. And quickly.

～ *Chapter Three* ～

Oversoul Seven Takes a Body and
Finally Meets the Right George

Cyprus was a speck of light in the office waiting room of George Brainbridge's twentieth-century residence. George was waiting in the office across the hall for the arrival of his new associate, Dr. Seven. George whistled under his breath, turned on the radio, squinted at the pigeons on the window ledge, and hoped to hell that the new arrangement was going to work out.

But Cyprus could tell that Seven was either waylaid or had taken a wrong turn in time or space; he wasn't in *this* space in this time. Slightly exasperated, she loosened her own consciousness from its precise orientation with time, but maintained the same space coordinates. From her present probable position her consciousness went whirling through the room's futures. Still no Seven! So Cyprus started to ruffle quickly through the past.

Almost at once she saw Seven wandering around, a good hundred years off—but in space hardly a few feet away. She materialized as the ancient-but-young woman teacher and stood beside him. George Brainbridge, glancing into the waiting room in *his* time, saw no one, of course.

"Seven, you're in the wrong time," Cyprus announced.

"I went back into the past," Seven cried, "and met George's grandfather." He was wearing his favorite fourteen-year-old male image.

Cyprus smiled; almost. "I didn't realize that you were methodical enough to do such background reference," she said.

Seven smiled modestly.

"I thought maybe you just got lost," Cyprus said.

Seven blushed. "Well, there must have been a reason why I ended up in the wrong time with the wrong George," he said defensively.

"Exactly," Cyprus replied. "Remember that later. But you don't even have a real body yet, and George expects you at any moment."

"You *do* mean a body, not just an image?" Seven asked.

"A *body*. I told you that before," Cyprus replied, laughing. "And you have to make it in the right time period, so it will fit properly. That means that we have to return to the twentieth century first."

Seven looked dejected. "How come you're so much better at time traveling than I am?" he asked plaintively. "Sometimes I have no problems, and then . . . well, I get confused."

"All right," Cyprus said. "Look at that chair beside you." Seven did as he was told, studying the red velvet Victorian armchair until it suddenly shimmered and became the leather rocker in George's twentieth-century waiting room. "That's the easiest way for you to do it now," Cyprus said. "There are better ways, and before long, you'll know what they are."

"Where *is* that guy?" George muttered from his office.

"Well? Where's your body?" Cyprus demanded. "Isn't it ready?"

Seven sighed. "I haven't even had time to think about a body, much less do anything about getting one," he said disconsolately.

"We just can't have your body suddenly appearing from nowhere in the middle of the room, either," said Cyprus. "Stop pouting, Seven. Come over here, around the corner, where George can't see you from his office."

They stood by a corner of the fireplace in the waiting room. "Now," Cyprus directed. "First, adopt the image you want. A young man is best; about twenty-six years old will do. As for the rest, use your imagination."

Rather regretfully, Seven dismissed his fourteen-year-old image entirely and started over. He stood six foot three. His hair was almost black, and bushy. He added a beard, then removed it. First his eyes were blue, then he changed them to brown. "What about the mouth?" he asked Cyprus.

"Hurry, Seven," she said scoldingly. "Decide on one clear image and let that be that."

So Seven changed his hair to a bushy dark brown, added a rather high forehead, a resolute jaw (so he'd look trustworthy). The mouth just seemed to come of itself; it belonged to the fourteen-year-old image he liked so well, except that its mischievous humor was modified by a slight turn downward. "That's it," Seven cried.

"All right, now," Cyprus said. "Try to keep your consciousness as clear and still as you can. This will just take a moment."

Seven wasn't sure exactly what Cyprus did then, but he felt his image slowly solidify. Invisible atoms rushed from the four corners of the earth to congregate within the form. He felt tremendous activity. Then, in a flash, he felt the activity from *inside*. A heart was pumping blood; the blood flowed through the brand-new veins. His pulse started like a tiny clock. Seven grinned, trying out his facial muscles. He'd been inside a few of his personalities' bodies before, to help them out for one reason or another, but this was different. A body of his own! A strange sense of possessiveness overtook him. This living parcel of earth belonged to him; let no one trespass!

"I see the experience isn't so undesirable after all," Cyprus said drily. "But there seems to be something you've forgotten."

"What?" Seven asked. He looked down at the elastic flesh, and felt within it the ambitious inner organs . . . all snapping to attention. "Everything's there, as far as I can see."

"Seven," Cyprus said, meaningfully.

Seven grinned brilliantly. "Oh, the clothes. I forgot the clothes," he said.

"Precisely." Cyprus shook her head. "I hope you've done your homework and know what garments you want," she said. "Now make an image of the clothes, and I'll fill them in."

Seven was actually quite proud of himself. He formed the image of undershorts figured with appletrees, and a black turtleneck undershirt. Cyprus quickly turned these from images into real items of clothing.

"How do you do that?" Seven asked.

"The same as with your body," Cyprus replied. "I haven't time to explain. I cause the . . . atoms in space to thicken . . . and congregate. But what else do you need?"

"The *pièce de résistance*," Seven answered proudly, and on top of the underclothes he formed the image of a dark green polyester suit, with the tiniest of green and white checks. "What do you think of that?" he asked. "Perfect late 1980's."

"Well, you *do* look like a young dental associate," Cyprus said, doubtfully.

"I hope so," Seven retorted. "I studied and studied and studied so that I'd be sure to fit in."

"It's just that I didn't realize that dentists in this century went barefoot," Cyprus said, laughing and staring into Seven's new bright and astonished brown eyes.

Instantly Seven formed the images of socks and black boots. "The socks are treated with deodorant," he said. "I saw some like them in George's dresser. Most of these clothes are based on his wardrobe . . . so he has to like the way I dress. . . . " When Cyprus continued to laugh, he said defensively, "Well, there's an awful lot to remember. Your humor's at my expense. . . . "

"You just look so . . . so *earthy,*" Cyprus replied, trying to control herself. "You have no idea; you look like a young dandy."

"I don't," Seven protested. "I look like a young dental associate. You said so yourself."

But suddenly Cyprus was serious. She filled in his socks and boots. "Remember, your body is only a temporary one," she warned. "And treat it kindly. There are some things you're used to doing that you can't do with it; and some places it won't go. But you'll learn all of that."

"What places?" Seven asked, a bit alarmed.

But Cyprus had no time to answer. Again George Brainbridge muttered loudly, "Damn, where is that guy?" This time he came out into the hallway. Cyprus said, "Quick, walk to the hall so it looks as if you came from the waiting room." And she vanished.

Dr. George Brainbridge (the Third) was thirty-nine, slightly stouter than he should be for his unimposing five feet, 6½″. In fact, Seven thought he was a trifle jowly, and his brown hair was nondescript. His moustache and eyebrows were both rather shaggy, but extremely expressive; both were moving, it seemed, all the while. And George Brainbridge's eyes, though small and a bit sunken, were—well, dynamic. People probably didn't notice George's eyes much, Seven mused, because he kept them half closed a good deal of the time. But then, whammo; they opened wide, all the way, usually to express an amazed appraisal of the person to whom he'd been talking so mildly. And sometimes the eyes grinned all by themselves.

Right now, George's eyes did their grinning act as he looked at the newly minted Seven. "Super," George said. "You must be my new assistant."

Young Dr. Seven smiled and stepped forward, extending his hand in the accepted Earth fashion.

"Super. Super, super," George Brainbridge said again, squeezing Seven's new hand so tightly and with such force that Seven almost felt like whimpering. "Tonight's garbage time, though. I have to stack the garbage cans outside. It'll only take a minute. And drive to the corner store for some pickles. Whole trip will only take two minutes. Then you and I can relax, have a few drinks and eat dinner. Make yourself at home. Be right back."

And before Seven could even answer, George bounded toward the rear of the house, leaving Seven flabbergasted—and a bit annoyed: All that rushing on his part just so George could pile the garbage!

And here he was alone in the house again. A house that just wasn't trustworthy, he thought. Then almost without thinking about it, he went into George's twentieth-century waiting room.

"I never should have called the house untrustworthy," he said later to Cyprus. "But of course I did. And it was."

~ *Chapter Four* ~

Up and Down the Time Staircase

Of course, Seven realized that the house had changed through the years since George-the-First's time. For one thing, there were two water marks indicated by small gold plaques showing how far up the walls the water had risen in the floods of 1948 and 1972. The two plaques were set about two feet apart, one above the other, just to the right of the marble fireplace in the waiting room. In the first George's time, this had been a parlor and the fireplace had been workable. Now it just sat, elegant but useless; a decoration. Above it was an innocuous still life of flowers. Oversoul Seven grimaced at it and looked out of the narrow floor-to-ceiling front windows. Set right before them were huge pots of plants that instantly took Seven's attention. He was only vaguely aware of the cars speeding by just past the front sidewalk, in a certain rhythm, as the traffic light at the corner by the bridge let swarms of traffic by. Then there was a pause until the light turned green again.

The house was built of the sturdiest red brick, so that even on this warm June day it was cool inside; and possibly the bricks muffled the traffic sounds, even though a window was open. In any case it was during one of the pauses in traffic that Oversoul Seven suddenly realized that something was wrong—again! There was a thick maroon rug on the dark wooden floor, but none in the entry way behind him. And Seven realized that he'd been hearing footsteps cross the tiled entry floor from the front door to the stairs. They'd been pacing, he realized, for some time, though no one but himself should have been in the house.

Seven whirled around, astonished, for he caught sight of George Brainbridge the *First,* just going up the stairs. Simultaneously, the sounds from the window seemed terribly different than they had only a moment ago. Seven spun around again. He stared, quite incredulous.

Both the nineteenth- and twentieth-century streets existed at once; or nearly. The automobiles were clearer than the horses and buggies, but only by a hair. The houses across the street shimmered back and forth from their nineteenth- to twentieth-century appearances, and back again. A new house kept disappearing and a lot took its place. The lot changed to the house again, so quickly that Seven blinked.

He turned back toward the room to rub his eyes, but to his dismay, the process hadn't been confined to the outdoors. Objects from the nineteenth-century drawing room kept appearing in the waiting room — or rather, the waiting room kept turning into the drawing room. One mohair chair suddenly appeared, bumping Seven in the knee. He leapt back. A huge fern sprang up in the far corner.

The coffee table beside Seven vanished and was replaced by a Victorian tea table, complete with a pot of tea, three cups and a bouquet of early summer roses from the yard. Actually, Seven saw, it was as if everything pulsated, but so quickly that he couldn't keep track. Everything shimmered and vanished, but not before a second group of objects already began to appear.

He stared and squinted. There was no time where there was nothing, but always at least the indication of an appearing or disappearing object. So when the roses appeared again, Seven grabbed the vase and held it to see what would happen.

"It wasn't a very bright move," he said later to Cyprus, who agreed. Because the vase and flowers trembled, shook, shimmered — and so did everything else in the entire room. Then, as if the room had made up its mind, the vase and roses settled down to be themselves. The Victorian tea table stayed. The flood watermarks were gone. The room didn't change back again, and Seven found himself standing in the wrong place and the wrong time.

Seven gulped. Surely, he thought, this must be happening only to his own perception. That is, the twentieth-century house would be there for George the Third when he came home from stacking the garbage and buying the pickles. Wouldn't it? But there was no time to consider George the Third because Seven suddenly heard someone come in the back door—

and anyone who came in *that* door would find him, physical body and all, where he didn't belong. In his consternation, Seven dropped the vase. It crashed into pieces on the floor.

In a flash, Oversoul Seven rushed to the stairs, running on tiptoe as quickly and quietly as possible, heading for George the First's private attic study. Seven's heart was pounding. He was sweating. He thought that at any moment someone would come out of a bedroom to see him racing down the dark hall of the second story. It surprised him that a body could move so fast, but he was panting by the time he reached the door to the attic steps. He opened it, overcome by relief, and stood resting against it on the other side.

It was then that he heard George the First laughing.

Seven was all ready to go through the door to George's study when he remembered that he had a real body, even if it *was* in the wrong time. He lifted his hand to knock at the door, then just stood there, pondering: George probably wouldn't let him in; and worse — he wouldn't recognize him because when they'd met before, Seven was in a wise-old-man image.

"Oh. Ah. Haaaa, haaa. . . ." The sounds from the closed door drove Seven to distraction. He had to talk to George and find out what the connection was between his sniffing gas and the time changes. "And then, the solution came," he told Cyprus again later. "I saw the closet, and from then on I knew what to do." Seven went quickly into a small closet to the left of George's door, sat his body nicely down, hidden and out of the way. And then, pleased with his resourcefulness, he just left his body, took an astral image of a wise old man, and walked through George's door.

George Brainbridge the First giggled slightly and said, "So you've come back! Here, have a sniff. I've made the most astounding discovery."

"How come you always see my astral form when you're sniffing gas?" Seven demanded. "And what have you been up to? I just saw you downstairs a few minutes ago and — "

"Hush, hush, hush, now," George said. Then in a happy singsong voice he went on: "I saw . . . I saw . . . the future. I saw this house in the future. . . . I even saw a book on dentistry that's in the library where it can't be, of course. But it is."

"Well it won't be there for you now," Seven replied glumly. "We're back in your time now. What did you do to . . . make it happen? I'm supposed to be in the other time, the future one."

"Zounds. A problem," George said, in the same singsong voice. "That is, I haven't the faintest inkling of how or why it all happened."

Really worried now, Seven sat down on the cot beside George. The late afternoon sunlight filtered through the lace curtains and glinted here and there on the rose petal pattern of the wallpaper. The carriage house door had been left open and the carriage was gone. The maple trees were full of singing birds. The white doily on George's old bureau moved gently at the edge by the window as the soft breeze blew in. George lifted the small canister, took another sniff of gas, and said dreamily, "I hardly ever get to come up here during the day, but several patients canceled their appointments . . . ah, how lovely . . . a day in June it is." His moustache quivered, his brown eyes smiled fondly at Seven, and he snapped his suspender straps gently back and forth. "Whoever you are, welcome again and again," he murmured.

And Seven thought: The carriage was gone from the carriage house, just as George the Third's car was gone from the garage. Did that mean that George was still at the store?

"I'm going to write down the name of the book I saw, too," the George beside him said. "It will prove that I *was* in the future somehow. Maybe I'll even inform that personage, William James, about my story. . . . "

"You can't prove anything," Seven said, crossly. "The book won't be discovered in your time by others—" As soon as he said this, Seven figuratively bit his tongue, because George's eyes suddenly glistened. "You're right," he said, "I'll have to steal it somehow; and bring it back with me. If the time change happens again, that's what I'll do."

"No, no, no, you mustn't do that," Seven cried. "I grabbed ahold of a vase of flowers in your parlor when the times were changing back and forth, and when I held the vase, I got the time that went along with it."

"My mind is clear as space," George said, wonderingly. "You're saying that if I steal the future book, I might wind up there."

"Exactly," Seven said, reminding himself of Cyprus.

George half-closed his eyes, leaned backward, and negligently played with the tassels on the belt of his maroon dressing gown. He wiggled his shoeless black stockinged feet and said smugly, "That would be most auspicious."

"Auspicious! It would be disastrous," Seven cried. Just as he spoke, a sound from below caught his attention.

"Zounds, it's the carriage," said George. "The housekeeper, Mrs. Norway, must be returning from her visit with her aunt. I suppose I'll have to make myself presentable and—"

"Will you be quiet!" Oversoul Seven cried. He was thinking as fast as he could. If the carriage was returning in *this* time, then just possibly the car was pulling into the driveway in 1985—with the right George Brainbridge in it. Seven ran to the window.

The carriage came slowly past the peony bushes. Seven waited until the horses drew up to the carriage house—apparently Mrs. Norway was taking them all the way inside the barn, ignoring the hitching post. Then with all his might, Seven imagined George's small Porsche car. He saw every detail in his mind and he kept trying mentally to transpose the desired shape of the car over the carriage. One of the horses neighed, distracting him, and behind him George the First muttered dreamily, "What are you doing now?"

The carriage shimmered, the horses disappeared, the car came into position, and then the horses and carriage (and Mrs. Norway) returned. Seven gasped because the Porsche *also* remained. Mrs. Norway got out of the carriage, apparently without seeing the automobile. George Brainbridge leapt out of his car, slammed the door, started whistling, and ambled up the sidewalk. And then, both he and Mrs. Norway went in the back door.

Seven didn't know what to do. Beside him, George the First stood up, straightened out his dressing gown and shoved the gas canister under the cot. When he turned around Seven was gone. George shook his head, said, "Zounds" beneath his breath, and thought that there was no telling how long the effects of sniffing lasted.

Seven was afraid to go out into the hall; he hoped against hope that when he left George's study, somehow he'd be back in the twentieth-century house. No such luck, he thought, finding the hall as it had been before. He stepped into the small closet where his body was sleeping comfortably. He dove into his body as quickly as he could, even though several questions instantly came to mind.

Who would see his body, for example? If Mrs. Norway saw him, in the nineteenth-century house — well, he was in trouble. He reeked of the twentieth century, decked out as he was in a summer polyester suit whose style and material would be quite strange to her. To say nothing of the digital watch — a nice touch, he thought, though that at least he could hide in his pocket. He couldn't change into either of the Georges' clothes, because both Georges were too short and pudgy for the body Seven had decided upon. While he was thinking about all this, Oversoul Seven very gingerly walked down the stairs to the second floor, which was *still* nineteenth-century. And then, with his heart in his throat he started down the front stairs that came out in the front entry.

Or suppose George the Third saw him, Seven wondered; then that would mean that George would experience the house in the *past* as Seven was. Didn't it? Or — he shuddered — suppose both George the Third and Mrs. Norway saw him simultaneously. Or suppose. . . .

He stepped onto the slate floor of the entryway. At the same time, both Mrs. Norway and George the Third approached, though the room itself was solid nineteenth-century. "Back," George announced. "Chores all done. Super!" he said, bounding across the room. He loosened his tie, tossed his light summer jacket over what appeared to be a nineteenth-century arm-chair, and said, "I've got some great new jokes, though."

"Ah, zounds," Seven said.

"What?" George asked, surprised.

"Uh, I mean, super," Seven replied, blushing and realizing his mistake. "Uh, do you see anything different about the house? Or that chair?"

Seven felt dizzy. As he spoke to George, who obviously saw him, Mrs. Norway (who obviously saw neither Seven nor George) was bending over the broken vase on the rug and murmuring, "Now how did *that* happen?" Seven closed his eyes a moment in true despair.

"What's wrong with the chair? It looks okay to me," George said. "Every-thing looks okay to me. It's been a super day, garbage or no garbage." He grinned at Seven, sat down (in the mohair chair, as far as Seven was con-cerned), and said, "Well, what have *you* been up to?"

Seven shook his head, and suddenly began laughing. Tears fell down his face. George Brainbridge the Third was so pragmatic, so focused in his time and place that, well, anything else would seem an impossibility. And as Seven laughed, a part of his consciousness merged momentarily with George's, and through George's eyes Seven saw the twentieth-century room just as it had always been as far as George was concerned. And in that instant, George the Third unknowingly endeared himself to Seven forever after.

"What's so funny?" George asked, beginning to laugh too. "Is there egg on my face or something? Did you sniff some laughing gas from my canister?"

Seven laughed louder; here was the down-to-earth George in the pre-sent, perceiving his usual environment, come hell or high water, while up-stairs and ninety-five years away, his grandfather couldn't even begin to keep his times straight.

"I don't know," Seven gasped. "You made me laugh, something you said or didn't say. . . . As George's face broke into a new cheerful grin, Mrs. Norway vanished, the tea table disappeared, and Seven was back in George's twentieth century, where he belonged.

~ *Chapter Five* ~

A Would-Be Thief in the Night

*T*hey sat at the kitchen table. "We have this whole second floor as our living quarters," George said. "Usually it's noisy as hell, but with Jean and the three boys at the cottage, it sure gets quiet."

Seven grinned, imagining George surrounded by young sons.

"Shit," George said. "Last weekend I started enlarging two rooms at the cottage, but you could *still* put the whole place in the middle of *this* house and have room left over! No one builds houses like this one any more."

Thank Heaven, Oversoul Seven thought, enjoying his own joke. But the dinner was excellent. George half considered himself a gourmet cook. In fact he wore an old apron over the summer shorts he'd put on after work. Seven stared at George's thick thighs with some begrudging admiration, and wondered if he should have made his own thighs larger.

"My parents and their parents must have had thousands of suppers in this same spot," George said, musingly.

Seven almost said, "I wish you hadn't said that," because as soon as George mentioned his grandparents, Seven imagined them sitting at the 1890 summer table.

"I'll say," George answered. "It's spooky in a way to think of it. And these old houses. They're being torn down through the city all the time. This one

448

has really been kept up, though. So has the neighborhood. But it *is* decaying. The town would love to make it into an urban renewal project."

Seven nodded but he wiggled uncomfortably. A sense of menace suddenly assailed him. He looked around. The back dining room was brightly lit. Beyond it, out the second story windows, the yard was disappearing in twilight. Then someone said, "Here's the smartassed dude's place," and Seven looked up in surprise. "What?" he asked.

George raised his bushy brows. "Nobody said anything."

"Uh. I must be hearing things," Seven replied, and he smiled brilliantly.

In his confusion it took Seven a minute to realize what had happened. He'd forgotten that humans heard only spoken conversation, though he tried to keep it in mind; and according to the rules, he had paid attention only to words. But in the instant that he forgot, he'd picked up someone's thoughts — and they didn't belong to George. . . .

"Uh, I thought I heard something downstairs," Seven said finally.

"Naw. It's just the house; it makes noises all the time," George replied, helping himself to some dessert.

"What would anyone want to steal down there?" Seven asked, insistent.

"A few drugs in my office, is all. Now and then some joker breaks into a dentist's or doctor's office." Unconcerned, George said, "Come on. There's no one down there. Besides the car's out there. So anybody could tell that we were home. . . ."

But Seven was now following the menacing thoughts from room to room downstairs, from the back to the front of the house. He finally located them in George's office.

And for once, Oversoul Seven didn't have the slightest inkling of what to do. The thoughts he "heard" told him that the man downstairs was full of hate and rage; but also full of indecision, scared to death. If he told George about the intruder, Seven thought anxiously, he'd have to play by physical rules. The police would be called, the thief caught; for he *was* a thief . . . even now he was picking the lock of George's drug cabinet. Seven started coughing to hide his confusion, and to give himself time to think.

"Oh, I'll get you some water," said George. Seven coughed harder. George stood up and slapped him on the back. Seven, suddenly realizing what a body felt like when it was slapped, stopped coughing. "Uh. I'm all right," he said, blushing.

"Look," George said. "Let me do up the dishes. You go down and relax. Got a bedroom for the night all ready. Then we'll have a couple of beers."

"*Super,*" Seven exclaimed, getting up so quickly that George looked startled. But Seven was still aware of the intruder.

Rather pleased with himself for dispatching George so cleverly, Seven started very quietly and somewhat cockily down the stairs toward the first floor. Surely he could take care of the culprit in some ingenious fashion. Then suddenly Seven stood still with dismay and foreboding. For one thing, a suspicious shifting was taking place in the air; innocuous paintings lined the staircase and they were . . . dissolving at the edges or trying to; and the old nineteenth-century oils were peeking through. While Seven was thinking, "What an awful time for time to start shifting again," he remembered something vital that he'd forgotten in his desire to protect George's mortal frame. He, Seven, had a physical body now, too, which meant that dealing with the unknown culprit wouldn't be as easy as he'd hoped.

That thought came to mind just as Seven came to the entryway and saw a young man hastily going through George's desk in the office. The door was open; and the thief worked with a flashlight that he turned off as soon as he heard Seven's now-hesitant footsteps.

Again, the house's contents seemed to shimmer. The young man crouched down and Seven saw him clearly in the glare of the streetlight — before it turned into a dimmer gaslight; and Seven made an inaudible moan. He was about to advance in any case when he heard new footsteps pounding down the stairway behind him. "Zounds. Who's here?" thundered George the First, descending the stairs with a hunting rifle.

As quickly as he could, Seven turned on the light switch, and the gaslights lit up the room. In the office, Gregory Diggs stared, mouth open, too astounded to move or speak. The room looked like a movie set, and the man who stood at the bottom of the stairs was completely unbelievable. He wore a dressing robe with tasseled belt, pince-nez glasses that looked a hundred years old — and he had a rifle.

"Oh wow, this is screwy," said Gregory, shaking his head from side to side. "I don't want no trouble. . . ."

"You blackguard," George shouted, advancing. "What's in that bag?" He rushed over, yanked Gregory aside, and pulled out the bottles and vials that stuffed the bag to the brim.

Dazed, Oversoul Seven watched; how could George the First see the thief in the twentieth century? How could the thief see George? And why didn't *either* of them see him?

"Sit right down, there," George Brainbridge demanded, pointing to the dentist's chair.

Gregory was shaking. "I came to the wrong place, I guess. I was trying to get even with a guy."

"Even with a guy, huh. What kind of talk is that?" George thundered.

"I didn't know anybody had *gaslights* no more," Gregory murmured, staring at them. "And that outfit; man, where are you at?" He was feeling a bit more confident now, because George had put the gun aside, though it was still within his easy reach.

"Don't either of you see or hear me at all?" Seven asked, looking into George's face.

"You got everything back," Gregory stammered. "I was just gonna sell the stuff."

"Open your mouth," George demanded.

"What?"

"Open your mouth," George said. "Your breath smells: There's something wrong in there. A man's house is his castle, you young whippersnapper. Don't you know that? Open wider!"

"You gonna torture me?" Gregory cried. "You're some kind of pervert. Oh, Jesus." He was near tears.

Oversoul Seven gave up. He sat down in the corner as George shouted, "Hell, no. I'm a man of good will when I'm not crossed. Look at that! What kind of meals do you eat anyhow? Your gums are a mess."

"My gums?" Gregory gasped. It was hard to talk with George's fingers in his mouth, and Gregory still wasn't sure the guy wasn't going to pull his teeth out by the roots or something.

"Come from a poor family, do you?" George demanded.

"Uh."

"Nobody's all bad. That's my policy," George said, warming up to the subject.

"This is no time for a sermon!" Oversoul Seven yelled, but George didn't hear him.

Catching on, Gregory Diggs said sadly, "Very poor family. We don't have nothing." But he was feeling more sure of himself now that he had a handle on George. A bleeding heart liberal was a pushover.

Testing, Oversoul Seven tried to pick up a pair of scissors from a small table. His hands went through them. But the thief had a body—and he was from the *twentieth* century. Seven had to figure out how George and the thief could see each other at all.

"This will make you feel better," said George, taking a bottle from a drawer. He took the top off and the smell of cloves almost took Seven's breath away.

"Hey!" Gregory cried but George smeared some all over his gums, the competent fingers pressing in, so that Gregory shrank back in the chair. He was thoroughly scared again. Here he was in a dentist's chair like one he'd never seen before — with a gaslight shining in his face — and the pressure from some nutty dentist's fingers driving his gums mad. Besides he felt saliva gathering all over his mouth and his eyes stung. "Tender, huh!" George said.

Seven was getting panicky. He didn't seem to be able to affect either environment, and his own body felt strange and disconnected.

∼ *Chapter Six* ∼

A Challenge of Probabilities

Seven kept trying to speak, but again no one heard or saw him. Worse, an odd shifting seemed to take hold of everything — not just the furniture as before, but the very house itself. It was as if space speeded up through time . . . or as if time speeded up through space; Seven couldn't decide which. But the walls themselves began to flutter almost like wooden curtains, and then to break up into beads, and then into dots.

Seven realized that the walls had vanished. He stood alone, on a grassy knoll, in a warm dark night. The house and Dr. Brainbridge and the thief — indeed, the entire neighborhood — were gone. Yet Seven was sure he was in the same place, though he wasn't sure just how he knew this. A soft wind blew past his face, and then he saw that the river (the same river?) was still approximately the same distance away.

Seven was more upset than he wanted to admit, because his experiences thus far had seemed to lack any kind of organization — or rather, while he could perceive some order, he didn't seem to know how it worked at all. Before, the house had given *some* orientation. Now it was gone. Besides this, Cyprus seemed to have abandoned him, at least for the present; *any* present, he thought, dejected.

He looked about. As far as he could see, the area was entirely wooded except for the small clearing on which he stood. Where or when was he? "Cyprus?" he called, mentally. But there was no answer.

Was this the spot on which the Brainbridge house stood? If so, from the viewpoint of the house's existence, was he in the future or the past? Seven looked up. Three globes glittered in the far distance above the earth. He groaned and tried to recall earth history. The first floating city was in operation in the twenty-third century; he remembered because one of his personalities—Proteus—lived there. The second floating city came around the twenty-fifth century and the third wasn't habitable until . . . until the late twenty-eighth century. Oversoul Seven let himself drop down on the uneven but grassy ground as he recognized his unhappy predicament. By his reckoning, it was about 2985 give or take a couple of centuries; so even if he was in the right space, he was a thousand years off his target!

Worse, Seven didn't dare walk outside of the area where the house was—or had been—because that must be the focus of whatever was happening. If he just sat there and thought back to the twentieth-century house, perhaps time would reverse itself. But the environment itself was rather unsettling. There were no ground lights at all, and from his position, the floating cities were no brighter than stars. A very fine rain was falling, so fine that it was more like a mist, and the grass was wet, and the trees made a murmuring sound as the water fell from one leaf to another. Otherwise, silence.

Why a thousand years in the future, where before he'd only bounced back and forth between the nineteenth and twentieth centuries? "Cyprus," he called, and again there was no reply.

Seven shivered. His body was wet, and though the air was warm enough, the rain had soaked through his polyester suit. No wonder mortals carried umbrellas, he thought, miserably. Nor did he dare leave his body while it dried out, for fear a time reversal might come and whisk his body off without *him*. But how was it that all of this happened when he still had a body on?

Cyprus existed in every time, and so did he, Seven mused, so he couldn't be lost. But he *felt* very lost indeed. If he remembered his history properly, in one probability, the earth in this century was a largely uninhabited planetary reservation area designed to protect nature, with visitors restricted. In another probability, though, the planet was nearly dead, bearing the lethal debris of countless nuclear wars. And in still another probability, it was just in the process of developing a new civilization.

But Seven had no way of knowing *which* future he was in, except that it "grew out of" the Brainbridges' presents—both of them!

Despite himself, Oversoul Seven noticed that the area was bathed in a soft mysterious air that now seemed enhanced by the rainy mist. In some strange way, the landscape seemed enchanted *and* enchanting. On the other hand, it also possessed a quiet waiting quality—as if it were a stage, in the few moments before a play was to begin. . . . Or, Seven thought suddenly, as if he were witnessing a probability-in-the-making.

And was this the Brainbridges' earth?

Before Seven could even begin to answer his own question, the sky exploded with images, and he saw a picture of such multidimensional proportions that he didn't know where to look first—much less how to interpret what he was seeing. The vision was so vast and astounding that he felt his consciousness struggling to expand its reach to contain it. The entire scene was one world with areas laid out in various time periods. The architectures and agricultures and technologies were changing in each segment and the people were all wearing the unique clothes of their times—and yet (Seven saw) they moved from time to time as mortals now moved from place to place.

There were dazzling cities and the most primitive huts, all in glowing mosaics; there were factories and stone tools—and the emblems and flags of countries and religions and causes of which he'd never known.

Then—abruptly—a particular person's figure would take prominence in a particular mosaic. The person (sometimes a male, sometimes a female) would make a simple motion—lift a vase, raise an arm, turn away. And as if in response, all of the other segments would change, too. Different kinds of buildings would appear, or an army or a vast parade would rush into action. But as these persons executed their simple motions, the entire panorama was completely altered in one way or another.

As Oversoul Seven tried to interpret his experience, he almost lost himself in his concentration. In one mosaic, for example, a woman in 13,000 B.C. picked up a simple tool—and in another mosaic, a spaceship took off. *Then,* however, the order of motion was reversed. The astronaut pushed a simple button on an instrument panel—and as if in response, the woman picked up her tool.

Then, so quickly that Seven couldn't follow, he saw George Brainbridge the First in his private attic study; a miniature, but glowing with intensity. And the Victorian George was peering out of the attic window at the very scene Seven was witnessing. At the same time, George the Third appeared, also in miniature, the antiseptic white dentist's office like a tiny brilliant white closet against the sky; and George was looking down into the face of Gregory Diggs, the thief. The two of them were seemingly frozen in the same position forever, even while Seven had the feeling that the relationships between them were constantly changing. And again simultaneously, in another mosaic the patient at the mental institution who thought he was Christ suddenly held up his hand, as if to stop the entire cosmic production. And at once everything vanished — except for the landscape, which was again filled with mist.

The wind had an unusual murmuring sound as if voices were hidden in it somewhere — a hypnotizing, compelling, yet distant sound. Seven listened, knowing that whatever he was "hearing" wasn't sound as he was used to thinking of it; but an inner molecular rustling as if the atoms of the rocks and trees and grass were all trying to speak, or manufacture tongues, at once. The "sounds" changed several times until Seven finally made out their message: *The Codicils.* But what did that mean? The inner sounds were more like vibrations that he translated into words, so that the very ground beneath Seven's feet vibrated; and so did the misty trees; until from everywhere those inner words, *The Codicils,* came rushing into Seven's mind.

"What are *they*?" Seven asked mentally. But the moment he asked, the vibrations ceased. And Cyprus stood beside him.

Cyprus looked more radiant than he'd ever seen her. Besides this, she seemed to have a kaleidoscope of images at her command, so that as she appeared, other images of herself cascaded from the main one; images of men and women of all ages and countries and times sparked out onto the landscape and then exploded like firecrackers. Seven was almost abashed at Cyprus' abilities. He felt quite powerless in the midst of such a display, as he stood there in his polyester permanent-press suit, now more than slightly damp in the night mists that had returned.

In fact, by the time Cyprus settled upon one image — the ancient woman with young appearance, or the young woman with ancient knowledge — Seven felt quite dejected.

"I certainly am glad to see you," he said. "But I haven't the slightest idea of what's been happening. Even with a body, I can't seem to stay in the right time. And you saw the world vision I just saw?"

"I saw it," Cyprus said gently. "You perceived more of it than I thought you would. Part of it you'll interpret as you go along."

"But none of my experiences seem *orderly* lately," Seven cried. "There's order there, I know! But I keep losing it. . . ."

"You don't lose it," Cyprus said softly. "It's there. You put off perceiving it, for reasons you'll remember later. But I have some important clues to help you.

"There's an important dilemma, or rather, an important period of change approaching . . . Now on the one hand, this change has happened, of course, and on the other hand, from the standpoint of George Brainbridge in the twentieth century, it hasn't. He's approaching a vital intersection of probabilities, and *you* must learn to help your personalities in the probable areas of their lives as well as with the problems they're aware of. . . . "

But Seven was truly dismayed. "You don't mean I have to handle a group of probable Georges?" he cried.

Cyprus smiled and ignored the outburst. "Remember your vision," she urged, in a tone he'd learned to pay attention to. "Important clues are there, too. Remember the personalities you saw in it, Diggs in particular. And remember, even for mortals, not all experience is physically manifest. Each person, Seven, is partially responsible for the birth of probable worlds . . . There, don't frown. You're doing very well. Your suit is most appropriate too — exquisite twentieth century; quite quaint."

"You're just saying that to cheer me up," Seven protested. But before he could finish, Cyprus said, "Get back to your main-line century for now though, or you'll end up more confused than ever. And don't forget, there's a reason why George the First perceived Diggs."

"I'm more confused than ever," Seven complained under his breath. "And how come my body travels through all those probabilities?"

"You'd better get that young thief out of the house before the twentieth-century George catches on," Cyprus said. "Worry about the rest later."

Cyprus vanished, and so did the thirtieth-century night landscape. Seven stood (fully visible, he realized) in front of George Brainbridge and the twentieth-century thief. The house still had its Victorian appearance. "Who in thunder are you?" yelled George Brainbridge the First, seeing him this time.

This time Seven concentrated with all his might. "Out, out," he shouted at Gregory Diggs, and he shoved Gregory out of the twentieth-century door. This time, he really felt his own muscles move.

Almost at the same time he turned to George the First and commanded him to rush back up the nineteenth-century stairs. Eyes ablaze with astonishment, George did as he was told.

~ *Chapter Seven* ~

The Transformation of Gregory Diggs

*G*regory Diggs crossed the street outside of George Brainbridge's house, walked the half block to the river by cutting through back yards, and sat down on the grassy riverbank to think. A few cars passed above him to the right, sweeping over the bridge, but the night was quiet. The air was still warm though damp, with a mist rising from the water. Way to the left was the soft glimmer of downtown lights. Gregory smoked a cigarette and debated.

He'd planned to steal the dentist's drugs and sell them for some ready cash; and *that* hadn't panned out. Not that it was his fault. Even a genius couldn't have anticipated the nut who'd discovered him — and thinking of it, Gregory started laughing so hard that he rolled on the ground. A house with gas lights, yet, and a clown who dressed like a dude from another century. Oh, God! He gasped. Now that it was all over, the comedy struck him. The guy who sent the other one upstairs must have been his keeper or something, Gregory decided.

But he stopped laughing — even if he didn't get the drugs after all, he was damned lucky he got off so easily. Only he *did* need some cash, and if it wasn't for his goddamned gums hurting him all the time, he'd just take off. The social worker had told him that the clinic would fix him up, but all the stupid dentist said was, "Too bad." A lot of good that did, Gregory thought, getting angry as he remembered; he'd still rip the bastard off if he knew where the hell he lived. Both men must have the same name. At least the nutty dentist put cloves on his gums, which helped some.

Gregory started walking, rather dejectedly, toward downtown, on his way to the health complex beyond. He had no other place to go, he mused; so what the hell? He wasn't even sure of his status there; he wasn't an outpatient but he wasn't an . . . inmate either. He'd sneak back in, he decided, and after breakfast, maybe take off for good. So he was out on bail. Caught stealing from a supermarket. What was that? All the judge said was that he had to stay under observation for a few days . . . Observation?

He grinned. Nobody paid any attention to him. He wasn't in any security area, though they had one. And in the day the place was mobbed with outpatients. All he had to do was just walk out again, if he wanted to.

He passed the backs of the downtown buildings, looking up at the rickety fire escapes that rose from the riverbank, thinking that those places would be easy to rip off—but would hardly be worth the bother. Nobody who lived there had anything worth stealing.

Two more blocks, and the grounds of the mental health complex were visible: low buildings, some with outside patios, trees in front planted in geometric patterns, a playground, a huge hospital-like structure with decorated bars at the upper windows. It all looked like some ideal neat modern village, Gregory thought, suddenly catching his breath because the whole place was bathed in the soft light from downtown that diffused through the clouds.

"Dirty bastards," Gregory muttered not knowing exactly who he was thinking of, but the peaceful uncluttered area with its trees and shaded small pathways sure as hell seemed to offer something that wasn't being delivered.

In his mind's eye, Gregory already saw himself walking across the back expanse of lawn, right up to the building he'd left so secretly, and right through the bottom window to the small room and cot they'd given him. Maybe they hoped that he *would* run off, to another town—one less problem for the town officials.

"Shit," Gregory said. Despite himself, the softness of the June night was reviving his spirits. He sat down on one of the red benches by a small bed of flowers, and smelled the moist air that rose from the river. It was a crappy life, he thought, even as he felt his spirits rise. Still, the night was so comforting that he decided to stay where he was. If anyone questioned him, he'd say he couldn't sleep and came out for a walk. Now he was drowsily aware of his gums again, but suddenly he was too tired to care and he fell asleep on the bench.

When he awakened, it was sometime just after dawn. Not only did his gums hurt now, but two gumboils had apparently developed during his sleep, and the tip of his tongue was sore. Gregory grinned, and tried to ignore his difficulties, though, as he remembered the events of the night before. Best of all, he hadn't stolen anything, even if he *had* intended to, so nobody new was after him. And he was on the honors system at the clinic division of the mental-health place. He grinned again, ambled over to the main building, climbed in his window, and sat down on the bed.

There were early noises from the security section of the building where the mentally disturbed were kept; and from somewhere, the smell of coffee. Gregory got up, went down the corridor whose walls featured glossy snapshots of the city and valley, and came out finally in a large room. The new sunlight poured through five east windows, leaving five brilliant paths upon the linoleum floor. In one corner, a television set was turned on, though no one was watching it. There were various kinds of chairs about the room, some upholstered in floral patterns, a few bean chairs, several tables, and lamps.

At first Gregory thought he was alone, but then a noise at the further end of the room caught his attention. The sun was so bright that he could hardly see, but in the glare he made out a man's thin figure. "Uh, hi," Gregory said. "Any idea where I could get some coffee or aspirin around here?"

The figure came closer. The man, in his forties, wore dungarees, shirt, sneakers, and carried a broom. "Custodian," he said.

"They start you working early, huh?" Gregory asked.

"Verily," the man answered.

"Verily? That's a funny thing to say," Gregory replied. "Cigarette?"

"Don't mind if I do," the man said, setting the broom aside.

Gregory grinned: he'd been lonely, he thought; and this guy seemed engaging in a way he liked at once. He lit the man's cigarette. "Keep the joint clean, do you?" he asked.

They sat down facing each other, a small table beside them. "I'm Gregory Diggs," said Gregory, amazed at his own politeness.

"My real name is John Window, but I think I'm Christ," the man said, smiling. "You might as well know right off."

"Aw, you're putting me on?" Gregory said, blushing despite himself. "I mean He's dead, for one thing. And you don't look dead to me."

"That's a fact," the man answered.

"You don't look like you're nearly two thousand years old, either," Gregory said, with a jerky laugh. But he was fascinated. "Hey, I heard about you a few days ago," he said. "Why do you think you're Christ? What do the psychologists say? How come they let you around like this? I mean, you could just walk out of this place."

"Where would I go to?" the man, Christ asked. "I have an advantage on myself. I know Christ's history. They'll crucify me if I leave here, and the doctors know I won't go any place. Besides, I have jobs to do here."

Gregory's eyes had never been wider. "Yeah, like what?" he asked. The sun hit his eyes again, and he had to turn his head.

"Oh, I go about my father's business," the man answered. There was a sly hint to his voice, or so Gregory thought, so he turned back to look closer at the man's face.

The sunlight hit it almost directly as the man also turned; and for a moment the custodian's face looked hazy, unformed, glimmering. Gregory sprang up without a word and snapped down each shade to the bottom of each window, then went back to his chair. "Couldn't see," he muttered.

"Blessed are the blind, for they shall see God," the man said sweetly.

"Now, see here, that's enough of that," cried Gregory, feeling a trifle uneasy by now. "Do you know where I can get aspirin? My gums are killing me. They got some disease, the dentist here says."

"He took out a tooth of mine," the custodian said sympathetically, and Gregory started laughing, no longer frightened. "Well, that proves you aren't Christ," he said. "Christ could fix his own teeth, couldn't he? So you can go out in the world now and not worry about being crucified." Suddenly, though, Gregory's tone changed. "They won't hang you to any damned cross anyhow. But they'll get anybody they can. You don't have to be Christ, you know, to be crucified in this world."

"That's a fact too, I guess," the custodian answered, and for a moment Gregory felt that he and this odd stranger were united in some way, or at least understood the world in the same terms, or *something*. The momentary rapport between them made him uneasy too, so he said in a brusquer voice, "My gums . . . I guess my damned teeth are going to fall out."

And Gregory was never sure exactly what happened next, or who spoke first, he or the custodian. He only knew that once again, the sun nearly blinded him. Colors of all kinds kaleidoscoped through his inner vision; yet at the same time, there was a whiter-than-white pattern as well. . . . Through all of this, he glimpsed — or thought he glimpsed — the custodian's face, close up, with the most compassionate smile imaginable.

The custodian spoke, and Gregory felt the words, but couldn't understand them with his ears. In the next moment a tingling warmth spread through his face, gums, jaws, and eyes. The warmth was somehow almost dizzying, and he felt — he *felt* his teeth tighten in his head.

There was the warmest pressure as each root dug itself in deeper; and tiny hot snaps as the gums tightened around them. Gregory was caught up in so many emotions that he could hardly identify them. His tongue slid across his gums — no gumboils! And the tip of his tongue didn't hurt. He opened his eyes. Then he saw that the light wasn't nearly as bright as it had seemed only a moment before, because he had, after all, pulled the shades. Then where *had* that light come from? "The . . . the . . . light," he muttered.

"Not as bright as it was a minute ago. The sun just dimmed some," said the custodian, looking more or less, Gregory thought, like any man in his forties; no halo, for Christ's sake, no . . . *power* such as he'd just sensed.

"Feel better? Gums okay, huh?" the custodian asked. And when Gregory heard his voice this time, there was no doubt in his mind that somehow or other this man had completely healed his gums. "How . . . did you do that?" he stuttered. "I don't know what to say. Nobody ever does anything decent for me, much less. . . ."

"Now and then I *can* work miracles," the custodian said. "I don't mean to brag, though, it's just my way. Now I have to finish my chores. Don't tell anyone, though. Miracles always cause trouble for me." He picked up his broom and began vigorously sweeping the floor.

"But . . . but you shouldn't be here doing *that*," Gregory shouted. "You healed my gums! You could make a million dollars. You could . . . My God, how did you do that? I feel fantastic all over. . . ."

"Do what?" the custodian asked, blinking now as if the sun suddenly hurt his eyes. "Aspirin and coffee can be got two doors down."

"Hell, who needs aspirin?" Gregory shouted happily. "I never felt better in my life. You healed me, or something." Again he said, "But how did you do that?" He couldn't hide the awe in his voice.

"Shush. I'm just the custodian now," John Window said, almost in a drawl. There was a sly closed look about his face; and yet a secret smile belied his proclaimed ignorance. He moved rather loosely toward the television set and stood watching the program in progress.

"You thought you were Christ a minute ago," Gregory yelled, scandalized. "You just . . . did the impossible. How can you pretend nothing happened?" In his bafflement, Gregory grabbed Window's arm and half swung him about.

There was no doubt that Window was suddenly frightened. "Don't tell anyone," he said, in a new, low, quavering voice. "When I think I'm Christ, sometimes I do things that can't be done. But I know who I am now. I'm John Window, and that's a fact."

The sunlight now had a hard yellow cast, an objectionable glare. Gregory backed away from Window scowling. It was a game Window was playing, he realized — and not a nice one. Window was terrified of . . . well, whatever . . .

power he had. So Gregory said, "That's all right. I'll play it any way you want. Don't you worry, everything will be okay. Cool it. Don't get upset."

John Window's eyes fluttered just slightly. It seemed to Gregory that one powerful ray of strength or understanding or compassion—traveled from Window's eyes to his before the custodian turned his back and ambled away. No, Gregory thought, watching. Window was shuffling, where before his steps had been quick and sure.

Gregory couldn't believe what had happened, and he couldn't *not* believe it either. What was Window so frightened of? he wondered, because he recognized real fear when he saw it; he felt it himself a good deal of the time. Window wasn't feigning *that.* But what was he so scared of, and why should someone with such . . . *power* fear anything?

He watched until Window disappeared into another room off the main corridor and then, forgetting he'd wanted coffee, Gregory drifted out to the lawn. The mental changes in himself weren't at first obvious, though the physical ones *were;* and he tested these at once. Grinning, he tugged at his teeth, *tugged,* and they were as firm in their sockets as teeth could be.

He still couldn't get over it. The soreness had been with him for several years, too; and without it he felt almost giddy and light. But more, he felt like running, really running—not away from anyone as usual, but just for the joy of it. So he stood up and ran as fast as he could across the street, behind the buildings, to the riverbank. It seemed that in some way he couldn't fathom, the trees and sky and riverbank were all his—his and everyone else's, too. He ran up and down so buoyantly that he was laughing out loud until finally he felt drained—and ready to think. He hardly remembered crossing the street again and sitting down on the same bench on the psych center lawn.

By now it was nearing 8 o'clock. Outpatients and center attendants began arriving for the day, parking their cars in the lot to the left. Gregory stared at the people; they looked okay on the outside, he thought, but they wouldn't be there if they didn't have troubles. And inside, unknown to the doctors or psychologists or *dentists,* was some guy they all thought was a nut. Only that nut could do things that could make people right.

Gregory tested his teeth again; what would he do if they suddenly wobbled? But they wouldn't, he thought triumphantly, remembering and still feeling the unique sense of certainty that he'd experienced when . . . when the custodian did whatever it was he did. There it was, Gregory realized, the thought he'd been putting to the back of his mind: He wasn't exactly sure if the man had actually touched him, or only looked at him. But what difference did that make? This Christ had credentials!

He breathed deeply, freely, noticing something else. Until up to right now, he'd always breathed tightly. It felt as if he had more room in his lungs, or as if his lungs had more room in his ribs, or. . . . And that thought clued Gregory in to a further realization: his fear was gone. Here he was, sitting on a bench like anyone else, not wondering what people thought of him, or if he looked like a bum, or if some cop was going to challenge him just because he always looked as if he'd slept in his clothes for a week, which he usually had. He even found himself smiling at a passersby; not faking it, either.

This almost awed him as much as the tight teeth. When he thought *that*, a delayed reaction set in to a change of mind that had been going on ever since he left the custodian. Now Gregory *was* dizzy with elation: for the first time in his life, he thought, someone had done something great for him . . . and without wanting anything back . . . and without his asking. He'd always taken it for granted that the worst would most likely happen unless you did something to prevent it, and his twenty-one years of experience seemed to prove his point — up to now. He felt half embarrassed, but there was no doubt of it; the universe or God or chance or just the fates had unquestioningly somehow blessed his presence. And not just with a trifling pat on the back, but by giving him suddenly proof of. . . . His thoughts boggled. Proof of what? He didn't believe the guy was Christ, for instance . . . but when *Window* believed he was Christ — wow!

And the guy responsible, Gregory thought, was locked up inside the psych center, frightened, probably afraid that the authorities would find out about his abilities, and do what? What could they do? he wondered. Kick him out on his ass, Gregory supposed. Then he remembered: When he believed he was Christ, the custodian also was sure he'd be crucified.

Well, he wouldn't be — not in any way, shape, or manner, Gregory told himself resolutely. And in that moment, Gregory felt the first strong purpose of his life; he was going to help the custodian somehow, someway. It didn't occur to him that he was thinking of someone else for the first time in his life, too. The big question in his mind was, *How* could he help?

"I'll just walk right into the newspaper once and tell my story," he thought, imagining an awed reception, the reporters interviewing Window, Window healing the masses of people who came to see him. . . . But then Gregory's smile faded; *that* would scare the custodian to death. "Shit," he muttered. It was then that he felt almost inspired — or at least the solution came instantly to mind. Before anything else, he had to show the dentist the change in his mouth. Oh, Christ! Tears of laughter fell from his eyes as Gregory imagined Dr. Brainbridge when he saw those tight teeth in the healed gums. What could he say? What could the poor bastard say?

~ *Chapter Eight* ~

Dr. Brainbridge Is Confronted with
Proof of the Impossible: Or Is He?

Gregory Diggs found out that Dr. Brainbridge worked at the psych center only two mornings a week, so it was two days later that Gregory stood waiting in front of the dentist's office in the center's main building. He was nervous, he realized, no doubt about it. He suffered from a bad conscience, knowing that this was the man he'd intended to rob only a few days earlier. He still didn't know if he'd been in the right place or not, or if the odd character in old-fashioned clothes was a demented relative of this dentist's or what. Gregory fidgeted: and who was the younger man who had finally let him go? For all of Gregory's desire to tell his story and prove John Window's abilities, he hadn't dared go back to Brainbridge's house. So now he waited impatiently as Dr. Brainbridge walked down the corridor, with Seven stepping smartly beside him.

Seven and Gregory recognized each other at once. Gregory started to bolt, certain that the story of the attempted robbery must be out — but in a flash, Seven grinned, put out his hand and said, "A patient who can't wait to get in, huh?"

Confused, Gregory managed a smile half guilty and half filled with gratitude.

Dr. George Brainbridge said, "You aren't on my appointment list today, are you?"

Brainbridge opened the door at the same time, and Gregory pushed in past Seven. "I have to talk to you. Just a minute. You've got to see something."

He was almost pleading, and his manner toward George was so deferential that George grinned quizzically and said, with a half laugh: "Not out to get me today?"

"I'm done with all of that. Look at this," Gregory cried, opening his mouth as wide as he could.

George shrugged, adjusted his glasses, started to say, "What happened? Lose a tooth?" when, looking, he gasped, cried "Jesus Christ, sit down there," and shoved Gregory over to the dental chair.

"Open wider," he demanded. Gregory did. George let out a long whistle and said to Seven: "Look in this kid's mouth, will you? Tell me what you see."

Wonderingly, Seven looked. "All fine and dandy," he said. "Uh, super."

And George Brainbridge, his face flushed, said, "That's what I was afraid you'd say."

"Surprised, I bet?" Gregory said. He laughed as George put his hand into his mouth and started tugging at the tight teeth.

"Jesus," George said. "A few days ago these teeth were damn near ready to fall out; so bad in fact I figured the kindest thing to do for Greg here was to let them do just that." He shook his head, and looked at Gregory. "What happened?" he asked. "I've never in my entire career seen anything like this. Once started, the tissue just gets more diseased, and in the condition you were in, the thing was way past any reversing. It just doesn't happen."

"So you told me," Gregory said with relish.

Oversoul Seven let his consciousness dip toward George's and found himself astounded at George's inner reaction. It was as if Gregory's healed gums had set off a series of psychological quakes in George's mind. He believed what he saw in Gregory's mouth and yet he couldn't; he kept looking for ways of dismissing the evidence obviously before him. His stubborn denial completely baffled Seven.

And Gregory, after laughing out loud triumphantly, now found himself feeling sorry for the dentist.

"What happened?" George demanded again. He was red-faced.

"You probably won't believe me," Gregory began.

"After this, I'll believe anything," George muttered.

Now when it actually came time to tell his story, Gregory found himself embarrassed. Only his determination to help the custodian kept him from running from the room. "I don't really know," he started. "My gums hurt like hell. I got two new gum boils from when I saw you. Then yesterday morning, I met this custodian in the entertainment room. He was sweeping up and we talked. . . ." Gregory gulped, and looked directly into George's eyes. His voice went high and scared and wavery. "This guy looked at me or did something, and suddenly I felt my teeth tighten in my head. I mean I *felt* them tighten. I got hot all over and saw lights. . . . " He broke off, his telling of the story finally making him aware of its impact; of its impossibility—and of its definite truth. Briefly he lifted his head and cried, "It's that guy I told you about, the one who thinks he's Christ. He did it, I mean, he really did."

Oversoul Seven tried to look impressed, but he kept his mouth shut so he wouldn't say the wrong thing. A body and a polyester suit didn't necessarily make you human, he thought, rather confused. And it certainly didn't make some human views any easier to understand. He wanted to shout, "Miracles, as you call them, happen all the time. That's nature unimpeded," but he said nothing of the sort. Instead he tried to understand why George and Gregory Diggs both seemed so shocked, and why Gregory was almost near tears.

George Brainbridge rubbed the corner of his nose, blew his nose, adjusted his glasses for the tenth time in ten minutes, sat down, and threw out his nearly pudgy arms in astounded dismay. "Well, if it happened, it happened! I mean, no dentist could have fixed those gums in ten years, much less two days. There's no way you could have tricked me." He said this last to Gregory, but with a desperate question in his voice as if wishing that he *was* being tricked. Indeed he said, "I'd almost rather it *was* a trick than face —well, what those healed gums imply. . . . " He took the cellophane off a fresh patient's glass, filled it with water, and drank it down quickly.

Gregory just watched him. He was trying to recover his own composure. Then he said, almost apologetically, "That's not really all. But my whole body's felt terrific since. I mean, fantastic. And well, I'm not so, you know, paranoid about people." He looked embarrassed.

With a sudden rush of despairing humor George said, "Well, every silver lining has a cloud."

Gregory managed a wan grin and glanced toward Seven. "I've done some things I'm not so proud of," he said, with a slight question in his own voice.

Now that he'd told his story, he began worrying that Seven might tell Brainbridge about the attempted robbery. . . . But Seven gave Gregory a brilliant grin and said, "Put all that behind you."

Seven had been so quiet that George almost forgot he was there. Rather startled, brought back from his own thoughts, he said emphatically, "Right, right." Then, after a pause, he shook his head again with new perplexity. "Had to be suggestion. It's the only answer. I mean, that guy John Window is a nut. At least he certainly isn't Christ. But suggestion—shit— how can suggestion heal gums in a minute that were in the shape yours were in? It can't."

With more courage than he knew he had, Gregory said, "That guy may not be Christ, but he's okay. I mean, he *knows* that he thinks he's Christ sometimes. And he's harmless. But not only *that,* man, think of how many people he could cure. Maybe he could even cure cancer!"

"Whoa, whoa. Super!—a whisk of the hand and you're cured—" George planked his hands on his hips. "I can't quite see that," he said, almost vehemently. Then, with true exasperation, "Open your mouth again, will you? And Seven, get me this kid's dental records from the file there. I want to see that diagnosis in black and white. . . ."

Seven got out the records. George flipped through them, holding up Gregory's with the tip of his fingers as if it were made of fire; he eyed it gingerly, unbelievingly. He shook his head again and said, "Well, there you are. Dated four days ago. Advanced periodontal disease."

Looking at the record, his worst fears confirmed—that something impossible *had* happened—George determined to face the impossible with determination, vigor, and a sense of humor. His pragmatism made him face the fact of . . . a most unusual event! That's what it amounted to, he decided, just as Gregory asked, in a worried tone, "What are you going to do?"

"Do?" George repeated. "Hell, what's to do? It's done. I might like a little talk with that custodian though. Or then again, maybe not. Give me a bit of time to think about it. I'd like to see those gums of yours tomorrow, anyhow. . . ."

"You won't get Window in any trouble, will you?" Gregory asked, sounding more worried than before. "I mean, well, his abilities challenge the authorities, don't they?"

"They sure as hell do," George answered. He was caught, because though he was nominally a member of the establishment, his sympathies were usually with the underdog—which was one of the reasons he helped out at the center to begin with. But . . . his conventional knowledge of medicine and dentistry made him scandalized at the apparent healing—it flew in the face of all common sense knowledge. Moreover, he was beginning to remember his own encounter with the Christ patient. This made him more nervous than before. "Look, I've got three patients lined up for this morning," he said. "I'll think about this and I'll get in touch with you. We'll put this thing in some kind of perspective. . . ." Gregory didn't want to budge, but Seven gave him a friendly shove, and led him to the door.

"I'll be in touch. I promise," George assured him. After Gregory left, George did two extractions and a filling without saying another word to Seven except for, "Just hand me that thing-a-majig," pointing to an instrument for which Seven had learned the proper name but not George's pet designation. So Seven was kept hopping, anticipating what George would want next, and following the gesture of George's arm as his fingers pointed generally to the area in which the instrument could be found.

"Now, the digger," he said, and when Seven promptly handed him the tool, he murmured, "Super," but in a distracted, automatic way. Even his reminders to the patients to open wider were made without his usual accompanying smile.

When the last patient left, George looked at Seven and shook his head. "I am truly mystified. For the first time in my life, I just do not know how to react. What's your opinion on all of this. . . ?"

This time Seven forgot himself in his desire to help, so he said, "What's the problem? The boy's gums were definitely healed. Miracles are nature, unimpeded."

George's eyes snapped open. "That's an odd thing to say. Miracles are nature unimpeded, huh? Bullshit! Something's going on beside just the healing of gums. Come on now, do you think we've been hypnotized?"

"Hypnotized?" Seven asked, astounded. Where could George ever get an idea like that?

"Or maybe we're hallucinating?" George went on lamely. "Nope. Well, I don't know about you, but I'm hooked. I've got to find out what happened. Some kind of gimmick's got to be involved."

As they talked, George and Seven locked the office and left the building and headed for the parking lot. The June afternoon was warm, the day a soft green-gray. Every time he visited the center, George passed the playground, but this afternoon, talking with Seven, he paused and sat down on a swing. Seven sat on the swing beside him. There were no children around this time of the day, and only a few patients strolled the grounds. The sounds of traffic from the nearby main street were partially muted by all the shrubbery, and Seven and George sat, not speaking for a moment.

Then George said, "You're an odd one. You know? You're taking all this damn calmly."

"What is is, is," Seven said lightly.

"Maybe it's because you're younger. I don't know, but at least when I went to dental school, they taught us that some things were absolutely irreversible; certain conditions. Hell, I'm chairman of the cancer drive."

"The drive for cancer?" Seven said incredulously, "Who wants that?"

"It's no time for jokes," George replied. "If *one* cure like that can happen, it shafts the entire medical profession. Instead of drives for dollars for technological advances, we'd have to . . . hell, *I* don't know, reexamine our ideas about the entire body, or find healers, for Christ's sake, or. . . ."

"Well, you know where *one* healer is," Seven said innocently.

"Yeah, in a nut house, where I'd say he belonged—if I hadn't seen that kid's gums for myself." Suddenly George sat bolt upright. "I've got it," he shouted. "There are two kids. Yes, that's it! They're twins, one with good gums and one with lousy ones. It's a goddamned con game!

"Twins," he gasped, laughing so heartily that he was half bent over, sitting in the swing.

Seven just stared.

"Oh, Christ! How could I have fallen for that?" George shouted, between laughs. "That little bugger's out to get me just because I couldn't fix his damn gums. I mean, he thinks we're all shitheads, members of the establishment, and that we couldn't care less; we get paid anyhow."

As hard as he tried, Oversoul Seven couldn't understand George's reaction. Why would George prefer that fraud was involved in the first place? And why was George growing more jovial by the minute? Finally Seven said, "You don't think there was any miracle at all, then?"

"Hell no, you're too gullible and well-meaning," George said, still laughing, but more softly. He swung back and forth gently, studying the toe of his right shoe as if the answers were contained within it. "Look," he said. "That Christ chap had to be in on this, too. Twin One shows me his lousy gums, then Twin Two shows me his healthy ones and says that that "Christ" healed him. But where do they expect to go with it from here? Miracles! Boy, was I ever taken in."

"I don't suppose you believe in the soul either, huh?" Seven asked, a trifle plaintively.

George stood up to stretch his legs. "I believe in teeth and gums," he said, grinning. "And they don't lie."

Within the context of the relationship between himself and George, Seven could only say so much; and he didn't even know how to say that, he thought miserably. But he looked at George with just the slightest touch of severity and replied, "There's more to life than teeth and gums, though."

And at once he saw that he'd hurt George's feelings, because George sat back down on the swing, slapped Seven lightly but disapprovingly on the shoulder and said, "Yeah? Well, listen. Being a dentist may not be the most heroic profession in the world—as you'll find out yourself before too long. But I'll tell you one thing: People are damn grateful when a bad tooth is extracted, or you get rid of a pain. And that's real. It may not be philosophic, but it's a very practical help to people when they're suffering. So I leave the question of souls to the ministers or priests or whatever. And I still say that gums are honest. They don't lie."

Again Seven just stared; he was learning more about George every minute.

George grinned and said, "You surprised? Anyhow, that's why a con game like that makes me mad—giving people false hopes. Though hell, I can understand the motives involved! I think I'll just play along to see what they plan next before I lower the boom."

"You'll have to find Gregory's twin first," Seven said.

"And I was thinking how great it was that the kid's attitude had changed so for the better, miracle or no," said George, starting to laugh again. "Instead —two kids. Well, the joke's on me, I guess."

But then, suddenly George's mood changed. He dug his foot into the sand beneath the swings and said, in a harder voice, "Except that it's not such a funny joke, when you come right down to it. Hell, I don't know. But I worked on that custodian's teeth the other day; he told me he was Christ, all right. He seemed like a nice enough guy. When I was finished he said, "God bless you," or something like that. . . ." George broke off, obviously embarrassed.

Seven said, "And—?"

"Shit," George went on, grinning self-deprecatingly. "But for just a few moments there I felt great, renewed, vigorous, full of life or whatever. The attendant said that kind of thing happened now and then, and laid it to suggestion. And it *had* to be—suggestion. But goddammit, I'm not particularly suggestible, or I didn't think I was.

Momentarily George seemed to forget that Seven was even there. He mused, aloud but to himself, "I thought of all kinds of things that I haven't thought about, in years . . . and now this. It's a dirty shame when people take advantage like that—"

"Like what?" Seven asked, unable to remain quiet.

"Like, well, hell, raise false hopes like that," George cried, throwing up his arms in the air. "Well, let's get going," he said. "Life's no playground, I'll tell you that. . . . And I'm going to catch that bunch red-handed."

Resolutely George got up and began striding toward the parking lot. Beside him, feeling some alarm, Oversoul Seven almost shouted, "You might be in for more surprises than you're counting on. . . . "

But George didn't answer. He was filled with righteous indignation; his brown eyes blazed, his arms swung vigorously at his sides. "A joke is a joke and enough is enough," he said. And Seven thought that George suddenly bore an uncomfortable resemblance to his grandfather, George Brainbridge the First.

~ *Chapter Nine* ~

George Hears Further Disclosures:
His Dilemma Deepens

George was to meet Gregory Diggs in the center's dental office, where they'd have some privacy. Diggs was a few minutes late for their appointment, and George muttered to Seven, "Want to bet that he doesn't come? He probably guesses we're on to him. Damn! How can life get so complicated?"

"Maybe he's on the up and up though," Seven offered, grinning as if this possibility was the furthest from his mind. "After all, we didn't find records of any twin. I mean, the records the police checked couldn't have been tampered with."

"Records or no, it's the only possible explanation," George said stubbornly. "Unless you believe in miracles."

"Maybe miracles are events we just don't understand," Seven ventured. "Science admits there's lots of phenomena that can't be explained—"

"But gums are gums!" George said, as if that ended all possible discussion.

Before Seven could answer, Gregory Diggs walked in and closed the door behind him. George didn't even wait for Diggs to sit down. He advanced, demanding, "All right, where's your twin? We know you have one."

"Twin?" exclaimed Gregory, completely confused.

"The guy with the bad gums," George said, meaningfully. "There's two of you. You show me your good gums and tell me some crazy story about a healing. And I fall for it — or I almost did. We found the records of your twin," he said, lying with a sense of true virtue.

Gregory Diggs stared at George with an honest outrage that even George could see was beyond manufacture; so that George, who was basically good-hearted, felt instantly guilty.

"I don't have any goddamned twin," Gregory Diggs said, in a sputtering completely disbelieving voice. "How could you come up with *that*? I mean, maybe I haven't always played cricket with the world, but I swear I've been completely above board in all this. I tell you, the guy healed my gums. It's true, I left a few details out, but they didn't have anything to do with my gums," Gregory said, guiltily. He looked at Seven.

In some alarm, Seven said, "Forget it. Dr. Brainbridge has had enough to put up with today. I'll tell him tomorrow."

"No. I want to get it over with," Gregory Diggs insisted, sounding as stubborn as George had earlier. "I told you, I'm starting over. The world's just different for me now."

"Tell me what?" George asked, with a silly quizzical look as if not sure he wanted to know at all.

So Seven just threw up his hands, telling himself that he'd ad-lib some explanations along the way, and Gregory began, in a hesitant, somewhat defensive voice:

"This was before my gums got healed. I saw you in the morning, and you said nothing could be done for them. They hurt like hell, and I was mad. I figured like I used to, that nobody gave a damn. Anyhow that night I decided to skip town, only I didn't have any money. So I looked up your address in the phone book and went over." Diggs stopped, glanced almost imploringly at the wide-eyed George and continued, "Well, I figured on stealing some drugs and selling them on the street for cash. I figured you probably got them free anyhow. Well. . . ." He broke off, looking twice as uneasy as he had before.

"You may as well tell it all," said George. He kept shaking his head and staring inquiringly at Seven.

"Hell, I don't know," Gregory said, almost stammering. "I went inside. The downstairs was dark. A car was in the garage, and there were lights on upstairs in the back. I reckoned that the downstairs office was closed for the night. If I was quiet, I could get away with it. The back door wasn't even locked, so I went in. . . ."

"Where I found him," Oversoul Seven said briskly.

"Why didn't you tell me?" George's eyebrows leapt upward.

"Well, he didn't take anything, that's the important thing," Seven said. "We had a talk. So I didn't want him to get in more trouble than he was. . . ."

"For Christ's sake," George said.

"So when you left," Seven said, brightly, "I went downstairs to see what was going on, and found Gregory here pawing around looking for drugs."

George, looking awed, just stared at Seven. "My God, that was a brave thing to do," he said. "Dumb. But brave."

Seven had the grace to blush, and George said, "But why? I'd have been able to handle it okay."

Seven did not answer, leaving George to figure things out for himself. "Yeah . . . ," George said, still confused.

Gregory, who had been just standing there, then said, "That isn't all, though. This last is wild."

"*This last,*" Seven was sure, was going to consist of Gregory's story about finding the gaslights turned on, the house appearing in the time of George's grandfather, and worse — of Gregory's confrontation with George the First. Seven braced himself and eyed George uneasily.

"Wild?" George thundered, sounding quite a bit like his grandfather. "That's *all* these last few days have been. Wild. So get on with it."

Gregory gulped. "Well, before Seven found me, somebody else did — a gentleman dressed in an old-fashioned red dressing gown, carrying an ancient rifle. He aimed it right at me. First, though, he switched on the lights, only they weren't electric. There were gaslights all over. I yelled I wasn't armed at all."

Silence. George's mouth dropped open. He rubbed his brow and said, "I just don't believe what I'm hearing."

"I didn't believe it either," Gregory nearly shouted. He was more and more agitated, remembering. "He sat me down and gave me a lecture, and he was a dentist, too. He put cloves on my gums. Only . . . everything looked like a movie set, like the room was out of the last century or something. I thought . . . it was some crazy relative of yours or something. He said *he* was Dr. George Brainbridge. I was trying to figure out what to do when Dr. Seven, here, came in. He yelled, and the guy in the dressing gown picked up his rifle and went upstairs. Then Seven let me go. I ran back to the psych center without being caught. The next morning, Window healed my teeth."

George Brainbridge's eyes were a study in the expression of utter amazement. He started to laugh, certain that Seven and Gregory were playing a trick. Then, staring at Gregory's obvious resoluteness, George caught back the laugh and gasped instead. "You've got to be putting me on!" he exclaimed, knowing beyond all hope that he'd heard the second most amazing story of his life — and that it was the rockbottom truth.

Seven said, "Uh, maybe Gregory was frightened and hallucinated the man with the rifle."

"*You* told him to go away," Gregory cried.

"Uh, exactly," Seven replied, redfaced.

George Brainbridge sat down, put his head in his arms and groaned. Then, lifting his head, grinning, he said, "Okay. Suppose I pretend for a minute that anything's possible. Describe the man in the dressing gown. "

"He had sandy hair—bushy brows—thinnish, about six feet," Gregory said promptly. "His dressing gown was velvet—I couldn't believe it—with tassels on the belt. And wait—sure, it had a monogram, G.B."

George just stared. His face grew pale, while incongruously his grin still lasted. "My grandfather looked like that when he was alive. And he had a dressing gown like that. I remember it from when I was a kid."

Gregory stared back incredulously. "Oh no. Uh-uh. This wasn't any ghost," he said in a shaking voice. "I couldn't see through him, or anything. But he put cloves on my gums. No ghost could do that. I could show you where he kept them."

"There's no oil of cloves in *my* office," George said clearly. "My grandfather *was* a dentist. He used cloves. I remember the smell—"

"That's it!" Gregory cried. "The smell burnt my eyes."

"And you don't have a twin? Those were *your* gums?" George asked in a quiet voice.

Gregory nodded. "The man I saw was solid, though," he objected. "Dr. Seven saw him. And the gaslights, too."

"I've seen him before," Seven admitted, blushing. Then to George: "He *does* seem to be your grandfather."

"You too?" George shouted. "Why didn't you tell me? Never mind; you didn't think I'd believe you, I suppose. Well, I don't." He plunked down in his own dentist's chair and glanced out the small window. "At least I wouldn't have, a few days ago. I do now, though God knows why. Do either of you realize what this does to my life? My grandfather's ghost . . . and a man who thinks he's Christ healing diseased gums? What am I supposed to do with this? I ask you, quite honestly."

"Accept the events as part of reality," Seven said quickly. "Since they happened, they're legitimate, whether or not they're supposed to happen or not. You've never been a quitter."

"How do you know?" George asked, suspiciously.

"Well, you sure don't act like one," Seven amended hastily.

"You happen to be right," George replied. "And if these things happened—well, they happened. Only why to *me*, for Christ's sake?"

"What about me?" Gregory Diggs exclaimed. Then, slowly, "You know, I've done a lot of thinking lately and I might have found an answer to that, sort of."

He paused, and George said, "Well, come on, out with it. Hell, I'm really interested."

Gregory looked at the floor, then said, "Well, I'm not looking for sympathy, but my childhood was crummy. Poor. Father was a drunk. Mother not much better. Five kids. I didn't think anyone cared a shit about me; I mean nobody . . . And for a bunch of years at night sometimes I used to — I don't know how to say this — stare at the sky and think, 'You sunabitchin' universe, you could do some tiny nice thing just for me if you wanted.' I didn't care how small it was; but I wanted some tiny miracle at least that was just for me, to let me know that life or the universe or something knew I was alive. And cared."

Gregory muttered the last sentences, yet spoke them so quickly that George and Seven had difficulty understanding him. When Gregory was finished, George said, "Hell, I'm sorry. . . ."

"But don't you see?" Gregory interrupted, speaking firmly now. "I think that was it, somehow. I mean, back then I wanted a miracle so bad. So maybe it just took this long for one to catch up with me."

Forgetting himself, Seven cried, "Of course! I forgot how important *you* are in all of this. Now I see why. Your intent — "

"I wish somebody would explain it all to me," George said, interrupting. Then, to Gregory, "Gaslights, you said?"

Gregory just nodded.

"So what's to be done?" Seven asked briskly.

George Brainbridge stood up, his face full of resoluteness, his eyes narrowed with intentness, his hands on his hips. "I'm going to check out John Window," he declared. "And if he *can* heal gums or anything else, the world, or somebody should know about it. The medical society. God knows who."

"No, you can't do that," Gregory protested. "They'd make his life a living hell. You don't understand. When Window thinks he's Christ, he can heal, at least he healed me, but he's paranoid. He's afraid that . . . he'll be crucified. I mean he really gets panicky. I admit it sounds screwy, but to tell the authorities would scare Window to death."

"Well, what do you suggest, then?" George asked, exasperated. "I thought you wanted publicity."

"I don't know what to do. Nothing, maybe," Gregory said, in a subdued tone.

"And if the guy *has* been healing, say, other patients, how come it isn't out by now?" George asked.

"They're all supposed to be nutty to one extent or another," Gregory said, almost shouting. "I mean, you didn't want to believe me. Who'd believe one of the patients?"

"Yeah. Well—" George said.

"Man, I sure am sorry I said *anything*," Gregory murmured. "I just wanted to prove you wrong in the beginning. Now I'm really sorry I did. I sure don't want to make it hard on the very guy . . . that helped me. It wasn't just my gums, you know. My whole world is better now. My whole life. . . ." He looked to be near tears.

"Look," George said, reassuringly, "I'll just talk to Window's doctor, and Window; nobody else without checking with you. Okay?"

"Yeah," Gregory said, sounding unconvinced.

"Do you trust my word?" George asked.

"Yeah," Gregory replied, surprising himself. He realized that he liked George Brainbridge, and Dr. Seven, and anyway he felt as if he'd found real friends for the first time in his life. Only—Window was a friend, too. And he wouldn't let anything hurt him.

"Of course, there's no proof that was my grandfather," George said with an embarrassed laugh. "I'm just taking you both at your word, but for the life of me I can't see why you'd want to lie. Can you describe the room?"

"I sure can," Gregory said. "It was all old-fashioned. So was the dentist's office. I mean, it had weird little wooden tables in it and lace curtains at the window, and a funny dentist's chair not like the one here at all. There was, uh, Victorian furniture, I guess you'd call it. And in particular a gigantic fern set in a pot by the window—in the dentist's office. I hid behind it, but I was caught anyway."

As evenly as he could, George said, "I have a photo in an old album of my grandfather's office, there was a plant just like that by the window." He shook his head. "This thing is beginning to make its own peculiar sense, I feel. But I can't really get a handle on it. What about you, Seven?"

"I don't believe he's a ghost," Seven replied, deciding that it was time for George to know a few more facts of life. "I think that somehow or other, when you aren't there, time changes and the past appears. Or something like that."

"You mean, I go out and close the door and bango—inside the house it's 1900 or something?"

Seven thought that George was going to snort or laugh in disbelief, but instead his face went from initial astonishment to relief.

George took his glasses off, cleaned them with a tissue, and shook his head. "I used to be afraid I was going crazy sometimes when I was a kid. Damn, I forgot the whole thing until now. Or shoved it out of my mind anyhow. I never got along with my father, but my grandfather was an idol of mine. He died when I was nine. Sometimes I thought I saw him, upstairs usually. But several times it happened in the waiting room, downstairs, in broad daylight. But as a kid coming down the front stairs, I had the weirdest impression that the rooms at the foot of the stairs were . . . different, and that if I was careful, I could catch them the way they were before. . . . Before what? Hell, I didn't know. But I used to sneak down the stairs at odd hours, and one night I swear I saw the waiting room as it was when my grandfather was in his prime. And there were gaslights. As I grew up I convinced myself that it was all my imagination. . . ."

George's eyes were half closed. His voice grew dreamy. "Granpa was known as a sort of odd nut. Adored by his patients. He was the best of the Victorian do-gooders, up to his neck in humanitarian work and so forth. He left an old journal. It's in the attic somewhere, I suppose. But he was into . . . expansion of consciousness or something like that, and he followed all the works of William James. He carried on some weird experiments and wrote to James about them, I guess. My father said he was dotty and told me to rid my mind of my grandfather's nonsense." Coming back to himself, George's face reddened and he said, "So I grew up to be a good red-blooded American boy." Then, "Hell, I don't know what I'm apologizing for. I'm a damn good dentist."

"So was your grandfather," said Seven, grinning. "And when I've seen him, he's been sniffing laughing gas. . . ."

At Seven's remark, George Brainbridge leapt to his feet. "That does it," he cried. "That's a family secret. I mean, it was considered a really deep dark secret. My father told me never to speak of it. I caught Granddad sniffing laughing gas fairly often. Summers my parents went abroad; my dad was a dandy of sorts, to be frank, a social climber. We had a housekeeper, and summers I stayed home with her and my grandfather up until the year of his death. Later I went with my parents, or to summer camp. It *must* have been my grandfather you saw one way or the other; hell, he let me sniff once, too; he was fairly old by then. I had a ball."

"Then we *did* see a ghost?" Gregory Diggs asked. "Now you're putting *me* on. He was solid, I tell you."

"It must have to do with relativity," George exclaimed. "Or timewarps. That must be involved. Einstein's theory of relativity, not that I understand it. Something about time and space being relative. Anyhow, there's got to be a scientific explanation. Shit, I'm not going to take all of this lying down. I'm going to get to the bottom of it. Weren't you pretty shaken, Seven, when you saw my grandfather strolling around?"

Seven grinned. "No. I liked him. I take things as they are. That means I'm a pragmatist, doesn't it? I mean, what happens, happens. It's silly to try and pretend it away."

"Super, super," George said, in a booming voice. "My position exactly. If people don't like it, they can go to hell." But then he shook his head again.

"That sounds great," he said. "Only why did this have to happen to me? It's going to be impossible to explain to anyone else, yet we can't just ignore it. Particularly Gregory's healing . . . I can still see those damn diseased gums as they were—and then whammo, they're perfectly healthy. I've got to see John Window's therapist."

"Maybe he won't let you see Window," Gregory said, almost hopefully.

But George said, "I'd like to see him stop me. Now that I'm convinced, we're going to see this thing through."

"That's what I'm afraid of," said Gregory. And Oversoul Seven was beginning to feel the same way.

∼ *Chapter Ten* ∼

Seven and George Meet Dr. Josephine Blithe,
and Christ Disappears

G eorge Brainbridge felt at a definite disadvantage. For one thing, he
was sweaty and hot. It was his afternoon off, but he'd already gone to
the homes of two patients who couldn't get to the office, and now he was
dying for a cold beer. He wore shorts and a short-sleeved sportshirt, plus the
old sneakers he always put on the minute his office hours were over.

On the other hand, Dr. Josephine Blithe of the Psych Center obviously
went in for appearances. Her blue summer suit was impeccably neat; her
black hair didn't show a spot of perspiration at the temples, and her
armpits were dry. Mentally George groaned; she was probably one of those
professional women who had to prove that they were, well, professional.
Her smile was social, polite, cool, and guarded.

"Dr. Brainbridge? Right on time," she said, with a hint of a raised eye-
brow as she glanced at his rather hairy, almost but not quite pudgy, thighs.
"I understand you want to discuss one of the patients, a Mr. John Window."

She hadn't said, "Sit down" yet, but George did, sitting in the upholstered chair facing her desk. He crossed his thighs, and grinned engagingly,
"Now as a dentist, I know about teeth. No mystery there. The mind's something else, though. And that's your field."

"Uh, hold it," she said. "And this is?" She indicated Oversoul Seven who
had entered diffidently behind George. George grinned, again engagingly.

"Uh, my associate. I didn't think you'd mind, but if you do, of course. . . ." He'd asked Seven at the last moment. He still didn't know why. And Seven hadn't been included in the appointment.

Josephine Blithe stared hard at Seven, then smiled as if she meant it and said, "Okay, you can stay," and George grinned inwardly, thinking that for some damn reason, everyone seemed to like Seven. Seven just nodded politely and sat down.

Then Josephine said to George, "There's always the matter of confidentiality, of course."

"Always," George said, settling himself a bit more comfortably. Josephine seemed to shrink back slightly, a fact George noticed at once. What was the matter with her? he wondered, with slight irritation. Hadn't she seen a man in shorts before?

"The patient you're interested in is John Window. On the phone you didn't tell me anything more. So suppose you fill me in?" Josephine said in a prim, distant voice.

"Hell, I was hoping you could fill *me* in," George replied, lighting a cigarette. "I admit I'm stumped, or I wouldn't be here. This guy thinks he's Christ, right? Well, that's one thing. But I've another problem, and before I tell you about it, I'd like to ask you a few rather off-beat questions."

"Oh?" she said.

"Has this guy ever . . . healed anyone of anything? Hell, I don't know any other way to put it," George said, so embarrassed that he felt himself sweating more profusely than before.

"*Healed* anyone? Oh, that's rich." Her sudden laugh was so brittle and falsely brilliant that George almost leapt to his feet in alarm. She was terrified, the laugh told him that.

He was accustomed to people's behavior under the stress of dental work. Some laughed one moment and were hysterical the next. And Josephine Blithe was laughing that kind of laugh. But why? And what was she frightened of? She caught herself, though, and went from the fake humor right into an equally fake simplistic explanation that anyone could see she didn't believe herself.

"Oh, forgive me," she said, daintily wiping away the tears of laughter with a linen handkerchief. "You've heard those delightful impossible *stories!* Honestly." She leaned forward in her chair, smiling across the desk with assumed frankness. "In a place like this, the line between fact and fiction frequently gets confused," stated Josephine in her brisk, professional manner. "People imagine things, of course. And with someone around who believes he's Christ, well, the rumors fly. Suggestion is an important *culprit* in this respect, I'm afraid. But is that why you wanted to talk about John Window? He's harmless enough, I assure you; in fact, he's a custodian here. . . ."

She was out of breath. George saw with some not unkind satisfaction that there were sweat beads above her lips. "I don't think you believe that," he said.

Her eyes flew open. They turned defiant. "I beg your pardon," she said.

Seven had purposely remained silent. Now he said, "I think George means that you're perceptive and knowledgeable enough to wonder yourself about John Window's behavior. Uh, we aren't here in any kind of official context," Seven added, in a conspiratorial tone, "We understand that you have to be careful in your capacity as psychologist here."

George shook his head. Careful about what? He wondered. What was Seven getting at? Whatever it was, Josephine Blithe certainly responded. She suddenly relaxed, and the strain went out of her shoulders. "Yes, I *do* have to be careful," she replied. "Thank you for recognizing that fact."

"I always put my foot in my mouth," said George with that self-deprecating grin. "Seven, here, is more diplomatic, I guess. So anyhow I'll put this question to you. Do you think that Window is capable of perpetrating a fraud, or taking part in a con game of any kind?"

She was honestly shocked; scandalized. "I definitely do not," she said, her voice severe again. "Now maybe you'd better tell me what you really have in mind." She half turned, glancing out the window. Then decisively she swung around again. "Well?" she demanded.

"Okay, what we have is this," George replied, staring at his hands. "I have a patient whose gums were in a state of advanced deterioration. Two days later, those same gums were perfectly healthy and the teeth were tight. The patient said that John Window healed him, here, in this institution. Now I just don't know what to do with this."

Seven said softly, "At first George thought fraud might be involved, that the one patient was actually a set of identical twins, one with good gums and one with bad. But now we understand that there *was* no fraud."

Again George shook his head. It must be the heat, he thought, because he was having trouble distinguishing Seven's words, but their tone was instantly comforting. Moreover, this reassuring effect carried over to Dr. Blithe, too, because the muscles of her face relaxed again.

"We aren't accusing Window of anything," Seven said, in that same voice. "If Window *does* have any extraordinary abilities, we thought you'd be aware of it, and George thought that this would put you in a very uneasy position."

The words were getting through to George, and he stared at Seven with abashed admiration. Seven was a natural psychologist!

So George said, "That's why we decided to bring this thing to you, rather than to anyone else."

"I knew it, I knew it would happen someday," Josephine Blithe cried. Then, in a rush, "If you knew the strain I've been under. It's a wonder *I'm* in my right mind! I knew this thing would get out sometime, that John would heal the wrong person — somebody who would talk to the authorities, or something. Actually, I guess I'm relieved. At least I can share this incredible burden with someone else." She paced the floor.

George was completely astonished. His face had a rosy, sweaty, quizzical grin. "Share what? What burden? Are you telling us that Window *does* heal? I mean, he really does this?" Now George was scandalized by the turn of events. How could an accredited psychologist say such a thing? "I thought surely you'd convince me that suggestion was somehow responsible," he said, almost shouting. "I couldn't see how on earth it could be, but I thought a psychologist would — " He stopped in mid-sentence, ashamed of himself.

Josephine Blithe moved, standing right in front of him, and said in a hard resentful voice; "You're not going to get out of this now, even if you want to, because I'm going to tell you more than you want to know."

Silence.

Dr. Josephine Blithe stood in the center of her office, staring at George Brainbridge. Her stance was alive with challenge. In the sudden quiet, bees buzzed loudly in the shrubs outside the open window, through which George saw patients and visitors walking the shaded paths. Oversoul Seven coughed.

George said, "I have the damnedest feeling that I should just get out of here while the going's good." He paused, glanced quizzically at Seven, and wiped his sweating face with a Kleenex. "What do you think, pal?" he asked.

"Why not see it through?" Seven answered, but he was uneasy on George's behalf. Besides that, he felt intriguing comprehensions skirt around the corners of his mind, but he couldn't seem to catch them.

"Well? Make up your mind," Josephine said. Her hands were on her hips, and her dark eyes were wide with either anticipation or anger, George couldn't tell which.

"Okay," he said, grinning. "I'll probably regret it, but what the hell."

With that, Dr. Blithe sat down and almost seemed to go into a reverie.

"I really don't know where to start, don't you know," she said in a soft, distant voice. "So I'll tell you about my first meeting with John Window, and fill in the details later." She raised her dark brows with a jerky, nervous motion, paused, and went on quickly as if afraid that she'd never tell the whole story unless she did it now.

"This is a small community institution. Clients get a fair amount of attention, but the emphasis is on getting the less disturbed ones into decent shape so they can get back out into the world. We have 'half-way houses' for them. Sometimes they become outpatients. But John and a few others caused no problems here; they had jobs of a kind within the institution and for various reasons, no one figured they'd be able to make it outside. So I suppose they ended up with less attention. Anyway, I'd been here several weeks before I got to check John's chart and set up an appointment.

"Well, I had a miserable migraine headache that day. I'd taken medication, but nothing seemed to help much. It was just after lunch. I felt vaguely sick to my stomach. Then John Window came for his first appointment with me. I'd read his file. Later I'll show it to you, but that doesn't matter now. Have you met him? Oh, of course, you worked on his teeth. Well, there he was, a quite ordinary man, medium everything, medium height, coloring, weight. Nothing distinctive. I found myself wondering that he was imaginative enough to ever believe he was Christ. I introduced myself. He sat where you're sitting now, Dr. Brainbridge. May I call you George?"

George nodded.

"George," she said. "Anyway, we didn't mention Christ. He said he was John Window. In my first interviews with clients, I go gently to set up a good rapport if possible, so we talked briefly about innocuous subjects. I must have glanced out the window or perhaps checked my watch, because I didn't catch the transition at all. When I looked up, well, something happened. He said, mildly enough, 'Christ, here. Now let's get rid of that headache. You see? It's quite gone.' And everything about him had changed. The very *ordinariness* of his appearance magnified, so that he seemed to represent all men. It was as if *ordinariness* was raised to an incredible degree. So that it wasn't ordinary at all, of course." (She wet her lips.) "And in that instant my headache vanished. And mind you, I hadn't even told him I had a headache."

George Brainbridge stood up and started pacing the room. Seven felt sorry for him and for Josephine Blithe, too; how difficult it must be, he thought, when you found miracles so hard to accept.

Josephine paused. Her face reddened. "I was shocked. I mean, wouldn't you think I would have been delighted first of all? But my first thought was, 'This is awful; he can't do that.' And he — John Window or Christ or whoever — smiled exactly as if he knew what I was thinking. Even as all that went through my head, though, John was John again. He seemed not to know what had happened. I thought he was pretending, but he wasn't. His face was guileless. But I was — unbelievably I guess — almost in a fury. I told him that we'd have to cut the interview short; that I'd forgotten another appointment, and I really hustled him to the door."

She stopped; out of breath. The bees in the shrubs sounded loudly again. George looked embarrassed and shook his head.

"Now *that* could have been suggestion," George said. "I don't know much about it, but aren't migraines emotionally based?"

Josephine glared at him, placed her hands on her hips and stood up, legs spread out, the tips of her summer sandals pointing in almost opposite directions. "I'm aware of the emotional aspects of migraine," she said in a cold, even voice. "And up to that point, mine had always lasted several days. I used to get them every other week or so. Well, I haven't had one since, and that was six months ago." Her voice softened. She brought her feet together almost primly and said, "I shouldn't blame you, though. I was so upset about the whole thing that I avoided John Window like the plague for a while. I kept making excuses for not seeing him until finally I couldn't stand myself, of course. . . ."

She lowered her voice again. "There are other incidents too, but for now, here are the main points. I'd be passing through the corridors and find a small group around Window, or maybe he'd be standing there with just one patient. They protect him, I've had evidence of that, I'll tell you later . . . But *some* patients that I'd worked with, without any discernible results— well, they suddenly improved remarkably well; well enough to be released. And I'd seen John talking to those same patients. I can't tell you how I knew what he was doing, but there'd be a circle of secrecy or *conspiracy* about all of them when I found them. In each case — it happened three times — John would be Christ while they talked. He reverted to Window the minute I came by, looking at me with that same damned ignorance or innocence. . . ."

"Nothing you could prove one way or the other," George muttered.

Without warning, Dr. Blithe almost bent over with laughter. Tears ran down her face. George sprang forward, wondering what the devil she was up to. Eyes half closed, she reached for her linen handkerchief. "Oh, I'm sorry. I've held all this in for so long. You understand? I haven't told any- one. But—" She looked George straight in the face for a moment before she started laughing again, and in between gasps, she cried, "Proof? Uh. No proof at all. But since John's been here we have one of the highest rates of cures in the East. Patients spend less time in here and are released to soci- ety far quicker than at institutions with far greater facilities and professional staffs. And . . ." Her laughing stopped at once. "Before too long, some- body's going to wonder how come."

George stared at her unbelievingly. "You're not trying to tell me that this guy . . . cures mental patients?"

She nodded vigorously. "Not only that, but embarrassingly enough, I get a good deal of the credit. I'm the only full-time psychologist in this wing of the center. We're dealing with disturbed people here, of course; the really bad cases are in another wing entirely. So we're not talking about severe psychotics."

George and Josephine had nearly forgotten Seven, as he'd hoped they would. He just sat quietly, listening, growing more amazed at human reactions with each moment. Just why did George and Josephine consider Window's miracles so disrupting and unwelcome?

Couldn't they see that they were manufacturing a problem where none existed? Obviously they couldn't, so somewhere he himself had failed to understand their reasoning or motivation.

If he weren't so confused about all this, Seven thought, he'd probably also know why George and Josephine were ignoring so much else that was happening around them. Like the fantastic June afternoon, in which Seven almost kept losing himself. What a delightful corner of the universe! he kept thinking, whenever he took his mind off the conversation for an instant. The air in the room smelled of the roses that climbed up the decorative iron filigrees just outside the window. The shrubs were alive with insects, bees, and birds. The damp yet sweet odor of the river swirled invisibly, and appreciating all of this, Seven almost forgot George's and Josephine's predicament.

Not for long, though. When he came to himself again, Seven saw that Josephine was near tears, though controlling herself with obvious difficulty. George stood nearby, looking concerned and embarrassed. So Seven leapt to his feet, all crisp efficiency. "This can all be figured out," he said to Dr. Blithe. "Certainly science doesn't have all the answers yet." Josephine instantly brightened, causing George Brainbridge to think, "That was exactly the thing to say." He was again astonished at Seven's sensitivity.

"I know," Josephine replied. "That's what's kept me going, of course, the chance of discovering something. . . . Perhaps some psychological mechanism that would lead to healing. And when Window thinks he's Christ, he heals. Window himself can't heal anything. So how could his obsession release abilities . . . ?" Her voice trailed off in confusion.

"You're kidding," George Brainbridge thundered. Then *he* started laughing. "I've got the solution, then. Get rid of Window's obsession, and we don't have any problems!" He grinned with feigned wickedness, leered, then added slowly, "Hey, that's not a bad idea. Could you do it?"

Oversoul Seven was so scandalized by the suggestion that he just stared at George with true horror.

"I . . . just couldn't do that," Josephine said, frowning. "I thought of it . . . of trying, I mean." She paused, threw her head back defiantly, and again her glance was full of challenge. "He *does* have some kind of healing ability.

Your experience with the boy's gums proves that. What right have any of us to rob him of that, just so he'll fit into our preconceived ideas of normality? That's why I've been stymied . . . and you're talking as if science really knew how to cure obsession."

"Yeah," George said. His face reddened. He felt ashamed of himself and at a disadvantage again. His pragmatism came to his aid: "Well, if that's what we're faced with, we may as well admit it," he said, in a hearty almost blustery way. "As long as we know our feet are on the ground. *Any* ground. Can I see this Window? I've got to start someplace."

By now Dr. Josephine Blithe looked considerably subdued. She nodded. "There's one thing, though. I want to be there, too," she said. "And we have to be very careful. When John is Christ, he's quite paranoid."

"Jesus . . . " George muttered in a long drawn-out voice.

"Wait here," Josephine directed. "I'll check and see when I can slate Window for an appointment. Actually I'm relieved. I didn't want to talk to him alone." She left the room.

George lit a cigarette and shook his head at Seven. "I just don't believe this," he said.

"Why not?" Seven asked in an oddly clear voice that somehow made George uncomfortable. Why not? He began listing all of the reasons that made the entire affair seem quite unbelievable when Dr. Josephine Blithe came hurriedly back into the room. Her face was white.

"Window isn't around anywhere," she cried. "No one's seen him since early morning."

"Jesus!" George said.

"He won't even go out on the plaza, though he's allowed to. He's too afraid of strangers," Josephine said with a very worried air. "I'll have to report this, of course. But where would he go? And why? I mean, he liked it here."

"Yeah?" George replied ironically. "Well we'd better find him fast." Without knowing exactly why, George Brainbridge was a very frightened man. He felt as if some remarkable crisis had emerged in his life, one that threatened all of his beliefs and values.

~ *Chapter Eleven* ~

The Museum of Time

While Oversoul Seven was concentrating on George Brainbridge's problems he was, of course, simultaneously involved with all of his other personalities as well. Since he had a body to contend with, too, this demanded a multiplication of focuses that Seven was still in the process of perfecting. He was also having experiences with his teacher, Cyprus, who was monitoring his actions from her own impeccable viewpoint.

For example, even as George Brainbridge was saying to Dr. Josephine Blithe, "Maybe we can find John Window before anyone realizes he's missing," Oversoul Seven suddenly heard Cyprus' voice; and when he did, he managed to stay in Josephine's office (nodding his head, he hoped, in the right places) while his main consciousness formed a small bit of light that played on the ceiling. Cyprus was another spot of light, dancing at the top of the window.

"None of this will do at all," Cyprus said. She moved at the speed of light, of course, as did Seven, so their conversation took hardly any time at all.

"I know it won't do," Seven cried. "Where have you been? Just tell me where Window is, that's all, and I'll straighten things out somehow."

Cyprus sighed. "You *know* I can't tell you," she said. "That would be cheating —"

"So cheat," Seven replied. "Look at George. He's half out of his mind. He doesn't even understand miracles."

Cyprus smiled, looking down at the rumpled George, who was wiping the perspiration from his face and saying, "I bet that damn Gregory Diggs took Window somewhere to protect him."

The physical Seven nodded vigorously, yet to Cyprus' and Seven's consciousnesses, the motions and sounds of the room were incredibly slow.

"But why?" Josephine asked.

"I see what you mean," Cyprus said sympathetically. "I'll give you some hints. First, remember the message you received earlier about the Codicils. They're vitally important. And remember that all of your personalities are involved in one way or another with the activities of any *one* of them. And in earth terms of course, you do have a deadline."

"A deadline?" Seven asked, more uneasy than ever.

"Oh, Seven, just find Window," Cyprus said, softly. "I'll give you another clue; follow your impulses. And in physical terms, hurry! You *do* know where he is."

"I do?" Seven said, wonderingly. But instantly he was fully back in his body, which George Brainbridge was nudging with his elbow.

"Come on, let's get going," George demanded.

Almost teetering on her high-heeled sandals, Josephine Blithe said, with bitter amusement, "Yeah, we're off to see the Wizard of Oz."

"Super," Seven said, complimenting himself on making a suitable reply under somewhat confusing conditions.

The conditions became even more confused — and disorganized, Seven thought, as the afternoon progressed. First they searched the Psych Center — as nonchalantly as possible — for Window or for Gregory Diggs. When this failed, they all piled into George's Porsche and began driving up and down the streets in the hopes of sighting one or the other.

"If we drive up and down past this shopping center one more time, I'll go crazy," Josephine said finally. "We've been everywhere around town with no sign of either of them. For all we know, they're on a bus to Timbuktu or somewhere. We don't even know for sure if they're together." She sighed. Her makeup was caking from the heat; her shoes hurt, and she didn't like being crowded so close to George Brainbridge in the car's front seat.

From the small back seat, Seven said, "Let's park and talk a minute. Maybe we can think of a plan of action. Park in front of your place, George, why don't you? Where it's cool." Seven didn't know why he mentioned parking in front of George's, but the minute he did, he remembered the odd time-transfers that had happened in the spot where George's house stood. Follow your impulses, Cyprus had said. Was that what she meant?

"It's okay with me," George replied with weary resignation.

Josephine eased one shoe off and rubbed one heel with the other one. They pulled up in front of George's house. "I don't see the point of this," Josephine said with a worried air. "We're just not getting anyplace."

Seven was tempted to agree.

"Hell, we'll find him sometime," George replied, without conviction. "If he's in town, that is."

But Seven was suddenly alert; George's words made brilliant sense — "We'll find him some *time*" — Seven thought. Of course!

"Your car windows need a good washing," Josephine said for something to say, and Seven stared at her. Did she realize what else her words meant besides what they were saying? Probably not. But when Josephine said the word "windows" Seven was suddenly reminded of someone he'd entirely forgotten. ("Well, not entirely of course," he said later to Cyprus.) He remembered another man, one whose name was Window — a personality of his, who was in the twenty-third century, the last time Seven checked. And John Window was like an unclear version of the twenty-third-century Window. He was, Seven thought with sudden inspiration, like a window that needed cleaning because it was distorting a view. . . .

"Yeah, I know. I'll clean 'em before Jean comes home," George said. "She always complains about that, too."

In that moment Seven knew that something was going to happen, and he didn't want George or Josephine around when it did. On impulse, he opened the car door and squeezed himself out. "I think I'll sit on the porch a while," he said, a bit apologetically. "The heat's really getting to me. It's getting toward suppertime, but I'm not even hungry. Why don't you two get a bite and pick me up afterward? In the meantime, 'I'll think a lot,'" he said, borrowing one of George's pet phrases.

Josephine shook her head. "No food for me. But I think we should check the center again. George can look outside, and I'll go in on some pretext or other. . . ."

Seven nodded impatiently because he could already feel times changing. The car turned the corner just as the road itself disappeared.

Seven sprang to his feet, as the house behind him disappeared; so did just about everything else. In a bewildering display, objects again appeared, disappeared, and were replaced by others.

Finally Seven remembered a knack of dealing with such events, one that he'd learned (somewhere? when?) and forgotten. He stared directly ahead, and when the next object — a small tree — appeared there, Seven kept his gaze riveted on the spot. Everything disappeared again, and now the tree was taller. So he was going into the future; at least he had *that* settled, he thought. And he wanted to find Window of the twenty-third century to see what connections there were between him and his namesake in the twentieth century. If he found the future Window . . . would he automatically find the twentieth-century one?

Seven was blinking furiously. The tree was full-grown, then dead; then the spot was vacant. A hut appeared, then the spot was empty again. Then new growth . . . Seven groaned; the spot looked more or less the way it had when he'd found himself in the twenty-fifth century with the floating cities. If so, he'd gone two centuries too far. But before he could think of anything to do about this, the environment began to stabilize. He looked up, his suspicions confirmed. The landscape looked more or less deserted, and in the sky the floating cities caught the rays of the sun like glittering, round kites.

Seven gulped; something decidedly unpleasant had happened in this latest time change. Instead of grass, the ground was covered with a sickly brown layer of vegetation that almost looked like the thin wisps of hair on a bald man's head. And beneath, the ground was almost gray in color. The only trees were dwarfed crooked ones, hardly three feet tall at most; and though the air was warm enough (meaning it was still summer), there were no flowers or birds or — Seven listened intently — or insects; or if there were, they were ominously still.

As he looked about, Oversoul Seven felt a deepening sense of desolation. Here, in the very spot where George Brainbridge's house stood in easy hearing distance of the busy traffic of Water Street; where the busy twentieth-century air was full of activity — now, in the twenty-fifth century, all of that had vanished; the Earth for all purposes was a deserted, sterile world. Seven let his consciousness roam. While he stood disconsolately, his mind traveled over the nearly blank landscape. In the flash of a human eye, Seven's consciousness leapt from continent to continent. Even the seas were sluggish, and the vegetation had sloughed off the mountains so that only here or there one lonely dwarfed tree remained. What had happened?

Seven was almost overwhelmed by the desolation; he was an Earth soul after all. So what if some mortals dwelled in the manufactured cities above the earth? What heritages had been lost? What physical echoes no longer sounded in the blood?

Window wouldn't be found here, Seven realized suddenly. This world had no inhabitants. Then where was the precise future probability that Window belonged in? Besides, wasn't Window in the twenty-third century, not the twenty-fifth?

Then why had he come *here*? Seven wondered. Cyprus, he knew, would say, "Trust yourself, even your seeming mistakes." But what good would *that* do? Seven nervously looked around again. He wanted to get out of *this* probability as quickly as possible. But maybe the century was somehow right, even though he was positive that Window had been in the twenty-third century last time he remembered.

Scowling, Seven stared directly before him again, this time at a spindly, dead gray twig. Probabilities, he knew, were like tangents out from a certain time . . . they were horizontal extensions, sort of. So he stared at the twig and stared and stared. Finally it began to blur just a bit. At the same time, he felt as if he were just looking through his right eye, or tipping very gently sidewards to the right, or leaning psychologically to the right. At least this is how he tried to explain it to himself as everything — ground, sky, Seven, and all his thoughts — suddenly took a turn in one probability and shifted into another. The time was still the twenty-fifth century, for the three floating cities still hung in the sky. The twig (or its double? or triple?) was now infinitesimally to the right of the first one. The distance was so small it could never be physically measured. But Seven knew he was in a different world.

This became apparent at once as new objects kept appearing everywhere, so quickly that Seven leapt back. When he did, something struck his leg or his leg struck something, and he spun around, rubbing his eyes with momentary disbelief.

There stood what looked at first to be George Brainbridge's house in the twentieth century, and what he'd brushed up against was the hitching post that George had kept from his grandfather's time, as a decoration. Only now, it was to the right of the porch, just by the steps, instead of out by the curb. The house itself was even more confusing for it resembled George's so completely, and yet glaring distortions or differences were everywhere. It looked to be of brick, yet at the same time, it appeared to be made of some much lighter material. The three windows were right in the front waiting room, but there were also three windows on the left side, where Seven was sure George's house had only two. Besides that, though, *this* house looked newly constructed, or too good to be true, or somehow unused.

Seven stepped back to get a better look, and then saw the neat sign. It read: "The Ancient House of Many Windows: believed to be a perfect replica of a structure that actually stood in this spot roughly from 1860 to 2010. The original tell, explored in the twenty-third century, delivered artifacts that led historical designers to begin their detailed assessment of the structure. Later excavations gave further data. The discovery of the *original* Codicils was made only five years ago when an ancient bomb shelter was evacuated at a deeper level. This peoples' museum is open to the public. Further information on the Codicils inside."

The Codicils? Seven could hardly contain his excitement. Yet he was uneasy because no one was about. He sat down on the steps, looking toward the river.

The riverbank had changed; the old dikes built in George's time were now buried under new topsoil. The river must have flooded many times and then widened somehow, for now it ran deeper and wider below a high bank of planted shrubbery and trees. Seven saw no roads, only natural, well-tended paths, and he realized that he was in the middle of a park area. The surroundings were so pleasant that he was almost tempted to walk down to the river, but he sighed, and walked up the steps to the museum's porch.

Hesitantly he opened the front door. It was far lighter in weight than George's twentieth-century door, even though the material looked the same. No sooner had the door opened and Seven glimpsed the layout of the rooms off the hall, than a man's figure appeared coming down the front stairwell.

"Good afternoon," the man said. "You've missed the tour scheduled for the past hour. I can give you a private tour, however, although it won't be as extensive as the group one. Will you follow me, please?"

Seven was confused, at least momentarily. The man vaguely reminded him of the twenty-third-century Window, with his long, severe nose and intent eyes. But there was no consciousness involved at all with this figure, even though it was three-dimensional.

Before Seven could comment, the man came closer, turned in a graceful circle so that Seven could see his back, faced Seven again and said with quiet authority, "I am Monarch, appearing as a hologram and acting as your guide."

"A hologram! I should have known at once," Seven said. It was impossible not to admire the hologram: the skin, hair, eyes—everything in fact—was perfect, and the illusion of depth was flawless. Seeing Monarch's face (or rather, the image of it), Seven was almost certain that the hologram's original was also Window of the twenty-third century. Not that the features were the same, but that Seven kept seeing Window's features superimposed over the hologram's.

When Seven didn't move to follow him, the hologram-man said, "Have you a question? Technology has advanced so that I can answer almost any question that a tourist might ask, though—"

"Where is the real Window, I mean Monarch?"

"In his study. He's the force behind the evacuations and the construction of this museum. Appointments may be arranged. His administration building is a mile away, taking the western footpath which is clearly marked.

Now, if you'll step into the next room, this, it is believed, was an ancient dentist's office — "

Seven took one startled glance at the open doorway through which he saw what was supposed to be a reconstructed version of George's dentist's chair. At once he saw that it was the mismatched combination of such chairs from at least four different historical periods, all put together in one. Just inside the door was a table bearing dental tools from both the nineteenth and twentieth centuries, and the label by them read: "Dental instruments."

Seven paused. "Sir?" said the hologram-man.

"I haven't time for a tour," Seven said impatiently. "I have to find Window. Uh, thanks for your attention. Super."

"I beg your pardon?" said the hologram-man. "I'm not familiar with the meaning of the last term in that context . . . " But Seven was gone, and when the door closed, the hologram-man was deactivated as the laser beams that formed his image disappeared.

As he left the museum, Seven wondered if he should have found out what the Codicils were. He knew Cyprus had said that they were vitally important. But it was imperative that he find John Window. And if he was right — a big if, Seven reminded himself — then *maybe* Window (or Monarch) in this future probability would somehow help him find the twentieth-century Window.

Seven found the western path with no difficulty. As he walked along as fast as he could, he couldn't forget that this same spot of footpaths and tall shady trees existed in the space where Water Street and Walnut Street intersected. No, he realized: in the twentieth-century reality, he would have already turned and walked up Walnut Street. And somewhere in that area, George Brainbridge and Dr. Josephine Blithe were cruising around in George's car, looking for John Window.

Seven hoped he kept the whole thing straight. He could hear himself later telling Cyprus that this had been the most complicated venture she'd ever sent him on. The fantasy in his mind faded, though, as he finally approached a large stone building with many verandas. Seven shook his head . . . this was a beautiful but hardly faithful replica of the old Christian Science church that sat on the corner of Church and Walnut Streets in George's time. A small plaque read: "Administration Building."

Was Window — Seven caught himself — Monarch inside? There was only one way to find out. Seven walked up the steps . . . and the door automatically opened.

As Seven stepped over the doorsill, he saw Monarch sitting at the end of a long, wide corridor. Seven quickly recognized him as the model of the hologram-man. But more than that, Seven's consciousness merged at once with Monarch's and, joyfully, Seven realized that Monarch and Window *were* the same and yet different. They were counterparts of each other, living in different times and yet more connected than brothers. And that meant . . . of course! Seven thought. John Window was also one of *his own* personalities, a counterpart of the others—and he had let himself forget these connections so that the various personalities would be free to seek their own ways unless or until they needed his help. And now they did.

But as soon as Seven recognized Monarch as the twenty-fifth-century Window and made other connections—and even as Monarch looked up with a glance of polite inquiry—the objects and space itself began to shimmer again, wrinkle into itself, blink off and on until, blinking himself, Seven found himself standing inside the twentieth-century Christian Science church, in the reading room, staring at a startled John Window and Gregory Diggs.

"How on earth did you find us *here?* I've never even been in a church in my life before," Gregory Diggs said, as Seven appeared in the doorway.

"It's a long story," Seven replied. He felt relieved, surprised, and out of breath.

"Verily," Window replied.

"He's Christ again," Gregory said, "and I'm going to see that nobody takes advantage of him."

Seven shook his head. It was still hot, and his polyester suit wasn't even wrinkled. "What *are* you doing here?" he asked.

Diggs scowled defensively. "I'm showing Christ here that some people believe that healing is natural. He doesn't have to be afraid either because . . . well, these people say there isn't no evil either. They left bulletins at the center, so I thought we'd see what they had to offer. Nobody's going to crucify you either, because. . . ." Diggs said this last to John Window, who now believed he was Christ again. And Window stared sorrowfully at Oversoul Seven and said, "Are you Judas? Have you come to betray me?"

"Jesus Christ," Diggs said under his breath, to Seven. "Now see what you've done! Will you get out of here?"

"Hurry. Run to the door and drag Window with you," Seven cried. "If my deductions are right, George's car should be passing this place right now."

Diggs, grunting, pushed the unhappy John Window to the door. Seven threw it open. And George's car was right out front—in the very spot where Monarch's door opened in the twenty-fifth century.

Josephine saw the trio at once and told George to stop the car. They all piled in and drove off.

~ Chapter Twelve ~

Window Speaks for Monarch,
and Seven Is Worried

Window, who still thought he was Christ, kept staring sadly at George and asking, "Are you Judas?" even as Seven hustled him and Gregory Diggs into the small sportscar.

"No he's a friend," Gregory kept repeating each time Window asked. They were all crowded in the car together. Josephine wrinkled her nose at George's hairy and sweaty thighs and yelled over the sound of the motor: "I borrowed John's files." She waved a folder.

The car windows were all open, but it was still stifling. George looked anxious. Window's Christ face was calm but resigned. George started driving up Church Street and asked rhetorically, "Well, what now?"

"Let's eat," Seven said. "Why not give Window a good meal in a restaurant? He missed supper at the Center, didn't he? And then we can figure out what to do next."

"I don't know," Josephine said dubiously.

"Why not?" Gregory demanded. "He could stand a treat. He's not going to embarrass anyone, if that's what you're afraid of."

"Yeah. What the hell," George said, grinning. "I've never had dinner with Christ before."

Josephine glared at him. Seven grinned. Window in his Christ voice said, "I hope it's not the Last Supper. It's not easy being Christ in this day and age."

"You just think you're Christ," Gregory said reproachfully. "I thought we settled that when we had our talk."

"Well, that isn't easy, either," Window said, intelligently enough, Seven thought. "You all eat," Window continued, cordially. "I'm fasting."

George was relieved when everyone decided on the next restaurant they came to. He was tired, wondering what on earth he was getting into, and John Window disconcerted him. For one thing, Window looked innocuous enough, and George had rather expected a more wild-eyed man, even though in the dentist's chair he'd been mild enough. But George hadn't heard of the healing then, and knowing about it now made him expect Window to demonstrate some bizarre behavior. (Damn, he thought, anybody could *say* he was Christ. If Window believed it, why didn't he do something now while George had his eye on him?)

They filed into the restaurant. The minute they sat down, they were all gripped by an air of expectancy—all but Window, who smiled amiably and said to Gregory Diggs: "I knew taking me away from the Center wouldn't work; that they'd find us."

"Yeah," Diggs replied, dourly.

"Let's decide on dinner and then talk," Seven said, with a brisk smile, because he was uneasy himself and wanted to discover why before anything happened that he couldn't control.

They were silent, reading their menus. The restaurant was quiet, with only a few patrons. "It's quiet in all the local restaurants," George said, too loudly. "Everybody's at their cottages."

Josephine Blithe ignored the statement, wet her lips, smiled earnestly, and said to Window, "John, do you believe you're Christ right now?"

"*John?*" George muttered; grinning suddenly.

"Of course, John, no need for formality. We're friends aren't we, John? You remember, we've talked before."

And suddenly, with Josephine's question, the area of interest shifted to John Window. He had the floor and he knew it. He even smiled in acknowledgment. Until this point, he had been almost unreal to them, hardly a person at all. ("In a funny fashion, he seemed almost anonymous, particularly for someone causing so much fuss," Seven told Cyprus later. And she replied, "Of course. It's too bad you didn't understand why, then.")

"Verily," John Window said, "I'm John Window who thinks he's Christ. Or I'm Christ who thinks he's John Window. This *is* a dilemma to me and, I understand, to others. I am a man of strange education; that is, what I've learned seems to have been taught to me someplace else. And I am quite articulate. Gregory has taught me to come out of the closet, as they say; I've been a closet Christ. Or a closet John Window. I'm not sure which. Does any of this answer any of your questions?" He started to eat his meal. He'd ordered fish and chips after Gregory talked him into fasting tomorrow instead.

Dr. Josephine Blithe smiled professionally. "You're doing fine, just fine," she said.

George was quite taken aback. "You don't sound crazy to me," he said. "You sure as hell sound strange. But you make it sound as if there's sense there someplace."

"I've considered all of this often," Window said, looking at George. "It's a peculiar position to be in particularly since I think that Christianity has done as much harm as good. It's seen its time. So why would anyone want to be Christ in this day and age?"

"You tell me," George said, a trifle embarrassed. Window's eyes never left George's face. Finally George blew his nose.

They'd all heard John Window speak at least briefly before, but now all of them at the same time were struck by a clear transparent quality in his voice, as if each word he spoke was somehow inevitable, and meant for them alone. Josephine struggled to maintain her professional, superior stance. "*Very* good, John," she said, in a condescending voice.

George muttered, "Damn."

Gregory Diggs said to all of them, "What did I tell you?"

John Window wore jeans, a sportshirt, and sandals. George stared at him: He didn't look any different from any other male in the room. Indeed, looking at the male patrons, then back to Window, George had the weird feeling that something in each of the other men's faces was somehow reflected in Window's. Yet Window had his own features; light blue eyes, medium complexion, rather thinnish lips; and the proportions were all normal. Yet granting this, George thought stubbornly, Window's face still had a quality he'd never seen before — and that was why he couldn't get a handle on it.

Window was saying, "I know when I think I'm Window, and I know when I think I'm Christ. What really gets me thinking, though, is this: Who is the me that thinks I'm either Christ or Window?"

"Probing question, John!" Josephine said in a bubbling voice. But it was no use to pretend; whoever or whatever he was, John Window was beyond today's psychology. It couldn't explain him. She frowned. Something else was odd, too. They'd finished their suppers. Usually a waitress would come over, but their table seemed isolated in some fashion that she couldn't explain. She almost wanted to pinch the table to see if it was alive.

"Another thing," Window said. "Christ is able to heal people — but he's paranoid. He really believes he'll be crucified. Window can't heal, but he knows that somehow he has access to that ability through Christ. And Window is sane enough. He's scared, but he isn't paranoid."

"Who's speaking now?" Oversoul Seven asked quickly before anyone could interrupt. "You spoke of Christ *and* Window. So who are *you?*"

Complete silence. George held his breath. Josephine nervously scratched her stockinged leg. Window-Christ looked the most astonished of any of them. He started to speak, faltered, began again. "I'm not sure. I think my name is Monarch. Or I think it could be. Now and then I think to myself as this person."

Monarch? Seven gulped. Of course. It was possible that, with psychological bleed-throughs, such a thing could happen. Josephine opened her mouth to speak, and Seven's suddenly commanding glance stopped her. He said, "All right, Monarch, can you help Window or Christ?"

George and Gregory Diggs were so fascinated that they couldn't take their eyes from Window's face.

George muttered, "You mean he's somebody else, *too?*"

"Shush," said Gregory, urgently. "Listen."

"I *am* Window and Christ," Monarch said, in a distant voice. And suddenly Window's face did have a "someplace else" look. "Or I was. Christ is a Window who heals." Now the voice was hesitant, as if the words were coming from far away and had to be translated; and yet, again, each individual word was clear and oddly transparent — so transparent, Seven thought (too late), that they could all fall through the voice if they didn't watch out.

No one was completely sure exactly what happened next, although Seven had a very good idea, but it was one that even he had trouble accepting.

First of all, there were changes in perception. The things in the environment remained the same. Yet to George, Josephine, Gregory and Seven, each detail in the restaurant seemed suddenly more emphatic, more itself, brighter, more separate on the one hand, yet impossibly more a part of the entire environment. George happened to be looking at a glass sugar bowl, for example, and his eyes widened as it seemed to attain a different reality than it had only the moment before. The sugar glistened — tiny dazzling crystals, each individual and somehow perfect, mixed in with each other; each crystal touching another, flowing into another while retaining its own sparkling apartness. Besides this, the reflections on the sugar bowl itself became almost dazzling, seeming to belong to the bowl, to stain the glass, while simultaneously dancing above or even within it. George felt as if he were being hypnotized.

Diggs had been looking at the toe of his right shoe. Suddenly he saw it as he never had before, as if it was the most significant thing in the world, simply because it existed. The shoe seemed planted in time, in space, solid leather resting on the wooden floor. Yet it also seemed composed of thousands of specks of light, each separate yet making up the entire structure; lights interlacing and dancing within themselves, and moving with the reflections from the restaurant lights, which also seemed somehow to belong to the shoe.

Josephine's eyes had been on an edge of a menu sticking out between a napkin holder and a ketchup dispenser. Before she realized what was happening, the letters on the menu seemed to leap upward, almost as if they were written in the air above the paper. She even swore that she saw shadows fall behind the letters for an instant, before the perspective of the entire menu changed. That is, the menu now appeared to form itself about the letters so that the word *bacon* not only seemed alive in the strangest fashion, but seemed to form the rest of the menu around itself. Each word made the menu pucker or change, as in turn each word became prominent and the others faded from view almost completely. Then — she gasped — all the words came into prominence at once, so vividly that she could hardly bear to look, and each word had a hand in forming the menu upon which it was written.

George Brainbridge had been staring rather impolitely at the spot in the front of John Window's mouth where he'd removed the bad tooth. The gap was quite noticeable, and George was idly thinking that after he took out the one beside it, he'd fit Window with a bridge. Just about then, his eye roamed toward a good tooth on the other side of the gap in Window's mouth, and what happened next left George literally breathless. ("I almost peed in my pants," he said later to Josephine, who wrinkled her lips distastefully.)

That one tooth instantly took all of George's attention. He felt the life of the roots beneath, of the nerves, the rich bed of the gums, but more . . . the tooth seemed to form the gums as much as the other way around. No, that wasn't it, he thought, struggling to understand. It was as if the tooth had a part in forming the gums that would later hold it so snugly . . . as if ahead of time the tooth, knowing its reality, demanded a mouth to hold it.

All of these changes began as the man who now called himself Monarch said, "Christ is a Window who heals." And to Seven, it was as if the man had two sets of eyes, or rather, double vision. Seven saw the restaurant, precise and definite, yet the effect was as if he were looking through the small end of a telescope — one that probed into time instead of space. At the other wide end, the full-sized, flesh-and-blood Monarch of the twenty-fifth century looked out at the expanse of landscape outside the museum; he was talking to himself. Except that it was John Window's "Monarch" in the restaurant who spoke the actual words Seven heard:

"How strange to find myself in such a place and time! I feel that I lived in Christ's era and in the twentieth century and in the twenty-fifth all at once, as if I'm a set of different selves, but with one slightly out of focus. I wonder how many other people have felt this way?'

A pause. Through the double vision that Seven saw in Window's eyes, he saw Monarch smile, just as Window's seemingly miniature face did at the same time. "Maybe Monarch is a future self to other portions of my entire selfhood. Maybe Christ and Window made my existence possible."

"And vice versa," Seven whispered, wondering if both or only one Monarch would hear him.

"Of course," said "Monarch" in the restaurant, mouthing the words of the twenty-fifth-century Monarch who now mused to himself, "Perhaps I even had a hand in initiating the Codicils that I uncovered in my own time."

"The Codicils," Seven said urgently. "Quickly, tell me about them."

"They're the basis of our civilization. Without them, the world would never have survived," mused Monarch in front of the museum, as "Monarch" in the restaurant spoke the words.

A feeling of panic almost washed over Seven as he saw the implications of Monarch's answer. He asked quickly, "When? When did they originate?"

The answer came: "In the time of 'The George.' "

With those words, the alterations of perception vanished. John Window said, "I forgot what I was doing."

George Brainbridge just shook his head and muttered, "What the hell just happened?" He was staring at Window's mouth, which now appeared quite normal.

"I don't know," said Josephine, blinking at the menu which also looked quite ordinary now. And Gregory Diggs shook his head wonderingly as the tip of his shoe lost its magic.

Window thought he was Christ again. He said morosely, "This could be a modern version of the Last Supper, don't you know? I know you're my dentist, Dr. Brainbridge. But are you certain you're not Judas too?"

"Now cut that out," George muttered, but softly, not wanting to make a scene, "I'm sure. Take my word for it, will you?"

"Verily," Christ said.

"Super," George replied, with a sigh.

"Do you remember saying you were Monarch?" Seven asked. He tried not to look worried, but he had an idea that there were more time bleed-throughs than he knew what to do with, and he wanted to question Window or Christ or Monarch while he still could.

"I think Window must be a catalyst of some kind," Josephine said to George. "I've got to tell you what just happened to me."

"Ditto," George said. "I mean, you won't believe — "

"Window, did you do something to my shoe just now?" Gregory Diggs asked.

Seven tried to cut in on the conversation, or rather to put a temporary end to it so he could question Window, but Window promptly answered Gregory. "No, you just saw it the way it is," he saiᴅ, almost apologetically. "Things were complicated enough. I mean, they are. But sometimes I think I'm a future man named Monarch. When I think I'm him, people sometimes see things as they really *are.* Sometimes," he said slowly, "I suspect I have to go beyond Christ to something else."

"But you should have said something," Josephine said. "I'd have, uh, understood. Honestly, John." She reached over and touched his hand.

Window looked momentarily disconcerted. He lifted his other hand in the air, as if unsure what to do with it, then he gently placed it quickly and lightly on top of Josephine's. Her face got so red that George thought she'd suddenly developed a fever. She gave a funny muffled gasp, pulled her hand back, and just stared at Window, who said, "I was just trying to help."

"Well, I don't need your help," she whispered fiercely. "*Now* what the hell is going on?" George asked.

"Touch fire and you get burned," Gregory Diggs replied, grinning, but good-naturedly.

"Now do you see?" Window said. "I've hurt her feelings. That's another thing. Sometimes when I touch people, they touch themselves or get in touch with themselves, and it makes them angry. And I never know when that's going to happen."

Josephine grabbed her white-beaded pocketbook, sprang to her feet, and walked as quickly as she could to the door. It was obvious that she was holding back tears. George Brainbridge, looking bewildered, followed her. "Now what?" he said, as she opened the door.

She leaned against the outside of the building, dabbing at her eyes with a handkerchief. "He just did it again," she gasped. "Only this time, well, he . . . picked up a secret of mine, and told me not to worry about it. . . . "

"But he didn't *say* anything," George protested. "Just touched your hand."

"Yeah? Well, that was enough," she said, in an almost harsh voice, abandoning her lady-like manner. George grinned. "And there's more. What are we going to do with him? I'm humiliated. I've learned more about him tonight than I have in our three official appointments. And I can *see* now how I put him down . . . and programmed him to say what I wanted. George — he isn't crazy! *That's* what frightens me. And I could tell when he touched me — he was . . . sorry for *me* for not knowing how to handle it all; for being scared when he healed me of that damn headache."

"Uh. I'd forgotten that part," George admitted. "What the hell, though, that was super."

"Gregory thinks that about his gums, too. But it makes me nervous. If someone can heal you — well, they must have some kind of power over you, mustn't they? *That* scares me too."

"Come on! Healing a headache can't be all that bad," George said, jokingly. Then with a playful leer: "What's the secret he discovered?"

"It isn't funny," she said glumly. "And something else. He's only been at the Center three months, since I was appointed. His records say he committed himself. His parents are dead. I don't know where he came from, what section of the country or anything. I just think it's damn weird."

They stood in the summer night darkness, watching the traffic speed by the parking lot. The air was somewhat cooler; Josephine pulled her summer jacket tighter, and George's legs were getting goose pimples, the tiny hairs sticking up like wires. "Damn, I'm getting chilly," he said. "I don't know what the hell to do with Window. We have to get him back before eleven, though, didn't you say?"

Josephine blushed. "Actually, I signed him out as a guest at your place to cover his absence," she said. "I mean, he's a man . . . I didn't want to sign him out to my place, because people might talk."

"You're devious," George said, grinning. "What are you saying? We should take him to my place? I mean, we're covered."

She nodded.

"I hope Jean doesn't decide to surprise me, and show up. The fewer who know about this, the better," replied George, looking worried.

"You mean, you haven't told your wife?" Josephine asked, disapprovingly.

"Told her? Hell, I haven't seen her in three days. She and the kids are at the cottage," George answered. His eyes widened. For the first time he found himself wondering about that old arrangement. "They go every summer," he said, almost defensively.

In his mind's eye he saw his wife's face, and at the same time he was uncomfortably aware of his growing pleasure with Josephine Blithe's company. "Uh. We better go get the others and get out of here, then."

"Mmm," she answered. "There's something else. I don't know what happened to you in there, but I had some changes in perception that I'd assign to drugs, except that I didn't have any. God, my peers would think I was out of my mind if they heard this!"

"Peer power, huh?" George replied, but he was growing more aware of her closeness, so he swung around almost brusquely and opened the door.

Seven's face told George that something was happening; he'd never seen Seven look so serious before. Gregory Diggs was obviously listening intently to whatever was going on. George pulled out Josephine's chair for her (for the first time) and sat down himself.

Gregory Diggs whispered, "Window is Monarch again. It's wild. Listen."

Window, as Monarch, had a bemused expression on his face. He looked at Seven and looked *through* him at the same time, as if caught up in a spectacular daydream. The twenty-fifth-century Monarch began to stroll in the direction of the museum. He felt an odd disquiet. He wondered, for the hundredth time, what had given him the idea to dig at this particular tell in the first place. And as he thought, Window as Monarch spoke the words, in the restaurant: "I wonder what actually gave me the idea for digging at this particular tell to begin with?"

"What's he talking about?" George asked Gregory. Diggs shushed him. In the background, a waitress was clearing the tables, and George leaned closer so that he could hear better.

"The Codicils' origin could have remained a mystery," Monarch mused, growing still more uneasy. "Or worse, I suppose they could have never been discovered. But what about our world, then? Without the Codicils, God knows what fate would have befallen the species." And again, in the restaurant, his eyes looking nowhere, Window as Monarch spoke the same words.

Then his words suddenly became urgent. "I've got to check the Codicils again. I don't know why," Monarch said, and he began walking as quickly as he could toward the museum. Even the Monarch speaking to Oversoul Seven grew agitated—And so did Seven. The museum in the twenty-fifth century correlated with George's house. Seven knew that he had to go there right away—and that Window had to go with him.

"It's all right," Seven said, to Window, who now was silent. "We'll work it all out. We have to."

"Work what out?" asked George, sounding irritated.

Seven had been concentrating on "Monarch's" words so intently that he hadn't even realized that George and Josephine had returned. Now he looked up at them all in sudden dismay. How could he explain what he'd just learned? What delightful human companions they were—he looked at them with a fondness that surfaced so surely that its expression was obvious. George looked embarrassed. Gregory somehow understood. Josephine blushed. But the expression of such emotion frightened George, so he said, alarmed, "What's wrong?"

"Not a thing," Seven said briskly. "Only we have to go back to your house. Quickly. I'll explain later. Right now we haven't any time to lose."

George shrugged and said, "Lead on: Nothing would surprise me now." Josephine picked up her purse. Diggs took Window's arm protectively, and, though he was still trying to look unperturbed, Oversoul Seven was almost beside himself with worry. If they didn't find the Codicils in time, this world of Josephine's, George's, Gregory's and Window's might not exist at all — or it might turn into another probability, or lead to a future probable world in which the earth lay in ruins and Monarch himself did not exist.

Window walked along docilely enough. But would he be strong enough, Seven wondered, to do what must be done?

All of Seven's sense of urgency couldn't keep the group together much longer, though. Josephine Blithe insisted they rest for a while. She went home in a taxi.

George took everyone else to his place. He went to his bedroom purposefully. Oversoul Seven fidgeted and waited while Diggs and Window drank coffee in the kitchen. So everything was quiet. But not for long.

∼ *Chapter Thirteen* ∼

A Complicated Out-of-Body Experience
and a Full House

While George Brainbridge the Third slept and Seven talked to Window and Diggs in the twentieth-century kitchen, George Brainbridge the First sat in his red silk dressing gown on the side of his cot, looking out the attic window at the carriage house and drive and lawn below. His mind felt deliciously clear and unruffled — as still, he thought, as the June night sky whose moonlight illuminated the scene outside his window with such delicate artistry. He was trying to get out of his body.

It's 1892, he told himself. And no matter how definite and authoritative that date sounded to him, no matter how perfectly his sense data confirmed it, he had to try to realize that other times — other years, seasons, and even centuries, somehow coincided in this moment. He *had* learned that much. And, he reminded himself, no matter that his wife and son would be home in a short week from Europe, he had to understand that the remaining time could be as "lengthy" as he wanted, despite the fact that when they returned, his experiments would be drastically reduced — if not entirely curtailed.

The thought reminded him of the distractions he had to avoid; he had to keep a clear, open mental focus. "Forget everything but this present moment as you experience it," he told himself. He stared gently, gently, out the window. He watched the white lace curtain move softly in the night June air.

He watched the moonlight blink and tremble on the back hitching post . . . and on the dark leaves of the lilac bushes, and . . .

George frowned and nervously twirled the edges of his fine moustache: everything was quiet, yet he *felt* things stirring beneath it all. He stared at the rolltop desk in the corner—or rather, he stared at where he knew it was; for it was mostly invisible in the darkness. His journal was in the desk drawer. He wanted to make some notations and yet he didn't want to move, lest he break the spell that he was trying to get himself into. It seemed that the soft air pulsated with urgency, as if there was something he was supposed to do. And he had no idea what it could be.

Patiently and stubbornly he tried another tactic, one that often worked. He'd largely given up sniffing laughing gas ever since he discovered that he could do things with his consciousness without it and control events better, besides. So now he tried to get out of his body using what he called Method One.

He lay down, relaxed himself completely, closed his eyes and felt around inside himself for what he called the invisible muscles of his astral body. Then, he tried to sit up—while his body lay still; to move inner arms while his physical ones lay crossed on his chest, to walk on astral legs while his physical ones lay flat against the bed.

"Uh, ug." He groaned with the effort. The sound was like thunder. His body shuddered. "Thunderation," he cried; realizing that he'd used too much effort, tried too hard. Now he'd have to start all over again! At the same time, he was growing sleepy. He yawned, annoyed with himself. Then another idea came to him. He'd use Method Five if he could remember it. He'd use his own sleepiness to advantage.

Usually George Brainbridge was all for the importance of will power, resolution and effort. He was learning, though, that sometimes these got in the way of his very special mental activities. So now, grudgingly, he gave in and tried a method of getting out of his body that took full advantage (or so it seemed to him) of the body's slavish need for sleep. He let his sleepiness come on. Trickily, he courted it. He yawned deeply, as if to tempt sleep to come closer. His eyes were closed; his bony body heavy on the cot's surface.

He let sleep come on, let sleep have its way. And this was the trick: at the same time he conjured up an image of himself in the hall outside his room. When he fell asleep—at that very precise moment—just before his consciousness "went under," he'd transfer it (and himself) to that other waking image.

His breathing was getting deeper. Was it time yet? His mind was getting . . . wavery; yet it was still . . . too alert; just a touch of wakefulness of the wrong kind. His breathing was even deeper — and deeper — he was *so* near sleep. Yet at the same time, craftily, he held the image of himself intact in his mind's eye. He mentally watched it. It was perfect: thinning brown hair, hawk-like nose, red dressing gown. He avoided getting sidetracked by details, though, and felt his consciousness gently begin a rolling motion that by now he'd learned to recognize. It was as if his consciousness were about to roll off a hill, into sleep's oblivion. And just when he got that feeling, George (Eureka! he shouted mentally) rolled his consciousness into the image, in which he was now fully awake. He congratulated himself and avoided the temptation to go back and look at his body because sometimes when he did, he just fell right back into it, so to speak, and that was that.

"Now then. What now?" he mused, listening and watching. Was everything as it should be? It was still night. He was still in the hall, so he went down to the second floor.

What a delicious secret triumph, to be walking around out of his body! George thought of indulging in his favorite sport — walking or flying around the block at night out of his body. The only thing that stopped him was that once he went through the front door, the outside environment frequently changed, and then he had to be very alert and in good shape to handle the situation. As he mused, he walked down the hall of the second floor and paused. The bedroom doors were closed. Suddenly he knew that he wasn't alone.

Cautiously, George Brainbridge walked through the first door into the western bedroom. The moon shone through the window, and George noted several things at once. The familiar bedroom furniture was gone. The gas lamps were gone from the walls, and lamps without wicks sat on the bedside tables.

Now what was going on? George wondered. Excited, he bent down to get a closer look. Wires running from the lamps led to an outlet of some kind in the baseboards; he had to be in the future. These must be future electric lights, amplifications of the simple models he'd read of in his journals. What a boon to dentistry!

He almost chortled. Yet at the same time, he knew that if he got too excited, he might lose control and be swept back to his body. Was this his house, in the future? Then who was sleeping in the bed that stood where his own should be? He bent closer. The moonlight shone on a man's face, and George Brainbridge stared; there was definitely a family resemblance. This man looked more like him than his own son did. Zounds! He bent closer.

Too late he noticed the wires leading from the light blanket. He touched the blanket gently — tiny shocks went through him, and the shocks were somehow translated into those weird crackling sounds that he found so curious. There must be electricity — in the *blanket?* In his consternation, George swore. But if he was out of his body, why should electricity bother him, if that *was* electricity? His consciousness started to stray. The scene began to get dim.

In desperation, George concentrated on the bedside table in front of his eyes, trying to keep it in focus. The smell of the late lilacs rushed up from the yard. The bedside table became increasingly visible. Then George heard a strange buzzing in his ears, or the sound of fire crackling, and suddenly a dizzying shift in his consciousness almost made him stagger. He felt as if he were flying through immense distances, even though he could plainly see that he hadn't moved an inch.

This time George's excitement nearly *did* sweep him back to his body, but his curiosity was even stronger; it kept him rooted to the spot, though for a moment his consciousness twanged like a rubber band, trying to be snapped in two places at once.

The room was the same, but again the furniture was different. Soft lights emerged from the ceiling, though George couldn't see their source. A group of people, looking as if they were on a tour, stood looking at the room in which he stood. There were ohs and ahs, but no one saw him. Was he hallucinating all this? George wondered. "Let all hallucinations vanish," he commanded mentally, with more confidence than he felt.

Nothing happened. George gasped; if he was right, then the people and room would have vanished if he were creating them himself. So he must have outdone himself. But where was he, and what was going on?

A voice came out of the walls, and George leapt back. "This is a replica of The George's bedroom, containing artifact copies found or reconstructed from the original tell. The exact age is uncertain, but certainly these furnishings were in vogue before the mid-1900s. You'll notice the ancient electric blanket, of course, plugged into wall sockets. Lamps that were turned off and on by hand."

This was the most vivid out-of-body experience George had ever had. He was jubilant. He tried to see and hear everything he could, for later notation in his journal. At the same time, the clarity of the affair frightened him, too. Everything was almost *too* clear. Suppose . . . he couldn't get back?

But before he could really worry about that, George noticed something else that shocked him to the core. The visitors, or whoever they were, men and women alike, wore short colorful tunics, with bare arms and legs everywhere flashing, and no one showed the slightest embarrassment. For a moment he wondered if he'd somehow traveled to some weird brothel. But no; the visitors obviously were staring at the room as if it were . . . a museum piece.

The invisible voice went on: "Who knows how many evenings The George spent back in those ancient times, experimenting with various states of consciousness until finally he came upon the Codicils? And without the Codicils, our world surely would not exist. Mankind's beliefs to that point were so self-destructive that only annihilation could have resulted."

"*The* GEORGE?" George felt dizzy again, and when he heard the word *Codicils,* more shocks went through his dream body. Every portion of his consciousness became super alert; the word seemed to fill his mind. CODICILS. . . .

More crackling sounds. Darkness, light. Then darkness. The next thing George knew, he snapped back to his body. Physically he was shouting, "The Codicils! The Codicils!" The sound of his own voice was so loud that it frightened him.

He looked around and checked the clock. It was 11 P.M. He was wide awake, and more excited than he could remember being in years. Quickly he put on his slippers, went out into the hall and down to the second floor. He opened the door to the western bedroom. Everything was the way it should be. His familiar bed sat there, empty. The gaslamps were in their accustomed places on the wall. He stroked his moustache and sighed. "Maybe the house is haunted," he thought.

George Brainbridge the Third was thinking exactly the same thing as his grandfather closed the door. George woke up with his scalp prickling. He shook his head, bemused; he could have sworn that someone was in the room for a minute. Shit. He sat up, turned off the electric blanket which was set at its lowest summer temperature because the old house got damp even on the warmest nights, put his pants on over his naked body, plunged his feet into his shoes, and headed for the kitchen. He'd never experienced a crazier week in his life, he thought. He wished Jean and the kids were back so that life could become commonplace again.

The light was on. George heard voices. Shit again, he thought. All he wanted was a sandwich and a moment's peace, and instead Seven must be talking to that damn Window, because now he heard voices clearly.

"*What's* going on down here?" he called, with joking peevishness, as he approached the kitchen door.

∼ *Chapter Fourteen* ∼

Dire Probability

"Hi," Seven said, brightly.

"Who's that with you? Window, Monarch, or Christ?" asked George, grinning.

"Verily. I'm Christ just now," Window said. "That's just super," George exclaimed brusquely. "All we need, I'd say." Then to Seven, "What the hell is really going on around here? Do you know? I'll be so glad to get back to my 'Tooth and Gums Business' tomorrow that I'm tempted to pay the patients."

Seven grinned sympathetically, but George said, "No kidding. I mean it. All this shit is driving me out of my mind. None of it *should* have happened —Christ healing Diggs; all those hallucinations or whatever they were at the restaurant; Window thinking he's two people, Christ and some guy in the future. Tomorrow he goes back to the Center. That's that!"

"Are you Judas?" Christ asked, with mild curiosity.

"No, godammit," George replied. "I'm just a poor bemused tooth doctor."

"If they crucify me. . . ." Christ began.

"Will you stop that?" George interrupted, "They don't crucify people in this country anyhow. . . ."

"Bless you," Christ answered.

"Hell," George replied, "I like you better when you're Window."

At the same time, George's voice turned quizzical: When Window thought he was Christ — aside from the pat phrases about Judas and getting crucified — there *was* an aura about him. Suddenly George leaned forward and said dramatically, "You aren't *really* afraid of being crucified, are you? And you *know* I'm not Judas. What in the hell are you trying to pull? I'm mystified, I admit it."

"Well," demanded a voice, "are you going to tell him or not?"

George started with surprise as Gregory Diggs came in through the open back porch door. "What is this, a convention?" George said. "I suppose you couldn't sleep, either."

"I wasn't about to leave you guys alone with Mr. Window here," said Gregory, leering. Then to Seven, "Well?"

"Uh, it's sort of a wild story," Seven said, dubiously.

"Try me," George responded dryly. He sat down at the kitchen table, sighing with mock despair; then grinning. "Come on, guys. Give. This is an elaborate put-on."

This time Seven sighed. He put down his peanut butter sandwich, spread out his hands, and said, "This is it, the truth as we understand it after talking to Window-Christ-Monarch half the night. Ready?"

"Shoot," George said. He crossed his legs. "Nothing will surprise me," he added.

"Okay," Seven answered. "Window, interrupt me if I say anything you don't agree with. But it looks like this. That person" (he pointed to Window) "is the combination of the characteristics that belong to Window, Christ, and Monarch. Only for some reason, the characteristics are separate; he hasn't put them together. Now he *can* heal. We know that. He claims to come from the future or to see into it when he's Monarch."

"Yeah?" George said, with a silly unbelieving grin.

"I *am* Monarch," Window said suddenly and gently.

"Oh, Christ," George sputtered, before Seven shushed him.

At the same time, Diggs poked George and pointed to his own lap where a small cassette recorder was balanced on his knees. He turned it on to record.

Window-Monarch's face was grave. He said softly, "I'd like to believe that somehow or other I was speaking with George, The George, who initiated the Codicils into the world. Are you *The* George?"

George couldn't rid his face of its embarrassed perplexity. He wanted to say, "No, and I'm not Judas either!" But with some surprise he heard his voice respond differently: "Hell, I know about the Codicils," he said.

As he spoke, George heard Seven gasp. At the same time, Window's eyes certainly seemed to belong to someone else. They stared urgently at George. "I had the worst feeling that . . . something had happened in the past," Monarch said softly. "As if probabilities were changing. As if I had to contact you in your present time . . . I'll try again soon. I'm not as good at this as I should be — " As the words faded, Window's eyes lost the intentness. Himself again, he said, "That time I almost saw something . . . through someone else's eyes — "

But Seven was on his feet. "George, what do you know about the Codicils?" he asked. "Quickly."

"What is this?" asked George, bewildered. "When he said 'Codicils,' I just remembered seeing the word on the title page of one of my grandfather's old journals in the attic someplace. That's all — *The Codicils*. That was the title of one of his journals. He labeled them all; I don't even know if they're still up there."

And Seven cried, "They've got to be."

When Seven was with mortals, he had to act like them as much as possible so as not to give himself away. It was with considerable relief then that he rushed up to the attic, after getting George's permission to search for his grandfather's old journals. George, Window, and Diggs were off to bed in the second floor bedrooms.

Seven went into the attic, turned on the light, and closed the door behind him. The steady thumping of his heart distracted him ("All that racket," he cried), so he stepped out of his twentieth-century body after arranging it neatly on the old cot that stood by the window. He wondered if that cot was in another time occupied by another body — George the First's, for example?

Seven looked around. What he saw was the dirty, cluttered twentieth-century attic, with boxes stashed all over, antique furniture standing at odd angles, and the smell of dust mingling with the scent of lilacs that came in through the opened window. It was then that Seven spied the old desk. It was the same one that had stood polished and gleaming in the attic study of George the First. Quickly Seven went rummaging through the drawers until finally he found what he was looking for. It was too much to ask for, he thought, grinning, as he came upon the neat stack of old journals.

Still, Seven paused before opening the one at hand. Was their author, George the First, invisibly there? And if he was, would *his* desk drawers open as if by an invisible hand? Or would his journals and desk drawers remain motionless? Because as Seven thought of opening the first journal, he felt very close to George the First — close enough to touch him, in fact.

Seven paused, staring. He studied the positions of the old journals, now scattered on the floor and looked at the dusty surface of the desk. Everything seemed complete twentieth-century except—Seven squinted his eyes—except for one tiny circle of air. Well, the circle wasn't tiny exactly, he thought, and he wasn't even sure how he knew it was different from all of the other air in the attic room, but it *was.*

Seven stared at the shiny segment of space suspiciously and hopefully at the same time. He simply had to discover what George the First knew about the Codicils! Was that odd super-transparent circle of space somehow connected with the same space in the 1890s? Because now Seven felt closer than ever to George the First—and more than that, he smelled a difference between that significant spot of air, and all the rest in the room.

Seven grinned: he had it! His inner senses were much more acute than the physical ones that came with his body, of course, and now he realized that the smell of dust and lilacs was everywhere else in the attic—*except* in that circle of space he was staring at. He stepped closer, thinking that here, for some reason, the times of both Georges must intersect.

In the next moment, though, Seven stepped back so quickly that he almost fell over, because suddenly a very real and solid red-sleeved lower arm and red-cuffed hand appeared in the center of the circle of space; it reached out and picked up the nearest journal that Seven hadn't yet placed with the others. And as the hand (surely George the First's) grabbed the journal, the dust instantly vanished from it; its color brightened, and the journal looked quite new.

"George? George?" Seven yelled—mentally, since he was out of his body. No one answered. Instead the hand flipped open the journal and began to write with a fountain pen. "George, what do you know about the Codicils?" Seven cried, again getting no response.

At the same time almost, Seven gasped as he saw what was happening. The effect was somewhat like looking at a round television screen, whose stations automatically synchronized places and times. That is, the round circle in space shimmered. George's hand and the journal disappeared. There were wavy lines and warps in the circle, and then George's hand appeared again, only this time it was obvious that the hand was part of a statue—one of George that must stand in the twenty-fifth-century museum.

Seven's head was swimming. He concentrated as hard as he could on George in the 1890s, and after some more wavy lines, the circle in space changed. There was George's hand again, already having written several sentences in the open journal.

The picture stabilized. As quickly as he could, Seven began to read the sentences even as George's hand wrote on in neat script:

June 2, 1892

> *Tonight, having finally achieved an out-of-body condition, I first found myself in the western bedroom, only the time seemed to be somewhere in the future. I'm convinced that some electrical devices were in evidence, far superior to our current knowledge of that new field; though I wasn't quick enough to discover their workings. In a strange vision, I also saw a man sleeping in a bed where my bed should be. My intuitions told me that be was a future relative, and surely there was a family resemblance. This episode reminds me that a few days ago, in an altered state of consciousness while sniffing gas, I encountered a man who told me I bad a grandson. Obviously I do not, and my son isn't married. Yet . . . Is it possible that I actually saw a future grandson sleeping in the room that is now my bedroom (when I use it)? When Sarah is away of course, I practically live in this attic hideaway except for handling my patients very nicely I must admit, in the morning hours.*

Seven frowned. That was as far as George got on the page, and his hand was now in the way. What about the Codicils? And where was Cyprus? It was obvious that she'd simplified his mission considerably. He was worried about everything.

George's hand moved down a few lines. Impatiently, Seven read:

> *The other adventure was equally mysterious, and I'm not sure how much hallucination was involved. I found myself again, it seemed, in the western bedroom in some distant future, only the room was a museum piece. The furniture was an odd mixture of what is now in my bedroom, and the furniture that I saw in it in the previous instance. People who certainly seemed alive were staring at the room. They were dressed in the flimsiest of apparel, and though I'm far from being narrowly moralistic, I was somewhat shocked, and at first thought I might be in a brothel.*

George's hand was in the way again, and Seven almost cried with impatience. If *he* saw George's hand, did George sense that someone was watching *him*? Could he, Seven, reach into that magic space and pull the journal back? Seven grinned, imagining George's startled reaction (He'd probably scream, "Zounds."). And anyway, what good would that do? Seven wondered. None. So he waited.

George's hand was trembling. He began to write in a faster, agitated manner.

> *Now we come to the heart of the matter. A man's voice came out of the walls in some way unknown to me, but surely some future development of the gramophone was involved. The voice spoke about "the Codicils" with a significance of tone that gave the phrase "the Codicils" great import. Something was said, if I remember correctly, about "The George" or "in the time of George," or words to that effect. But the impact of those words upon myself was unprecedented. I felt them to the core of my soul. The entire affair may be symbolic rather than literal, of course, and I've had enough experience with states of consciousness to know how insidious hallucinations can be — if you accept them as real. But ever since* [and here, the handwriting became very agitated] *I began my adventures in consciousness, I felt that there was a reason for them. And tonight I knew that I have to discover The Codicils, whatever they are.*
>
> *My only clue is in the distant future just mentioned. And I have no assurance that I can return there. I tried several out-of-body methods before achieving success last time. Did the last one I used somehow propel me into other times as well? Of course I'll experiment further, for even as I write, a sense of urgency that I do not understand overtakes me. And in a week my wife and son will return from Europe, in which case my opportunities for experimentation will be drastically reduced.*

And, Seven thought, in a week Jean and the kids would return to George the Third. . . .

Seven couldn't believe what he was reading. George hadn't discovered the Codicils yet! And Seven had hoped to learn them from George, to give to Window in the twentieth century. With dismay, Seven stared again at the journal page. The circle in space barely contained it, and again George's hand was in the way. But again Seven managed to glimpse the date at the top of the page — *June 2, 1892* — and he shook his head in confusion. It was June 2, 1982, in the attic, and in the world of George, Josephine, Gregory, and Window. Then apparently George the First had had his out-of-body encounters while Window and Diggs sat with Seven in the kitchen just a short "time" ago; and before George got out of bed to see what was going on.

These thoughts came and went, but since Seven realized that George hadn't discovered the Codicils, a sense of foreboding began to assail him.

At first his dismay merely grew sharper. Then, however, the circle of space in which the journal appeared began to darken, shimmer, and tremble until finally it seemed to whirl into darkness altogether. It became a black circle of space darker than the space about it and somehow threatening. If the Codicils weren't discovered 'in time' Seven wondered, what probable worlds might vanish? Could they actually disappear? And how could the Codicils appear in the twenty-fifth century and form the basis of a world, if they hadn't *already* been planted in the past? Seven looked around anxiously. The black circle was . . . expanding, while at the same time it grew even blacker, and more concentrated. And compelling.

Seven thought he heard Cyprus cry, "Seven, look away. Quick." But it was too late. Events began to happen and unhappen with such rapidity that Seven instinctively knew he was in trouble. In a flash he dismissed his own mental image of himself, so that he was invisible consciousness. (And just in time, as he said to Cyprus later, "Because that circle or hole or whatever was like a multidimensional meatgrinder; any kind of form at all would be . . . well, ground up.")

His consciousness actually twirled topsy-turvy, turned inside out, side-ways . . . if consciousness had a shape, it was pulled out of it, so that Seven first felt long, then short, then big, then small, then absolutely "not there." The circle that had opened up through the universe itself, it seemed, was like an eternally ravenous animal-of-space. Seven felt as if he was falling down some infinite tunnel. Even that idea didn't fit, though, because Seven felt that time was so scrambled that while he was falling through the tunnel on the one hand, on the other hand, another part of him was poised eter-nally on its threshold—staring, unable to move. And that part didn't know about this tumbling-through-the-tunnel-self at all.

And worse: As fast as these events kept happening, they kept unhap-pening at the same time, so that yet another part of him felt as if he was tumbling back the other way through the hole he'd just entered. Not only that, but somewhere along the way, space had vanished; that is, it felt as if space knotted up into itself . . . or he himself was knotting up into space, so that even his thoughts had no psychological room between them but kept bumping into one another, sticking to each other like glue until there was just one clump of thoughts like porcupine quills—and then *that* vanished.

Psychological silence.

Seven knew he was thinking at an incredibly fast rate—but somehow no thoughts registered. He was himself, and he felt oddly cool and quiet, though he had nothing to judge himself against. He existed . . . in reference to nothing. So how did he know he existed? He thought the question, but it didn't register, and all Seven knew was that . . . his thinking seemed to exist apart from himself, with no connection to himself. And "at the same time" in this silence he felt that unendurable energy surrounded him, making energy-falls instead of say, waterfalls; and that this energy felt solid even though its motion blurred the edges of his consciousness.

This particular experience seemed endless. He kept falling through this chute with the moving walls of energy; yet knowing this, he didn't feel as if he were falling. Or rather, he felt suspended, unmoving and moving at once. Even the darkness around him moved, varied in intensity, trembled, formed shapes of darkness within darkness.

Seven was beyond fear. He even began to feel a part of whatever strange process was occurring, as if he and the process were one.

His thoughts had felt compressed and inaccessible to him. Now they began to gyrate within his consciousness; to swirl. Simultaneously, he felt a fantastic pull from some distance "in front of him" and suddenly he *did* feel as if he was falling. And falling fast. In the next "moment" Seven saw a rim of light so bright that he thought physical eyes could never stand it. And before he could even begin to wonder about this, there was a light, floating sensation, an odd popping sound — and Seven found himself standing in what he knew at once was another universe altogether.

Seven gulped, figuratively speaking. He was definitely in another universe or *un*universe, he thought, for he sensed negation everywhere. The atmosphere was peculiarly suffocating; the air heavy and motionless. Yet the environment was physical enough. There were ugly dwarf bushes every-where; miles of grayish sand, and the sky was a threatening purple-gray, with fog reaching from a few feet above the ground, hanging almost motionless for what seemed to be miles, at least, before the thick levels of purple-gray sky began.

It was difficult to say whether it was night or day; the place seemed to exist in an eternal twilight. The mountains in the distance were devoid of growth, their naked rock and dirt ledges looking like eerie steps to nowhere. The longer Seven stood where he was, the more aware he became of the heavy atmosphere. Even though he was without a body, he felt as if he weighed tons. Or — no, he felt as if his *thoughts* weighed tons; as if his very psychological being was too heavy a burden to bear.

Anxious, he looked more closely around him. He was on some kind of ancient fortification, on the second or third floor, for above him now he saw half-destroyed floors; and he was standing only on a fairly small ledge, obviously all that was left of this part of the fortress. It was made of wood; much of it now rotten and as Seven squinted in the distance he realized that the ruins of hundreds of such structures lay in piles and heaps on the gray ground, blending in so well with this weathered world, that he hadn't distinguished them as structures at all.

A glint of metal at Seven's feet caught his eye. He squinted down at it sideways. It was a broken-off metal plaque. Seven read the weathered lettering: "Skirmish 541. World War V."

World War Five? The implications made Seven dizzy. The structures or their remains *were* fortresses, then. When he thought *that,* Seven's inner senses showed him a sudden scene: thousands of men and women, living and fighting in this area thousands of years ago, building and rebuilding the fortresses; literally a decayed species, dying of—

Of despair. The emotion was so strong that Seven cried out, as he realized what this world, this universe was. Created by man's despair, it was a future probable universe in which man answered none of the questions that plagued him in George's time.

Seven looked up again; there were no floating cities in that sky, either, no evidence of man's technology or adventuresomeness. In *this* reality, the species didn't last that long. It was then that Seven noticed the silence. Not one bird call or insect sound. No murmuring of the wind. He looked down: no anthills. It was a final version of the dire visions he'd seen earlier.

And Seven knew that no one could withstand that atmosphere of despair. It caught at his own consciousness; he felt his own thoughts darkening. Desolation stained even his inner vision until he feared that his spiritual sight would be forever dimmed by a cast of darkness. Was this what mortals felt, when they experienced despair? Did George feel that way? Or Window? Or Diggs or Josephine? As if nothing mattered and no meaning existed? They never *said* that to themselves or to each other, Seven thought, confused. And Monarch?

And the instant Seven thought of Monarch, he remembered *the* Codicils. This he realized was a universe in which the Codicils didn't exist and were never discovered; in which they remained psychologically invisible to man. But what about Christianity? Seven wondered, even as he struggled against the growing closeness of the air. *What about Christianity?*

Suddenly, brightly, in his mind's eye Seven saw Window speaking as Christ as he had done in George's kitchen earlier, and then speaking for Monarch. And as he saw this inner vision, Seven cried out. For Window . . . *was* himself Window and yet a personification of the people of George's time. Christianity as it had been known was deadended. The twentieth-century world still wasn't big enough to accept miracles as fact; and so Christ became a delusion. And man had to take the steps that would lead him beyond what he was—to become . . . Monarch. Man had to find the Codicils.

Seven felt more helpless and forlorn than he ever remembered being. How could one soul, even a Seven, discover such a vital message—when he didn't even know what the Codicils said exactly, or how to find them? And if he didn't, did it mean that *this* terrible world would be the future of George's Earth? The sense of responsibility felt crushing, yet Seven told himself that he'd accept it—if he had to; if there was no other way, if. . . .

"I'll find the Codicils," he shouted; and as he did, he gasped in astonishment. He'd felt the air get closer, but now it had collected tightly around him so that it formed a circle filled, it seemed, with new magnetic darkness. And before he could understand what was happening, he began to fall once more through the tunneling dimensions from which he'd only shortly emerged.

Space turned into time, time into space. Seven's thoughts suddenly had incredible mass—and then seemed to disappear altogether. In between, he told himself that he didn't care what happened; he'd find the Codicils. Only once, when his thoughts appeared clearly, did he wonder nostalgically where George's world was now; and the attic room where his body still lay neatly on the twentieth-century couch.

Did George's world even exist?

Was it there, to return to?

∼ *Chapter Fifteen* ∼

Cyprus Introduces Seven to Framework Two,
and George the First Visits the Museum of Time

"**O**f course George's world exists," Cyprus said.
As he heard Cyprus' words, Seven felt as if he were being pulled (by the hair of his head) out through the other end of the mysterious chute in which he'd found himself. Once again, times and places came together and made sense, just as his thoughts once more came in clear sentences.

"You just haven't learned the grammar of energy yet," Cyprus said. Seven heard her, but he couldn't yet sense her presence.

"Grammar of energy!" Seven cried, mentally. "That experience was awful."

"You just got caught in the middle of a process, the process by which energy speaks its atomic structure," Cyprus' voice answered.

"But where are you?" Seven asked quarrelsomely. "And where am I? I just feel suspended. . . ." Seven broke off, for suddenly he felt . . . portions of himself coming together and joining him, like thousands of glowing bolts of energy hopscotching to join his own consciousness. "Oh," he said, in a small voice. "Oh. Now I remember."

"Well, remember more, and you'll be in Framework Two with me," Cyprus replied.

"Remember what?" Seven thought, but even as he asked the question, the returning bolts of energy joined with his consciousness so quickly that he forgot the question. He didn't need it any longer. As the energy mixed and merged with his own awareness, Seven cried, "Of course," and instantly a group of images appeared. At the same time, Seven saw Cyprus waiting for him — and he gasped as Framework Two formed about him.

They were standing in a natural garden in which each flower seemed to be the most beautiful one that Seven had ever seen in any space or time. Each leaf also seemed to be itself, and more than a leaf at the same time. Surrounding the garden grew the liveliest forest that Seven could imagine; each tree more supple and delightful than any Seven had ever seen. He could hardly begin to examine the environment. Even the air had the sweetest odor, as if it were the essence from which all summer air was distilled.

Cyprus said, "Seven, because you're an earth soul, I thought you'd like Framework Two to look like this," and Seven was so enchanted that he could hardly answer. At the same time, the landscape was constantly changing as if a million summers were forming.

Cyprus had also outdone herself as far as her image was concerned, but exactly *what* she'd done was almost impossible for Seven to discover. It wasn't just that she looked like the model from which all female and male elements were first drawn — being at the same time handsome and beautiful, athletic and supple, combining all of the characteristics of each sex in one form — but that these characteristics seemed intensified to an incredible degree. . . .

"You're on the right track," Cyprus said.

"But . . . everything looks . . . brand-new," Seven cried. "As if it were all created this instant. I mean, that one rose — look, there, the third one in from the first row. It's a bud, so of *course* it looks new. But beside it is a much bigger rose, with all of its petals opened, and it looks brand-new too!"

"Precisely," Cyprus replied, with the most innocent and yet the most enigmatic smile.

"And the older trees look as fresh or . . . new, anyhow, as the younger ones," continued Seven, even more puzzled.

"Exactly," Cyprus said, smiling more mysteriously than ever. "You almost have it."

With that Seven shouted, "And you're always magnificent when you want to be. But now, now you're so much . . . *more* like yourself . . . that you're almost like a Model for yourself — " Seven's thoughts swirled. His intuitions made connections that left him breathless. He cried, "You *are* . . . the source from which the usual you emerges!"

And Cyprus said very gently, "And here, Seven, so are you." As she spoke, Seven realized that her words were literally true. He felt himself . . .

growing out of his own larger source, and at the same time, he was the source from which he was ever emerging.

In that instant, Oversoul Seven felt himself turn into pure awareized energy—his identity stamping itself upon the universe; energy turning into who he was, in a process unending. His awareness was vast, yet with each detail sharp and clear as if it alone existed. And within his awareness, Seven saw George the First and George the Third, and Window who was also Monarch in the twenty-fifth century.

"They're separate! Inviolately themselves, each like no one or anything else in the universe," Seven called out in exaltation to Cyprus. "But . . . they're counterparts of each other, too."

"There's more," said Cyprus' voice, and it turned into waves of energy, flowing all about them. The waves turned into sparkling images. Seven gasped, figuratively speaking, for there before him stood both of the Georges, and Window, and Monarch . . . and—he gasped—Josephine and Gregory Diggs. Only these mortals—all his personalities, he realized—were more than mortals, as the roses and trees were more than roses and trees. They were multidimensional models of themselves, brilliant with infinite potentials and abilities; they were personal psychological banks sources from which they drew the personified energy of the universe.

As this was happening, Seven's own consciousness took form after sparkling mental form. *He* was Window and Josephine and Diggs. *His* energy automatically, splendidly, and spontaneously formed their lives. Even now he felt a portion of himself nestled in a cell in the crook of Gregory Diggs' arm as Gregory slept in the twentieth-century world—

"And more," Cyprus said. And Oversoul Seven felt his identity swept up into a new, different vastness—he was couched in a clear psychological universe in which he was everywhere supported. His memory instantly refreshed itself; of course, he thought, without thinking in our terms at all. Now he remembered his own birth—and his constant rebirth—in this inner indescribable universe that automatically formed itself into individuation, Framework Two. And he felt himself intact, with more powers and potentials and desires and purposes than he knew he had, and Seven knew that he was within the mental reality that was Cyprus'.

He didn't think he could comprehend anything beyond this, but even as he thought *that,* Cyprus' reality opened up and he sensed even more magnificence of which she herself was but a part. Yet in all of this, his identity rode securely, jubilantly, safely—boldly and exuberantly. He felt as if he was the youngest being in the universe, and that he was being shown the model for his own future growth.

"But there's more," Cyprus said. "Watch closely." And for a moment, everything vanished except for a small earthen hut on a hillside that suddenly sprang out of nowhere. Almost instantly, on the same spot, a million other buildings seemed to be transposed over the hut, and its environment steadily expanded. Seven counted at least a hundred cities, each one beginning from the hut or springing out of it; and then, from each sparkling building he saw, another new structure sprang into being. There were too many styles and cultures to count. He saw Byzantine palaces and their boulevards; the twenty-fifth-century floating cities, splendid European and Indian castles, temples, and Medieval villages as well as Arabian bazaars. And in each case, these separate civilizations remained themselves, while in each of them, all of the others were somehow implied.

"The models for every possible civilization exist here," Cyprus said. "And each possible eccentric variation is given freedom."

"The Codicils," Seven shouted. "They have to be models for civilization —"

Smiling, Cyprus answered, "Exactly."

"Well, then, I've got to find them," Seven cried. "And at once."

"Shush," Cyprus said. "I'll make this easy for you by cutting out anything that doesn't apply to the problem. Look."

And Seven saw George the First in his attic study, trying another "out-of-body." The picture was clear and detailed, fully sensed, so that Seven even smelled the lilacs out in George's back yard.

George was out-of-body. He kept muttering, "I've got to find the Codicils, whatever they are, before it's too late." His dream body wore a mental version of his favorite red dressing gown. He half-walked and half-floated down the hallway, thinking, "I've got to get to the future where I saw the museum."

And as George thought *that,* Seven held his breath in surprise (figuratively speaking), because George disappeared from the 1890s picture and suddenly appeared in an adjacent twenty-fifth-century one. *There* he stood in front of the museum.

"I admit I'm startled," Seven said. "But from here, it's so easy to see how it's done. I didn't have to worry about juggling time, or going through space atom by atom so to speak; you just . . . state your intent —"

"And in Framework Two, you can move through any time period that exists in Framework One, which is all the earthly dimensions," Cyprus added.

George shook his dream head with happy puzzlement. "Now how did I do that?" he wondered. "And — zounds — what do I do next?"

Seven grinned; there was the museum — the twenty-fifth-century version of George's house. And to Seven, the walls suddenly became transparent. In an upper room, supposed to be a replica of George's study, a statue stood staring out the window. Seven saw all the rooms, each more or less bearing a resemblance to the twentieth-century ones he knew. But he noticed something else—a lower room, in the cellar. As soon as he wanted to examine the details, the picture zoomed in closer. A gold plaque read, "Ye old bomb shelter." And just inside there were some glass cases. Seven peered closer. The sign read: "Replica of the Codicil microfilm, discovered in the tell of 2550."

Seven started to cry, "Microfilm?" when he noticed another larger plaque, filled with writing and headed: "The Codicils." "There they are," he shouted to Cyprus. "All I have to do is—"

Cyprus shook her head. "You can't do it *for* George. He has to find them himself . . . and sift their message back to his own version of them."

Now what does *that* mean? Seven wondered, but mentally he yelled out to George: "Go down to the basement."

George pulled his dressing robe tighter about him. "I think I'll go downstairs first, if I ever get inside," he thought. But his consciousness was wavering. He thought of his body with a touch of fear: had he been away from it too long? No—resolutely, he told himself that everything was all right. "It's *all* all right," he muttered for the tenth time, but something told him that it wasn't all right at all.

George realized that he had a headache—out of his body. How was that possible? he wondered. He started to float through the museum's front door. At the same time, he became aware of a white light, seemingly in his head. The light frightened him, and as this happened, his consciousness flashed back to his body.

But damnation! George thought. It had taken him forever to get in decent out-of-body condition; he couldn't—wouldn't—miss the opportunity! He had to find the Codicils! Even his sense of urgency didn't surprise him. Since he'd first heard the words, they'd obsessed him. He concentrated as hard as he could.

Now he stood inside the museum. "Go downstairs," he told himself; wavering. The light came again, this time much more intense than before— and his inner mental space seemed to . . . expand in the oddest, quite frightening fashion, and the headache returned with double strength. Such a thing had never happened to him before.

He drifted downward; stairs were beneath him. He gritted his dream teeth—if he could just make it further . . . After all, what could happen? At the worst, he'd just plunge back into his body. Wouldn't he? Or had he really been gone too long?

Oversoul Seven was mentally yelling, "Go back to your body," but George never heard him, lost as he was in his resolute determination to reach the

Codicils. "He *has* been out too long," Seven said to Cyprus. "Why doesn't he take the warning?"

"Because he's stubborn, like someone else I know," Cyprus said.

George saw a plaque. The light became almost blinding. For a moment, he was afraid that he could somehow disappear in its sensed vastness. His consciousness felt as if it were being pulled back to his body at an incredible rate. He looked down . . . his dream body gyrated over his physical one, then he blanked out for a moment, and blinking, sat up.

Cyprus and Seven turned into two bits of light on George's brass gaslamp.

"Well, he's all right now," Seven said. "But *I'm* not stubborn, if that's what you mean."

George sat up and lit his pipe.

"We'll discuss that later," Cyprus said. "Right now, I want to be sure that you understand what you have to do about the Codicils."

"Right-o," said Seven, grinning. "At least I think I do. Somehow even though George failed this time, I have to help him get the Codicils in the twenty-fifth-century museum and bring them back to the 1890s —"

"He can't bring back the plaque," Cyprus interrupted. "That object can't exist in George's time, but the ideas *can*. . . ."

"You mean, he has to memorize them?" Seven cried.

"Not necessarily."

"But he'll *never* memorize all the stuff I saw on that plaque," Seven protested. "He's bound to forget some things and distort others, and —"

"He'll be translating them into his own time scheme," Cyprus said gently. "After that, though, the Codicils have to be discovered in the time of George's grandson."

George put out his pipe, lay down, promptly fell asleep, and started snoring.

"But how?" Seven cried. "I'm really confused now. And if I don't get it all right, that awful probable Earth will come into being in George's world's future." He sighed. "Cyprus, you've given me too much to handle this time."

"Nonsense," Cyprus answered, looking nowhere in particular. "You can always do more than you think you can. You know about Framework Two now. It's really quite simple. George has to find the Codicils in the twenty-fifth-century museum, and write them down in his journal in the 1890s so that his grandson can find them in the attic in the twentieth century and put them on microfilm in the bomb shelter. *Then* they can be found by Monarch in the twenty-fifth century, as they *are* in that probable future. Nothing could be simpler!"

"But if I can't, what happens then? And it sounds impossibly complicated to me," Seven cried. He took on his fourteen-year-old male image to emphasize his lack of experience in such matters, and stood there, looking dismayed and put-upon. "And what about John Window and Josephine Blithe and Gregory Diggs and their problems?" he said glumly. "What do they have to do with all this?"

Cyprus took on her favorite image of the woman teacher, her face changing from an ancient, knowing one to a young one that nevertheless shone with the wisdom of age. She smiled and said softly, "Seven, I'm not going to give you *all* of the answers. And if I were you, I'd get busy. You left your body in the twentieth-century attic for one thing, and for another, probabilities are really spinning at this moment because George the Third is about to open up this attic door. So you'd better get back to the right time in a hurry."

"Now I'm so confused that I don't know how to," Seven protested. "I certainly don't want to go through that tunnel again either, if I don't have to."

Cyprus sighed. "Think of Framework Two," she directed. "It's the Inside of every time and place. Concentrate on the time you want, and you'll come out there."

"You're sure?" Seven asked, dubiously. "And why didn't you tell me about Framework Two before?"

"I can't explain right now, but yes, I'm sure about the directions I just gave you. They won't work, though, unless you're sure, too."

"I'm sure," Seven said promptly. He imagined Framework Two as being the Insideness of all times and places, and then said mentally, "I want this room and time of night, but on June 2, 1982."

To help himself concentrate, he'd closed his mental eyes and when nothing seemed to be happening, he opened them. It worked! There was his nifty twentieth-century body, lying empty on the old cot. Seven grinned, and dived into the physical form — just in time.

The attic door opened, and George Brainbridge the Third stuck his head inside the room and bellowed, "Well, it's dawn. Did you find the damned journals?"

~ *Chapter Sixteen* ~

Brothers of the Mind, a Dream Investigation,
and Paranoia from the Past

T he Codicils were such a part of Monarch's mental life, and so self-
explanatory, that it was extremely difficult for him to imagine what
the world must have been like without them. He knew that the historians
had left huge gaps in their story of man's progress. At the same time, as he
prepared for the 500th anniversary, the cinquecentennial celebration of
the Codicils' origin, Monarch found himself considering the pre-Codicil
world with feelings of strong disquiet.

He'd been thinking how spectacular The George's achievement truly
was, considering the background of his times; the fact that few if any people
then embarked in any serious mental travel, and the fact that all of The
George's previous training and belief systems must have been directly contrary to his own intuitive discoveries.

And, as always, standing in the museum's front hallway, Monarch felt
the familiar thrilling sensations that indicated he was picking up information through an alternate neurological sequence. He could almost sense
the presence of The George; still learning the inner mechanics of mental
locomotion, wandering in a world none of his compatriots could find, until
finally he came upon the Codicils. But how? That question had never been
answered. It was a vital question, Monarch mused, because if the Codicils
hadn't appeared in that ancient past, then surely he, Monarch, and all of

the earth people, would have known an entirely different world. *If* mankind had even been able to survive at all without the Codicils, which didn't seem too likely.

Monarch shivered suddenly. The museum seemed almost eerie in the silence. Waiting. The workers had all left, after cleaning the place from top to bottom, touching up, washing the windows. Fresh flowers stood in vases on all of the tables. Only now, the vacuum cleaner turned itself off after soundlessly going over all of the floors. The place was supposed to represent The George's twentieth-century house — its ancient domestic arrangements, its stationary windows instead of moving window-walls, its boxed-in yet cozy interior. Monarch noted the fresh flowers, native species that, had perhaps once grown in The George's back yard.

Yet there was no doubt about it, Monarch thought uneasily, the flowers themselves had a different air than the house itself; they seemed . . . strangely modern. It was almost as if faded flowers would be more appropriate. Monarch smiled to himself, and at the same time he felt a stronger surge of . . . alienness enter the immaculate hall in which he stood.

His prominent narrow nose wiggled. He shivered again with mild surprise. "Is there anyone here?" he asked mentally.

At the same time he felt around inside his own consciousness for any patterns of sensation, however faint; for any information that seemed to be coming through those neural passageways with which he did not usually identify his consciousness. Faint whisperings. Strange — for he began to hear words, which then mentally appeared as letters that took the shape of a man. So! Monarch speculated: A man with that shape must be *speaking* the words.

A window frame appeared transposed over the man's figure. All of this was very faint, and even with the training given everyone throughout life, Monarch had trouble holding the images intact long enough to study them. Why the unaccustomed difficulty? he wondered. He closed his eyes to see the images better, then sighed as he interpreted the message: A man called Window was speaking. But to whom? About what? And how did the event have any connection with himself?

But there was . . . something! Monarch suddenly felt weak and leaned against the hallway table. The channel that had opened had a different feel to it . . . a vacant quality, as if some important ingredient were lacking. A message from a dank world — and Monarch's head suddenly snapped up — a world *before* the Codicils; a world seeking for them; and a personality living in that world . . . who was . . . another aspect of himself!

There was no doubt of it. Monarch knew the feel of his own essence. And if the Codicils had taught man anything, it was the multidimensionality of the self, which was seeded throughout the centuries. And he recognized that peculiar yet definite *alter-essence* that represented his own psychological acknowledgment of "another self." A self, Monarch thought, that would always be "other" to him as he would be "other" to it. Yet they were connected through neurological pathways that appeared ghostily, roaming through the worlds of their individual thoughts.

But why in a world prior to the Codicils?

What was that ancient self trying to tell him? Monarch broke off, correcting himself: That self existed simultaneously with his own life — the twentieth and twenty-fifth centuries coexisted.

"Brother of my mind, speak," Window said mentally.

No answer; only a steadily growing sense of anxiety. But about what? This time Monarch heard the words, "the Codicils," repeated several times, in a warning or at least highly anxious mental voice that now he accepted as his own. Were they about to be stolen? The Codicils themselves *couldn't* be stolen, Monarch thought; they were in the people's minds. The precious ancient microfilms could, but why? Monarch frowned again. It couldn't be that. He must be wrong.

Still pondering and uneasy, he walked up the front stairs, taking some comfort in his own muscular activity, automatically checking to see if everything was in readiness. How perfect it all looked; The George's house — preserved, as if he might return to it at any time. *At any time!* In another frame of reference, The George *was* here, Monarch thought suddenly. The idea had come to him many times before, but as a pleasant theoretical fantasy. It now occurred to him that fantasy or no, according to the principles laid down by the Codicils themselves, The George lived in this house or its facsimile in the twentieth century even as he, Monarch, climbed the steps in the twenty-fifth. Then, what was The George doing now? And who was worried about the Codicils, and why? Surely they were safe enough, but what would anyone possibly gain by stealing them? The people would lose a vital artifact, a beloved symbol. . . .

Astonished with himself, Monarch broke off his line of thought and, almost dazed, reached the top of the stairs. His thoughts had actually been paranoid! He'd actually, seriously, been considering the possibility that someone would really steal the Codicils — and in a world where such social diseases had been completely eliminated for over a century! Whatever possessed him? To his knowledge, not one act of thievery had been committed in his lifetime; the causes had been eradicated almost naturally, as the Codicils taught man about his own potentials and abilities. The resentments and hatreds that had caused individual crimes no longer existed in the same way. Not that men were saints, but they were at least acting like members of a dignified species. They respected themselves and others.

Then how could he have seriously considered the possibility that the Codicils would be stolen, and felt such an intense anxiety? Of course, Monarch thought: The ideas hadn't been his own. When would he really learn to recognize the messages that rose up through his own familiar consciousness? That paranoia wasn't of his own time. Perplexed, Monarch sat down on the Victorian period chair at the top of the stairs. He knew that there were psychic correlations between himself and his "other" selves — invisible psychological intersections. And that fear about the Codicils had come from just such a channel. But why had he picked up that particular message now, just before the celebration of the finding of the microfilm at the dig? In two hours, the entire area would be mobbed with visitors from all over the world.

In two hours, the Codicils would be on view, of course.

The Holograph Players would perform the ceremonial drama — the history of the finding of the Codicils — and depict the life of The George.

Monarch sighed and decided to check with his mate, Leona, to see if her latest dream work had yielded any results that might throw light on this odd anxiety of his. He and Leona were both dream archeologists. But Leona had always been the best dreamer, Monarch thought. Sometimes at the last minute, she *had* come up with excellent dream data, as if a crisis stimulated her abilities. He frowned. His abilities didn't work that way; he liked peace and quiet. But there wouldn't be any until the celebration was over . . . and as he walked down the museum's hall, Monarch tried to throw aside the sudden nagging thought that the celebration itself was somehow threatened.

He opened the door to The George's bedroom; Leona spent her dreaming time there, in the hopes that the location might stimulate new information. She was looking out the windows and turned, almost anxiously, as Monarch entered.

"I'm done," she said, "and the room is in order — "

"But?" Monarch asked. He knew her so well that her anxiety was apparent, even as she tried to soften its expression by a reassuring smile.

"Well, I may have received some new facts . . . disturbing ones. Or at least, I may have some information that contradicts other things we think we know. I hate it when that happens." Her large brown eyes still carried hints of their dream visions. She seemed bathed in the softness of an alternate consciousness; not blurred, but carrying the look a child does when roused from sleep. Even her anxiety was softened by this aura of subjective refreshment. "The dreams are already recorded," she said. "I taped them at once." Her toes wiggled in her sandals; she tapped her right foot gently so that her ankle bracelets tinkled, and her short skirt rippled with the graceful motion. "Just think. These windows opened once. Or the originals did." Again she stared out at the museum's grounds.

"And let in all the dirt of traffic," Monarch said, laughing despite himself. It was a game they usually loved to play. They'd stand there, using their inner senses, trying to bring up to awareness's threshold all of the sounds of the ancient automobiles, the squeal of tires. . . . "Don't put me off, though. You're the best dreamer of the two of us. What did you come up with?"

She swung around. "*I* am? And whose dreaming led to this dig and resulted in the museum to begin with? Yours!"

"True," Monarch said. "But I've always felt that something was incomplete. . . ."

"Maybe it was," Leona said seriously. "You can check my dream records later. But there were *three* separate, clear dreams. In one, I stood in an ancient kitchen, much like the museum's, and there was a man named Window who was trying to look into our world."

Monarch's face almost drained of color.

"What's wrong?" asked Leona, alarmed.

"Go on," responded Monarch, "I'll tell you when you're through."

"Well," she said doubtfully, "I'll tell you the second one in sequence, though it's somewhat complicated. This dream was almost like a nightmare. In a terribly vivid series of events I saw . . . what the world would be like now if we didn't have the Codicils. It really was somewhat frightening, but I kept my head and my critical functions throughout. . . ." She paused, then continued quickly. "Some — most — of the ideas were sheer insanity. It was hard to understand, but in the dream, wars were considered a method of achieving peace. I mean, countries had armies, and the greater the war machines, the greater the chances of peace were considered to be! Idiocy, I told you. And in the dream, mankind hadn't learned how to handle technology at all. Somehow it was used to build up a country's arsenal of possible retaliatory equipment." Leona shook her head almost angrily. "The entire affair was most distasteful, and I was really amazed to find myself encountering such nonsense so directly. There was more," she went on, "but the third dream was the one I thought most significant."

Monarch nodded, knowing that they'd checked dream details and crosschecked them a thousand times in their ten years of keeping records.

"Well, in the third dream I was a woman, connected with the man Window, of the first dream. And my name was Josephine." Leona paused, then spelled out the name meaningfully.

Monarch stared at her. "You're saying that there's been an error in the legends? That the man we have as The George's closest friend was a woman?"

Leona answered slowly, "Not 'Joseph Ine' at all. But *Josephine,* a woman. I'm really quite sure . . . though where the man Window, fits in, I don't know."

"I can tell you that," Monarch replied. From a brief experience I had on the way up here, I think that Window was — is — one of my own aspects in the twentieth century."

"And if Josephine was an aspect of me, if I'm right — "

"Then somehow both of us were involved with The George. In some capacity at least," Monarch said. And more slowly: "That could be why I picked up the location of this dig to begin with."

Leona looked forlorn. "Then why have you had these dreadful feelings lately about the Codicils being in danger?"

Monarch sighed. "I don't know. The entire museum, the environment, the grounds and the river sometimes lately seem . . . transitory, as if they could vanish in a moment."

"Then we have to conduct a Together Dream!" Leona cried.

"There's nothing else to do. We'll be our own dreamguides, we'll sleep in this bed . . . and try to dreamt ravel into the past clearly — "

"There's so many variables," Monarch said. "I don't do my best dream travel under pressure, either, like you do . . . and there's not much time before the celebration, either. The technicians must be gathering in the basement and downstairs rooms even now."

She grinned at him.

He started laughing. "Of course you're right. And who knows what we'll find? Maybe we'll even have more new data for the celebration."

They took off all of their clothes and lay down in the replica of The George's bed. They let their thoughts melt: then they let their thoughts melt *together,* and they felt their bodies dissolving into the bedding — becoming the bedding as far as sensation was concerned, though both of their physical forms lay there, cool and quiet as sleeping stones. Their minds met where their thoughts merged together, and their dream-selves rose up like forms of smoke. The forms faded together into the room's past — into the pasts of the room — disappearing in numberless autumns and summers, floating through immeasurable winters and springtime . . . following the beckoning focuses of their individual and joint intents.

Monarch and Leona were naturally gifted dream travelers, their abilities tuned and developed through their university training. They loved working together, and now they maintained their separate critical consciousnesses carefully, clearly, easily, letting them ride atop the deeper, steadier dream consciousnesses that supported them. Their love for each other was a further support, adding to their closeness, so that now the dream consciousness of one of them could intermingle with the other's. But always their intent steered them in one direction: toward The George's ancient world.

Now and then, their dream bodies passed through utter darkness. There were bursts of flame and the chattering, it seemed, of a million voices, but both of them knew enough not to become distracted—not to investigate, not to be touched by such dream-atmospheric conditions.

"I love you," Monarch said mentally. "I love *you,*" she mentally replied. Then they both felt that sudden exhilaration, that focusing of energy, that surge of triumph as the dream trip zoomed them in precisely on the desired location in time and space; incredibly finding the target from an infinity of probabilities.

Now was a time of special care.

~ *Chapter Seventeen* ~

A Together Dream

*T*he sense of motion ceased. Monarch and Leona tried to hold their consciousnesses as steady as possible, but even then there was a momentary mental blackout. It lasted barely a second. Then there was a jumble of half-formed images as their dreamsight began to operate.

At first Monarch just saw shapes but gradually they gained object status, though everything was gray. All of his other dream senses operated fully, though, so that he stood solidly enough in the corner of "the landing room."

Beside him, Leona gasped. She saw color brilliantly. Testing, she tried to smell the air—nothing! So she wasn't quite focused yet, she thought. Preparing to take a few steps, she rose in the air several tumbling feet. Monarch smiled, and she floated down, apologizing. "I'm sorry. I'm all right now. Can you tell anything?"

They stood quietly, staring. Gradually the contents of the room became clear. There were several people seated at a table. "If we're right, our aspects should be here. We'd be attracted to them," Monarch said. And as he uttered those words, his consciousness fluctuated, surged, and pulled him toward a man who was speaking. Monarch stood invisibly beside the man's chair; and as he did, that individual's mind opened up to him, almost as if it was his own. It wasn't, of course, yet the sense of familiarity and strangeness was extremely intoxicating. . . .

"Watch yourself," Leona cried. "Don't double in on yourself and him that way, Monarch!"

Monarch heard and didn't hear. Why, he wondered, did this man and this room seem so familiar, so intimate? As if he'd been here (and not in dreams) before?

Before he could even begin to answer his own question, Monarch almost panicked as some assaulting audio data suddenly blotted out everything else. The thunderous, throbbing rush of sound was followed by squeaking, squealing higher frequencies that hurt Monarch's dream ears, even while the rhythm of the two kinds of sound seemed to be translated into an unwieldy anxiety. For a moment the sounds seemed everywhere. Then, suddenly, they stopped.

Dazed, Monarch opened his dream eyes again. Leona was staring at him incredulously; she'd obviously heard the noises, too.

There was still some static, but gradually, as they stood invisibly in the room, Monarch and Leona identified the specific sounds of the persons speaking. The earlier barrage had propelled Monarch's consciousness away from the man who so intrigued him, and now Monarch made cautious attempts to establish some kind of rapport. "I'm Monarch," he said mentally.

"I'm Monarch," John Window said, seated in George's twentieth-century kitchen.

"Again?" George asked, grinning.

"I've *always* been Monarch," Monarch replied mentally with astonishment. And again, John Window spoke his words.

"There's some other consciousness here," Seven said.

"Will you cut that out? You're as bad as Window. It's positively spooky," George said, quickly finishing a beer. "He's a . . . split personality—"

Seven turned to Window and said, "If you're really Monarch, then you must know what the Codicils are."

Silence.

Monarch was so excited that he didn't dare speak, not even mentally. Beside him, Leona said, "One of them isn't really physical! Look, that body doesn't have a history; it's flat at this level. Be careful. The room and other people seem real, though."

Just then, the dreadful combination of sounds set up a new uproar, knocking all thoughts from Monarch's head. This time the volume was greater than before, and the sounds rattled around Monarch's dream head like sharp rocks. Then once again, unaccountably, the noises stopped.

One man was saying, "You can't hear a thing with that goddamn traffic." Monarch was able to make out the words. He grinned weakly at Leona. *Traffic!* So that's what *traffic* was. . . .

George closed the window.

Seven really wanted to get out of his body so that he could deal with this new group of events, but he didn't dare. Again he said gently, "If you're Monarch, we know the Codicils are in your world, in your probability. But in *our* probability, in your past, we haven't put them there yet. Do you understand?"

Monarch tried to concentrate on the words he heard, but the floor of his consciousness kept shifting. There was only one thing to do, he thought — if he could manage it. "Bail me out if I need it," he told Leona mentally. And in the next moment he let his consciousness lean closer and closer to Window's.

At a certain psychological level, a subjective attraction took over, and Monarch felt as if he went twirling through worlds of emotions and sensations until finally he opened his eyes — to look out upon the strange room from Window's viewpoint. Yet he was still himself, and this body's senses kept the sense data clear and untangled. "I think I understand," he said with Window's voice.

But for a moment Monarch could say nothing more as he tried to orient himself. Window's consciousness was . . . truly spacious! Monarch symbolically experienced the aspects of Window's personality as separate large rooms at whose doorways he stood, staring. The twentieth-century Window faced his own time — that was certain. But in a reflection form, Monarch saw his own personality in still another room (where his own characteristics operated as Window's unconscious? Could that be? he wondered). And between the two stood Window's Christ. Really astonished, but understanding, Monarch through Window spoke out:

"Window *can* heal. I understand now. Before the Codicils, you didn't realize that you could heal yourselves or others without . . . medicine." Monarch was overwhelmed with compassion as Window's memory-images glowed in his own consciousness: Window as a child being punished for healing a cat, the child trying to use his abilities against the greatest constraints. . . . "Oh," Monarch cried, half with exasperation, "Window identified with Christ, because gods at least could *heal.* And Window wouldn't have to bear the guilt . . ." Monarch felt woozy. He struggled to control his own subjective stance.

"It's all right. I'm here, helping," Leona said.

"Hell, that makes sense," said George, wiping the perspiration from his face. "It makes sense, you know." And then to Seven: "But why does he have to go into one of those damn trances to find it out?"

"Be quiet, George," Seven whispered, "you'll distract him."

"*George?*" Monarch asked, incredulously. "You're George? *The* George?"

George was always embarrassed for Window when he spoke for Christ or Monarch; he couldn't look him in the face. Grinning, he said, "*The* George? Well, I'm George anyhow."

"I'm deeply honored," Monarch said.

"He *is* The George," Leona whispered mentally, "and he isn't. I can tell. Something's . . . distorted."

"And then, obviously you aren't trying to steal the Codicils," Monarch replied to George, with relief.

Seven interrupted, "We're trying to make sure that the Codicils *do* appear in your time. You must be dream travelers. I sense someone else with Monarch . . ."

But Monarch gasped. The room's walls were fading, the objects falling away into images and the images into shapes that gently disintegrated. "Leona, are you with me?" he called mentally. He felt her presence — even as his body called him back to the bedroom at the museum.

For an instant, all expression vanished from John Window's eyes as Monarch's consciousness fled from his counterpart's mind; and Window felt as if he'd suddenly wakened in a new world without knowing which world it was. But no, he thought, the world was the same. George, Seven and Diggs were still staring at him; only *he* had changed. Christ was gone!

Almost incredulous, Window rummaged through his inner awareness. The paranoid Christ was nowhere to be found. "I'm not Christ any more," he said. "He's gone for good — "

Awed, George just muttered, "Yeah," because there was no doubt about it: Before his eyes, Window was turning into . . . someone else. Or into himself. Even Seven gasped. Window's eyes seemed to go click, click, click, as if changing or reflecting several different focuses before settling on one . . . and that one focus represented Window's characteristics reshuffled, put together in a new way. Then Window's eyes were calm, resolute, sure of themselves; no longer sifting or listless or frightened.

The process hardly took a moment. When Window's eyes started their transformation, Gregory Diggs had started to say, "My God," and by the time he'd completed the two words, the process was over.

But as if in response, innumerable vital yet individually minute alterations took place in John Window's posture, manner, in his lips and nose and ears . . . as if the man called Window was suddenly put together right, and all of the tensions and struggles that divided him had been resolved. Quite simply, George, Diggs, and Seven all knew that Window was now completely sane whether or not he had been before; and that this man *was* Window, regardless of the status of Christ or Monarch.

"What's going on?" Diggs asked, staring. "What do you mean, you're not Christ any more? *Ever?* You can't heal?"

Window grinned, shaking his head from one side to the other with relief. "I know what I experienced," he said. "You'll have to fill me in on what I don't remember. But anyhow, when it was over, I knew that I've always been able to heal, and that unconsciously I formed the Christ personality to make the whole thing reasonable — as crazy as it seemed to others. But there's so much more."

Seven felt Cyprus somewhere at the outskirts of his own consciousness, and it seemed to him that there was psychological motion all about; so powerful that he wanted to join it, and leave his body . . . which he kept forgetting now and then, not that anyone noticed. He said quickly, "Tell us what happened as far as you're concerned, Window."

Window grinned again. "I'm just getting used to being . . . myself," he answered. "And what I'm going to say does sound crazy, I guess. But I know it isn't."

George shook his own head. He knew that whatever Window would say was true. But *how* did he know?

Window began: "I used to speak for a personality called Monarch — as you know. Well, suddenly that consciousness and mine merged. I knew Monarch's life, and he knew mine. But his was a world that makes ours really look sick. I've never been so happy in my life as when I glimpsed pictures of that world through his mental images. And his world was based on completely different ideas than ours is. . . ."

While Oversoul Seven was so concerned with finding the Codicils, the words "the Codicils" kept sounding through Josephine's mind. She sensed some odd familiarity, as if she herself had run across that particular phrase in some significant way before. That is, she thought, the words meant "appendages to a will." Yet suppose in this connotation, they meant "appendixes to *the* will" — to man's will?

With no particular destination in mind, she walked up the stairs to her small study and found herself examining the piles of books stacked so neatly on the bookshelves. "The Codicils," she muttered angrily, anxiously. As if by themselves, her hands began rummaging through the books, fingering the pages. Yet she had the odd feeling that her fingers knew what they were doing, that she had in mind some particular goal beyond her conscious knowing.

There was a window above the bookcase. She glanced up at it, and as if the window were a clue, suddenly her fingers flew nervously past book after book, sorting through pages. She'd never felt such a strange pressure in her mind, in her fingers, in her entire being. Then the moment came that she would always remember. She yelled out suddenly in triumph and exaltation as she found the phrase, the particular phrase, that was so vital. It was in an old book, *Psychic Politics,* by a Jane Roberts, written many years before. There it was — the blueprint for mankind's future, the blueprint that she was now completely sure was also written in the tissues and cells of the species itself. She read quickly, triumphantly:

CODICILS

(Alternate hypotheses as a base for private and public experience.)

1. All of creation is sacred and alive, each part connected to each other part, and each communicating in a creative cooperative commerce in which the smallest and the largest are equally involved.

2. The physical senses present one unique version of reality, in which being is perceived in a particular dimensionalized sequence, built up through neurological patterning, and is the result of one kind of neurological focus. There are alternate neurological routes, biologically acceptable, and other sequences so far not chosen.

3. Our individual self-government and our political organizations are by-products of sequential perception, and our exterior methods of communication set up patterns that correlate with, and duplicate, our synaptic behavior. We lock ourselves into certain structures of reality in this way.

4. Our sequential prejudiced perception is inherently far more flexible than we recognize, however. There are half steps — other unperceived impulses — that leap the nerve ends, too fast and too slow for our usual focus. Recognition of these can be learned and encouraged, bringing in perceptive data that will trigger changes in usual sense response, filling out potential sense spectra with which we are normally not familiar.

5. This greater possible sense spectrum includes increased perception of inner bodily reality in terms of cellular identity and behavior; automatic conscious control of bodily processes; and increased perception of exterior conditions as the usual senses become more vigorous. (Our sight, for example, is not nearly as efficient as it could be. Nuances of color, texture, and depth could be expanded and our entire visual area attain a brilliance presently considered exceptional or supernormal.)

Josephine's glance slid down the page. The Codicils were followed by comments by the author. There was a paragraph called Comments on Codicils.
It seemed to apply to Codicil 1, and to the five Codicils in general at the
same time. She read the pertinent passages quickly and impatiently.

COMMENTS ON CODICILS

Acceptance of these first codicils would expand practical knowledge
of the self, break down barriers that are the result of our prejudiced
perception, and restructure personal, social, and political life.

Concepts of the self and practical experience of the self must be
broadened if the species is to develop its true potentials. Only an
evolution of consciousness can alter the world view that appears to
our official line of consciousness.

COMMENT ON CODICIL 2

This next step is as important as the birth of Christianity was in the
history of mankind. It will present a new structure for civilization to
follow. Christianity represented the human psyche at a certain point,
forming first inner patterns for development that then became
exteriorized as myth, drama, and history, with the Jewish culture of
the Talmud presenting the psyche's direction. The differences
between Jewish and Christian tradition represented allied but
different probabilities, one splitting off from the other, but united by
common roots and actualized in the world to varying degrees.

The traditional personified god concept represented the mass
psyche's one-ego development; the ego ruling the self as God ruled
man; man dominant over the planet and other species, as God was
dominant over man — as opposed to the idea of many gods or the
growth of a more multifocused self with greater nature identification.

Neurological patterning of the kind we know began with the early
old-Testament Jews (known, then, as God's people), looking forward
through time to a completely one-ego focused self: Before,
neurological functioning was not as set; and in our world today some
minority peoples and tribes still bold to those alternate neurological
pulses. These will not appear to our measuring devices because we are
literally blind to them.

The Jewish prophets, however, utilized these alternate focuses of
perception themselves, and were relatively unprejudiced neurologically.

They were therefore able to perceive alternate visions of reality. Yet their great work, while focusing the energy of an entire religion, and leading to Christianity, also resulted in limiting man's potential perceptive area in important ways.

The prophets were able to sense the potentials of the mass psyche, and their prophecies charted courses in time, projecting the Jewish religion into the future. The prophecies gave the people great strength precisely because they gave their religion a future in time, providing a thread of continuity and a certain immortality in earthly terms.

The prophecies were psychic molds to be filled out in flesh. Some were fulfilled and some were not, but the unfulfilled ones were forgotten and served their purpose by providing alternate selections and directions. The prophecies ahead of time charted out a people's probable course, foreseeing the triumphs and disasters inherent in such an adventure through time.

They provided psychic webworks, blueprints, and dramas, with living people stepping into the roles already outlined, but also improvising as they went along. These roles were valid, however, chosen in response to an inner reality that foresaw the shape that the living psyche of the people would take in time.

But as a snake throws off old skin, the psyche throws off old patterns that have become rigid, and we need a new set of psychic blueprints to further extend the species into the future, replete with great deeds, heroes, and challenges; a new creative drama projected from the psyche into the three-dimensional arena. For now we no longer view reality through original eyes, but through structures of beliefs that we have outgrown. These structures are simply meant to frame and organize experience, but we mistake the picture for the reality that it represents. We've become neurologically frozen in that respect, forced to recognize the one sequential pattern of sense perceptions, so that we think that the one we've chosen is the only one possible.

COMMENT ON CODICIL 3

Thus far we've projected the unrecognized portions of our greater selfhood outward into God, religion, government, and exteriorized concepts. In this existence, selfhood is dependent upon sense perceptions, so that our neurological prejudice and rigid focus have limited our concepts of identity. When we do become aware of unofficial information, coming through other than recognized channels then it seems to come from "notself," or outside.

A great deal of energy has been used to repress levels of selfhood and to project these into religious and nationalistic heroes and cultural organizations. Government and religion try to preserve the status quo, to preserve their own existences, not for political or religious reasons, but to preserve the official picture of the self around which they are formed.

But the structured reality in which that kind of a self can exist is breaking down. The official picture no longer fits or explains private experience which is growing out of it. There is a momentary rift between the inner psyche and its creations.

Besides this, the experienced self is not the same through the ages. The experienced self is a psychic creation, responsive to exterior conditions which it creates as the psyche dives into the waters of experienced earthly selfhood. Only a portion of the potential self is experienced, but different portions as intents and purposes change. It is possible, though, to actualize more of our potential.

COMMENT ON CODICILS 4 AND 5

The answers and solutions lie in using levels of consciousness now considered eccentric or secondary. This includes far greater utilization of the dream states and altered conditions thus far thought to be exceptions of consciousness. These "exceptions" represent other kinds of focuses, greatly needed to broaden our concepts of the self; and our experience of personal selfhood by increasing conceptualization, giving direct experience of alternate views, and bringing other kinds of data to bear upon the world we know. In the past, the attitudes surrounding such perceptions brought about their own difficulties. The perceptions are biologically acceptable, however, and will lead to a clearer relationship between mind and body.

Josephine felt like crying with joy and relief. It was as if the Codicils had always been in the back of her consciousness, about to be retrieved. And what about the book? She'd found it a year or so ago in a secondhand book-shop, and had never read it through. She had read those few pages, though, never recognizing their importance, and surely not realizing that they would one day change her life. Because her life was being changed—no doubt about it. She felt suddenly that she should return to George's at once.

At the same time, Josephine felt some portion of her own mind reach outward in a new and wonderful fashion. She sat down in the one armchair, almost dazed. What was happening? she wondered, because a part of her consciousness already was at George's: That portion of her mind dimly saw the kitchen, and the name LEONA started to appear in her mind in block letters and flashing lights. Now what could *that* mean?

And as Josephine wondered, Leona in her dream body in George's kitchen sensed Josephine's presence. In her dream body Leona cried out to Monarch, "I can almost sense still another person—a woman who is a counterpart of mine, a woman who possesses knowledge of the Codicils. I'm not sure what is happening, but I know the Codicils are safe. We can go home now. It's all right. The Codicils are safe."

Her consciousness fluctuated. She and Monarch joined their minds together once again. They looked once more around the ancient kitchen, knowing that the Codicils had been planted firmly back in time. The rhythms of mind-travel reasserted themselves, and they started their mental journey home, satisfied, joyful, ready for the cinquecentennial.

In her study, Josephine picked up the book again and glanced at those significant paragraphs, and as she did, they flashed into Leona's mind, and Window's and Monarch's, and into Gregory Diggs' mind and into the minds of both the Georges, and into Oversoul Seven's mind.

But it was Seven alone who saw Cyprus. She was smiling the most serene smile Oversoul Seven had ever seen. Seven was trying to keep track of everything at once. He was so excited and relieved that he could hardly speak.

At the same time Cyprus said, "Seven, look here." And Seven saw the thin hand of George the First begin scribbling on the page of the old journal. And Oversoul Seven saw George's hand begin to write down those vital words: "The Codicils."

George the First cried out: "Zounds, what luck!"

"You'll never know," Seven whispered to George mentally. "Goodbye, dear friend, at least for now." He grinned and added, "It's been a—uh—super relationship. You succeeded in your pursuits far better than you know."

And Seven knew that it was all right, that everything was all right, always *had* been all right, that it had only been their own anxieties and doubts that ever made it all seem wrong. They were all couched and safe, forever secure, forever jubilant at the heart of their own beings. There was never anything to be afraid of, if only they trusted the great sweet security that forever held the vitality of their beings, for they were all truly splendid, a part of a loving universe that cradled them forever in a safety and love literally beyond all comprehension.

Seven cried out to Cyprus, "That love is a part of all of us now. I can sense it if I don't try. Trying makes it difficult, because it's there all of the time. It's always here"—Seven smiled incredulously—"or there. Anyhow, it's everywhere, and it couches and protects the very heart of our beings. So it's all right. Everything's all right and always has been."

And Cyprus answered. "What have I been telling you?"

Seven said aloud to George and Gregory Diggs. "I have to go now, or pretty soon at least. But even if you don't see me, I'll be around, and in a way I'll be a part of each one of you."

He felt inside his consciousness, and saw Josephine driving more quickly than she should have down the dark streets toward George's house. "Do take life easier," he said gently to her. "You're accomplishing more than you realize, and as I told the others, everything really is all right. . . ." Seven sensed the night air and the smell of lilacs, and knew that Josephine was pulling into the back yard below. He whispered good-bye once again, and Josephine smiled to herself and drove up to George's garage. She straightened her dress as she got out of the car.

Seven felt a catch in his physical throat. He said to George, "I sort of liked this physical body. The eyes and hands and hair, the ears and all, fit me really well. But I don't really belong here this way, you know—and I think, George, you've always known that in a way. I wish you all the very best of luck, but I'm afraid you won't remember me. Not consciously. I'll be around, anyway. . . ." Seven looked at all of them and grinned the best, gayest smile he could conjure up.

Cyprus said gently, "It's time now, Seven. They won't remember, but they will."

"Won't remember what?" asked George.

"What?" asked Gregory Diggs.

"Gee, I don't know," George replied. "I just had the feeling that something important had come and gone, yet not gone. And don't ask me what the hell I mean by that."

Tiny rays of light glittered and sparkled high in the upper corners of the room, and moved to the windowsill and outside the windowsill. They danced and gyrated in the transparent air. Then they disappeared.

"What's next?" Seven asked Cyprus.

"Who knows?" she answered.

"Do you know?"

"I know. And you know, and all of your personalities really know," Cyprus said in the sweetest, clearest mental voice imaginable.

And Seven said, "I know—or I almost know." He grinned, and waited to see what would happen next.

THE SETH AUDIO COLLECTION

RARE RECORDINGS OF SETH SPEAKING through Jane Roberts are now available on audio cassette. The Seth Audio Collection consists of selections of Seth, recorded by Jane's student, Rick Stack, during Jane's classes in Elmira, New York in the 1970s. The majority of these selections have never been published in any form and represent the best of Seth's comments gleaned from over 120 Seth sessions.

Volume I of The Seth Audio Collection consists of six (1-hour) cassettes plus a 34-page booklet of Seth transcripts. Topics covered in Volume I include:

- Creating your own reality — how to free yourself from limiting beliefs and create the life you want
- Dreams and out-of-body experiences
- Reincarnation and simultaneous time
- Connecting with your inner self
- Spontaneity — letting yourself go with the flow of your being
- Creating abundance in every area of your life
- Parallel (probable) universes and exploring other dimensions of reality
- Spiritual healing, how to handle emotions, overcoming depression, and much more.

FOR A FREE CATALOGUE of Seth-related products including a detailed description of The Seth Audio Collection, please send your request to the address below.

ORDER INFORMATION:

If you would like to order a copy of The Seth Audio Collection Volume I, please send your name and address, with a check or money order payable to New Awareness Network, Inc. in the amount of $59.95 plus shipping charges.

New York residents please add appropriate sales tax.

Shipping charges: U.S. – $3.75, Canada – $6, Europe – $10, Australia – $14

Please allow 2 weeks for delivery.

Mail to: NEW AWARENESS NETWORK, INC.
P.O. Box 192
Manhasset, New York 11030

SETH NETWORK
INTERNATIONAL

Seth Network International (SNI) is a nonprofit network of Seth/Jane Roberts readers from around the globe. The group publishes a quarterly magazine, *Reality Change: The Global Seth Journal,* and offers conferences and other activities. For information, contact:

Seth Network International
P.O. Box 1620
Eugene, OR 97440 USA
(503) 683-0803   Fax (503) 683-1084

Vereinigung der Seth-Freunde

The Association of the Friends of Seth, founded in 1980, was created as a meeting point and forum for Seth/Jane Roberts readers in Europe. They publish a newsletter, *Multidimensionale Wirklichkeit,* and hold an annual conference. They can be reached at:

Verinigung der SETH-Freunde
Postfach 3337
CH–8031 Zurich, Switzerland
Tel: 01-721-22 04

SUGGESTED READING

The Nature of Personal Reality: Specific, Practical Techniques for Solving Everyday Problems and Enriching the Life You Know by Jane Roberts. In this perennial best-seller, Seth challenges our assumptions about the nature of reality and stresses the individual's capacity for conscious action. Included are excellent exercises for applying these theories to any life situation. (Trade Paperback)

Seth Speaks: The Eternal Validity of the Soul by Jane Roberts. One of the most powerful of the Seth books, this is an essential guide to conscious living. It clearly and powerfully articulates the furthest reaches of human potential, and the concept that we all create our own reality according to our individual beliefs. (Trade Paperback)

The Magical Approach: Seth Speaks About the Art of Creative Living by Jane Roberts. In this brand new volume of original material, Seth invites us to look at the world through another lens—a magical one. Seth reveals the true, magical nature of our deepest levels of being, and explains how to live our lives spontaneously, creatively, and according to our own natural rhythms. (Trade Paperback)

Amber-Allen Publishing is dedicated to publishing books and cassettes that help improve the quality of our lives.

For a catalog of our fine books and cassettes, please contact:

AMBER-ALLEN PUBLISHING
P.O. Box 6657
San Rafael, California 94903

Or call toll free: (800) 227-3900